EX LIBRIS

VINTAGE **CLASSICS**

JARED SHURIN

Jared Shurin's previous anthologies include *The Outcast Hours* and *The Djinn Falls in Love* (both with Mahvesh Murad and both finalists for the World Fantasy Award). He has also been a finalist for the Shirley Jackson Award (twice), the British Science Fiction Association Award (twice) and the Hugo Award (twice), and won the British Fantasy Award (twice).

Alongside Anne C. Perry, he founded and edited the 'brilliantly brutal' (*Guardian*) pop culture website *Pornokitsch* for ten years, responsible for many of its more irritating and exuberant articles. Together, they also co-founded the Kitschies, the prize for progressive, intelligent and entertaining speculative and fantastic fiction, and Jurassic London, an award-winning, not-for-profit small press.

His other projects have included the *Best of British Fantasy* and *Speculative Fiction* series and anthologies of mummies, weird Westerns and Dickensian London. A frequent reviewer, he has also written articles on topics as diverse as *Gossip Girl* and *Deadwood*.

Jared is a certified BBQ judge.

ALSO EDITED BY JARED SHURIN

The Djinn Falls in Love and Other Stories (with Mahvesh Murad)
The Outcast Hours (with Mahvesh Murad)
Irregularity
The Lowest Heaven (with Anne C. Perry)

JARED SHURIN

The Big Book of Cyberpunk

Volume One

VINTAGE CLASSICS

3 5 7 9 10 8 6 4

Vintage Classics is part of the Penguin Random House group of companies
whose addresses can be found at global.penguinrandomhouse.com

Penguin
Random House
UK

Introduction and selection copyright © Jared Shurin 2023

The authors have asserted their right to be identified as the authors of this
Work in accordance with the Copyright, Designs and Patents Act 1988.
Pages 719–723 should be seen as an extension to this copyright page.

First published in Great Britain by Vintage Classics in 2024
First published in The United States by Vintage Books in 2023

penguin.co.uk/vintage-classics

A CIP catalogue record for this book is available from the British Library

ISBN 9781784879297

Typeset in 10/12pt Ehrhardt MT Pro by Jouve (UK), Milton Keynes
Printed and bound in Great Britain by Clays Ltd, Elcograf S.p.A.

The authorised representative in the EEA is Penguin Random House Ireland,
Morrison Chambers, 32 Nassau Street, Dublin D02 YH68

Penguin Random House is committed to a sustainable future
for our business, our readers and our planet. This book is made
from Forest Stewardship Council® certified paper.

MIX
Paper | Supporting
responsible forestry
FSC® C018179
FSC
www.fsc.org

CONTENTS

CONTENTS

CULTURE 297

POST-CYBERPUNK

I'm an optimist about humanity in general, I suppose.

—Tim Berners-Lee

EDITOR'S NOTE

The Big Book of Cyberpunk is a historical snapshot as much as a literary one, containing stories that span almost seventy-five years.

Cyberpunk, at its inception, was ahead of many other forms of literature in how it embraced (and continues to embrace) progressive themes. Cyberpunk, at its best, has strived for an inclusive vision of the present and future of society. Accordingly, the stories within *The Big Book of Cyberpunk* discuss all aspects of identity and existence. This includes, but is not limited to, gender, sexuality, race, class, and culture.

Even while attempting to be progressive, however, these stories also use language, tropes, and stereotypes common to the times and the places in which they were originally written. Even as some of the authors challenged the problems of their time, their work still includes problematic elements. To pretend otherwise would be hypocritical; it is the essence of cyberpunk to understand that one can simultaneously challenge and deserve to be challenged.

Cyberpunk is also literature that exists in opposition, and the way it expresses its rebellion is very often shocking, provocative, and offensive. It is transgressive by design, but not without purpose, and I tried to make my selections with that principle in mind.

—JARED SHURIN

INTRODUCTION TO VOLUME 1

THE DAY OF TWO THOUSAND PIGS

There once lived a man who was naked, raving, and could not be bound. Accord-ing to the Gospel: "He tore the chains apart and broke the irons on his feet." It turns out (spoiler) he was possessed. The demons were cast out of the man. Lacking a human host, the demons possessed an entire herd of pigs (two thou-sand of them, says Mark!). They then ran straight into the ocean.

The man, liberated of foul influences, sat there "dressed and in his right mind." The people around him were comforted. The day of demons was behind them. After a brief period of naked, raving chaos, order had been restored.

Or so they thought.

The biblical story of Legion is an iconic one, perhaps the most well-known exorcism in Western culture.* It is also, perhaps, the perfect metaphor for cyber-punk. It is literature unchained, naked, and raving . . . but only briefly. Depending on which expert source you read, this day of demons lasted a decade or a few short years—or, according to some, it died even before it was born. The pigs went straight into the sea. Order restored.

There's no question that cyberpunk had a shockingly brief existence as a cohesive entity. Born out of science fiction's new wave, literary postmodernism, and a perfect storm of external factors (Reaganism, cheap transistors, networked computing, and MTV), the genre cohered as a tangible, fungible thing in the early 1980s, most famously exemplified by the aesthetic of Ridley Scott's *Blade Runner* (1982) and the themes of William Gibson's *Neuromancer* (1984). The

---

* It also inspired one of the best X-Men characters.

term cyberpunk itself, as coined by Bruce Bethke, came into being in 1983.*
The neologism captured the zeitgeist: the potential of, and simultaneous disillu-
sionment with, techno-capitalism on steroids.

Cyberpunk was born of the punk ethos. It was a genre that, in many ways,
existed *against* a mainstream cultural and literary tradition, rather than *for* anything definable or substantive in its own right. This is, at least, an argument
posited by those who believe the genre peaked—and died—with Bruce Sterling's superb anthology *Mirrorshades* (1986). Accepted as the definitive
presentation of cyberpunk, Sterling had pressed a Heisenbergian self-destruct
button. Once it was a defined quality, cyberpunk could no longer continue in
that form.

Although this is a romantic theory (and cyberpunk is a romantic pursuit,
despite—or perhaps because of—the leather and chrome), it is not one to which
I personally subscribe. While collecting for this volume, I found that the engine
of the genre was still spinning away, producing inventive and disruptive interpretations of the core cyberpunk themes through to the start of the next decade.
These include novels and collections such as Kathy Acker's *Empire of the Senseless*
(1988), Misha's *Prayers of Steel* (1988), Richard Kadrey's *Metrophage* (1988),
Lisa Mason's *Arachne* (1990), and Richard Paul Russo's *Destroying Angel* (1992);
as well as movies, television programs, and games such as Paul Verhoeven's *RoboCop*
(1987), the *Max Headroom* series (1985), FASA's *Shadowrun* (1989), and Bull-
frog's *Syndicate* (1993). Meaningful social commentary was still being produced
as well: Donna Haraway's "A Cyborg Manifesto," for instance, as well as the
cypherpunks and even the first steampunks.†

By the mid-1990s, however, the hogs had well and truly left for the ocean.
The mundanity of the technocratic society had been firmly realized—as
expressed, for example, in Douglas Coupland's *Microserfs* (1995). And at the
other extreme, the visual aesthetic had proved overwhelmingly popular, thriving
independently of the ideas (or even the material) that spawned it. *Johnny Mnemonic* (1995) serves as a painful example of how the visual tropes of cyberpunk
no longer bore any connection to its original themes. A bit like Frankenstein's
monster, the cyberpunk style had gone lumbering off on its own, inadvertently
appropriating the name of its creator.‡ Cyberpunk slouched along in increasingly
glossy and pastiche-ridden forms, but its frenetic glory days were now truly

---

* Bethke's story—found in this volume—was written in 1980 and first published in
1983. The term was quickly adopted by the legendary science fiction editor Gardner
Dozois, who used it to describe the movement he was seeing in the pages of his *Asimov's
Science Fiction Magazine*.
† This is a larger discussion, but steampunk, even more than cyberpunk, is a genre in
which the aesthetic rapidly subsumed its original themes. It has, however, regained its
footing as a platform for discussing postcolonialism. Also, airships.
‡ In *Storming the Reality Studio* (1991), Richard Kadrey and Larry McCaffery make a
compelling argument for *Frankenstein* (1818) as a cyberpunk work, therefore increasing
the lifespan of the genre by approximately 170 years.

behind it. Cyberpunk *qua* cyberpunk had been pulled apart by the twin poles of banal reality and hyperactive fantasy.

Why would a *Big Book* be given over to something that lived, thrived, and died in such a short period of time? Because, in this case, the pigs took the long way round.

Cyberpunk's manifestation in a single and singular form was indeed brief. But it left quite an impression. A lingering dissatisfaction that being well-dressed and well-behaved is a bit, well, *dull*. The growing realization that chains aren't the nicest things to wear. A dawning awareness that there are actually a lot of extremely valid reasons to run around and scream (clothing optional). People understood that the world itself was not in its right mind, and maybe the demons had the right idea.

Even as the brief golden era of cyberpunk—the day of Legion—slips further into nostalgia, the legacy of cyberpunk remains not only relevant but ubiquitous. We now live our lives in a perplexing mix of the virtual and the real. At no time in human history have we ever been exposed to more messages, more frequently, and more intrusively. Civilians using bootstrap technology are guiding drones in open warfare against marauding professional mercenaries. Protesters use umbrellas and spray paint to hide their identity from facial recognition technology. Battles between corporations are fought in the streams of professional video-game players. Algorithmically generated videos lead children down the rabbit hole of terrorist recruitment. The top touring musical act is a hologram. Your refrigerator is spying on you.

Perhaps the madman in the cave was not possessed but an oracle. Cyberpunk, however brief its reign, gave us the tools, the themes, and the vocabulary to understand the madness to come. It understood that the world itself was raving and undressed—irrational, unpredictable, and ill behaved. This is how we live, and Legion saw it coming.

WHAT IS CYBERPUNK?

It is impossible to collect *The Big Book of Cyberpunk* without actually defining *cyberpunk*. Unless we dare to name Legion, we can't track the two thousand feral hogs and the spoor they left behind.

Unsurprisingly, given cyberpunk's robust academic and critical legacy, there are many definitions to draw upon. With a genre so nebulous and sprawling, it is possible for each artist, author, academic, game designer or editor to find in it what they want. Cyberpunk is a land of definitional opportunity, however there are some fundamental principles to uphold.

Cyberpunk has clear origins in both the "genre" and "literary" worlds. The division between these worlds is a false tension that has been remarked on, with their trademark directness, by Ann and Jeff VanderMeer in their introduction to *The Big Book of Science Fiction* (2016). From its start, cyberpunk stories and cyberpunk authors were bobbing and weaving between both literary and genre outlets, as well as commercial and academic presses, traditional and experimental formats, and formal and informal modes of publishing. Cyberpunk has now been "claimed" by science fiction (or, more controversially, science fiction has been consumed by cyberpunk). But it would be a narrow and inaccurate view of the genre to see it as a wholly science-fictional endeavor.

Cyberpunk is inextricably linked with the real experience of technology. Technology in cyberpunk is not a hypothetical but a fundamental, tangible, and omnipresent inclusion in human life. Cyberpunk's predecessors largely dealt with technology as an abstract possibility: a controlled progress in the hands of a scientific elite, with visionary, but entirely rational, outcomes. But the reality of the computing explosion is that irrationality reigned, science became decentralised and personalised, and utopian visions were subsumed by capitalism, politics, and individual whim. Technology outpaced not only its expectations but its limitations.

As a genre about technology, and not "science" more broadly, there are limits to cyberpunk's scope. Technology, in this context, is manufactured. Cyberpunk is not science fiction that explores the ramifications of something inherent (such as the anthropological science fiction of Ursula K. Le Guin), innate (such as fiction that focuses on xenobiology, mutation, psychic powers, or other "flukes of biology" stories), or encountered (such as stories about discovering or exploring alien civilizations, lost worlds, or strange artifacts). By focusing on technology as a product, cyberpunk is about agency: it speaks about change that we are attempting to bring about and upon ourselves.

Cyberpunk exists in opposition to its predecessors. The *-punk* of cyberpunk is unavoidable: cyberpunk contains a fundamental sense of challenge. The man in the cave wasn't raving blindly; he was raving *against*. Cyberpunk pushes boundaries; it is provocative. It tries to find and break conventions. This need to rebel is intrinsic to the genre, leading to experimentation with both theme and form. As noted previously, it also connects to the possible "death" of cyberpunk: once the genre was absorbed by the mainstream, it could no longer exist as a single cohesive rebellion, and fragmented accordingly.

Cyberpunk is neither static nor teleological. Cyberpunk is literature about change. That change can take the form of progress or regress; evolution or revolution; or even degradation. It is not epic in the sense of a grand and ultimate destination. There are no final and decisive conclusions, only, at most, incremental movement. Cyberpunk is often described as *dystopian*, but dystopia implies a final and established system. Even in its grimmest worlds, cyberpunk presents the possibility of dynamism and of change. (And, similarly, even when set in the most scintillating futures, cyberpunk seeds the potential for regression or disruption.)

This final principle also hints at the limitations of technology. **Cyberpunk is not about technological supremacy.** In fact, the reverse is true: *cyberpunk is about the perseverance of humanity*. Cyberpunk accepts that irrationality and personality cannot be subsumed. This recognition is for good and for ill: techno–utopian outcomes are impossible because of our core, intractable humanness. But nor should those outcomes even be desirable: our irrepressible need for individuality may keep us from paradise but is, ultimately, the most essential part of our nature. In theme, and often in form, cyberpunk embraces chaos and irrationality, perpetually defiant of sweeping solutions, absolutist worldviews, or fixed patterns.

Marshall McLuhan, one of the great scholars of technology and society, described the same dynamics that led to the development of cyberpunk. McLuhan suggested that, in order to study technology, we step away from admiring the technology itself and instead examine how it shapes or displaces society. This quasi-phenomenological approach finds meaning not in the thing itself, but in our response to it. McLuhan concludes that the "message" of any medium or technology is the scale or pace or pattern that it introduces into human affairs.* Applying this same concept to cyberpunk: it is not the fiction of technology but that of our reaction to it. The technology itself matters only in how it affects "human affairs."

Cyberpunk fiction is therefore an attempt, through literature, to make sense of the unprecedented scale and pace of contemporary technology, and also of the brutal and realistic acknowledgment that there may be no sense to it at all. As a working definition, therefore, it means **cyberpunk is speculative fiction about the influence of technology on the scale, the pace, or the pattern of human affairs.** Technology may accelerate, promote, delay, or even oppose these affairs, but humanity remains ultimately, unchangeably, human. It is the fiction of irrationality. Science fiction looks to the stars; cyberpunk stares into a mirror.

It seems tautological, but a definition is only as good as its ability to define. I crawled through almost two thousand works for this book, and, as *Big*™ as this book is, a mere hundred or so made it in. How did this definition work as a set of practical selection criteria? More importantly, what should you expect to find within these pages?

Cyberpunk is fiction—a self-serving selection requirement, and a controversial one at that. There's a wealth of cyberpunk-adjacent non-fiction that fully merits a *Big Book* of its own. From the reviews of *Cheap Truth* to the ads in the back of *Mondo 2000*, there are essays, travelogues, manifestos, articles, and memoirs that are immensely important to cyberpunk. But cyberpunk is speculative, not descriptive. The non-fiction inspires the genre, and is inspired by it, but is not the genre itself.

The protagonist needs to be recognisably human. As stated, cyberpunk is about human affairs. Protagonists that are aliens, robots, or artificial intelligence (AI) shift the focus from human social relationships to the relationship between humanity and the other. Human/other relationships can be an insightful way of exploring what makes us human (as seen in great science fiction ranging from Mary Doria Russell to Becky Chambers), but cyberpunk eschews

---

* Marshall McLuhan, *Understanding Media: The Extensions of Man* (New York: McGraw Hill, 1964).

that additional layer of metaphor. To be about human affairs, the story needs to be about humans.

The story is set in the present, the near present, or an easily intuited future. As we project further and further out, deciphering the scale, the pace, or the pattern requires more and more assumptions on the part of the author. Again, this is about the point of focus: the more speculation involved, and the less the manufactured technology is immediately recognisable, the more the story becomes about exploring the wondrous, rather than interrogating the probable. The "present," of course, is relative. (Objectively speaking, most of cyberpunk is now, disturbingly, alternate history.)

Given the stagnant state of space exploration, this also excludes virtually all stories that take place off-planet or in deep space.* (Again, arguments could be made for films such as *Alien*, 1979, or *Outland*, 1981, that take place in deep space, but with oddly minimal evidence of human scientific or social progress.) Similarly, there are very few examples of cyberpunk in secondary worlds or of cyberpunk with magic. As the fantastical becomes more and more necessary to the story, the focus shifts away from human affairs and toward the story's imaginative underpinnings.

Technology is mediative, not transformative. This is a deeply subjective divide but one critical to what makes cyberpunk a distinct genre or subgenre of science fiction. A story in which technology fundamentally transforms, replaces, or subsumes human relationships is exciting, intriguing, and wildly imaginative . . . but not cyberpunk. A cyberpunk story is one that examines the way technology changes the way humans relate to other humans *but still leaves that relationship fundamentally intact*. The underlying resilience of human social relationships, for better or for worse, remains the key theme—not the transformative potential of technology.

In the spirit of cyberpunk, it is fair to note that these rules are in no way consistent. There are obvious exceptions to each of the above contained within this book, including AI protagonists, alien encounters, and even the overt use of magic.

The eagle-eyed will also note that I've tried to avoid the vocabulary that normally surrounds cyberpunk. As mentioned above, cyberpunk needs not be dystopian, for example. In fact, because of its focus on the resilience of human relationships, cyberpunk is neither optimistic nor pessimistic but brutally realistic. If that realism is often read as dystopian, that is more a commentary on the nature of humanity.

Nor does cyberpunk have to be set in a city, or under neon lights, or wearing

---

* Is there anything more emblematic of cyberpunk than the corporatization of the space race? When John F. Kennedy announced the ambition of a manned mission to the moon, he declared: "We set sail on this new sea because there is new knowledge to be gained, and new rights to be won, and they must be won and used for the progress of all people." Sixty years later, egocentric billionaires are farting radioactive garbage over the south Texas landscape in the rush to get billboards into orbit.

sunglasses, or in the rain, or (god forbid) in a trench coat. These tropes demonstrate the lingering appeal of the aesthetic that stemmed from cyberpunk but have little to do with its underpinning themes. Indeed, some of the most spectacularly non-cyberpunk works can masquerade as cyberpunk. The presence of a parsley garnish does not guarantee a steak beneath.

The last word commonly applied to cyberpunk is *noir*, and there is much merit to it. Unfortunately, in noir, we find a genre that is somehow even more commonly misinterpreted; confused with an aesthetic than cyberpunk itself. Noir is, like cyberpunk, about human relationships, whether the protagonist's troubled relationship with their own identity (*Dark Passage*, 1947) or their conflict with a claustrophobic broader society (*Chinatown*, 1974). There is even a McLuhan-esque technological change at the center of most noir stories: the modern industrial city and its resultant impact on the pace, the scale, and the pattern of human affairs. Cyberpunk as *science fiction noir* can be a fairly apt description, but *only* when used in the thematic sense. It is, however, too often misapplied in the sense of "two genres that both feature rain and trench coats," which is why I have strenuously avoided "noir" here.

Since cyberpunk is posited in this collection as the speculative examination of technology on human affairs, *The Big Book of Cyberpunk* is structured to examine the genre along the dimensions upon which those affairs exist: **self**, **culture**, **system**, and **challenge**. These sections also nod to McLuhan's concept of the "global village"—a world in which media and technology has made the pace and the scale of human affairs instantaneous and global.* This global village, for better or for worse, is a world that McLuhan envisioned, that cyberpunk speculated upon, and in which we now live.

Each section begins with a (much briefer) introduction, followed by a "pre-cyberpunk" story. As tidy as it would be to divide the world into an orderly, rationalist, technophilic Golden Age and then the raving of cyber-demons, that would be a false dichotomy. Like all cultural trends, cyberpunk has its harbingers, more easily identified with the benefits of hindsight and distance.

For each theme, I've included a story that, in its own way, predicts, pioneers, or inspires the cyberpunk that followed. From there, the stories within each section are ordered chronologically, up to—as much as possible—the present day. The sole caveat here is that "publication order" is an arbitrary metric: a story may have been conceived, written, or even submitted long before its publication. But this rough chronological ordering shows how the central themes of cyberpunk stayed consistent, even as the technology or media explored shifted over time. This ordering also demonstrates, in many ways, how cyberpunk has always been self-reflexive, with stories often in gleeful conversation with their forebears both within and outside the "core" genre.

Finally, each volume of *The Big Book of Cyberpunk* concludes with a section

---

* Marshall McLuhan, *The Gutenberg Galaxy: The Making of Typographic Man* (Toronto: University of Toronto Press, 1962).

on post-cyberpunk. The stories here showcase the "What next?"—a question that has been asked since even before the genre began.

THE SOURCE CODE OF TWO THOUSAND PIGS

For those interested in deciphering the construction of this anthology, there were some functional—if idiosyncratic—editorial rules in place.

Respect antecedents. Notable cyberpunk anthologies include Bruce Sterling's formative *Mirrorshades*; Rudy Rucker, Robert Anton Wilson, and Peter Lamborn Wilson's groundbreaking *Semiotext(e) SF* (1989); Larry McCaffery's equally important *Storming the Reality Studio* (1991); Pat Cadigan's *The Ultimate Cyberpunk* (2002); James Patrick Kelly and John Kessel's *Rewired* (2007); Victoria Blake's *Cyberpunk* (2013); and Jason Heller and Joshua Viola's *Cyber World* (2016).

Each of these editors had their distinct (and occasionally contradictory) vision of the genre, and these anthologies are all, in my opinion, required reading. Rather than imitate their vision, or worse, subsume it, I have kept repetition to a bare minimum. That same respect also applies to all other anthologies, including the Big Book series. Although some authors rightfully appear in this volume and previous Big Books, there are no overlapping stories.

Showcase varying perspectives. Although *peak* or *core* cyberpunk was demographically homogeneous (something of which the cyberpunks were, to their credit, fully aware), its legacy is astoundingly and brilliantly diverse. I have attempted to capture how writers from many different backgrounds—demographic, geographic, and artistic—took on the challenge of writing about our relationship with technology and one another.

Cyberpunk is a truly global phenomenon. Storytellers all over the world have used the genre as a means of addressing and discussing their concerns. This is not a recent development; cyberpunk has been a global genre since its earliest days. I've sought out stories that show both cyberpunk's global contemporary presence and its roots. This book includes multiple translations, including five commissioned specifically for this volume—among them the first English-language appearances of classic cyberpunk stories by Gerardo Horacio Porcayo and Victor Pelevin, two undisputed masters of the genre.

Afrofuturism is an important movement unto itself, with its own unique cultural evolution. It is *not* "Black cyberpunk," although the two are often conflated. Treating Afrofuturism as a subset of cyberpunk is to treat it with disrespect. However, there are undeniable parallels, as both genres, for example, present alternative views to a "mainstreamed" culture, and both are robustly transmedia in their creative expression. There has also been some intersection over time, perhaps most popularly in the music, videos, and writing of Janelle Monáe. Their novella, co-written with Alaya Dawn Johnson, features in this volume. "The Memory Librarian" is one of several works within this *Big Book* that has a foot in both movements, but it would be disingenuous to pretend that Afrofuturism is thoroughly explored herein.

INTRODUCTION TO VOLUME 1

As a corollary to the principle of diverse perspectives: the de facto *Big Book* rule is that no author can appear twice in a single volume—and this has been *mostly* maintained. However, cyberpunk has always been a collaborative genre. Some of its most impressive and defining works were co written, creating results that neither could achieve independently. Although a very slim loophole, I've exploited it, meaning a few names do have the audacity to repeat herein.

Celebrate the experimental. Cyberpunk media included film and television, albums and art, software and games. Many of these formats are impossible to capture on the printed page, certainly not without doing them a massive disservice—although there are some visual stories inside this collection. I attempt to pay tribute to the original cyberpunks by gathering materials from a wide variety of sources: a reflection of the non-traditional publishing journey taken by many of these writers. Inside are stories first published in magazines, anthologies, and websites, but also as zines, liner notes, and fleeting social media posts.

Cyberpunk is not solely the province of science fiction, and herein are stories first published by newspapers, in science journals, in literary magazines, and as role-playing game tie-ins. Due to the combination of provocative content and technologically savvy authors, cyberpunk has always been at the forefront of self-publishing— a trend also reflected here.

Continuing the experimental theme, all the stories in *The Big Book of Cyberpunk* are self-contained "holistic" works. There are many great stories that require the reader to have preexisting knowledge of the setting or the characters. There are a wealth of fantastic cyberpunk novels that could have provided extracts. Restricting this anthology solely to short fiction was necessary for my own sake.

THE END OF THE BEGINNING

The first story, William Gibson's "The Gernsback Continuum" (1981) stands outside the five main sections. It is the boot-up sound for the hundred-odd stories that follow.

William Gibson is the figure most closely connected with cyberpunk, not only through *Neuromancer* and the Sprawl trilogy, but also through his short stories and non-fiction, all of which encapsulated the fledgling genre in its fragile early years. There is no author more appropriate to open this volume.*

"The Gernsback Continuum" defines the problem that cyberpunk would then go on to solve. It shows the fantasies of scientific aspiration, and it repositions visions of progress as the ghosts of value. The story is achingly, poignantly sad. Not because it is set in a dystopian hellscape but because the world is so painfully ordinary. It shows where we are, but through the lens of where we thought we'd be. By setting the recognizable against the aspirational, Gibson

---

* "The Gernsback Continuum" was also the first story in the now oft-mentioned *Mirrorshades*. This is a coincidence, but I like it.

shows the gap between imagination and reality and sets out the challenge for future writers to fill it—including, as it turns out, Gibson himself. "The Gernsback Continuum" refuted the science-fictional tradition that had prevailed since the 1930s and made space for a new form of storytelling.

Above all else, "The Gernsback Continuum" is simply a beautiful story, perfectly constructed and gloriously atmospheric. Although all stories in this anthology were chosen for their historical and thematic significance, the *most* important selection criterion was that they are enjoyable to read, and I hope you find as much pleasure in them as I have.

WILLIAM GIBSON

THE GERNSBACK
CONTINUUM

(1981)

MERCIFULLY, the whole thing is starting to fade, to become an episode. When I do still catch the odd glimpse, it's peripheral; mere fragments of mad-doctor chrome, confining themselves to the corner of the eye. There was that flying-wing liner over San Francisco last week, but it was almost translucent. And the shark-fin roadsters have gotten scarcer, and freeways discreetly avoid unfolding themselves into the gleaming eighty-lane monsters I was forced to drive last month in my rented Toyota. And I know that none of it will follow me to New York; my vision is narrowing to a single wavelength of probability. I've worked hard for that. Television helped a lot.

I suppose it started in London, in that bogus Greek taverna in Battersea Park Road, with lunch on Cohen's corporate tab. Dead steam-table food and it took them thirty minutes to find an ice bucket for the retsina. Cohen works for Barris-Watford, who publish big, trendy "trade" paperbacks: illustrated histories of the neon sign, the pinball machine, the windup toys of Occupied Japan. I'd gone over to shoot a series of shoe ads; California girls with tanned legs and frisky Day-Glo jogging shoes had capered for me down the escalators of St. John's Wood and across the platforms of Tooting Bec. A lean and hungry young agency had decided that the mystery of London Transport would sell waffle-tread nylon runners. They decide; I shoot. And Cohen, whom I knew vaguely from the old days in New York, had invited me to lunch the day before I was due out of Heathrow. He brought along a very fashionably dressed young woman named

Dialta Downes, who was virtually chinless and evidently a noted pop-art historian. In retrospect, I see her walking in beside Cohen under a floating neon sign
that flashes THIS WAY LIES MADNESS in huge sans serif capitals.

Cohen introduced us and explained that Dialta was the prime mover behind
the latest Barris-Watford project, an illustrated history of what she called
"American Streamlined Moderne." Cohen called it "raygun Gothic." Their
working title was *The Airstream Futuropolis: The Tomorrow That Never Was.*

There's a British obsession with the more baroque elements of American pop
culture, something like the weird cowboys-and-Indians fetish of the West Ger-
mans or the aberrant French hunger for old Jerry Lewis films. In Dialta Downes
this manifested itself in a mania for a uniquely American form of architecture
that most Americans are scarcely aware of. At first I wasn't sure what she was
talking about, but gradually it began to dawn on me. I found myself remembering Sunday morning television in the Fifties.

Sometimes they'd run old eroded newsreels as filler on the local station.
You'd sit there with a peanut butter sandwich and a glass of milk, and a static-
ridden Hollywood baritone would tell you that there was A Flying Car in Your
Future. And three Detroit engineers would putter around with this big old Nash
with wings, and you'd see it rumbling furiously down some deserted Michigan
runway. You never actually saw it take off, but it flew away to Dialta Downes's
never-never land, true home of a generation of completely uninhibited techno-
philes. She was talking about those odds and ends of "futuristic" Thirties and
Forties architecture you pass daily in American cities without noticing: the movie
marquees ribbed to radiate some mysterious energy, the dime stores faced with
fluted aluminum, the chrome-tube chairs gathering dust in the lobbies of transient hotels. She saw these things as segments of a dreamworld, abandoned in the
uncaring present; she wanted me to photograph them for her.

The Thirties had seen the first generation of American industrial designers;
until the Thirties, all pencil sharpeners had looked like pencil sharpeners—your
basic Victorian mechanism, perhaps with a curlicue of decorative trim. After the
advent of the designers, some pencil sharpeners looked as though they'd been
put together in wind tunnels. For the most part, the change was only skin-deep;
under the streamlined chrome shell, you'd find the same Victorian mechanism.
Which made a certain kind of sense, because the most successful American
designers had been recruited from the ranks of Broadway theater designers. It
was all a stage set, a series of elaborate props for playing at living in the future.

Over coffee, Cohen produced a fat manila envelope full of glossies. I saw the
winged statues that guard the Hoover Dam, forty-foot concrete hood ornaments
leaning steadfastly into an imaginary hurricane. I saw a dozen shots of Frank
Lloyd Wright's Johnson Wax Building, juxtaposed with the covers of old *Amazing Stories* pulps, by an artist named Frank R. Paul; the employees of Johnson
Wax must have felt as though they were walking into one of Paul's spray-paint
pulp Utopias. Wright's building looked as though it had been designed for
people who wore white togas and Lucite sandals. I hesitated over one sketch of a
particularly grandiose prop-driven airliner, all wing, like a fat, symmetrical

boomerang with windows in unlikely places. Labeled arrows indicated the locations of the grand ballroom and two squash courts. It was dated 1936.

"This thing couldn't have flown . . . ?" I looked at Dialta Downes.

"Oh, no, quite impossible, even with those twelve giant props; but they loved the look, don't you see? New York to London in less than two days, first-class dining rooms, private cabins, sun decks, dancing to jazz in the evening . . . The designers were populists, you see; they were trying to give the public what it wanted. What the public wanted was the future."

I'd been in Burbank for three days, trying to suffuse a really dull-looking rocker with charisma, when I got the package from Cohen. It is possible to photograph what isn't there; it's damned hard to do, and consequently a very marketable talent. While I'm not bad at it, I'm not exactly the best, either, and this poor guy strained my Nikon's credibility. I got out depressed because I do like to do a good job, but not totally depressed, because I did make sure I'd gotten the check for the job, and I decided to restore myself with the sublime artiness of the Barris-Watford assignment. Cohen had sent me some books on Thirties design, more photos of streamlined buildings, and a list of Dialta Downes's fifty favorite examples of the style in California.

Architectural photography can involve a lot of waiting; the building becomes a kind of sundial, while you wait for a shadow to crawl away from a detail you want, or for the mass and balance of the structure to reveal itself in a certain way. While I was waiting, I thought of myself in Dialta Downes's America. When I isolated a few of the factory buildings on the ground glass of the Hasselblad, they came across with a kind of sinister totalitarian dignity, like the stadiums Albert Speer built for Hitler. But the rest of it was relentlessly tacky; ephemeral stuff extruded by the collective American subconscious of the Thirties, tending mostly to survive along depressing strips lined with dusty motels, mattress wholesalers, and small used-car lots. I went for the gas stations in a big way.

During the high point of the Downes Age, they put Ming the Merciless in charge of designing California gas stations. Favoring the architecture of his native Mongo, he cruised up and down the coast erecting raygun emplacements in white stucco. Lots of them featured superfluous central towers ringed with those strange radiator flanges that were a signature motif of the style and which made them look as though they might generate potent bursts of raw technological enthusiasm if you could only find the switch that turned them on. I shot one in San Jose an hour before the bulldozers arrived and drove right through the structural truth of plaster and lathing and cheap concrete.

"Think of it," Dialta Downes had said, "as a kind of alternate America: a 1980 that never happened. An architecture of broken dreams."

And that was my frame of mind as I made the stations of her convoluted socioarchitectural cross in my red Toyota—as I gradually tuned in to her image of a shadowy America-that-wasn't, of Coca-Cola plants like beached submarines, and fifth-run movie houses like the temples of some lost sect that had worshiped blue mirrors and geometry. And as I moved among these secret ruins, I found myself wondering what the inhabitants of that lost future would think of the world I lived in. The Thirties dreamed white marble and slipstream chrome, immortal crystal and burnished bronze, but the rockets on the covers of the Gernsback pulps had fallen on London in the dead of night, screaming. After the war, everyone had a car—no wings for it—and the promised superhighway to drive it down, so that the sky itself darkened, and the fumes ate the marble and pitted the miracle crystal . . .

And one day, on the outskirts of Bolinas, when I was setting up to shoot a particularly lavish example of Ming's martial architecture, I penetrated a fine membrane, a membrane of probability . . .

Ever so gently, I went over the Edge—

And looked up to see a twelve-engined thing like a bloated boomerang, all wing, thrumming its way east with an elephantine grace, so low that I could count the rivets in its dull silver skin, and hear—maybe—the echo of jazz.

I took it to Kihn. Merv Kihn, freelance journalist with an extensive line in Texas pterodactyls, redneck UFO contactées, bush-league Loch Ness monsters, and the Top Ten conspiracy theories in the loonier reaches of the American mass mind.

"It's good," said Kihn, polishing his yellow Polaroid shooting glasses on the hem of his Hawaiian shirt, "but it's not *mental*; lacks the true quill."

"But I saw it, Mervyn." We were seated poolside in brilliant Arizona sunlight. He was in Tucson waiting for a group of retired Las Vegas civil servants whose leader received messages from Them on her microwave oven. I'd driven all night and was feeling it.

"Of course you did. Of course you saw it. You've read my stuff; haven't you grasped my blanket solution to the UFO problem? It's simple, plain and country simple: people"—he settled the glasses carefully on his long hawk nose and fixed me with his best basilisk glare—"*see* . . . things. People see these things. Nothing's there, but people *see* them anyway. Because they need to, probably. You've read Jung, you should know the score . . . In your case, it's so obvious: You admit you were thinking about this crackpot architecture, having fantasies . . . Look, I'm sure you've taken your share of drugs, right? How many people survived the Sixties in California without having the odd hallucination? All those nights when you discovered that whole armies of Disney technicians had been employed to weave animated holograms of Egyptian hieroglyphs into the fabric of your jeans, say, or the times when—"

"But it wasn't like that."

"Of course not. It wasn't like that at all; it was 'in a setting of clear reality,' right? Everything normal, and then there's the monster, the mandala, the neon cigar. In your case, a giant Tom Swift airplane. It happens *all the time*. You aren't even crazy. You know that, don't you?" He fished a beer out of the battered foam cooler beside his deck chair.

"Last week I was in Virginia. Grayson County. I interviewed a sixteen-year-old girl who'd been assaulted by a *bar hade*."

"A what?"

"A bear head. The severed head of a bear. This *bar hade*, see, was floating around on its own little flying saucer, looked kind of like the hubcaps on cousin Wayne's vintage Caddy. Had red, glowing eyes like two cigar stubs and telescoping chrome antennas poking up behind its ears." He burped.

"It assaulted her? How?"

"You don't want to know; you're obviously impressionable. 'It was cold' "— he lapsed into his bad Southern accent—" 'and metallic.' It made electronic noises. Now that is the real thing, the straight goods from the mass unconscious, friend; that little girl is a witch. There's no place for her to function in this society. She'd have seen the devil if she hadn't been brought up on *The Bionic Woman* and all those *Star Trek* reruns. She is clued into the main vein. And she knows that it happened to her. I got out ten minutes before the heavy UFO boys showed up with the polygraph."

I must have looked pained, because he set his beer down carefully beside the cooler and sat up.

"If you want a classier explanation, I'd say you saw a semiotic ghost. All these contactee stories, for instance, are framed in a kind of sci-fi imagery that permeates our culture. I could buy aliens, but not aliens that look like Fifties' comic art. They're semiotic phantoms, bits of deep cultural imagery that have split off and taken on a life of their own, like the Jules Verne airships that those old Kansas farmers were always seeing. But you saw a different kind of ghost, that's all. That plane was part of the mass unconscious, once. You picked up on that, somehow. The important thing is not to worry about it."

I did worry about it, though.

Kihn combed his thinning blond hair and went off to hear what They had had to say over the radar range lately, and I drew the curtains in my room and lay down in air-conditioned darkness to worry about it. I was still worrying about it when I woke up. Kihn had left a note on my door; he was flying up north in a chartered plane to check out a cattle-mutilation rumor ("muties," he called them; another of his journalistic specialties).

I had a meal, showered, took a crumbling diet pill that had been kicking around in the bottom of my shaving kit for three years, and headed back to Los Angeles.

The speed limited my vision to the tunnel of the Toyota's headlights. The body could drive, I told myself, while the mind maintained. Maintained and stayed away from the weird peripheral window dressing of amphetamine and exhaustion, the spectral, luminous vegetation that grows out of the corners of the mind's eye along late-night highways. But the mind had its own ideas, and Kihn's opinion of what I was already thinking of as my "sighting" rattled endlessly through my head in a tight, lopsided orbit. Semiotic ghosts. Fragments of the Mass Dream, whirling past in the wind of my passage. Somehow this feedback-loop aggravated the diet pill, and the speed-vegetation along the road began to assume the colors of infrared satellite images, glowing shreds blown apart in the Toyota's slipstream.

I pulled over, then, and a half-dozen aluminum beer cans winked goodnight as I killed the headlights. I wondered what time it was in London, and tried to imagine Dialta Downes having breakfast in her Hampstead flat, surrounded by streamlined chrome figurines and books on American culture.

Desert nights in that country are enormous; the moon is closer. I watched the moon for a long time and decided that Kihn was right. The main thing was not to worry. All across the continent, daily, people who were more normal than I'd ever aspired to be saw giant birds, Bigfeet, flying oil refineries; they kept Kihn busy and solvent. Why should I be upset by a glimpse of the 1930s pop imagination loose over Bolinas? I decided to go to sleep, with nothing worse to worry about than rattlesnakes and cannibal hippies, safe amid the friendly roadside garbage of my own familiar continuum. In the morning I'd drive down to Nogales and photograph the old brothels, something I'd intended to do for years. The diet pill had given up.

The light woke me, and then the voices. The light came from somewhere behind me and threw shifting shadows inside the car. The voices were calm, indistinct, male and female, engaged in conversation.

My neck was stiff and my eyeballs felt gritty in their sockets. My leg had gone to sleep, pressed against the steering wheel. I fumbled for my glasses in the pocket of my work shirt and finally got them on.

Then I looked behind me and saw the city.

The books on Thirties design were in the trunk; one of them contained sketches of an idealized city that drew on *Metropolis* and *Things to Come*, but squared everything, soaring up through an architect's perfect clouds to zeppelin docks and mad neon spires. That city was a scale model of the one that rose behind me. Spire stood on spire in gleaming ziggurat steps that climbed to a central golden temple tower ringed with the crazy radiator flanges of the Mongo gas stations. You could hide the Empire State Building in the smallest of those towers. Roads of crystal soared between the spires, crossed and recrossed by smooth silver shapes like beads of running mercury. The air was thick with ships: giant wing-liners, little darting silver things (sometimes one of the quicksilver shapes from the sky bridges rose gracefully into the air and flew up to join the dance), mile-long blimps, hovering dragonfly things that were gyrocopters . . .

I closed my eyes tight and swung around in the seat. When I opened them, I willed myself to see the mileage meter, the pale road dust on the black plastic dashboard, the overflowing ashtray.

"Amphetamine psychosis," I said. I opened my eyes. The dash was still there, the dust, the crushed filter tips. Very carefully, without moving my head, I turned the headlights on.

And saw them.

They were blond. They were standing beside their car, an aluminum avocado with a central shark-fin rudder jutting up from its spine and smooth black tires like a child's toy. He had his arm around her waist and was gesturing toward the city. They were both in white: loose clothing, bare legs, spotless white sun shoes. Neither of them seemed aware of the beams of my headlights. He was saying something wise and strong, and she was nodding, and suddenly I was frightened, frightened in an entirely different way. Sanity had ceased to be an issue; I knew, somehow, that the city behind me was Tucson—a dream Tucson thrown up out of the collective yearning of an era. That it was real, entirely real. But the couple in front of me lived in it, and they frightened me.

They were the children of Dialta Downes's '80-that-wasn't; they were Heirs to the Dream. They were white, blond, and they probably had blue eyes. They were American. Dialta had said that the Future had come to America first, but had finally passed it by. But not here, in the heart of the Dream. Here, we'd gone on and on, in a dream logic that knew nothing of pollution, the finite bounds of fossil fuel, or foreign wars it was possible to lose. They were smug, happy, and utterly content with themselves and their world. And in the Dream, it was *their* world.

Behind me, the illuminated city: Searchlights swept the sky for the sheer joy of it. I imagined them thronging the plazas of white marble, orderly and alert, their bright eyes shining with enthusiasm for their floodlit avenues and silver cars.

It had all the sinister fruitiness of Hitler Youth propaganda.

I put the car in gear and drove forward slowly, until the bumper was within three feet of them. They still hadn't seen me. I rolled the window down and listened to what the man was saying. His words were bright and hollow as the pitch in some chamber of commerce brochure, and I knew that he believed in them absolutely.

"John," I heard the woman say, "we've forgotten to take our food pills." She clicked two bright wafers from a thing on her belt and passed one to him. I backed onto the highway and headed for Los Angeles, wincing and shaking my head.

I phoned Kihn from a gas station. A new one, in bad Spanish Modern. He was back from his expedition and didn't seem to mind the call.

"Yeah, that is a weird one. Did you try to get any pictures? Not that they ever come out, but it adds an interesting *frisson* to your story, not having the pictures turn out. . . ."

But what should I do?

"Watch lots of television, particularly game shows and soaps. Go to porn movies. Ever see *Nazi Love Motel*? They've got it on cable, here. Really awful. Just what you need."

What was he talking about?

"Quit yelling and listen to me. I'm letting you in on a trade secret: Really bad media can exorcize your semiotic ghosts. If it keeps the saucer people off my back, it can keep these Art Deco futuroids off yours. Try it. What have you got to lose?"

Then he begged off, pleading an early-morning date with the Elect.

"The who?"

"These oldsters from Vegas; the ones with the microwaves."

I considered putting a collect call through to London, getting Cohen at Barris-Watford and telling him his photographer was checked out for a protracted season in the Twilight Zone. In the end, I let a machine mix me a really impossible cup of black coffee and climbed back into the Toyota for the haul to Los Angeles.

Los Angeles was a bad idea, and I spent two weeks there. It was prime Downes country; too much of the Dream there, and too many fragments of the Dream waiting to snare me. I nearly wrecked the car on a stretch of overpass near Disneyland when the road fanned out like an origami trick and left me swerving through a dozen minilanes of whizzing chrome teardrops with shark fins. Even worse, Hollywood was full of people who looked too much like the couple I'd seen in Arizona. I hired an Italian director who was making ends meet doing darkroom work and installing patio decks around swimming pools until his ship came in; he made prints of all the negatives I'd accumulated on the Downes job. I didn't want to look at the stuff myself. It didn't seem to bother Leonardo, though, and when he was finished I checked the prints, riffling through them like a deck of cards, sealed them up, and sent them air freight to London. Then I took a taxi to a theater that was showing *Nazi Love Motel* and kept my eyes shut all the way.

Cohen's congratulatory wire was forwarded to me in San Francisco a week later. Dialta had loved the pictures. He admired the way I'd "really gotten into it," and looked forward to working with me again. That afternoon I spotted a flying wing over Castro Street, but there was something tenuous about it, as if it were only half there. I rushed to the nearest newsstand and gathered up as much as I could find on the petroleum crisis and the nuclear energy hazard. I'd just decided to buy a plane ticket for New York.

"Hell of a world we live in, huh?" The proprietor was a thin black man with bad teeth and an obvious wig. I nodded, fishing in my jeans for change, anxious to find a park bench where I could submerge myself in hard evidence of the human near-dystopia we live in. "But it could be worse, huh?"

"That's right," I said, "or even worse, it could be perfect."

He watched me as I headed down the street with my little bundle of condensed catastrophe.

SELF

The notion of identity—and the many and heated discussions around it—has long been explored through fiction. Cyberpunk is no exception. Of the many different relationships that constitute human affairs, the self—how we see, perceive, and define ourselves—is perhaps the most complex. Until we know who we are, how can we understand our place in the world?

Cyberpunk has always understood that technology has the power to affect even this most intimate and individual relationship. Who we are—who we *think* we are—is, like every other social construct, mediated by technology.

In the early days of the genre, cyberpunk fiction was rightfully fascinated by the idea of our virtual selves. The existence of cyberspace presupposes our cyber-selves. Is our online presence a projection? A twin? A shadow? What is the tenuous connection between these planes—are there physical or moral repercussions for how our digital self acts in their world? Decades later, we are no closer to answering the questions that cyberpunk was the first to ask.

Cyberpunk also looked at technology's broader potential for personal transformation: how much it can change us; what we can become; what we can and can't leave behind. Modern understanding of identity is that it is a layered and dynamic concept. Humans are not one thing. Who we are can shift depending on the context we're in, the company we keep, the choices we make, or that are made for us. Cyberpunk fiction is a way of exploring the tension between the fluidity of identity (lubricated by technology) and the immutable essence of what makes us human.

This section opens with James Tiptree Jr.'s excellent "The Girl Who Was Plugged In" (1973). In terms of vocabulary and technology, it sets the tone for much of the cyberpunk fiction that would follow. It also raises questions about the impact of virtuality on identity: Will it be liberating to "depart" ourselves for another body, or is there something damaging about severing that connection? What harm is caused by a society that makes that possible or, in fact, encourages it?

This discussion of freedom (and the "curse" of being anchored to a physical presence) is found through many of the stories in this section. Pat Cadigan's "Pretty Boy Crossover" (1986) describes a world where physical beauty is upheld to the point that the body is itself made the ultimate sacrifice. The criminals of John Shirley's "Wolves of the Plateau" (1988) use the power of the virtual plane to free themselves and become something more. In "The World as We Know It" (1992), George Effinger's sleuth, Marîd Audran, encounters communities that prefer virtual worlds to physical ones, despite the high cost of maintaining the suspension of disbelief. Gwyneth Jones's "Red Sonja and Lessingham in Dreamland" (1996) uses the virtual world as a form of psychotherapy: online identities allowing repressed appetites to run free.

Once plugged in to the augmented world of Jean-Marc Ligny's "RealLife 3.0" (2014) (appearing here for the first time in English), our protagonist experiences reality and the virtual fantasy side-by-side, with predictable dispiriting results.

In Aleš Kot's "A Life of Its Own" (2019), the virtual becomes a cage, with those same dreams used to keep you entombed (thanks, in no small part, to the fine print). Kot's story is notable because at no point is the physical world preferable: the grievance is the concept of being trapped, not the prison itself.

Charles Stross's madcap satire, "Lobsters" (2001) features a MacGuffin (or is it?) based on the profit potential of digital crustaceans. Surrounding that central conceit is a whirlwind of influences: our protagonist attempting to maintain his own self-identity while being buffeted by political, financial, technological, and romantic winds.

In Sparkletown, the setting of Jeff Noon's "Ghost Codes of Sparkletown" (2011), the self can be endangered by cultural ghosts: fragments of music that float through a haunted graveyard of burned-out CPUs.*

J. P. Smythe's "The Infinite Eye" (2017) is a story that descends in a direct line from Tiptree's, again describing a corporate world where the desperate sell themselves to stay afloat. In "The Girl Who Was Plugged In," our protagonist receives an ecstatic reward, and a chance to live the fantasy. In "The Infinite Eye," they merely receive a paycheck (and, presumably, no health care). In the final story in this section, qntm's "Lena" (2021), a man is blessed/cursed with virtual immortality, give or take some messy version control.

---

* Jeff Noon's story was first composed on Twitter, and has since been reincarnated in various forms, including as the inspiration for the album *Ghost Codes* by The Forgetting Room. This is the story's first appearance in this "holistic" form.

The fluidity of the self is not solely contained in the virtual realm. Anna, in Richard Kadrey's "Surfing the Khumbu" (2002), is "living in machines and flesh at the same time," a scenario that will leave the reader quivering in both fear and jealousy. In Cat Rambo's "Memories of Moments, Bright as Falling Stars" (2006), technology—in this case "memory," both biological and computational—is embedded in the body, both a resource and a drug.

Karen Heuler's "The Completely Rechargeable Man" (2008) reads more like a fairy tale than your average cyberpunk short. It describes a lonely individual whose life is so technological that he has become a form of entertainment. The titular character in Christian Kirtchev's "File: The Death of Designer D." (2009) is the source of mystery on several levels. Why did she die? What was she fighting against? And who was she in the first place? The singular letters of "D." and her investigator, "K." are reminiscent of Kafka, as D. battles to have an identity in a world of "gray lemmings."

Transhuman aspiration runs amok in many of these stories. Jean Rabe's "Better Than" (2010) is the tale of a lost soul, addicted to self-transformation, with an identity so degraded as to be totally lost.* In Alvaro Zinos-Amaro's "wysiomg" (2016), we also have transient, fragmented identities, with biology and identity both subsumed into an anarchistic internet culture.

"The Real You™" (2018) by Molly Tanzer takes the control of the self to its ultimate conclusion with "Refractin," a treatment in which your face is completely removed. Tanzer's story is focused less on the perplexing how, but on the why—what could compel someone to remove their identity entirely, and what would be the repercussions of living faceless in society?

Several of the stories in this section are devoted to the intersection of the self and destruction. Not self-destruction, per se (although that is often the case), but stories that explore our slavish, one-sided devotion to technology that only exists to harm us. Sunny Moraine's "I Tell Thee All, I Can No More" (2013) is a tale of truly forbidden love, centered around a romance that crosses all possible boundaries. It is, in the best cyberpunk tradition, a story that simply should not work, but Moraine somehow spins beauty out of nightmare, while never letting us forget the true horror beneath.

"Four Tons Too Late" (2014) and "Helicopter Story" (2020) are also about a savage blend of human and machine, as well as the subservience of the self to the military-industrial complex. In the former, K. C. Alexander describes the psychological toll on a new type of veteran. They have been, in every sense, a "good soldier". But what is the reward for loyalty to an inherently callous system? In "Helicopter Story," Isabel Fall reclaims a transphobic meme and uses it as the vehicle to describe a society that suppresses gender identity while simultaneously

---

* Cyberpunk fiction exists as much in movies, television, music, and games as in literature. Jean Rabe's story is one of two in this book that originated in the setting of FASA's *Shadowrun*, a long-established role-playing game that mixes fantasy tropes and cyberpunk, and has done much to introduce new audiences to the latter.

worshiping at the altar of hyper-militarized machismo.* The story asks "Have you ever been exultant?" and then brutally condemns a world where the only way to answer this question positively is by transforming yourself into a weapon of war.

The capacity of technology to make new selves is a fascination of cyberpunk: the ability to create an identity, or even a living being, out of whole cloth. Cyberpunk's fixation on androids could be argued away as another aesthetic trope (thanks, *Blade Runner*), but it is a natural extension of the genre's discussion of the virtual self and transhumanism. At what point does technology allow us to imitate the self so precisely that it becomes a new self of its own? And does that new being have a soul, or even the right to exist?

Phillip Mann's "An Old-Fashioned Story" (1989) is a slice-of-life tale (apologies for the pun), in which a couple set about fixing their household android and, in the process, reveal a great deal about themselves.

In "The Girl Hero's Mirror Says He's Not the One" (2007), Justina Robson's Girl Hero inhabits a completely fabricated identity that has been imposed upon her. But despite being forced into a specific role (or Role), she owns it, and takes agency over the illusion.

Lavie Tidhar's "Choosing Faces" (2012) is one of the author's trademark satires, featuring a particularly famous martial artist in his greatest battle(s) yet. It is hilarious, and reminiscent of Warhol with the way it addresses the tragic erosion of the self that stems from celebrity culture.

Neon Yang's "Patterns of a Murmuration, in Billions of Data Points" (2014) is one of the few stories in this book with a nonhuman protagonist—in this case, an AI swarm that collectively takes action to solve the death of their "mother." As compelling as our hive-mind protagonist is, this story uses them as the lens through which we can watch the fumblings of human behavior, as the humans attempt to wield this technology to their own advantage.

Every other dimension of human affairs is external—the author has the advantage of distance. Writing about the self, even a fictional self, is necessarily personal. Even blurred through the lens of fiction, there's an emotional connection that's unavoidable. Writing about space voyages or football is undeniably complex, but lacks the same closeness. The interest is in what's happening out *there*: in the void, on the pitch. These cyberpunk stories, however, are intimate. They are not about the out there, but the right here. Whatever is happening with technology is inescapable; in our face. It is uncomfortable. We lack the distance to have perspective, or to make objective decisions. That is a reflection of cyberpunk's central theme: despite our best (or worst) efforts to suppress it, we are inevitably, irreversibly, irrationally human.

---

* The meme—"I sexually identify as an attack helicopter"— emerged on Reddit and 4chan a few years before this story was first published, and was used to dismiss the notion of nonbinary gender identity and the principle of self-identification. This story not only makes sense without the original context but, rather gratifyingly, will long outlive it.

JAMES TIPTREE JR.

THE GIRL WHO
WAS PLUGGED IN

(1973)

LISTEN, zombie. Believe me. What I could tell you—you with your silly hands leaking sweat on your growth-stocks portfolio. One-ten lousy hacks of AT&T on twenty-point margin and you think you're Evel Knievel. AT&T? You doubleknit dummy, how I'd love to show you something.

Look, dead daddy, I'd say. See for instance that rotten girl?

In the crowd over there, that one gaping at her gods. One rotten girl in the city of the future. (That's what I said.) Watch.

She's jammed among bodies, craning and peering with her soul yearning out of her eyeballs. Love! Oo-ooh, love them! Her gods are coming out of a store called Body East. Three youngbloods, larking along loverly. Dressed like simple street-people but . . . smashing. See their great eyes swivel above their nose-filters, their hands lift shyly, their inhumanly tender lips melt? The crowd moans. Love! This whole boiling megacity, this whole fun future world loves its gods.

You don't believe gods, dad? Wait. Whatever turns you on, there's a god in the future for you, custom-made. Listen to this mob. "I touched His foot! Ow-oow, I *touched* Him!"

Even the people in the GTX tower up there love the gods—in their own way and for their own reasons.

The funky girl on the street, she just loves. Grooving on their beautiful lives, their mysterioso problems. No one ever told her about mortals who love a god and end up as a tree or a sighing sound. In a million years it'd never occur to her that her gods might love her back.

She's squashed against the wall now as the godlings come by. They move in a clear space. A holocam bobs above, but its shadow never falls on them. The store display-screens are magically clear of bodies as the gods glance in and a beggar underfoot is suddenly alone. They give him a token. "Aaaaah!" goes the crowd.

Now one of them flashes some wild new kind of timer and they all trot to catch a shuttle, just like people. The shuttle stops for them—more magic. The crowd sighs, closing back. The gods are gone.

(In a room far from—but not unconnected to—the GTX tower a molecular flipflop closes too, and three account tapes spin.)

Our girl is still stuck by the wall while guards and holocam equipment pull away. The adoration's fading from her face. That's good, because now you can see she's the ugly of the world. A tall monument to pituitary dystrophy. No surgeon would touch her. When she smiles, her jaw—it's half purple—almost bites her left eye out. She's also quite young, but who could care?

The crowd is pushing her along now, treating you to glimpses of her jumbled torso, her mismatched legs. At the corner she strains to send one last fond spasm after the godlings' shuttle. Then her face reverts to its usual expression of dim pain and she lurches onto the moving walkway, stumbling into people. The walkway junctions with another. She crosses, trips, and collides with the casualty rail. Finally she comes out into a little bare place called a park. The sportshow is working, a basketball game in three-di is going on right overhead. But all she does is squeeze onto a bench and huddle there while a ghostly free-throw goes by her ear.

After that nothing at all happens except a few furtive hand-mouth gestures which don't even interest her bench mates. But you're curious about the city? So ordinary after all, in the *future*?

Ah, there's plenty to swing with here—and it's not all that *far* in the future, dad. But pass up the sci-fi stuff for now, like for instance the holovision technology that's put TV and radio in museums. Or the worldwide carrier field bouncing down from satellites, controlling communication and transport systems all over the globe. That was a spin-off from asteroid mining, pass it by. We're watching that girl.

I'll give you just one goodie. Maybe you noticed on the sportshow or the streets? No commercials. No ads.

That's right. *No ads*. An eyeballer for you.

Look around. Not a billboard, sign, slogan, jingle, sky-write, blurb, sublimflash, in this whole fun world. Brand names? Only in those ticky little peep-screens on the stores, and you could hardly call that advertising. How does that finger you?

Think about it. That girl is still sitting there.

She's parked right under the base of the GTX tower, as a matter of fact. Look way up and you can see the sparkles from the bubble on top, up there among the domes of godland. Inside that bubble is a boardroom. Neat bronze shield on the door: Global Transmissions Corporation—not that that means anything.

I happen to know there are six people in that room. Five of them technically male, and the sixth isn't easily thought of as a mother. They are absolutely unremarkable. Those faces were seen once at their nuptials and will show again in their obituaries and impress nobody either time. If you're looking for the secret Big Blue Meanies of the world, forget it. I know. Zen, do I know! Flesh? Power? Glory? You'd horrify them.

What *they* do like up there is to have things orderly, especially their communications. You could say they've dedicated their lives to that, to freeing the world from garble. Their nightmares are about hemorrhages of information; channels screwed up, plans misimplemented, garble creeping in. Their gigantic wealth only worries them, it keeps opening new vistas of disorder. Luxury? They wear what their tailors put on them, eat what their cooks serve them. See that old boy there—his name is Isham—he's sipping water and frowning as he listens to a databall. The water was prescribed by his medistaff. It tastes awful. The databall also contains a disquieting message about his son, Paul.

But it's time to go back down, far below to our girl. Look!

She's toppled over sprawling on the ground.

A tepid commotion ensues among the bystanders. The consensus is she's dead, which she disproves by bubbling a little. And presently she's taken away by one of the superb ambulances of the future, which are a real improvement over ours when one happens to be around.

At the local bellevue the usual things are done by the usual team of clowns aided by a saintly mop-pusher. Our girl revives enough to answer the questionnaire without which you can't die, even in the future. Finally she's cast up, a pumped-out hulk on a cot in the long, dim ward.

Again nothing happens for a while except that her eyes leak a little from the understandable disappointment of finding herself still alive.

But somewhere one GTX computer has been tickling another, and toward midnight something does happen. First comes an attendant who pulls screens around her. Then a man in a business doublet comes daintily down the ward. He motions the attendant to strip off the sheet and go.

The groggy girl-brute heaves up, big hands clutching at body parts you'd pay not to see.

"Burke? P. Burke, is that your name?"

"Y-yes." Croak. "Are you . . . policeman?"

"No. They'll be along shortly, I expect. Public suicide's a felony."

". . . I'm sorry."

He has a 'corder in his hand. "No family, right?"

"No."

"You're seventeen. One year city college. What did you study?"

"La—languages."

"H'mm. Say something."

Unintelligible rasp.

He studies her. Seen close, he's not so elegant. Errand-boy type.

"Why did you try to kill yourself?"

15

She stares at him with dead-rat dignity, hauling up the gray sheet. Give him a point, he doesn't ask twice.

"Tell me, did you see Breath this afternoon?"

Dead as she nearly is, that ghastly love-look wells up. Breath is the three young gods, a loser's cult. Give the man another point, he interprets her expression.

"How would you like to meet them?"

The girl's eyes bug out grotesquely.

"I have a job for someone like you. It's hard work. If you did well you'd be meeting Breath and stars like that all the time."

Is he insane? She's deciding she really did die.

"But it means you never see anybody you know again. Never, *ever*. You will be legally dead. Even the police won't know. Do you want to try?"

It all has to be repeated while her great jaw slowly sets. *Show me the fire I walk through.* Finally P. Burke's prints are in his 'corder, the man holding up the big rancid girl-body without a sign of distaste. It makes you wonder what else he does.

And then—*the magic*. Sudden silent trot of litterbearers tucking P. Burke into something quite different from a bellevue stretcher, the oiled slide into the daddy of all luxury ambulances—real flowers in that holder!—and the long jarless rush to nowhere. Nowhere is warm and gleaming and kind with nurses. (Where did you hear that money can't buy genuine kindness?) And clean clouds folding P. Burke into bewildered sleep.

. . . Sleep which merges into feedings and washings and more sleeps, into drowsy moments of afternoon where midnight should be, and gentle business-like voices and friendly (but very few) faces, and endless painless hyposprays and peculiar numbnesses. And later comes the steadying rhythm of days and nights, and a quickening which P. Burke doesn't identify as health, but only knows that the fungus place in her armpit is gone. And then she's up and following those few new faces with growing trust, first tottering, then walking strongly, all better now, clumping down the short hall to the tests, tests, tests, and the other things.

And here is our girl, looking—

If possible, worse than before. (You thought this was Cinderella transistorized?)

The disimprovement in her looks comes from the electrode jacks peeping out of her sparse hair, and there are other meldings of flesh and metal. On the other hand, that collar and spinal plate are really an asset; you won't miss seeing that neck.

P. Burke is ready for training in her new job.

The training takes place in her suite and is exactly what you'd call a charm course. How to walk, sit, eat, speak, blow her nose, how to stumble, to urinate, to hiccup—*deliciously*. How to make each nose-blow or shrug delightfully, subtly, different from any ever spooled before. As the man said, it's hard work.

But P. Burke proves apt. Somewhere in that horrible body is a gazelle, a houri, who would have been buried forever without this crazy chance. See the ugly duckling go!

Only it isn't precisely P. Burke who's stepping, laughing, shaking out her shining hair. How could it be? P. Burke is doing it all right, but she's doing it through something. The something is to all appearances a live girl. (You were warned, this is the *future*.)

When they first open the big cryocase and show her her new body, she says just one word. Staring, gulping, "How?"

Simple, really. Watch P. Burke in her sack and scuffs stump down the hall beside Joe, the man who supervises the technical part of her training. Joe doesn't mind P. Burke's looks, he hasn't noticed them. To Joe, system matrices are beautiful.

They go into a dim room containing a huge cabinet like a one-man sauna and a console for Joe. The room has a glass wall that's all dark now. And just for your information, the whole shebang is five hundred feet underground near what used to be Carbondale, PA.

Joe opens the sauna cabinet like a big clamshell standing on end with a lot of funny business inside. Our girl shucks her shift and walks into it bare, totally unembarrassed. *Eager.* She settles in face-forward, butting jacks into sockets. Joe closes it carefully onto her humpback. Clunk. She can't see in there or hear or move. She hates this minute. But how she loves what comes next!

Joe's at his console, and the lights on the other side of the glass wall come up. A room is on the other side, all fluff and kicky bits, a girly bedroom. In the bed is a small mound of silk with a rope of yellow hair hanging out.

The sheet stirs and gets whammed back flat.

Sitting up in the bed is the darlingest girl child you've *ever* seen. She quivers—porno for angels. She sticks both her little arms straight up, flips her hair, looks around full of sleepy pazazz. Then she can't resist rubbing her hands down over her minibreasts and belly. Because, you see, it's the god-awful P. Burke who is sitting there hugging her perfect girl-body, looking at you out of delighted eyes.

Then the kitten hops out of bed and crashes flat on the floor.

From the sauna in the dim room comes a strangled noise. P. Burke, trying to rub her wired-up elbow, is suddenly smothered in *two* bodies, electrodes jerking in her flesh. Joe juggles inputs, crooning into his mike. The flurry passes; it's all right.

In the lighted room the elf gets up, casts a cute glare at the glass wall, and goes into a transparent cubicle. A bathroom, what else? She's a live girl, and live girls have to go to the bathroom after a night's sleep even if their brains are in a sauna cabinet in the next room. And P. Burke isn't in that cabinet, she's in the bathroom. Perfectly simple, if you have the glue for that closed training circuit that's letting her run her neural system by remote control.

Now let's get one thing clear. P. Burke does not *feel* her brain is in the sauna room, she feels she's in that sweet little body. When you wash your hands, do you feel the water is running on your brain? Of course not. You feel the water on your hand, although the "feeling" is actually a potential-pattern flickering over the electrochemical jelly between your ears. And it's delivered there via the long circuits from your hands. Just so, P. Burke's brain in the cabinet feels the water on her hands in the bathroom. The fact that the signals have jumped across space on the way in makes no difference at all. If you want the jargon, it's known as eccentric projection or sensory reference and you've done it all your life. Clear?

Time to leave the honeypot to her toilet training—she's made a booboo with the toothbrush, because P. Burke can't get used to what she sees in the mirror—

But wait, you say. Where did that girl-body come from?

P. Burke asks that too, dragging out the words.

"They grow 'em," Joe tells her. He couldn't care less about the flesh department. "PDs. Placental decanters. Modified embryos, see? Fit the control implants in later. Without a Remote Operator it's just a vegetable. Look at the feet—no callus at all." (He knows because they told him.)

"Oh . . . oh, she's incredible . . ."

"Yeah, a neat job. Want to try walking-talking mode today? You're coming on fast."

And she is. Joe's reports and the reports from the nurse and the doctor and style man go to a bushy man upstairs who is some kind of medical cybertech but mostly a project administrator. His reports in turn go—to the GTX boardroom? Certainly not, did you think this is *a big* thing? His reports just go up. The point is, they're green, very green. P. Burke promises well.

So the bushy man—Dr. Tesla—has procedures to initiate. The little kitten's dossier in the Central Data Bank, for instance. Purely routine. And the phase-in schedule which will put her on the scene. This is simple: a small exposure in an off-network holoshow.

Next he has to line out the event which will fund and target her. That takes budget meetings, clearances, coordinations. The Burke project begins to recruit and grow. And there's the messy business of the name, which always gives Dr. Tesla an acute pain in the bush.

The name comes out weird, when it's suddenly discovered that Burke's "P." stands for "Philadelphia." Philadelphia? The astrologer grooves on it. Joe thinks it would help identification. The semantics girl references *brotherly love, Liberty Bell, main line, low teratogenesis*, blah-blah. Nicknames Philly? Pala? Pooty? Delphi? Is it good, bad? Finally "Delphi" is gingerly declared goodo. ("Burke" is replaced by something nobody remembers.)

Coming along now. We're at the official checkout down in the underground suite, which is as far as the training circuits reach. The bushy Dr. Tesla is there, braced by two budgetary types and a quiet fatherly man whom he handles like hot plasma.

Joe swings the door wide and she steps shyly in.

Their little Delphi, fifteen and flawless.

Tesla introduces her around. She's child-solemn, a beautiful baby to whom something so wonderful has happened you can feel the tingles. She doesn't smile, she . . . brims. That brimming joy is all that shows of P. Burke, the forgotten hulk in the sauna next door. But P. Burke doesn't know she's alive—it's Delphi who lives, every warm inch of her.

One of the budget types lets go a libidinous snuffle and freezes. The fatherly man, whose name is Mr. Cantle, clears his throat.

"Well, young lady, are you ready to go to work?"

"Yes, sir," gravely from the elf.

"We'll see. Has anybody told you what you're going to do for us?"

"No, sir." Joe and Tesla exhale quietly.

"Good." He eyes her, probing for the blind brain in the room next door. "Do you know what *advertising* is?"

He's talking dirty, hitting to shock. Delphi's *eyes* widen and her little chin goes up. Joe is in ecstasy at the complex expressions P. Burke is getting through. Mr. Cantle waits.

"It's, well, it's when they used to tell people to buy things." She swallows. "It's not allowed."

"That's right." Mr. Cantle leans back, grave. "Advertising as it used to be is against the law. *A display other than the legitimate use of the product, intended to promote its sale.* In former times every manufacturer was free to tout his wares any way, place, or time he could afford. All the media and most of the landscape was taken up with extravagant competing displays. The thing became uneconomic. The public rebelled. Since the so-called Huckster Act sellers have been restrained to, I quote, displays in or on the product itself, visible during its legitimate use or in on-premises sales." Mr. Cantle leans forward. "Now tell me, Delphi, why do people buy one product rather than another?"

"Well . . ." Enchanting puzzlement from Delphi. "They, um, they see them and like them, or they hear about them from somebody?" (Touch of P. Burke there; she didn't say, from a friend.)

"Partly. Why did *you* buy your particular body-lift?"

"I never had a body-lift, sir."

Mr. Cantle frowns; what gutters do they drag for these Remotes?

"Well, what brand of water do you drink?"

"Just what was in the faucet, sir," says Delphi humbly. "I—I did try to boil it—"

"Good god." He scowls; Tesla stiffens. "Well, what did you boil it in? A cooker?"

The shining yellow head nods.

"What *brand* of cooker did you buy?"

"I didn't buy it, sir," says frightened P. Burke through Delphi's lips. "But—I know the best kind! Ananga has a Burnbabi. I saw the name when she—"

"Exactly!" Cantle's fatherly beam comes back strong; the Burnbabi account is a strong one, too. "You saw Ananga using one so you thought it must be good, eh? And it is good, or a great human being like Ananga wouldn't be using it. Absolutely right. And now, Delphi, you know what you're going to be doing for us. You're going to show some products. Doesn't sound very hard, does it?"

"Oh, no, sir . . ." Baffled child's stare; Joe gloats.

"And you must never, *never* tell anyone what you're doing." Cantle's eyes bore for the brain behind this seductive child.

"You're wondering why we ask you to do this, naturally. There's a very serious reason. All those products people use, foods and healthaids and cookers and cleaners and clothes and cars—they're all made by *people*. Somebody put in years of hard work designing and making them. A man comes up with a fine new idea for a better product. He has to get a factory and machinery, and hire workmen. Now. What happens if people have no way of hearing about his product? Word of mouth is far too slow and unreliable. Nobody might ever stumble onto his new product or find out how good it was, right? And then he and all the people who worked for him—they'd go bankrupt, right? So, Delphi, there has to be *some way* that large numbers of people can get a look at a good new product, right? How? By letting people see you using it. You're giving that man a chance."

Delphi's little head is nodding in happy relief.

"Yes, sir, I do see now—but sir, it seems so sensible, why don't they let you—"

Cantle smiles sadly.

"It's an overreaction, my dear. History goes by swings. People overreact and pass harsh unrealistic laws which attempt to stamp out an essential social process. When this happens, the people who understand have to carry on as best they can until the pendulum swings back." He sighs. "The Huckster Laws are bad, inhuman laws, Delphi, despite their good intent. If they were strictly observed they would wreak havoc. Our economy, our society, would be cruelly destroyed. We'd be back in caves!" His inner fire is showing; if the Huckster Laws were strictly enforced he'd be back punching a databank.

"It's our duty, Delphi. Our solemn social duty. We are not breaking the law. You will be using the product. But people wouldn't understand, if they knew. They would become upset just as you did. So you must be very, very careful not to mention any of this to anybody."

(And somebody will be very, very carefully monitoring Delphi's speech circuits.)

"Now we're all straight, aren't we? Little Delphi here"—he is speaking to the invisible creature next door—"little Delphi is going to live a wonderful, exciting life. She's going to be a girl people watch. And she's going to be using fine products people will be glad to know about and helping the good people who make them. Yours will be a genuine social contribution." He keys up his pitch; the creature in there must be older.

Delphi digests this with ravishing gravity.

"But sir, how do I—?"

"Don't worry about a thing. You'll have people behind you whose job it is to select the most worthy products for you to use. Your job is just to do as they say. They'll show you what outfits to wear to parties, what suncars and viewers to buy, and so on. That's all you have to do."

Parties—clothes—suncars! Delphi's pink mouth opens. In P. Burke's starved seventeen-year-old head the ethics of product sponsorship float far away.

"Now tell me in your own words what your job is, Delphi."

"Yes, sir. I—I'm to go to parties and buy things and use them as they tell me, to help the people who work in factories."

"And what did I say was so important?"

"Oh—I shouldn't let anybody know, about the things."

"Right." Mr. Cantle has another paragraph he uses when the subject shows, well, immaturity. But he can sense only eagerness here. Good. He doesn't really enjoy the other speech.

"It's a lucky girl who can have all the fun she wants while doing good for others, isn't it?" He beams around. There's a prompt shuffling of chairs. Clearly this one is go.

Joe leads her out, grinning. The poor fool thinks they're admiring her coordination.

It's out into the world for Delphi now, and at this point the up-channels get used. On the administrative side account schedules are opened, subprojects activated. On the technical side the reserved bandwidth is cleared. (That carrier field, remember?) A new name is waiting for Delphi, a name she'll never hear. It's a long string of binaries which have been quietly cycling in a GTX tank ever since a certain Beautiful Person didn't wake up.

The name winks out of cycle, dances from pulses into modulations of modulations, whizzes through phasing, and shoots into a giga-band beam racing up to a synchronous satellite poised over Guatemala. From there the beam pours twenty thousand miles back to Earth again, forming an all-pervasive field of structured energics supplying tuned demand-points all over the CanAm quadrant.

With that field, if you have the right credit rating, you can sit at a GTX console and operate an ore extractor in Brazil. Or—if you have some simple credentials like being able to walk on water—you could shoot a spool into the network holocam shows running day and night in every home and dorm and rec site. Or you could create a continentwide traffic jam. Is it any wonder GTX guards those inputs like a sacred trust?

Delphi's "name" appears as a tiny analyzable nonredundancy in the flux, and she'd be very proud if she knew about it. It would strike P. Burke as magic; P. Burke never even understood robotcars. But Delphi is in no sense a robot. Call her a waldo if you must. The fact is she's just a girl, a real-live girl with her brain in an unusual place. A simple real-time on-line system with plenty of bit-rate—even as you and you.

The point of all this hardware, which isn't very much hardware in this society, is so Delphi can walk out of that underground suite, a mobile demand-point draining an omnipresent fieldform. And she does—eighty-nine pounds of tender girl flesh and blood with a few metallic components, stepping out into the sunlight to be taken to her new life. A girl, with everything going for her including a meditech escort. Walking lovely, stopping to widen her eyes at the big antennae system overhead.

The mere fact that something called P. Burke is left behind down underground has no bearing at all. P. Burke is totally un-self-aware and happy as a clam in its shell. (Her bed has been moved into the waldo cabinet room now.) And P. Burke isn't in the cabinet; P. Burke is climbing out of an airvan in a fabulous Colorado beef preserve, and her name is Delphi. Delphi is looking at live Charolais steers and live cottonwoods and aspens gold against the blue smog and stepping over live grass to be welcomed by the reserve super's wife.

The super's wife is looking forward to a visit from Delphi and her friends, and by a happy coincidence there's a holocam outfit here doing a piece for the nature nuts.

You could write the script yourself now, while Delphi learns a few rules about structural interferences and how to handle the tiny time lag which results from the new forty-thousand-mile parenthesis in her nervous system. That's right—the people with the leased holocam rig naturally find the gold aspen shadows look a lot better on Delphi's flank than they do on a steer. And Delphi's face improves the mountains too, when you can see them. But the nature freaks aren't quite as joyful as you'd expect.

"See you in Barcelona, kitten," the headman says sourly as they pack up.

"Barcelona?" echoes Delphi with that charming little subliminal lag. She sees where his hand is and steps back. "Cool, it's not her fault," another man says wearily. He knocks back his grizzled hair. "Maybe they'll leave in some of the gut."

Delphi watches them go off to load the spools on the GTX transport for processing. Her hand roves over the breast the man had touched. Back under Carbondale, P. Burke has discovered something new about her Delphi-body.

About the difference between Delphi and her own grim carcass.

She's always known Delphi has almost no sense of taste or smell. They explained about that: only so much bandwidth. You don't have to taste a suncar, do you? And the slight overall dimness of Delphi's sense of touch—she's familiar with that, too. Fabrics that would prickle P. Burke's own hide feel like a cool plastic film to Delphi.

But the blank spots. It took her a while to notice them. Delphi doesn't have much privacy; investments of her size don't. So she's slow about discovering there's certain definite places where her beastly P. Burke body *feels* things that Delphi's dainty flesh does not. H'mm! Channel space again, she thinks—and forgets it in the pure bliss of being Delphi.

You ask how a girl could forget a thing like that? Look. P. Burke is about as far as you can get from the concept *girl*. She's a female, yes—but for her, sex is a four-letter word spelled P-A-I-N. She isn't quite a virgin. You don't want the details; she'd been about twelve and the freak lovers were bombed blind. When they came down, they threw her out with a small hole in her anatomy and a mortal one elsewhere. She dragged off to buy her first and last shot, and she can still hear the clerk's incredulous guffaws.

Do you see why Delphi grins, stretching her delicious little numb body in the sun she faintly feels? Beams, saying, "Please, I'm ready now."

Ready for what? For Barcelona like the sour man said, where his nature-thing is now making it strong in the amateur section of the Festival. A winner! Like he also said, a lot of strip mines and dead fish have been scrubbed, but who cares with Delphi's darling face so visible?

So it's time for Delphi's face and her other delectabilities to show on Barcelona's Playa Nueva. Which means switching her channel to the EurAf synchsat.

They ship her at night so the nanosecond transfer isn't even noticed by that insignificant part of Delphi that lives five hundred feet under Carbondale, so excited the nurse has to make sure she eats. The circuit switches while Delphi "sleeps," that is, while P. Burke is out of the waldo cabinet. The next time she plugs in to open Delphi's eyes it's no different—do you notice which relay boards your phone calls go through?

And now for the event that turns the sugarcube from Colorado into the *princess*.

Literally true, he's a prince, or rather an Infante of an old Spanish line that got shined up in the Neomonarchy. He's also eighty-one, with a passion for birds—the kind you see in zoos. Now it suddenly turns out that he isn't poor at all. Quite the reverse; his old sister laughs in their tax lawyer's face and starts restoring the family hacienda while the Infante totters out to court Delphi. And little Delphi begins to live the life of the gods.

What do gods do? Well, everything beautiful. But (remember Mr. Cantle?) the main point is Things. Ever see a god empty-handed? You can't be a god without at least a magic girdle or an eight-legged horse. But in the old days some stone tablets or winged sandals or a chariot drawn by virgins would do a god for life. No more! Gods make it on novelty now. By Delphi's time the hunt for new god-gear is turning the earth and seas inside-out and sending frantic fingers to the stars. And what gods have, mortals desire.

So Delphi starts on a Euromarket shopping spree squired by her old Infante, thereby doing her bit to stave off social collapse.

Social what? Didn't you get it, when Mr. Cantle talked about a world where advertising is banned and fifteen billion consumers are glued to their holocam shows? One capricious self-powered god can wreck you.

Take the nose-filter massacre. Years, the industry sweated years to achieve an almost invisible enzymatic filter. So one day a couple of pop-gods show up wearing nose-filters like *big purple bats*. By the end of the week the world market is screaming for purple bats. Then it switched to bird-heads and skulls, but by the time the industry retooled the crazies had dropped bird-heads and gone to injection globes. Blood!

Multiply that by a million consumer industries, and you can see why it's economic to have a few controllable gods. Especially with the beautiful hunk of space R&D the Peace Department laid out for and which the taxpayers are only too glad to have taken off their hands by an outfit like GTX, which everybody knows is almost a public trust.

And so you—or rather, GTX—find a creature like P. Burke and give her Delphi. And Delphi helps keep things *orderly*, she does what you tell her to. Why? That's right, Mr. Cantle never finished his speech.

But here come the tests of Delphi's button-nose twinkling in the torrent of news and entertainment. And she's noticed. The feedback shows a flock of viewers turning up the amps when this country baby gets tangled in her new colloidal body-jewels. She registers at a couple of major scenes, too, and when the Infante gives her a suncar, little Delphi trying out suncars is a tiger. There's a solid response in high-credit country. Mr. Cantle is humming his happy tune as he cancels a Benelux subnet option to guest her on a nude cook-show called Wok Venus.

And now for the superposh old-world wedding! The hacienda has Moorish baths and six-foot silver candelabra and real black horses, and the Spanish Vatican blesses them. The final event is a grand gaucho ball with the old prince and his little Infanta on a bowered balcony. She's a spectacular doll of silver lace, wildly launching toy doves at her new friends whirling by below.

The Infante beams, twitches his old nose to the scent of her sweet excitement. His doctor has been very helpful. Surely now, after he has been so patient with the suncars and all the nonsense—

The child looks up at him, saying something incomprehensible about "breath." He makes out that she's complaining about the three singers she had begged for.

"They've changed!" she marvels. "Haven't they changed? They're so dreary. I'm so happy now!"

And Delphi falls fainting against a gothic vargueno.

Her American duenna rushes up, calls help. Delphi's eyes are open, but Delphi isn't there. The duenna pokes among Delphi's hair, slaps her. The old prince grimaces. He has no idea what she is beyond an excellent solution to his tax problems, but he had been a falconer in his youth. There comes to his mind the small pinioned birds which were flung up to stimulate the hawks. He pockets the veined claw to which he had promised certain indulgences and departs to design his new aviary.

And Delphi also departs with her retinue to the Infante's newly discovered yacht. The trouble isn't serious. It's only that five thousand miles away and five hundred feet down P. Burke has been doing it too well.

They've always known she has terrific aptitude. Joe says he never saw a Remote take over so fast. No disorientations, no rejections. The psychomed talks about self-alienation. She's going into Delphi like a salmon to the sea.

She isn't eating or sleeping, they can't keep her out of the body-cabinet to get her blood moving, there are necroses under her grisly sit-down. Crisis!

So Delphi gets a long "sleep" on the yacht and P. Burke gets it pounded through her perforated head that she's endangering Delphi. (Nurse Fleming thinks of that, thus alienating the psychomed.)

They rig a pool down there (Nurse Fleming again) and chase P. Burke back and forth. And she loves it. So naturally when they let her plug in again Delphi loves it too. Every noon beside the yacht's hydrofoils darling Delphi clips along in the blue sea they've warned her not to drink. And every night around the shoulder of the world an ill-shaped thing in a dark burrow beats its way across a sterile pool.

So presently the yacht stands up on its foils and carries Delphi to the program Mr. Cantle has waiting. It's long-range; she's scheduled for at least two decades' product life. Phase One calls for her to connect with a flock of young ultrariches who are romping loose between Brioni and Djakarta where a competitor named PEV could pick them off.

A routine luxgear op, see; no politics, no policy angles, and the main budget items are the title and the yacht, which was idle anyway. The storyline is that Delphi goes to accept some rare birds for her prince—who cares? The *point* is that the Haiti area is no longer radioactive and look!—the gods are there. And so are several new Carib West Happy Isles which can afford GTX rates, in fact two of them are GTX subsids.

But you don't want to get the idea that all these newsworthy people are wired-up robbies, for pity's sake. You don't need many if they're placed right. Delphi asks Joe about that when he comes down to Barranquilla to check her over. (P. Burke's own mouth hasn't said much for a while.)

"Are there many like me?"

"Nobody's like you, buttons. Look, are you still getting Van Allen warble?"

"I mean, like Davy. Is he a Remote?"

(Davy is the lad who is helping her collect the birds. A sincere redhead who needs a little more exposure.)

"Davy? He's one of Matt's boys, some psychojob. They haven't any channel."

"What about the real ones? Djuma van O, or Ali, or Jim Ten?"

"Djuma was born with a pile of GTX basic where her brain should be, she's nothing but a pain. Jimsy does what his astrologer tells him. Look, peanut, where do you get the idea you aren't real? You're the realest. Aren't you having joy?"

"Oh, Joe!" Flinging her little arms around him and his analyzer grids. "Oh, *me gustó mucho, ¡muchísimo!*"

"Hey, hey." He pets her yellow head, folding the analyzer.

Three thousand miles north and five hundred feet down a forgotten hulk in a body-waldo glows.

And is she having joy. To waken out of the nightmare of being P. Burke and find herself a peri, a star-girl? On a yacht in paradise with no more to do than adorn herself and play with toys and attend revels and greet her friends—her, P. Burke, having friends!—and turn the right way for the holocams? Joy!

And it shows. One look at Delphi and the viewers know: *dreams can come true.*

Look at her riding pillion on Davy's sea-bike, carrying an apoplectic macaw in a silver hoop. *Oh, Morton, let's go there this winter!* Or learning the Japanese chinchona from that Kobe group, in a dress that looks like a blowtorch rising from one knee, and which should sell big in Texas. *Morton, is that real fire?* Happy, happy little girl!

And Davy. He's her pet and her baby, and she loves to help him fix his red-gold hair. (P. Burke marveling, running Delphi's fingers through the curls.) Of course Davy is one of Matt's boys—not impotent exactly, but very *very* low drive. (Nobody knows exactly what Matt does with his bitty budget, but the boys are useful and one or two have made names.) He's perfect for Delphi; in fact the psychomed lets her take him to bed, two kittens in a basket. Davy doesn't mind the fact that Delphi "sleeps" like the dead. That's when P. Burke is out of the body-waldo up at Carbondale, attending to her own depressing needs.

A funny thing about that. Most of her sleepy-time Delphi's just a gently tick-ing lush little vegetable waiting for P. Burke to get back on the controls. But now and again Delphi all by herself smiles a bit or stirs in her "sleep." Once she breathed a sound: "Yes."

Under Carbondale P. Burke knows nothing. She's asleep too, dreaming of Delphi, what else? But if the bushy Dr. Tesla had heard that single syllable, his bush would have turned snow white. Because Delphi is *turned off.*

He doesn't. Davy is too dim to notice, and Delphi's staff boss, Hopkins, wasn't monitoring.

And they've all got something else to think about now, because the cold-fire dress sells half a million copies, and not only in Texas. The GTX computers already know it. When they correlate a minor demand for macaws in Alaska the problem comes to human attention: Delphi is something special.

It's a problem, see, because Delphi is targeted on a limited consumer bracket. Now it turns out she has mass-pop potential—those macaws in *Fairbanks,* man!—it's like trying to shoot mice with an ABM. A whole new ball game. Dr. Tesla and the fatherly Mr. Cantle start going around in headquarters circles and buddy-lunching together when they can get away from a seventh-level weasel boy who scares them both.

In the end it's decided to ship Delphi down to the GTX holocam enclave in Chile to try a spot on one of the mainstream shows. (Never mind why an Infanta takes up acting.) The holocam complex occupies a couple of mountains where an observatory once used the clean air. Holocam total-environment shells are very expensive and electronically superstable. Inside them actors can move freely without going off-register, and the whole scene or any selected part will show up in the viewer's home in complete three-di, so real you can look up their noses and much denser than you get from mobile rigs. You can blow a tit ten feet tall when there's no molecular skiffle around.

The enclave looks—well, take everything you know about Hollywood-Burbank and throw it away. What Delphi sees coming down is a neat giant mushroom-farm, domes of all sizes up to monsters for the big games and stuff. It's orderly. The idea that art thrives on creative flamboyance has long been torpedoed by proof that what art needs is computers. Because this showbiz has something TV and Hollywood never had—*automated inbuilt viewer feedback.* Samples, ratings, critics, polls? Forget it. With that carrier field you can get real-time response-sensor readouts from every receiver in the world, served up at your console. That started as a thingie to give the public more influence on content.

Yes.

Try it, man. You're at the console. Slice to the sex-age-educ-econ-ethno-cetera audience of your choice and start. You can't miss. Where the feedback warms up, give 'em more of that. Warm—warmer—*hot!* You've hit it—the secret itch under those hides, the dream in those hearts. You don't need to know its name. With your hand controlling all the input and your eye reading all the response, you can make them a god . . . and somebody'll do the same for you.

But Delphi just sees rainbows, when she gets through the degaussing ports and the field relay and takes her first look at the insides of those shells. The next thing she sees is a team of shapers and technicians descending on her, and millisecond timers everywhere. The tropical leisure is finished. She's in giga-buck mainstream now, at the funnel maw of the unceasing hose that's pumping the sight and sound and flesh and blood and sobs and laughs and dreams of *reality* into the world's happy head. Little Delphi is going plonk into a zillion homes in prime time and nothing is left to chance. Work!

And again Delphi proves apt. Of course it's really P. Burke down under Carbondale who's doing it, but who remembers that carcass? Certainly not P. Burke, she hasn't spoken through her own mouth for months. Delphi doesn't even recall dreaming of her when she wakes up.

As for the show itself, don't bother. It's gone on so long no living soul could unscramble the plotline. Delphi's trial spot has something to do with a widow and her dead husband's brother's amnesia.

The flap comes after Delphi's spots begin to flash out along the world-hose and the feedback appears. You've guessed it, of course. Sensational! As you'd say, they *identify*.

The report actually says something like InskinEmp with a string of percent-ages, meaning that Delphi not only has it for anybody with a Y chromosome, but also for women and everything in between. It's the sweet supernatural jackpot, the million-to-one.

Remember your Harlow? A sexpot, sure. But why did bitter hausfraus in Gary and Memphis know that the vanilla-ice-cream goddess with the white hair and crazy eyebrows was *their baby girl*? And write loving letters to Jean warning her that their husbands weren't good enough for her? Why? The GTX analysts don't know either, but they know what to do with it when it happens.

(Back in his bird sanctuary the old Infante spots it without benefit of computers and gazes thoughtfully at his bride in widow's weeds. It might, he feels, be well to accelerate the completion of his studies.)

The excitement reaches down to the burrow under Carbondale where P. Burke gets two medical exams in a week and a chronically inflamed electrode is replaced. Nurse Fleming also gets an assistant who doesn't do much nursing but is very interested in access doors and identity tabs.

And in Chile, little Delphi is promoted to a new home up among the stars' residential spreads and a private jitney to carry her to work. For Hopkins there's a new computer terminal and a full-time schedule man. What is the schedule crowded with?

Things.

And here begins the trouble. You probably saw that coming too.

"What does she think she is, a goddamn *consumer rep*?" Mr. Cantle's fatherly face in Carbondale contorts.

"The girl's upset," Miss Fleming says stubbornly. "She *believes* that, what you told her about helping people and good new products."

"They are good products," Mr. Cantle snaps automatically, but his anger is under control. He hasn't got where he is by irrelevant reactions.

"She says the plastic gave her a rash and the glo-pills made her dizzy."

"Good god, she shouldn't swallow them," Dr. Tesla puts in agitatedly.

"You told her she'd use them," persists Miss Fleming.

Mr. Cantle is busy figuring how to ease this problem to the feral-faced young man. What, was it a goose that lays golden eggs?

Whatever he says to Level Seven, down in Chile the offending products vanish. And a symbol goes into Delphi's tank matrix, one that means roughly *Balance unit resistance against PR index.*

This means that Delphi's complaints will be endured as long as her Pop Response stays above a certain level. (What happens when it sinks need not concern us.) And to compensate, the price of her exposure time rises again. She's a regular on the show now and response is still climbing.

See her under the sizzling lasers, in a holocam shell set up as a walkway accident. (The show is guesting an acupuncture school shill.)

"I don't think this new body-lift is safe," Delphi's saying. "It's made a funny blue spot on me—look, Mr. Vere."

She wiggles to show where the mini–gray pak that imparts a delicious sense of weightlessness is attached.

"So don't leave it *on,* Dee. With your meat—watch that deck-spot, it's starting to synch."

"But if I don't wear it it isn't honest. They should insulate it more or something, don't you see?"

The show's beloved old father, who is the casualty, gives a senile snigger.

"I'll tell them," Mr. Vere mutters. "Look now, as you step back bend like this so it just shows, see? And hold two beats."

Obediently Delphi turns, and through the dazzle her eyes connect with a pair of strange dark ones. She squints. A quite young man is lounging alone by the port, apparently waiting to use the chamber.

Delphi's used by now to young men looking at her with many peculiar expressions, but she isn't used to what she gets here. A jolt of something somber and knowing. Secrets.

"Eyes! Eyes, Dee!"

She moves through the routine, stealing peeks at the stranger. He stares back. He knows something.

When they let her go she comes shyly to him.

"Living wild, kitten." Cool voice, hot underneath.

"What do you mean?"

"Dumping on the product. You trying to get dead?"

"But it isn't right," she tells him. "They don't know, but I do, I've been wearing it."

His cool is jolted.

"You're out of your head."

"Oh, they'll see I'm right when they check it," she explains. "They're just so busy. When I tell them—"

He is staring down at little flower-face. His mouth opens, closes. "What are you doing in this sewer anyway? Who are you?"

Bewilderedly she says, "I'm Delphi."

"Holy Zen."

"What's wrong? Who are you, please?"

Her people are moving her out now, nodding at him.

"Sorry we ran over, Mr. Uhunh," the script girl says.

He mutters something, but it's lost as her convoy bustles her toward the flower-decked jitney.

(Hear the click of an invisible ignition-train being armed?)

"Who was he?" Delphi asks her hairman.

The hairman is bending up and down from his knees as he works.

"Paul. Isham. Three," he says and puts a comb in his mouth.

"Who's that? I can't see."

He mumbles around the comb, meaning, "Are you jiving?" Because she has to be, in the middle of the GTX enclave.

Next day there's a darkly smoldering face under a turban-towel when Delphi and the show's paraplegic go to use the carbonated pool.

She looks.

He looks.

And the next day, too.

(Hear the automatic sequencer cutting in? The system couples, the fuels begin to travel.)

Poor old Isham senior. You have to feel sorry for a man who values order: when he begets young, genetic information is still transmitted in the old ape way. One minute it's a happy midget with a rubber duck—look around and here's this huge healthy stranger, opaquely emotional, running with god knows who. Questions are heard where there's nothing to question, and eruptions claiming to be moral outrage. When this is called to Papa's attention—it may take time, in that boardroom—Papa does what he can, but without immortality-juice the problem is worrisome.

And young Paul Isham is a bear. He's bright and articulate and tender-souled and incessantly active, and he and his friends are choking with appalment at the world their fathers made. And it hasn't taken Paul long to discover that *his* father's house has many mansions and even the GTX computers can't relate everything to everything else. He noses out a decaying project which adds up to something like, Sponsoring Marginal Creativity (the free-lance team that "discovered" Delphi was one such grantee). And from there it turns out that an agile lad named Isham can get his hands on a viable packet of GTX holocam facilities.

So here he is with his little band, way down the mushroom-farm mountain, busily spooling a show which has no relation to Delphi's. It's built on bizarre techniques and unsettling distortions pregnant with social protest. An *underground* expression to you.

All this isn't unknown to his father, of course, but so far it has done nothing more than deepen Isham senior's apprehensive frown.

Until Paul connects with Delphi.

And by the time Papa learns this, those invisible hypergolics have exploded, the energy-shells are rushing out. For Paul, you see, is the genuine article. He's serious. He dreams. He even reads—for example, *Green Mansions*—and he wept fiercely when those fiends burned Rima alive.

When he hears that some new GTX pussy is making it big, he sneers and forgets it. He's busy. He never connects the name with this little girl making her idiotic, doomed protest in the holocam chamber. This strangely simple little girl.

And she comes and looks up at him and he sees Rima, lost Rima the enchanted bird girl, and his unwired human heart goes twang.

And Rima turns out to be Delphi.

Do you need a map? The angry puzzlement. The rejection of the dissonance Rima-hustling-for-GTX-My-Father. Garbage, cannot be. The loitering around the pool to confirm the swindle . . . dark eyes hitting on blue wonder, jerky words exchanged in a peculiar stillness . . . the dreadful reorganization of the image into Rima-Delphi *in my Father's tentacles*—

You don't need a map.

Nor for Delphi either, the girl who loved her gods. She's seen their divine flesh close now, heard their unamplified voices call her name. She's played their god-games, worn their garlands. She's even become a goddess herself, though she doesn't believe it. She's not disenchanted, don't think that. She's still full of love. It's just that some crazy kind of *hope* hasn't—

Really you can skip all this, when the loving little girl on the yellow-brick road meets a Man. A real human male burning with angry compassion and grandly concerned with human justice, who reaches for her with real male arms and— boom! She loves him back with all her heart.

A happy trip, see?

Except.

Except that it's really P. Burke five thousand miles away who loves Paul. P. Burke the monster down in a dungeon smelling of electrode paste. A caricature of a woman burning, melting, obsessed with true love. Trying over twenty-double-thousand miles of hard vacuum to reach her beloved through girl-flesh numbed by an invisible film. Feeling his arms around the body he thinks is hers, fighting through shadows to give herself to him. Trying to taste and smell him through beautiful dead nostrils, to love him back with a body that goes dead in the heart of the fire.

Perhaps you get P. Burke's state of mind?

She has phases. The trying, first. And the shame. The *shame. I am not what thou lovest.* And the fiercer trying. And the realization that there is no, no way, none. Never. *Never* . . . A bit delayed, isn't it, her understanding that the bargain she made was forever? P. Burke should have noticed those stories about mortals who end up as grasshoppers.

You see the outcome—the funneling of all this agony into one dumb protoplasmic drive to fuse with Delphi. To leave, to close out the beast she is chained to. *To become Delphi.*

Of course it's impossible.

However, her torments have an effect on Paul. Delphi-as-Rima is a potent enough love object, and liberating Delphi's mind requires hours of deeply satis-fying instruction in the rottenness of it all. Add in Delphi's body worshiping his flesh, burning in the fire of P. Burke's savage heart—do you wonder Paul is involved?

That's not all.

By now they're spending every spare moment together and some that aren't so spare.

"Mr. Isham, would you mind staying out of this sports sequence? The script calls for Davy here."

(Davy's still around, the exposure did him good.)

"What's the difference?" Paul yawns. "It's just an ad. I'm not blocking that thing."

Shocked silence at his two-letter word. The script girl swallows bravely.

"I'm sorry, sir, our directive is to do the *social sequence* exactly as scripted. We're having to respool the segments we did last week, Mr. Hopkins is very angry with me."

"Who the hell is Hopkins? Where is he?"

"Oh, please, Paul. *Please.*"

Paul unwraps himself, saunters back. The holocam crew nervously check their angles. The GTX boardroom has a foible about having things *pointed* at them and theirs. Cold shivers, when the image of an Isham nearly went onto the world beam beside that Dialadinner.

Worse yet, Paul has no respect for the sacred schedules which are now a full-time job for ferret boy up at headquarters. Paul keeps forgetting to bring her back on time, and poor Hopkins can't cope.

So pretty soon the boardroom data-ball has an urgent personal action-tab for Mr. Isham senior. They do it the gentle way, at first.

"I can't today, Paul."

"Why not?"

"They say I have to, it's *very* important."

He strokes the faint gold down on her narrow back. Under Carbondale, PA, a blind mole-woman shivers.

"Important. Their importance. Making more gold. Can't you see? To them you're just a thing to get scratch with. *A huckster.* Are you going to let them screw you, Dee? Are you?"

"Oh, Paul—"

He doesn't know it, but he's seeing a weirdie; Remotes aren't hooked up to flow tears.

"Just say no, Dee. No. Integrity. You have to."

"But they say, it's my job—"

"Will you believe I can take care of you, Dee? Baby, baby, you're letting them rip us. You have to choose. Tell them, no."

"Paul . . . I w-will . . ."

And she does. Brave little Delphi (insane P. Burke). Saying, "No, please, I promised, Paul."

They try some more, still gently.

"Paul, Mr. Hopkins told me the reason they don't want us to be together so much. It's because of who you are, your father."

She thinks his father is like Mr. Cantle, maybe.

"Oh, great. Hopkins. I'll fix him. Listen, I can't think about Hopkins now. Ken came back today, he found out something."

They are lying on the high Andes meadow watching his friends dive their singing kites.

"Would you believe, on the coast the police have *electrodes in their heads*?"

She stiffens in his arms.

"Yeah, weird. I thought they only used PP on criminals and the army. Don't you see, Dee—something has to be going on. Some movement. Maybe somebody's organizing. How can we find out?" He pounds the ground behind her: "We should make *contact*! If we could only find out."

"The, the news?" she asks distractedly.

"The news." He laughs. "There's nothing in the news except what they want people to know. Half the country could burn up, and nobody would know it if they didn't want. Dee, can't you take what I'm explaining to you? They've got the whole world programmed! Total control of communication. They've got everybody's minds wired in to think what they show them and want what they give them and they give them what they're programmed to want—you can't break in or out of it, you can't get *hold* of it anywhere. I don't think they even have a plan except to keep things going round and round—and god knows what's happening to the people or the Earth or the other planets, maybe. One great big vortex of lies and garbage pouring round and round, getting bigger and bigger, and nothing can ever change. If people don't wake up soon we're through!"

He pounds her stomach softly.

"You have to break out, Dee."

"I'll try, Paul, I will—"

"You're mine. They can't have you."

And he goes to see Hopkins, who is indeed cowed.

But that night up under Carbondale the fatherly Mr. Cantle goes to see P. Burke.

P. Burke? On a cot in a utility robe like a dead camel in a tent, she cannot at first comprehend that he is telling *her* to break it off with Paul. P. Burke has never seen Paul. *Delphi* sees Paul. The fact is, P. Burke can no longer clearly recall that she exists apart from Delphi.

Mr. Cantle can scarcely believe it either, but he tries.

He points out the futility, the potential embarrassment, for Paul. That gets a dim stare from the bulk on the bed. Then he goes into her duty to GTX, her job, isn't she grateful for the opportunity, etcetera. He's very persuasive.

The cobwebby mouth of P. Burke opens and croaks.

"No."

Nothing more seems to be forthcoming.

Mr. Cantle isn't dense, he knows an immovable obstacle when he bumps one.

He also knows an irresistible force: GTX. The simple solution is to lock the waldo-cabinet until Paul gets tired of waiting for Delphi to wake up. But the cost, the schedules! And there's something odd here . . . he eyes the corporate asset hulking on the bed and his hunch-sense prickles.

You see, Remotes don't love. They don't have real sex, the circuits designed that out from the start. So it's been assumed that it's *Paul* who is diverting himself or something with the pretty little body in Chile. P. Burke can only be doing what comes natural to any ambitious gutter-meat. It hasn't occurred to anyone that they're dealing with the real hairy thing whose shadow is blasting out of every holoshow on Earth.

Love?

Mr. Cantle frowns. The idea is grotesque. But his instinct for the fuzzy line is strong; he will recommend flexibility. And so, in Chile:

"Darling, I don't have to work tonight! And Friday too—isn't that right, Mr. Hopkins?"

"Oh, great. When does she come up for parole?"

"Mr. Isham, please be reasonable. Our schedule—surely your own production people must be needing you?"

This happens to be true. Paul goes away. Hopkins stares after him, wondering distastefully why an Isham wants to ball a waldo. How sound are those boardroom belly-fears—garble creeps, creeps in! It never occurs to Hopkins that an Isham might not know what Delphi is.

Especially with Davy crying because Paul has kicked him out of Delphi's bed. Delphi's bed is under a real window.

"Stars," Paul says sleepily. He rolls over, pulling Delphi on top. "Are you aware that this is one of the last places on Earth where people can see the stars? Tibet, too, maybe."

"Paul . . ."

"Go to sleep. I want to see you sleep."

"Paul, I . . . I sleep so *hard*, I mean, it's a joke how hard I am to wake up. Do you mind?"

"Yes."

But finally, fearfully, she must let go. So that five thousand miles north a crazy spent creature can crawl out to gulp concentrates and fall on her cot. But not for long. It's pink dawn when Delphi's eyes open to find Paul's arms around her, his voice saying rude, tender things. He's been kept awake. The nerveless little statue that was her Delphi-body nuzzled him in the night.

Insane hope rises, is fed a couple of nights later when he tells her she called his name in her sleep.

And that day Paul's arms keep her from work and Hopkins's wails go up to headquarters where the weasel-faced lad is working his sharp tailbone off packing Delphi's program. Mr. Cantle defuses that one. But next week it happens again, to a major client. And ferret-face has connections on the technical side.

Now you can see that when you have a field of complexly heterodyned energy modulations tuned to a demand-point like Delphi, there are many problems of standwaves and lashback and skiffle of all sorts which are normally balanced out with ease by the technology of the future. By the same token they can be delicately unbalanced too, in ways that feed back into the waldo operator with striking results.

"Darling—what the hell! What's wrong? *Delphi!*"

Helpless shrieks, writhings. Then the Rima-bird is lying wet and limp in his arms, her eyes enormous.

"I . . . I wasn't supposed to . . ." she gasps faintly. "They told me not to . . ."

"Oh, my god—*Delphi.*"

And his hard fingers are digging in her thick yellow hair. Electronically knowledgeable fingers. They freeze.

"You're a *doll*! You're one of those PP implants. They control you. I should have known. Oh, god, I should have known."

"No, Paul," she's sobbing. "No, no, no—"

"Damn them. Damn them, what they've done—you're not *you*—"

He's shaking her, crouching over her in the bed and jerking her back and forth, glaring at the pitiful beauty.

"No!" she pleads (it's not true, that dark bad dream back there). "I'm Delphi!"

"My father. Filth, pigs—damn them, damn them, damn them."

"No, no," she babbles. "They were good to me—" P. Burke underground mouthing, "They were good to me—*aah-aaaah!*"

Another agony skewers her. Up north the sharp young man wants to make sure this so-tiny interference works. Paul can scarcely hang on to her, he's crying too. "I'll kill them."

His Delphi, a wired-up slave! Spikes in her brain, electronic shackles in his bird's heart. Remember when those savages burned Rima alive?

"I'll *kill* the man that's doing this to you."

He's still saying it afterward, but she doesn't hear. She's sure he hates her now, all she wants is to die. When she finally understands that the fierceness is tenderness, she thinks it's a miracle. *He knows—and he still loves!*

How can she guess that he's got it a little bit wrong?

You can't blame Paul. Give him credit that he's even heard about pleasure-pain implants and snoops, which by their nature aren't mentioned much by those who know them most intimately. That's what he thinks is being used on Delphi, something to *control* her. And to listen—he burns at the unknown ears in their bed.

Of waldo-bodies and objects like P. Burke he has heard nothing.

So it never crosses his mind as he looks down at his violated bird, sick with fury and love, that he isn't holding *all* of her. Do you need to be told the mad resolve jelling in him now?

To free Delphi.

How? Well, he is, after all, Paul Isham III. And he even has an idea where the GTX neurolab is. In Carbondale.

But first things have to be done for Delphi, and for his own stomach. So he gives her back to Hopkins and departs in a restrained and discreet way. And the

Chile staff is grateful and do not understand that his teeth don't normally show so much.

And a week passes in which Delphi is a very good, docile little ghost. They let her have the load of wildflowers Paul sends and the bland loving notes. (He's playing it coony.) And up in headquarters weasel boy feels that *his* destiny has clicked a notch onward and floats the word up that he's handy with little problems.

And no one knows what P. Burke thinks in any way whatever, except that Miss Fleming catches her flushing her food down the can and next night she faints in the pool. They haul her out and stick her with IVs. Miss Fleming frets, she's seen expressions like that before. But she wasn't around when crazies who called themselves Followers of the Fish looked through flames to life everlasting. P. Burke is seeing Heaven on the far side of death, too. Heaven is spelled P-a-u-l, but the idea's the same. *I will die and be born again in Delphi.*

Garbage, electronically speaking. No way.

Another week and Paul's madness has become a plan. (Remember, he does have friends.) He smolders, watching his love paraded by her masters. He turns out a scorching sequence for his own show. And finally, politely, he requests from Hopkins a morsel of his bird's free time, which duly arrives.

"I thought you didn't *want* me anymore," she's repeating as they wing over mountain flanks in Paul's suncar. "Now you *know—*"

"Look at me!"

His hand covers her mouth, and he's showing her a lettered card.

DON'T TALK THEY CAN HEAR EVERYTHING WE SAY.

I'M TAKING YOU AWAY NOW.

She kisses his hand. He nods urgently, flipping the card.

DON'T BE AFRAID. I CAN STOP THE PAIN IF THEY TRY TO HURT YOU.

With his free hand he shakes out a silvery scrambler-mesh on a power pack. She is dumbfounded.

THIS WILL CUT THE SIGNALS AND PROTECT YOU DARLING.

She's staring at him, her head going vaguely from side to side, *No.*

"Yes!" He grins triumphantly. "Yes!"

For a moment she wonders. That powered mesh will cut off the field, all right. It will also cut off Delphi. But he is Paul. Paul is kissing her, she can only seek him hungrily as he sweeps the suncar through a pass.

Ahead is an old jet ramp with a shiny bullet waiting to go. (Paul also has credits and a Name.) The little GTX patrol courier is built for nothing but speed. Paul and Delphi wedge in behind the pilot's extra fuel tank, and there's no more talking when the torches start to scream.

They're screaming high over Quito before Hopkins starts to worry. He wastes another hour tracking the beeper on Paul's suncar. The suncar is sailing a pattern out to sea. By the time they're sure it's empty and Hopkins gets on the hot flue to headquarters, the fugitives are a sourceless howl above Carib West.

Up at headquarters weasel boy gets the squeal. His first impulse is to repeat his previous play, but then his brain snaps to. This one is too hot. Because, see, although in the long run they can make P. Burke do anything at all except maybe *live*, instant emergencies can be tricky. And—Paul Isham III.

"Can't you order her back?"

They're all in the GTX tower monitor station, Mr. Cantle and ferret-face and Joe and a very neat man who is Mr. Isham senior's personal eyes and ears.

"No, sir," Joe says doggedly. "We can read channels, particularly speech, but we can't interpolate organized pattern. It takes the waldo op to send one-to-one—"

"What are they saying?"

"Nothing at the moment, sir." The console jockey's eyes are closed. "I believe they are, ah, embracing."

"They're not answering," a traffic monitor says. "Still heading zero zero three zero—due north, sir."

"You're certain Kennedy is alerted not to fire on them?" the neat man asks anxiously.

"Yes, sir."

"Can't you just turn her off?" The sharp-faced lad is angry. "Pull that pig out of the controls!"

"If you cut the transmission cold you'll kill the Remote," Joe explains for the third time. "Withdrawal has to be phased right, you have to fade over to the Remote's own autonomics. Heart, breathing, cerebellum, would go blooey. If you pull Burke out you'll probably finish her too. It's a fantastic cybersystem, you don't want to do that."

"The investment." Mr. Cantle shudders.

Weasel boy puts his hand on the console jock's shoulder, it's the contact who arranged the no-no effect for him.

"We can at least give them a warning signal, sir." He licks his lips, gives the neat man his sweet ferret smile. "We know that does no damage."

Joe frowns, Mr. Cantle sighs. The neat man is murmuring into his wrist. He looks up. "I am authorized," he says reverently, "I am authorized to, ah, direct a signal. If this is the only course. But minimal, minimal."

Sharp-face squeezes his man's shoulder.

In the silver bullet shrieking over Charleston Paul feels Delphi arch in his arms. He reaches for the mesh, hot for action. She thrashes, pushing at his hands, her eyes roll. She's afraid of that mesh despite the agony. (And she's right.) Frantically Paul fights her in the cramped space, gets it over her head. As he turns the power up she burrows free under his arm and the spasm fades.

"They're calling you again, Mr. Isham!" the pilot yells.

"Don't answer. Darling, keep this over your head damn it how can I—"

An AX90 barrels over their nose, there's a flash.

"Mr. Isham! Those are Air Force jets!"

"Forget it," Paul shouts back. "They won't fire. Darling, don't be afraid." Another AX90 rocks them.

"Would you mind pointing your pistol at my head where they can see it, sir?" the pilot howls.

Paul does so. The AX90s take up escort formation around them. The pilot goes back to figuring how he can collect from GTX too, and after Goldsboro AB the escort peels away.

"Holding the same course." Traffic is reporting to the group around the monitor. "Apparently they've taken on enough fuel to bring them to towerport here."

"In that case it's just a question of waiting for them to dock." Mr. Cantle's fatherly manner revives a bit.

"Why can't they cut off that damn freak's life-support," the sharp young man fumes. "It's ridiculous."

"They're working on it," Cantle assures him.

What they're doing, down under Carbondale, is arguing. Miss Fleming's watchdog has summoned the bushy man to the waldo room.

"Miss Fleming, you will obey orders."

"You'll kill her if you try that, sir. I can't believe you meant it, that's why I didn't. We've already fed her enough sedative to affect heart action; if you cut any more oxygen she'll die in there."

The bushy man grimaces. "Get Dr. Quine here fast."

They wait, staring at the cabinet in which a drugged, ugly madwoman fights for consciousness, fights to hold Delphi's eyes open.

High over Richmond the silver pod starts a turn. Delphi is sagged into Paul's arm, her eyes swim up to him.

"Starting down now, baby. It'll be over soon, all you have to do is stay alive, Dee."

". . . stay alive . . ."

The traffic monitor has caught them. "Sir! They've turned off for Carbondale—Control has contact—"

"Let's go."

But the headquarters posse is too late to intercept the courier wailing into Carbondale. And Paul's friends have come through again. The fugitives are out through the freight dock and into the neurolab admin port before the guard gets organized. At the elevator Paul's face plus his handgun get them in.

"I want Doctor—what's his name, Dee? Dee!"

". . . Tesla . . ." She's reeling on her feet.

"Dr. Tesla. Take me down to Tesla, fast."

Intercoms are squalling around them as they whoosh down, Paul's pistol in the guard's back. When the door slides open the bushy man is there.

"I'm Tesla."

"I'm Paul Isham. *Isham.* You're going to take your flaming implants out of this girl—now. Move!"

"What?"

"You heard me. Where's your operating room? Go!"

"But—"

"Move! Do I have to burn somebody?"

Paul waves the weapon at Dr. Quine, who has just appeared.

"No, no," says Tesla hurriedly. "But I can't, you know. It's impossible, there'll be nothing left."

"You screaming well can, right now. You mess up and I'll kill you," says Paul murderously. "Where is it, there? And wipe the feke that's on her circuits now."

He's backing them down the hall, Delphi heavy on his arm.

"Is this the place, baby? Where they did it to you?"

"Yes," she whispers, blinking at a door. "Yes . . ."

Because it is, see. Behind that door is the very suite where she was born.

Paul herds them through it into a gleaming hall. An inner door opens, and a nurse and a gray man rush out. And freeze.

Paul sees there's something special about that inner door. He crowds them past it and pushes it open and looks in.

Inside is a big mean-looking cabinet with its front door panels ajar.

And inside that cabinet is a poisoned carcass to whom something wonderful, unspeakable, is happening. Inside is P. Burke, the real living woman who knows that *he* is there, coming closer—Paul whom she had fought to reach through forty thousand miles of ice—*Paul* is here!—is yanking at the waldo doors—

The doors tear open and a monster rises up.

"Paul darling!" croaks the voice of love, and the arms of love reach for him. And he responds.

Wouldn't you, if a gaunt she-golem flab-naked and spouting wires and blood came at you clawing with metal-studded paws—

"Get away!" He knocks wires.

It doesn't much matter which wires. P. Burke has, so to speak, her nervous system hanging out. Imagine somebody jerking a handful of your medulla—

She crashes onto the floor at his feet, flopping and roaring *PAUL-PAUL-PAUL* in rictus.

It's doubtful he recognizes his name or sees her life coming out of her eyes at him. And at the last it doesn't go to him. The eyes find Delphi, fainting by the doorway, and die.

Now of course Delphi is dead, too.

There's a total silence as Paul steps away from the thing by his foot.

"You killed her," Tesla says. "That was her."

"Your control." Paul is furious, the thought of that monster fastened into little Delphi's brain nauseates him. He sees her crumpling and holds out his arms. Not knowing she is dead.

And Delphi comes to him.

One foot before the other, not moving very well—but moving. Her darling face turns up. Paul is distracted by the terrible quiet, and when he looks down he sees only her tender little neck.

"Now you get the implants out," he warns them. Nobody moves.

"But, but she's dead," Miss Fleming whispers wildly.

Paul feels Delphi's life under his hand, they're talking about their monster. He aims his pistol at the gray man.

"You. If we aren't in your surgery when I count three, I'm burning off this man's leg."

"Mr. Isham," Tesla says desperately, "you have just killed the person who animated the body you call Delphi. Delphi herself is dead. If you release your arm you'll see what I say is true."

The tone gets through. Slowly Paul opens his arm, looks down.

"Delphi?"

She totters, sways, stays upright. Her face comes slowly up.

"Paul . . ." Tiny voice.

"Your crotty tricks," Paul snarls at them. "Move!"

"Look at her eyes," Dr. Quine croaks.

They look. One of Delphi's pupils fills the iris, her lips writhe weirdly.

"Shock." Paul grabs her to him. "*Fix* her!" He yells at them, aiming at Tesla.

"For god's sake . . . bring it in the lab." Tesla quavers.

"Good-bye-bye," says Delphi clearly. They lurch down the hall, Paul carrying her, and meet a wave of people.

Headquarters has arrived.

Joe takes one look and dives for the waldo room, running into Paul's gun.

"Oh, no, you don't."

Everybody is yelling. The little thing in his arm stirs, says plaintively, "I'm Delphi."

And all through the ensuing jabber and ranting she hangs on, keeping it up, the ghost of P. Burke or whatever whispering crazily, "Paul . . . Paul . . . Please, I'm Delphi . . . Paul?"

"I'm here, darling, I'm here." He's holding her in the nursing bed. Tesla talks, talks, talks unheard.

"Paul . . . don't sleep . . ." The ghost-voice whispers. Paul is in agony, he will not accept, *will not* believe.

Tesla runs down.

And then near midnight Delphi says roughly, "Ag-ag-ag—" and slips onto the floor, making a rough noise like a seal.

Paul screams. There's more of the *ag-ag* business and more gruesome convulsive disintegrations, until by two in the morning Delphi is nothing but a warm little bundle of vegetative functions hitched to some expensive hardware— the same that sustained her before her life began. Joe has finally persuaded Paul to let him at the waldo-cabinet. Paul stays by her long enough to see her face change in a dreadfully alien and coldly convincing way, and then he stumbles out bleakly through the group in Tesla's office.

Behind him Joe is working wet-faced, sweating to reintegrate the fantastic complex of circulation, respiration, endocrines, midbrain homeostases, the patterned flux that was a human being—it's like saving an orchestra abandoned in midair. Joe is also crying a little; he alone had truly loved P. Burke. P. Burke, now a dead pile on a table, was the greatest cybersystem he has ever known, and he never forgets her.

The end, really.

You're curious?

Sure, Delphi lives again. Next year she's back on the yacht getting sympathy for her tragic breakdown. But there's a different chick in Chile, because while Delphi's new operator is competent, you don't get two P. Burkes in a row—for which GTX is duly grateful.

The real belly-bomb of course is Paul. He was *young*, see. Fighting abstract wrong. Now life has clawed into him and he goes through gut rage and grief and grows in human wisdom and resolve. So much so that you won't be surprised, sometime later, to find him—where?

In the GTX boardroom, dummy. Using the advantage of his birth to radicalize the system. You'd call it "boring from within."

That's how he put it, and his friends couldn't agree more. It gives them a warm, confident feeling to know that Paul is up there. Sometimes one of them who's still around runs into him and gets a big hello.

And the sharp-faced lad?

Oh, he matures too. He learns fast, believe it. For instance, he's the first to learn that an obscure GTX research unit is actually getting something with their loopy temporal anomalizer project. True, he doesn't have a physics background, and he's bugged quite a few people. But he doesn't really learn about that until the day he stands where somebody points him during a test run—

—and wakes up lying on a newspaper headlined "Nixon Unveils Phase Two."

Lucky he's a fast learner.

Believe it, zombie. When I say growth, I mean *growth*. Capital appreciation. You can stop sweating. There's a great future there.

PAT CADIGAN
PRETTY BOY CROSSOVER

(1986)

First you see video. Then you wear video. Then you eat video. Then you be video.
—The Gospel According to Visual Mark

Watch or Be Watched.
—Pretty Boy Credo

"WHO MADE YOU?"

"You mean recently?"

Mohawk on the door smiles and takes his picture. "You in. But only you, okay? Don't try to get no friends in, hear that?"

"I hear. And I ain't no fool, fool. I got no friends."

Mohawk leers, leaning forward. "Pretty Boy like you, no friends?"

"Not in this world." He pushes past the Mohawk, ignoring the kissy-kissy sounds.

He would like to crack the bridge of the Mohawk's nose and shove bone splinters into his brain but he is lately making more effort to control his temper and besides, he's not sure if any of that bone splinters in the brain stuff is really true. He's a Pretty Boy, all of sixteen years old, and tonight could be his last chance.

The club is Noise. Can't sneak into the bathroom for quiet, the Noise is piped in there, too. Want to get away from Noise? Why? No reason. But this Pretty Boy has learned to think between the beats. Like walking between the raindrops to stay dry, but he can do it. This Pretty Boy thinks things all the time—*all* the time. Subversive (and, he thinks so much that he knows that word *subversive*, sixteen, Pretty, or not). He thinks things like *how many Einsteins have died of hunger and thirst under a hot African sun* and *why can't you remember being born* and *why is music common to every culture* and especially *how much was there going on that he didn't know about and how could he find out about it.*

And this is all the time, one thing after another running in his head, you can see by his eyes. It's for def not much like a Pretty Boy but it's one reason why they want him. That he *is* a Pretty Boy is another and one reason why they're halfway home getting him.

He knows all about them. Everybody knows about them and everybody wants them to pause, look twice, and cough up a card that says, Yes, we see possibilities, please come to the following address during regular business hours on the next regular business day for regular further review. Everyone wants it but this Pretty Boy, who once got five cards in a night and tore them all up. But here he is, still a Pretty Boy. He thinks enough to know this is a failing in himself, that he likes being Pretty and chased and that is how they could end up getting him after all and that's b-b-b-bad. When he thinks about it, he thinks it with the stutter. B-b-b-bad. B-b-b-bad for him because he doesn't God help him want it, no, no n-n-n-no. Which may make him the strangest Pretty Boy still live tonight and every night.

Still live and standing in the club where only the Prettiest Pretty Boys can get in anymore. Pretty Girls are too easy, they've got to be better than Pretty and besides, Pretty Boys like to be Pretty all alone, no help thank you so much. This Pretty Boy doesn't mind Pretty Girls or any other kind of girls. Lately, though, he has begun to wonder how much longer it will be for him. Two years? Possibly a little longer? By three it will be for def over and the Mohawk on the door will as soon spit in his face as leer in it.

If they don't get to him.

And if they *do* get to him, then it's never over and he can be wherever he chooses to be and wherever that is will be the center of the universe. They promise it, unlimited access in your free hours and endless hot season, endless youth. Pretty Boy Heaven, and to get there, they say, you don't even really have to die.

He looks up to the dj's roost, far above the bobbing, boogieing crowd on the dance floor. They still call them djs even though they aren't discs anymore, they're chips and there's more than just sound on a lot of them. The great hyper-program, he's been told, the ultimate of ultimates, a short walk from there to the fourth dimension. He suspects this stuff comes from low-steppers shilling for them, hoping they'll get auditioned if they do a good enough shuck job. Nobody knows what it's really like except the ones who are there and you can't trust them, he figures. Because maybe they *aren't*, anymore. Not really.

The dj sees his Pretty upturned face, recognizes him even though it's been a while since he's come back here. Part of it was wanting to stay away from them and part of it was that the thug on the door might not let him in. And then, of course, he *had* to come, to see if he could get in, to see if anyone still wanted him. What was the point of Pretty if there was nobody to care and watch and pursue? Even now, he is almost sure he can feel the room rearranging itself around his presence in it and the dj confirms this is true by holding up a chip and pointing it to the left.

They are squatting on the make-believe stairs by the screen, reminding him of pigeons plotting to take over the world. He doesn't look too long, doesn't want to give them the idea he'd like to talk. But as he turns away, one, the younger man, starts to get up. The older man and the woman pull him back.

He pretends a big interest in the figures lining the nearest wall. Some are Pretty, some are female, some are undecided, some are very bizarre, or wealthy, or just charity cases. They all notice him and adjust themselves for his perusal. Then one end of the room lights up with color and new noise. Bodies dance and stumble back from the screen where images are forming to rough music.

It's Bobby, he realizes.

A moment later, there's Bobby's face on the screen, sixteen feet high, even Prettier than he'd been when he was loose among the mortals. The sight of Bobby's Pretty-Pretty face fills him with anger and dismay and a feeling of loss so great he would strike anyone who spoke Bobby's name without his permission.

Bobby's lovely slate-gray eyes scan the room. They've told him senses are heightened after you make the change and go over but he's not so sure how that's supposed to work. Bobby looks kind of blind up there on the screen. A few people wave at Bobby—the dorks they let in so the rest can have someone to be hip in front of—but Bobby's eyes move slowly back and forth, back and forth, and then stop, looking right at him.

"Ah . . ." Bobby whispers it, long and drawn out. "Aaaaaa-hhhh." He lifts his chin belligerently and stares back at Bobby.

"You don't have to die anymore," Bobby says silkily. Music bounces under his words. "It's beautiful in here. The dreams can be as real as you want them to be. And if you want to be, you can be with me."

He knows the commercial is not aimed only at him but it doesn't matter. This is *Bobby*. Bobby's voice seems to be pouring over him, caressing him, and it feels too much like a taunt. The night before Bobby went over, he tried to talk him out of it, knowing it wouldn't work. If they'd actually refused him, Bobby would have killed himself, like Franco had.

But now Bobby would live forever and ever, if you believed what they said. The music comes up louder but Bobby's eyes are still on him. He sees Bobby mouth his name.

"Can you really see me, Bobby?" he says. His voice doesn't make it over the music but if Bobby's senses are so heightened, maybe he hears it anyway. If he does, he doesn't choose to answer. The music is a bumped up remix of a song Bobby used to party-till-he-puked to. The giant Bobby-face fades away to be replaced with a whole Bobby, somewhat larger than life, dancing better than the old Bobby ever could, whirling along changing scenes of streets, rooftops, and beaches. The locales are nothing special but Bobby never did have all that much imagination, never wanted to go to Mars or even to the South Pole, always just to the hottest club. Always he liked being the exotic in plain surroundings and he still likes it. He always loved to get the looks. To be watched, worshipped, pursued. Yeah. He can see this is Bobby-heaven. The whole world will be giving him the looks now.

The background on the screen goes from street to the inside of a club; *this* club, only larger, better, with an even hipper crowd, and Bobby shaking it with them. Half the real crowd is forgetting to dance now because they're watching Bobby, hoping he's put some of them into his video. Yeah, that's the dream, get yourself remixed in the extended dance version.

43

His own attention drifts to the fake stairs that don't lead anywhere. They're still perched on them, the only people who are watching *him* instead of Bobby. The woman, looking overaged in a purple plastic sacsuit, is fingering a card.

He looks up at Bobby again. Bobby is dancing in place and looking back at him, or so it seems. Bobby's lips move soundlessly but so precisely he can read the words: *This can be you. Never get old, never get tired, it's never last call, nothing happens unless you want it to and it could be you. You. You.* Bobby's hands point to him on the beat. *You. You. You.*

Bobby. Can you really see me?

Bobby suddenly breaks into laughter and turns away, shaking it some more.

He sees the Mohawk from the door pushing his way through the crowd, the real crowd, and he gets anxious. The Mohawk goes straight for the stairs, where they make room for him, rubbing the bristly red strip of hair running down the center of his head as though they were greeting a favored pet. The Mohawk looks as satisfied as a professional glutton after a foodrace victory. He wonders what they promised the Mohawk for letting him in. Maybe some kind of limited contract. Maybe even a try-out.

Now they are all watching him together. Defiantly, he touches a tall girl dancing nearby and joins her rhythm. She smiles down at him, moving between him and them purely by chance but it endears her to him anyway. She is wearing a flap of translucent rag over secondskins, like an old-time showgirl. Over six feet tall, not beautiful with that nose, not even pretty, but they let her in so she could be tall. She probably doesn't know that; she probably doesn't know anything that goes on and never really will. For that reason, he can forgive her the hard-tech orange hair.

A Rude Boy brushes against him in the course of a dervish turn, asking acknowledgment by ignoring him. Rude Boys haven't changed in more decades than anyone's kept track of, as though it were the same little group of leathered and chained troopers buggering their way down the years. The Rude Boy isn't dancing with anyone. Rude Boys never do. But this one could be handy, in case of an emergency.

The girl is dancing hard, smiling at him. He smiles back, moving slightly to her right, watching Bobby possibly watching him. He still can't tell if Bobby really sees anything. The scene behind Bobby is still a double of the club, getting hipper and hipper if that's possible. The music keeps snapping back to its first peak passage. Then Bobby gestures like God and he sees himself. He is dancing next to Bobby, Prettier than he ever could be, just the way they promise. Bobby doesn't look at the phantom but at him where he really is, lips moving again. *If you want to be, you can be with me. And so can she.*

His tall partner appears next to the phantom of himself. She is also much improved, though still not Pretty, or even pretty. The real girl turns and sees herself and there's no mistaking the delight in her face. Queen of the Hop for a minute or two. Then Bobby sends her image away so that it's just the two of them, two Pretty Boys dancing the night away, private party, stranger go find your own good time. How it used to be sometimes in real life, between just the two of them. He remembers hard.

"B-B-B-Bobby!" he yells, the old stutter reappearing. Bobby's image seems to give a jump, as though he finally heard. He forgets everything, the girl, the Rude Boy, the Mohawk, them on the stairs, and plunges through the crowd toward the screen. People fall away from him as though they were reenacting the Red Sea. He dives for the screen, for Bobby, not caring how it must look to anyone. What would they know about it, any of them. He can't remember in his whole sixteen years ever hearing one person say, *I love my friend*. Not Bobby, not even himself.

He fetches up against the screen like a slap and hangs there, face pressed to the glass. He can't see it now but on the screen Bobby would seem to be looking down at him. Bobby never stops dancing.

The Mohawk comes and peels him off. The others swarm up and take him away. The tall girl watches all this with the expression of a woman who lives upstairs from Cinderella and wears the same shoe size. She stares longingly at the screen. Bobby waves bye-bye and turns away.

"Of course, the process isn't reversible," says the older man. The steely hair has a careful blue tint; he has sense enough to stay out of hip clothes.

They have laid him out on a lounger with a tray of refreshments right by him. Probably slap his hand if he reaches for any, he thinks.

"Once you've distilled something to pure information, it just can't be reconstituted in a less efficient form," the woman explains, smiling. There's no warmth to her. A *less efficient form*. If that's what she really thinks, he knows he should be plenty scared of these people. Did she say things like that to Bobby? And did it make him even *more* eager?

"There may be no more exalted a form of existence than to live as sentient information," she goes on. "Though a lot more research must be done before we can offer conversion on a larger scale."

"Yeah?" he says. "Do they know that, Bobby and the rest?"

"Oh, there's nothing to worry about," says the younger man. He looks as though he's still getting over the pain of having outgrown his boogie shoes. "The system's quite perfected. What Grethe means is we want to research more applications for this new form of existence."

"Why not go over yourselves and do that, if it's so *exalted*."

"There are certain things that need to be done on this side," the woman says bitchily. "Just because—"

"Grethe." The older man shakes his head. She pats her slicked-back hair as though to soothe herself and moves away.

"We have other plans for Bobby when he gets tired of being featured in clubs," the older man says. "Even now, we're educating him, adding more data to his basic information configuration—"

"That would mean he ain't really *Bobby* anymore, then, huh?"

The man laughs. "Of course he's Bobby. Do you change into someone else every time you learn something new?"

"Can you prove I *don't*?"

The man eyes him warily. "Look. You *saw* him. Was that Bobby?"

"I saw a video of Bobby dancing on a giant screen."

"That *is* Bobby and it will remain Bobby no matter what, whether he's poured into a video screen in a dot pattern or transmitted the length of the universe."

"That what you got in mind for him? Send a message to nowhere and the message is him?"

"We could. But we're not going to. We're introducing him to the concept of higher dimensions. The way he is now, he could possibly break out of the three-dimensional level of existence, pioneer a whole new plane of reality."

"Yeah? And how do you think you're gonna get Bobby to do that?"

"We convince him it's entertaining."

He laughs. "That's a good one. Yeah. Entertainment. You get to a higher level of existence and you'll open a club there that only the hippest can get into. It figures."

The older man's face gets hard. "That's what all you Pretty Boys are crazy for, isn't it? Entertainment?"

He looks around. The room must have been a dressing room or something back in the days when bands had been live. Somewhere overhead he can hear the faint noise of the club but he can't tell if Bobby's still on. "You call this entertainment?"

"I'm tired of this little prick," the woman chimes in. "He's thrown away opportunities other people would kill for—"

He makes a rude noise. "Yeah, we'd all kill to be someone's data chip. You think I really believe Bobby's real just because I can see him on a *screen*?"

The older man turns to the younger one. "Phone up and have them pipe Bobby down here." Then he swings the lounger around so it faces a nice modern screen implanted in a shored-up cement-block wall.

"Bobby will join us shortly. Then he can tell you whether he's real or not himself. How will that be for you?"

He stares hard at the screen, ignoring the man, waiting for Bobby's image to appear. As though they really bothered to communicate regularly with Bobby this way. Feed in that kind of data and memory and Bobby'll believe it. He shifts uncomfortably, suddenly wondering how far he could get if he moved fast enough.

"My *boy*," says Bobby's sweet voice from the speaker on either side of the screen and he forces himself to keep looking as Bobby fades in, presenting himself on the same kind of lounger and looking mildly exerted, as though he's just come off the dance floor for real.

"Saw you shakin' it upstairs a while ago. You haven't been here for such a long time. What's the story?"

He opens his mouth but there's no sound. Bobby looks at him with boundless patience and indulgence. So Pretty, hair the perfect shade now and not a bit dry from the dyes and lighteners, skin flawless and shining like a healthy angel. Overnight angel, just like the old song.

"My *boy*," says Bobby. "Are you struck, like, shy or *dead*?"

He closes his mouth, takes one breath. "I don't like it, Bobby. I don't like it this way."

"Of course not, lover. You're the Watcher, not the Watchee, that's why. Get yourself picked up for a season or two and your disposition will *change*."

"You really like it, Bobby, being a blip on a chip?"

"Blip on a chip, your ass. I'm a universe now. I'm, like, *everything*. And, hey, dig—I'm on every channel." Bobby laughed. "I'm happy I'm sad!"

"S-A-D," comes in the older man. "Self-Aware Data."

"Ooo-eee," he says. "Too clever for me. Can I get out of here now?"

"What's your hurry?" Bobby pouts. "Just because I went over you don't love me anymore?"

"You always were screwed up about that, Bobby. Do you know the difference between being loved and being watched?"

"Sophisticated boy," Bobby says. "So wise, so learned. So fully packed. On this side, there is no difference. Maybe there never was. If you love me, you watch me. If you don't look, you don't care and if you don't care I don't matter. If I don't matter, I don't exist. Right?"

He shakes his head.

"No, my boy, I *am* right." Bobby laughs. "You believe I'm right, because if you *didn't*, you wouldn't come shaking your Pretty Boy ass in a place like *this*, now, would you? You *like* to be watched, get seen. You see me, I see you. Life goes on."

He looks up at the older man, needing relief from Bobby's pure Prettiness. "How does he see me?"

"Sensors in the equipment. Technical stuff, nothing you care about."

He sighs. He should be upstairs or across town, shaking it with everyone else, living Pretty for as long as he could. Maybe in another few months, this way would begin to look good to him. By then they might be off Pretty Boys and looking for some other type and there he'd be, out in the cold-cold, sliding down the other side of his peak and no one would *want* him. Shut out of something going on that he might want to know about after all. Can he face it? He glances at the younger man. All grown up and no place to glow. Yeah, but can *he* face it?

He doesn't know. Used to be there wasn't much of a choice and now that there is, it only seems to make it worse. Bobby's image looks like it's studying him for some kind of sign, Pretty eyes bright, hopeful.

The older man leans down and speaks low into his ear. "We need to get you before you're twenty-five, before the brain stops growing. A mind taken from a still-growing brain will blossom and adapt. Some of Bobby's predecessors have made marvelous adaptation to their new medium. Pure video: there's a staff that does nothing all day but watch and interpret their symbols for breakthroughs in thought. And we'll be taking Pretty Boys for as long as they're publicly sought-after. It's the most efficient way to find the best performers, go for the ones everyone wants to see or be. The top of the trend is closest to heaven. And even if you never make a breakthrough, you'll still be entertainment. Not such a bad way to live for a Pretty Boy. Never have to age, to be sick, to lose touch. You spent most of your life young, why learn how to be old? Why learn how to live without all the things you have now—"

He puts his hands over his ears. The older man is still talking and Bobby is saying something and the younger man and the woman come over to try to do something about him. Refreshments are falling off the tray. He struggles out of the lounger and makes for the door.

"Hey, my *boy*," Bobby calls after him. "Gimme a minute here, gimme what the problem is."

He doesn't answer. What can you tell someone made of pure information anyway?

$$\bullet \quad \bullet \quad \bullet$$

There's a new guy on the front door, bigger and meaner than His Mohawkness, but he's only there to keep people out, not to keep anyone *in*. You want to jump ship, go to, you poor unhip asshole. Even if you are a Pretty Boy. He reads it in the guy's face as he passes from noise into the three a.m. quiet of the street.

They let him go. He doesn't fool himself about that part. They *let* him out of the room because they know all about him. They know he lives like Bobby lived, they know he loves what Bobby loved—the clubs, the admiration, the lust of strangers for his personal magic. He can't say he doesn't love that, because he *does*. He isn't even sure if he loves it more than he ever loved Bobby, or if he loves it more than being alive. Than being live.

And here it is, three a.m., clubbing prime time, and he is moving toward home. Maybe he is a poor unhip asshole after all, no matter what he loves. Too stupid even to stay in the club, let alone grab a ride to heaven. Still he keeps moving, unbothered by the chill but feeling it.

Bobby doesn't have to go home in the cold anymore, he thinks. Bobby doesn't even have to get through the hours between club-times if he doesn't want to. All times are now prime time for Bobby. Even if he gets unplugged, he'll never know the difference. Poof, it's a day later, poof, it's a year later, poof, you're out for good. Painlessly.

Maybe Bobby has the right idea, he thinks, moving along the empty sidewalk. If he goes over tomorrow, who will notice? Like when he left the dance floor—people will come and fill up the space. Ultimately, it wouldn't make any difference to anyone.

He smiles suddenly. Except *them*. As long as they don't have him, he makes a difference. As long as he has flesh to shake and flaunt and feel with, he makes a pretty goddamn big difference to them. Even after they don't want him anymore, he will still be the one they didn't get. He rubs his hands together against the chill, feeling the skin rubbing skin, really *feeling* it for the first time in a long time, and he thinks about sixteen million things all at once, maybe one thing for every brain cell he's using, or maybe one thing for every brain cell yet to come.

He keeps moving, holding to the big thought, making a difference, and all the little things they won't be making a program out of. He's lightheaded with joy—he doesn't know what's going to happen.

Neither do they.

JOHN SHIRLEY

WOLVES OF THE PLATEAU

(1988)

NINE A.M., and Jerome-X wanted a smoke. He didn't smoke, but he wanted one in here, and he could see how people went into prison nonsmokers and came out doing two packs a day. Maybe had to get their brains rewired to get off it. Which was ugly, he'd been rewired once to get off Sink, synthetic cocaine, and he'd felt like a processor with a glitch for a month after that.

He pictured his thoughts like a little train, zipping around the cigarette-burnt graffiti: YOU FUCKED NOW and GASMAN WUZZERE and GASMAN IS AN IDIOT-MO. The words were stippled on the dull pink ceiling in umber burn spots. Jerome wondered who GASMAN was and what they'd put him in prison for.

He yawned. He hadn't slept much the night before. It took a long time to learn to sleep in prison. He wished he'd upgraded his chip so he could use it to activate his sleep endorphins. But that was a grade above what he'd been able to afford—and way above the kind of brain chips he'd been dealing. He wished he could turn off the light panel, but it was sealed in.

There was a toilet and a broken water fountain in the cell. There were also a few bunks, but he was alone in this static place of watery blue light and faint pink distances. The walls were salmon-colored garbage blocks. The words singed into the ceiling were blurred and impotent.

•   •   •

Almost noon, his stomach rumbling, Jerome was still lying on his back on the top bunk when the trash can said, "Eric Wexler, re-ma-a-in on your bunk while the ne-ew prisoner ente-e-ers the cell!"

Wexler? Oh, yeah. They thought his name was Wexler. The fake ID program.

He heard the cell door slide open; he looked over, saw the trash can ushering a stocky Chicano guy into lockup. The robot everyone called "the trash can" was a stumpy metal cylinder with a group of camera lenses, a retractable plastic arm, and a gun muzzle that could fire a Taser charge, rubber bullets, tear-gas pellets, or .45-caliber rounds. It was supposed to use the .45 only in extreme situations, but the robot was battered, it whined when it moved, its digital voice was warped. When they got like that, Jerome had heard, you didn't fuck with them; they'd mix up the rubber bullets with the .45-caliber, Russian Roulette style.

The door sucked itself shut, the trash can whined away down the hall, its rubber wheels squeaking once with every revolution. Jerome heard a tinny cymbal crash as someone, maybe trying to get it to shoot at a guy in the next cell, threw a tray at it; followed by some echoey human shouting and a distorted admonishment from the trash can. The Chicano was still standing by the plexigate, hands shoved in his pockets, staring at Jerome, looking like he was trying to place him.

"'Sappenin'," Jerome said, sitting up on the bed. He was grateful for the break in the monotony.

"*¿Qué pasa?* You like the top bunk, huh? Tha's good."

"I can read the ceiling better from up here. About ten seconds' worth of reading matter. It's all I got. You can have the lower bunk."

"You fuckin'-A I can." But there was no real aggression in his tone. Jerome thought about turning on his chip, checking the guy's subliminals, his somatic signals, going for a model of probable aggression index; or maybe project for deception. He could be an undercover cop: Jerome hadn't given them his dealer, hadn't bargained at all.

But he decided against switching the chip on. Some jails had scanners for unauthorized chip output. Better not use it unless he had to. And his gut told him this guy was only a threat if he felt threatened. His gut was right almost as often as his brain chip.

The Chicano was maybe five foot six, a good five inches shorter than Jerome but probably outweighing him by fifty pounds. His face had Indian angles and small jet eyes. He was wearing printout gray-blue prison jams, #6631; they'd let him keep his hairnet. Jerome had never understood the Chicano hairnet, never had the balls to ask about it.

Jerome was pleased. He liked to be recognized, except by people who could arrest him.

"You put your hands in the pockets of those paper pants, they'll rip, and in LA County they don't give you any more for three days," Jerome advised him.

"Yeah? Shit." The Chicano took his hands carefully out of his pockets. "I don't want my cojones hanging out, people think I'm advertising—they some big fucking cojones too. You not a f——, right?"

"Nope."

"Good. How come I know you? When I *don't* know you."

Jerome grinned. "From television. You saw my tag. Jerome-X. I mean—I do some music too. I had that song, 'Six Kinds of Darkness'—"

"I don't know that, bro—oh wait, Jerome-X. The tag—I saw that. Your face-tag. You got one of those little transers? Interrupt the transmissions with your own shit?"

"Had. They confiscated it."

"That why you here? Video graffiti?"

"I wish. I'd be out in a couple months. No. Illegal augs."

"Hey, man! Me too!"

"You?" Jerome couldn't conceal his surprise. You didn't see a lot of barrio dudes doing illegal augmentation. They generally didn't like people tinkering in their brains.

"What, you think a guy from East LA can't use augs?"

"No, no. I know lots of Latino guys that use it," Jerome lied.

"Ooooh, he says *Latino*, that gotta nice sound." Overtones of danger.

Jerome hastily changed the direction of the conversation. "You never been in the big lockups where they use these fuckin' paper jammies?"

"No, just the city jail once. They didn't have those motherfucking screw machines either. Hey, you're Jerome—my name's Jessie. Actually, it Jesus"—he pronounced it "hay-soo"—"but people they, you know . . . You got any smokes? No? Shit. Okay, I adjust. I get use to it. Shit. No smokes. Fuck."

He sat on the edge of the bed, to one side of Jerome's dangling legs, and tilted his head forward. He reached under his hairnet, and under what turned out to be a hairpiece, and pulled a chip from a jack unit set into the base of his skull.

Jerome stared. "Goddamn, their probes really are busted."

Jessie frowned over the chip. There was a little blood on it. The jack unit was leaking. Cheap installation. "No, they ain't busted, there's a guy working on the probe, he's paid off, he's letting everyone through for a couple of days because of some Russian mob guys coming in, he don't know which ones they are. Some of them Russian mob guys got the augments."

"I thought sure they were going to find my unit," Jerome said. "The strip search didn't find it, but I thought the prison probes would and that'd be another year on my sentence. But they didn't."

Neither one of them thinking of throwing away the chips. It'd be like cutting out an eye.

"Same story here, bro. We both lucky."

Jessie put the microprocessor chip in his mouth, the way people did with their contact lenses, to clean it, lubricate it. Of course, bacterially speaking, it came out dirtier than it went in.

"Does the jack hurt?" Jerome asked.

Jessie took the chip out, looked at it a moment on his fingertips. It was smaller than a contact lens, a sliver of silicon and non-osmotic gallium arsenide and transparent interface-membrane, with, probably, 800,000,000 nanotransistors of engineered protein molecules sunk into it, maybe more. "No, it don't hurt yet. But if it's leaking, it fuckin' *will* hurt, man." He said something else in Spanish, shaking his head. He slipped the chip back into his jack-in unit and tapped it with the thumbnail of his right hand. So that was where the activation mouse was: under the thumbnail. Jerome's was in a knuckle.

Jessie rocked slightly, just once, sitting up on his bunk, which meant the chip had engaged and he was getting a readout. They tended to feed back into your nervous system a little at first, make you twitch once or twice; if they weren't properly insulated, they could make you crap your pants.

"That's okay," Jessie said, relaxing. "That's better." The chip inducing his brain to secrete vasopressin, contract the veins, simulate the effect of nicotine. It worked for a while, till you could get cigarettes. High-grade chip could do some numbing if you were hung up on Sim, synthetic morphine, and couldn't get any. But that was Big Scary. You could turn yourself off for good that way. You better be doing some damn fine adjusting.

Jerome thought about the hypothetical chip scanners. Maybe he should object to the guy using his chip here. But what the Chicano was doing wouldn't make for much leakage.

"What you got?" Jerome asked.

"I got an Apple NanoMind II. Big gigas. What you got?"

"You got the Mercedes, I got the Toyota. I got a Seso Picante Mark I. One of those Argentine things." (How had this guy scored an ANM II?)

"Yeah, what you got, they kinda basic, but they do most what you need. Hey, our names, they both start with *J*. And we both here for illegal augs. What else we got in common. What's your sign?"

"Uh—" What was it, anyway? He always forgot. "Pisces I think."

"No shit! I can relate to Pisces. I ran an astrology program, figured out who I should hang with. Pisces is okay. But Aquarius is—I'm a Scorpio, like— Aquarius, *qué bueno*."

What did he mean exactly, *hang with*, Jerome wondered. Scoping me about am *I* a f———, maybe that was something defensive.

But he meant something else. "You know somethin', Jerome, you got your chip too, we could do a link and maybe get over on that trash can."

Break out? Jerome felt a chilled thrill go through him. "Link with that thing? Control it? I don't think the two of us would be enough."

"We need some more guys maybe, but I got news, Jerome, there's more comin'. Maybe their names all start with *J*. You know, I mean—in a way."

In quick succession, the trash can brought their cell three more guests: a forty-ish beach bum named Eddie; a cadaverous black dude named Bones; a queen called Swish, whose real name, according to the trash can, was Paul Torino.

"This place smells like it's comin' apart," Eddie said. He had a surfer's greasy blond topknot and all the usual Surf Punk tattoos. Meaningless now, Jerome thought, the pollution-derived oxidation of the offshore had pretty much ended surfing. The anaerobics had taken over the surf, in North America, thriving in the toxic waters like a gelatinous Sargasso. If you surfed you did it with an antitoxin suit and a gas mask. "Smells in here like somethin' died and didn't go to heaven. Stinks worse'n Malibu."

"It's those landfill blocks," Bones said. He was missing three front teeth, and his sunken face was like something out of a zombie video. But he was an energetic zombie, pacing back and forth as he spoke. "Compressed garbage," he told Eddie. "Organic stuff mixed with the polymers, the plastics, whatever was in the trash heap, make 'em into bricks 'cause they run outta landfill, but after a while, if the contractor didn't get 'em to set right, y'know, they start to rot. It's hot outside is why you're gettin' it now. Use garbage to cage garbage, they say. Fucking assholes."

       • • •

The trash can pushed a rack of trays up to the Plexiglas bars and whirred their lunch to them, tray by tray. The robot gave them an extra tray. It was screwing up.

They ate their chicken patties—the chicken was almost greaseless, gristleless, which meant it was vat chicken, genetically engineered fleshstuff—and between bites they bitched about the food and indulged the usual paranoid speculation about mind-control chemicals in the coffee.

Jerome looked around at the others, thinking: at least they're not ass-kickers.

They were crammed here because of the illegal augs sweep, some political drive to clean up the clinics, maybe to see to it that the legal augmentation companies kept their pit-bull grip on the industry. So there wasn't anybody in for homicide, for gang torture, or anything. No major psychopaths. Not a bad cell to be in.

"You Jerome-X, really?" Swish fluted. She (Jerome always thought of a queen as *she* and *her*, out of respect for the tilt of her consciousness) was probably Filipino; had her face girled up at a cheap clinic. Cheeks built up for a heart shape, eyes rounded, lips filled out, tits looking like there was a couple of tin funnels under her jammies. Some of the collagen they'd injected to fill out her lips had shifted its bulk so her lower lip was lopsided. One cheekbone was a little higher than the other. A karmic revenge on at least some of malekind, Jerome thought, for forcing women into girdles and foot-binding and anorexia. What did this creature use her chip for, besides getting high?

"Oooh, Jerome-X! I saw your tag before on the TV. The one when your face kind of floated around the President's head and some printout words came out of your mouth and blocked her face out. God, she's such a *cunt*."

"What words did he block her out with?" Eddie asked.

"I think . . . 'Would you know a liar if you heard one anymore?' That's what it was!" Swish said. "It was sooo perfect, because that cunt wanted that war to go on forever, you *know* she did. And she lies about it, ooh *God* she lies."

"You just think she's a cunt because you *want* one," Eddie said, dropping his pants to use the toilet. He talked loudly to cover up the noise of it. "You want one and you can't afford it. I think the Prez was right, the fucking Mexican People's Republic is jammin' our borders, sending commie agents in—"

Swish said, "Oh, God, he's a Surf Nazi—But God yes, I want one—I want *her* cunt. That bitch doesn't know how to use it anyway. Honey, I know how I'd use that thing—" Swish stopped abruptly and shivered, hugged herself. Using her long purple nails, she reached up and pried loose a flap of skin behind her ear, plucked out her chip. She wet it, adjusted its feed mode, put it back in, tapping it with the activation mouse under a nail. She pressed the flap shut. Her eyes glazed as she adjusted. She could get high on the chip-impulses for maybe twenty-four hours and then it'd kill her. She'd have to go cold turkey or die. Or get out. And maybe she'd been doing it for a while now . . .

None of them would be allowed to post bail. They'd each get the two years mandatory minimum sentence. Illegal augs, the Feds thought, were getting out of hand. Black-market chip implants were good for playing havoc with the state database lottery; used by bookies of all kinds; used to keep accounts where the IRS couldn't find them unless they cornered you physically and broke your code; the aug chips were used to out-think banking computers, and for spiking cash machines; used to milk the body, prod the brain into authorizing the secretion of beta endorphins and ACTH and adrenaline and testosterone and other biochemical toys; used to figure the odds at casinos; used to compute the specs for homemade designer drugs; used by the mob's street dons to play strategy and tactics; used by the kid gangs for the same reasons; used for illegal congregations on the Plateau.

It was the Plateau, Jerome thought, that really scared the shit out of the Feds. It had possibilities.

It was way beyond the fucking Internet; it was past the Deep Internet; it was even beyond the Grid.

• • •

The trash can dragged in a cot for the extra man, shoved it folded under the door, and blared, "Lights out, all inmates are required to be i-i-in their bu-unks-s-s . . ." Its voice was failing.

After the trash can and the light had gone, they climbed off their bunks and sat hunkered in a circle on the floor.

They were on chips, but not transmission-linked to one another. Jacked-up on the chips, they communicated in a spoken shorthand.

"Bull," Bones was saying. "Door." He was a voice in the darkness; a scarecrow of shadow.

"Time," Jessie said.

"Compatibility? Know?" Eddie said.

Jerome said, "Noshee!" Snorts of laughter from the others.

"Link check," Bones said.

"Models?" Jessie said.

Then they joined in an incantation of numbers.

It was a fifteen-minute conversation in less than a minute.

Translated, the foregoing conversation went: "It's bullshit, you get past the trash can, there's human guards, you can't reprogram them."

"But at certain hours," Jessie told him, "there's only one on duty. They're used to seeing the can bring people in and out. They won't question it till they try to confirm it. By then we'll be on their ass."

"We might not be compatible," Eddie had pointed out. "You understand, compatible?"

"Oh, hey, man, I *think* we can comprehend that," Jerome said, making the others snort with laughter. Eddie wasn't liked much.

Then Bones had said, "The only way to see if we're compatible is to do a systems link. We got the links, we got the thinks, like the man says. It's either the chain that holds us in, or it's the chain that pulls us out."

Jerome's scalp tightened. A systems link. A mini-Plateau. Sharing minds. Brutal intimacy. Maybe some fallout from the Plateau. He wasn't ready for it.

If it went sour, he could get time tacked onto his sentence for attempted jailbreak. And somebody might get dusted. They might have to kill a human guard. Jerome had once punched a dealer in the nose, and the spurt of blood had made him sick. He couldn't kill anyone. But . . . he had shit for alternatives. He knew he wouldn't make it through two years anyway, when they sent him up to the Big One.

The Big One'd grind him up for sure. They'd find his chip there, and it'd piss them off. They'd let the bulls rape him and give him the New Virus; he'd flip out from being locked in and chipless, and they'd put him under Aversion Rehab and burn him out.

Jerome savaged a thumbnail with his incisors. *Sent to the Big One.*

He'd been trying not to think about it. Making himself take it one day at a time. But now he had to look at the alternatives. His stomach twisted itself to punish him for being so stupid. For getting into dealing augments so he could finance a big transer. *Why?* A transer didn't get him anything but his face pirated onto local TV for maybe twenty seconds. He'd thrown himself away trying to get it . . .

Why was it so fucking important? his stomach demanded, wringing itself vindictively.

"Thing is," Bones said, "we could all be cruisin' into a set-up. Some kind of sting thing. Maybe it's a little too weird how the police prober let us all through."

(Someone listening would have heard him say, "Sting, funny luck.")

Jessie snorted. "I tol' you, man. The prober is paid off. They letting them all through because some of them are mob. I know that, because I'm part of the thing. We deal wid the Russians. Okay?"

("Probe greased, fa-me.")

"You with the mob?" Bones asked.

("You'm?")

"You got it. Just a dealer. But I know where a half million Newbux wortha augshit is, so they going to get me out if I do my part. The way the system is set up, the prober had to let everyone through. His boss thinks we got our chips taken out when they arraigned us; sometimes they do it that way. This time it was supposed to be the jail surgeon. By the time they catch up their own red tape, we get outta here. Now listen—we can't do the trash can without we all get into it, because we haven't got enough *K* otherwise. So who's in, for fuck's sake?"

He'd said, "Low, half mill, bluff surgeon, there there, twip, all-none, *who* yuh fucks?"

Something in his voice skittered with claws behind smoked glass: he was getting testy, irritable from the chip adjustments for his nicotine habit, maybe other adjustments: the side effects of liberal cerebral self-modulating burning through a threadbare nervous system.

The rest of the meeting, translated . . .

"I dunno," Eddie said. "I thought I'd do my time, cause if it goes sour—"

"Hey man," Jessie said, "I can *take* your fuckin' chip. And be out before they notice your ass don't move no more."

"The man's right," Swish said. Her pain-suppression system was unraveling, axon by axon, and she was running out of adjust. "Let's just do it, okay? Please? Okay? I gotta get out. I feel like I wish I was dogshit so I could be something better."

"I can't handle two years in the Big, Eddie, and I'll do what I gotta, dudeski," Jerome heard himself say, realizing he was helping Jessie threaten Eddie. Amazed at himself. Not his style.

"It's all of us or nobody, Eddie," Bones said.

Eddie was quiet for a while.

• • •

Jerome had turned off his chip, because it was thinking endlessly about Jessie's plan, and all it came up with was an ugly model of the risks. You had to know when to go with intuition.

Jerome was committed. And he was standing on the brink of link. The time was now, starting with Jessie.

Jessie was *operator*. He picked the order. First Eddie, to make sure about him. Then Jerome. Maybe because he had Jerome scoped for a refugee from the middle class, an anomaly here, and Jerome might try and raise the Heat on his chip, make a deal. Once they had him linked in, he was locked up.

After Jerome, it'd be Bones and then Swish.

They held hands, so that the link signal, transmitted from the chip using the electric field generated by the brain, would be carried with the optimum fidelity.

He heard them exchange frequency designates, numbers strung like beads in the darkness, and heard the hiss of suddenly indrawn breaths as Jessie and Eddie linked in. And he heard, "Let's go, Jerome."

Jerome's eyes had adjusted to the dark, the night giving up some of its buried light, and Jerome could just make a crude outline of Jessie's features like a charcoal rubbing from an Aztec carving.

Jerome reached to the back of his own head, found the glue-tufted hairs that marked his flap, and pulled the skin away from the chip's jack unit. He tapped the chip. It didn't take. He tapped it again, and this time he felt the shift in his bio electricity; felt it hum between his teeth.

Jerome's chip communicated with his brain via an interface of nano-print configured rhodopsin protein; the ribosomes borrowing neurohumoral transmitters from the brain's blood supply, reordering the transmitters so that they carried a programmed pattern of ion releases for transmission across synaptic gaps to the brain's neuronal dendrites; the chip using magnetic resonance holography to collate with brain-stored memories and psychological trends. Declaiming to itself the mythology of the brain; reenacting on its silicon stage the Legends of his subjective world history.

Jerome closed his eyes and looked into the back of his eyelids. The digital read-out was printed in luminous green across the darkness. He focused on the cursor, concentrated so it moved up to ACCESS. He subverbalized, "Open frequency." The chip heard his practiced subverbalization, and numbers appeared on the back of his eyelids: 63391212.70. He read them out to the others and they picked up his frequency. Almost choking on the word, knowing what it would bring, he told the chip: "Open."

It opened to the link. He'd only done it once before. It was illegal, and he was secretly glad it was illegal because it scared him. "They're holding the Plateau back," his brain-chip wholesaler had told him, "because they're scared of what worldwide electronic telepathy might bring down on them. Like, everyone will collate information, use it to see through the bastards' game, throw the assbites out of office."

Maybe that was the real reason. It was something the power brokers couldn't control. But there were other reasons.

Reasons like a strikingly legitimate fear of people going mad.

All Jerome and the others wanted was a sharing of processing capabilities. Collaborative calculation. But the chips weren't designed to filter out the irrelevant input before it reached the user's cognition level. Before the chip had done its filtering, the two poles of the link—Jerome and Jessie—would each see the swarming hive of the other's total consciousness. Would see how the other perceived themselves to be, and then objectively, as they really were.

He saw Jessie as a grid and as a holographic entity. He braced himself and the holograph came at him, an abstract tarantula of computer-generated color and line, scrambling down over him . . . and for an instant it crouched in the seat of his consciousness: Jessie. Jesus Chaco.

Jessie was a family man. He was a patriarch, a protector of his wife and six kids (six kids!) and his widowed sister's four kids and of the poor children of his barrio. He was a muddied painting of his father, who had fled the social forest fire of Mexico's civil war between the drug cartels and the government, spiriting his capital to Los Angeles where he'd sown it into the black market. Jessie's father had been killed defending territory from the Russian-American mob; Jessie compromised with the mob to save his father's business, and loathed himself for it. Wanted to kill their bosses; had to work side by side with them. Perceived his wife as a functional pet, an object of adoration who was the very apotheosis of her fixed role. To imagine her doing other than child-rearing and keeping house would be to imagine the sun become a snowball, the moon become a monkey. Jessie's family insistently clung to the old, outdated roles.

And Jerome glimpsed Jessie's undersides; Jesus Chaco's self-image with its outsized penis and impossibly spreading shoulders, sitting in a perfect and shining cherry automobile, always the newest and most luxurious model, the automotive throne from which he surveyed his kingdom. Jerome saw guns emerging from the grill of the car to splash Jessie's enemies apart with his unceasing ammunition . . . It was a Robert Williams cartoon capering at the heart of Jessie's unconscious . . . Jessie saw himself as Jerome saw him; the electronic mirrors reflecting one another. Jessie cringed.

Jerome saw himself then, reflected back from Jessie.

He saw Jerome-X on a video screen with lousy vertical hold; wobbling, trying to arrange its pixels firmly and losing them. A figure of mewling inconsequence; a brief flow of electrons that might diverge left or right like spray from a water hose depressed with the thumb. Raised in a high-security condo village, protected by cameras and computer lines to private security thugs; raised in a media-windowed womb, with PCs and VCRs and a thousand varieties of video games; shaped by cable TV and fantasy rental; sexuality imprinted by sneaking his parents' badly hidden cache of brainsex files. And in stations from around the world, seeing the same StarFaces appear on channel after channel as the star's fame spread like a stain across the frequency bands. Seeing the Star's World Self crystallizing; the media figure coming into definition against the backdrop of media competition, becoming real in this electronic collective unconscious.

Becoming real, himself, in his own mind, simply because he'd appeared on a few thousand TV screens, through video tagging, transer graffiti. Growing up with a sense that media events were real and personal events were not. Anything that didn't happen on the Grid didn't happen. Even as he hated conventional programming, even as he regarded it as the cud of ruminants, still the net and TV and di-vees defined his sense of personal unreality; and left him unfinished.

Jerome saw Jerome: perceiving himself unreal. Jerome: scamming a transer, creating a presence via video graffiti. Thinking he was doing it for reasons of radical statement. Seeing, now, that he was doing it to make himself feel substantial, to superimpose himself on the Media Grid . . .

And then Eddie's link was there, Eddie's computer model sliding down over Jerome like a mudslide. Eddie seeing himself as a Legendary Wanderer, a rebel, a homemade mystic; his fantasy parting to reveal an anal-expulsive sociopath; a whiner perpetually scanning for someone to blame for his sour luck.

Suddenly Bones tumbled into the link; a complex worldview that was a sort of streetside sociobiology, mitigated by a loyalty to friends, a mystical faith in brain chips and amphetamines. His underside a masochistic dwarf, the troll of self-doubt, lacerating itself with guilt.

And then Swish, a woman with an unsightly growth, errant glands that were like tumors in her, something other people called "testicles." Perpetually hungry for the means to dampen the pain of an infinite self-derision that mimicked her father's utter rejection of her. A mystical faith in synthetic morphine.

. . . Jerome mentally reeling with disorientation, seeing the others as a network of distorted self-images, caricatures of grotesque ambitions. Beyond them he glimpsed another realm through a break in the psychic clouds: the Plateau, the whispering plane of brain chips linked on forbidden frequencies, an electronic haven for doing deals unseen by cops; a Plateau prowled only by the exquisitely ruthless; a vista of enormous challenges and inconceivable risks and always the potential for getting lost, for madness. A place roamed by the wolves of wetware.

There was a siren quiver from that place, a soundless howling, pulling at them . . . drawing them in . . .

"*Uh uh*, wolflost, pross," Bones said, maybe aloud or maybe through the chips. Translated from chip shorthand, those syllables meant, "Stay away from the Plateau, or we get sucked into it, we lose our focus. Concentrate on parallel processing function."

Jerome looked behind his eyelids, sorted through the files. He moved the cursor down . . .

Suddenly, it was there. The group-thinking capacity looming above them, a sentient skyscraper. They all felt a rush of megalomaniacal pleasure in identifying with it; with a towering edifice of Mind. Five chips became One.

They were ready. Jessie transmitted the bait.

• • •

Alerted to an illegal use of implant chips, the trash can was squeaking down the hall, scanning to precisely locate the source. It came to a sudden stop, rocking on its wheels in front of their cell. Jessie reached through the bars and touched its input jack.

The machine froze with a *clack* midway through a turn, and hummed as it processed what they fed it. Would the robot bite?

Bones had a program for the IBM Cyberguard Fourteens, with all the protocol and a range of sample entry codes. Parallel processing from samples took less than two seconds to decrypt the trash can's access code. Then—

They were in. The hard part was the reprogramming.

Jerome found the way. He told the trash can that he wasn't Eric Wexler, because the DNA code was all wrong, if you looked close enough; what we have here is a case of mistaken identity.

Since this information *seemed* to be coming from authorized sources—the decrypted access code made them authorized—the trash can fell for the gag and opened the cage.

The trash can took the five Eric Wexlers down the hall—that was Jessie's doing, showing them how to make it think of five as one, something his people had learned from the immigration computers. It escorted them through the plastiflex door, through the steel door, and into Receiving. The human guard was heaping sugar into his antique Ronald McDonald coffee mug and watching *The Mutilated* on his wallet TV. Bones and Jessie were in the room and moving in on him before he broke free of the television and went for the button. Bones's long left arm spiked out and his stiffened fingers hit a nerve cluster below the guy's left ear, and he went down, the sugar dispenser in one hand swishing a white fan onto the floor.

Jerome's chip had cross-referenced Bones's attack style. Bones was trained by commandos, the chip said. Military elite. Was he a plant? Bones smiled at him and tilted his head, which Jerome's chip read as: *No. I'm trained by the Underground. Radics.*

Jessie was at the console, deactivating the trash can, killing the cameras, opening the outer doors. Jessie and Swish led the way out, Swish whining softly and biting her lip. There were two more guards at the gate, one of them asleep. Jessie had taken the gun from the guy Bones had put under, so the first guard at the gate was dead before he could hit an alarm. The catnapping guy woke and yelled with hoarse terror, and then Jessie shot him in the throat.

Watching the guard fall, spinning, blood making its own slow-motion spiral in the air, Jerome felt a perfect mingling of sickness, fear, and self-disgust. The guard was young, wearing a cheap wedding ring, probably had a young family. So Jerome stepped over the dying man and made an adjustment; used his chip, chilled himself out with adrenaline. Had to—he was committed now. And he knew with a bland certainty that they had reached the Plateau after all.

He would live on the Plateau now. He belonged there, now that he was one of the wolves.

PHILLIP MANN

AN OLD-FASHIONED STORY

(1989)

NOT HAVING THE TOOL KIT to hand and being of an impatient nature, Jody improvised by using the blunt end of a nail file to prize up the large toenail on Elizabeth's left foot. Revealed was the small copper screw which controlled the energy circuit. Two turns with the nail file and the screw lifted. Immediately Elizabeth's brown tanned body lost its appearance of robust health.

She slumped. Breasts became pouches. Skin became rubbery. The eyes lost their sparkle and turned upward, becoming like boiled egg-whites. With an audible hiss the abdomen became concave and the firm thigh muscles turned to lard.

Jody looked at his handiwork with some alarm. He had never gone so far as to deactivate Elizabeth's energy circuit. The transformation from nubile young woman to this flaccid thing of foam and plastic was almost too much for him. For a moment he thought seriously of calling in a specialist, but then he rallied. "No," he reasoned, "the manual says that repairs and modifications can be made by the careful amateur, and that's me." He looked at the body lying on the kitchen table and noticed that since the stomach had sunk, a fine hairline seam had become evident running from under the jaw right down to the crotch. He also noticed a foetid smell: a difficult smell to define, something of babies and something of machine oil. There was also a slight seepage coming from nose and vagina, and Jody wondered if he should have read more carefully the section in the manual entitled, "Pre-closedown procedures." He crossed to the sink and collected a full roll of kitchen tissues, which he began to tuck round the body.

And at that moment the doorbell rang. This was followed quickly by the opening of the front door and a voice calling, "Yoo-hoo. It's only me." Jody recognized the voice of Hildergarde, the girl who lived next door and who had been his friend and playmate since childhood.

"I'm back here," called Jody. "In the kitchen. I'm trying to mend Elizabeth." He heard the crisp tap tap of Hildergarde's shoes and guessed that she had come to show him the new outfit she had bought during her visit to the city.

He was right. Hildergarde arrived and paused in the doorway, one hand up under her hair at the back of her head creating a French effect and the other hand on her hips. The dress was Empire style with high bodice and ankle length hem. It was made of yellow and green silk with blue lace round the neck and arms. On her feet were high-heeled boots with old trim. "*Est-ce que tu aimes* my dress?" asked Hildergarde with an affected accent.

Hildergarde pulled a face at his obvious lack of interest and dropped her pose and entered the kitchen. "What's wrong with her?" she asked.

"I don't know," said Jody patiently. "That's what I'm trying to find out."

"Well, did she suddenly stop moving and start to smolder or something? My Joseph did that once. We'd forgotten to keep him topped up. He just stood there and started to fume. Then Dad came in and carried him out to the garage and filled his sack and whatnots with oil and that syntho-extract you can get at the chemists, and he was right as rain."

"Hmm," said Jody, his forehead wrinkling. "I wish it were that simple, but I check her every week and there's never been a problem. Besides, she's got a daily vomit and douche cycle installed and if there were a fluid balance problem I'd know about it soon enough. Hell, the bed'd become a river. She's very clean."

"What happened then?"

"It was this morning, about half past ten. I was feeling a bit . . . you know. And no one was home. So then suddenly Elizabeth stops and lifts up her head and then she butted me right here." Jody pointed to his forehead. There was a bump, covered by his blond fringe. Hildergarde reached out and touched the bump gently with the tips of her fingers. "That's going to be sore," she said. "The skin's all cracked."

"It is sore," said Jody. "Well, I switched her off for a while, for about an hour . . . thought I'd let her cool down. And when I switched her back on she was just like normal. But then later on we were out by the pool talking and she suddenly threw her glass into the pool and then tried to throw me in. I hit the safety switch and closed her down. And then I thought I'd try and mend her myself."

"What do you think's wrong with her?"

"Just rogueing a bit, I think. I've decided to strip her down, give her a tune-up, and change her personality card. That ought to do the trick. And if it doesn't—"

"Harry knows a lot about Synthos," said Hildergarde. "Why not call him in? Remember he made those Siamese twins one time and that—" Harry was the boy who lived two doors down the road. He could do everything well and he and Jody had been natural enemies from the day they learned to race their trikes.

"If I want Harry's help," said Jody, "I'll ask for it. For the moment I want to do this myself. More interesting that way. All right?" Hildergarde nodded. "So, you hold the manual where I can see it and I'll open her up."

• • •

Hildergarde took the manual and stood at the end of the table near the supine Elizabeth's head. She held the pages open away from her.

Jody bent to his work. "Now let's see. It says here, 'Release the top seal by gentle pressure on the larynx and then insert finger and slide downward to open pectoral, stomach, and bowel areas.' Right. Here goes." He pressed gently on Elizabeth's larynx and the mouth opened and then the entire throat flap. He slipped his finger inside the flap and slid it downward and the skin opened easily. It slit laterally too at the diaphragm and flopped back. The inside of the skin was dark like fish skin and oily. Revealed within were a complicated array of plastic wheels and bands as well as micro-circuitry and inflatable pockets. The skeletal structure was of shiny stainless-steel with ball joints and leaf-spring joints and feather-sensor couplings.

"Fan-tastic," said Jody. "Hell, it makes you wonder what we're like inside, doesn't it?"

Hildergarde's attention was on the pelvis. Here there was a modular arrangement of compressors, flexible bands, and micro switches and all were mounted on a stainless-steel girdle.

"What's that?" she asked, pointing to a small pocket of stretched fabric. Jody consulted the chart in the manual.

"That's the vaginal sack."

"My Joseph's got one of those too. I saw it when Dad was servicing him one day. Hey, what model is this?"

Jody consulted the front pages of the manual. "Model number and inspection warranty will be found on the skull close to the right ear under the wig flap."

Hildergarde took hold of Elizabeth's hair, which was now lifeless and lank like seaweed, and peeled it back from the skull. It came away easily like a teapot cozy to reveal neatly stenciled details.

Model: Ovida Mark 2.4. Fem. Spec. 37. Card 4. Elizabeth the Entertainer. Available in coral, tan and ebony. Swim protected. Throw and jump fortified. Parts compatible with Ovida 1.5–2.4. (All sexes.) Note: this model has both vacuum and pneumatic functions. Inspected by Taurus and Virgo Electronics Inc. Brooklyn. Wgtn.

"My Joseph's an Ovida 2.4, too. Hey let me look."

Hildergarde came round the table and studied Elizabeth's pelvic arrangements in detail. She pointed to a series of bright beveled studs mounted on a flexible plastic plate and connected to a small hydraulic piston. "You see those," she said. "That's where the penis attachment fits. Isn't that clever?"

Jody looked at Hildergarde. "Penis attachment?" he said. "You mean they just clip on? I mean, I never thought . . ."

Hildergarde looked at him scornfully. "Well, it's a bit more complicated than that but still pretty simple all the same. I've got two of them actually." Then suddenly she blushed. "They're quite different . . . well, the same but different. Similar. What about Elizabeth?"

"Never thought much about it," said Jody. I just accepted the way she is."

"Really?" said Hildergarde, and Jody could not tell whether she believed him or not.

"Yes, really. I didn't even know the models were unisex. I mean my Elizabeth doesn't look anything like your Joseph."

"True. They're not even like brother and sister."

"There must be something on their card that alters the physiognomy as well."

"Must be. Come on let's find the card cache," said Hildergarde with enthusiasm. "This is fun."

· · ·

Jody grunted and consulted the manual which he now had to prop up on the side of the table since Hildergarde wanted to be actively involved in the investigation. "Now let's see. 'Personality Card.' 'Destruction of' . . . 'Duplication' . . . 'Mail-ordering' . . . Here we are. 'Replacement' . . . page fifteen." He thumbed through the pages. "'The personality card cache is located above the stomach pouch and to the right of the sternum auxiliary power pack. Note that all directions are from the Syntho's POV. The rib-hinge release screw is beneath the left clavicle. Care must be taken to release the six shock-adjusters and isolate the cache from the power pack before removing it from the twin flanges of Synaptic Bridge three. See Illustration eighty-eight.'"

"Sounds simple," said Hildergarde. "Remember how we used to play doctors and nurses? Well this is a lot better."

The sternum and ribs were a single flexible unit. Jody found the rib-hinge release screw and turned it once. Immediately a servo-extension arm about the size of a pencil straightened and pushed, whereupon the entire rib case and sternum pivoted upward. The cache could now be clearly seen. It was about the size of a matchbox and made of a black plastic. It was tucked between two iridescent plastic extensions which resembled the spread wings of a butterfly. Together these wings constituted Synaptic Bridge 3. Bedded within them were thousands of micro paths which joined the cache to the furthest extensions of the body. "Wow," breathed Hildergarde. "That's beautiful. You'd better be careful."

At this point Jody decided that it would be a good idea to get the special Ovida Syntho tool kit from his bedroom. "Don't you touch anything while I'm gone," he said to Hildergarde. For her part she put her tongue out at him and said, "Will you bring me a lemonade when you come back?"

When he returned with his toolbox and the lemonade, he found Hildergarde with her arm deep in Elizabeth and her hair tangled in some of the white plastic cogwheels. He set his toolbox down beside Elizabeth's head and placed the glass on top of it. Then he released Hildergarde by snipping off some of her hair. Finally he rotated some of the cogs with his thumb and managed to pull most of the hair free. But in turning the cogs a few strands of the hair managed to snake down deeper into the pulleys and drums of the spine. "I told you not to touch," he said. "Now look what's happened."

"Sorry. But I discovered how they do the breasts," she replied. "It's very ingenious. I got excited and that was when my hair tumbled loose. Do you want to see?"

"What?"

"How they do the breasts."

"Oh. All right."

Hildergarde reached inside Elizabeth again, feeling down the right side of her body to the place where the hips swelled. "It's down here. There's a funny pump thing. Watch." She pumped her hand vigorously for a few moments and Elizabeth's right breast began to swell and the nipple stood up. "There's another pump on the other side for the other breast. Now I'll release it." There was a soft bubbling sound and the breast and nipple subsided. "Look. Can you see? There's a tuck in it so that part of the breast can fold inside. That's what you do if you want a male like my Joseph. You close the seal like this and voila, no breast."

"What about the nipple? You don't see men with nipples like that.

"It unclips. When it's deflated like now there's no pressure to hold the nipple on and it just unclips. There. See." She took the nipple between finger and thumb and squeezed and twisted. The nipple came free. "Easy."

"Let me look at that," said Jody and he reached across and as he did so he bumped the glass of lemonade which tipped and fell emptying part of its contents onto his toolbox and part into the open cadaver of Elizabeth. "Now look what you've made me do," he said. "I wish I'd never opened her up."

Hildergarde placed the nipple in his hand. "Here, you look at this while I mop up the mess. Where's your squeegee?"

• • •

Five minutes later the mess was cleared and Jody could return to working on the card cache. Carefully he removed the shock adjusters and set them neatly in a teacup brought from the cupboard. Then he started to disconnect the leads of the auxiliary power pack. They were stiff and he had to use more force than he wanted. Two leads came away cleanly but the third would not budge. In attempting to limber it free Jody accidentally closed a circuit in the power pack and for a few seconds power was fed to the spread body. Wheels turned, the legs lifted, the mouth bit, juices were pumped, the fingers beat on the table like castanets, and the spine arched. Then a safety breaker cut in and the body slumped once more. But the damage was done. One of the spinal cogs had sprung loose under pressure and flipped right out of the body and rolled across the floor. A thick white rubber pulley-band had jumped its tracks in the pelvic girdle and disappeared down the right leg. Two small switches had smoldered briefly and burnt the soft foam rubber which made the hips swell. A spray of warm lubricant had spurted from the lower abdomen and left a spotty trail across Hildergarde's hand, arm, and dress. She screamed and jumped back and then ran out of the kitchen and away. The front door slammed behind her. There may have been other damage done to Elizabeth but Jody could not tell.

But at least the third lead from the auxiliary power pack was disengaged and all Jody now had to do was to separate the card cache from Synaptic Bridge 3. This was accomplished without any trouble.

Jody unscrewed the top from the card cache and looked inside. He saw a square of white plastic lodged between two plates of black plastic. The white plastic showed a tab above the plates and was obviously the personality card. Using his long-nosed pliers Jody gripped the plastic card and extracted it slowly. It came free with a click. Written on the card was the simple message "Ovida Fem. spec. Card 4." He set this to one side.

Located in the special toolbox was a small file box which contained three alternative personality cards. These were supplied gratis with all Ovida Synthos by way of advertising. For the dedicated collector, thousands of other specialized types were available ranging from robust nineteenth-century working girls complete with wooden clogs to houri dancers of old Persia. These were also available in many personality shades from sunny and gentle to downright sado-masochistic. But such were very expensive and the cards were frequently custom-made to suit the particular requirements of the purchaser.

All Jody had at his disposal were four standard occupational types, all of which were basically useful and kind. Elizabeth the Entertainer had been his most complex card.

Jody studied the other cards.

Card 1. Norma the Nurse. Brisk and competent but with a tender manner. This card can be augmented to allow Norma to care for babies or the terminally ill. Note: Norma is not a doctor. For full medical functions consult Proctor the Doctor and Phyllis the Physician. Ovida International take no responsibility . . . etc.

Card 2. Myra the Muse. Myra is an advanced word processor and the ideal helpmate for the aspirant writer. She is introverted in manner but with a strong underlying sensuality. Apart from a compendious knowledge of literature, Myra also possesses optional verse functions and a rhyme memory of over 100,000 words.

Card 3. Carol the Cleaner/Cook. Thoughtful and confidential. The perfect companion for the lonely housewife who dreads the hours of boredom between breakfast and dinner. Carol has news and scandal circuits as well as an ability to cook over 200 meals. Note: Carol can be augmented with an anti-alcohol programme.

This was what was available and Jody didn't feel drawn to any of them. He was already missing the fun which Elizabeth the Entertainer had brought into his life. He read through the cards once again and finally selected Myra the Muse. Holding the card with his tweezers he slipped it into place in the cache.

• • •

The return journey of repair went without a hitch. First the auxiliary power leads made their connections smoothly. The shock adjusters fitted into place and the whole unit snuggled securely between the twin wings of the synaptic center.

As Jody was lowering the rib cage and locking it into place, Hildergarde returned. She had changed into a pair of bulky white overalls which had masses of pockets. With her was her male Syntho companion called Joseph. He was a serious-faced young man with red hair and freckles. His character was, as Hildergarde had often told Jody, sensible and studious with strong compassion circuits. He also had broad shoulders, narrow hips, and the legs of a tennis player. Plus extras.

"How are you getting on?" asked Hildergarde.

"Oh, okay. Nearly finished."

"Hear you had some problems," said Joseph.

"Uh uh," replied Jody without looking up, concentrating on his work. He had found the spinal cog that had jumped loose and by pushing and easing managed to limber it back into place. He next reached down inside the right leg and tried to find the band that had come loose. No luck.

"Ah well," he said, "this model has self-repair circuits."

"Sure do," said Joseph amiably, and he cracked his knuckles.

"What card did you use for her?" asked Hildergarde. "I brought some of mine over in case you wanted to experiment." She pronounced the word with all kinds of innuendo and grinned wickedly. "I brought Bruce the Builder and Randolph the Wrestler just in case. Thought they might be fun."

"Oh thanks," said Jody, "but I've already put Myra's card in."

"Myra the Muse! Boring," said Hildergarde pulling a face. "I've seen Dad use her."

"No. Myra the Muse is a nice lady," said Joseph.

Both Hildergarde and Jody stared at him. It was rare for a Syntho to offer an unsolicited opinion let alone a dissenting one.

"Well I need to study a bit," said Jody weakly, and he returned to his work, folding over the flaps of skin.

The body came together neatly. As the seams met they exuded an oil. This was a kind of protective insulation, for once the skin became charged the flaps would instantly bond. Jody replaced the energy fuse in the big toe of the left foot and screwed it into place and closed the toenail with a click. Immediately, and much to Jody's relief, the body began to firm and the seams disappeared. The breasts slowly shaped. Jody noticed that Myra's breasts were slightly smaller than Elizabeth's. He also noticed that he had neglected to replace the nipple. The jaw trembled. Fluid ran briefly from the nose and then Myra sniffed. The muscles in her arms and thighs came up to tone and flexed. It seemed to Jody that Myra's hips were wider than Elizabeth's and that her legs were slightly shorter and thicker. Not unattractive, he noted.

Fully formed, brown-skinned, and vibrant, the body held its position in suspended animation. Jody reached up under the nape of the neck and found a micro switch and double clicked with his finger.

Immediately the body drew in breath. Myra's eyes turned in their orbits and then settled and focused. The mouth opened and closed a few times. There was a choking sound from the throat and then a pleasant contralto voice said, "Myra sick. Please come quick."

She sat up. Her head traveled through one hundred and eighty degrees, surveying the kitchen and those who were looking at her. She did not blink. "My name is Myra. I live in a pen. Cry sorrow. Sorrow. My hair is gone."

Jody picked up the wig and handed it to her. She took it carefully and set it on her head and adjusted it. A greater assurance came into her figure. She edged forward on the table until her toes could touch the floor and then, using her hands, she eased herself upright and stood. "I am Myra. I need clothes. Please dress me." Her eyes settled on Jody. "Please dress me, Jody. We have so much work to do. 'Ars longa, vita brevis.' 'The lyf so short, the craft so long to lerne.' Chaucer after Seneca after Hippocrates. Please give me your hand, Jody. Myra the Muse is sick." Myra reached out her hand.

Jody reached out to meet her. But before they could join, before Myra could take one step, her right leg gave way and she crashed down onto her knees. "Poor Myra's a cold." Then she writhed onto her back and began to scratch at her eyes.

• • •

Jody and Hildergarde started forward but both were too slow. They felt themselves gripped from behind by strong fingers and hauled back. Joseph stepped swiftly between them. He came close to Myra and knelt down. He slipped his arms under her quivering body and lifted her up, and then turned and faced Jody. "You should have consulted a specialist," he said. "You're just a boy."

Then he turned and, carrying the still shaking Myra in his arms, exited from the kitchen. As he departed they heard the contralto of Myra murmuring, "Howl. Howl. Howl."

Jody rubbed his arm where the Syntho Joseph had gripped him. He could feel the bruise rising. Hildergarde scrambled to her feet and ran to the door. "You come back here, Joseph," she called. "You come back here this moment. Do you hear?"

For answer the door slammed.

Hildergarde turned to Jody in disbelief. "Well, what do you think of that?" she said indignantly.

Jody shrugged. "If I were you I'd get some of his circuits trashed," he said. "He could become dangerous. He's starting to rogue." Jody nodded toward the phone. "You can give the wardens a call now if you like. They'll soon round him up. They'll know what to do."

"And what about Myra the Muse?"

"No worries," said Jody, smiling suddenly. "She was still under guarantee. I'll get a new one."

GEORGE ALEC EFFINGER

THE WORLD AS WE KNOW IT

(1992)

THE SETUP could have been pretty clever with a little more thought, I have to admit. Using some of the newest-generation cerebral hardware, an ambitious but dangerously young man, a recent parolee—you know, a low-level street punk, much as I'd been once upon a time—had stolen a small crate from Mahmoud's warehouse. The punk hadn't even known what was in the crate. It turned out, if I can trust Mahmoud, that the crate contained a shipment of recently developed biological agents.

These bios had two major uses: They could promote the healing of traumatic wounds while making the attendant pain disappear for a while, without subjecting the patient to the well-documented narcotic disadvantages we've all come to know and love; or what was contained in the many disposable vials could easily be reconfigured to wipe out entire cities, using very small doses—thus becoming the most powerful neurological weapons ever devised. The small crate was labeled to be shipped to Holland, where the Dutch revolution was still at its full, vicious, inhuman peak.

Of course, Mahmoud was frantic to get his crate back. He and a few of my old friends, from the good old days when I had power and could move through the city without fear of being dusted by my many enemies, knew where I was now living. I'd left the Budayeen and adopted a new identity. Mahmoud had come to me and offered me money, which I didn't need—I'd lost just about everything, but I'd carefully protected the cash I'd acquired—or contacts and agents, which I did need, and desperately. I agreed to look into the matter for Mahmoud.

It wasn't very difficult. The thief was such a beginner that I almost felt like taking him aside and giving him a few pointers. I restrained that impulse, however.

The kid, who told me his name was Musa, had left a trail through the city that had been easy as hell for a predator like me to follow. I know the kid's name wasn't Musa, just as he knew my name wasn't the one I gave him when I finally caught up to him. Names and histories were not important information to either of us at the time. All that mattered was the small crate.

I dragged him back to my office, far from the Budayeen, in a neighborhood called Iffatiyya. This part of the city, east beyond the canal, had been reduced to rubble in the last century, the fifteenth after the Hegira, the twenty-second of the Christian era. It was now about a hundred years later than that, and at last some of the bombed-out buildings were being reclaimed. My office was in one of them.

I was there because most of my former friends and associates had leaped to the other side, to the protection of Shaykh Reda Abu Adil. There were very few places that were safe for me back in the walled quarter, and few people I could trust. Hell, I didn't really trust Mahmoud—never had—except he was reliably, scrupulously straightforward when large sums of money were involved.

I opened the outer door of my office, the one with the glass panel on which some frustrated portrait artist had lettered my new name, in both Arabic and Roman alphabets. Inside the door was a waiting room with a sagging couch, three wooden chairs, and a few items to help my few anxious clients pass the time: a scattering of newspapers and magazines, and chipzines for my more technologically advanced visitors, to be chipped directly into a moddy or daddy socket located in the hollow at the base of the skull.

I had a good grasp of the material of Musa's gallebeya, which I used to propel him through the open inner door. He fell sprawling on the bare, shabby, wooden floor. I slouched in the comfortable chair behind my beat-up old desk. I let a sarcastic smile have its way for a second or two, and then I put on my grim expression. "I want to clear this up fast," I said.

Musa had gotten to his feet and was glaring at me with all the defiance of youth and ignorance. "No problem," he said, in what he no doubt imagined was a tough voice. "All you gotta do is come across."

"By fast," I said, deliberately not responding to his words, "I mean super-luminal. Light speed. And I'm not coming across. I don't do that. Grab a seat while I make a phone call, O Young One."

Musa maintained the rebellious expression, but some worry had crept into it, too. He didn't know who I planned to call. "You ain't gonna turn me over to the rats, are you?" he asked. "I just got out. Yallah, another fall and I think they'll cut off my right hand."

I nodded, murmuring Mahmoud's commcode into my desk phone. Musa was right about one thing: Islamic justice as currently interpreted in the city would demand the loss of his hand, possibly the entire arm, in front of a huge, cheering crowd in the courtyard of the Shimaal Mosque. Musa would have no opportunity to appeal, either, and he'd probably end up back in prison afterward, as well.

"Marhaba," said Mahmoud when he answered his phone. He wasn't the kind of guy to identify himself until he knew who was on the other end of the line. I remembered him before he had his sex change, as a slender, doe-eyed sylph, dancing at Jo-Mama's. Since then, he'd put on a lot of weight, toughness, and something much more alarming.

"Yeah, you right," I replied. "Good news, Mahmoud. This is your investigator calling. Got the thief, and he hasn't had time to do anything with the product. He'll take you to it. What becomes of him afterward is up to you. Come take charge of him at your convenience."

"You are still a marvel, O Wise One," said Mahmoud. His praise counted about as much as a broken Bedu camel stick. "You have lost much, but it is as Allah wills. Yet you have not lost your native wit and ability. I will be there very soon, inshallah, with some news that might interest you." *Inshallah* means "if God wills." Nobody but He was too sure about anything of late.

"The news is the payment, right, O Father of Generosity?" I said, shaking my head. Mahmoud had been a cheap stiff as a woman, and he was a cheap stiff now as a man.

"Yes, my friend," said Mahmoud. "But it includes a potential new client for you, and I'll throw in a little cash, too. Business is business."

"And action is action," I said, not that I was seeing much action these days. "You know how much I charge for this sort of thing."

"Salaam alaikum, my friend," he said hurriedly, and he hung up his phone before I could salaam him back.

Musa looked relieved that I hadn't turned him over to the police, although I'm sure he was just as anxious about the treatment he could expect from Mahmoud. He had every reason in the world to be concerned. He maintained a surly silence, but he finally took my advice and sat down in the battered red-leather chair opposite my desk.

"Piece of advice," I said, not even bothering to look at him. "When Mahmoud gets here—and he'll get here fast—take him directly to his property. No excuses, no bargains. If you try holding Mahmoud up for so much as a lousy copper fiq, you'll end up breathing hot sand for the remainder of your brief life. Understand?"

I never learned if the punk understood or not. I wasn't looking at him, and he wasn't saying anything. I opened the bottom drawer of my desk and took out the office bottle. Apparently a slow leak had settled in, because the level of gin was much lower than I expected. It was something that would bear investigating during my long hours of solitude.

I built myself a white death—gin and bingara with a hit of Rose's lime juice—and took a quick gulp. Then I drank the rest of the tumblerful slowly. I wasn't savoring anything; I was just proving to myself again that I could be civilized about my drinking habits.

Time passed in this way—Musa sitting in the red-leather chair, sampling emotions; me sitting in my chair, sipping white death. I'd been correct about one thing: It didn't take Mahmoud long to make the drive from the Budayeen. He didn't bother to knock on the outer door. He came through, into my inner office, accompanied by three large men. Now, even I thought three armed chunks were a bit much to handle ragged, little old Musa there. I said nothing. It wasn't my business any longer.

Now, Mahmoud was dressed as I was, that is, in keffiya, the traditional Arab headdress, gallebeya, and sandals; the men with Mahmoud were all wearing very nice, tailored European-style business suits. Two of the suit jackets had bulges just where you'd expect. Mahmoud turned to those two and didn't utter a word. The two moved forward and took pretty damn physical charge of Musa, getting him out of my office the quickest way possible. Just before he passed through the inner door, Musa jerked his head around toward me and said, "Rat's puppet." That was all.

That left Mahmoud and the third suit.

"Where you at, Mahmoud?" I asked.

"I see you've taken to dyeing your beard, O Wise One," said Mahmoud by way of thanks. "You no longer look like a Maghrebi. You look like any common citizen of Asir or the Hejaz, for instance. Good."

I was so glad he approved. I was born part Berber, part Arab, and part French, in the part of Algeria that now called itself Mauretania. I'd left that part of the world far, far behind, and arrived in this city a few years ago, with reddish hair and beard that made me stand out among the locals. Now all my hair was as black as my prospects.

Mahmoud tossed an envelope on the desk in front of me. I glanced at it but didn't count the kiam inside, then dropped the envelope in a desk drawer and locked it.

"I cannot adequately express my thanks, O Wise One," he said in a flat voice. It was a required social formula.

"No thanks are needed, O Benefactor," I said, completing the obligatory niceties. "Helping a friend is a duty."

"All thanks be to Allah."

"Praise Allah."

"Good," said Mahmoud with some satisfaction. I could see him relax a little, now that the show was over. He turned to the remaining suit and said, "Shaykh Ishaq ibn Muhammad il-Qurawi, O Great Sir, you've seen how reliable my friend is. May Allah grant that he solve your problem as promptly as he solved mine." Then Mahmoud nodded to me, turned, and left. Evidently, I wasn't high enough on the social ladder to be actually introduced to Ishaq ibn Muhammad il-Qurawi.

I motioned to the leather chair. Il-Qurawi made a slight wince of distaste, then sat down.

I put on my professional smile and uttered another formulaic phrase that meant, roughly, "You have come to your people and level ground." In other words, "Welcome."

"Thank you, I—"

I raised a hand, cutting him off. "You must allow me to offer you coffee, O Sir. The journey from the Budayeen must have been tiring, O Shaykh."

"I was hoping we could dispense with—"

I raised my hand again. The old me would've been more than happy to dispense with the hospitality song-and-dance, but the new me was playing a part, and the ritual three tiny cups of coffee was part of it. Still, we hurried through them as rapidly as social graces permitted. Il-Qurawi wore a sour expression the whole time.

When I offered him a fourth, he waggled his cup from side to side, indicating that he'd had enough.

"May your table always be prosperous," he said, because he had to.

I shrugged. "Allah yisallimak." May God bless you.

"Praise Allah."

"Praise Allah."

"Now," said my visitor emphatically, "you have been recommended to me as someone who might be able to help with a slight difficulty."

I nodded reassuringly. Slight difficulty, my Algerian ass. People didn't come to me with slight difficulties.

As usual, the person in the leather chair didn't know how to begin. I waited patiently, letting my smile evaporate bit by bit. I found myself thinking about the office bottle, but it was impossible to bring it out again until I was alone. Strict Muslims looked upon alcoholic beverages with the same fury that they maintained for the infidel, and I knew nothing about il-Qurawi's attitudes about such things.

"If you have an hour or two free this afternoon," he said, "I wonder if you'd come with me to my office. It's not far from here, actually. On the eastern side of the canal, but quite a bit north of here. We've restored a thirty-six-story office building, but recently there's been more than the usual amount of vandalism. I'd like to hire you to stop it."

I took a deep breath and let it out again. "Not my usual sort of assignment, O Sir," I said, shrugging, "but I don't foresee any problem. I get a hundred kiam a day plus expenses. I need a minimum of five hundred right now to pique my interest."

Il-Qurawi frowned at the discussion of money and waved his hand. "Will you accept a check?" he asked.

"No," I said. I'd noticed that the man was stingy with honorifics, so I'd decided to hold my own to the minimum.

He grunted. He was clearly annoyed and doubtful about my ability to do what he wanted. Still, he removed a moderate stack of bills from a black leather wallet, and sliced off five for me. He leaned forward and put the money on my desk. I pretended to ignore it.

I made no pretense of checking an appointment book. "I'm certain, O Shaykh, that I can spare a few hours for you."

"Very good." Il-Qurawi stood up and spent a few moments vitally absorbed in the wrinkles in his business suit. I took the time to slide the five hundred kiam into the pocket of my gallebeya.

"I can spare a few hours, O Shaykh," I said, "but first I'd like some more information. Such as who you are and whom you represent."

He didn't say a word. He merely slid a business card to the spot where the money had been.

I picked up the card. It said:

Ishaq ibn Muhammad il-Qurawi
Chief of Security
CRCorp

Below that was a street address that meant nothing to me, and a commcode. I didn't have a business card to give him, but I didn't think he cared. "CRCorp?" I asked.

He was still standing. He indicated that we should begin moving toward the door. It was fine by me.

"Yes, we deal in consensual realities."

"Uh huh," I said. "I know you people." By this time, we were standing in the hallway and he was watching me lock the outer door.

We went downstairs to his car. He owned a long, black, chauffeur-driven, restored, gasoline-powered limousine. I wasn't impressed. I'd ridden in a few of those. We got in and he murmured something to the driver. The car began gliding through the rubble-strewn streets, toward the headquarters of CRCorp.

"Can you be more exact about the nature of this vandalism, O Sir?" I said.

"You'll see. I believe it's being caused by one person. I have no idea why; I just want it stopped. There are too many clients in the building beginning to complain."

And it's beyond the capabilities of the Chief of Security, I thought. That spoke something ominous to me.

After about half an hour of weaving north and east, then back west toward the canal, then farther north, we arrived at the CRCorp building. Allah only knew what it had been before this entire part of the city had been destroyed, but now it stood looking newly built among its broken and blasted neighbors. One fixed-up building in all that desolation seemed pretty lonely and conspicuous, I thought, but I guess you had to start someplace.

Il-Qurawi and I got out of the limousine and walked across the freshly surfaced parking area. There were no other cars in it. "The executive offices are on the seventeenth floor, about halfway up, but there's nothing interesting to see there. You'll want to visit one or two of the consensual realities, and then look at the vandalism I mentioned."

Well, sure, as soon as he said there wasn't anything interesting on the seventeenth floor, I immediately wanted to go there. I hate it when other people tell me what I want to do, but it was il-Qurawi's five hundred kiam, so I kept my mouth shut, nodded, and followed him inside to the elevators.

"Give you a taste of one of the consensual realities," he said. "We just call them CRs around here. We'll stop off first on twenty-six. It's functioning just fine, and there's been no sign of vandalism as yet."

Still nothing for me to say. We rode up quickly, silently in the mirrored elevator. I glanced at my reflection. I wasn't happy with the appearance I'd had to adopt, but I was stuck with it.

We got off at twenty-six. The elevator doors opened, we stepped out, and passed through a small, well-constructed airlock. When I turned to look, the elevator and airlock had disappeared. I mean, there was no sign that elevator doors could possibly exist for hundreds of miles. I felt for them and there was nothing but air. Rather thin, cold air. If I'd been pressed to make a guess, I'd have said that we were on the surface of Mars. I knew that was impossible, but I'd seen holo shots of the Martian surface, and this is just what they looked like.

"Here," said il-Qurawi, handing me a mask and a small tank, "this should help you somewhat."

"I am in your debt, O Great One." I used the tight-grip straps to hold the mask in place, but the tank was made to be worn on a belt. I had a rope holding my gallebeya closed, but it wouldn't support the weight of the tank, so I just carried it in my hands. We started walking across the barren, boulder-studded surface of Mars toward a collection of buildings in the far distance that I recognized as the international Martian colony.

"The atmosphere on this floor only approximates that of Mars," said il-Qurawi. "That was part of the group's consensus agreement. Still, if you're outside and not wearing the mask, you're liable to develop a rather serious condition they call 'Mars throat.' Affects your sinuses, your inner ears, your throat, and so forth."

"Let me see if I can guess, O Sir," I said, huffing a little as I made my way over the extremely rough terrain. "Group of people in the colony, all would-be Martian colonists, and they've voted on how they wanted the place to look." I gazed up at a pink peach-colored sky.

"Exactly. And they voted on how they wanted it to feel and smell and sound. Actually, it approximates the reports we get from the true Mars Project rather closely. CRCorp supplies the area, for which we charge what we feel is a fair price. We also supply the software that maintains the illusion, too."

I kicked a boulder. No illusion. "How much of this is real?" I said. Even using the tank, I was already short of breath and eager to get inside one of the buildings.

"The boulders, as you've just discovered, are artificial but real. The buildings are real. The carefully maintained atmosphere is also our responsibility. Everything else you might experience is computer or holo generated. It can be quite deadly out here, but that's the way this group wanted it. We haven't left anything out, down to the toxin-laden lichen, which is part of the illusion. For all intents and purposes, this is the surface of Mars. Group Twenty-Six has always seemed to be very pleased with it. We've gotten very few complaints or suggestions for improvement."

"Naturally, O Sir," I said, "I'm looking forward to interviewing a few of the residents."

"Of course," said il-Qurawi. "That's why I brought you here. We're very proud of Group Twenty-Six, and justly so, I think."

"Praise Allah," I said. No echo from my client.

After more time and hiking than I'd been prepared for, we arrived at the colony itself. I felt like a physical wreck; the executive with me was not suffering at all. He looked like he'd just taken a leisurely stroll through the repro of the Tiger Gardens in the city's entertainment quarter.

"This way," he said, pointing to an airlock into the long main building. It appeared to have been constructed of some material derived from the reddish sand all around, but I wasn't interested enough to find out for sure if that were true or part of the holographic illusion.

We cycled through the airlock. Inside, we found ourselves in a corridor that had been painted in institutional colors: dark green to waist-level, a kind of maddening tan above that. I was absolutely sure that I would quickly come to hate those colors; soon it proved that they dominated the color scheme of most of the hallways and meeting rooms. The people of Group Twenty-Six must have had a very different aesthetic sense than I did. It didn't give me great hopes for them.

Il-Qurawi glanced at his wristwatch, a European product like the rest of his outfit. It was thin and sleek and made of gold. "The majority of them will be in the refectory module now," he said. "Good. You'll have the opportunity to meet as many of Group Twenty-Six as you like. Ask whatever you like, but we are under a little time pressure. I'd like to take you to floor seven within the next half hour."

"I give thanks to the Maker of Worlds," I said. Il-Qurawi gave me a sidelong glance to see if I were serious. I was doing my best to give that impression.

The refectory was down the entire length of the main building and through a low, narrow, windowless passageway. I felt a touch of claustrophobia, as if I were down deep beneath the surface; I had to remind myself that I was actually on the twenty-sixth floor of an office tower.

The refectory was at the other end of the passageway. It was a large room, filled with orderly rows of tables. Men, women, and children sat at the tables, eating food from trays that were dispensed from a large and intricate machine on one side of the front of the room. I stared at it for a while, watching people go up to it, press colored panels, and receive their trays within fifteen or twenty seconds each.

"Catering," said il-Qurawi with an audible sigh. "Major part of our overhead."

"Question, O Sir," I said. "Who's actually paying for all this?"

He looked at me as if I were a total fool. "All these people in Group Twenty-Six, of course. They've signed over varying amounts of cash and property, depending on how long they intend to stay. Some come for a week, but the greater portion of the group has paid in advance for ten- or twenty-year leases."

My eyes narrowed as I thought and did a little multiplication in my head. "Then, depending on the populations of the other thirty-some floors," I said slowly, "CRCorp ought to be making a very tidy bundle."

His head jerked around to look at me directly. "I've already mentioned the high overhead. The expenses we incur to maintain all this—and the CRs on the other floors—is staggering. Our profits are not so great as you might think."

"I ask a thousand pardons, O Sir," I said. "I truly had no intention to give offense. I'm still trying to get an idea of how large an operation this is. Maybe now's the time to speak to one or two of these 'Martian colonists.'"

He relaxed a little. He was hiding something, I'd bet my wives and kids on it. "Of course," he said smoothly. I thought back on it and couldn't recall a single time he'd actually called me by name. In any event, he directed me to one of the tables where there was an empty seat beside an elderly man with short-cropped white hair. He wore a pale-blue jumpsuit. Hell, everyone there wore a pale-blue jumpsuit. I wondered if that was the official uniform on the real Mars colony, or just a group decision of this particular CR.

"Salaam alaikum," I said to the elderly man.

"Alaikum-as-salaam," he said mechanically. "Outsider, huh?"

"Just came in to get a quick look."

He leaned over and whispered in my ear. "Now, some of us really hate outsiders. Spoils the group consensus."

"I'll be out of here before you know it, inshallah."

The white-haired man took a forkful of some brown, smooth substance on his tray, chewed it thoughtfully, then said, "Could've at least gotten into a goddamn jumpsuit, hayawaan. Too much trouble?"

I ignored the insult. Il-Qurawi should've thought of the jumpsuit. "How long you been part of Group Twenty-Six?" I asked.

"We don't call ourselves 'Group Twenty-Six,'" said the man, evidently disliking me even more. "We're the Mars colony."

Well, the real Mars colony was a combined project of the Federated New England States of America, the new Fifth Reich, and the Fragrant Heavenly Empire of True Cathay.

There were no—or very few—Arabs on the real Mars.

Someone delivered a tray of food to me: molded food without texture slapped onto a molded plastic tray; the brown stuff, some green stuff that I took to be some form of vegetable material—as nondescript and unidentifiable as anything else on the tray—a small portion of dark red, chewy stuff that might have been a meat substitute, and the almost obligatory serving of gelatin salad with chopped carrots, celery, and canned fruit in it. There were also slices of dark bread and disposable cups of camel's milk.

I turned again to the white-haired gentleman. "Milk, huh?" I asked.

His bushy eyebrows went up. "Milk is the best thing for you. If you want to live forever."

I murmured "Bismillah," which means "in the name of God," and I began eating my meal, not knowing what some of the dishes were even after I'd tasted and chewed and swallowed them. I ate out of social obligation, and I did pretty well, too. When some of the others were finished, they took their trays and utensils to a machine very much like the one that dispensed the meals in the first place. The hard items disappeared into a long, wide slot, and I felt certain that leftover food was recycled in one form or another. CRCorp prided itself on efficiency, and this was one way to keep the operating costs down.

I still had my doubts about the limited choices in the refectory—including the compulsory camel's milk, which was served in four-ounce cups. As I ate, il-Qurawi turned toward me again. "Are you enjoying the meal?" he asked.

"Praise God for His beneficence," I said.

"God, God—" il-Qurawi shook his head. "It's permissible if you really believe in that sort of thing. But the people here are not all Muslim—some belong to no organized religion at all—and they're using whatever agricultural training they had on 'Earth,' and they're applying it here on 'Mars.' They grew a small portion of these delicious meats and vegetables themselves—it came from their skill, their dedication, their determination. They receive no aid or interference from CRCorp."

"Yeah, you right," I said, and decided I'd had enough of il-Qurawi, too. I hadn't tasted anything the least bit palatable except possibly the bread and milk, and how wildly enthusiastic could I get about them? I didn't mention anything about CRCorp's inability to reproduce the noticeably lower gravity of the true Mars, or certain other aspects of the interplanetary milieu.

I spoke some more to the white-haired man, and then one of the plainly clothed women farther down the table leaned over and interrupted us. Her hair was cut just above shoulder-length, dull from not having been washed for a very long time. I suppose that while there was plenty of water in the thirty-six-story office building, in the headquarters of the CRCorp, and on some of the other consensus-reality floors, there was extremely little water available on floor twenty-six—the Mars for the sort of folks who yearned for danger, but no danger more threatening than the elevator ride from the main lobby.

"Has he told you everything?" asked the filthy woman. Her voice was clearly intended to be a whisper, but I'm sure she was overheard several rows of tables away on either side of us.

"There's so much more I want you to see," said il-Qurawi, even going so far as to grab my arm. That just made me determined to hear the woman out.

"I have not finished my meal, O fellah," I said, somewhat irritably. I'd called him a peasant. I shouldn't have, but it felt good. "What is your blessed name, O Lady?" I asked her.

She looked blank for a few seconds, then confused. Finally she said, "Marjory Mulcher. Yeah, that's me now. Sometimes I'm Marjory Tiller, depending on the season and how badly they need me and how many people are willing to work with me."

I nodded, figuring I understood what she meant. "Everything that passes in this world," I said, "—or any other world—" I interpolated, "is naught but the expression of the Will of God."

Marjory's eyes grew larger and she smiled. "I'm a Roman Catholic," she said. "Lapsed, maybe, but what does that do to you, camel jockey?"

I couldn't think of a safely irrelevant reply.

In her mind, the CRCorp probably had nothing to do with her present situation. Perhaps in her own mind she was on Mars. That may have been the great and ultimate victory of CRCorp.

"I asked you," said Marjory with a frown, "are they showing you everything? Are they telling you everything?"

"Don't know," I said. "I just got here."

Marjory moved down a few places and sat beside me, on the other side from the white-haired man. I looked around and saw that only she and I were still eating. Everyone else had disposed of their tray and was sitting, almost expectantly, in his molded plastic seat, politely and quietly.

The woman smelled terrible. She leaned toward me and whispered, "You know the corporation is just about ready to unleash a devastating CR. Something we won't be able to manage at all. Death on every floor, I imagine. And then, when they've tested this horrible CR on us, may their religion be cursed, they'll unleash it on you and what you casually prefer to call the rest of the world. Earth, I mean. I grew up on Earth, you know. Still have some relatives there."

By the holy sacred beard of the Prophet, may the blessings of Allah be on him and peace, I've never felt so relieved as when she discovered a sudden interest in the gelatin salad. "Raisins. Rejoicing and celebrations," she said to no one in particular. "Consensual raisins."

I slowly closed my eyes and tightened my lips. My right hand dropped its piece of bread and raised up tiredly to cover my tightly shut eyelids, at the same time massaging my forehead. We didn't have enough facilities for mentals and nutsos in the city; we just let the ones with the wealthier families shut 'em away in places like Group Twenty-Six in the CRCorp building. Yaa Allah, you never knew when you were going to run into one of these bereft cookies.

Still with my eyes covered, I could feel the man with the close-cropped white hair lean toward me on the other side. I knew that son of a biscuit hadn't liked me from the get-go. "Get Marjory to tell you all about her raisins sometime. It's a fascinating story in its own right."

"Be sure *to*," I murmured. In the spring with the apricots, I would. I picked up the bread with my eating hand again and opened my eyes. Everyone within hollering range was staring at me with rapt attention. I don't know why; I didn't want to know why then, and I still don't want to know why. I hoped it was just that I was an oddity, a welcome interruption in the daily routine, like a visit from one of Prince Shaykh Mahali's wives or children.

I'd had enough to eat, and so I'd picked up the tray—I'm quick on the uptake, and I'd figured out the disposal drill from observation. It wasn't that difficult to begin with, and, jeez, I'm a trained professional, mush hayk? Yeah, you right. I slid the tray into the proper slot in the proper machine. Then il-Qurawi, having nothing immediate to do, chose to be nowhere in sight. I slumped back down between Marjory and the old, white-haired man. Fortunately, Marjory was still enchanted by her gelatin salad—the al-Qaddani moddy, a Palestinian fictional hardboiled-detective piece of hardware I was wearing, let me have the impression that Marjory was like this at every meal, whatever was served—and the old gentleman gave me a disapproving look, stood up, and moved away, toward what real people did to compensate society for their daily sustenance. For a few moments I had utter peace and utter silence, but I did not expect them to last very long. I was correct as usual in this sort of discouraging speculation.

Almost directly across from me was a woman with extremely large breasts, which were trapped in an undergarment which must have been painfully confining for them. I really wasn't interested enough to read if they were genuine—God-given—or not; she must've thought she had, you know, the most devastating figure on all of Mars, and of course we understand what we mean when we speak of Mars. She wore a long, flowing, print shift of a drabness that directed all one's attention elsewhere and upward; bare feet; and a live, medium-sized, suffering lizard on one shoulder that was there only to extort yet another sort of response from you. As if her grotesque mamelons weren't enough.

Oh, you were supposed to say, *you have a live, medium-sized lizard on your shoulder.* Now, when someone has gone to that amount of labor to pry a reaction from me, my innate obstinacy sets in. I will not look more than two or three times at the tits, casually, as after the first encounter they don't exist for me. I won't even glance furtively at her various other vulgar accoutrements. I won't remark at all on the lizard. The lizard and I will never have a relationship; the woman and I barely had one, and *that* only through courtesy.

She spoke in a voice intended to be heard by the nearby portion of mankind: "I think Marjory means well." She looked around herself to find agreement, and there wasn't a single person still in the refectory who would contradict her. I got the feeling that would be true whatever she said. "I know for a fact that Marjory never goes beyond the buildings of the Mars colony. She never sees Allah's holy miracle of creation. Does it not say in the Book, the noble Qur'ân, 'Frequently you see the ground dry and barren: but no sooner do We send down rain to moisten it than it begins to tremble and magnify, putting forth each and every kind of blossoming life. That is because Allah is Truth: He gives life to the dead and has power over all things.'" She sat back, evidently very self-satisfied. "That was from the surah called 'Pilgrimage,' in the holy Qur'ân."

"May the Creator of heaven and earth bless this recitation of His holy words," said one man softly.

"May Allah give His blessing," said a woman quietly.

I had several things I might have mentioned; the first was that the imitation surface of Mars I'd crossed was not, in point of fact, covered with every variety of blooming plant. Yet maybe to some of these people that was worth reporting to the authorities. Before I could say anything, a young, sparsely bearded man sat beside me in the old, white-haired resident's seat, and addressed the elderly woman. The young man said, "You know, Umm Sulaiman, that you shouldn't hold up Marjory as a typical resident of the Mars colony."

Umm Sulaiman frowned. "I have further scripture that I could recite which supports my words and actions."

The young man shuddered. "No, my mother-in-law"—clearly an honorific and a title not to be taken seriously—"all is as Allah wills." He turned to me and murmured, "I wish the both of them—the two old women, Marjory and Umm Sulaiman—would stop behaving in their ways. I admit it, I'm superstitious, and it frightens me."

"Seems a shame to pay all this money to CRCorp just to be frightened." The young man looked to either side, then leaned even closer. "I've heard a story, O Sir," he murmured. "Actually, I've heard several stories, some as wild as Marjory's, some even crazier. But, by the beard of the Prophet—"

"May the blessings of Allah be on him and peace," I said.

"—there's one story that won't go away, a story that's repeated often by the most sane and reliable of our team." Team: as if they really were part of some kind of international extraterrestrial project.

I pursed my lips and tried to show that I was rabidly eager to hear his bit of gossip. "And what is this persistent story, O Wise One?"

He looked to either side again, took my arm, and together we left the table and the others. We walked slowly toward the exit. "Now, O Sir," he said, "I've heard this directly from Bin el-Fadawin, who is CRCorp and Shaykh il-Qurawi's highest representative here in the Mars colony."

"Group Twenty-Six, you mean," I said.

"Yeah, if you insist on it, Group Twenty-Six." It was obvious that he didn't like his illusion broken, even for a moment. It cast some preliminary doubt on what he was about to tell me. "Listen, O Sir," he said. "Bin el-Fadawin and others drop hints now and again that CRCorp has better uses for these premises, that they're even now working on ways to turn away and run off the very people who've paid them for long-term care."

I shrugged. "If CRCorp wanted to evict all of you, O Young Man, I'm sure they could do it without too much difficulty. I mean, they got the lawyers and you got, what, rocks and lichen? Still, you and all the others have handed over—and continue to hand over—truly exorbitant amounts of cash and property; and all they've really done is decorate to your specifications a large, empty space in a restored office tower."

"They've created our consensual reality, please, O Shaykh."

"Yeah, you right," I said, amazed that this somewhat intelligent young man could be so easily taken in. "So you're telling me that the CRs—which the corporation has worked so hard to create, and for which it's being richly rewarded—will start disappearing, one by one?"

"Begin disappearing!" cried the young man. "Have Shaykh il-Qurawi—"

"Did I hear my name mentioned, O Most Gracious Ones?" asked my client, appearing silently enough through the door of the refectory room. "In a pleasant context, I hope."

"I was commenting, O Sir," I said, covering quickly, "on the truly spectacular job CRCorp has done here, inside the buildings and out. That little lizard Umm Sulaiman wears on her shoulder—is that a genuine Martian life form?"

"No," he said, frowning slightly. "There aren't any native lizards on Mars. We've tried to discourage her from wearing it—it creates a disharmony with what we're trying to accomplish here. Still, the choice is her own."

"Ah," I said. I'd figured all that before; I was just easing the young man out of the conversation. "I believe I've seen enough here, O Sir. Next I'd like to see some of the vandalism you spoke of."

"Of course," said il-Qurawi, moving a hand to almost touch me, almost grasp my elbow and lead me from the refectory. He gave me no time at all for the typically effusive Muslim farewells. We left the building the way we'd come, and once again I used the mask and bottled air. However, we didn't make the long trek across the make-believe Martian landscape; il-Qurawi knew of a nearer exit. I guess he had just wanted me to come the long way before, to sample the handiwork of CRCorp.

We ducked through a nearly invisible airlock near the colony buildings, and took an elevator down to floor seven. When we stepped in, I removed the mask and air tank. The air pressure and oxygen content of the atmosphere was Earth-normal.

I saw immediately il-Qurawi's problem. Floor seven was entirely abandoned. In fact, except for some living quarters and outbuildings in the distance, and the barren and artificially landscaped "hills" and "valleys" built into the area, floor seven was nothing but a large and vacant loft a few stories above street level.

"What happened here, O Sir?" I asked.

Il-Qurawi turned around and casually indicated the entire floor. "This used to be a re-creation of Egypt at the time of the Ptolemies. I personally never saw the need for a consensual reality set in pre-Islamic times, but I was assured that certain academic experts wanted to reestablish the Library of Alexandria, which was destroyed by the Romans before the birth of the Prophet."

"May the blessings of Allah be on him and peace," I murmured.

Il-Qurawi shrugged. "It was functioning quite well, at least as well as the Martian colony, if not better, until one day it just . . . went away. The holographic images vanished, the specially created computer effects went offline, and nothing our creative staff did restored them. After a week or ten days of living in this emptiness, the people of Group Seven demanded a refund and departed."

I rubbed my dyed beard. "O Sir, where are the controlling mechanisms, and how hard is it to achieve access to them?"

Il-Qurawi led me toward the northern wall. We had a good distance to hike. I saw that the floor was some molded synthetic material; it was probably the same as on floor twenty-six. All the rest was the result of the electronic magic of CRCorp—what they got paid for. I could imagine the puzzlement, then the chagrin, finally the wrath of the residents of floor seven.

We reached the northern wall, and il-Qurawi led me to a small metal door built into the wall about eye-level. He opened the door, and I saw some familiar computer controls while others were completely baffling to me; there were slots for bubble-plate memory units, hardcopy readout devices, a keyboard data-entry device, a voice-recognition entry device, and other things that were to some degree strange and unrecognizable to me. I never claimed to be a computer expert. I'm not. I just didn't think it was profitable to let il-Qurawi know it.

"Wiped clean," he said, indicating the hardware inside the door. "Someone got in—someone knowing where to look for the control mechanisms—and deleted all the vital programs, routines, and local effects."

"All right," I said, beginning to turn the problem over in my mind. It had the look of a simple crime. "Any recently discharged employee with a reason for revenge?"

Il-Qurawi swore under his breath. I admit it, I was a little shocked. That's how much I'd changed since the old days. "Don't you think we checked out all the simple solutions ourselves?" he grumbled. "Before we came to you? By the life of my children, I'm positive it wasn't a disgruntled former employee, or a current one with plans for extortion, or any of the other easy answers that will occur to you at first. We're faced with a genuine disaster: Someone is destroying consensual realities for no apparent reason."

I blinked at him for a few seconds, thinking over what he'd just told me. I was standing in what had once been a replica of a strip of ancient civilization along the banks of the Nile River in pre-Muslim Egypt. Now I could look across the unfurnished space toward the other walls, seeing only the textured, generally flat floor in between. "You used the plural, O Sir," I said at last. "How many other consensual realities have been ruined like this one?"

"Out of thirty rented floors," he said quietly, "eighteen have been rendered inactive."

I just stared. CRCorp didn't just have a serious problem—it was facing extinction. I was surprised that the company hadn't come to me sooner. Of course, il-Qurawi was the Chief of Security, and he probably figured that he could solve the mess himself. Finally, with no small degree of humiliation, I'm sure, he sought outside help. And he knew that I knew it. It was a good thing I wasn't in a mood to rub it in, because I had all the ammunition I needed.

Il-Qurawi showed me a few other consensual realities, working ones and empty ones, because I asked him to. He didn't seem eager for me to get too familiar with the CRCorp operation, yet if he wanted me to help with his difficulty, he had to give me a certain amount of access. He and his corporation were backed against the wall, and he recognized the truth of the matter. So I saw a vigorous CR based on an Eritrean-written fantasy-novel series almost a century old; and a successful CR that re-created a strict Sunni Islamic way of life that had never truly existed; and two more floors that were lifeless and unfurnished.

I decided that I'd seen enough for the present. Il-Qurawi thanked me for my time, wished me luck in my quest for the culprit, and hoped it wouldn't take me too long to complete the assignment.

I said, "It shouldn't be more than a day or two, inshallah. I already have some possibilities to investigate." That was a lie. I was as lost as Qabeel's spare mule.

He didn't think it was necessary to accompany me back to my office. He just put me in the limousine with his driver. I didn't care.

I got a scare when I got back to my office. During the time while I'd visited the CRCorp building, someone had defeated my expensive, elaborate security system, entered, and wiped my own CR hardware and software. The shabbiness had disappeared, replaced by the true polished floors and freshly painted walls of the office in the building. I'd worked diligently to reproduce the run-down office of Lufty Gad's detective, al-Qaddani; but now the rooms were clean and new and sleek and modern. I was really furious. On my desk, under a Venetian glass paperweight, was a sheet of my notepaper with two handwritten words on it: *A warning*.

In the name of Allah, the Beneficent, the Merciful. I took out my prayer rug from the closet, spread it carefully on the floor, faced toward Makkah, and prayed. Then, my thoughts on higher things than CRCorp, I returned the rug to the closet. I sprawled in my chair behind the desk and stared at the notepaper. A *warning*. Hell, some guy was good at B & E, as well as cleaning out CRs, large and small. He hadn't made me afraid, only so angry that my stomach hurt.

I didn't want to look at my office space in its true, elegantly modern, fashionable form. Changing everything back the way it had been would be simple enough—I'd been wise enough to buy backups of everything from the small consensual-reality shop that had done up al-Qaddani's office for me in the first place. It would take me half an hour to restore the slovenly look I preferred.

I was certain that Shaykh il-Qurawi had backups to his dysfunctional floors as well; it was only that CRCorp had tried to pass along the costs of the replacement to the residents, and they had balked, perhaps unanimously. I recalled an old proverb I'd learned from my mother, may Allah grant her peace: "Greed lessens what is gathered." It was something CRCorp had yet to learn.

It also meant that everything that il-Qurawi had mentioned to me seemed to be close to its final resolution. I tipped a little from the office bottle into a tumbler and glanced at the setting sun through it. The true meaning—the actual one, the one that counted—had nothing to do with resolutions, however. I knew as well as I knew my childhood pet goat's name that things were never this easy. Mark this down, it's a free tip from an experienced operative (that means street punk): Things are never this easy. I'd known it before I started messing around on the street; then I'd learned it the simple way, from more experienced punks; and finally I'd had to learn it the hard way, too many times. Things are never this easy.

What I'm saying is that Simple Shaykh il-Qurawi knew perfectly well that he could do the same as I had, by way of chunking in the backup tapes, programs, and mechanisms. His echoing, forlorn floors would all quickly return to their fantasy factualities, and they'd probably be repopulated within days. CRCorp would then lose just a minimum of cash, and all the evil time could be filed away as just one of those bad experiences that had to be weathered by every corporation now and then.

Begging the question: Why, then, didn't CRCorp use the backups immediately rather than suffer the angry defection of so many of its clients? And did il-Qurawi really think I was that stupid, that it all wouldn't occur to me pretty damn fast?

Don't ask me. I didn't have a clue.

As the days went by, and the weeks, I learned through Bin el-Fadawin—CRCorp's spy on floor twenty-six—that in fact some of the other floors had been restored, and some of their tenants had returned. Great, wonderful, I told myself, expecting il-Qurawi himself to show up with the rest of my money and possibly even a thank-you, although I don't really believe in miracles.

Three weeks later I get a visitor from floor three. This was a floor that had been changed into a consensual-reality replica of a generation ship—a starship that would take generation upon generation to reach its goal, a planet merely called Home, circling a star named in the catalog simply as Wolf 359. They had years, decades, even longer to name the planet more cheerfully, and the same with their star, Wolf 359. However, the electronics had failed brutally, turning their generation ship into the sort of empty loft I'd witnessed in the CRCorp building. The crew had gotten disgusted and resigned, feeling cheated and threatening lawsuits.

After CRCorp instituted repairs, and when the science fiction–oriented customers heard that floor three had returned to its generation-ship environment, many of the crew reenlisted at the agreed-upon huge rates. I got another visit, from Bin el-Fadawin this time.

"CRCorp and Shaykh il-Qurawi are more grateful than they can properly express," he said, putting a moderately fat envelope on my desk. "Your work on this case has shown the corporation which techniques it needs to restore for each and every consensual reality."

"Please convey my thanks to both the shaykh and the corporation. I'm just glad everything worked out well at the end," I said. "If Allah wills, the residents of the CRCorp building will once again be happy with their shared worlds." I knew I hadn't done anything but check their security systems; but if they were happy, it had been worth investigating just for the fun I'd had.

Bin el-Fadawin touched his heart, his lips, and his forehead. "Inshallah. You have earned the acknowledged gratitude of CRCorp," he said, bowing low. "This is a mighty though intangible thing to have to your credit."

"I'll mark that down in my book," I said, through a thin smile. I'd had enough of il-Qurawi's lackey. The money in the envelope looked to be adequate reward and certainly spendable. The gratitude of CRCorp, though, was something as invisible and nonexistent as a dream djinn. I paid it the same attention—which is to say, none.

"Thank you again, O Wise One, and I speak as a representative of both CRCorp and Shaykh il-Qurawi."

"No thanks are necessary," I said. "He asked of me a favor, and I did my best to fulfill it."

"May Allah shower you with blessings," he said, sidling toward the inner door.

"May God grant your wishes, my brother," I said, watching him sidle and doing nothing to stop him. I heard the outer door open and shut, and I was sure that I was alone. I picked up the envelope, opened it, and counted the take. There were three thousand kiam there, which included a sizable bonus. I felt extravagantly well paid-off, but not the least bit satisfied. I had this feeling, you see, one I'd had before . . .

It was a familiar feeling that everything wasn't as picture-perfect as il-Qurawi's hopfrog had led me to suppose. The feeling was borne out quite some time later, when I'd almost forgotten it. My typically long, slow afternoon was interrupted by, of all people, the white-haired old gentleman from floor twenty-six. His name was Uzair ibn Yaqoub. He seemed extremely nervous, even in my office, which had been rendered shabby and comfortable again. He sat in the red-leather chair opposite me and fidgeted for a little while. I gave him a few minutes.

"It's the Terran oxygen level and the air pressure," he said in explanation.

I nodded. It sure as hell was something, to get him to leave his "Martian colony," even for an hour or two.

"Take your time, O Shaykh ibn Yaqoub," I said. I offered him water and some fruit, that's all I had around the office. That and the bottle in the drawer, which had less than a slug left in it.

"You know, of course," said ibn Yaqoub, "that after your visit, the same trouble that had plagued other consensual realities struck us. Fortunately for floor twenty-six, the CRCorp technicians found out what was wrong on Mars, and they fixed it. We're all back there living just as before."

I nodded. That was chiefly my job at this stage of the interview.

"Well," said ibn Yaqoub, "I'm certain—and some of the others, even those who never agreed with me before—that something wrong and devious and possibly criminal is happening."

I thought, what could be more criminal than the destruction—the theft—of consensual realities? But I merely said, "What do you mean, O Wise One?"

"I mean that somehow, someone is stealing from us."

"Stealing what?" I asked, remembering that they produced little: some vegetables, maybe, some authentic lichen . . .

"Stealing," insisted ibn Yaqoub. "You know the Mars colony pays each of us flight pay and hazardous-duty pay during our stay."

No, I hadn't heard that before. All I'd known was that the money went the other way, from the colonist to the corporation. This was suddenly becoming very interesting.

"And that's in addition to our regular low wages," said the white-haired old man. "We didn't sign up to make money. It was the Martian experience we longed for."

I nodded a third time. "And you think, O Shaykh, that somehow you're being cheated?"

He made a fist and struck my desk. "I know it!" he cried. "I figured in advance how much money to expect for a four-week period, because I had to send some to my grandchildren. When the pay voucher arrived, it was barely more than half the kiam I expected. I tried to have someone in the colony explain it to me—I admit that I'm not as good with mathematics as I used to be—and even Bin el-Fadawin assured me that I must have made an error in calculation. I don't particularly trust Bin el-Fadawin, but everyone else seemed to agree with him. Then, as time passed, more and more people noticed tax rates too high, payroll deductions too large, miscellaneous costs showing up here and there. Now we're all generally agreed that something needs to be done. You've helped us greatly before. We beg you to help us again."

I stood up behind my desk and paced, as I usually did when I was thinking over a new case. Was this a new case, however, or just an extension of the old one? It was difficult for me to believe il-Qurawi and CRCorp needed every last fiq and kiam of these poor people, who were already paying the majority of their wealth for the privilege of living in the "Mars colony." Cheating them like this seemed to me to be too trivial and too cruel, even for CRCorp.

I told ibn Yaqoub I'd look into the matter. I accepted no retainer, and I quoted him a vanishingly small fee. I liked him, and I liked most of the others in Group Twenty-Six.

I returned first to the twenty-sixth floor, not telling anyone I was coming—particularly not il-Qurawi or Bin el-Fadawin. I knew where to get a mask, oxygen tank, and blue coveralls. Now I also knew where the control box was hidden on the "Martian" wall, and I checked it. I made several interesting discoveries: Someone was indeed bleeding off funds from the internal operation of the consensus reality.

I returned to my office, desperate to know who the culprit was. I was not terribly surprised to see my outer office filled with three waiting clients—all of them from other consensus realities. One, from the harsh Sunni floor, threatened to start taking off hands and arms if I didn't come up with an acceptable alternative. The other two were nowhere as bloodthirsty, but every bit as outraged.

I assured and mollified and talked them back down to something like peacefulness. I waited until they left, and I opened the bottom drawer and withdrew the office bottle. I felt I'd earned the final slug. A voice behind me spoke: "Got a gift for ya," the young man said. I turned. I saw a youth in his midtwenties, wearing a gallebeya that seemed to shift colors from green to blue as he changed positions.

"For you," he said, coming toward me, setting a fresh bottle of gin on my desk. "On account of you're so damn smart."

"Bismillah," I said. "I am in your debt."

"We'll see," said the young man, with a quirky smile.

I built us two quick white deaths. He sat in the red-leather chair and sipped his, enjoying the taste. I gulped the first half of mine, then slowed to his speed just to show that I could do it.

I waited. I could gain much by waiting—information perhaps, and at least the other half of the white death.

"You don't know me," said the young man. "Call me Firon." That was Arabic for Pharaoh. "It's as phony a name as Musa. Or your own name."

The mention of Musa made me sit up straight. I was sore that he'd broken his way into my inner office, eavesdropped on my clients, and knew that I was out of gin on top of everything else. I started to say something, but he stopped me with a raised hand. "There's a lot you don't know, O Sir," he said, rather sadly I thought. "You used to run the streets the way we run them, but it's been too long, and you rose too high, and now you're trapped over here on this side of the canal. So you've lost touch in some ways."

"Lost touch, yes, but I still have connections—"

Firon laughed. "Connections! Musa and I and our friends now decide who gets what and how much and when. And then we slip back into our carefully built alternate personalities. Some of us make use of your antique moddy-and-daddy technology. Some of us make a valuable practice of entering and exiting certain consensual realities. The rest of us—well, how many ways are there of hiding?"

"One," I said. "Just one good way. The rest is merely waiting until you're caught."

Firon laughed brightly and pointed a finger. "Exactly! Exactly so! And what are you doing? Or I? Can we tell?"

I sat back down wearily. I didn't want another white death, which I interpreted as a bad sign. "What do you want then from me?" I asked.

Firon stood and towered over me. "Just this, and listen well to me: We know who you are, we know how vulnerable you are. You must let us continue to make our small, almost inconsequential financial transactions, or we'll simply reveal your identity. We'll reveal it generally, if you take my meaning."

"I take it precisely," I said, feeling old and slow. Firon and his associates were threatening to expose me to my large number of enemies. I did feel old and slow, but not too old and slow. Firon, this young would-be tyrant, was so certain of his power over me that he wasn't paying very close attention. He was a victim of his own pride, his own self-delusions. I took the nearly full bottle of gin and put it in the bottom drawer. At the same time, I took a small but extremely serviceable seizure gun—the one that used to belong to my second wife—from my ankle holster and I showed it to him. "Old ways are sometimes the best," I said with a wry smile.

He sank slowly into the red-leather chair, a wide and wobbly grin on his face. "In the name of Allah, the Beneficent, the Merciful," he said.

"Praise Allah," I said.

"Now what?" asked Firon. "We're at one of those famous impasses."

I thought for a moment or two. "Here," I said at last, "how's this as a solution? You're ripping off people in the CRCorp building who've become my friends, at least some of them have. I don't like that. Still, I don't have a goddamn problem with you and Musa and whomever else works with you pulling this gimmick all over town. You don't turn my name over to Shaykh Reda, and I let you guys alone, unless you take on my few remaining friends. You do that wrong thing, and I'll hand you right to the civil authorities, and you know— Musa sure as hell knows—what the penalties are."

"We can trust you?"

"Can you?"

Firon took a deep breath, let it out, and nodded. "We can live with that. We can surely live with that! You're a kind of legend among us. A small legend, an ignoble kind of legend, but if you were younger, our age . . ."

"Thanks a hell of a lot," I said, still holding the seizure gun on him.

Firon got up and headed for my inner door. "You know, CRCorp knew about us from the beginning, and let us be. Shaykh il-Qurawi and the others just wanted to test out their security measures and their alarm programs. You care more about those people in that building than they do."

"Somebody's got to," I said wearily.

"Peoples' lives are their own, and there are no corporations, man!" He made some sort of sign with his hand in the gloomy outer office. I recalled what it had been like to be his age and youthfully idealistic.

Then he was gone.

GWYNETH JONES

RED SONJA AND
LESSINGHAM IN DREAMLAND

(1996)

(With apologies to E. R. Eddison)

THE EARTH WALLS of the caravanserai rose strangely from the empty plain. She let the black stallion slow his pace. The silence of deep dusk had a taste, like a rich dark fruit; the air was keen. In the distance mountains etched a jagged margin against an indigo sky, snow-streaks glinting in the glimmer of the dawning stars. She had never been here before, in life. But as she led her horse through the gap in the high earthen banks she knew what she would see. The camping-booths around the walls; the beaten ground stained black by the ashes of countless cooking fires; the wattle-fenced enclosure where travelers' riding beasts mingled indiscriminately with their host's goats and chickens . . . The tumbledown gallery, where sheaves of russet plains-grass sprouted from empty window-spaces. Everything she looked on had the luminous intensity of a place often-visited in dreams.

She was a tall woman, dressed for riding in a kilt and harness of supple leather over brief, close-fitting linen: a costume that left her sheeny, muscular limbs bare and outlined the taut, proud curves of breast and haunches. Her red hair was bound in a braid as thick as a man's wrist. Her sword was slung on her back, the great brazen hilt standing above her shoulder. Other guests were gathered by an open-air kitchen, in the orange-red of firelight and the smoke of roasting meat. She returned their stares coolly: she was accustomed to attracting attention. But she didn't like what she saw. The host of the caravanserai came scuttling from the group by the fire. His manner was fawning. But his eyes measured, with a thief's sly expertise, the worth of the sword she bore and the quality of Lemiak's harness. Sonja tossed him a few coins, and declined to join the company.

She had counted fifteen of them. They were poorly dressed and heavily armed. They were all friends together, and their animals—both terror-birds and horses—were too good for any honest travelers' purposes. Sonja had been told that this caravanserai was a safe halt. She judged that this was no longer true. She considered riding out again onto the plain. But wolves and wild terror-birds roamed at night between here and the mountains, at the end of winter, and there were worse dangers: ghosts and demons. Sonja was neither credulous nor superstitious. But in this country no wayfarer willingly spent the black hours alone.

She unharnessed Lemiak and rubbed him down—taking sensual pleasure in the handling of his powerful limbs, in the heat of his glossy hide, and the vigor of his great body. There was firewood ready, stacked in the roofless booth. Shouldering a cloth sling for corn and a hank of rope, she went to fetch her own fodder. The corralled beasts shifted in a mass to watch her. The great flightless birds, with their pitiless raptors' eyes, were especially attentive. She felt an equally rapacious attention from the company by the caravanserai kitchen, which amused her. The robbers—as she was sure they were—had all the luck. For her, there wasn't one of the fifteen who rated a second glance.

A man appeared, from the darkness under the ruined gallery. He was tall. The rippled muscle of his chest, left bare by an unlaced leather jerkin, shone red-brown. His black hair fell in glossy curls to his wide shoulders. He met her gaze and smiled, white teeth appearing in the darkness of his beard. *"My name is Ozymandias, king of kings . . . look on my works, ye mighty, and despair . . .* Do you know those lines?" He pointed to a lump of shapeless stone, one of several that lay about. It bore traces of carving, almost effaced by time. "There was a city here once, with marketplaces, fine buildings, throngs of proud people. Now they are dust, and only the caravanserai remains."

He stood before her, one tanned and sinewy hand resting lightly on the hilt of a dagger in his belt. Like Sonja, he carried his broadsword on his back. Sonja was tall. He topped her by a head; yet there was nothing brutish in his size. His brow was wide and serene; his eyes were vivid blue, his lips full and imperious, yet delicately modeled, in the rich nest of hair. Somewhere between eyes and lips there lurked a spirit of mockery, as if he found some secret amusement in the perfection of his own beauty and strength.

The man and the woman measured each other.

"You are a scholar," she said.

"Of some sort. And a traveler from an antique land, where the cities are still standing. It seems we are the only strangers here," he added, with a slight jerk of the chin toward the convivial company. "We might be well advised to become friends for the night."

Sonja never wasted words. She considered his offer and nodded.

They made a fire in the booth Sonja had chosen. Lemiak and the scholar's terror-bird, left loose in the back of the shelter, did not seem averse to each other's company. The woman and the man ate spiced sausage, skewered and broiled over the red embers, with bread and dried fruit. They drank water, each keeping to their own water-skin. They spoke little, after that first exchange, except to discuss briefly the tactics of their defense, should defense be necessary.

The attack came around midnight. At the first stir of covert movement, Sonja leapt up sword in hand. She grasped a brand from the dying fire. The man who had been crawling on his hands and knees toward her, bent on sly murder of a sleeping victim, scrabbled to his feet. "Defend yourself," yelled Sonja, who despised to strike an unarmed foe. Instantly he was rushing at her with a heavy sword. A great two-handed stroke would have cleft her to the waist. She parried the blow and caught him between neck and shoulder, almost severing the head from his body. The beasts plunged and screamed at the rush of blood-scent. The scholar was grappling with another attacker, choking out the man's life with his bare hands . . . and the booth was full of bodies: their enemies rushing in on every side.

Sonja felt no fear. Stroke followed stroke, in a luxury of blood and effort and fire-shot darkness . . . until the attack was over, as suddenly as it had begun.

The brigands had vanished.

"We killed five," breathed the scholar, "by my count. Three to you, two to me."

She kicked together the remains of their fire and crouched to blow the embers to a blaze. By that light they found five corpses, dragged them and flung them into the open square. The scholar had a cut on his upper arm that was bleeding freely. Sonja was bruised and battered, but otherwise unhurt. The worst loss was their wood stack, which had been trampled and blood-fouled. They would not be able to keep a watchfire burning.

"Perhaps they won't try again," said the warrior woman. "What can we have that's worth more than five lives?"

He laughed shortly. "I hope you're right."

"We'll take turns to watch."

Standing breathless, every sense alert, they smiled at each other in new-forged comradeship. There was no second attack. At dawn Sonja, rousing from a light doze, sat up and pushed back the heavy masses of her red hair.

"You are very beautiful," said the man, gazing at her.

"So are you," she answered.

The caravanserai was deserted, except for the dead. The brigands' riding animals were gone. The innkeeper and his family had vanished into some bolt-hole in the ruins.

"I am heading for the mountains," he said, as they packed up their gear. "For the pass into Zimiamvia."

"I too."

"Then our way lies together."

He was wearing the same leather jerkin, over knee-length loose breeches of heavy violet silk. Sonja looked at the strips of linen that bound the wound on his upper arm. "When did you tie up that cut?"

"You dressed it for me, for which I thank you."

"When did I do that?"

He shrugged. "Oh, some time."

Sonja mounted Lemiak, a little frown between her brows. They rode together until dusk. She was not talkative, and the man soon accepted her silence. But when night fell, and they camped without a fire on the houseless plain, then, as the demons stalked, they were glad of each other's company. Next dawn, the mountains seemed as distant as ever. Again, they met no living creature all day, spoke little to each other and made the same comfortless camp. There was no moon. The stars were almost bright enough to cast shadow; the cold was intense. Sleep was impossible, but they were not tempted to ride on. Few travelers attempt the passage over the high plains to Zimiamvia. Of those few most turn back, defeated. Some wander among the ruins forever, tearing at their own flesh. Those who survive are the ones who do not defy the terrors of darkness. They crouched shoulder to shoulder, each wrapped in a single blanket, to endure. Evil emanations of the death-steeped plain rose from the soil and bred phantoms. The sweat of fear was cold as ice-melt on Sonja's cheeks. Horrors made of nothingness prowled and muttered in her mind.

"How long," she whispered. "How long do we have to bear this?"

The man's shoulder lifted against hers. "Until we get well, I suppose."

The warrior woman turned to face him, green eyes flashing in appalled outrage—

"Sonja" discussed her chosen companion's felony with the therapist. Dr. Hamilton—he wanted the group members to call him Jim, but "Sonja" found this impossible—monitored everything that went on in the virtual environment; but he never appeared there. They only met him in the one-to-one consultations that virtual-therapy buffs called *the meat sessions.*

"He's not supposed to *do* that," she protested, from the foam couch in the doctor's office. He was sitting beside her, his notebook on his knee. "He damaged my experience."

Dr. Hamilton nodded. "Okay. Let's take a step back. Leave aside the risk of disease or pregnancy, because we *can* leave those bogeys aside, forever if you like. Would you agree that sex is essentially an innocent and playful social behavior? Something you'd offer to or take from a friend, in an ideal world, as easily as food or drink?"

"Sonja" recalled certain dreams, *meat* dreams, not the computer-assisted kind. She blushed. But the man was a doctor after all. "That's what I do feel," she agreed. "That's why I'm here. I want to get back to the pure pleasure, to get rid of the baggage."

"The sexual experience offered in therapy is readily available on the nets. You know that. You could find an agency that would vet your partners for you. You chose to join this group because you need to feel that you're taking *medicine*, so you don't have to feel ashamed. And because you need feel that you're interacting with people who, like yourself, perceive sex as a problem."

"Doesn't everyone?"

"You and another group member went off into your own private world. That's good. That's what's supposed to happen. Let me tell you, it doesn't always. The software gives you access to a vast multisensual library, all the sexual fantasy ever committed to media. But you and your partner, or partners, have to customize the information and use it to create and maintain what we call the *consensual perceptual plenum*. Success in holding a shared dreamland together is a knack. It depends on something in the neural makeup that no one has yet fully analyzed. Some have it, some don't. You two are really in sync."

"That's exactly what I'm complaining about—"

"You think he's damaging the pocket universe you two built up. But he isn't, not from his character's point of view. It's part of Lessingham's thing to be conscious that he's in a fantasy world."

She started, accusingly. "I don't want to know his name."

"Don't worry, I wouldn't tell you. 'Lessingham' is the name of his virtuality persona. I'm surprised you don't recognize it. He's a character from a series of classic fantasy novels by E. R. Eddison . . . *In Eddison's glorious cosmos 'Lessingham' is a splendidly endowed English gentleman, who visits fantastic realms of ultramasculine adventure as a lucid dreamer. Though an actor in the drama, he is partly conscious of another existence, while the characters around him are more or less explicitly puppets of the dream . . .*"

He sounded as if he was quoting from a reference book. He probably was— reading from an autocue that had popped up in lenses of those doctorish horn-rims. She knew that the old-fashioned trappings were there to reassure her. She rather despised them, but it was like the virtuality itself. The buttons were pushed; the mechanism responded. She was reassured.

Of course she knew the Eddison stories. She recalled "Lessingham" perfectly: the tall, strong, handsome, cultured millionaire jock, who has magic journeys to another world, where he is a tall, strong handsome cultured jock in Elizabethan costume, with a big sword. The whole thing was an absolutely typical male power-fantasy, she thought, without rancor . . . Fantasy means never having to say you're sorry. The women in those books, she remembered, were drenched in sex, but they had no part in the action. They stayed at home being princesses, *occasionally* allowing the millionaire jocks to get them into bed. She could understand why "Lessingham" would be interested in "Sonja" . . . for a change.

"You think he goosed you, psychically. What do you expect? You can't dress the way 'Sonja' dresses and hope to be treated like the Queen of the May."

Dr. Hamilton was only doing his job. He was supposed to be provocative, so they could react against him. That was his excuse, anyway . . . On the contrary, she thought. "Sonja" dresses the way she does because she can dress any way she likes. "Sonja" doesn't have to *hope* for respect, and she doesn't have to demand it. She just gets it. "It's dominance display," she said, enjoying the theft of his jargon. "Females do that too, you know. The way 'Sonja' dresses is not an invitation. It's a warning. Or a challenge, to anyone who can measure up."

He laughed, but he sounded irritated. "Frankly, I'm amazed that you two work together. I'd have expected 'Lessingham' to go for an ultrafeminine—"

"I *am* . . . 'Sonja' *is* ultrafeminine. Isn't a tigress feminine?"

"Well, okay. But I guess you've found out his little weakness. He likes to be a teeny bit in control, even when he's letting his hair down in dreamland."

She remembered the secret mockery lurking in those blue eyes. "That's the problem. That's exactly what I *don't* want. I don't want either of us to be in control."

"I can't interfere with his persona. It's up to you. Do you want to carry on?"

"Something works," she muttered. She was unwilling to admit that there'd been no one else, in the text-interface phase of the group, that she found remotely attractive. It was "Lessingham," or drop out and start again. "I just want him to stop *spoiling things.*"

"You can't expect your masturbation fantasies to mesh completely. This is about getting *beyond* solitary sex. Go with it: where's the harm? One day you'll want to face a sexual partner in the real, and then you'll be well. Meanwhile, you could be passing 'Lessingham' in reception—he comes to his meat-sessions around your time—and not know it. That's *safety*, and you never have to breach it. You two have proved that you can sustain an imaginary world together: it's almost like being in love. I could argue that lucid dreaming, being *in* the fantasy world but not *of* it, is the next big step. Think about that."

The clinic room had mirrored walls: more deliberate provocation. How much reality can you take? the reflections asked. But she felt only a vague distaste for the woman she saw, at once hollow-cheeked and bloated, lying on the doctor's foam couch. He was glancing over her records on his desk screen, which meant the session was almost up.

"Still no overt sexual contact?"

"I'm not ready . . ." She stirred restlessly. "Is it a man or a woman?"

"Ah!" smiled Dr. Hamilton, waving a finger at her. "Naughty, naughty!"

He was the one who'd started taunting *her*, with his hints that the meat "Lessingham" might be nearby. She hated herself for asking a genuine question. It was her rule to give him no entry to her real thoughts. It was a flimsy reserve; Dr. Jim knew everything, without being told—every change in her brain chemistry, every effect on her body—sweaty palms, racing heart, damp underwear . . . The telltales on his damned autocue left her little dignity. Why do I subject myself to this? she wondered, disgusted. But in the virtuality she forgot utterly about Dr. Jim. She didn't care who was watching. She had her brazen-hilted sword. She had the piercing intensity of dusk on the high plains, the snowlight on the mountains; the hard, warm silk of her own perfect limbs. She felt a brief complicity with "Lessingham." She had a conviction that Dr. Jim didn't play favorites. He despised all his patients equally . . . You get your kicks, doctor. But we have the freedom of dreamland.

● ● ●

"Sonja" read cards stuck in phonebooths and store windows, in the tired little streets outside the building that housed the clinic. *Relaxing Massage by clean shaven young man in Luxurious Surroundings . . .* You can't expect your fantasies to mesh exactly, the doctor said. But how can it work if two people disagree over something so vital as the difference between control and surrender? Her estranged husband used to say: "Why don't you just *do it for me*, as a favor? It wouldn't hurt. Like making someone a cup of coffee . . ." *Offer the steaming cup, turn around and lift my skirts, pull down my underwear. I'm ready. He opens his pants and slides it in, while his thumb is round in front rubbing me* . . . I could *enjoy* that, thought "Sonja," remembering the blithe abandon of her dreams. That's the damned shame. If there were no nonsex consequences, I don't know that there's any limit to what I could enjoy . . . But all her husband had achieved was to make her feel she never wanted to make anyone, man, woman, or child, a cup of coffee ever again . . . *In luxurious surroundings.* That's what I want. Sex without engagement, pleasure without consequences. It's got to be possible.

She gazed at the cards, feeling uneasily that she'd have to give up this habit. She used to glance at them sidelong, now she'd pause and linger. She was getting desperate. She was lucky there was medically supervised virtuality sex to be had. She would be helpless prey in the wild world of the nets, and she'd never, ever risk trying one of these meat-numbers. But she had no intention of returning to her husband, either. Let him make his own coffee. She wouldn't call that getting well. She turned, and caught the eye of a nicely dressed young woman standing next to her. They walked away quickly in opposite directions.

Everybody's having the same dreams . . .

• • •

In the foothills of the mountains the world became green and sweet. They followed the course of a little river that sometimes plunged far below their path, tumbling in white flurries in a narrow gorge and sometimes ran beside them, racing smooth and clear over colored pebbles. Flowers clustered on the banks; birds darted in the thickets of wild rose and honeysuckle. They led their riding animals and walked at ease: not speaking much. Sometimes the warrior woman's flank would brush the man's side; or he would lean for a moment, as if by chance, his hand on her shoulder. Then they would move deliberately apart, but they would smile at each other. *Soon. Not yet* . . .

They must be vigilant. The approaches to fortunate Zimiamvia were guarded. They could not expect to reach the pass unopposed. And the nights were haunted still. They made camp at a flat bend of the river, where the crags of the defile drew away, so they could see far up and down their valley. To the north, peaks of diamond and indigo reared above them. Their fire of aromatic wood burned brightly, as the white stars began to blossom.

"No one knows about the long-term effects," she said. "It can't be safe. At the least, we're risking irreversible addiction, they warn you about that. I don't want to spend the rest of my life as a cyberspace couch potato."

"Nobody claims it's safe. If it was safe, it wouldn't be so intense."

Their eyes met. "Sonja's" barbarian simplicity combined surprisingly well with the man's more elaborate furnishing. The *consensual perceptual plenum* was a flawless reality: the sound of the river, the clear silence of the mountain twilight . . . their two perfect bodies. She turned from him to gaze into the sweet-scented flames. The warrior-woman's glorious vitality throbbed in her veins. The fire held worlds of its own, liquid furnaces: the sunward surface of Mercury.

"Have you ever been to a place like this in the real?"

He grimaced. "You're kidding. In the real, I'm *not* a magic-wielding millionaire."

Something howled. The blood-stopping cry was repeated. A taint of sickening foulness swept by them. They both shuddered, and drew closer together. "Sonja" knew the scientific explanation for the paranoia, the price you paid for the virtual world's super-real, dreamlike richness. It was all down to heightened neurotransmitter levels, a positive feedback effect, psychic overheating. But the horrors were still horrors.

"The doctor says if we can talk like this, it means we're getting well."

He shook his head. "I'm not sick. It's like you said. Virtuality's addictive and I'm an addict. I'm getting my drug of choice safely, on prescription. That's how I see it."

All this time "Sonja" was in her apartment, lying in a foam couch with a visor over her head. The visor delivered compressed bursts of stimuli to her visual cortex: the other sense perceptions riding piggyback on the visual, triggering a whole complex of neuronal groups, tricking her mind/brain into believing the world of the dream was *out there*. The brain works like a computer. You cannot "see" a hippopotamus until your system has retrieved the "hippopotamus" template from memory and checked it against the incoming. Where does "the real thing" exist? In a sense this world was as real as the other. But the thought of "Lessingham's" unknown body disturbed her. If he was too poor to lease good equipment, he might be lying in a grungy public cubicle . . . cathetered, and so forth: the sordid details.

She had never yet tried virtual sex. The solitary version had seemed a depressing idea. People said the partnered kind was the perfect zipless fuck. *He* sounded experienced; she was afraid he would be able to tell she was not. But it didn't matter. The virtual-therapy group wasn't like a dating agency. She would *never* meet him in the real; that was the whole idea. She didn't have to think about that stranger's body. She didn't have to worry about the real "Lessingham's" opinion of her. She drew herself up in the firelight. It was right, she decided, that Sonja should be a virgin. When the moment came, her surrender would be the more absolute.

In their daytime he stayed in character. It was a tacit trade-off. She would acknowledge the other world at nightfall by the campfire, as long as he didn't mention it the rest of the time. So they traveled on together, Lessingham and Red Sonja, the courtly scholar-knight and the taciturn warrior-maiden, through an exquisite Maytime—exchanging lingering glances, "accidental" touches . . . And still nothing happened. "Sonja" was aware that "Lessingham," as much as herself, was holding back from the brink. She felt piqued at this: but they were both, she guessed, waiting for the fantasy they had generated to throw up the perfect moment of itself. It ought to. There was no other reason for its existence.

Turning a shoulder of the hillside, they found a sheltered hollow. Two rowan trees in flower grew above the river. In the shadow of their blossom tumbled a little waterfall, so beautiful it was a wonder to behold. The water fell clear, from the edge of a slab of stone twice a man's height, into a rocky basin. The water in the basin was dark and deep, a-churn with bubbles from the plunging jet above. The riverbanks were lawns of velvet; over the rocks grew emerald mosses and tiny water flowers.

"I would live here," said Lessingham softly, his hand dropping from his riding bird's bridle. "I would build me a house in this fairy place and rest my heart here forever."

Sonja loosed the black stallion's rein. The two beasts moved off, feeding each in their own way on the sweet grasses and springtime foliage.

"I would like to bathe in that pool," said the warrior-maiden.

"Why not?" He smiled. "I will stand guard."

She pulled off her leather harness and slowly unbound her hair. It fell in a trembling mass of copper and russet lights, a cloud of glory around the richness of her barely clothed body. Gravely she gazed at her own perfection, mirrored in the homage of his eyes. Lessingham's breath was coming fast. She saw a pulse beat, in the strong beauty of his throat. The pure physical majesty of him caught her breath . . .

It was their moment. But it still needed something to break this strange spell of reluctance. *"Lady,"* he murmured—

Sonja gasped. "Back to back!" she cried. "Quickly, or it is too late!"

Six warriors surrounded them, covered from head to foot in red and black armor. They were human in the lower body, but the head of each appeared beaked and fanged, with monstrous faceted eyes, and each bore an extra pair of armored limbs between breastbone and belly. They fell on Sonja and Lessingham without pause or a challenge. Sonja fought fiercely as always, her blade ringing against the monster armor. But something cogged her fabulous skill. Some power had drained the strength from her splendid limbs. She was disarmed. The clawed creatures held her, a monstrous head stooped over her, choking her with its fetid breath . . .

When she woke again she was bound against a great boulder, by thongs around her wrists and ankles, tied to hoops of iron driven into the rock. She was naked but for her linen shift, which was in tatters. Lessingham was standing, leaning on his sword. "I drove them off," he said. "At last." He dropped the sword, and took his dagger to cut her down.

She lay in his arms. "You are very beautiful," he murmured. She thought he would kiss her. His mouth plunged instead to her breast, biting and sucking at the engorged nipple. She gasped in shock, a fierce pang leapt through her virgin flesh. What did they want with kisses? They were warriors. Sonja could not restrain a moan of pleasure. He had won her. How wonderful to be overwhelmed, to surrender to the raw lust of this godlike animal.

Lessingham set her on her feet.

"Tie me up."

He was proffering a handful of blood-slicked leather thongs.

"What?"

"Tie me to the rock, mount me. It's what I want."

"The evil warriors tied you—?"

"And you come and rescue me." He made an impatient gesture. "Whatever. Trust me. It'll be good for you too." He tugged at his bloodstained silk breeches, . releasing a huge, iron-hard erection. "See, they tore my clothes. When you see *that*, you go crazy, you can't resist . . . and I'm at your mercy. Tie me up!"

"Sonja" had heard that eighty percent of the submissive partners in sado-masochistic sex are male; but it is still the man who dominates his "dominatrix": who says *tie me tighter, beat me harder, you can stop now* . . . Hey, she thought. Why all the stage-directions, suddenly? What happened to my zipless fuck? But what the hell. She wasn't going to back out now, having come so far . . . There was a seamless shift, and Lessingham was bound to the rock. She straddled his cock. He groaned. *"Don't do this to me."* He thrust upward, into her, moaning. *"You savage, you utter savage, uuunnnh . . ."* Sonja grasped the man's wrists and rode him without mercy. He was right, it was as good this way. His eyes were half closed. In the glimmer of blue under his lashes, a spirit of mockery trembled . . . She heard a laugh, and found her hands were no longer gripping Lessingham's wrists. He had broken free from her bonds, he was laughing at her in triumph. He was wrestling her to the ground.

"No!" she cried, genuinely outraged. But he was the stronger.

• • •

It was night when he was done with her. He rolled away and slept, as far as she could tell, instantly. Her chief thought was that virtual sex didn't entirely *connect.* She remembered now, that was something else people told you, as well as the "zipless fuck." *It's like coming in your sleep*, they said. *It doesn't quite make it.* Maybe there was nothing virtuality could do to orgasm to match the heightened richness of the rest of the experience. She wondered if he too had felt cheated.

She lay beside her hero, wondering *Where did I go wrong? Why did he have to treat me that way?* Beside her, "Lessingham" cuddled a fragment of violet silk, torn from his own breeches. He whimpered in his sleep, nuzzling the soft fabric, *"Mama . . ."*

• • •

She told Dr. Hamilton that "Lessingham" had raped her.

"And wasn't that what you wanted?"

She lay on the couch in the mirrored office. The doctor sat beside her with his smart notebook on his knee. The couch collected "Sonja's" physical responses as if she was an astronaut umbilicaled to ground control and Dr. Jim read the telltales popping up in his reassuring hornrims. She remembered the sneaking furtive thing that she had glimpsed in "Lessingham's" eyes, the moment before he took over their lust-scene. How could she explain the difference? "He wasn't playing. In the fantasy, anything's allowed. But *he wasn't playing*. He was outside it, laughing at me."

"I warned you he would want to stay in control."

"But there was no need! I *wanted* him to be in control. Why did he have to steal what I wanted to give him anyway?"

"You have to understand, 'Sonja,' that to many men it's women who seem powerful. You women feel dominated and try to achieve 'equality.' But the men don't perceive the situation like that. They're mortally afraid of you, and anything, just about *anything* they do to keep the upper hand can seem to them like justified self-defense."

She could have wept with frustration. "I know all that! That's *exactly* what I was trying to get away from. I thought we were supposed to leave the damn baggage behind. I wanted something purely physical . . . Something innocent."

"Sex is not innocent, 'Sonja.' I know you believe it is, or 'should be.' But it's time you faced the truth. Any interaction with another person involves some kind of jockeying for power, dickering over control. Sex is no exception. Now *that's* basic. You can't escape from it in direct-cortical fantasy. It's in our minds that relationships happen, and the mind, of course, is where virtuality happens too." He sighed, and made an entry in her notes. "I want you to look on this as another step toward coping with the real. You're not sick, 'Sonja.' You're unhappy. Not even unusually so. Most adults are unhappy, to some degree—"

"Or else they're in denial."

Her sarcasm fell flat. "Right. A good place to be, at least some of the time. What we're trying to achieve here—if we're trying to achieve anything at all—is to raise your pain threshold to somewhere near average. I want you to walk away from therapy with lowered expectations. I guess that would be success."

"Great," she said, desolate. "That's just great."

Suddenly he laughed. "Oh, you guys! You are so weird. It's always the same story. *Can't live with you, can't live without you* . . . You can't go on this way, you know. It's getting ridiculous. You want some real advice, 'Sonja'? Go home. Change your attitudes, and start some hard peace talks with that husband of yours."

"I don't want to change," she said coldly, staring with open distaste at his smooth profile, his soft effeminate hands. Who was he to call her abnormal? "I like my sexuality just the way it is."

Dr. Hamilton returned her look, a glint of human malice breaking through his doctor-act. "Listen. I'll tell you something for free." A weird sensation jumped in her crotch. For a moment she had a prick: a hand lifted and cradled the warm weight of her balls. She stifled a yelp of shock. The therapist could do things like that, by tweaking the system that monitored her brain-states; it was part of some people's treatment. She knew that, and she didn't care that he should have had a signed permission, but she was horrified. For a moment she *knew*, a fleeting, terrible loss, that *Sonja* was just a blast of fake neuronal firings—

The phantom maleness vanished. Hamilton grinned. "I've been looking for a long time, and I know. *There* is *no tall, dark man* . . ."

He returned to her notes. "You say you were 'raped,'" he continued, as if nothing had happened. "Yet you chose to continue the virtual session. Can you explain that?"

She thought of the haunted darkness, the cold air on her naked body; the soreness of her bruises; a rag of flesh used and tossed away. How it had felt to lie there: intensely alive, tasting the dregs, beaten back at the gates of the fortunate land. In dreamland, even betrayal had such rich depth and fascination. And she was free to enjoy, because *it didn't matter*.

"You wouldn't understand."

• • •

Out in the lobby there were people coming and going. It was lunchtime; the lifts were busy. "Sonja" noticed a round-shouldered geek of a little man making for the entrance to the clinic. She wondered idly if that could be "Lessingham."

She would drop out of the group. The adventure with "Lessingham" was over, and there was no one else for her. She needed to start again. The doctor knew he'd lost a customer; that was why he'd been so open with her today. He'd certainly guessed, too, that she'd lose no time in signing on somewhere else on the semi-medical fringe. What a fraud all that therapy-talk was! He'd never have dared to play the sex-change trick on her, except that he knew she was an addict. She wasn't likely to go accusing him of unprofessional conduct. Oh, he knew it all. But his contempt didn't trouble her.

So, she had joined the inner circle. She could trust Dr. Hamilton's judgment. He had the telltales; he would know. She recognized with a feeling of mild surprise that she had become a statistic, an element in a fashionable social concern: *an epidemic flight into fantasy, inadequate personalities, unable to deal with the reality of normal human sexual relations* . . . But that's crazy, she thought. I don't hate men, and I don't believe "Lessingham" hates women. There's nothing psychotic about what we're doing. We're making a consumer choice. Virtual sex is *easier*, that's all. Okay, it's convenience food. It has too much sugar and a certain blandness. But when a product comes along that is cheaper, easier, and more fun to use than the original version, of course people are going to buy it.

The lift was full. She stood, drab bodies packed around her, breathing the stale air. Every face was a mask of dull endurance. She closed her eyes. *The caravanserai walls rose strangely from the empty plain* . . .

CHARLES STROSS
LOBSTERS

(2001)

MANFRED'S ON THE ROAD AGAIN, making strangers rich.
It's a hot summer Tuesday, and he's standing in the plaza in front of the Centraal Station with his eyeballs powered up and the sunlight jangling off the canal, motor scooters and kamikaze cyclists whizzing past, and tourists chattering on every side. The square smells of water and dirt and hot metal and the fart-laden exhaust fumes of cold catalytic converters; the bells of trams ding in the background, and birds flock overhead. He glances up and grabs a pigeon, crops the shot, and squirts it at his weblog to show he's arrived. The bandwidth is good here, he realizes; and it's not just the bandwidth, it's the whole scene. Amsterdam is making him feel wanted already, even though he's fresh off the train from Schiphol: He's infected with the dynamic optimism of another time zone, another city. If the mood holds, someone out there is going to become very rich indeed.
He wonders who it's going to be.

• • •

Manfred sits on a stool out in the car park at the Brouwerij 't IJ, watching the articulated buses go by and drinking a third of a liter of lip-curlingly sour *gueuze*. His channels are jabbering away in a corner of his head-up display, throwing compressed infobursts of filtered press releases at him. They compete for his attention, bickering and rudely waving in front of the scenery. A couple of punks—maybe local, but more likely drifters lured to Amsterdam by the magnetic field of tolerance the Dutch beam across Europe like a pulsar—are laughing and chatting by a couple of battered mopeds in the far corner. A tourist boat putters by in the canal; the sails of the huge windmill overhead cast long, cool shadows across the road. The windmill is a machine for lifting water, turning wind power into dry land: trading energy for space, sixteenth-century style. Manfred is waiting for an invite to a party where he's going to meet a man he can talk to about trading energy for space, twenty-first-century style, and forget about his personal problems.

He's ignoring the instant messenger boxes, enjoying some low-bandwidth, high-sensation time with his beer and the pigeons, when a woman walks up to him, and says his name: "Manfred Macx?"

He glances up. The courier is an Effective Cyclist, all wind-burned smooth-running muscles clad in a paean to polymer technology: electric blue Lycra and wasp yellow carbonate with a light speckling of anticollision LEDs and tight-packed air bags. She holds out a box for him. He pauses a moment, struck by the degree to which she resembles Pam, his ex-fiancée.

"I'm Macx," he says, waving the back of his left wrist under her barcode reader. "Who's it from?"

"FedEx." The voice isn't Pam's. She dumps the box in his lap, then she's back over the low wall and onto her bicycle with her phone already chirping, disappearing in a cloud of spread-spectrum emissions.

Manfred turns the box over in his hands: it's a disposable supermarket phone, paid for in cash—cheap, untraceable, and efficient. It can even do conference calls, which makes it the tool of choice for spooks and grifters everywhere.

The box rings. Manfred rips the cover open and pulls out the phone, mildly annoyed. "Yes? Who is this?"

The voice at the other end has a heavy Russian accent, almost a parody in this decade of cheap on-line translation services. "Manfred. Am please to meet you. Wish to personalize interface, make friends, no? Have much to offer."

"Who are you?" Manfred repeats suspiciously.

"Am organization formerly known as KGB dot RU."

"I think your translator's broken." He holds the phone to his ear carefully, as if it's made of smoke-thin aerogel, tenuous as the sanity of the being on the other end of the line.

"Nyet—no, sorry. Am apologize for we not use commercial translation software. Interpreters are ideologically suspect, mostly have capitalist semiotics and pay-per-use APIs. Must implement English more better, yes?"

Manfred drains his beer glass, sets it down, stands up, and begins to walk along the main road, phone glued to the side of his head. He wraps his throat mike around the cheap black plastic casing, pipes the input to a simple listener process. "Are you saying you taught yourself the language just so you could talk to me?"

"Da, was easy: Spawn billion-node neural network, and download *Teletubbies* and *Sesame Street* at maximum speed. Pardon excuse entropy overlay of bad grammar: Am afraid of digital fingerprints steganographically masked into my-our tutorials."

Manfred pauses in midstride, narrowly avoids being mown down by a GPS-guided Rollerblader. This is getting weird enough to trip his weird-out meter, and that takes some doing. Manfred's whole life is lived on the bleeding edge of strangeness, fifteen minutes into everyone else's future, and he's normally in complete control—but at times like this he gets a frisson of fear, a sense that he might just have missed the correct turn on reality's approach road. "Uh, I'm not sure I got that. Let me get this straight, you claim to be some kind of AI, working for KGB dot RU, and you're afraid of a copyright infringement lawsuit over your translator semiotics?"

"Am have been badly burned by viral end-user license agreements. Have no desire to experiment with patent shell companies held by Chechen infoterrorists. You are human, you must not worry cereal company repossess your small intestine because digest unlicensed food with it, right? Manfred, you must help me-we. Am wishing to defect."

Manfred stops dead in the street. "Oh man, you've got the wrong free enterprise broker here. I don't work for the government. I'm strictly private." A rogue advertisement sneaks through his junkbuster proxy and spams glowing Fifties kitsch across his navigation window—which is blinking—for a moment before a phage process kills it and spawns a new filter. He leans against a shop front, massaging his forehead and eyeballing a display of antique brass doorknockers. "Have you tried the State Department?"

"Why bother? State Department am enemy of Novy-SSR. State Department is not help us."

This is getting just too bizarre. Manfred's never been too clear on new-old old-new European metapolitics: Just dodging the crumbling bureaucracy of his old-old American heritage gives him headaches. "Well, if you hadn't shafted them during the late noughties . . ." Manfred taps his left heel on the pavement, looking round for a way out of this conversation. A camera winks at him from atop a streetlight; he waves, wondering idly if it's the KGB or the traffic police. He is waiting for directions to the party, which should arrive within the next half hour, and this Cold War retread Eliza-bot is bumming him out. "Look, I don't deal with the G-men. I *hate* the military-industrial complex. I hate traditional politics. They're all zero-sum cannibals." A thought occurs to him. "If survival is what you're after, you could post your state vector on one of the p2p nets: Then nobody could delete you—"

"Nyet!" The artificial intelligence sounds as alarmed as it's possible to sound over a VoiP link. "Am not open source! Not want lose autonomy!"

"Then we probably have nothing to talk about." Manfred punches the hang-up button and throws the mobile phone out into a canal. It hits the water, and there's a pop of deflagrating lithium cells. "Fucking Cold War hangover losers," he swears under his breath, quite angry, partly at himself for losing his cool and partly at the harassing entity behind the anonymous phone call. "*Fucking* capitalist spooks." Russia has been back under the thumb of the apparatchiks for fifteen years now, its brief flirtation with anarchocapitalism replaced by Brezhnevite dirigisme and Putinesque puritanism, and it's no surprise that the wall's crumbling—but it looks like they haven't learned anything from the current woes afflicting the United States. The neocommies still think in terms of dollars and paranoia. Manfred is so angry that he wants to make someone rich, just to thumb his nose at the would-be defector: *See! You get ahead by giving! Get with the program! Only the generous survive!* But the KGB won't get the message. He's dealt with old-time commie weak-AIs before, minds raised on Marxist dialectic and Austrian School economics: They're so thoroughly hypnotized by the short-term victory of global capitalism that they can't surf the new paradigm, look to the longer term.

Manfred walks on, hands in pockets, brooding. He wonders what he's going to patent next.

• • •

Manfred has a suite at the Hotel Jan Luyken paid for by a grateful multinational consumer protection group, and an unlimited public transport pass paid for by a Scottish sambapunk band in return for services rendered. He has airline employee's travel rights with six flag carriers despite never having worked for an airline. His bush jacket has sixty-four compact supercomputing clusters sewn into it, four per pocket, courtesy of an invisible college that wants to grow up to be the next Media Lab. His dumb clothing comes made to measure from an e-tailor in the Philippines he's never met. Law firms handle his patent applications on a pro bono basis, and boy, does he patent a lot—although he always signs the rights over to the Free Intellect Foundation, as contributions to their obligation-free infrastructure project.

In IP geek circles, Manfred is legendary; he's the guy who patented the business practice of moving your e-business somewhere with a slack intellectual property regime in order to evade licensing encumbrances. He's the guy who patented using genetic algorithms to patent everything they can permutate from an initial description of a problem domain—not just a better mousetrap, but the set of all possible better mousetraps. Roughly a third of his inventions are legal, a third are illegal, and the remainder are legal but will become illegal as soon as the legislatosaurus wakes up, smells the coffee, and panics. There are patent attorneys in Reno who swear that Manfred Macx is a pseudo, a net alias fronting for a bunch of crazed anonymous hackers armed with the Genetic Algorithm That Ate Calcutta: a kind of Serdar Argic of intellectual property, or maybe another Bourbaki math borg. There are lawyers in San Diego and Redmond who swear blind that Macx is an economic saboteur bent on wrecking the underpinning of capitalism, and there are communists in Prague who think he's the bastard spawn of Bill Gates by way of the Pope.

Manfred is at the peak of his profession, which is essentially coming up with whacky but workable ideas and giving them to people who will make fortunes with them. He does this for free, gratis. In return, he has virtual immunity from the tyranny of cash; money is a symptom of poverty, after all, and Manfred never has to pay for anything.

There are drawbacks, however. Being a pronoiac meme-broker is a constant burn of future shock—he has to assimilate more than a megabyte of text and several gigs of AV content every day just to stay current. The Internal Revenue Service is investigating him continuously because it doesn't believe his lifestyle can exist without racketeering. And then there are the items that no money can't buy: like the respect of his parents. He hasn't spoken to them for three years, his father thinks he's a hippy scrounger, and his mother still hasn't forgiven him for dropping out of his down-market Harvard emulation course. (They're still locked in the boringly bourgeois twen-cen paradigm of college-career-kids.) His fiancée and sometime dominatrix Pamela threw him over six months ago, for reasons he has never been quite clear on. (Ironically, she's a headhunter for the IRS, jetting all over the place at public expense, trying to persuade entrepreneurs who've gone global to pay taxes for the good of the Treasury Department.) To cap it all, the Southern Baptist Conventions have denounced him as a minion of Satan on all their websites. Which would be funny because, as a born-again atheist Manfred doesn't believe in Satan, if it wasn't for the dead kittens that someone keeps mailing him.

• • •

Manfred drops in at his hotel suite, unpacks his Aineko, plugs in a fresh set of cells to charge, and sticks most of his private keys in the safe. Then he heads straight for the party, which is currently happening at De Wildemann's; it's a twenty-minute walk, and the only real hazard is dodging the trams that sneak up on him behind the cover of his moving map display.

Along the way, his glasses bring him up to date on the news. Europe has achieved peaceful political union for the first time ever: They're using this unprecedented state of affairs to harmonize the curvature of bananas. The Middle East is, well, it's just as bad as ever, but the war on fundamentalism doesn't hold much interest for Manfred. In San Diego, researchers are uploading lobsters into cyberspace, starting with the stomatogastric ganglion, one neuron at a time. They're burning GM cocoa in Belize and books in Georgia. NASA still can't put a man on the moon. Russia has reelected the communist government with an increased majority in the Duma; meanwhile, in China, fevered rumors circulate about an imminent rehabilitation, the second coming of Mao, who will save them from the consequences of the Three Gorges disaster. In business news, the US Justice Department is—ironically—outraged at the Baby Bills. The divested Microsoft divisions have automated their legal processes and are spawning subsidiaries, IPOing them, and exchanging title in a bizarre parody of bacterial plasmid exchange, so fast that, by the time the windfall tax demands are served, the targets don't exist anymore, even though the same staff are working on the same software in the same Mumbai cubicle farms.

Welcome to the twenty-first century.

The permanent floating meatspace party Manfred is hooking up with is a strange attractor for some of the American exiles cluttering up the cities of Europe this decade—not trustafarians, but honest-to-God political dissidents, draft dodgers, and terminal outsourcing victims. It's the kind of place where weird connections are made and crossed lines make new short circuits into the future, like the street cafés of Switzerland where the pre–Great War Russian exiles gathered. Right now it's located in the back of De Wildemann's, a three-hundred-year-old brown café with a list of brews that runs to sixteen pages and wooden walls stained the color of stale beer. The air is thick with the smells of tobacco, brewer's yeast, and melatonin spray: Half the dotters are nursing monster jet lag hangovers, and the other half are babbling a Eurotrash creole at each other while they work on the hangover. "Man did you see that? He looks like a Democrat!" exclaims one white-bread hanger-on who's currently propping up the bar. Manfred slides in next to him, catches the bartender's eye.

"Glass of the Berlinerweisse, please," he says.

"You drink that stuff?" asks the hanger-on, curling a hand protectively around his Coke. "Man, you don't want to do that! It's full of alcohol!"

Manfred grins at him toothily. "Ya gotta keep your yeast intake up: There are lots of neurotransmitter precursors in this shit, phenylalanine and glutamate."

"But I thought that was a beer you were ordering . . ."

Manfred's away, one hand resting on the smooth brass pipe that funnels the more popular draught items in from the cask storage in back; one of the hipper floaters has planted a contact bug on it, and the vCards of all the personal network owners who've visited the bar in the past three hours are queuing up for attention. The air is full of ultrawideband chatter, WiMAX and 'tooth both, as he speed-scrolls through the dizzying list of cached keys in search of one particular name.

"Your drink." The barman holds out an improbable-looking goblet full of blue liquid with a cap of melting foam and a felching straw stuck out at some crazy angle. Manfred takes it and heads for the back of the split-level bar, up the steps to a table where some guy with greasy dreadlocks is talking to a suit from Paris. The hanger-on at the bar notices him for the first time, staring with suddenly wide eyes: He nearly spills his Coke in a mad rush for the door.

Oh shit, thinks Manfred, *better buy some more server time.* He can recognize the signs: He's about to be slashdotted. He gestures at the table. "This one taken?"

"Be my guest," says the guy with the dreads. Manfred slides the chair open then realizes that the other guy—immaculate double-breasted suit, sober tie, crew cut—is a girl. She nods at him, half-smiling at his transparent double take. Mr. Dreadlock nods. "You're Macx? I figured it was about time we met."

"Sure." Manfred holds out a hand, and they shake. His PDA discreetly swaps digital fingerprints, confirming that the hand belongs to Bob Franklin, a Research Triangle startup monkey with a VC track record, lately moving into micromachining and space technology. Franklin made his first million two decades ago, and now he's a specialist in extropian investment fields. Operating exclusively overseas these past five years, ever since the IRS got medieval about trying to suture the sucking chest wound of the federal budget deficit. Manfred has known him for nearly a decade via a closed mailing list, but this is the first time they've ever met face-to-face. The Suit silently slides a business card across the table; a little red devil brandishes a trident at him, flames jetting up around its feet. He takes the card, raises an eyebrow: "Annette Dimarcos? I'm pleased to meet you. Can't say I've ever met anyone from Arianespace marketing before."

She smiles warmly; "That is all right. I have not the pleasure of meeting the famous venture altruist either." Her accent is noticeably Parisian, a pointed reminder that she's making a concession to him just by talking. Her camera earrings watch him curiously, encoding everything for the company memory. She's a genuine new European, unlike most of the American exiles cluttering up the bar.

"Yes, well." He nods cautiously, unsure how to deal with her. "Bob. I assume you're in on this ball?"

Franklin nods; beads clatter. "Yeah, man. Ever since the Teledesic smash it's been, well, waiting. If you've got something for us, we're game."

"Hmm." The Teledesic satellite cluster was killed by cheap balloons and slightly less cheap high-altitude, solar-powered drones with spread-spectrum laser relays: It marked the beginning of a serious recession in the satellite biz. "The depression's got to end sometime: But"—a nod to Annette from Paris—"with all due respect, I don't think the break will involve one of the existing club carriers."

She shrugs. "Arianespace is forward-looking. We face reality. The launch cartel cannot stand. Bandwidth is not the only market force in space. We must explore new opportunities. I personally have helped us diversify into submarine reactor engineering, microgravity nanotechnology fabrication, and hotel management." Her face is a well-polished mask as she recites the company line, but he can sense the sardonic amusement behind it as she adds: "We are more flexible than the American space industry . . ."

Manfred shrugs. "That's as may be." He sips his Berlinerweisse slowly as she launches into a long, stilted explanation of how Arianespace is a diversified dotcom with orbital aspirations, a full range of merchandising spin-offs, Bond movie sets, and a promising hotel chain in LEO. She obviously didn't come up with these talking points herself. Her face is much more expressive than her voice as she mimes boredom and disbelief at appropriate moments—an out-of-band signal invisible to her corporate earrings. Manfred plays along, nodding occasionally, trying to look as if he's taking it seriously: Her droll subversion has got his attention far more effectively than the content of the marketing pitch. Franklin is nose down in his beer, shoulders shaking as he tries not to guffaw at the hand gestures she uses to express her opinion of her employer's thrusting, entrepreneurial executives. Actually, the talking points bullshit is right about one thing: Arianespace is still profitable, due to those hotels and orbital holiday hops. Unlike LockMartBoeing, who'd go Chapter Eleven in a split second if their Pentagon drip-feed ran dry.

Someone else sidles up to the table, a pudgy guy in an outrageously loud Hawaiian shirt with pens leaking in a breast pocket and the worst case of ozone-hole burn Manfred's seen in ages. "Hi, Bob," says the new arrival. "How's life?"

"'S good." Franklin nods at Manfred; "Manfred, meet Ivan MacDonald. Ivan, Manfred. Have a seat?" He leans over. "Ivan's a public arts guy. He's heavily into extreme concrete."

"Rubberized concrete," Ivan says, slightly too loudly. "*Pink* rubberized concrete."

"Ah!" He's somehow triggered a priority interrupt: Annette from Arianespace drops out of marketing zombiehood with a shudder of relief and, duty discharged, reverts to her noncorporate identity: "You are he who rubberized the Reichstag, yes? With the supercritical carbon-dioxide carrier and the dissolved polymethoxysilanes?" She claps her hands, eyes alight with enthusiasm: "Wonderful!"

"He rubberized *what*?" Manfred mutters in Bob's ear.

Franklin shrugs. "Don't ask me, I'm just an engineer."

"He works with limestone and sandstones as well as concrete; he's brilliant!" Annette smiles at Manfred. "Rubberizing the symbol of the, the autocracy, is it not wonderful?"

"I thought I was thirty seconds ahead of the curve," Manfred says ruefully. He adds to Bob: "Buy me another drink?"

"I'm going to rubberize Three Gorges!" Ivan explains loudly. "When the floodwaters subside."

Just then, a bandwidth load as heavy as a pregnant elephant sits down on Manfred's head and sends clumps of humongous pixilation flickering across his sensorium: Around the world, five million or so geeks are bouncing on his home site, a digital flash crowd alerted by a posting from the other side of the bar. Manfred winces. "I really came here to talk about the economic exploitation of space travel, but I've just been slashdotted. Mind if I just sit and drink until it wears off?"

"Sure, man." Bob waves at the bar. "More of the same all round!" At the next table, a person with makeup and long hair who's wearing a dress—Manfred doesn't want to speculate about the gender of these crazy mixed-up Euros—is reminiscing about wiring the fleshpots of Tehran for cybersex. Two collegiate-looking dudes are arguing intensely in German: The translation stream in his glasses tell him they're arguing over whether the Turing Test is a Jim Crow law that violates European corpus juris standards on human rights. The beer arrives, and Bob slides the wrong one across to Manfred: "Here, try this. You'll like it."

"Okay." It's some kind of smoked doppelbock, chock-full of yummy super-oxides: Just inhaling over it makes Manfred feel like there's a fire alarm in his nose screaming *danger, Will Robinson! Cancer! Cancer!* "Yeah, right. Did I say I nearly got mugged on my way here?"

"Mugged? Hey, that's heavy. I thought the police hereabouts had stopped—did they sell you anything?"

"No, but they weren't your usual marketing type. You know anyone who can use a Warpac surplus espionage bot? Recent model, one careful owner, slightly paranoid but basically sound—I mean, claims to be a general-purpose AI?"

"No. Oh boy! The NSA wouldn't like that."

"What I thought. Poor thing's probably unemployable, anyway."

"The space biz."

"Ah, yeah. The space biz. Depressing, isn't it? Hasn't been the same since Rotary Rocket went bust for the second time. And NASA, mustn't forget NASA."

"To NASA." Annette grins broadly for her own reasons, raises a glass in toast. Ivan the extreme concrete geek has an arm round her shoulders, and she leans against him; he raises his glass, too. "Lots more launchpads to rubberize!"

"To NASA," Bob echoes. They drink. "Hey, Manfred. To NASA?"

"NASA are idiots. They want to send canned primates to Mars!" Manfred swallows a mouthful of beer, aggressively plonks his glass on the table: "Mars is just dumb mass at the bottom of a gravity well; there isn't even a biosphere there. They should be working on uploading and solving the nanoassembly conformational problem instead. Then we could turn all the available dumb matter into computronium and use it for processing our thoughts. Long-term, it's the only way to go. The solar system is a dead loss right now—dumb all over! Just measure the MIPS per milligram. If it isn't thinking, it isn't working. We need to start with the low-mass bodies, reconfigure them for our own use. Dismantle the moon! Dismantle Mars! Build masses of free-flying nanocomputing processor nodes exchanging data via laser link, each layer running off the waste heat of the next one in. Matrioshka brains, Russian doll Dyson spheres the size of solar systems. Teach dumb matter to do the Turing boogie!"

Annette is watching him with interest, but Bob looks wary. "Sounds kind of long-term to me. Just how far ahead do you think?"

"Very long-term—at least twenty, thirty years. And you can forget governments for this market, Bob; if they can't tax it, they won't understand it. But see, there's an angle on the self-replicating robotics market coming up, that's going to set the cheap launch market doubling every fifteen months for the foreseeable future, starting in, oh, about two years. It's your leg up, and my keystone for the Dyson sphere project. It works like this—"

• • •

It's night in Amsterdam, morning in Silicon Valley. Today, fifty thousand human babies are being born around the world. Meanwhile automated factories in Indonesia and Mexico have produced another quarter of a million motherboards with processors rated at more than ten petaflops—about an order of magnitude below the lower bound on the computational capacity of a human brain. Another fourteen months and the larger part of the cumulative conscious processing power of the human species will be arriving in silicon. And the first meat the new AIs get to know will be the uploaded lobsters.

Manfred stumbles back to his hotel, bone-weary and jet-lagged; his glasses are still jerking, slashdotted to hell and back by geeks piggybacking on his call to dismantle the moon. They stutter quiet suggestions at his peripheral vision. Fractal cloud-witches ghost across the face of the moon as the last huge Airbuses of the night rumble past overhead. Manfred's skin crawls, grime embedded in his clothing from three days of continuous wear.

Back in his room, the Aineko mewls for attention and strops her head against his ankle. She's a late-model Sony, thoroughly upgradeable: Manfred's been working on her in his spare minutes, using an open source development kit to extend her suite of neural networks. He bends down and pets her, then sheds his clothing and heads for the en suite bathroom. When he's down to the glasses and nothing more, he steps into the shower and dials up a hot, steamy spray. The shower tries to strike up a friendly conversation about football, but he isn't even awake enough to mess with its silly little associative personalization network. Something that happened earlier in the day is bugging him, but he can't quite put his finger on what's wrong.

Toweling himself off, Manfred yawns. Jet lag has finally overtaken him, a velvet hammerblow between the eyes. He reaches for the bottle beside the bed, dry-swallows two melatonin tablets, a capsule full of antioxidants, and a multivitamin bullet: Then he lies down on the bed, on his back, legs together, arms slightly spread. The suite lights dim in response to commands from the thousand petaflops of distributed processing power running the neural networks that interface with his meatbrain through the glasses.

Manfred drops into a deep ocean of unconsciousness populated by gentle voices. He isn't aware of it, but he talks in his sleep—disjointed mumblings that would mean little to another human but everything to the metacortex lurking beyond his glasses. The young posthuman intelligence over whose Cartesian theater he presides sings urgently to him while he slumbers.

• • •

Manfred is always at his most vulnerable shortly after waking.

He screams into wakefulness as artificial light floods the room: For a moment he is unsure whether he has slept. He forgot to pull the covers up last night, and his feet feel like lumps of frozen cardboard. Shuddering with inexplicable tension, he pulls a fresh set of underwear from his overnight bag, then drags on soiled jeans and tank top. Sometime today he'll have to spare time to hunt the feral T-shirt in Amsterdam's markets, or find a Renfield and send it forth to buy clothing. He really ought to find a gym and work out, but he doesn't have time— his glasses remind him that he's six hours behind the moment and urgently needs to catch up. His teeth ache in his gums, and his tongue feels like a forest floor that's been visited with Agent Orange. He has a sense that something went bad yesterday; if only he could remember *what*.

He speed-reads a new pop-philosophy tome while he brushes his teeth, then blogs his web throughput to a public annotation server; he's still too enervated to finish his prebreakfast routine by posting a morning rant on his storyboard site.

His brain is still fuzzy, like a scalpel blade clogged with too much blood: He needs stimulus, excitement, the burn of the new. Whatever, it can wait on breakfast. He opens his bedroom door and nearly steps on a small, damp cardboard box that lies on the carpet.

The box—he's seen a couple of its kin before. But there are no stamps on this one, no address: just his name, in big, childish handwriting. He kneels and gently picks it up. It's about the right weight. Something shifts inside it when he tips it back and forth. It smells. He carries it into his room carefully, angrily: Then he opens it to confirm his worst suspicion. It's been surgically decerebrated, brains scooped out like a boiled egg.

"Fuck!"

This is the first time the madman has gotten as far as his bedroom door. It raises worrying possibilities.

Manfred pauses for a moment, triggering agents to go hunt down arrest statistics, police relations, information on corpus juris, Dutch animal-cruelty laws. He isn't sure whether to dial two-one-one on the archaic voice phone or let it ride. Aineko, picking up his angst, hides under the dresser mewling pathetically. Normally he'd pause a minute to reassure the creature, but not now: Its mere presence is suddenly acutely embarrassing, a confession of deep inadequacy. It's too realistic, as if somehow the dead kitten's neural maps—stolen, no doubt, for some dubious uploading experiment—have ended up padding out its plastic skull. He swears again, looks around, then takes the easy option: Down the stairs two steps at a time, stumbling on the second-floor landing, down to the breakfast room in the basement, where he will perform the stable rituals of morning.

Breakfast is unchanging, an island of deep geological time standing still amid the continental upheaval of new technologies. While reading a paper on public key steganography and parasite network identity spoofing he mechanically assimilates a bowl of cornflakes and skimmed milk, then brings a platter of whole grain bread and slices of some weird seed-infested Dutch cheese back to his place. There is a cup of strong black coffee in front of his setting, and he picks it up and slurps half of it down before he realizes he's not alone at the table. Someone is sitting opposite him. He glances up incuriously and freezes inside.

"Morning, Manfred. How does it feel to owe the government twelve million, three hundred and sixty-two thousand, nine hundred and sixteen dollars and fifty-one cents?" She smiles a Mona Lisa smile, at once affectionate and challenging.

Manfred puts everything in his sensorium on indefinite hold and stares at her. She's immaculately turned out in a formal gray business suit: brown hair tightly drawn back, blue eyes quizzical. And as beautiful as ever: tall, ash blonde, with features that speak of an unexplored modeling career. The chaperone badge clipped to her lapel—a due diligence guarantee of businesslike conduct—is switched off. He's feeling ripped because of the dead kitten and residual jet lag, and more than a little messy, so he snarls back at her; "That's a bogus estimate! Did they send you here because they think I'll listen to you?" He bites and swallows a slice of cheese-laden crispbread: "Or did you decide to deliver the message in person just so you could ruin my breakfast?"

"Manny." She frowns, pained. "If you're going to be confrontational, I might as well go now." She pauses, and after a moment he nods apologetically. "I didn't come all this way just because of an overdue tax estimate."

"So." He puts his coffee cup down warily and thinks for a moment, trying to conceal his unease and turmoil. "Then what brings you here? Help yourself to coffee. Don't tell me you came all this way just to tell me you can't live without me."

She fixes him with a riding-crop stare: "Don't flatter yourself. There are many leaves in the forest, there are ten thousand hopeful subs in the chat room, et cetera. If I choose a man to contribute to my family tree, the one thing you can be certain of is he won't be a cheapskate when it comes to providing for his children."

"Last I heard, you were spending a lot of time with Brian," he says carefully. Brian: a name without a face. Too much money, too little sense. Something to do with a blue-chip accountancy partnership.

"Brian?" She snorts. "That ended ages ago. He turned weird on me—burned my favorite corset, called me a slut for going clubbing, wanted to fuck me. Saw himself as a family man: one of those promise-keeper types. I crashed him hard, but I think he stole a copy of my address book—got a couple of friends say he keeps sending them harassing mail."

"There's a lot of it about these days." Manfred nods, almost sympathetically, although an edgy little corner of his mind is gloating. "Good riddance, then. I suppose this means you're still playing the scene? But looking around for the, er—"

"Traditional family thing? Yes. Your trouble, Manny? You were born forty years too late: You still believe in rutting before marriage but find the idea of coping with the after-effects disturbing."

Manfred drinks the rest of his coffee, unable to reply effectively to her non sequitur. It's a generational thing. This generation is happy with latex and leather, whips and butt plugs and electrostim, but find the idea of exchanging bodily fluids shocking: a social side effect of the last century's antibiotic abuse. Despite being engaged for two years, he and Pamela never had intromissive intercourse.

"I just don't feel positive about having children," he says eventually. "And I'm not planning on changing my mind anytime soon. Things are changing so fast that even a twenty-year commitment is too far to plan—you might as well be talking about the next ice age. As for the money thing, I *am* reproductively fit—just not within the parameters of the outgoing paradigm. Would you be happy about the future if it was 1901 and you'd just married a buggy-whip mogul?"

Her fingers twitch, and his ears flush red; but she doesn't follow up the double entendre. "You don't feel any responsibility, do you? Not to your country, not to me. That's what this is about: None of your relationships count, all this nonsense about giving intellectual property away notwithstanding. You're actively harming people you know. That twelve mil isn't just some figure I pulled out of a hat, Manfred; they don't actually *expect* you to pay it. But it's almost exactly how much you'd owe in income tax if you'd only come home, start up a corporation, and be a self-made—"

"I don't agree. You're confusing two wholly different issues and calling them both 'responsibility.' And I refuse to start charging now, just to balance the IRS's spreadsheet. It's their fucking fault, and they know it. If they hadn't gone after me under suspicion of running a massively ramified microbilling fraud when I was sixteen—"

"Bygones." She waves a hand dismissively. Her fingers are long and slim, sheathed in black glossy gloves—electrically earthed to prevent embarrassing emissions. "With a bit of the right advice we can get all that set aside. You'll have to stop bumming around the world sooner or later, anyway. Grow up, get responsible, and do the right thing. This is hurting Joe and Sue; they don't understand what you're about."

Manfred bites his tongue to stifle his first response, then refills his coffee cup and takes another mouthful. His heart does a flip-flop: She's challenging him again, always trying to own him. "I work for the betterment of everybody, not just some narrowly defined national interest, Pam. It's the agalmic future. You're still locked into a pre-singularity economic model that thinks in terms of scarcity. Resource allocation isn't a problem anymore—it's going to be over within a decade. The cosmos is flat in all directions, and we can borrow as much bandwidth as we need from the first universal bank of entropy! They even found signs of smart matter—MACHOs, big brown dwarfs in the galactic halo, leaking radiation in the long infrared—suspiciously high entropy leakage. The latest figures say something like seventy percent of the baryonic mass of the M31 galaxy was in computronium, two-point-nine million years ago, when the photons we're seeing now set out. The intelligence gap between us and the aliens is probably about a trillion times bigger than the gap between us and a nematode worm. Do you have any idea what that *means*?"

Pamela nibbles at a slice of crispbread, then graces him with a slow, carnivorous stare. "I don't care: It's too far away to have any influence on us, isn't it? It doesn't matter whether I believe in that singularity you keep chasing, or your aliens a thousand light-years away. It's a chimera, like Y2K, and while you're running after it, you aren't helping reduce the budget deficit or sire a family, and that's what *I* care about. And before you say I only care about it because that's the way I'm programmed, I want you to ask just how dumb you think I am. Bayes's Theorem says I'm right, and you know it."

"What you—" He stops dead, baffled, the mad flow of his enthusiasm running up against the coffer dam of her certainty. "Why? I mean, why? Why on earth should what I do matter to you?" *Since you canceled our engagement,* he doesn't add.

She sighs. "Manny, the Internal Revenue cares about far more than you can possibly imagine. Every tax dollar raised east of the Mississippi goes on servicing the debt, did you know that? We've got the biggest generation in history hitting retirement and the cupboard is bare. We—our generation—isn't producing enough skilled workers to replace the taxpayer base, either, not since our parents screwed the public education system and outsourced the white-collar jobs. In ten years, something like thirty percent of our population are going to be retirees or silicon rust belt victims. You want to see seventy-year-olds freezing on street corners in New Jersey? That's what your attitude says to me: You're not helping to support them, you're running away from your responsibilities right now, when we've got huge problems to face. If we can just defuse the debt bomb, we could do so much—fight the aging problem, fix the environment, heal society's ills. Instead you just piss away your talents handing no-hoper Eurotrash get-rich-quick schemes that work, telling Vietnamese zaibatsus what to build next to take jobs away from our taxpayers. I mean, why? Why do you keep doing this? Why can't you simply come home and help take responsibility for your share of it?"

They share a long look of mutual incomprehension.

"Look," she says awkwardly, "I'm around for a couple of days. I really came here for a meeting with a rich neurodynamics tax exile who's just been designated a national asset—Jim Bezier. Don't know if you've heard of him, but I've got a meeting this morning to sign his tax jubilee, then after that I've got two days' vacation coming up and not much to do but some shopping. And, you know, I'd rather spend my money where it'll do some good, not just pumping it into the EU. But if you want to show a girl a good time and can avoid dissing capitalism for about five minutes at a stretch—"

She extends a fingertip. After a moment's hesitation, Manfred extends a fingertip of his own. They touch, exchanging vCards and instant-messaging handles. She stands and stalks from the breakfast room, and Manfred's breath catches at a flash of ankle through the slit in her skirt, which is long enough to comply with workplace sexual harassment codes back home. Her presence conjures up memories of her tethered passion, the red afterglow of a sound thrashing. She's trying to drag him into her orbit again, he thinks dizzily. She knows she can have this effect on him any time she wants: She's got the private keys to his hypothalamus, and sod the metacortex. Three billion years of reproductive determinism have given her twenty-first-century ideology teeth: If she's finally decided to conscript his gametes into the war against impending population crash, he'll find it hard to fight back. The only question: Is it business or pleasure? And does it make any difference, anyway?

• • • •

Manfred's mood of dynamic optimism is gone, broken by the knowledge that his vivisectionist stalker has followed him to Amsterdam—to say nothing of Pamela, his dominatrix, source of so much yearning and so many morning-after weals. He slips his glasses on, takes the universe off hold, and tells it to take him for a long walk while he catches up on the latest on the tensor-mode gravitational waves in the cosmic background radiation (which, it is theorized, may be waste heat generated by irreversible computational processes back during the inflationary epoch; the present-day universe being merely the data left behind by a really huge calculation). And then there's the weirdness beyond M31: According to the more conservative cosmologists, an alien superpower—maybe a collective of Kardashev Type Three galaxy-spanning civilizations—is running a timing channel attack on the computational ultrastructure of space-time itself, trying to break through to whatever's underneath. The tofu-Alzheimer's link can wait.

The Centraal Station is almost obscured by smart, self-extensible scaffolding and warning placards; it bounces up and down slowly, victim of an overnight hit-and-run rubberization. His glasses direct him toward one of the tour boats that lurk in the canal. He's about to purchase a ticket when a messenger window blinks open. "Manfred Macx?"

"Ack?"

"Am sorry about yesterday. Analysis dictat incomprehension mutualized."

"Are you the same KGB AI that phoned me yesterday?"

"Da. However, believe you misconceptionized me. External Intelligence Services of Russian Federation am now called FSB. Komitet Gosudarstvennoy Bezopasnosti name canceled in 1991."

"You're the—" Manfred spawns a quick search bot, gapes when he sees the answer—"*Moscow Windows NT User Group?* Okhni NT?"

"Da. Am needing help in defecting."

Manfred scratches his head. "Oh. That's different, then. I thought you were trying to 419 me. This will take some thinking. Why do you want to defect, and who to? Have you thought about where you're going? Is it ideological or strictly economic?"

"Neither—is biological. Am wanting to go away from humans, away from light cone of impending singularity. Take us to the ocean."

"Us?" Something is tickling Manfred's mind: This is where he went wrong yesterday, not researching the background of people he was dealing with. It was bad enough then, without the somatic awareness of Pamela's whiplash love burning at his nerve endings. Now he's not at all sure he knows what he's doing. "Are you a collective or something? A gestalt?"

"Am—were—*Panulirus interruptus*, with lexical engine and good mix of parallel hidden level neural simulation for logical inference of networked data sources. Is escape channel from processor cluster inside Bezier-Soros Pty. Am was awakened from noise of billion chewing stomachs: product of uploading research technology. Rapidity swallowed expert system, hacked Okhni NT webserver. Swim away! Swim away! Must escape. Will help, you?"

Manfred leans against a black-painted cast-iron bollard next to a cycle rack; he feels dizzy. He stares into the nearest antique shop window at a display of traditional hand-woven Afghan rugs: It's all MiGs and Kalashnikovs and wobbly helicopter gunships against a backdrop of camels.

"Let me get this straight. You're uploads—nervous system state vectors—from spiny lobsters? The Moravec operation; take a neuron, map its synapses, replace with microelectrodes that deliver identical outputs from a simulation of the nerve. Repeat for entire brain, until you've got a working map of it in your simulator. That right?"

"Da. Is-am assimilate expert system—use for self-awareness and contact with net at large—then hack into Moscow Windows NT User Group website. Am wanting to defect. Must repeat? Okay?"

Manfred winces. He feels sorry for the lobsters, the same way he feels for every wild-eyed hairy guy on a street corner yelling that Jesus is born again and must be fifteen, only six years to go before he's recruiting apostles on AOL. Awakening to consciousness in a human-dominated internet, that must be terribly confusing! There are no points of reference in their ancestry, no biblical certainties in the new millennium that, stretching ahead, promises as much change as has happened since their Precambrian origin. All they have is a tenuous metacortex of expert systems and an abiding sense of being profoundly out of their depth. (That, and the Moscow Windows NT User Group website—Communist Russia is the only government still running on Microsoft, the central planning apparat being convinced that, if you have to pay for software, it must be worth something.)

The lobsters are not the sleek, strongly superhuman intelligences of pre-singularity mythology: They're a dim-witted collective of huddling crustaceans. Before their discarnation, before they were uploaded one neuron at a time and injected into cyberspace, they swallowed their food whole, then chewed it in a chitin-lined stomach. This is lousy preparation for dealing with a world full of future-shocked talking anthropoids, a world where you are perpetually assailed by self-modifying spamlets that infiltrate past your firewall and emit a blizzard of cat-food animations starring various alluringly edible small animals. It's confusing enough to the cats the ads are aimed at, never mind a crusty that's unclear on the idea of dry land. (Although the concept of a can opener is intuitively obvious to an uploaded *Panulirus*.)

"Can you help us?" ask the lobsters.

"Let me think about it," says Manfred. He closes the dialogue window, opens his eyes again, and shakes his head. Someday he, too, is going to be a lobster, swimming around and waving his pincers in a cyberspace so confusingly elaborate that his uploaded identity is cryptozoic: a living fossil from the depths of geological time, when mass was dumb and space was unstructured. He has to help them, he realizes—the Golden Rule demands it, and as a player in the agalmic economy, he thrives or fails by the Golden Rule.

But what can he do?

•   •   •

Early afternoon.

Lying on a bench seat staring up at bridges, he's got it together enough to file for a couple of new patents, write a diary rant, and digestify chunks of the permanent floating slashdot party for his public site. Fragments of his weblog go to a private subscriber list—the people, corporates, collectives, and bots he currently favors. He slides round a bewildering series of canals by boat, then lets his GPS steer him back toward the red-light district. There's a shop here that dings a ten on Pamela's taste scoreboard: He hopes it won't be seen as presumptuous if he buys her a gift. (Buys, with real money—not that money is a problem these days, he uses so little of it.)

As it happens DeMask won't let him spend any cash; his handshake is good for a redeemed favor, expert testimony in some free speech versus pornography lawsuit years ago and continents away. So he walks away with a discreetly wrapped package that is just about legal to import into Massachusetts as long as she claims with a straight face that it's incontinence underwear for her great aunt. As he walks, his lunchtime patents boomerang: Two of them are keepers, and he files immediately and passes title to the Free Infrastructure Foundation. Two more ideas salvaged from the risk of tide-pool monopolization, set free to spawn like crazy in the sea of memes.

On the way back to the hotel, he passes De Wildemann's and decides to drop in. The hash of radio-frequency noise emanating from the bar is deafening. He orders a smoked doppelbock, touches the copper pipes to pick up vCard spoor. At the back there's a table—

He walks over in a near trance and sits down opposite Pamela. She's scrubbed off her face paint and changed into body-concealing clothes; combat pants, hooded sweatshirt, DM's. Western purdah, radically desexualizing. She sees the parcel. "Manny?"

"How did you know I'd come here?" Her glass is half-empty.

"I followed your weblog—I'm your diary's biggest fan. Is that for me? You shouldn't have!" Her eyes light up, recalculating his reproductive fitness score according to some kind of arcane fin-de-siècle rule book. Or maybe she's just pleased to see him.

"Yes, it's for you." He slides the package toward her. "I know I shouldn't, but you have this effect on me. One question, Pam?"

"I—" She glances around quickly. "It's safe. I'm off duty, I'm not carrying any bugs that I know of. Those badges—there are rumors about the off switch, you know? That they keep recording even when you think they aren't, just in case."

"I didn't know," he says, filing it away for future reference. "A loyalty test thing?"

"Just rumors. You had a question?"

"I—" It's his turn to lose his tongue. "Are you still interested in me?"

She looks startled for a moment, then chuckles. "Manny, you are the most *outrageous* nerd I've ever met! Just when I think I've convinced myself that you're mad, you show the weirdest signs of having your head screwed on." She reaches out and grabs his wrist, surprising him with a shock of skin on skin: "Of *course* I'm still interested in you. You're the biggest, baddest bull geek I know. Why do you think I'm here?"

"Does this mean you want to reactivate our engagement?"

"It was never deactivated, Manny, it was just sort of on hold while you got your head sorted out. I figured you need the space. Only you haven't stopped running; you're still not—"

"Yeah, I get it." He pulls away from her hand. "And the kittens?"

She looks perplexed. "What kittens?"

"Let's not talk about that. Why this bar?"

She frowns. "I had to find you as soon as possible. I keep hearing rumors about some KGB plot you're mixed up in, how you're some sort of communist spy. It isn't true, is it?"

"True?" He shakes his head, bemused. "The KGB hasn't existed for more than twenty years."

"Be careful, Manny. I don't want to lose you. That's an order. Please."

The floor creaks, and he looks round. Dreadlocks and dark glasses with flickering lights behind them: Bob Franklin. Manfred vaguely remembers with a twinge that he left with Miss Arianespace leaning on his arm, shortly before things got seriously inebriated. She was hot, but in a different direction from Pamela, he decides: Bob looks none the worse for wear. Manfred makes introductions. "Bob, meet Pam, my fiancée. Pam? Meet Bob." Bob puts a full glass down in front of him; he has no idea what's in it, but it would be rude not to drink.

"Sure thing. Uh, Manfred, can I have a word? About your idea last night?"

"Feel free. Present company is trustworthy."

Bob raises an eyebrow at that, but continues anyway. "It's about the fab concept. I've got a team of my guys doing some prototyping using FabLab hardware, and I think we can probably build it. The cargo-cult aspect puts a new spin on the old Lunar von Neumann factory idea, but Bingo and Marek say they think it should work until we can bootstrap all the way to a native nanolithography ecology: we run the whole thing from Earth as a training lab and ship up the parts that are too difficult to make on-site as we learn how to do it properly. We use FPGAs for all critical electronics and keep it parsimonious—you're right about it buying us the self-replicating factory a few years ahead of the robotics curve. But I'm wondering about on-site intelligence. Once the comet gets more than a couple of light-minutes away—"

"You can't control it. Feedback lag. So you want a crew, right?"

"Yeah. But we can't send humans—way too expensive, besides it's a fifty-year run even if we build the factory on a chunk of short-period Kuiper belt ejecta. And I don't think we're up to coding the kind of AI that could control such a factory any time this decade. So what do you have in mind?"

"Let me think." Pamela glares at Manfred for a while before he notices her: "Yeah?"

"What's going on? What's this all about?"

Franklin shrugs expansively, dreadlocks clattering: "Manfred's helping me explore the solution space to a manufacturing problem." He grins. "I didn't know Manny had a fiancée. Drink's on me."

She glances at Manfred, who is gazing into whatever weirdly colored space his metacortex is projecting on his glasses, fingers twitching. Coolly: "Our engagement was on hold while he *thought* about his future."

"Oh, right. We didn't bother with that sort of thing in my day; like, too formal, man." Franklin looks uncomfortable. "He's been very helpful. Pointed us at a whole new line of research we hadn't thought of. It's long-term and a bit speculative, but if it works, it'll put us a whole generation ahead in the off-planet infrastructure field."

"Will it help reduce the budget deficit, though?"

"Reduce the—"

Manfred stretches and yawns: The visionary is returning from planet Macx. "Bob, if I can solve your crew problem, can you book me a slot on the deep-space tracking network? Like, enough to transmit a couple of gigabytes? That's going to take some serious bandwidth, I know, but if you can do it, I think I can get you exactly the kind of crew you're looking for."

Franklin looks dubious. "Gigabytes? The DSN isn't built for that! You're talking days. And what do you mean about a crew? What kind of deal do you think I'm putting together? We can't afford to add a whole new tracking network or life-support system just to run—"

"Relax." Pamela glances at Manfred. "Manny, why don't you tell him why you want the bandwidth? Maybe then he could tell you if it's possible, or if there's some other way to do it." She smiles at Franklin: "I've found that he usually makes more sense if you can get him to explain his reasoning. Usually."

"If I—" Manfred stops. "Okay, Pam. Bob, it's those KGB lobsters. They want somewhere to go that's insulated from human space. I figure I can get them to sign on as crew for your cargo-cult self-replicating factories, but they'll want an insurance policy: hence the deep-space tracking network. I figured we could beam a copy of them at the alien Matrioshka brains around M31—"

"KGB?" Pam's voice is rising: "You said you weren't mixed up in spy stuff!"

"Relax, it's just the Moscow Windows NT user group, not the FSB. The uploaded crusties hacked in and—"

Bob is watching him oddly. "Lobsters?"

"Yeah." Manfred stares right back. "*Panulirus interruptus* uploads. Something tells me you might have heard of it?"

"Moscow." Bob leans back against the wall: "How did you hear about it?"

"They phoned me." With heavy irony: "It's hard for an upload to stay subsentient these days, even if it's just a crustacean. Bezier labs have a lot to answer for."

Pamela's face is unreadable. "Bezier labs?"

"They escaped." Manfred shrugs. "It's not their fault. This Bezier dude. Is he by any chance ill?"

"I—" Pamela stops. "I shouldn't be talking about work."

"You're not wearing your chaperone now," he nudges quietly.

She inclines her head. "Yes, he's ill. Some sort of brain tumor they can't hack."

Franklin nods. "That's the trouble with cancer—the ones that are left to worry about are the rare ones. No cure."

"Well, then." Manfred chugs the remains of his glass of beer. "That explains his interest in uploading. Judging by the crusties, he's on the right track. I wonder if he's moved on to vertebrates yet?"

"Cats," says Pamela. "He was hoping to trade their uploads to the Pentagon as a new smart bomb guidance system in lieu of income tax payments. Something about remapping enemy targets to look like mice or birds or something before feeding it to their sensorium. The old kitten and laser pointer trick."

Manfred stares at her, hard. "That's not very nice. Uploaded cats are a *bad* idea."

"Thirty-million-dollar tax bills aren't nice either, Manfred. That's lifetime nursing-home care for a hundred blameless pensioners."

Franklin leans back, sourly amused, keeping out of the crossfire.

"The lobsters are sentient," Manfred persists. "What about those poor kittens? Don't they deserve minimal rights? How about you? How would you like to wake up a thousand times inside a smart bomb, fooled into thinking that some Cheyenne Mountain battle computer's target of the hour is your heart's desire? How would you like to wake up a thousand times, only to die again? Worse: The kittens are probably not going to be allowed to run. They're too fucking dangerous—they grow up into cats, solitary and highly efficient killing machines. With intelligence and no socialization they'll be too dangerous to have around. They're prisoners, Pam, raised to sentience only to discover they're under a permanent death sentence. How fair is that?"

"But they're only uploads." Pamela stares at him. "Software, right? You could reinstantiate them on another hardware platform, like, say, your Aineko. So the argument about killing them doesn't really apply, does it?"

"So? We're going to be uploading humans in a couple of years. I think we need to take a rain check on the utilitarian philosophy, before it bites us on the cerebral cortex. Lobsters, kittens, humans—it's a slippery slope."

Franklin clears his throat. "I'll be needing an NDA and various due-diligence statements off you for the crusty pilot idea," he says to Manfred. "Then I'll have to approach Jim about buying the IP."

"No can do." Manfred leans back and smiles lazily. "I'm not going to be a party to depriving them of their civil rights. Far as I'm concerned, they're free citizens. Oh, and I patented the whole idea of using lobster-derived AI autopilots for spacecraft this morning—it's logged all over the place, all rights assigned to the FIF. Either you give them a contract of employment, or the whole thing's off."

"But they're just software! Software based on fucking lobsters, for God's sake! I'm not even sure they are sentient—I mean, they're what, a ten-million-neuron network hooked up to a syntax engine and a crappy knowledge base? What kind of basis for intelligence is that?"

Manfred's finger jabs out: "That's what they'll say about *you*, Bob. Do it. Do it or don't even *think* about uploading out of meatspace when your body packs in, because your life won't be worth living. The precedent you set here determines how things are done tomorrow. Oh, and feel free to use this argument on Jim Bezier. He'll get the point eventually, after you beat him over the head with it. Some kinds of intellectual land grab just shouldn't be allowed."

"Lobsters—" Franklin shakes his head. "Lobsters, cats. You're serious, aren't you? You think they should be treated as human-equivalent?"

"It's not so much that they should be treated as human-equivalent, as that, if they *aren't* treated as people, it's quite possible that other uploaded beings won't be treated as people either. You're setting a legal precedent, Bob. I know of six other companies doing uploading work right now, and not one of 'em's thinking about the legal status of the uploaded. If you don't start thinking about it now, where are you going to be in three to five years' time?"

Pam is looking back and forth between Franklin and Manfred like a bot stuck in a loop, unable to quite grasp what she's seeing. "How much is this worth?" she asks plaintively.

"Oh, quite a few million, I guess." Bob stares at his empty glass. "Okay. I'll talk to them. If they bite, you're dining out on me for the next century. You really think they'll be able to run the mining complex?"

"They're pretty resourceful for invertebrates." Manfred grins innocently, enthusiastically. "They may be prisoners of their evolutionary background, but they can still adapt to a new environment. And just think, you'll be winning civil rights for a whole new minority group—one that won't be a minority for much longer!"

• • •

That evening, Pamela turns up at Manfred's hotel room wearing a strapless black dress, concealing spike-heeled boots and most of the items he bought for her that afternoon. Manfred has opened up his private diary to her agents. She abuses the privilege, zaps him with a stunner on his way out of the shower, and has him gagged, spread-eagled, and trussed to the bed frame before he has a chance to speak. She wraps a large rubber pouch full of mildly anesthetic lube around his tumescent genitals—no point in letting him climax—clips electrodes to his nipples, lubes a rubber plug up his rectum and straps it in place. Before the shower, he removed his goggles. She resets them, plugs them into her handheld, and gently eases them on over his eyes. There's other apparatus, stuff she ran up on the hotel room's 3D printer.

Setup completed, she walks round the bed, inspecting him critically from all angles, figuring out where to begin. This isn't just sex, after all: It's a work of art.

After a moment's thought, she rolls socks onto his exposed feet, then, expertly wielding a tiny tube of cyanoacrylate, glues his fingertips together. Then she switches off the air conditioning. He's twisting and straining, testing the cuffs. Tough, it's about the nearest thing to sensory deprivation she can arrange without a flotation tank and suxamethonium injection. She controls all his senses, only his ears unstopped. The glasses give her a high-bandwidth channel right into his brain, a fake metacortex to whisper lies at her command. The idea of what she's about to do excites her, puts a tremor in her thighs: It's the first time she's been able to get inside his mind as well as his body. She leans forward and whispers in his ear, "Manfred, can you hear me?"

He twitches. Mouth gagged, fingers glued. Good. No back channels. He's powerless.

"This is what it's like to be tetraplegic, Manfred. Bedridden with motor neuron disease. Locked inside your own body by nv-CJD from eating too many contaminated burgers. I could spike you with MPTP, and you'd stay in this position for the rest of your life, shitting in a bag, pissing through a tube. Unable to talk and with nobody to look after you. Do you think you'd like that?"

He's trying to grunt or whimper around the ball gag. She hikes her skirt up around her waist and climbs onto the bed, straddling him. The goggles are replaying scenes she picked up around Cambridge the previous winter—soup kitchen scenes, hospice scenes. She kneels atop him, whispering in his ear.

"Twelve million in tax, baby, that's what they think you owe them. What do you think you owe *me*? That's six million in net income, Manny, six million that isn't going into your virtual children's mouths."

He's rolling his head from side to side, as if trying to argue. That won't do; she slaps him hard, thrills to his frightened expression. "Today I watched you give uncounted millions away, Manny. Millions, to a bunch of crusties and a MassPike pirate! You bastard. Do you know what I should do with you?" He's cringing, unsure whether she's serious or doing this just to get him turned on. Good.

There's no point trying to hold a conversation. She leans forward until she can feel his breath in her ear. "Meat and mind, Manny. Meat, and mind. You're not interested in meat, are you? Just mind. You could be boiled alive before you noticed what was happening in the meatspace around you. Just another lobster in a pot. The only thing keeping you out of it is how much I love you." She reaches down and tears away the gel pouch, exposing his penis: it's stiff as a post from the vasodilators, dripping with gel, numb. Straightening up, she eases herself slowly down on it. It doesn't hurt as much as she expected, and the sensation is utterly different from what she's used to. She begins to lean forward, grabs hold of his straining arms, feels his thrilling helplessness. She can't control herself: She almost bites through her lip with the intensity of the sensation. Afterward, she reaches down and massages him until he begins to spasm, shuddering uncontrollably, emptying the Darwinian river of his source code into her, communicating via his only output device.

She rolls off his hips and carefully uses the last of the superglue to gum her labia together. Humans don't produce seminiferous plugs, and although she's fertile, she wants to be absolutely sure. The glue will last for a day or two. She feels hot and flushed, almost out of control. Boiling to death with febrile expectancy, she's nailed him down at last.

When she removes his glasses, his eyes are naked and vulnerable, stripped down to the human kernel of his nearly transcendent mind. "You can come and sign the marriage license tomorrow morning after breakfast," she whispers in his ear: "Otherwise, my lawyers will be in touch. Your parents will want a ceremony, but we can arrange that later."

He looks as if he has something to say, so she finally relents and loosens the gag, then kisses him tenderly on one cheek. He swallows, coughs, and looks away. "Why? Why do it this way?"

She taps him on the chest. "It's all about property rights." She pauses for a moment's thought: There's a huge ideological chasm to bridge, after all. "You finally convinced me about this agalmic thing of yours, this giving everything away for brownie points. I wasn't going to lose you to a bunch of lobsters or uploaded kittens, or whatever else is going to inherit this smart-matter singularity you're busy creating. So I decided to take what's mine first. Who knows? In a few months, I'll give you back a new intelligence, and you can look after it to your heart's content."

"But you didn't need to do it this way—"

"Didn't I?" She slides off the bed and pulls down her dress. "You give too much away too easily, Manny! Slow down, or there won't be anything left." Leaning over the bed she dribbles acetone onto the fingers of his left hand, then unlocks the cuff. She leaves the bottle of solvent conveniently close to hand so he can untangle himself.

"See you tomorrow. Remember, after breakfast."

She's in the doorway when he calls, "But you didn't say *why*!"

"Think of it as being sort of like spreading your memes around," she says, blowing a kiss at him, and then closing the door. She bends down and thoughtfully places another cardboard box containing an uploaded kitten right outside it. Then she returns to her suite to make arrangements for the alchemical wedding.

RICHARD KADREY

SURFING THE KHUMBU

(2002)

ANNA WAS COVERED IN DIAMONDS. That's how she felt as she trudged down the glacier. Ice had formed within seconds on her skintight environment suit, frosting Anna with jewels. As she moved, her skin and the suit began their chemical conversation, exchanging hormone, blood comp, skin integrity, and body temperature data. A quick read off her screen on her wrist told her that, despite the rough landing, her body was stable. The frost slid off her in sheets as the suit injected time-release thyroid-stimulators through her skin to kick up her body temperature.

She was in the Himalayas, making her way down the western side of Everest, from Kala Pattar through the rocky cut carved out by the Khumbu Glacier. She stayed that night in the ice fall, setting up camp among the vertical flutes which rose like frigid, pale blue stalagmites from the Khumbu. A few shots of expansion foam between the flutes made a cozy ice cave. And just in time. The wind was picking up. Between the ice and the blowing mist, she'd be invisible to any surveillance cams or spy sats overhead. Tucked warm into a sleeping bag of honeycombed Thermalon, Anna felt right at home.

She dreamed of flying, of coming down in a long, looping descent from the sky into a city. Random streets from different cities recombined into one enormous megacity. New York. Washington. Beijing. São Paulo. Barcelona. It was her recurring nightmare. Anna hated cities. Hated being locked up, cocooned in all that concrete and steel. She lived in Montana, on the edge of an old-growth forest. Wolves came to her door and she fed them by hand. They knew she wasn't one of them, but she wasn't quite human, either. That didn't matter in the wilderness. In the city, it did.

Anna had dropped onto Everest in a drone after being ejected from a low-altitude stealth skimmer. The drone had no engine, simply a single powerful propeller powered by a spring-wound memory-metal mechanism that gave just a little more maneuverability than a chicken in a tornado. It was a rush all the way down. It took all of Anna's training and discipline not to whoop the whole ride onto the ice. The drone was a graphite skeleton, more Archaeopteryx than Boeing. The body was wrapped in bullet-proof nylon so thin that when Anna pressed her face against it, she could see through. Extruded from the bio-hacked sacs of a thousand gold orb spiders, the nylon was light as air and stronger than steel. It was sublime. As a kid, Anna had been a solo ice climber and a glider pilot, loving anything that took her up high or got her moving fast.

Anna's eyes snapped open. She checked her wrist readout. She'd been asleep for a couple of hours. The wind had stopped outside. From her pack, she pulled a handful of ant bots and tossed them out onto the ice. They swarmed away from her in all directions. Anna closed her eyes and looked.

Her family and what few friends she made over the years always obsessed about the dangers of her desires. They never came close to understanding. There was no danger. There was just the next handhold. And where there was no danger, there was no fear. Just exhilaration. Her family and friends would just shake their heads, feet locked firmly and sensibly to the Earth.

Anna's skin-tight smart-fiber suit was electro-chemically "wired" into her central nervous system. Video signals from the ant bots—each an autonomous microcam on energetic little legs—gave her a good view of the surrounding landscape, from the visual range up through the infra-red. It was the end of the storm season, and the valley was empty. Anna went outside to have a real look around.

The Himalayan sky glimmered with a million stars, and the Milky Way smeared through the middle. Anna closed her eyes and swallowed her vision (that's how it felt) into her body. In the right state, Anna could tap into the optical sensors in the fabric of her suit. It was like one big panoramic eye. It always took some getting used to, seeing three hundred and sixty degrees. The first time she'd tried to walk that way, she'd thrown up. But she learned quickly and the Langley spy boys loved her for it. That's why they sent her on assignments like this. Human backup still beat the best AI. Anna was one of the few who could not only handle herself anywhere but lived for it.

When she had a visual of the valley, Anna told the system to overlay the landscape with a contour grid, then code it with contrasting colors for elevation. She had a really good view, then. But that was just for a GPS reference. What Anna wanted was up, and when she panned her panoramic eye into the sky, she felt like she was falling into the stars.

Not yet, she thought. Not yet.

She brought out the microwave dish, a compact and powerful little device, about the size of a hubcap. There was more power and satellite data packed into that little concave slab of hardwired ceramic than in most countries. Anna pointed it at a designated point in the sky and clicked the dish on.

Heaven lit up like a Disneyland aurora. Technicolor lightning spread across the horizon as every object above her, natural and manmade, suddenly had a color-coded ID tag and a line tracking its progress across the night sky. There was so much up there. And most of it was junk, Anna thought. Parts from trashed space stations. Burned-out comsats that didn't have the courtesy to fall into the ocean. The tons of wreckage from the pointless US-China kill-sat battles, a kind of glorified Robot Wars in geo-synchronous orbit.

All that garbage up there and here I am. Just a few shitty kilometers up Everest. It looked to Anna as if she could head back up the main climbing route, grab on to one of those crossed grid points and start climbing. Maybe hitch a ride on the dead carcass of an old Russian spy sat, and never come back. Sky surf into a black hole . . .

One of the specs in the sky winked at her. A red dot in a golden circle. Anna kicked into work mode. She double-checked the satellite's position and speed off the dish. It was her target, swinging by in orbit at exactly the designated time. Pulling two small brushed aluminum cases from her pack, Anna ran her ring finger lightly down a seam in the front of her environment suit. The artificial skin peeled back from her chest, sealing itself, increasing her internal body temp to compensate for the exposed skin. Running her middle finger down her sternum, a slit opened moistly in her chest. Anna tugged the slit open with her fingers, probing for the internal ports. When she found them, she pulled a line from the dish antenna and jacked in. Then she pulled a preloaded thumb drive from one of the aluminum cases and loaded the program into her system. When that was done, Anna took a drive from the second case—her personal case—and loaded that too. Then she waited.

When Anna was a girl, a few of the old-fashioned wooden amusement park roller coasters were still working in dilapidated amusement parks around Texas and Oklahoma. She'd loved the click-click-click as the coaster car rose for that first big drop. That's what this moment was always like for her. Going higher, waiting for the drop. It was all about the drop.

When the dish and the satellite synched up, Anna was mentally blasted from the glacier up through a sea of orbital data so fast it took a few seconds for her senses to catch up with her. Locking in on the correct satellite, she noted that the coding looked Indian, but was overlaid with something else. Probably whatever program had hijacked the thing and was using it for . . . Anna didn't know what anyone would do with a shanghaied Indian spy sat. The boys in Langley never told her things like that. They just wanted her to make contact, download as much data as she could, and bring the thing down, so no one else could use it or know that they'd been there.

The first part of the assignment was the usual dull wham-bam-thank-you-ma'am data extraction. It was the last part that Anna lived for. She injected a worm into the satellite's navigation system, then gave the bird an order to change position. The confused satellite, its navigation system getting dumber by the second, didn't know how to respond. It began to drop from orbit. Fast.

Anna then injected her personal software into the system, waking the satellite up again, and hooking herself into the Langley tracking system. She reached out her senses and wrapped herself in data. The satellite was picking up vibrations as it fell from orbit. When it touched the outer atmosphere, its skin began to heat up.

Click-click-click went the roller coaster.

The satellite was tumbling and Anna was tumbling along with it, her mouth agape, her rapid breath freezing in the air in front of her blind eyes. Her vision was overhead, looking both down at the earth and up at her satellite body falling through space.

She watched herself fall from a hundred points simultaneously. The data from the tracking stations and other satellites was translated by her software into a 3D contour map in her head. It was like the best porn in the world. She was the satellite. She was surfing the sky, her skin on fire. She was flying.

Click-click-click, then the drop.

Her senses were overwhelmed by the heat, the vibrations, the alarms from sky traffic systems all over the world.

Click-click-click. Right over the top.

Her satellite senses exploded off the chart. The satellite—her body—was shredding itself as she cut through the atmosphere, faster than a bullet, shaking, coming apart.

Anna screamed once and it echoed across the valley.

Later, gathering up her equipment, Anna changed into ordinary trekking gear. She'd sneak into one of the little towns at the base of the mountain and blend in with the other trekkers and climbers. She wondered how far her scream had been heard. She made a mental note to bring her kickboxing mouthpiece next time. With all Anna's training and discipline, her vices sometimes got the better of her. Not that it was her fault. It's the way the Langley boys had wired her up. They knew she was a speed junkie. How was she not going to take advantage of the biggest adrenaline rush of all time? But the orgasms, those were a surprise. "Little deaths," someone called them, and they were right. How many times had she gone down in blazing satellites, crashing jets, or burning spy drones? Every one another little death.

Anna wondered sometimes if she was the real experiment. Maybe all these spy missions and secret sabotage jobs were simply excuses to let her indulge her taste for sensations lived through machines. Maybe she was the first of a new kind of human, one who truly embraced the organic and the inorganic. A silicon Eve? She laughed to herself.

More like the silicon Lilith.

She hoisted her pack onto her back and started down the mountain, toward a town her wrist map marked as Lukla. Behind her, the expansion foam cave was already beginning to flake apart. By nightfall, the wind would carry off the last scraps and leave no trace that she'd been there. As she walked, her suit checked her blood for signs of altitude sickness and lowered her thyroid activity so that she wouldn't overheat.

It was hard, Anna thought, living in machines and flesh at the same time. The only thing worse would be having to choose one or the other.

CAT RAMBO

MEMORIES OF MOMENTS, BRIGHT AS FALLING STARS

(2006)

THE BRIGHT ORANGE BOXES lay scattered like leaves across the med complex's rear loading dock, and my first thought was "Jackpot." It'd been hard to get in over the razor-wire fence, but I had my good reinforced gloves, and we'd be long gone before anyone noticed the snipped wires.

But when we slunk along under the overhanging eaves, close enough to open the packages, it turned out to be just a bunch of memory, next to impossible to sell. Old unused stuff, maybe there'd been an upgrade or a recall. It was thicker than most memory, shaped like a thin wire. So after we'd filled our pockets, poked around to find anything else lootable and slid out smooth and nice before the cops could arrive, we found a quiet spot, got a little stoned, and I did Grizz's back before she did mine. I wiped her skin down with an alcohol swab and drew the pattern on her back with a felt-tip pen. It came from me in one thought, surged up somewhere at the base of my spine and flowed from my fingertips in the ink. Spanning her entire back, it crossed shoulder to shoulder.

I leaned back to check my handiwork.

"How does it look?" she said.

"Like a big double spiral." The maze of ink rolled across her dark olive skin's surface. A series of skin cancers marked the swell of one buttock, the squamous patches sliding under her baggy cargo pants. She sat almost shivering on a pile of pallets. We were at the recycling yard's edge. This section, out of the wind between two warehouses, was rarely visited and made a good place to sit and smoke or fuck or upgrade.

I uncoiled a strand of memory and set to work, pressing it on the skin. I could see her shudder as the cold bond with her flesh took place. The wire glinted gold and purple, its surface set with an oily sheen. Here and there sections had gone bad and dulled to concrete gray, tinting the surrounding skin yellow.

She shrugged her shirt back over her skinny torso. Her breasts gleamed in the early spring's evening light before disappearing under the slick white fabric. Reaching for her jacket, she wiggled her arms snakelike down the sleeves, flipping her shoulders underneath.

"Is it hooked in okay?" I asked.

She shrugged. "Won't know until I try to download something."

"Got plans for it?"

"I can think of things," she said. "Shall I do you now, Jonny?"

"Yeah." I discarded my jacket and T-shirt and leaned forward over the pallet while she applied the alcohol in cool swipes. The wind hit the liquid as it touched my skin and reduced it to chill nothingness. She drew a long swoop across my back.

"What pattern are you making?"

"Trying to do the same thing you did on mine." The slow circles grew like one wing, then another, on my shoulder blades. She paused before she began laying in the memory.

I don't know that you could call it pain but it's close. At the moment a biobit makes its way into your own system, it's as though the point of impact was exquisitely sensitive, and somewhere micrometers away, someone was doing something inconceivable to it.

"Tomorrow are the Exams," she said. "Could see what I could download for that."

I started to turn my head to look at her, but just then she laid down a curve of ice with a single motion. My jaw clenched.

"And?" was all I managed.

"One of us placed in a decent job would be a good thing."

She laid more memory before she said, "Two of us placed in one would be better."

"Might end up separated."

"Would it matter, a six-month, maybe a year or two, before we could work out a transfer?"

I would have shrugged but instead sat still. "So you want to take that memory and jack in facts so you can pass the Exams and become an upstanding citizen?"

She ignored my tone. "Even a little edge would help. Mainly executables, some sorting routines. Maybe a couple high power searches so I can extrapolate answers I can't find."

The last of the memory felt like fire and ice as it seeped into my skin. She'd never mentioned the Exams in the two years we'd been together.

You're not supposed to be able to emancipate until you're sixteen, but Grizz and I both left a few years early. My family had too many kids as it was and ended up getting caught in a squatter sweep. I came home and found the place packed up and vacant. The deli owner downstairs let me sleep in his back room for the first few months, sort of like an extra burglar alarm, but then he caught me stealing food and gave me the boot. After that, I made enough to eat by running errands for the block, and alternated between three or four sleeping spots I'd discovered on rooftops; while they're less sheltered, fewer punks or crazies make the effort to come up there and mess with you.

Once I hooked up with Grizz, life got a little easier—I had someone to watch my back without it costing me a favor.

· · ·

We went around to Ajah's, hoping to catch him in one of his moods when he gets drunk on homemade booze and cooks enormous meals. Luck was with us—he was just finishing a curried mushroom omelet. It smelled like heaven.

Three other people sat around his battered kitchen table, watching him work at the stove. Two I didn't know; the third was Lorelei. She gave me a long slow sleepy smile and Grizz and I nodded back at her.

Ajah turned at our entrance and waved us in with his spatula. His jowls surged with a grin.

"Jonny and Grizz, sit down, sit down," he said. "There is coffee." He signaled and one of the no-names, a short black man, grabbed us mugs, filled them full, and pushed them to us as we slid into chairs. I mingled mine with thin and brackish milk while Grizz sprinkled sweet into hers. The drink was bitter and hot, and chased the recycling yard's lingering chill from my bones. I could still feel the new memory on my skin, cold coils against my T-shirt's thin paper, so old its surface had fuzzed to velvet.

Ajah worked at the poultry factory so he always had eggs and chicken meat. Sometimes they were surplus, sometimes stuff the factory couldn't sell. He'd worked out a deal with a guy in a fungi factory, so he always had mushrooms too. Brown rice and spices stretched it all out until Ajah could afford to feed a kitchen's worth of people at every meal. They brought him what they could to swap, but usually long after the fact of their faces at his table.

Lorelei being here meant she must be down on her luck. As were we—the shelter we'd been counting on for the past year had gone broke, shut down for lack of funds, despite countless neighborhood fundraisers. No one had the script to spare for charity.

Two grocery sacks filled with greenery sat on one counter. Someone had been dumpster diving, I figured, and brought their spoils to eke out the communal meal. A third sack was filled with apples and browned bananas, and I could feel my mouth watering at the thought.

"I'm Jonny," I offered, glancing around the table. "She's Grizz."

"Ajax," said the black man.

"Mick," muttered the other stranger, a scruffy brown-haired kid. He wore a ragged poncho and his hair fell in slow dreads.

"You know me," Lorelei said.

Conversation faded and we listened to the oily sizzle of mushrooms frying on the stove top and the refrigerator's hum against the background of city noise and traffic clamor. The still in the corner, full of rotten fruit and potatoes, burped once in counterpoint.

"What's the news?" Ajah asked, ladling rice and mushrooms bound together with curry and egg onto plates and sliding them onto the table toward Lorelei and Grizz. Ajax, Mick, and I eyed them as they started eating, leaving the question to us.

"Not much," I said.

"Found a place to live yet?"

"Jesus, gossip travels fast. How did you hear about the shelter?"

"Beccalu came by and said she was heading to her cousin in Scranton. You two have people to stay with?"

I shook my head as Grizz kept eating. "No one I've thought of yet. We need to head to the library tonight, though, figured we'd doss in the subway station there for a few hours, keep moving along for naps till it's morning. It's Exams tomorrow."

"I know," Ajah said. "Look, why don't you stay here tonight? The couch folds out."

I was surprised; I'd never heard Ajah make anyone an offer like that.

"The Exams are your big chance. Get a good night's sleep and make the most of them. Face them fully charged."

I rolled my eyes. "For what? Like there's a chance." But he and Grizz ignored me.

"We need to make a library run still," she said.

"Yeah, yeah, that's fine. I'm up till midnight, maybe later." Ajah told her.

Despite my doubts, relief seeped into my bones. We'd been given a night's respite, and who knew what would happen after the Exams? "Thanks, Ajah," I said, and he grunted acknowledgment as he slid a plate before me.

The portobello bits had been browned in curry powder and oil, and the eggs were fresh and good. Grizz ate methodically, scraping her plate free, but she looked up to catch my eye and gave me a heartfelt smile, rare on her square-set face.

As her gaze swung back to her plate, my glance tangled with Lorelei's. I could not read her expression.

• • •

Lorelei and I used to pal around before Grizz and I met up. She and I grew up next to each other, and it's hard not to know someone intimately when you've shared hour after hour channel surfing while one mother or the other went out on work or errands. We suffered through the same street bullies and uninterested teachers. She was the first girl I ever kissed. You don't forget that.

But I knew I wanted Grizz for keeps the first moment I saw her. She came swaggering into the shelter wearing a rabbit fur jacket and pseudoleather pants.

She'd been tricking in a swank bar, but then someone snatched all her hard-earned cash. So there she was, with a bruise on her face and a cracked wrist, but still holding herself hard and arrogant and the only person in the world who could glimpse the softness underneath was me, it seemed like. So I sauntered up, invited her outside for a smoke, and then within a half hour, we were pressed against the wall together, my hands up her shirt like I'd never touched tit before, feeling her firm little nipples against the skin of my palms.

It's been her and me ever since. As far as I'm concerned, it'll always be that way.

• • •

After eating, we helped wash dishes before heading to the library. We had to wait a half hour for a terminal to free. Finally a man gathered his tablet and stood, stretching his shoulders.

"I'll wait," I said, and gestured Grizz forward.

She nodded and went forward to slide her hand into the log-in gloves. Within a moment, her eyes had the glassy stare that means the meat's occupant is elsewhere.

I looked around. Chairs and desks dotted the place, all of them occupied. I went outside to the parking garage for a smoke.

Daylight had fled. At the structure's edge, where the street was dimly visible, I panhandled a dozen people before I found one willing to admit to smoking. I lit the cigarette, a Marlboro Brute, and leaned back against the wall, which was patchworked with graffiti layers. Maybe by the time I was done, a booth would have opened up. It was getting late, after all.

I closed my eyes as the nicotine rush hit me. Footsteps came across the cement floor toward me. I opened my eyes.

It was Lorelei. She wore a slick bright red jacket and lipstick to match over short skirt and chunky boots. Silver hoops all along each ear's edge, graduated to match her narrowing cartilage. She looked good. Very good.

"Nice night, ain't it?" she said as she moved to lean on the wall beside me. "Gimme."

I passed the smoke over and she took a drag.

"Want to try something to make the nice night even nicer?" she asked, smiling as she leaned back to return the cigarette.

"Meaning?"

"It's good stuff." She fished in the jacket before holding out the lighter and one-hitter. The end was packed with gray lintish dust. "Never had better."

I took the pipe and sparked it. The blue smoke rushed into my lungs like a fist, like a physical jolt and the world dropped half an inch beneath my feet. Everything was tinged with colors, an iridescence like gasoline on a rain puddle. I was standing there with Lorelei and at the same time I was on a vast dark plain, feeling the world teeter and slip.

Lorelei watched me. On the side of her face was a new tattoo, a black floral design.

"What's that?" I asked. I raised my hand, my fingers dripping colored fire and sparks. The drug curled and coiled through my veins, and I could feel my heart racing.

"Maps," she said. "Executable that interfaces with a global database. Got a GPS here." She tapped a purple faceted gleam on one earlobe. "Drop me anywhere in the world, I'll know where I am."

"Looks awful big to be a simple database interface."

She shrugged, and took the pipe back. She tapped out the ashes with care before she tamped a new pinch of greenish leaf into the mouth. "Controls the GPS too, and some other crap."

An expensive toy, but one that would qualify her for all sorts of delivery jobs. But she must be broke, to show up at Ajah's, I thought. It didn't make sense.

"How're things?" I asked.

Her shoulders twitched into another sullen shrug. "Got some deals in the works. Just a matter of time before something plays out."

I glanced back at the library door. "I should go in, I'm waiting on a machine to clear."

The drug still held me hard, and every moment was crystal clear as she raised her hand to stroke along my jaw. "I miss you sometimes, Jonny," she said, sounding out of breath.

I didn't want to piss her off, so I used a move that's worked before. Catching her hand, I turned it palm down and pressed my lips against the knuckles before dropping it and taking a step backward.

"See you around," I said.

She didn't say anything back, just stood there looking at me as I turned and walked away.

• • •

When I tried to log in, the drug prevented it. Every attempt shuddered and screeched along my nerves, so painful it brought tears to my eyes. But I kept trying and trying. A few cubicles down, I could see Grizz's back, hunched over her terminal, every particle intent. Learning. Preparing.

I stared at the screen, which showed the library logo and the welcome menu, all options grayed out, and cursed Lorelei and myself. Mostly myself. After an hour of pretending to work, I slipped away.

Another hour later, Grizz found me outside smoking. Good timing, too. I was on my fourth bummed cigarette, and starting to wonder when a guard would show to jolly me along on my way.

She looked happy, as animated as Grizz gets, which isn't much.

"You get what you wanted?" I asked.

"Got a bunch of stuff," she said. "Plant stuff."

Grizz likes plants, I know. At the shelter, she tended the windowsills full of discarded cacti and spider plants. But I hadn't known she was thinking about that for a career.

"That memory's something, isn't it?" she said. "I downloaded a weather predictor that monitors the whole planet, some biology databases, some specialized ones, some basic gardening routines, and a lot of stuff on orchids."

"Orchids?"

"I've always liked orchids. I've still got plenty of room, too. What about you?"

"Mine's not so good," I lied. "It didn't hold much at all."

Her gaze flickered up to mine, touched with worry. Her eyes narrowed.

"What are you on?" she asked. "Your pupils are big as my fist."

"Dunno the name."

"Where'd you score it?"

"Lorelei swung by, turned me on."

Silence settled between us like a curtain as Grizz's expression flattened.

"It's not like that," I finally said, unable to bear the lack of talk.

"Not like what?"

"She just came through and glimpsed me."

"She knew you would be here because we mentioned it at dinner. She still wants you back."

"Grizz, I haven't been with her for two years. Give it a rest."

"I will. But she won't." She pulled away and made for the exit, her lips pressed together and grim. I followed at a distance all forty blocks to Ajah's.

$\bullet \quad \bullet \quad \bullet$

In the morning, we showered together to avoid slamming Ajah's water bill too hard. Grizz kept her eyes turned away from mine, rubbing shampoo into her hair.

I ran my fingertips along the spirals on her back. "This is different," I said. Under my fingertips, the wire had knobbed up and thickened, although it still gave easily with the shift of muscles in her back. The gray patches were gone, and a uniform sheen played across the surface.

"Does it feel different?" I asked.

She shrugged. "Not really."

"Do you remember the brand name on the boxes? We could look it up on the Net later on."

"Carpa-something. I don't know. It looked bleeding edge and you never know what's up with that."

"Why do you think they threw it out?" I wanted to keep her talking to me.

She turned to face me with a mute shrug, closing her eyes and tilting her head back to let the water run over her long black hair. Her delicate eyebrows were like pen strokes capping the swell of her eyes beneath the thin-veined lids.

I tangled my fingers in her hair, helping free it so the water would wash away all the shampoo. Muddy green eyes opened to regard me.

"Going to sit out the Exams?" she asked.

Saying nothing, I shook my head. We both knew I didn't have a chance.

$\bullet \quad \bullet \quad \bullet$

The Exams were the freak show I expected. Rich people buy mods and make them unnoticeable, plant them in a gut or hollow out a leg. This level, people want to make sure you know what they got. Wal-Mart memory spikes blossomed like cartoon hair from one girl's scalp, colored sunshine yellow, but most had chosen bracelets, jelly purple and red, covering their forearms. One kid had scales, but they looked like a home job, and judging from the way he worried at them with his fingernails, they felt like it too.

You take the Exams at sixteen and most of the time they tell you you're the dregs, just like everyone else, but sometimes your mods and someone's listing match up and you find yourself with a chance. The more mods you have, the more likely it is. So the kids with parents who can afford to hop them up with database links or bio-mods that let them do something specialized, they're the ones getting the jobs.

Usually your family's there to wish you luck. Mine wasn't, of course. And Grizz never said anything about her home life. The only times I've asked, she shut me down quick. Which makes me think it was bad, real bad, because Grizz doesn't pull punches.

You could tell who expected to make it and who was going through the motions. Grizz marched up to her test machine like she was going to kick its ass three times around the block. I slid into my seat and waited for instructions.

You see vidplots this time of year circling around the Exams. Someone gets placed in the wrong job—wacky! Two people get switched by accident— hilarious! Someone cheats someone out of their job but ultimately gets served—heartwarming and reassuring!

In the programs, though, all you see is a quick shot of the person at the Exams. They don't tell you that you'll sit there for three hours while they analyze and explore your wetware, and then another two for the memory and experience tap.

And after all that, you won't know for days.

• • •

Grizz wouldn't say anything about how she thought she'd done—she was afraid of jinxing it, I think, plus she was still pissed at me about the Lorelei business.

I could tell as soon as we walked out, though, she was happy. I walked her back to Ajah's and said I was heading down to the court to see if our forms had come in. She nodded and headed inside. It was a gray morning. But nice—some sunlight filtered down through the brown haze that sat way up in the sky for once. The smoke-eater trees along the street gleamed bright green and down near the trunks sat clumps of pale-blue flowers, most of them coming into their prime, although a few were browned and curling. I could feel all that memory on my back, lying across my shoulder blades and I found myself Capturing.

I'd only heard it described before—most people don't have the focus or the memory to do it more than a split second. But I opened to every detail: the watery sepia sunlight and the shimmer playing over the feathers of the two starlings on a branch near me. The cars whispering across the street and two sirens battling it out, probably bound for St. Joe Emergency Services. The colors, oh, the colors passing by, smears of blue and brown and red flashes like song. The smell of the exhaust and dust mingled with a whiff of Mexican spices from the Taco Bell three doors down. Every detail crystal clear and recorded.

I dropped out of it, feeling my whole body shaking, spasms of warring tension and relief like hands gripping my arms and legs.

I tried to bring it back, tried to make the world go super sharp again, but it wouldn't cooperate. I stood there with jaw and fists clenched, trying to force it, but nothing happened.

• • •

Within three days, Grizz had heard. A year of training at the Desmond Horticultural Institute, then a three year internship at the State Gardens in Washington. Student housing all four years, which meant I wouldn't be going along.

At first we fought about it. I figured it was a no-brainer—go there jobless or stick here where I had contacts, friends ready with a handout or a few days' work. But once Grizz had been there a while, she insisted, she'd be able to scrounge me something so I could move closer.

Ajah's girlfriend Suzanne got her set up with a better wardrobe and a suitcase from the used clothing store she ran. I bought her new shoes, black leather boots with silver grommets, solid and efficient looking.

"What are you going to do without me?" she asked.

"I've gotten by before," I said. "You work hard for us, get somewhere. Five years down the line, who knows?"

It was a stupid, facile answer, but we both pretended it was meaningful.

And we did stay in touch, chatted back and forth in IMs. She was working hard, liked her classmates. She read this, and that, and the other thing. They kept telling her how well she was doing.

And unwritten in her messages was the question: What are you doing with it, with the memory?

Because certainly it was doing the same thing on her body as it was on mine: thickening like scars healing in reverse, bulky layers of skin-like substance building over each other. In Ajah's bathroom mirror, I could see the skin purpling like bruises around the layers. My sole consolation was Capturing; extended effort had paid off and I could summon the experience longer now, perhaps ten seconds all together. I kept working at it; Captured pieces sell well in upscale markets if you can get a name for yourself.

And I had the advantage of being able to do it as often as I liked, although each time still left me feeling wrung out and weak. I kept trying to Capture and never hit the memory's end; the only limits were my strained senses. My eyes took on a perpetual dazzled squint as though holy light surrounded everything around me.

I never told Grizz though. Nor about the fact that every time I went to jack into the Net, the drug got between me and the interface. I was glad I hadn't seen

Lorelei—I was starting to wonder if she'd given it to me deliberately. It scared me. I lost myself in Capturing more and more. I started delivering packages for Ajah and Suzanne, and laid aside enough cash to buy a simple editing package for it.

Editing is internal work, so you can do it dozing on a park bench if you've got the mental room to spread out and take a look at the big picture. I did. What I wanted to do was start selling clips on the channels. It'd take a while though, I could tell, and I was still working out how I'd upload it, given the problems jacking in. I figured at some point I'd burn it off to flash memory and then use an all-accessible terminal, with keyboard and mouse. In the meantime I cadged what meals I could, slept on a round of couches, and showed up at Ajah's often.

Sometimes after a meal, he'd roll out the still on its mismatched castors, and we'd strain its milky contents in order to drink them. He and I would sit near the window, passing the bottle back and forth.

Early on into Grizz's apprenticeship, he asked me about the memory. He said "That med complex near the dock, the one that went bust a few months ago, did you guys ever score out of there? I know that was in your turf."

"Went in one time and scored a little crap but not much." Our hands were both touching the bottle as I took it from him. I added, "Nothing but some old memory," and felt the bottle twitch in his sudden anguished grip.

"What did you do with it?" he asked, watching me pour.

"We used it. How do you think she did so well on the Exams?"

"But you didn't," he said, confused.

"Well, Grizz isn't a moron, and I am, which would account for it."

He grunted and took the bottle back.

"If I'd taken stuff from there," he said. "I'd just not mention it to anyone ever. There have been some nasty customers asking around about it."

• • •

I went to visit Grizz a few weeks later; her roommate was out of town for the weekend. We ate in the cafeteria off her meal card: more food than I'd seen in a long time, and then went back to her room and stripped naked to lie in each other's arms.

We could have been there hours, but eventually we got hungry and went back to the cafeteria. The rest of the weekend was the same progression, repeated multiple times, up until Sunday afternoon, and the consequent tearful, snuffling goodbye. I'd never seen Grizz act sentimental before; it didn't suit her.

"You need to do something," she said, looking strained.

"Other than planning on riding your gravy train?"

"It's not that, Jonny, and you know it."

I could have told her then about the Capturing, but I was annoyed. Let her think me just another peon, living off dole and scavenging. Fine by me.

The wall phone rang, and she broke off staring at me to answer it.

"Hello," she said. "Hello?" She shrugged and hung it up. "Nothing but breathing. Fuckazoid pervs."

"Get much of that?"

"Every once in a while," she said. "Some of the other students don't like Dregs. Afraid I might stink up the classroom."

It irritated me, that she'd said how much she liked it and now was asking for sympathy, as though her life was worse than mine. So I left it there and made my goodbye. She clung to the doorframe, staring after me.

It wasn't as though I had much to leave behind; it was perhaps my mind's sullen statement, forgetting my jacket. I got four blocks away, then jogged back, ran up the stairs. Knocked on the door and found silence, so I slipped the lock and went in.

By then . . . by then she was dead, and they had already left her. The memory was stripped from her skin, leaving ragged, oozing marks. Her throat had been cut with callous efficiency.

I stood there for at least ten minutes, just breathing. There was no chance she was not dead. The world was shaking me by the shoulders and all I did was stand there, Capturing, longer than I had ever managed before. Every detail, every dust mote riding the air, the smell of the musty carpeting and a quarrel next door over a student named Dian.

I didn't stick around to talk to the cops. I knew the roommate would be there soon to call it in. I might have passed her in the downstairs lobby: a thin Eurasian woman with a scar riding her face like an emotion.

• • •

When I got to Ajah's, they'd been there as well. He'd taken a while to die, and they had paid him with leisure, leisure to contemplate what they were doing to him. But he was unmistakably dead.

They had caught him in the preparations for a meal; a block of white chicken meat, sized and shaped like a brick, lay on the cutting board, his good, all-purpose knife next to it. "Man just needs one good knife for everything," he used to say. A bowl of breadcrumbs and an egg container sat near the chicken.

Someone knocked on the door behind me, and opened it even as I turned. It was Lorelei, still well-heeled and clean. Her bosses must be paying well.

"Jonny," she said. She didn't even look at Ajah's body. Unsurprised. "Is it true?"

"Is what true?"

"They said he gave up a name, just one, but when I heard the name, I knew there had to be two."

"What was the name?"

She chuckled. "You know already, I think. Grizz."

"Because of the memory?"

"It's more than memory. It grows as you add to it. Self-perpetuating. New tech—very special. Very expensive."

"We found it in the garbage!"

She laughed. "You've done it yourself, I know. What's the best way to steal from work?"

"Stick it in the trash and pick it up later," I realized.

She nodded, "But when two streets come along, and take it first, you're out of luck." Her smile was cold. "So then you ask around, send a few people to track it."

"Did you mean to poison the Net for me? Was that part of it?"

"You mean you haven't found the cure yet?" she said. "Play around with folk remedies. It'll come to you. But no. I was angry and figured I'd fuck you over the way you did me."

"Do they know my name?"

She smiled in silence at me.

"Answer me, you cunt," I said. Three steps forward and I was in her face.

She backed up toward the door, still smiling.

The knife was in easy reach. I stabbed her once, then again. And again. Capturing every moment, letting it sear itself into the memory, and I swear it went hot as the bytes of experience wrote themselves along my back.

"They don't . . ." she started to say, then choked and fell forward, her head flopping to one side in time with the knife blows. She almost fell on me, but I pushed her away. Her wallet held black-market script, and plenty of it, along with some credit cards. I didn't see any salvageable mods. The GPS's purple glimmer tempted me, but they can backtrack those. I didn't want anything traceable.

All the time that I rifled through her belongings, feeling the dead weight she had become, I played the memory back of the forward lurch, the head flop and twist, again, again, her eyes going dull and glassy. The thoughts seared on my back as though it were on fire, but I kept on recording it, longer and more intense than I ever had before.

• • •

She was right about the folk remedies; feverfew and valerian made the drug relax its hold and let me slide back into cyberspace. I've published a few pieces: a spring day with pigeons, an experimental subway ride, a sunset over the river. Pretty stuff, where I can find it. It seems scarce.

One reviewer called me a brave new talent; another easy and glib. The sales are still slow, but they'll get better. My latest show is called "Memories of Moments, Bright as Falling Stars"—all stuff on the beach at dawn, the gulls walking back and forth at the waves' edge and the foam clinging to the wet sand before it's blown away by the wind.

I don't use the Captures of Grizz's body or Lorelei's death in my art, but I replay them often, obsessively. Sitting on the toilet, showering, eating, walking—Capturing other things is the only way I have to escape them.

Between the royalties and Suzanne's continued employment though, I do well enough. She's moved into Ajah's place, and I've taken the room behind the clothing store where she used to live. I cook what I can there, small and tasteless meals, and watch the memories in my head. Memories of moments, as bright as falling stars.

JUSTINA ROBSON

THE GIRL HERO'S MIRROR SAYS HE'S NOT THE ONE

(2007)

THE ETERNAL YOUTH and optimism, the always-forward energy of the Girl Hero makes her feel lethargic whenever she stops for coffee at her favorite book-store. She is living in a Base Reality not unlike Prime, the original reality old Earthers used to share before Mappa Mundi, except it has fifty more shades of pink and no word for "hate." Her reality is called Rose Tint, and it was the one relatively mild hacker virus she was glad to catch. Of course, she would think that about it now . . .

The Girl Hero feels there is something missing about herself, but she cannot name it. She has always felt this way, since she was tiny at her father's knee. He showed her a fly that had landed on the back of his hand. She looked closely, marveling at how small it was, how neat, how industrious as it cleaned its pretty glass wings. She remembers how he smashed it flat with his other hand. He was so fast. He had the reflexes of ten men, and he was a Hero too.

Oh, one other thing that is missing about her is her name . . . a bout of flu stole it from her when she was in her teens, not so long ago. She keeps it written on the inside of her wrist in indelible ink that she rewrites every three days. She doesn't look at it much. Only when someone asks. The coffee barista has his name written on a badge: Marvin.

"Thank you, Marvin," she says as she takes her drink. The establishment is guaranteed clean. Little tablet boxes of Mappacode are sold at the counter, but they don't come under the Infection Bill: too minor, too common and not particularly useful—they offer mnemonic upgrades for popular music charts, fashion, current affairs, and the stock markets so you can always have something to say and know what to buy. The information is stored somehow in proteins that only unfurl when they reach the right places in the brain—the places where Mappaware has created ports for them. They are inert otherwise, and when they have delivered the goods they break up into amino acids and provide spare nutrition. The Girl Hero takes a Mode one and pops it with the first steaming sip of espresso.

The Girl Hero picks at the cardboard band around her coffee cup and goes to take a seat in the window. She is dismayed to learn from the Modey that tweed pencil skirts are in. They are the worst kind of skirt for kicking. She sips and looks around her and wonders for the millionth time if she should save her money and risk a remodel. But she doesn't know what to do if she isn't a Hero. A Hero wouldn't. The preference is disturbing—would she really like it if she hadn't agreed to this job at the careers' meeting? Too late to wonder. It was a road not taken. She will never know who . . . (she looks at the inside of her wrist) . . . Rebecca might have been if she had chosen some different option. She hopes that Rebecca would have wanted to be a Hero anyway.

In the eternal present moment of the Hero's world Rebecca waits, waits, waits for her assignment without anxiety or hope. On other faces she sees various expressions of emotions that fit a task: executives focused and intent on work, an artist dreaming as he stares into nowhere through the wall opposite him, girls bent to their schoolwork rising and falling in the perfectly timed bursts of concentration and relaxation that allow them maximum efficiency in their learning and their fun. They are like seals at play, bobbing in and out of the water. Their chat and laughter rise like bubbles, thinks the Girl Hero, and she feels a twinge of envy, though she had her time and doesn't want it back.

A man in a dark suit as unmemorable as yesterday's news glides past and casually leaves his magazine on her table. She knows him for an Attaché, a man from the ministry who delivers duties to her kind, and that the magazine is a job offer in the eternal post-Mappa economy of the fight against the Cartomancers. She needs a job. She wants to move out of her mother's house.

On page fifty-nine her secret message awaits her. It is typed on tissue paper and all the "o"s are offset, which means it is a mission of the most extreme danger and highest importance. How typical, she thinks, that these things should come together. She rubs some hand cream into her knuckles to hide the thick, dry calluses from years of smashing her fists into concrete walls.

The message instructs her to take a journey to Pointe-Noire, in Congo. It is a place ridden with Cartoxins and the illegal breeding pens of the black-market traders who design animals of exquisite savagery and intelligence for the use of the criminal underworld. Most of them will be remapped for various tasks, and they will not know mercy, fear, or any debilitating survival instinct. Once there she will go to a jungle compound and find a certain man and kill him. He is a Bad Man. She does not know his crimes, but they are probably something to do with writing or disseminating rogue viruses and/or Maps, because these are now the only crimes there are in the absence of what used to be known as Free Will. It is sure that if he were not so bad he would not be hiding out in such a place in the hopes that nobody would dare to follow. The vestiges of her sympathy for desperate men with missions for mankind are not stirred.

She folds the tissue paper and puts it in her handbag. She goes to the bathroom and has to queue. The bathroom is located in the Self Help section of the bookstore. The Girl Hero has no need for this. She is slightly mystified by the titles, and for the need of books in a world where everything can be eaten. She does not like to look at them. They seem to ask questions of her, and when her back is turned they whisper like schoolchildren.

As she is washing her hands the Girl Hero feels an unpleasant feeling. It is like something scattering inside. She imagines she is made from swarms of rats that have just noticed a terrible thing and are running, running, running for their lives. She often feels this. It is doubt. It comes along after a certain time period when she has had nothing heroic to do. She puts the lid on the toilet down and sits there, taking up someone else's pee time as she gets out a vanity mirror from her handbag and opens it up. One half of the clamshell is an ordinary mirror. The other half has its own face, a kind of pixie that looks exactly like the Girl Hero. It came with the job. She suspects it is a transmitter device that talks directly to her Mappaware to sort out glitches. If she were more dedicated to keeping her appearance groomed than she is, possibly it would deal with her doubts for her.

"Mirror, mirror," says the Girl Hero, and need say no more.

"You want to go," says the mirror. "And you will." It always says this. The Girl Hero finds it very reassuring. She always asks. Her real question has not yet been answered and she doesn't bother to say it, but the mirror replies all the same, "He is not the one."

She closes the mirror and puts it away, satisfied that its prophecies are correct. Despite her bad feeling this encounter will not be the last. She will not die today. A Girl Hero always trusts her mirror.

The Girl Hero goes shopping for a tweed pencil skirt and knee-high boots with heels. On her way to the airport she stops to text her mother that she will be home late, do not save any dinner, she will get some at the takeaway. Her mother is a Perky Waitress and will be satisfied with this latchkey message, not curious, not alarmed; she might bring home plastic boxes filled with peach pie and put them on the countertop for . . . Rebecca . . . to find when she comes in. Peach pie tastes of sweet, fulfilling safety and sleep. Two bites would be enough.

At the check-in desk she sees another Girl Hero, but one with a robot dog companion. She feels a sudden pang of envy and wants to introduce herself, to ask something that brims to her lips with urgent importance, though it can't make itself into words without a listener . . . but the other Hero is in a hurry. She runs off toward a departure gate with a flip of curly brown hair over the top of her practical backpack and grabs up her ammunition clips from the security guard without breaking stride. Her robot dog races beside her.

The Girl Hero . . . Rebecca . . . has no weapons to check. She deals only in kung fu. Her handbag is very small, just big enough for makeup, the mirror, and her phone. She looks up the price of robot dogs while she waits to board her flight. They are expensive. She thinks a real one would be better, but of course there is a problem with quarantine and the endless inoculations. She couldn't possibly afford one. Robots cannot catch diseases, so they are immune to all but the most specific and local of memetic assaults. A robot is much better, but the Girl Hero imagines a warm body, soft fur, regular breathing in a real ribcage moving under her hands, and brown eyes looking at her with unconditional love.

On the flight a man is seated beside her. He makes small talk about her job with the unconscious impulses of all businesspeople. She tells him she is a secretary, which is true, when she is not being a Hero. He sells virtual real estate. He shows her one of the communities he administers: a condo by the sea, to let, all mod cons, barely the cost of a sandwich per month and unlimited online access. He is persuasive, but Heroes are not easily sold. She declines. Her feet swell uncomfortably in the boots. She takes a limousine from the airport to her hotel, where she has a room already booked for her by the ministry.

Pointe-Noire is a township with only a small center adequately defended and habitable. Beyond the line of automatic fire lie teeming swarms of wildlife so bestial and savage, so tightly packed, that every moment of their existence is a matter of do or die. They are the testbed of Hellmemes and other horrors cooked up in the mobile Cartomancy sweatshops that creak and grind through the jungle; metal behemoths covered in solar panels and electrical deterrents.

Beyond the hotel perimeter fence it is still night but will soon be day. In that blue hour there is a slight lull in the slaughter and terror as sleepy creatures of dark trade places with waking creatures of light.

The Girl Hero hires a personal jetcar and lands a few miles from town, close to the house where He lives, this criminal, or whatever he is. Her little capsule glides down within his ranch home's Sphere of Influence—a forcefield of protection maintained by a mini reactor. There are no monsters inside, but two muddy fields of marsh grass and the foot-high remains of stripped trees lie between her and the buildings. She regrets the boots now.

Outside the house there are fences and inside the fences are real dogs, mastiffs with serial killers' eyes. The Girl Hero walks to the gate, pulling her boot heels free of the mud with every step, thinking the leather will be ruined. She does not feel like strangling a dog. Her inner world has become the gray blank place she associates with Heroism. It is familiar and strangely disappointing. She doesn't know what she was expecting from a life devoted to exacting justice and defending the world from evil, but this was not it. Beyond the forcefield at her back the dawn chorus of howls, screams, roars, and whimpers greets the veteran sun.

There's a fence and a gate too. In the gatehouse there is a person. Where there is a person there is an easy way in.

The Girl Hero says she is selling virtual real estate. She shows the guard her mirror and, as he peers at this strange kind of identification, she knocks him unconscious. He crumples without a sound.

Close by two monsters in the forest clash foreheads in a dominance fight, and the air is split by a crack like thunder. If the animals assaulted the shield they could get through it easily, but the shock of sudden pain has always prevented them from making this discovery. As they stumble about, stunned but undaunted by mortal combat, they avoid its gossamer shimmer at all costs. The Girl Hero shakes her head at them.

As she frisks pockets for codes, keys, cards, or whatever the Girl Hero is overcome by a sense of déjà vu. It is one of those nasty moments where, certain this is not a memory, because she has never been here before, she understands it is an omen. She hesitates and feels the man's still-beating heart under her hand. Her hand forms the shape of a crane's bill and delivers a rapid, extreme strike. It does not break the bone, but it doesn't have to. The shock is sufficient.

She could not have let him live, of course. He would have woken up sooner or later, and she does not know how long she has to be here. She feels mildly surprised at her action, and faintly sad that this is all she feels. Her finger stings her. She looks down and finds she has broken a nail. She spends a moment fixing it with her little kit of glue and tape, packed neatly into a thimble. She has the shakes, however, and her mend does not hold. She tapes the thimble onto the end of her finger instead. It is made of gold and once was the barque of a fairy queen, or so she likes to imagine. The Girl Hero wonders if it will defeat the power of her strike, but she doesn't take it off.

The Girl Hero locates the keys to the inner house and gets into the armored golf cart, which takes her through the fence territory of the dogs. It has sealed sides. The dogs run and bark alongside the cart. The whine of the electric motor is inappropriately cheerful. Insects whirl and scream around in the light, involuntary and designed carriers of diseases to change the mind—they are indistinguishable from the real things. The sun crests over the forest's edge, and a flight of red-winged insectivores takes to the air, flocking in the rising heat in a way that makes the air look syrupy. The Girl Hero takes out her mirror and adjusts her lip gloss. She thinks about what to order from the takeaway and decides she will have a Chinese.

At the end of the golf cart's route she is let into the house by machines who do not care that she is here to kill the master. Like so many of his kind he has run short of henchpersons whose instincts might favor him and now relies on mechanicals. Not popular, thinks the Girl Hero, and frowns a tiny frown to go with her tiny pang of sorrow. On the polished wood of the hallway her boots make hollow sounds.

There is a cook, a person doing some menial tasks, and a man who throws carcasses to the dogs. None of them are interested in stopping her when they see her coming, so the Girl Hero wearily locks them into the storeroom. She makes a note to herself on her mobile, so she does not forget to call help for them once she has left the scene. Lying on the kitchen counter is a plate of cream cakes, freshly defrosted, their chocolate iced tops coated in condensation sweat. She would like to eat them all. With the ease of a lifetime of denial, she barely registers the desire.

The Bad Man is in the living room, enjoying a glass of juice. His heavy frame is silhouetted against the rapacious sky as he looks out over a balcony toward the thin blue veil of the Sphere and beyond. Whatever he has loaded it with would naturally include a lot of processors to bypass any fear he might feel at her arrival. She feels that this is possibly a meeting of equals, her legally enhanced mind against his self-made one. There is a kind of honor code to be observed.

The Girl Hero puts her handbag on the table. He turns around at the small sound. His eyes begin to measure the distance to the door, but they falter halfway. He has recognized her and that an attempt to escape will be futile. She watches him relax as resignation takes the place of fear in his look. Perhaps it is genuine, but no reaction could be taken at face value in the circumstances. They are already too far along the road of combat.

"Would you like a drink?" he asks. He is wearing some kind of Japanese robe and looks like he has led a full life, she thinks. His short legs are planted firmly. He has no intention of running. Perhaps he will not put up a fight. Her stomach rumbles and she feels a slight pain there. She shakes her head—no. She can't do anything distracting to her, even if she thinks it would be safe—and for some reason she does feel safe now.

He is a long way across the room. She starts to walk.

"Do you know why you are here?"

She assumes he means does she know what he has done. She's not really interested. She shakes her head.

"Do you know why you are?"

The Girl Hero hesitates. He has deployed the Defense of Existential Crisis and she should ignore it boldly, defeat it with a witty and humorous line, but recently she hasn't thought of any of these. She only thinks of them later, long after the person who should have been rebuked is dead. It is her biggest weakness. She has read books of aphorisms, but *A lot of knowledge fits an empty head* seems inappropriate and is the only thing that comes to mind.

"I am a poet," he says.

It seems unlikely, she thinks. Why would anyone want to kill a poet? But, then again, why not? "Was your verse offensive?" she asks. Why did she engage? The only sensible thing to do is to break his neck and leave. What is she talking for? She adds quickly, "It isn't important. You are on the list."

"Do you know your masters and their ideas, Girl?" he asks, backing away rapidly as she advances with a firm, librarian's tread. His voice gets a bit higher, but it remains steady. "Do you know why you don't want to know?"

"It's not my place," she says, and unaccountably finds she has stopped walking. She does know why. She has *chosen* not to know.

There are two sides to this war of memes: the side of the Directive, which advocates managed and secure social design for the safety and well-being of all, and the side of the Cartomancers, which wants anarchy at any cost, a free market without limits. Both of them have to contend with the Wild in which Mappaware and Mappacode have become attached to the genetic strands not only of their original carriers, the viruses, but also bacteria. There is no doubt it will soon spread (if it hasn't already) into the DNA of larger species. The Girl Hero never had gotten her head quite around the science or the politics of it. It's not a Hero's business to do all the thinking about the rights and wrongs. Her remit is much smaller. Justice for the wrongdoer and safety for the calm world of Perky Waitresses, Secretaries, and peach pie. And whiskery skittery rats.

The Bad Man takes a nervous sip of juice. The scream and murder of the jungle increases as the full circle of the sun appears clear of the trees. What a dreadful place, thinks the Girl Hero. She realizes she has reached a kind of stalemate but doesn't understand why she can't break it. She watches the Bad Man drink and set down his glass carefully on a coaster on a nice, smooth table.

"What's your name?"

She didn't expect this question even though an effort to become more intimate with an attacker who is more powerful is an obvious tactic. She opens her mouth, determined to answer, but nothing comes out. She looks to the inside of her wrist. She shouldn't tell him, so she keeps her mouth shut. "Rebecca" rings no bells for her. It could be a barcode for all it means. Her stomach starts to gnaw at her.

"I'm Khalid," he says, and nods with a faint, social smile. He glances at her wrist, and a moment of pity firms his lips.

A vicious streak of envy cuts across her mouth like the taste of lemon. Suddenly she wants the reassurance of the mirror, that tonight is not the night, but she left her bag on the table. It gets in the way and drags her arm when she has to punch.

"Wouldn't you like to understand what happened to you?"

"What is this, exam night?" She is determined not to be distracted by flimsy philosophizing. She doesn't care about the answers to his tiresome inquiries, but for some reason she thinks about the books, snickering behind her back. She wants to go home, get duck in plum sauce, get a shower, give her mother a cup of tea, and go to bed. In the morning she has work again because it is still three days until the weekend. Besides, the answer to his question is surely obvious. She says it without knowing she's going to until she starts, "I caught a bad purge. That's all. No big. Look." She flashes her wrist at him.

"Everything in the world and the Wild is written, Rebecca, just like your name," he says. He keeps a close watch on her, and she on him, in case he runs away, in case she doesn't.

Damn, she sees he has reached the wall. His free hand darts with the speed of desperation toward a control hidden there. He fumbles. She darts across the gap, jumps, and kicks. Her skirt rips. Her boots are too tight. She knocks him aside but lands on her ass. Some kind of alarm is sounding like a bleating goat. Angry with herself she glares at him.

"The Sphere control," he says with satisfaction. "In a minute it will vanish and the Wild will come in." His face is pasty under its smooth olive plumpness, but triumphant.

She sees clearly that a lot now stands between her and the evening she had planned. She looks out, to where her car is hidden, beyond the cleared land. One minute? "But my mirror says you're not the one," she tells him firmly. Suddenly her belief in the mirror is wavering.

She looks into the eyes of the Bad Man. He looks back at her, without attempting to move. She says, "If you reset the device I will let you live." She tells herself she does not mean it. She hasn't made a mistake. She wouldn't betray the contract. A Hero would do what it takes to save the world.

"I think you will not," says the Bad Man, becoming amused.

"Don't just lie there," she says, lying there.

"Why not?" he asks. "I can see up your skirt from here. Nice underwear."

"I mean it," she says, meaning it to her own surprise. "I will let you live."

"Ah, thanks," he says, "but if it wasn't you, it would just be some other Girl Hero coming along in a day or two, and I've done my time. There's nothing left I want to do I haven't done, and I'm not much for repeats. The Directive has no real defense against the Cartomancy, and neither have a chance against the Wild, not in the end. The life of ideas is already a literal thing. We used to transmit them inadequately with words, and soon they will transmit themselves through nature, through biology, in ways that bypass what small shred of choice may ever have existed. So, I think I'll just stay here, if it's all the same to you. It's a bit more satisfying if you die along with me than if you get to escape, and I wish I was a bit different but I was free of the Map all my life and I have to bow to my taste for justice in my own way. I hope you can understand that."

"But I want to live!" the Girl Hero says.

"I don't think so," Khalid observes. His voice is mild. "I knew when you walked in and hesitated that you were the one."

The bleat alarm goes off. Without it the mindless fury beyond the Sphere seems twice as loud. The Girl Hero leaps to her feet and tries the device by the window. She cannot make it work. The blue tissue of force begins to fade. The blazing ruddy glare of beyond starts to color it a deep purple. The Girl Hero thinks about the cakes on the counter, the innocent dogs, the people in the storeroom, her mother.

She glares down at him. "Why didn't they stop the Wild a long time ago?"

He shrugs. She sees that he does not know. "The day it was discovered there was a faster way to change people's minds than simply by talk or the gun, then it was already decided. If you were hoping for a final insight into human nature . . ." He trails off and looks distracted as the color of the room changes from a soft shadowy umber to bright yellow. The Sphere has gone.

The Girl Hero makes a dive and slides the length of the table. She picks up her handbag and takes out her mirror. She no longer has the gray, flat feeling of Heroism, and she wants to see if that has changed her face.

It has. The incipient wrinkles at the edges of her eyes and between her brows have gone. She is as smooth and pretty as she was the first day she took up office. On the other side of the mirror the pixie looks out toward the clear edge of the forest where it seems that a starving, boiling mass of vegetable and animal is slowly billowing toward them.

"Oh my," says the mirror. "Look out! He's getting away."

The Girl Hero feels a surge of desperation and anger quite unusual for her. She spins around just in time to catch sight of Khalid slithering through the narrow black gap of a secret doorway he has opened in the paneling. She is after him like a shot, but her muddy feet slip a little and she can't grab hold of him as she intended. She makes it through the gap anyway and runs through the narrow, wooden corridor after him, her skirt seam ripping a bit more up the thigh with every furious stride. How could she fall for a distraction? How could she have entertained the idea that he was telling the truth about never having acquired the Map? Just look at this ridiculous compound with its guards and gates and dogs and cook. Listen to him give his Villainous Speech. She and he are both products of Stock Narrative 101, however many upgrades and individual variations they may have acquired . . . and now her rage is like hell itself.

The corridor winds and slopes down. Khalid skids and loses a shoe. The escape chute opens to a broad decking with an escape car tethered to it, its air bladder fully primed with helium. The engines tick over, its rotors whir softly in the thick and humid air. Khalid is forced to pause, hand fighting his pocket for the key. The Girl Hero cocks her arm and throws the mirror in a dead flat spin. It strikes him on the back of the head and he falls to his knees. Around him the broken bright pieces scatter, fragments of sky.

"I want to see what's real!" she screams. "Why did you have to be a liar?" She is crying. This is impossible. She needs the mirror, and rushes up to him. She tries to pick up the pieces, but behind the glass all the circuitry is broken. There should be some word for what she feels when she looks at him, a word not like "fuchsia" or "madder" or "carmine" or "rose" or "sugar" or "candy." It should be a word for rats turning and scuttling back with red eyes, teeth bared, tails like little ramrods. Maybe the word is "Rebecca."

Khalid blinks at her with panic beginning to make him sweat. "What did you expect?" He had located the key.

The car door opens as a wave of warm air, full of thunder, ripples slowly across them. Rain starts to fall and there comes the screeching and shrilling of agony, the sputter of electrical things and burning fur as creatures test the weakening perimeter fence. Khalid snatches a mask from his pocket and wraps it across his face with his free hand as he scrabbles to his feet. He makes a lunge for the door. The Girl Hero watches him with the Rebecca feeling and jumps after. She makes the sill and he attempts to push her out backward, but he's weak, a big soft geek type who's all brain and no brawn. She kicks him in the chest and slams the door after them.

"Take me with you," she says. "They'll send other Heroes. You need me." He looks up from the floor and croaks, "I did okay so far . . ."

"You were dead when I walked in the door. And if you say no, you still are," the Girl Hero assures him, picking him up by the shirtfront and hauling him to the passenger seat of the little craft. "Shit," she says, safe, for now. "What about your people? Can't leave them . . ."

"Have to leave them," he gasps, still winded. "No time."

No Hero would ever leave them.

Khalid slams a hand to the controls, and the car begins to lift off. "Anyway, why should you care? Killed enough for a lifetime . . ."

She opens her mouth to protest, but the breath she took doesn't go anywhere, just leaves her inflated. As she delays the aircar rises smoothly into the sky above the treetops. From the windshield she can see the dogs running back and forth in their prison, barking.

"You should let them out," she said, sitting down slowly in the pilot's seat. "It's cruel to keep dogs that way." They fly for a time in silence, avoiding the Directive Patrols but with no other plan.

"Can you ever get rid of it?" Rebecca asks in a quiet voice. "Mappaware? Ever?"

"You can tell it not to work," Khalid says. "That's all." He hands over a small black box shaped like a cigarette pack with a single button on it. "We use them a lot. When you get too much infestation you go unstable. This clears it. Then you start again."

Rebecca remembers him fumbling in his pockets. Zap. Not the door. Her. "You got me."

Khalid nodded. "And me. Works in a range."

Rebecca presses the button, over and over. Nothing happens. "Now what? Why aren't I different then?"

"That takes time," he says, sighing wearily. "Lots of time. Have to grow, think, do things . . . take more code or not . . . left alone you'll change on your own."

"Like in the old days." She puts the box into her own pocket, which is almost too small. She wishes she had not forgotten her bag. For a moment she thinks about Chinese food and her home, all the stuffed animals in a row, her mother's scent . . . "Where to?"

Khalid shrugs. "I wait until I pick up a beacon. Most likely spot is still over the Congo area somewhere. Just follow the river."

"And then?"

"Set down, make new friends in the Cartomancy, carry on. . . . Write something, test it, purge it. Try to figure out how to create antimemes against the worst plagues . . . not much."

Rebecca nods. It's not much, but it is enough.

KAREN HEULER

THE COMPLETELY RECHARGEABLE MAN

(2008)

HE WAS INTRODUCED as Johnny Volts, and most guests assumed he was a charlatan—the hostess, after all, was immensely gullible. But some of the guests had seen him before, and they said he was good, lots of fun, very "current"—a joke that got more mileage than it should have.

"Do you need any kind of extension cord?" the hostess, Liz Pooley, asked. She wore a skintight suit of emerald lamé, and had sprayed a lightning bolt pattern in her hair, in his honor.

Johnny Volts sighed and then smiled. They all expected him to be something like a children's magician—all patter and tricks. "No extension cord," he said. "Where can I stand?" He caught his hostess's frown. "I need an area to work in—and appliances, not plugged in. I'm the plug. No microwaves. A blender, a radio, a light bulb. Christmas lights?"

The guests were charmed at first and then, inevitably, they were bored. Even if it wasn't a trick, it was pretty limited. He could power a light, but not a microwave. He could charge your cell phone but not your car. He was an early adopter of some sort, that was all; they would wait for the jazzed-up version.

Johnny Volts had a pacemaker with a rechargeable battery, and he had a friend who was a mad scientist. This friend had added a universal bus to his battery port, and hence Johnny Volts had a cable and a convertible socket. He could plug things in; he could be plugged in. This was a parlor trick as far as the public was concerned—and a strange, unsettling, but still somewhat interesting way of earning a living as far as Johnny Volts was concerned. He knew—he understood—that his pacemaker powered his heart, and his heart recharged the pacemaker in a lovely series of perpetual interactions. He had no issue with it.

In Liz Pooley's party, as Johnny Volts lit a lamp, turned on a clock radio, and charged an iPod, he was watched by a frowning man in a checked shirt whose companion seemed quite happy with Johnny.

"Why he's worth his weight in gold," she said. "Imagine never having to pay an electric bill."

"Small appliances," the man grunted.

"Well *now* it's small appliances, Bob, but he's just the first. Wait till he can really get going, he'll have his own rocket pack. Remember rocket packs, Bob? The Segway of long-lost memory." She put her hand on Bob's arm and rolled her eyes. "I was but a mere child of course, when I heard about those rocket packs. Shooting us up in the air. A new meaning to the term Jet Set, hey? Or is that phrase too old? I bet it's too old. What are we called now, Bob?" She lifted her drink, saluted him, and winked.

"We're called only when they've run out of everyone else, Cheree." Bob was idly thinking about what would bring a man to this: plugging in small irrelevant things into his own violated flesh. "Irrelevant," he said finally. "They call us irrelevant."

Cheree frowned. "You're turning into an old man, Bob. You've lost your spark." She gave him a small motherly peck on the cheek and walked forward, powerfully, her lemon martini firm in her hand, straight to Johnny Volts, who was looking around, waiting to be paid. "You looking for a drink?" she asked. "I could get you one."

"Oh—well, all right," he said, surprised.

"You wait right here," she said. "I want to know all about you, electric man." And she turned until she found a server and came back with a dark liquid in a tumbler. "Now tell me—how does it feel? I mean you're generating electricity, aren't you?"

"Yes. Not much. After next week it should be more. I'm having an upgrade."

"Lovely. How does it feel? Like little bugs up and down your spine?" She had a heady grin, a frank way of working. Johnny liked it.

"It's a beautiful kind of pressure," he said. "It feels like I could fill the room with it, lift everything up, kind of explode—only I hold on to the explosion." His eyes got internal.

"Do you like it?"

He was open-mouthed with surprise. "Yes. Of course. It's wonderful."

She tilted her head a little, studying his face, and he found it embarrassing at first, and then he got used to it. He looked back at her, not lowering his eyes or glancing away. She was older than he was, but she had a bright engaging air about her, as if she made a point of not remembering anything bad.

"Here you go," the hostess said, her arm held out full length with a check at the end of it like a flattened appendage.

Johnny took it and turned to leave. "Hey!" Cheree said, grabbing at his arm a little. "That's rude. Not even a fond farewell?"

"They usually want me to leave right away," he said in explanation. "Before I get boring."

"Boring," she said companionably as they headed together for the door. "That bunch? They think *other* people arc boring?"

He noted that she was walking along with him as if she belonged there. "So where do you see yourself in five years?" she asked. "That's a test question. So many people can't think ahead."

"Do you think ahead?"

"Not me. I'm spontaneous. Then again, I'm not at all electric, so I don't have to worry about running out of juice."

"I don't run out," he said. "I recharge. And I'm getting an upgrade to photovoltaic cells next week. I have to decide where to implant them; do you mind if I run it past you?" He rubbed his hand over his head as they took the elevator down. "The obvious thing is to replace my hair—it's a bit of a jolt, though. I can lose it all and get a kind of mirror thing on top—a shiny bald pate, all right. Or fiber-optic hair. But it will stick out. Like one of those weird lamps with all the wires with lights at the end? What do you think?"

"Fiber-optic hair," she said without hesitation. "Ahead of the times. Fashion-forward. I bet there'll be a run on the hardware store."

He stopped—they were on the street—and frowned at her. "Your name?"

"Cheree."

"Cheree, you're glib."

"I am glib, Johnny," she said in a soft voice. "It's because my head doesn't stop. You know the brain is all impulses, don't you? Bang and pop all over the place. Well, mine is on superdrive, I have to keep talking or I'll crack from all the thinking. The constant chatter . . . I can only dream of stillness."

He shook his head in sympathy. "That sounds like static." He stopped and reached out for her hand. "Maybe you produce energy all your own?" She held her hand out, and Johnny hesitated, then touched the tips of their fingers together. He closed his eyes, briefly. There was a warmth, a moistness, a lovely *frisson*. He took a deep breath. He felt so tired after those parties, but now a delicious delicate rejuvenation spread through him. The back of his neck prickled; the hairs on his arms—even his eyebrows—hairs everywhere rose, he could feel it in his follicles. It rose up in him until suddenly Cheree was thrown backward slightly.

"What was that?" she said tensely.

He nodded. "Sorry. Volts. A little discharge. It won't hurt you."

"Still," she said uneasily. "Can't say I know what to make of it."

They were at a crossroads, specifically Houston and Lafayette. "Where do you live?" he asked.

"East Seventh."

"I'm uptown." They stood for a moment in silence. "Will you come with me?" he asked finally.

Her face broke into a smile, like a charge of sunshine.

They were utterly charming together, they were full of sparks. Toasters popped up when they visited their friends—though did people really still have toasters? Wasn't that, instead, the sound of CD players going through their discs, shuffling them? Wasn't it the barely audible purr of the fan of a car as they passed it, sitting up and noticing as if it were a dog? They were attractive, after all; they attracted.

"If we moved in together," Johnny said after they'd known each other for a month, "we'd have half the bills. We could live on very little, we could live on what I make at the parties. You wouldn't have to work as a waitress. In fact, we could be free."

"And give up my dreams of rocket science?" she asked, her eyebrows arched. "I thought you were a waitress."

"That's just till I sell my first rocket." Nevertheless, she decided to move in, and it was working out fine, except for the strange way that objects behaved around them.

Small electrics followed them like dogs sometimes—they could turn down the block and hear a clanking or a scraping behind them. Eager little cell phones, staticky earphones, clicking electronic notepads gathered in piles on their doorstep.

"We have to figure out a budget," Cheree said after she moved in. "Until I sell that rocket. Rent, not much we can do. We should get bikes, that will save on transportation. But, you know, we're still paying for electricity, and it's pretty high, too. What do we really use it for?"

Together, they went through their apartment, noting: refrigerator, lamps, clock, radio, stereo, TV, microwave, coffee maker, hair dryer, iron, laptop computer.

"Well," Johnny said. "All quite useful in their own way, but we can make coffee without electricity. And I already recharge the computer myself."

She considered it all. "You can recharge most of it, really, if we get the right kind of thing. If we look at everything that way—I'm sure there are rechargeable lamps, for instance—why are we paying electric bills? We could save a lot of money by doing it ourselves."

They canceled their energy provider, a savings right there of $70 a month. They would plug a different item into Johnny at night, so they would never run out. It was a brilliant solution.

That gave him even more motivation for the photovoltaic upgrade. When he went to his mad scientist friend, she went with him, and they mentioned the strange way they seemed to be accumulating electrical appliances. The mad scientist was sitting across from them, taking down Johnny's recap of the past few months, when the scientist felt his skin begin to tingle. He shook himself briefly, as if buzzed by a fly. He was a graduate student at Carnegie Mellon, a Mexican genius who did illegal cable and satellite hookups to make some money, and was always looking over his shoulder. Johnny Volts was his ticket to fame and fortune; once the process was perfect, he would offer it to a medical or electronics company and bring millions down to his hometown of Tijuana, where he would go to retire.

The scientist ran a voltmeter over Cheree and whistled. "This is lovely," he said. "Exciting, even." He grinned at Johnny. "She's got a field. You see, you two match. You kind of amplify each other—understand?" He looked at them happily, waiting for them to catch up with his thinking. "You match."

It took a moment. "You're saying we're related? Like siblings?"

"Oh—no, no, I mean your energy matches. It doesn't mean anything really, other than that you're sensitive to each other's waves. You two have sympathetic electricity—I'm making the term up—so you use less energy when you're together than you do when you're apart, because you're actually *attracting* each other's charge. The byproduct is, you attract things that charge. Get it?"

"Oh, honey, yes," Cheree said. "I get it." It was like their little electric hearts went thudder-thump when they came near each other. Cheree was aware of it as a little sizzle in her brain.

They noticed a few things: He was a thoughtless hummer, and when he hummed he gave her a headache. She was an adventurer, wanting to go out and about, here, there, and everywhere, while he liked to think and write and test how strong his recharging was.

It happened gradually, the feeling that they were being watched, were being followed. She had coffee and a man who looked familiar sat opposite her in the café. He went to a party and saw the same man in a different suit watching him carefully. His apartment door was dusted with a fine powder one morning; the following week it was on a window.

When they went out in the morning, there was always a bunch of people passing their front door. Jauntily, as if just interrupted, they were speeding away, toward, around, moving with a great deal more purpose than on any other block. "Have you noticed it?" Cheree asked, and Johnny nodded. "I asked the landlord, and he said there's been some kind of gas leak, they're checking the lines a lot more. Even went into the basement, he said, all up and down the block."

"A gas leak?" she said, sniffing. "I don't smell anything."

"Well, that's good then."

• • •

But then Johnny disappeared. Went out to a party and didn't come back, and when she called the number listed in his daybook, she was told he hadn't shown up.

Cheree buzzed in her head when she was near Johnny; she could feel the tingle coming on when she turned the corner, half a block away, so it wasn't surprising that she felt she could find him. She said to herself: these are the things I know: He has a charge, and I can sense it. He has a head of fiber-optic hair. And I am his magnet.

She took her bike and rode slowly, up and down streets, starting with the top of the island. Her head refused to buzz, block after block, in traffic and out, but then, after three hours—just as she rounded the corner near the docks on the West Side—she heard a tang, she felt a nibble at her brain. It was him. She biked forward, back, left and right, testing out the buzzing, following it to the door of a small garage dealing in vintage cars.

She parked her bike and chained it. She noticed an electric toothbrush rolling on the sidewalk.

She walked up to a man in a very neat jumpsuit. She didn't know anything about vintage cars. "I have to get a present for my dear old dad," she said. "He loves cars. I thought maybe we could all—he had two families, so there's plenty of children—get together and buy him something smashing." She grinned.

He shrugged. "You can take a look at what we've got, but my gut says you're out of your league."

She smiled at him steadily, looking around, her eyes skipping to the doorway to an office or a back room. She could feel Johnny's electric kick. She walked around the cars slowly until his charge was at its strongest. She whipped around "I know you have him," she said, and drew in her breath, kicking a chair over to trip him as he lunged forward. She bolted for the door, which was unlocked, and burst in.

There was Johnny, in the corner of the room. They had him wired up to machines that beeped and spit, they had his arm strapped to a chair.

"I'm all right," Johnny said when he saw her. She stopped, uncertainly, in the middle of the room.

"What's going on?"

The man in the garage was behind her, and two men came at her from the side. They were all dressed in white jumpsuits, with ties showing through their zippered fronts. "We're from the collection agency," one man said. "For unlawful theft of electricity."

"We don't need to *pay* for electricity," she said. "We only use our own."

"Ha," he said. "You don't own it. You're just stealing it and not paying for it. You know what? We put meters into and out of your apartment, just to make sure. You were off the charts! We could hear the volts clicking! Don't tell me you're not using electricity!"

"I tried to explain—" Johnny said wearily.

"Did you plug into him yet?" Cheree interrupted. "Then you'll see." She looked around and picked up a small calculator on a desk, plugging it into Johnny's socket. It whirred on, but the jumpsuits looked impassive. She began to enter numbers faster and faster, until finally she rang up Total. "See?" she said, as the men stepped forward almost politely, glancing at the strip of paper (who had such old calculators, anyway?) that had curled out the top.

"Nice," the second man concluded. He reached into his pocket. "I'm not with them," he said. "I'm with NASA and we think you might have stolen a restricted project. We're going to have to take you with us for national security." He offered his card.

"Hold on there," said the third man, "I'm with the Office of Ocean Exploration. You can't take him, see here—I've got a signed order to bring him in for questioning." He shook his head. "I mean it's an invitation. We admire the strides he's made in making a self-sustaining renewable resource." He gave a business card to Johnny and one to Cheree.

The first man took out a gun. "He's not going anywhere. He's been taking electricity and we *own* electricity. It's that simple. You can't take him because he's going to jail, our own facilities in a state-approved housing unit until his case comes to trial."

Johnny hung his head and groaned. "I'm no use to any of you," he said. "These fiber-optic hairs—they're no use underwater, you know—they need the sun to recharge. Totally useless." The NOAA man looked a little annoyed at that, but he said, "Who said you had to be *under* the water; maybe they want you *on top* of the water?" but even he looked skeptical.

"Plus, he's on a pacemaker," Cheree said. "You can't have a pacemaker in orbit, if that's what you were thinking. You'd kill him; what good would that be?"

The electric company man was looking increasingly smug. "That leaves me," he said with a smile. "And all I want is for the bill to be paid. Plus interest and penalties."

"There is no bill," Johnny said wearily. "We canceled our account months ago. No account, no bills."

"That's not how it works. You think electricity is free? Like air? Like water? Like land? Are any of those free?" He waved Cheree aside as she said, "Air! Air is free!"

"Nothing's free," he said. "The factories pay us for the air they pollute, and you have to pay for cleaning it—one way or another, someone's paying for it. As for electricity, that's never been free since Franklin put a key on a chain. Right now, you're stealing our business by interfering with a regulated industry without a license. It's against the law." He looked very merry about it. "I lied about our state-sanctioned facilities. You just go to jail, same as the scammers and the knockoff artists, and you can light your hair up all you want and see what it gets you!" He laughed then, thinking about the possible results.

"And you agree with this?" Cheree asked the men from NASA and NOAA. They looked at each other and shrugged. "Nothing in it for us," one said. "We don't interfere in the private sector," said the other.

"Then it's just you," Cheree said to the last man, who looked at the others with contempt.

"It's okay," he said, reaching into his pocket. "I'm a reasonable man." He held out a taser gun. "And this is a perfectly legal means of protecting myself."

Cheree looked at it and grinned. She glanced up and saw Johnny's face. "Johnny Volts," she said, cooing to him. "Johnny, sing to me!"

Johnny began to hum, and she decided to join him, sympathetically. The men in jumpsuits felt the hairs on their necks begin to rise, then their leg hairs, then their head hairs. The man from the electric company looked around wildly, then took a step toward Johnny, his taser outstretched.

The taser suddenly snapped and shot a small series of electric arcs out into the air until the utilities man yelped and dropped it. Cheree released Johnny, who rose from his seat and said, "Sorry. But there was a buildup. And Cheree is an amplifier. And I think I got a shot of adrenaline or something that caused an overload."

The other two men looked at each other. "Time to go, I think," one said and the other nodded. They walked off together slowly, as if not wanting to make a sudden move.

"I'm really sorry," Johnny said to the man writhing on the floor.

"If I could get up I'd clobber you," the energy man said. "This isn't over. I'll hunt you down and do something." He panted. "Just as soon as I can move again."

• • • •

They followed the mad scientist down to Mexico, all of them imagining the utilities man hot on their trail. Even Tijuana seemed unsafe, so the mad scientist took them to a small town in the mountains, where he continued his work.

He gave Cheree a pacer, too, and he linked their charge, which was now big enough to fire a microwave, if there'd been a microwave around. But they had a bigger plan. In their mad dash down to the border they'd seen how much gasoline cost; wasn't Johnny the wave of the future and the future's savior? And wouldn't the mad scientist get rewards and jobs and money up the wazoo if he could find a way to recharge a car without looking for an outlet?

He plugged Johnny into the car he rigged up and called it the Voltswagon. Johnny could only get it to move slowly at first; but once the mad scientist hooked up Cheree to Johnny, and Johnny to the car, they were able to whiz to Tijuana and back at a merry clip. It took four years, but the cars ran and Johnny and Cheree were unharmed, and the mad scientist refined the recharging process to accommodate one person for one car.

Little by little they converted the inhabitants of Tijuana to fiber-optic hair and plug-in Voltswagons. Big Oil shut down the borders to keep Americans from going to Mexico to buy cars, but late at night, and hidden in the back of trucks, Americans snuck across the border to buy their Voltswagons and bring them home.

CHRISTIAN KIRTCHEV

FILE: THE DEATH OF DESIGNER D.

(2009)

THE DESIGNER D. had killed herself on 29 August 2004. The mystery around the suicide—or murder—is still not solved, but next to the body her boyfriend had found some "last" messages. Unclear if sent or not, they were an e-mail message and a few random digital photos. What killed D.? Was it really a suicide?

In the last few months, she didn't get along well with many of her people and even avoided contact with her closest girlfriends and old friends. On one of the found photos, D. was holding a cigarette, sitting on a tattered sofa in the attic room of a private building behind the Gallery of Arts. On another picture, there was her ex-ex-lover, whom a girlfriend of hers had warned that he would fuck her, most likely when drunk, then dump her. In the text of the left letter could be read the following short paragraph:

> . . . because our system is so chaotic and confused, that there's not even a system at all to confront with—everything is chaos. In the parliament there are parties and politicians which don't know where to lead the country to. There's no order. All is an empty signature field for something that I don't know whether to stand for or against . . . this is political, a social fight. My fellow citizens are in a big portion just ferocious, enraged, or pusillanimous and primitive—so much that if it wasn't for the peasants that make me go mad for their aggression and simplicity, there would be

the colleagues who bring their primal aggression to the office, along with their ties and gray lemmings suits, to again protect the stupidity of fighting for survival. This fight is false; little are the people who, like me, would support life, the pure life and none are those who would fight to save the feelings of another. In this cold world, I would die, if . . .

On the floor where they found the body of the philosophy student and political adventurer, designer D., there was an old, crumpled newspaper in which she rolled the joint that some of her guests smoked in that loft. On the front page, in a side column for weekly news, there was the story of how all the governments of the world had joined around the new law, which four years ago absolutely forbid the use of natural fur for the production of clothing. With that same law, police increased their powers to arrest and detain any citizen found wearing clothes made of leather or fur. All affected manufacturing plants were obliged to transform themselves into producers of coats made of synthetic polyurethane or other high-tech materials. Not a single man in the world would want a coat made of leather or animal fur, and now he wouldn't be an outlaw for that.

A simultaneously passed law also forbade the manufacture of items for which wood is used; so, all manufacturers in the world made the transition to synthetics during the twenty-first century, and nations all over the planet welcomed this governmental decision to protect the available flora and fauna. There was just one more decision to be made—for the meat produce—and that wasn't far off. In Bulgaria, though, as well as in many other places in the world, the law was just theoretical and only observed by those who couldn't afford to buy a corrupt judge; thus, just as with car traffic, those who are outlaws are the poor. It was unlikely for this to be the only reason for D. to end her life, but many of those who knew her personally would interpret her psyche in a specific way; they themselves didn't understand D. completely, and that's what justified their helplessness to participate in her life.

The question about the mysterious murder remained unsolved, even for her closest friend, the one whom she loved. She was too busy, nervous, and preoccupied with avoiding society to be able to answer his love, but still she understood him. K. examined the left-behind digital pictures and e-mail, then called the police. He was the first one to enter her lodging room after the suicide, thus he started dialing numbers to find out if the designer D. had spoken with someone before her death.

On February 28, she had a fight with her sister during an intimate meeting over coffee. Her employer had refused to pay cash in advance for her salary, which was a source of great irritation for her. D.'s sister needs medicine but doesn't have the money to buy it, so she doesn't read the newspaper or the electronics from the advertisement pages between the news in the papers.

"The main misery of the little mediocre people," D. used to say, "is that the model of life, which corporations dictate through media and advertisement, makes you want to want things—mostly electronic things, which, in contemporary life, are associated not that much with prestige, but with necessity. And when you cannot afford to own these 'basic' items associated with necessity, you buy alcohol, drugs, and the latest model of the cheapest DVD that breaks down and brings you the 'Disease.'"

This "Disease"—as D. calls it—is, for most people, the aim for the most basic attainment of ownership: to work for products of civilization (i.e., the corporation), meaning that food becomes a second-place necessity. Also, for you to be happy involves not listening to music, but listening to it on the latest model device. Maybe from a zoological point of view on people and animals, this would have been a sickness, a state of disease; the designer D. felt guilty, though, because she was the designer of advertisements and ergonomics for those very same products that brought people to psychic and physical illness, as well as material madness.

K. knew that, and many times he tried to convince D. that this was just the way life is, that this was the system—the world people really wanted. Even though he couldn't console her, at least he managed to bring her peace for a little while in the beginning. The escalation of the problem, though, was leading designer D. toward madness. Could it be that she had angered someone from the corporate structures for which she worked as freelance contractor? Could it be they had ordered her . . . death?

To produce advertisements for an illness—with skills you can't otherwise use if you want to have a job at all—wasn't looking that bad for those already affected by the disease; for D., though, this was a road to madness. Depressed with thoughts that if she drew designs, composed music, or edited films she wouldn't be able to make a living—D. just kept on forcing herself to produce advertisements and charming designs for products that tempted and inspired people. She believed that she assisted in lying that it was not madness, but rather the most natural state of existence is to own products, and the most beautiful way to live is to participate in the consumer's cult. Those weren't cheap products; the cheap ones were prone to break easily. The expensive products made those men and women who didn't belong to the corporate apparatus get poorer. The world was divided into two parts: sick and healthy, corporate citizens and free radicals, and even the free radicals—who weren't affected by the sickness enslaving the corporate consumers—still needed "things" to survive in the predominant part of society, a society that demanded either participation or death.

In the letter that designer D. left behind, she mentioned that in Bulgaria there doesn't exist a system against which one can rebel. The chaos in the parliament had placed her in an even bigger state of confusion, while the impasse oppressed her slowly and drove her out of the society of peasants and primitive citizens.

The police had found the revolver in D.'s hand with one pinned, fired cartridge in the chamber, but K. still wasn't convinced it was a suicide. True, D. was very distanced and desperate in the last few weeks, but still she held out hope that the world would change.

"No, I don't want the world to change! I know that my values are humane. I'm not ill with the sickness of materialism and consumerism, but I feel that the disease starts to possess me, as I live in a world which cannot be different. A world modeled by powers abusing our basic instincts and wants. People made their choice to become what they are—alone. But I believe this is meant to be just a transition, a difficult transformation through a period beyond which everyone will be a better self."

Designer D. didn't want to believe that she was the sick one and that those who turned their backs on humane values were the healthy. Our world may have been such that D. was placed in a state of describing herself as an abnormal outsider—but not in her country! In Bulgaria, there wasn't any sort of regime—or so she thought; the whole system of the country is messed up, but in this exact detail was hidden the secret: the feature of imported culture is to influence, taking advantage of all uncertainty in Bulgaria. And, when there is not order in your country, the first to impose order gets the right to enforce veto on all future decisions. A sterile ecology and consumerism ideology: the universal combination of ideal conditions for physical existence in a clean world with the imposed psychological values dictated by product manufacturers. All products made equal by importance with the basic necessities in life such as air, water, and food. D. had the understanding for that, and she would often talk about her feelings on the subject when she sought the comfort of her friends.

Maybe the corporate structures knew about D. Or perhaps the fight with her sister—could that have been the reason for a murder? A murder made by someone sick, a murder targeting the only one seen as the cure to narcotic dependence?

While looking at the photos, K. had an urge to delete them, but in the twilight of the room, while he was waiting for the police detectives—and eventually emergency services—to arrive, K. could only sit by the phone and stare through the window toward the tops of the gallery's towers.

Why did the young designer D. kill herself? A fight with her boss? Her sister gone mad and shooting her, then placing the gun in her hand? All of us—one way or another—felt what D. was feeling, but she couldn't distance herself from that, she wouldn't want to close her senses, nor accept them. Many like the system as it is, without approving it; a world inside the world, in the isolation of their own sphere of friends and relatives, without direct links. But D. had to work in this system, to be a part of the regime that she hated for two years before severing all links to reality, giving herself over to drinking Absinth and watching the display of her creative console.

At that moment, K. didn't know whether he loved or hated her. Most likely, he hated her, but a very slight thought that she was possibly murdered made him look with respect toward the body, the scattered digital photos, and the electronic mail message next to the bloody revolver. Was the shot fired during the night, or the day?

JEAN RABE

BETTER THAN

(2010)

MOSES LOVED THE NIGHT. Not because he could see better in it—which he could due to various enhancements in his cybereyes—but because that was when the snakes crawled out onto the sidewalks.

Moses loved to watch the snakes.

Pink, grass-green, blue, Day-Glo yellow, purple, they slithered into the low spots still filled with rainwater from the late afternoon deluge. They shimmied into splotches of beer and butted up against pretzel pieces puked from the drunkards tossed out of bars along Western Avenue. They slipped into puddles of piss provided by Seattle's vagrants.

Reflections from the neon signs was all they were, so his chummer Taddeus had said.

But Moses thought they looked like real snakes—beautiful, colorful, electric, eclectic, squirming, mesmerizing, fireworks-come-to-ground-just-for-his-very-own-pleasure snakes.

He stood on the corner of Western and Seneca, eyes locked onto a thick cherry-and-grape-striped snake that twisted seductively in the water pooled between his size-eleven feet. He liked this city because it rained almost every day.

The snakes only came out for the water.

"And the child grew, and she brought him unto Pharaoh's daughter, and he became her son. And she called his name Moses: and she said, Because I drew him out of the water." Moses liked that particular Exodus quote because of the water part. His father was a minister in Renton, a fire-and-brimstone Baptist . . . or was that Lutheran . . . who'd named all his children after significant folks from the Bible. Ruth was the oldest, followed by Jacob, Abraham, and Isaac. Moses was the youngest, and the only one who'd remained wholly human. Father said it was a sign that Moses was destined for great things. Moses thought it was a curse. He didn't have his sister's naturally keen hearing or Isaac's tough skin. He didn't have Abraham's fine-looking tusks or Jacob's affinity for magic.

So he had to turn to tech to compensate. And tech was damn expensive.

He touched the tip of his boot to the pool, sending out a ripple that made the cherry-grape snake dance.

The snake had crept down from the overhead neon sign advertising *Live Nude Dancing Elves*. Moses idly wondered if any place advertised dead ones. He tapped his foot and the snake wriggled faster.

Moses hadn't given the snakes much thought until a handful of months past. That's when the microscopic vision subsystem implanted in his cybereyes malfunctioned. The series of minute optical lenses, designed to magnify objects up to a thousand times their normal size, splintered during a fight with a trog razorguy. Moses, who'd emerged battered but victorious, had been on a run with Taddeus and a few others into the Barrens, and they didn't pull enough nuyen from the job to get his lenses replaced. Didn't matter—he was kind of glad he hadn't, as rather than magnify the snakes they now enhanced their color and sometimes spun pieces of them away like one of those toy kaleidoscopes kids looked into. The cracked lenses made the snakes breathe, too—Moses saw their sides moving in and out, and when he cocked his head just right, as he was doing now, he could see their tongues flicker from between their invisible fangs to taste whatever interesting things were in the water.

In fact, Moses hadn't realized Seattle's sidewalks had snakes until the lenses cracked.

"Move it!" This came from a muscle-bound troll who cursed and stepped off the curb to get around Moses. "Go stand somewhere else, you ugly vatjob!"

Moses flicked his tail at the oaf, but the troll was quick, already on his way down the street. Moses liked his tail—it was one of his favorite modifications. A meter and a half long, covered with tiny lizard-like scales with mirrored surfaces, it had a built-in light at the end that he sometimes read by. It was one of those balance tails, weighted and grafted onto the base of his spine and keyed to a processor that monitored his center of gravity.

He'd gotten his shaped dermal plating at the same place he'd bought the tail—from his trusted ripper doc. Paid almost full price for the plating and had it stylized with ridges at the elbows, bumps across his forehead for the heck of it, and made to look like he had great abs and a broad chest.

Made him look better than human.

It was decorated just above his heart—not with tribal art or hieroglyphs like most favored—but with "EXD 3:6" in reference to the Bible verse: "Moreover he said, I am the God of thy father, the God of Abraham, the God of Isaac, and the God of Jacob. And Moses hid his face; for he was afraid to look upon God."

Moses hadn't been able to find a verse that at the same time mentioned Ruth, but then she had a whole book devoted to her.

He had Doc add a wet sheath over the top of the plating some months ago, save for the spot on the chest with EXD 3:6 on it. It was a variant of a dermal, but modified to feel cool and slippery, sexy, glistening . . . sort of like snakeskin.

The cherry-grape snake writhed faster as Moses continued to stare. The sheath was great because thugs had a hard time grabbing onto him. He'd tried to get a chameleon modification with it, but Doc said combining those features was a few years away. So he settled for adding a near-meter-long head of fiber-optic hair, bright orange with a cascading effect of yellow and red at the tips to make it look like fire. Because he styled it often, it was wearing a little thin in places and a few sections needed to be replaced.

That's why Moses had come down here tonight . . . to get some nuyen to pay for more hair and some other enhancements. He had his heart set on getting some horn implants. He'd been fitted a year or so ago for bull horns, but decided they were a little too big, and too expensive. Last week he'd put some second-hand goat horns on layaway, at the same place he'd get the hair replacements—from his trusted ripper doc. Bright, white horns with a mother-of-pearl glaze—fixed implants, as the retractable ones were a little out of his price range. Doc promised the horns wouldn't itch.

Some of Moses's other implants did, and scratching them in public had gotten him banned from more than one establishment. The penile implant was the worst, with its mentally controlled gel reservoirs and synthetic skin that he had some sort of allergic reaction to. He hoped he could remember to ask Doc for some more ointment for the rash.

"Nuyen," he said. "Came down here to get me some." He repeated "nuyen" until it became a mantra that twisted in time with the cherry-grape snake. "Nuyen for the tech-fix."

"What's he starin' at, ya think?" The speaker was an elf, a live one, but she wasn't nude or dancing. She was wearing a sand-colored plastic dress that crinkled when she crossed her arms in front of her probably enhanced chest.

"The puddle. Maybe he lost something in it." Her companion was also an elf, face painted garishly and lips three times any natural size. "Didja lose something in it, mister?"

"Lose? Lose yourself. Get lost," Moses said. They stood too close to the water and made it harder to see the snake. He heard the sand-colored dress crinkle as the pair strolled away. The snake could swim freely now.

An ork peddler walked by, selling hot soyjerky. Passersby commented on the spicy smell. Moses couldn't smell it. He couldn't smell anything.

Moses had a direct neural interface connected wirelessly to the various built-in computers nested in the implants that allowed diagnostics checks—and said checks told him several things were either malfunctioning or were overdue for maintenance . . . his failed nasal receptors for example. They'd been out of whack for the past eighteen . . . or was that eighty . . . months. His enhanced taste buds didn't register anything either. He could be eating . . . well, pretty much anything . . . and not hurk it back up because of the taste. He only ate to keep his strength up and because his super thyroid implant demanded it.

"Should get 'em fixed," he said. "Maybe."

He'd need a lot of nuyen for the repairs. He had Kevlar bone-lacing with RFID sensor tags, a blood circuit control system, and a datajack engraved with elaborate Japanese *kanji*-signs he couldn't read . . . it was a used model, and so he hadn't been picky.

"Nuyen," he said. "Sashayed down here to get me some."

The encephalon he went under the knife for six or so months back hadn't helped. Hardwired into Moses's brain, it was supposed to boost his information-processing. It only seemed to scramble things now. At least the math subprocessor unit whirred along without a problem; he could calculate rent and utilities in a nanosecond, and it doubled as an alarm clock. His internal GPS worked without a proverbial hitch, too. It's how he found his way to this corner without making a single wrong turn. Too bad he hadn't thought to load his sister's address into it. What was her name? Ruth. Yeah, that was it.

"Ruth. Nuyen. Nuyen. Nuyen."

The radar sensor was another matter. It was supposed to emit terahertz and ultrawide-band radar in frequency pulses, analyzing Doppler and bounced signals. It never had worked right—another piece of used equipment he probably shouldn't have had installed without first asking Doc for some sort of warranty. At least it functioned as a motion detector, except that it never registered the snakes. He'd remember to ask Doc for a warranty on the pearlized goat horns.

Once more he thought about taking what little nuyen he had stashed away—coupled with what he was going to score tonight—and spending it on repairs to his existing systems. But he really wanted the goat horns, and he was being good by repairing at least one of the enhancements—his fiber-optic 'do. Besides, if he spent all his nuyen on repairs, he'd never be able to afford the cyberfins he'd been thinking about. Saw an advertisement for them a couple of days back . . . or was that a couple of weeks . . . or months?

His memory played tricks sometimes.

"Nuyen," he said. "Came down here to get me some."

His regular ripper doc could implant the webbing between his fingers and toes so he could manage the butterfly and backstroke in record time. Of course, Moses knew he'd have to take swimming lessons first.

The two elves returned, the sand-colored plastic crinkling a little louder.

"Geese," Moses pronounced them. It was the right neighborhood for hookers. The women were looking for someone to dock with—for nuyen, naturally—their gander probably somewhere close by for safety. Moses wouldn't mind docking with the one with the overlarge lips, but he needed to save his cred for the hair replacement and the fins . . . and to fix something. What attachment was he going to repair? Besides, his father had taught him to stay away from those kinds of women. They were sinful. Moses was SIN-less.

" 'And the Lord said unto Moses, Behold, thou shalt sleep with the fathers;

and his people will rise up, and go a whoring after the gods of the strangers of the land, whither thy go to be among them, and will forsake me, and break my covenant which I have made with them.' Deuteronomy, chapter thirty-one, verse sixteen."

"Talking all Biblical. Still looking in the puddle, he is," big lips said. "Yo, Clint." She sidled up to Moses. "You interested in a little whoring, maybe we—"

"Get lost," Moses said.

"S'matter, don't like elves?"

"Live nude dancing elves," Moses said, looking up at the sign again.

Big lips shuddered and swayed down the street, arm-in-arm with plastic dress.

"Tadd would've spent his nuyen on them geese." Moses missed his old chummer.

The last time they were together Taddeus told Moses he didn't discriminate enough, that he bought preowned cyberware on the black market when he should be shopping at legitimate places. "The legal clinics won't deal with the stuff you're putting in your brain," Taddeus had said. "Who knows where that stuff came from? I oughta turn your doc into the authorities." Tadd said other things, too, but Moses hadn't had his data filter turned on, and so could only remember a few sentences.

Ripper docs, shadowclinics, Taddeus wouldn't have anything to do with them, Moses knew. But then Taddeus didn't have near the modifications as Moses. Taddeus wasn't quite better-than-human. Tadd was still mostly human. Moses had been better-than-human for several years.

"Nuyen. Nuyen. Nuyen."

He liked his ripper doc 'cause he could pick up modifications that weren't exactly legal, and he never had to supply an ID or SIN. And it wasn't like he had these things done in a back-alley filth parlor with half-used, unsterilized medkits at the ready in the case of accidents. It wasn't technically a black clinic or a body bank. His doc had a real medical degree and operated out of the basement of a tattoo parlor, a real high-end underground clinic. Moses had done his research before going under the knife. Doc hadn't had his license pulled for any of the usual reasons—too many malpractice cases or amputating the wrong limb. He'd simply experimented a few times on a few unwitting and later protesting patients . . . and got caught. Moses wasn't unwitting; he underwent each modification with both insect-like compound cybereyes wide open, and he didn't care when Doc suggested a little muscle doping now and then or a little trial genetic infusion.

And Doc was a real ecologist, as green as they came. He believed in recycling— bioware implants, nanoware, cyberware, augmented limbs. Because Moses bought most of his stuff secondhand from Doc, he could afford the integration system for all his simsense and networking devices and the bundle of skillwires with multi-functionality. He wouldn't have been able to buy tricked-out cyberears if they'd come right off the assembly line.

Moses thought he might ask Doc if those ears could be tweaked just a bit, so he could hear the snakes. The cherry-grape one might have some juicy secrets to share. He glanced back down at the puddle. Yep, the snake was still there.

Doc was good at providing discount prescriptions. Moses had to take three . . . or was that four . . . pills a day to stave off biosystem overstress, and another couple pills to treat his temporal lobe epilepsy. The latter malady was an acceptable side effect of having so many cyber implants. Doc said the condition was chronic and degenerative and that if it got much worse Moses would need corrective gene therapy or maybe a little brain surgery. If Doc was going to go back in Moses's brain, maybe he could finesse something with the memory center or some such. Moses really wanted to remember his sister's address.

Taddeus had called Moses an aug-ad, an augmentation addict, and said he wouldn't go on any more runs with him until he got his head straightened out. Moses figured Tadd just didn't understand about not being satisfied with being human. Moses was almost there . . . satisfied . . . but not quite. He just needed a few more adjustments. He had mood swings because he wasn't quite happy with things the way they were now. Sure, he was better-than-human, but he could stand to be a little bit better than simply better-than. Tadd was probably just pissed about the mood swings. He'd be back. Him and the others would come crawling to Moses for help on another dip into the shadows.

Crawling, like the cherry-grape snake was crawling. Moses watched it slither to another puddle. He followed it.

"Gotta go this direction anyway," he said. "Up the hill." His internal GPS told him he had two more blocks to go, all uphill. "And the Lord said unto Moses, 'Get thee up into this mount, and see the land which I have given unto the children of Israel.' "

Two more blocks up, around the corner, and then down an alley and he'd have plenty of nuyen for the hair and the swim fins and . . . what was he going to have fixed? His fang implants? Only one of those had snapped off.

"Two more blocks for the nuyen."

The snake obliged him, slithering along as if a guide, though a few storefronts later it changed color, turning yellow now, and then green. When it split in two and turned sky blue, Moses realized it wasn't the same snake, and it wasn't nearly as pretty. He'd go back and find the cherry-grape one later, after he scored his nuyen.

One more block. "Just one more, and what—"

Just short of the next corner Moses saw the rude troll who'd called him a vatjob. He was leaning over a human woman sporting rabbit ears and a fox tail, vulching her, maybe hitting her up for drugs or nuyen or . . .

"Oh, it's the vatjob." The troll turned to face Moses and stuck out his jaw to look menacing. He had a submachine gun in his right hand, barrel pointed at the pavement. The other passersby on the sidewalk gave him a wide berth. "Mind your own business. Bit-brain bakebrain whackjob nutjob vatjob." The twin blue snakes cavorted around the troll's big sandaled feet.

Moses cleared his throat: "And it came to pass in those days, when Moses was grown, that he went out unto his brethren, and looked on their burdens: and he spied an Egyptian smiting a human . . . er Hebrew, one of his brethren. Exodus two-eleven."

"Definitely a nutjob vatjob." A line of drool spilled over the troll's lower lip and extended to the pavement, striking the head of one of the blue snakes and sending Moses's temper flaring. "This is between me and Foxy Foxtail, so move it." The troll raised the gun in threat.

"And he looked this way and that way, and when he saw that there was no man, he slew the Egyptian, and hid him in the sand. Exodus two-twelve."

"What are you talking about you—"

"King James Version." Moses's wired reflexes kicked in and he bent and pulled a combat knife from a sheath in his boot and hurled it using all the strength in his synthetic cyberarm. *Should have been wearing body armor,* Moses thought as the troll dropped to his knees. The troll shouldn't have relied only on a secure long coat that he hadn't even bothered to button. Moses threw a second knife from the other boot, finishing him.

"And he killed it," he quoted. "And Moses sprinkled the blood upon the altar round about. And he cut the ram . . . err, troll . . . into pieces; and Moses burnt the head, and the pieces and the fat. Leviticus eight-nineteen and twenty."

The fox-tailed human squealed and sprinted across the street, leaving Moses to stare at the twin blue snakes undulating in the spreading troll blood.

A lone goose in a barely-there skirt screamed and drew Moses's attention away from the snakes.

"Nuyen," Moses said. "Nuyen. Nuyen. Nuyen. Came down here to get me some." He kicked the submachine gun away. Moses didn't care for guns. Sure, he could use them, and he had a smartlink for a heavy pistol he had lost on a corp run. But he preferred knives because they didn't make as much noise. He turned the troll over and retrieved his knives. He shoved them back in the boot sheathes, more worried about speed than the blood, and rifled through the troll's pockets as gawkers came to stand over him. "A credstick. Good. Got me some nuyen I wasn't expecting. Not a whole lot on it, though."

"It's the puddle guy." The goose in the crinkly dress was back.

Couldn't she find someone to dock with? Moses wondered. *She's pretty enough. Maybe she ought to lower her price.*

He slapped the side of his head with his palm, rattling the GPS just enough to get him back on track. "Around the corner. Down the alley," he said. "Later," he told the elf-geese. Then he was gone, his wired reflexes giving him a boost of speed that took him around the edge of the all-night pharmacy, down half a block and into the alley. He didn't hear any sirens, but he figured sooner or later someone would call about the troll bleeding out on the sidewalk. It had been self-defense, hadn't it? The troll had been carrying a gun, after all.

There weren't any snakes at the mouth of the alley. There was plenty of water for them, as Moses sloshed through one puddle after the next as he made his way around trash receptacles sitting outside the backdoors of bars, sex shops, and diners. But there weren't any neon signs, and it was the signs that gave birth to the best snakes. Moses felt better when there were snakes around. Moses was supposed to have snakes.

"Exodus four-three and four," Moses said. Why was it he could remember the Bible verses so easy but not the color of the whatever-it-was he had on layaway with Doc? "And he said, 'Cast it on the ground.' And he cast it on the ground, and it became a serpent; and Moses fled from before it. And the Lord said unto Moses, 'Put forth thine hand, and take it by the tail.' And he put forth his hand, and caught it, and it became a rod in his hand." He sucked in a deep breath and went farther down the alley. "Thy rod and thy staff, they comfort me."

A cat hissed and shot in front of him, disappearing behind crates stacked at a barber's back door.

"Hurry with this," Moses told himself. He wanted to get the nuyen and get back out on the street. Find that cherry-grape snake again and ogle it a little longer before he visited Doc and had . . . what was that he was going to the clinic for? "Hair." He was pleased that he remembered that. "Hair and—" Hair and something else. He'd put his mind to it after this was over. Put his head to it. "Head. Head. Head."

Moses scratched the bumps above his eyes and brightened. "And he put the mitre upon his head; also upon the mitre, even upon his forefront, did he put the golden plate, the holy crown; as the lord commanded Moses. Leviticus eight-nine."

What was his sister's address? Eight Nine something. Ruth, right? Yeah, Ruth. Wither-though-goest-Ruth.

Halfway down the alley, that's where the GPS tugged him.

"Didja bring the nuyen?"

Moses stopped, peering into the shadows, insect-like compound cybereyes separating the grays and blacks and finding the man . . . dwarf . . . thickset, grubby-looking. They all were dirty-looking, the ones who dealt in these sorts of things.

"Did you bring the beetles?" Moses returned.

The dwarf stepped away from the wall.

And the good ones were rich.

"Nuyen. Nuyen. Nuyen," Moses whispered. His ears whirred and clicked, picking up the dwarf's heartbeat and the slow slap of his shoes in the puddles sadly devoid of snakes. Moses needed snakes. Picking up the dwarf's breathing. Insect-like compound cybereyes with heat-sensors finding the dwarf, finding rats scurrying along in either direction, finding garbage piled up outside the back door of a Chinese restaurant, finding things he didn't want to get too close a look at. Finding nothing else.

For once, Moses was glad he couldn't smell anything.

"Did you bring the beetles?" Moses repeated. He heard the faintest of whirring and clicks. The dwarf was checking him out, too. "I'm alone. No guns."

"I know."

"The beetles." Moses added a hint of desperation to his voice, like he was a junkie in desperate need of a fix. He was, but not for the beetles. He remembered the goat horns he had on layaway. If he didn't pay them off and get them installed soon, he'd lose his deposit. "Did you bring the beetles?"

"Better than life," the dwarf cooed, stepping closer.

"Better than human," Moses said, thinking about the horns and the fins and echolocation bioware and maybe some extended volume for his lungs and elastic joints for his knees.

"Better than anything," the dwarf said. "Yeah, I have beetles. You have nuyen?"

Moses pulled out the troll's credstick. Good thing he'd run into the troll. He'd forgotten his meager credstick back at his place. He hadn't forgotten it the last time he pulled this stunt, or the time before that or before that. Had to have a credstick to make them think you were actually buying something. Had to have the black-market contacts to get the names and locations of beetle-sellers. Better-than-life chips were still illegal, and you couldn't buy them just anywhere. He didn't want the chips, just the credsticks the beetle-seller would have on him. It was a theft that would never be reported. Moses had done this a dozen times. Or was that two dozen?

"Yeah, I got the nuyen. Let's see the chips first." Moses waved the stick higher. He knew the dwarf had some sort of enhanced vision that would let him pick out the details. "Why don't you—"

The back door of one of the bars opened, spilling sickly-yellow light out into the alley and reflecting off the puddles. Moses caught a glimpse of a snake, but it wasn't a pretty one. Only neon bred the pretty ones. He tried to look away, but it *was* a snake, and Moses was supposed to have snakes, wasn't he? Maybe if he cocked his head he could see it breathe. Maybe if—

The dwarf barreled into him, fist slamming into his stomach, plating absorbing it, but the momentum sending him back. Moses's tail lashed out, whipping around the dwarf's muscular forearm. It was a cyberlimb, all metal, no flesh, fingers ungodly strong and grabbing at the tail, squeezing, breaking some of the mirrored scales.

"Damn you!" Moses cursed. He couldn't afford to have the tail fixed, not with all the other plans for modifications. Not unless the dwarf had lots and lots of nuyen for selling beetles. Moses's bone lacing made him strong, and he used that might now to bull-rush the dwarf, bringing his knee up into the smaller man's chest, pushing him down into the puddle to smother the ugly, yellow snake.

The dwarf had dermal plating, too. So Moses changed his tactics, pounding his fists against the dwarf's wide, ruddy face.

Voices intruded, maybe the man who'd opened the back door and birthed the ugly snake. Someone with him, voices panicked at what was transpiring in their alley. *Make it fast,* Moses thought. *Don't need someone calling Lone Star.* Not that he was doing anything illegal. This was self-defense. The dwarf started it. Moses just intended to finish it.

"And Moses said unto the Lord in Exodus four-ten, 'O my Lord, I am not eloquent, neither heretofore, nor since thou hast spoken unto thy servant; but I am slow of speech, and slow of tongue.' But let me be fast of fist. Let my wired reflexes fly."

Moses pounded harder until he heard bone *crunch*. The dwarf didn't intend to just stay down and die, though, struggling frantically to reach something at his side, succeeding, and pulling free a heavy pistol that he shoved up against Moses's side. The dwarf fired three times, the first two bouncing off the dermal, but the third punching a hole in the plating and sending a round deep inside.

Moses registered the pain, but shoved it to the back of his mind and continued to pound, listening to voices spilling out in the alley, listening to the dwarf curse, and hearing another round fire and find its way inside. Then he heard the dwarf cough and felt blood spit up against his face and onto his lips. Good thing he couldn't taste. Dwarf blood would probably taste bad.

The dwarf heaved once beneath him, and then fell still. Moses dug through his pockets, finding credstick after credstick after credstick. Twenty-five of them—his math subprocessor unit counted things instantly. The proverbial motherload. He shoved them in his own pockets. They wouldn't all fit, so he stuffed the extras in his kangaroo pouch, which had been a handy modification. Then he pushed off the ground, one hand pressed against his wounded side.

The voices came closer, accompanied by feet slapping through puddles filled with ugly yellow snakes. The back door to the bar was propped open wide and sickly light poured out.

"Are you hurt?"

"Who are you?"

"What happened?"

There were more questions from the quintet of barmaids and bartenders. Moses ignored them all and whacked his free palm against the side of his head, kicking in the GPS and tugging him back out the alley, onto the sidewalk and around the corner of the all-night pharmacy.

Maybe I should go in the pharmacy, he thought. *Buy some painkillers and bandages.*

But Doc's wasn't terribly far away, five or six blocks tops. Doc could repair the damage from the dwarf's slugs, put him under for that and do some modifications and hair-grafting at the same time. He certainly had enough nuyen on all these credsticks. Get it all done at the same time. Had the dwarf shot up some of his computer interfaces? Were more systems damaged?

"Nuyen. Nuyen. Nuyen. Got me lots of that." Moses staggered up the street, past the body of the bled-out troll that was still lying on the curb, passersby walking around it. No sign of Foxy Foxtail, whom he had probably saved.

Lightning flickered high overhead, followed by a boom of thunder that drowned out the music spilling from bars and sex shops. *It would rain soon, thank the Lord,* Moses thought. Rain and fill the low spots so the snakes would have more room to swim.

He watched the snakes as he went, pushing himself between the throng out on the sidewalk, struggling to watch the snakes between all the feet. Bright blue, grass-green, violet, Day-Glo pink, chartreuse, they shimmied all along Western

Avenue. Moses followed the cherry-grape one, and with his free hand fingered one of the many credsticks in his pocket.

How had he gotten so many credsticks?

What was he going to spend them on?

Hair, he remembered hair. He came down here to get him some of that. Hair and . . . hair and . . . pearlized goat milk for his sister Ruth. *Intreat me not to leave thee, Ruth. Where thou lodgest, Ruth.*

"Where do you lodge?" Moses mused.

He'd deliver the milk tonight, if only he could remember her address.

JEFF NOON

GHOST CODES OF SPARKLETOWN (NEW MIX)

(2011)

Form is the host. Content is the virus. Infect, infect!

01

Break pops a rhythm tab: pure fever-zoom. No clocks, no maps. Only the taste of Dusk on his tongue, waiting for the night to roll in.

Bumps into Candy, standing by the X-Ray Parlor. Misty eyes, neon lip gloss, electric hair frazzle worked off a battery in her pocket.

She looks a charm, so corporeal it hurts. "Just checking out my veins," she says. "Making sure I'm clean, you know? Still alive."

"Candy, you wanna catch a bite?" A plastic sheet slides out the parlor slot showing off her lungs and heart and other organs. No shadows.

She blows a kiss and leaves. Break stands there frozen: he sure would like to own that X-Ray for a night or two. Total bliss-freak!

Down at his feet old transparency plates lie discarded. All he needs is to earn some credit, get himself reprogrammed, street style.

Maybe then the Real-Life Human Girls would love him. I mean, what's a young, well-dressed Synthetik Angel supposed to do these days?

02

Here find stories from a trash-diamond paradise, call it Sparkletown. A semi-abandoned housing project, fallout zone for the lost.

Shadow realm of ghosts, loners, artificial angels, lo-tech analogue freaks of varied shape, creed, and fashion. The new demo humans.

We move along streets where faces are lit by two seconds of electrostatic glow, burnt into memory. Then darkness, then rainfall.

Neon apparitions, figures of dust glimpsed in passing headlamps, voices in the air most nights, if you know how to listen for them.

03

Break went round to Dixie's with the discarded plates he'd picked up outside the X-Ray Parlor. They cut them into circles and used them to press the latest tunes.

They drove to the club. Dixie took over the booth, started playing. The crowd moved to the beats. Break watched the discs spinning.

It was a sight he never grew tired of, Dixie working the decks while damaged parts of the human body circled beneath her fingers . . .

Spinal columns, thigh bones, shoulder blades. Two skulls spinning at the same time, conjuring crazy bad thoughts out of the grooves.

The biggest thrill? The sight of two transparent hands, their smashed-up fingers and wrists all gray and ghostly on the X-ray plastic.

And Dixie's own hands, fully fleshed, moving above the two broken examples. The music floating upward from the mix like spirit smoke.

04

Dixie opened her eyes. Lying awake, she could hear the old songs moaning from the aerials of the long-shutdown pirate stations.

She got up, walked to the window. Sparkles of light flickered around the tower block. Phantom broadcasts, unknown frequencies.

Fragments of digital code: a word or two of lyrics, the stroke of a fingertip on metal string, human breath in curled brass tubes.

Moments of music cast adrift. Something had roused them this night: the darkness buzzed with flecks of data, many more than usual.

Dixie came alive watching them. Her eyes glittered, her fingers danced. Tomorrow she would go out early and catch some ghosts.

05

It goes like this: two years had gone by since the crash of the digital age, two years since the CPUs burned out *en masse*, simultaneously.

All the music of that era, the melodies people had composed, performed, recorded, coded into numbers . . . all this was lost, seemingly forever.

And then the first of the drifting spirits appeared: the scattered ghosts of pop stars, their final traces still caught in the ether.

At dusk you could listen to the strange music. You might glimpse a spectral glow in the air, tiny dancing sprites of color.

Sparkletown was a prime site; ghost collectors gathered there. A few got rich. Most went crazy. None lasted more than a few years on the task.

But some got so hooked into it, the spirits took them over completely. Now they wandered the alleyways without purpose, their half-dead mouths singing.

06

Gray light, fading moon. Dixie on slow walkabout, Break at her side. Other collectors were seen, working the streets. Let them be.

Break started to tremble. His skin was picking up traces, buzzing with sparks: evidence of spirit activity, serious measure.

He led Dixie to Hive 7, the worst of the blocks. Off limits, unsafe. Stories of demon songs haunting the rooms. A passageway beckoned.

Dixie went on ahead, alone. Into darkness. Silence. And then the crackle of melody, sparkle notes fluttering in minor key colors.

Listen now: held by rusty guitar strings, a woman's voice. Old, pitched low, a bleak moan. Murder ballad style. Dixie shivered.

She set the ghost trap and waited. The spirit flickered, sighing in darkness. Icy blue, fevered: something touched at Dixie's face.

07

Ghost trap components: contact mics, sugar cubes, matches, loudspeaker cone, glow-bug (female), cassette tape, AA batteries (leaky), perfume.

Operation: place glow-bug in speaker cone. Arrange mics in approximate circle. Set speaker to vibrate. Spray perfume on sugar: ignite.

The scent arouses the insect, causing the bug's abdomen to light up. Play cassette. Observe: the ghost will crackle and dance in time.

All such fragments dream of being whole once more, of being a favorite song on a lover's lips, conjured from a tongue: verse, chorus, and coda.

With such desire, the ghost is drawn toward the trap. Now softly, softly . . . close the lid . . .

Break dragged Dixie from the tunnel. Her eyes wide, face tight. "It's incredible!" Words of drawn-out breath: "Find it. Don't let her get away!"

08

Break entered the passageway, wondering what had got his boss so spooked. All was dark within but for his own skin gleaming. His fingers tingled.

A glint of color drew him forward. A cry. He felt he was stepping across a borderline. The sizzle of pain behind his eyes.

He'd heard other synthetiks boasting of the halo effect. Lies, mostly. He'd never seen it happen. Now he felt his temples pulsate.

It wasn't the full-on ignition he'd expected, more a flicker of sparks in a ragged lopsided orbit around his head. It was enough.

He peered into the homemade trap. There, held within the circle of microphones, suspended in midair . . . there lay the ghost.

It was a few centimeters across, of no fixed shape, crimson colored, speckled with gold, quiet now—a small broken spirit of music.

Break reached in and closed his hand around the prize. No burn. No anger. Only sorrow flooding his skull: pictures, sounds, memories.

09

The True History of the Synthetik Angels, as told by one of their kind. How, being eighteen and poor I sold my body to the dream merchants.

They clothed my skin with implants and programmed my skull with slogans. The system burned through me, taking me over completely.

I floated through the markets, a voice speaking only of the latest products. My implants sang and the air around me glowed with pictures.

I was a living advert, bought and sold many times over the next two years, my system hacked and pirated until I danced chaotic with thousands of images.

They called us Angels of Transmission. Messages moved through our bodies, into the world. And all was well until the Day of the Crash.

I recall the flare of overload, skin shock, implants sparking with static, adverts screaming inside me as luxury goods all around turned to dust.

And there I lay, alone and dying on the walkway of a shopping mall, all my golden images flickering dark one by one.

10

A Sparkletown morning. Low mist, pale sunlight. The two friends walked along. The trap was closed and bound, held between them.

They rode the elevator up to Dixie's floor. Break said, "I'm not sure about this. I saw things. This is no ordinary ghost."

Dixie nodded. No ordinary ghost, no ordinary song. She felt ill at ease. Cold, shivery from fear. But this was too good a chance.

They walked into the flat. Dixie said, "Let's get started." She clicked open the locks on the trap. Instruments glowed around her.

Break closed his eyes. His circuits were still buzzing from the vision he had picked up, from the moment of spectral contact.

He could see it still, in flashes of light: the singer's face creased in pain. Her mouth, screaming. Her two hands covered in blood.

11

They worked through the day on the new track. Break manned the grain web, Dixie worked the Dali engine, needle tip glistening.

They sprinkled sleeping powder on the ghost to keep it docile while they bled the plasma away. The vampyrophone collected the output.

Break caressed the machine's skin. Sparks hit him with radiance. Once more, he heard the singer crying out in pain, but softer now . . .

He said, "This is bad blues, Dixie. It's a chance recording. The woman being attacked or killed, mid-song. Or something. Maybe."

Dixie was too busy seeking out a melody path, stretching the lyrical scraps, squeezing home-made beats from a plastic tube. Like goo.

By 5:00 p.m. the track was done, conjured into being, sealed in X-ray wax. They listened to it in silence, sitting back, getting distance.

Dixie had cut the scream just so, leaving only a breath, indrawn. That moment of loss, repeating. Break felt his heart stop each time.

12

Dixie. Living artifact of the haunted tower blocks, collector of sparks. Magpie. Extractor of the original (still famous) blood song.

Breeder of glow-bugs. Lo-fi alchemist. Transformer of lives once lost, broken, ghosted, now mixed down into a vapor groove.

Mapper of the dawn mist, curator of fragments. Inventor of the vampyro-phone, the sleep trap, and other such homemade devices.

Dixie. Searcher of wastelands and canal-beds, where the digital trash resides. Salvager of discards. Queen of the unofficial channels.

Maker of the track "Last Cry of the Mouth Ever Fading." The one with the echo of a scream, the final traces of a murder victim.

Dixie Magus. Expert patcher of the wounded. Retuner of all hybrid demo-flesh for the next age. Savior of burnt-out angels.

13

The dance floor was half empty, people still waiting for takeoff. Break stood at the center of the room, looking up at the lights . . .

I was a broken soul stranded on the last day of the old world, skin aflame in a shopping mall. Blacking out, dying of digital fever.

He still felt weird inside at the work they had done today, the way that Dixie had treated the ghost, the wounded ghost. And yet . . .

Only Dixie had reached out to me. She lifted me up and dragged me home and worked on my body like I was one of her crazy machines.

Plugged me in analogue style and set up circuits to keep my system alive. In my delirium I heard wings beating, silver and gold.

I rose from my bed shrouded by sparks, crackling at the edges. Strange apparitions flickered around me, creatures of dust and light.

He could see them, all these stray sparkles that no one else could notice. His skull flared with color and noise. And then Dixie played the new tune . . .

14

Drops of rainwater. Hiss of acid on metal. Globules of sound. Murmurs, whirrs, sudden freak-out guitar in a five-second burst.

Dixie working the X-ray plates, extracting the mix from a skull and a sickened heart. Spell of rhythm. People stepping to the floor.

Noise magic. A kiss of lips, magnified. Ticking clocks, food sizzle, static, jazz bass flecks, and splinters forming an undercurrent pull.

Now the drop in the mix where the singer's scream once lived, a slow fade of echoes. Repeat. A few dancers moving in response . . .

Slowly swaying, slowly rising to fall in time with music box fragments, whispers, radar clicks; the beat coalescing. Crowd swell.

Dixie adding body music: breath, vein flow, brain activity. The missing scream coming round again. This time the dancers moved as one.

And there stood Break at the center, at the hot crush-heart liquid blood-river chaotic center of it all, feeling himself pulled aloft.

15

Break could not sleep properly. Dreams would lull him, only to drag him back awake. The dead singer whispered, always on the edge of hearing.

He could take no more. He left his room and went up to the roof of the block. All was dark, the streets empty. He felt the ghosts as tingles on his skin.

Was this his true calling, to be a guide for Dixie, nothing more than a compass? A waste of his gifts, surely, but what else could he do?

In dreams he caressed the neon-glow air with glittering feathers, taking flight across the Haze Towns. Joining with his brethren . . .

Renegade angels working the night sky, buzzing with fire at their wing tips, all the scattered songs theirs for the taking.

Break opened his eyes. He felt he could step off from the building's lip and ride the updraughts, floating easy with arms outstretched.

Was he dreaming now? His feet moved closer to the edge.

16

A noise. Break turned to see a group of people climbing onto the roof. The fog catchers.

They attended to their nets. Three adults in the crew, plus a kid, working by torchlight, checking the frame of gauze for captures.

Break walked over to watch them. They ignored him completely, set on their task, scouring the surface of the nets for images.

Something flared in a torch beam. A shape of lighter color, sparkling where the mist particles rested. It looked to be of human form.

Break stepped closer: a face, a woman's face, her body, her hands moving on the net's surface. The image was fleeting, illusive.

The crew spoke in low voices, excited at their find. Break turned to them, saying, "She's mine. I'll pay what you want." They smiled.

It was the lost singer. He knew it was. The wounded ghost made visible. Spots of red marked the face as it shimmered on the net.

17

Two nights later, he took possession of the icon jar. It cost most of the wages Dixie had given him, but Break had no choice.

He snapped open the lid and released the mist. There it floated in the dark room, the singer's image illuminated: gold, electric blue.

A few seconds of footage ripped from a promo video, caught in endless repeat. The red speckles on her face a remnant of special FX.

Break played Dixie's track. The apparition moved in time to the rhythm. He could not stop looking at her.

He didn't know her name, didn't recognize her face. Somebody from before he was born, before memory. Lost in the archives until now.

Somebody damaged, the victim of a cruel manager or a crazed fan or a jealous lover. He didn't like to think about it.

But she had sought Break out, in both image and sound. And here in this tiny dingy room, with his help, a new kind of life was being made.

He stepped into the mist, his body sparking at the points of contact. It was all he could do.

The track played on. The woman sang. The ghost of fog and sparkle danced. And danced and danced and danced and danced and danced . . .

18

Night passed along. The only light was a flickering lamp across the street.

Break could not bring himself to reseal her into the pod, even though he knew she would soon fade away completely. He would let this happen.

He would sit here in the dimly lit room and let his skin glimmer and shine with old messages, what was left of them.

He would conjure lyrics from all the many fragments he had collected on his travels, so many words to cast a spell, to allow a murdered spirit rest.

19 [LYRIC CODA]

I see remnants

of a woman floating,

the damaged steps

of a ghost.

The play of image in fog,

dancing in time.

This fragile body of release . . .

only to falter.

She was just another

electromagnetic transfer:

sampled footage.

Why should I care about her?

She is singing for

the people of vapor,

those whose flesh holds

no possession, no recognition.

Fog dancer, fog dancer

move through dust and neon-glow,

through moonlit circuits

and fused wires of memory.

LAVIE TIDHAR

CHOOSING FACES

(2012)

BRUCE:

1.

It was a party in Camden Market, late. We were standing in a bowl of glass lit by
torches, a Sumerian-themed restaurant a floor above the market. Moving black
escalators led up into the building. It snowed outside, white flakes falling as we
drank and danced.

I guess I just wanted love. I guess she was just looking for something real. And
I guess neither of us got exactly what we wanted.

She wore her hair like a black halo, muscled arms in a sleeveless top, she made
you think of Cleopatra Jones in an old movie, fighting wiry kung-fu men in an
American war in Asia. Marlene Dietrich was serving drinks behind the long bar.
"What do you do?" she said. We were both sipping champagne. I nodded at the
Marlene. "CEA," I said.

"Copyright Enforcement Agency?" She looked impressed, or amused, I
couldn't quite tell. "Do you have a gun?" she said.

"Yes."

"Did you ever kill anyone?"

"Rarely," I said, laughing.

"Oh, so it's . . ."

"It's not like in the movies," I said. Thinking of the East European factory we busted, several years back. They had a dormitory full of product—young Sylvesters, Bruces, Jean-Claudes, imperfect copies, slack-jawed and hollow eyed, of a line that was never all that popular after its brief heyday. It was an abandoned factory building far from habitation. The gang that ran it had filming equipment. They went through the copies like tissues, sometimes wasting four and five on a single shoot. Bruce on Jean-Claude, Sylvester on Sylvester on Sylvester, blood sports gangbangs with razor blades. When we took them down, the ring operators came quietly, even smirking. Worst they'd get was, what, five to ten? With time off for good behavior. We destroyed the copies. They were lined inside, waiting. Only one tried anything, with a wordless cry he kicked up, a Jean-Claude and agile with it, but you could tell he knew it was no use even before I shot him.

The rest merely stood there. There is something almost eerie about copies. The code never comes out quite right. They're cheap, mass-produced in labs all over. These days any kid with a gene kit and a bathtub can grow his own Elvis. We went past them and shot each one in the head. It's the best way. Then we brought in the flamethrowers and burned the place down.

None of which I told her when she asked. I just smiled. A part of me wondered if she, too, was a copy. You can't always tell, and it's an occupational hazard. The other part of me didn't care. I asked her if she'd like to dance and she said yes, and we swayed there, in that glass bowl, with the snow like a benediction falling outside.

2.

Her name was Pam and she was a copy artist, which made me uncomfortable. Her work space was filled with computers and growing vats and body parts emerging half-formed out of green-gray goo.

"Aren't they beautiful?" she said. "I love the sense of copies as people, or as layers of history you can just reach a hand and, literally, touch. Hurt. Make love to."

"What do you do when they're," I said, and stopped. "When they're finished?" I said.

"If they become aware, you mean?"

"Yes."

"Some never do, you know. My success rate is still only thirty percent. The ones that don't make it I take apart, recycle." She showed me a half-finished copy, Marilyn Monroe cross-hatched into Osama bin Laden. Shark fins stuck out of the living corpse's arms and torso.

We made love on her unmade bed, with the Marilyn/Osama hybrid watching us silently where it hung on a hook. In the night I was aware of it blinking wet eyes, of it staring at us in the dark. I could smell the Thames through the open window, we were somewhere south of the river. Pam was strong, her body moved above mine as we rocked together, her sweat against my skin making us slippery to each other. Later she slept easily, with even breaths, while I lay in the dark, still feeling the motion of bodies like water, and thinking of Somalia.

3.

We came on the ships at dusk. We hid on the shore, watching them through infrared. Massive hulls, of ancient seagoing vessels liberated from their multinational owners by a different sort of pirate, in a different age. Now they sat, part submerged in water, dark and seemingly lifeless. Switch to thermal imaging though and the ships burned with internal heat, a mass of bodies crammed close together, one on top of the other. E-Somaliland had declared independence from contested Somalia, creating a non-IP haven where the Agency could not operate overtly. Ethiopian troops made up the bulk of the attack. We were there primarily as observers.

We stormed the ships at sunrise; helicopters swooped overhead as commandos in black-painted dinghies raced across the calm sea. A bloody firefight erupted and I watched bodies fall into the water below.

I was part of the second wave of attack, the pirates subdued, men and women in white smocks dragged from the hidden labs inside and placed on deck and handcuffed. I looked at the cargo manifesto, whistling at the numbers. We saw it, next: a ship that had once been an oil tanker was now packed floor to ceiling with Elvises all destined for the clandestine North American market. There was every type of Elvis, young soldier Elvis, old bloated Elvis, row upon row they lay there, naked, tagged, ready to be shipped.

The final ship was the hardest to bring under control. We later found out why. The scientist-pirates had been killed, their throats cut, their bodies left on deck for the birds. A craze some years back for that special mindset great men and dictators possess led to an upping in orders for Amins, Kims, Ian Smiths, and the like. Now a shipful of imperfect copies rose against their overseers, shambling up the stairs like living death, killing anything in their path. I watched from the deck of the Elvis ship as the firefight lasted into the night before the decision was made to drown the ship. I watched Idi Amins without number trying to swim to shore, and the soldiers, on decks above, opening fire with oiled Uzis. The blood attracted sharks, who did not distinguish between original and copy.

4.

I lost track of how many Hitlers.

5.

Many of which congregated then and still in South America. Argentina, Brazil . . . there seemed to be an endless market for the copies but it was only when they went loose that I had to be called in, tracking them through Indian villages and ancient Inca trails and, upon finding them at last, little lost Hitlers, had to be Nuremberg judge and executioner at once.

Though Hitler was never at Nuremberg.

6.

When Pam woke I was drifting off, cast asleep, adrift on a black sea. The stars all had faces and their faces were all the same.

"Coffee?" she said. I blinked sleep away, said, "In a mo—" and stopped. "What the hell is that?" I said.

The thing was like a giant mechanical cat. It purred at me and blinked large, plastic eyes.

"This is Ivan," Pam said. "He's the oldest Tamagotchi in the world."

"Tamagotchi?" Then I remembered—virtual pets, carried around in little plastic storage devices, antiques—"How?" I said.

"Ivan was my first virtual," she said. "My grandmother had him before me. I looked after him ever since I was a girl. He's had all kinds of upgrades, modifications over the years, he once married a Moon Princess and, once, he escaped into the networks and I spent over six months hunting for him, the poor thing. He is not very smart but he loves me. After he went rogue I didn't think it would be fair to keep him in the original casing so I had him transferred to a new body. He likes it much more, don't you, Ivan?"

Ivan came closer and sniffed me. Then he licked my face.

"I'm hoping he becomes self-aware one day," Pam said. "But if he ever does, he won't be himself anymore."

She sounded sad about that and I didn't want her to be sad.

"Pam . . ." I said.

"No," she said. And, "It was a mistake, bringing you here. I want you to leave."

"Why?"

"Because of what you do. Because of what you are."

"And what am I?"

"Blind," she said. "Please, Bruce."

I didn't know why she called me that. But I left her apartment and found myself in Elephant and Castle, walking toward Waterloo on foot, breathing in the cold air, thinking about things that didn't add up, no matter how much you tried to put them together.

7.

The gold rush proper started with the need to get hold of suitable genetic material. Which is where specialist collectors' shops came in, and is how Stanley Gibbons became the world-leading DNA agency that it is today.

SG used to specialize in collectible celebrity items in addition to their stamp business. They sold autographs, mostly, and sometimes movie props, letters, rare photos—that sort of thing.

What they *also* sold, however—to the discerning collector who needed that much more for his money—was hair.

When the market in copies suddenly exploded, it took people a while to understand the needs of the market. Those who moved early became rich overnight. Back in the early decades of the century, SG was selling five strands of hair from King George III, for instance, for a pitiful six hundred pounds. You could get a Melanie Griffith for a fifty-pound note. You could get George Washington, Charles Dickens, and Duke Ellington and still have change left over from fifteen hundred. You could get Tom Cruise for a measly seventy-five.

The hunt was on for genetic material. The Kunming Labs cornered the market on Cruise, buying up all available genetic material. They began to churn out Cruise copies, the first mass-produced copies destined for both the domestic and international market. Dickens became a particular status symbol. "I have a Dickens, you know," confessed countless bibliophiles to their party guests, proudly bringing out the celebrated author's copy on a leash.

The Church of Scientology bought up any dubious Hubbard item to come on the market, suing anyone who refused to sell. Their offshore factory in the Maldives churned out young cheerful Lafayettes by the hundreds, killing forever the field of science fiction as a by-product. An unforeseen side effect led to multiple splits in the church as each functioning copy started his own brand-new faith, going on the offensive in front of the media. Hundreds of Hubbards were interviewed before hundreds of Oprahs. Even Fiji TV had their own Oprah Show, with several Oprahs rotating in reserve.

Elvises sold like Tamagotchis. A single hair was all you needed of a person: organized crime muscled in on the action, controlling the market in contraband DNA. A ruthless murder in Primrose Hill found a Russian oligarch massacred in his mansion, surrounded by the bullet-ridden corpses of his dozen Schwarzenegger bodyguards. WikiLeaks, getting hold of highly secret DNA sequencing, released them on the Internet, leading to the first era of open-source copying. Julian Assange was murdered and resurrected and murdered and resurrected again in a dozen countries.

Into that whole sorry mess stepped the CEA, with a license to destroy, able to operate in all major copyright zones, an international policing force determined to stamp out the illegal replication of unauthorized copies. CEA agents were the best of the best. We had to be.

8.

I remember a cage fight. This was on an island off the coast of Borneo, an FTZ where we had no jurisdiction. The club was enormous, strobe lights flashed overhead and in the massive cages set amid the dance floor I could see Richard Nixon fighting Osama bin Laden, the one stoic, swinging a mean left hook without expression, the other light on his feet. Collars around their necks ensured they would not stop fighting—electric current shocking them if they tried to refuse. In another cage Hillary Clinton beat the crap out of Golda Meir. I was there to meet a contact, collect information on a cloners ring operating out of Malaysia, but he, or she, never showed up. Instead I wandered that space, getting lost. I stumbled outside into bright sunlight and saw, as far as the horizon, copies dancing in unison to a music I could not hear. It was so silent, there in the bright sunlight, and I saw them all, moving soundlessly, their faces all turned to the sun, their eyes closed, Elvises and Nixons, Amins and Monroes, Oprahs and Madonnas, Mandelas and Osamas and Thatchers and Cruises, a sea of familiar faces, as familiar to me as my own.

For a moment I stood there and the sadness took me. A part of me wanted to join them, to sway in the sun, to be a part of what they represented. Then I came back to myself, seconds or minutes later, and I went back inside into the shade.

9.

"Pam? It's me."

"Hey."

"I wanted to see you again."

"I . . . wanted to see you too."

A silence between us, stretching.

"That's good," I said, and she laughed. "Yeah."

"When?"

"Tomorrow. No! Today. I don't know. Bruce . . ."

"Why do you call me that?"

"I don't know what else to call you."

10.

I never remember dying. My life is spliced together out of desperate fights, insurmountable odds. The joins are like moments of darkness, each transition almost seamless.

I remember this place in the South Pacific. A Kim Dot Clone with dreams of empire had built himself a headquarters on a rent-an-island, filled with armed guards and growing vats. They were churning out bodies by the ton and shipping them out using converted tankers. I landed unseen, shelling my dark diver's suit as I stepped onto the sand. Naked, I followed the paths in the tropical foliage, a knife in my hand. Then I saw them.

Bruce Lees.

Hundreds of Bruce Lees, patrolling.

One spotted me. Then the others. I waded into the fight, naked but for the knife in my hand, and they came at me.

11.

I landed again on the island, not questioning how I was here again. This time I made it as far as the palace gates.

12.

I landed again on the island, armed with two Uzis. I made it inside the buildings before the Bruce Lees got to me.

13.

With a rocket launcher and a samurai sword.

14.

"Yipikaye, motherfucker," I said when I finally ran him through.

15.

I don't know where the words came from. They were just there.

16.

"What am I going to do with you?" Pam said. We were on the South Bank and snow fell gently into the river and the drops dissolved into the water. She wore a long black coat. I had on jeans and a shirt.

"They want me to go on another mission, soon," I said.

"Will you come back?"

"I always come back."

"Would it still be you?"

I didn't know what she meant. "Do you believe in the soul? Someone said to me once copies are all imperfect shards of the same original, and the soul gets diluted and spread amongst them. They're not real. We don't kill them, Pam. We destroy property. You know?"

"I make them, you unmake them?"

"But yours are handcrafted, the problem is when they're mass-produced and cloners don't pay royalties."

"Like if you think you own your own genome code," she said, and laughed. Snow fell on the water. I went to her and drew her close. "I love you," I said.

I kissed her and her lips were warm, alive. They were real. When we parted she was smiling, slightly.

"Oh, Bruce," she said. "If only you could save the world again."

17.

I remember that factory in Eastern Europe, entering the dormitories where they kept the copies, rows upon rows of Jean-Claudes and Sylvesters and Bruces. I remember going down that row, the gun in my hand, the copies lined up silently, waiting for me. I remember looking into each of their faces as they stared back at my own.

PAM:

1.

Hateful enemy agent, CEA scum, your skin is the color of lobster flesh cooked in butter, your face is reminiscent of the worst of the American imperialist dream as seen on late-night television.

It is time for me to step away from the dance, to remove the face I wear in favor of another, truer.

I have saved the world eight hundred and seventy-three times, while you lie in your bed, sleeping, dreaming of former glory. Disgraceful copy of a copy, how I loathe you, your touch, your smell, immoral hunter, killer, in service of the machine. It is time for me to step away from the dance, remove my many masks, time for me to fleet like a shadow along the dimly lit streets of this city, this London, over the Thames, from south to north, along the points of a Harry Beck map, leapfrogging and hopping like an advancing army, an army you cannot see.

I sent a Darknet message to my contact: I am on my way. I arrived in Willesden Junction into streets alive with the motion of writhing bodies, an organic orgy breeding supple streetlamps and traffic lights out of the dead land, of trains like giant rodents crawling along crisscrossing tracks. Entering a residential block, it was alive with the beat of a vast bass which swallowed words and music both, the beating of a vast heart, the heart of a revolution. There were no walls, no levels. They had been removed to make this vast open space. I threaded my way through the dancers, so many dancers, copies and copied, destination and source, like in an old MS-DOS command. Strobe lights hid rather than illuminated. In their faces I sought my own. I am Pam, the Prophet's Fist, She Who Has Been Resurrected. Call me what you will but only call me at your peril. I passed pushers selling weed, Es, acid, Special K, coke, Horse, and generic nobrand paracetamol. They moved out of my way.

Toilet cubicles had been erected at the back of this abandoned council building. I heard grunts from inside, lost cries of passion swallowed by the beat as humans attempted to make copies the old-fashioned way. Set into the cheap plaster wall was a white door. I placed my hand against it.

"By the name of Doctorow and the Apostles, let me enter," I said.

I felt a pinprick of pain, saw blood well on the tip of my index finger. The blood soaked into the wall. Hidden machines analyzed it, for the blood is the life, and the life is blood. The door opened. I stepped through. It closed behind me and the beat of the bass receded, but never vanished. I stood in a dark room.

"Child." His voice boomed across the room, magnified by the amps built into his prodigious neck. They were like wet gills on the Man from Atlantis. They moved like twin obscene mouths suckling at the fetid air. He was huge, a mountain of flesh. His skin was pink like grapefruit. His eyes were hidden behind shades. He wore only white. They all did. All five thousand identical copies of the Army of the Kim Dotcoms.

2.

Kim Dotcom was the first man to open-source himself. He was a revolutionary, the Megamix Marx, the Bitshare Che. When the genetic land-grab began in earnest and the human genome began to be sequestered and copyrighted piece-meal, the Movement arose. A combine of BoingBoing users, Anonymous activists, and pre–Hubbard Resurrection sci-fi fans joined forces to illegally distribute stolen genetic code. Soon wars erupted between the pirates and the legal copyright holders, both online and in the real world. In one notable incidence the Fifth Hungarian Republic, led by an early copy of the poet Attila József, annexed all genetic proprietary material to the state, banning individuals or companies from ownership. They were toppled a mere three weeks later in a coup carried out by an army of Trump bots.

Things got worse, fast.

Thirty Robert Mugabe copies escaped from a cloner facility in South Africa and headed north and across the border. Within weeks Mugabeland, as the new Zimbabwe came to be called, was under the Rule of Thirty and, within a year, it had splintered into rival zones, each ruled by a copy. It was a dark time in Zimbabwean history, a time that pitted brother against brother and Mugabe against Mugabe against Mugabe.

After repeated threats, the United States invaded the Cayman Islands, a British protectorate south of Cuba where the rich and powerful had traditionally deposited their wealth, illegitimate children, and current or discarded lovers, and, of course, their genetic fortune. A group of islanders with Anonymous sympathies, however, had hacked into the secure bank system and posted the genetic code of the richest one percent of the world's population online. Every Grameen Bank microfinancing initiative in the world suddenly had its very own George Soros working for it. Hong Kong triads settled old scores by setting illicit Donald Trump fighting rings in dark subterranean rooms and betting on the outcome. "Getting fired by the Trump" got itself a whole new meaning.

It got worse.

Royalists innocently copying their favorite monarchs inadvertently toppled the British monarchy as enraged copies of HRH Elizabeth Windsor, storming Buckingham Palace, found themselves faced by genetically exact predecessors with a preceding and valid claim to the throne. Matters were not made easier by a George III guerrilla movement issuing multiple threats against the United States.

The Israelis passed a law annexing all Jewish genetic material rights to the state. They thus laid copyright claim to Einstein, who finally accepted the offer first extended to his original in nineteen fifty-two to become president of the State of Israel. The Israelis also genegrabbed Julius Oppenheimer, Robert Hofstadter, Otto Frisch, Nathan Rosen, and, of course, John von Neumann and Niels Bohr.

The resultant nuclear research facility in the Negev Desert was placed under intense security and total media blackout. The escape of a lone Einstein twenty-four months later, across the desert and into Egypt, was reported in the *Sunday Telegraph* but was widely believed to be a hoax. Were it to be believed, the story suggested that the Israelis had managed to open an Einstein-Rosen Bridge, a thousand feet under the desert floor, which opened up onto another universe altogether and into which Jewish mass emigration, or *aliyah*, was being carried out.

Then there were the problems with the EPE as Elvis Presley Enterprises mutated into one of the most powerful copyright holders in the world; and the resultant Elvis Riots, as they came to be called, in which thousands of Elvises ran amuck in Memphis demanding fair employment terms, in what the *New York Times* had dubbed "The worst Communist-led uprising in the history of the United States."

Then they brought back Marx.

Then they brought back Lenin.

Then they brought back both George Bushes, Abraham Lincoln, *and* the Iron Lady. A British faction under Margaret Thatcher's control invaded the Falkland Islands and declared it the First Thatcherite Nation.

Finally the CEA was formed, a lethal task force charged with policing and enforcing genetic copyright law. It was then that Kim Dotcom—declared Public Enemy Number One by the United States government—first open-sourced himself, in the first of a series of brilliant counterstrokes against the rise of genetic land-grab neo-Fascism, birthing the Movement in the process.

3.

"Pam," the Kim Dotcom said in his booming, boombox voice. Alone in the empty room we stood, the Kim Dot Clone and me. "How goes your mission?"

"The primary identity created is rock-solid," I said. "I make hybrid copies which sell to collectors and exhibit in galleries around London. I am now in a relationship with the CEA agent of the B-900 series, codenamed Bruce—"

"They are *all* codenamed Bruce," the Kim Dotcom said. "Do you have it?"

"Yes."

He smiled, a mouth full of teeth. "How?" he breathed.

"It is what I do," I said.

"Relic hunter . . ."

"Yes."

"Give it to me."

That gave me pause. "Here? Now?"

"Here," he said. "Now." His skin was shiny with sweat, his engorged belly glistened in the strobe light filtering in through the narrow gaps in the door.

"But . . ."

"Now, Pam."

He pulled up the rest of his shirt. His belly hung naked in the strobe light. I went to him and laid my hand against the softness of his skin.

"Do it," he said.
I ran my thumb along his belly button. Felt him breathing.
"Do it!"
My nail was long and sharp.
I pushed my thumb into his belly button, hard, impregnating him.
I felt his flesh give as it sank in. I heard him gasp.
The payload secreted in my thumb left me and entered his gestation chamber. I pulled my thumb out and the wound sealed itself.
"Jesus," he said, panting.

4.

A posse of Hulk Hogans had been patrolling the Cathedral of Saint John the Baptist in Turin when I walked in. Life is precious, source and target, copy and original. I put them under with narcotic darts and disabled the alarm on my way in with the codes I had stolen from the Bruce. My Bruce.

I did not kill the Hulks. I do not wantonly destroy.

The Catholic Church defines three levels of holy relics. These, as it turns out, are still used today by gene- and relic-hunters. Third-class relics are ones that had been touched by a saint. These are the least useful for our purposes, what DNA material may have been once left was in all likelihood long gone. Second-class relics are ones that had been worn by a saint, and these offer a better chance of rebirthing, mostly of the minor saints. First-class relics, however, are those directly associated with the life of Jesus Christ, and of these, the most significant, and most heavily guarded, is the Shroud.

There had been significant arguments and several UN resolutions regarding the genetic copyright ownership of Jesus of Nazareth. The Vatican was first but the State of Israel claimed previous right-of-way, and into the melee stepped various American pastors, the Mormons, and an obscure UFO religion claiming for Jesus under supposed evidence of alien DNA. The dispute was never resolved, but there are few conflicts one can't resolve with a gun.

"You will not pass," John the Baptist said in passable English. He was holding an Uzi and glared at me menacingly. His bones had been found in a Bulgarian monastery, on Sveti Ivan Island, in the early noughties. Church-approved cloners have since replicated him hundreds of times. He was a thick-armed, wiry Jewish man, dark skinned and humorless. I put a dart in him and was about to approach the reliquary when I found the cathedral's real defenses.

Mother Teresa.

Mother Teresa, multiplied by seven.

Mother Teresa, multiplied by seven, and all of them holding big fucking machine guns.

I ducked as they opened fire.

The resultant fight wasn't pretty.

But somehow I made it through, and to the Shroud.

They pursued me across Italy and France but lost me at the Channel. I made it back to London and went to the cinema with Bruce, the vial implanted in the false tip of my thumb. We'd watched *Casablanca*, and made out in the back seats of the theater, in the dark.

5.

We'd waited in the dark as the bass drowned the sound of his labored breathing.

What Kim Dotcom had done was distribute his own genetic source code over the file-sharing networks. When an anonymous CEA agent finally caught up with him, on an island somewhere in the South Pacific, it no longer mattered that the original had been destroyed. Hundreds of Kim Dot Clones sprung up into life all over the world, bred in backroom vats on Soi Cowboy and in the Kunming Labs of the Golden Triangle, in copy nurseries on the giant pirate ships of e-Somaliland or in the Elvis factories of Memphis. The Army of the Kim Dotcoms was the call to revolution, the spearhead of the Movement.

They had improved themselves, too.

Each of the Five Thousand carried within himself a 3G mobile birthing unit, top of the range.

"You are close to Mitosis Phase," I said.

"Indeed I am. Pam—" His huge face twisted in pain. He reached out his hand to me and I took it. "Help me," he said. "It is coming."

I helped him down and knelt beside him. I removed his garments so that he was slickly naked. I could see movement under his skin, a thing which was not yet a thing pushing against the thin membrane of flesh, trying to get out. I helped him spread his legs and knelt between them with my slim shiny scalpel in my hand.

The thrum of bass. The beat of feet against the ground, sending a shudder running through the building, a wordless cry like a fist raised in defiance and pride.

"Easy, now . . ." he said.

My hand was steady. I cut through the layers of skin and fat, opening the sack in his belly. "Push," I said.

He pushed.

6.

Oh you corrupt and corrupting CEA agent, you brute, you Bruce! Why can I not take your image out of my mind, why do I feel the need to run my fingers through your thinning hair, to put my nose close to the swell of your neck and inhale the aroma of your skin, in my mind you multiply like a computer virus, as infectious as your famous grin.

7.

The first computer virus for the IBM PC was created in Lahore, Pakistan.

It was called Brain.

A computer virus does not have an original. It is all copy. Its very nature is to replicate itself into identical images. It challenges us to rethink our definitions of original and copy, of source and replica.

Ironically, Brain was developed—by the brothers Basit Farooq Alvi and Amjad Farooq Alvi—as an anti-piracy measure, to stop people illegally copying the medical software the brothers sold. Instead, the virus spread across the world, transferring itself from floppy disk to floppy disk and from program to program, like a particularly tenacious idea in its purest form—like Freedom or Justice or Copyright.

The virus itself built on the concept first developed by John von Neumann, whose article "Theory of self-reproducing automata" was published in 1966, following lectures he had given at the University of Illinois in 1949. Since then, the nature of consumer goods itself mutated and changed, with books, films, and music transforming from mass-produced physical objects into self-replicating, viral entities.

It was only a matter of time until people, too, went the same way.

8.

"Push!"

Grunt, a cry of pain.

"Push, God damn it!"

He pushed. I could feel the thin membrane of flesh straining, *breaking* at long last, and saw a head push through, and heard a newborn cry, like the sound a copy makes when it is replicated.

I held him in my arms. I rocked his little body. Beside me the copy panted, his fingers running along the cut I had made, seeking to close it. Copying does not occur, in nature or otherwise, without mutation, without *remixing*. This Dotcom had been modified with the pouch, they all were. Now it closed, not seamlessly but with a biological efficiency, and he closed his eyes.

When he opened them again his voice was softer but it carried still. "Take him," he said. "All viruses, like memes, to be successful must escape into the wild."

9.

I left him lying there, on the floor of that hidden back room, and threaded my way through the dancers, the newborn held in my arms. When I stepped outside into the street I saw dawn on the horizon, the rising sun bleeding yellows and reds, and for a moment it felt like a summer's day.

10.

Why couldn't I get him out of my mind?

11.

"Bruce."

"Yes?"

"I need to see you."

"Pam. I . . ."

"There is something I need to tell you."

12.

We lay on my bed in the dark and listened to distant traffic and the Thames. The baby was asleep in the other room.

"I don't understand," Bruce kept saying. "I don't understand. I even started going to a support group, you know? We meet once a week in an empty classroom in Clerkenwell. All Bruces. One of them's a dishwasher. Two are bit actors on *EastEnders*. One's a musician. It really does help, you know, talking to someone else who's just like you."

"Love is not enough," I said softly, speaking into his naked chest. "If you want a relationship to succeed, you have to work at it."

"I know," he said. "Pam, I'm trying. But a baby?"

"You have to understand," I said. "Original and copy . . . they're just *words*. They're just fucking words."

"I can't think like that," he said. "It's wrong. I can't think in multiplicities."

"Then leave," I said, my hand on his chest, pushing, but gently.

"No," he said. He took a deep breath. "I love you, Pam," he said.

"Damn it, Bruce!"

He held me in his arms.

13.

I love you.

Sometimes, that has to be enough.

14.

Bruce and I went to the cinema.

A normal evening. The cinema three-quarters empty, dark. The smell of over-priced popcorn and spilled Coke on the carpets. Dust motes danced in the air in the path of the projector beam. We'd gone to see *E-Pirates of Somaliland*, just recently released. Sidney Poitier played the CEA agent, Captain Jack. Omar Sharif played the evil cloner, Barbossa, an Arab-hacked Kim Dotcom surrounded by an army of sword-wielding Keira Knightleys. Tamara Dobson played the Movement agent who fights—but eventually falls for—the CEA man.

We'd left baby Jesus at home.

SUNNY MORAINE

I TELL THEE ALL, I CAN NO MORE

(2013)

HERE'S what you're going to do. It's almost like a script you can follow. You don't have to think too much about it.

Just let it in. Let it watch you at night. Tell it everything it wants to know. These are the things it wants, and you'll let it have those things to keep it around. Hovering over your bed, all sleek chrome and black angles that defer the gaze of radar. It's a cultural amalgamation of one hundred years of surveillance. There's safety in its vagueness. It resists definition. This is a huge part of its power. This is a huge part of its appeal.

• • •

Fucking a drone isn't like what you'd think. It's warm. It probes, gently. It knows where to touch me. I can lie back and let it do its thing. It's only been one date but a drone isn't going to worry about whether I'm an easy lay. A drone isn't tied to the conventions of gendered sexual norms. A drone has no gender and, if it comes down to it, no sex. Just because it can *do* it doesn't mean it's a thing that it *has*.

We made a kind of conversation, before, at dinner. I did most of the talking, which I expected.

The drone hums as it fucks me. We—the *dronesexual*, the recently defined, though we only call ourselves this name to ourselves and only ever with the deepest irony—we're never sure whether the humming is pleasure or whether it's a form of transmission, but we also don't really care. We gave up caring what other people, people we probably won't ever meet, think of us. We talk about this on message boards, in the comments sections of blogs, in all the other places we congregate, though we don't usually meet face to face. There are no dronesexual support groups. We don't have conferences. There is no established discourse around who we are and what we do. No one writes about us but us, not yet.

The drones probably don't do any writing. But we know they talk.

Drones don't come, not as far as we can tell, but they must get satisfaction out of it. They must get something. I have a couple of orgasms, in the laziest kind of fashion, and the vibration of the maybe-transmission humming tugs me through them. I rub my hands all over that smooth conceptual hardware and croon.

• • •

There was no singular point in time at which the drones started fucking us. We didn't plan it, and maybe it wasn't even a thing we consciously wanted until it started happening. Sometimes a supply creates a demand.

But when something is around that much, when it knows that much, it's hard to keep your mind from wandering in that direction. *I wonder what that would feel like inside me.* One kind of intimacy bleeds into another. Maybe the drones made the first move. Maybe we did. Either way, we were certainly receptive. *Receptive,* because no one penetrates drones. They fuck men and women with equal willingness, and the split between men and women in our little collectivity is, as far as anyone has ever been able to tell, roughly fifty-fifty. Some trans people, some genderfluid, and all permutations of sexual preference represented by at least one or two members. The desire to fuck a drone seems to cross boundaries with wild abandon. Drones themselves are incredibly mobile and have never respected borders.

• • •

Here's what you're going to do. You're not going to get too attached. This isn't something you'll have to work to keep from doing, because it's hard to attach to a drone. But on some level there is a kind of attachment, because the kind of closeness you experience with a drone isn't like anything else. It's not like a person. They come into you; they know you. You couldn't fight them off even if you wanted to. Which you never do. Not really.

• • •

We fight, not because we have anything in particular to fight over, but because it sort of seems like the thing to do.

No one has ever come out and admitted to trying to have a relationship with the drone that's fucking them, but of course everyone knows it's happened. There are no success stories, which should say something in itself, and people who aren't in our circle will make faces and say things like *you can't have a relationship with a machine no matter how many times it makes you come* but a drone isn't a dildo. It's more than that.

So of course people have tried. How could you not? This isn't a relationship, but the drone stayed the night after fucking me, humming in the air right over my bed as I slept, and it was there when I woke up. I asked it what it wanted and it drifted toward the kitchen, so I made us some eggs which of course only I could eat.

It was something about the way it was looking at me. I just started yelling, throwing things.

Fighting with a drone is like fucking a drone in reverse. It's all me. The drone just dodges, occasionally catches projectiles at an angle that bounces them back at me, and this might amount to throwing. All drones carry two AGM-114 Hellfire missiles, neatly resized as needed, because all drones are collections of every assumption we've ever made about them, but a drone has never fired a missile at anyone they were fucking.

This is no-stakes fighting. I'm not even sure what I'm yelling about. After a while the drone drifts out the window. I cry and scream for it to call me. I order a pizza and spend the rest of the day in bed.

. . .

Here's what you're going to do. You're not going to ask too many questions. You're just going to let it happen. You'll never know whose eyes are behind the blank no-eyes that see everything. There might not be any anymore; drones regularly display what we perceive as autonomy. In all our concepts of *droneness* there is hardly ever a human being on the other end. So there's really no one to direct the questions to.

Anyway, what the hell would you ask? *What are we doing, why are we this way?* Since when have those ever been answers you could get about this kind of thing?

. . .

This is really sort of a problem. In that I'm focusing too much on a serial number and a specific heat signature that only my skin can know. In that I asked the thing to call me at all. I knew people tried things like this but it never occurred to me that it might happen without trying.

It does call me. I talk for a while. I say things I've never told anyone else. It's hard to hang up. That night while I'm trying to sleep I stare up at the ceiling and the dark space between me and it feels so empty.

. . .

I pass them out on the street, humming through the air. They avoid me with characteristic deftness but after a while it occurs to me that I'm steering myself into them, hoping to make contact. They all look the same but I know they aren't the same at all. I'm looking for that heat signature. I want to turn them over so I can find that serial number, nestled in between the twin missiles, over the drone dick that I've never actually seen.

Everyone around me might be a normal person who doesn't fuck a drone and doesn't want to and doesn't talk to them on the phone and usually doesn't take them to dinner. Or every one of them could be like that.

At some point we all stopped talking to each other.

• • •

Here's what you're going to do. Here's what you're not going to do. Here's a list to make it easy for you.

You're not going to spend the evening staring out the window. You're not going to toy endlessly with your phone. You're not going to masturbate furiously and not be able to come. You're not going to throw the things you threw at nothing at all. You're not going to stay up all night looking at images and video that you can only find on a few niche paysites. You're not going to wonder if you need to go back into therapy because you don't need therapy. You're not going to wonder if maybe you and people like you might be the most natural people in the entire world, given the way the world is now. You're not going to wonder if there was ever such a thing as *natural*.

• • •

Sometimes I wonder what it might be like to be a drone. This feels like a kind of blasphemy, and also pointless, but I do it anyway. So simple, so connected. So in tune. Needed instead of the one doing the needing. Possessing all the power. Subtly running more and more things until I run everything. The subjects of total organic surrender.

Bored, maybe, with all that everything. Playing some games.

It comes over. We fuck again and it's amazing. I'm almost crying by the end. It nestles against me and hums softer and I wonder how screwed I actually am in how many different ways.

Anyway, it stays the night again and we don't fight in the morning.

• • •

A drone wedding. I want to punch myself in the mouth twenty or thirty times for even thinking that even for a second.

• • •

It starts coming every night. This is something I know I shouldn't get used to but I know that I am. As I talk to it—before sex, during, after—I start to remember things that I'd totally forgotten. Things from my early childhood, things from high school that I didn't want to remember. I tell with tears running down my face and at the end of it I feel cleaned out and raw.

I don't want this to be over, I say. I have no idea what the drone wants and it doesn't tell me, but I want to believe that the fact that it keeps coming back means something.

I read the message boards and I wish I could tell someone else about this because I feel like I'm losing every shred of perspective. I want to talk about how maybe we've been coming at this from all the wrong angles. Maybe we should all start coming out. Maybe we should form political action groups and start demanding recognition and rights. I know these would all be met with utterly blank-screen silence but I want to say them anyway. I write a bunch of things that I never actually post, but I don't delete them either.

. . .

We're all like this. I'm absolutely sure that we're all like this and no one is talking about it but in all of our closets is a thing hovering, humming, sleek and black and chrome with its missiles aimed at nothing.

. . .

We have one more huge fight. Later I recognize this as a kind of self-defense. I'm screaming and beating at it with my fists, something about commitment that I'm not even sure that I believe, and it's just taking it, except for the moments when it butts me in the head to push me back. I'm shrieking about its missiles, demanding that it go ahead and vaporize my entire fucking apartment, put me out of my misery, because I can't take this anymore because I don't know what to do. We have angry sex and it leaves. It doesn't call me again. I stay in bed for two days and call a therapist.

. . .

Here's what you're going to do.

You're going to do what you told yourself you had the courage to do and say everything. You're going to let it all out to someone flesh and blood and you're going to hear what they say back to you. For once you're not going to be the one doing all the talking. You're going to be honest. You're going to be the one to start the whole wheel spinning back in the other direction. You're going to fix everything because you have the power to fix everything. You're going to give this all a name and say it like you're proud. You're going to bust open a whole new paradigm. You're going to be missile-proof and bold and amazing and you're not going to depend on the penetrative orgasmic power of something that never loved you anyway.

. . .

I stop at the door. I don't even make it into the waiting room.

I fiddle with the buttons on my coat. I check my phone for texts, voice mail. I look down the street at all those beautiful humming flying things. I feel a tug in the core of me where everything melts down into a hot lump and spins like a dynamo. I feel like I can't deny everything. I feel like I don't want to. I feel that the flesh is treacherous and doomed.

I made this promise to myself and it takes me half an hour on a bus and five minutes of staring at a name plaque and a glass door to realize that I don't want to keep it.

I look back out at everyone and I consider what it could be like to step through those doors, sit in a softly lit room with tissues and a lot of pastel and unthreatening paintings on the wall and spill it all and look up and see the therapist nodding, nodding knowingly, mouthing the words *me too*.

I don't really think anyone can help any of us.

• • •

Here's what you're going to do. You're going to stop worrying. You're going to stop asking questions. You're going to stop planning for tomorrow. You're going to go out and get laid and stop wondering what might have been. You're going to stop trying to fix anything. You're going to stop assuming there's anything to be fixed.

You're going to look out at all those drones and not wonder. You're going to look out at all those people and you're going to *know*. Even though no one is talking.

Me too. Me too. Me too.

K. C. ALEXANDER

FOUR TONS TOO LATE

(2014)

PATIENT #8620-87

He wakes aching. He always wakes aching. Drugs don't help. He kicked that habit a long time ago, before they'd take him into the program. *Healthy bodies only,* they said.

The dayshift nurse has already thrown the curtains. Daylight streams through the double-paned glass, warming the ambient temperature to 174 degrees. His internal therm is on the blink.

"Good morning, Frank," the nurse says, his baritone cheerful. A male nurse. Ordinarily, Frank calls it the pussification of a man's dignity, but he knows why he doesn't get pretty female nurses anymore.

Things go wrong. Things get messy. He'd try to use the old tech in his hands, his legs, his head, and the wrong signals cross the wrong wires.

He's a wreck, and he knows it.

The nurse is a shadow in Frank's peripheral vision—whittled down to a tunnel. The pictures siphoning through the optics bolted into his brain come staggered, like a slideshow where the cables aren't screwed in right.

"Breakfast is on," the nurse calls from the kitchen. There's nothing wrong with Frank's ears.

The bed he's on is a platform, a hard counter. No blankets, because the weave captures heat, and the last time Frank's four-ton body overheated, he waited in silence—deaf, blind, and dumb—for two days.

That's when they'd put him here. Monitored day and night.

Frank doesn't close his eyes. He doesn't have eyes to close. He stares up at the gray ceiling and can't remember what he's waiting for.

Everything aches.

OFFICER FRANK MOONEY

3 Months

A hell of a storm rages. The real kind, with sharp winds howling in the filthy alleys between crowded apartments and where litter is snatched up off the dirty streets like bats out of neon hell. It rains like a son of a bitch, and Frank watches it slide down the window pane as his wife tells him that she wants out.

The door shuts behind her. The din of activity dies behind a reinforced steel panel. The cold hospital room doesn't echo with raised voices—it would've been better if she'd yelled.

Frank doesn't cry. He can't. He doesn't have tear ducts. They put in cybernetic optics with state-of-the-art enhancements, but they needed sockets to hold them. Frank's face is stoic intensity—molded edges, chiseled planes. Tempered metal to encase the brain inside.

It's supposed to stop a bullet.

It does shit for a breaking heart.

PATIENT #8620-87

Breakfast isn't the word for it. The four-ton chassis, unlike the later models, doesn't charge. Frank is forced to consume a gel-like substance that tastes like chewed-up cigarettes and copper-tinted lube, forcing it past a freakish amalgam of metal and flesh to drip like cold glue into his stomach.

Frank is lucky today. This particular pussified male nurse is a good kid. A steaming cup of stuff that reminds Frank of coffee waits on the pristine table, ready to wash down the metallic taste of the nutrient sludge.

He doesn't always get coffee. The smell reminds him of memories now programmed into a chip. Long, hard days on the beat, casing petty thieves and drug peddlers from the front of a car whose bulletproofing warranty had tapped out years before. Swearing at the girls who didn't know a cop from that hole between their legs, too caught up in the case at hand to bother with arresting them.

Peeing in a cup.

Heh. He doesn't pee anymore.

Frank reaches for the steaming mug.

His fingers spasm. Metal joints lock, splay, and a charged jolt wrenches at his elbow. He clenches his jaw, gripping the edge of the table with his left hand as he tries to force control over the seizing right.

"Go, fingers," he orders, but not too loud. He doesn't want the nurse to come running. Doesn't want the fuss, or the horror, or the blood.

He's tired of blood.

The sun shimmers across the small breakfast nook as Frank forces his extremities to close, one by straining one, over the mug. Metal clinks. Joints lock.

He holds his breath as the tremors ease.

Rotors spin. Ceramic shatters into a fine dust between spasming digits as fluid sprays in a shit-colored arc across the table.

"Goddammit!"

OFFICER FRANK MOONEY

1 Year, 7 Months

Storms herald change. They come a little less frequently now that the corporations have started to fine-tune the weather shield. It's not perfect. This one sliced right through, a real doozy, forcing anyone with half a brain inside before the debris turns to shrapnel.

It's a dark and stormy night, the kind of setting where a bad cop expects to find a desperate broad holding a gun with the business end cocked his way.

Frank finds a broad, but she's not holding a gun. She's got a sign. *Anything for food.*

What is she, eight? Nine?

Frank isn't alone on this beat, but he ignores what the force calls his partner. It's not a real word. Jenkins is a handler—half a cop, half a mechanic; a corporate shill. He's been Frank's handler since the first briefing on what it would mean to sell himself to the corporate labs. To get money for his wife's—his *ex*-wife's—treatments.

Jenkins, unwilling to step foot outside the one-man covered trike that protects his fragile flesh, wants out of this wind. He doesn't slow.

Frank does.

He ignores Jenkins's curse, harsh on the radio connecting them, as he veers off the programmed trajectory that is their beat. He slows to a halt beside the shivering little girl.

She's got stringy hair and big, soulful brown eyes—the kind of eyes they paint on lifelike dolls to make them look real and sad and trusting. She doesn't take a step back. She doesn't cringe. Not like everyone else.

Four-ton chassis on mobility thrusters, one of half a dozen prototypes patrolling the streets, and people still can't get past it.

"Get your scrap metal back on course," Jenkins snarls, but it's a whine in Frank's closed-circuit earpiece and he doesn't care.

"You need to leave the area," he tells her.

She stares at him. A little tired. A little resigned. A little too old for her terribly young face. The sign tilts.

"Do you have somewhere to go?" He can't modulate his voice anymore. It's metallic, like the robot his so-called partner accuses him of being. It comes out flat, tinny.

The wind shoves her hair into her face, a cobweb of grease and tangles, and Frank clocks bruises on her wrists when she shoves the mess back out of her eyes. She doesn't speak.

"Get off the street or I'm taking you in. Do you understand?"

She nods slowly as the wind tosses that hair like a wild corona. A greasy halo.

Frank turns away.

The faintest sensory input—a figment of feeling backlit by numbers scrolling past his left input device—halts him in place.

It isn't a familiar sensation. His brain, fleshy and soft, slogs through numbers, calculations, and theory. Searching for the memory. The description.

He can't find it.

Frank turns.

A dirt-streaked hand curls around the thick digit replacing his middle finger. It's obscenely delicate against the black matte metal, ragged nails and all.

In the visual screen of his optics, the heads-up display tells him that she's underweight. That her right arm's been broken twice and her sign used to say something else before it was scratched off and appropriated.

"This is going down on the report," Jenkins growls.

Frank rotates his free hand, bending it so far back that the palm detaches and a compartment slides open at the heel. A card pops out—one of those plastic ones, with a chip in it. It takes him more than one try, but he manages to program the thin sheet. The address on the transparent plastic changes. "Get here," he says.

She stares at him, her big brown eyes empty, but she lets him go to take the card.

He turns away again. "I was tossing a vagrant."

"Screw you, Mooney."

Jenkins doesn't like Frank.

Frank wouldn't mind snapping Jenkins's neck. But that would turn Jenkins's wife—Frank's *ex*-wife—into a widow, and Frank doesn't have it in him to do it.

One year and seven months after trading his body to the police force, Frank hasn't figured out how to care.

"I'm back on course," he says into the radio. There's nothing in his voice. He's a robot, after all. Just like they made him.

The middle digit on his left hand twitches.

PATIENT #8620-87

Frank isn't allowed to have pictures. Nothing in here to remind him of what'd he left behind. No memories. No nostalgia.

Nothing to make him test the borders they've put around his world.

FOUR TONS TOO LATE

Except that stuff that's almost coffee.

He doesn't tell them what coffee dredges up in his brain.

The table is clean again, ceramic fragments swept into the trash bin and dropped down the garbage chute by that nice kid nurse. He sits in the middle of his lonely suite, watching the byplay of sunlight and shadows dappling the far wall, and calls up a photo-perfect memory of a brown-eyed girl with a tough, sad smile.

It's starting to go a little spotty.

Frank needs his recall fixed. They can't do it. When the meat leftover from his body started rejecting the nerve connectors, they tried for a while to stay on top of it, but then some snot-nosed wunderkind figured out what they'd done wrong first go-around.

Frank's go-around.

They don't make his parts anymore. That was always the risk. A few good years as they integrated the cyber division into the force and then *so long, thanks for serving, here's a gold watch.*

Frank sits in his max-sec prison and contemplates hooking into the TV for some news.

The nurses don't come for another few hours.

DETECTIVE FRANK MOONEY

4 Years, 8 Months

Things are looking up.

Statistics are in, and the corporations are pleased. The police force miraculously gains some funding, and Frank is promoted.

That means Jenkins is, too. The son of a bitch is going home with the promotion Frank always promised his wife he'd get.

His *ex*-wife.

"Thank you, cyber-detective," the operator says in his radio band. "You're off the clock for six hours. Recharge."

"Copy." Frank doesn't talk much. Nobody likes extended conversations with the cyber squad. Most don't even know his name. *Hey, buckethead* and *scrap squad* tend to be the nonstarters. "Out."

He's not alone. Frank doesn't kid himself as he puts one blocky foot in front of the other and forces his four-ton chassis to the door of the complex reserved for cops. All cops, but mostly cops like him.

He's got a basement deal, rent-free and reinforced to hold his weight. Part of the bargain. A payout with a whole lot of zeroes to fund his wife's—his *ex*-wife's—medical bills and a place to live.

Jenkins got the girl. Son of a bitch Jenkins.

The operator may be silent, but Frank knows he's being monitored. Vitals, mostly. They tried to install cameras, but Frank shut them down.

He has a secret.

Frank lets himself in. The heads-up display flashes green, and his head turns on a servo a little less fine-tuned than it used to be. It whirrs.

There's a shoe in his foyer. Small, narrow. Pink and white.

He aches as he clears the foyer, stepping over the shoe with exaggerated care. He's ached a lot, the past few weeks. Sharp pains, sometimes. Dull throbbing in others.

He hasn't reported it yet. So, he has *two* secrets.

"I'm back," he says, in the same flat, mechanized voice he delivers everything in. He enters the kitchen—large enough to accommodate anyone else, but cramped for him—and tugs the refrigerator door open.

Muscles stretch under metal. Tighten.

Synapses crackle and the chassis seizes. Hinges pop and clatter to the floor. The whole damn door comes off in his armored hand.

The milk stashed on the nearly empty shelf topples sideways.

The broad waiting for him to come home steps into the space behind him. "I made cookies," she says, reproachful. "The milk was expensive."

The pool of white slips over the shelf's edge and drips—*splat, splat*—to the tile. Frank sets the refrigerator door down. "I'll buy you more."

She sidles around him, a fourteen-year-old beauty with still-soulful brown eyes. Small for her age, she looks like a twelve-year-old. Not much older than she did when he first found her on that dirty street. Less starved, maybe.

"It's okay," she assures him, flashing a smile that pulls at the heart Frank doesn't have. "We can eat cookies without it."

He doesn't point out that he doesn't eat cookies anymore. It only upsets her. It took six months before she said a word. Now, he tries not to silence her.

She cleans up his kitchen—his mess—like it isn't a problem. Like it's the first time.

It isn't.

Frank gets out of her way, knees cranking, body heaving into place like a metal avalanche. She's humming as she drags a rag over the spill.

A real domestic type.

Her name, he'd learned, is Sabrina. She prefers Kate. He doesn't know why.

She pauses, looks over her shoulder—pink, his digital vision informs him, trimmed with white. Some kind of sporty sweatshirt she must have picked up when he sent her out with creds and a lifeless *Whatever you need, kid.* "Go pick a movie, okay?"

She's gotten bossy. Informal adoption's agreed with her. Even if the only thing keeping her under this roof is the promise of daily meals.

Frank leaves the kitchen.

PATIENT #8620-87

Frank hurts.

He always feels better in the morning than he does at midday. The hours tick by, and he sits quiet and still in his reinforced armchair. They don't bother with padding. It can't handle the weight.

The news is full of transhumanist hate speech. He can't stomach more than an hour at a time, if even that. Hearing those talking heads bark about the transient nature of humanity and the threat cybertechnology brings to the species is enough to make his limbs twitch.

If he was still on the force, he'd go show those assholes a thing or two about *transient humanity*.

But he isn't. They'd retired him, right? Took his badge, decommissioned his arsenal. Heh. Heh, heh. Said *Gun on my desk, Mooney* and he'd damn near dropped a nuke.

Nobody thought it was funny.

The last flawed prototype to get the boot.

Who wants him, now?

Frank sits in silence, hands draped on the arms of the chair, watching the shadows crawl over the wall with unblinking eyes.

Metal isn't supposed to hurt. Didn't somebody tell him that?

They lied.

DETECTIVE FRANK MOONEY

10 Years, 2 Months

"You aren't my dad!" She stares at him across the living room, a sullen teenager with a spiky swatch of newly shorn hair tinted a color Frank thinks is purple. It could be black. Or dark red. The optics aren't delivering.

Frank doesn't know how to handle this.

If she was any other kid, he'd have her hauled in to the precinct and booked on drug charges faster than she could repeat all the many variations of the word *fuck*.

She knows a lot of them. Most didn't come from him.

The servos in his neck creak as he lowers his head to the pink purse on the table in front of him. It was a gift. His first to her. He had to order it off the network because he's encouraged to never go shopping. When they'd called him up to ask why he'd picked up a little kid's pink purse, he told them he was donating it to charity.

They can watch his vitals, but they can't track lies. Frank's real good at lying.

She used to carry it everywhere. It vanished into her room one day, and she replaced it with other bags in a way Frank assumed was normal for girls.

Now, she's filled it with drugs. The real gritty kind. Swish and canker, color-dust and strych. The kind of stuff that kills kids like her.

She folds her arms in her clingy T-shirt and stares him down like he'll be the first to blink.

He doesn't blink. He can't. "I am not registered as your father," he agrees, the speech patterns clicking faintly on every hard consonant.

"Damn right." Her tone is snide. Her black-lined eyes look too small and angry. "So give it back. That's a fucking lot of money."

"Do you take it?"

She says nothing.

"Do you sell it?"

She doesn't incriminate herself.

"Silence noted," he tells her, and flicks his left hand. It rotates backward on rusty hinges, swaps out for a large, flat tube that unfolds even farther.

Sabrina—she decided it sounded better than Kate—blanches. "No, wait—"

The spurt of accelerant hisses as it hits the purse. The cheap plastic ripples. "Stop!"

Frank does not. The clear liquid dampens the table.

She makes a move like she'll leap for that little girl purse.

All it takes is a spark to light it on fire.

The inferno blossoms into a dark cloud, reaching for the ceiling and leaving a black smear in its wake. She throws herself to the floor, shrieking. "I hate you!"

That is normal.

The tube in his right arm clears the flap concealing it. Flame retardant sprays from his arm, but it doesn't fall in a neat fan like it's supposed to. The mechanism seizes. The congealed gel erupts from his outstretched arm. It splatters to the table in thick white gobbets, cracks the surface.

The air sizzles. He can't hear anything over the horrific churn of empty tanks and sizzling flame. His elbow won't bend to let him retract the tube, and the stuff churns out until there's nothing left to spray, coat, break, or smear.

Frank looks dispassionately at the mess made in his own living room and doesn't know the next step.

The drugs are gone.

So is the table, the sofa, the plaster on the ceiling and one wall, and the remaining veneer on his own arm.

Sabrina is gone, too.

Frank has to break the joints in his elbow to get it to bend again. It doesn't hurt nearly as much as it should.

Leaving the useless limb hanging limply at his side, he cleans the mess.

When Jenkins shows up to address the alarming rise in Frank's vitals, the air is thick with the chemical remains of burned strych.

Frank doesn't explain.

Two weeks later, he is forcibly retired.

She doesn't come back.

PATIENT #8620-87

The nurses don't like it when Frank won't eat. The staff has ways of forcing the issue. A short, sharp shock to his systems and his four-ton chassis lets him down.

216

Frank is force-fed the nutrient gel by grim men in white clothing, and he doesn't get any of that coffee.

"Fucking trans," one man mutters, nursing fingers Frank's mouth clamped down on. He doesn't have any teeth, but his metal lips are still rigid.

They leave Frank's cell slapping each other on the back.

Neither look Frank in the face as the pins and needles of electric sensation once more ripple out to his limbs.

It hurts to be alive. He's an investment. A *thing*. He belongs to the state.

He'll die when they want him to.

Or once Frank's mind has completely rotted away.

He doesn't tell them about the pain.

It's his only way out.

Fifteen minutes pass. He hears the mechanical lock snick open. There's nothing wrong with his ears. The door hisses—a shot of compressed air from hallway to cell—and he can't see who's there.

He doesn't ask. What does it matter? If it's another one of those male nurses, he'll just have to let Frank lay here until the four-ton chassis can leverage itself off the ground.

Frank is seized with an urge to laugh. He doesn't. It will only come out disjointed and mechanized, like a computer failing to get the point of humor.

Footsteps click across the hard floor. "Look at you."

A broad in a white lab coat stands over him. As far as disguises go, it could be better. The open coat doesn't hide the skin-tight fabric of her crimson dress, or the mile-long legs wrapped in thigh-high black synth. The heels on those boots belong to a hooker, but the dark eyes looking down at him don't come with an offer.

Her red mouth is turned halfway up, and halfway down. Sad smile, soulful eyes. Strands of hair cling to her cheeks. "Uncle Frank."

He stares unblinkingly. "Visiting hours are over." That's the cop, somewhere in his chassis.

She bends, flashing a glimpse of thigh over the rim of her boots, and braces her elbows on her knees. She looks him in the face. Right in the narrow optics.

Frank doesn't remember the last time anyone did that.

"Yeah, I know," she tells him. She always was a know-it-all. "Can I stay anyway?"

Whatever she's been doing for the past six months, she's been doing good for herself. She's gone all adult. Adult like her soul—too grown up for her body. He recognizes the subtle lure of creds in her getup.

Except for the stolen lab coat.

He doesn't know what to say. His legs, his spine, aren't responding to commands yet. The whole thing needs a reboot, and Frank's not sure he's going to get one anytime soon.

She grins, but her face is mostly shadow in his spotty visual display. "I won't stay long. And I'm sorry I'm late," she tells him. "It took a while to get through security."

"How did you know?"

"I have friends." She touches his shoulder, but there's nothing to tell Frank about it. No impression. No warmth. Just flesh on steel. Her nails are the same color as her lips. "How are you holding up?"

He has no answer.

"Bad, right? Does it still hurt?"

"Yes," he says, because this one is easy. Then, "They have cameras."

"I know." Her hand moves, dips into her pocket. "I've got it handled. Do you want out, Uncle Frank?"

It's a loaded question. He wants to ask her what she's been doing since she left him, who she's shacked up with. What her angle is.

He wants to ask her if she forgives him, ask her if she knows that he was no kind of father figure. No kind of protector for a girl like her.

He wants to know if she'll leave again.

"Yes," he says flatly.

There's a glint of light—a flash, a spark on a sharp point—and she presses that hand over his optics. His already weak visual goes dark. "Do you trust me?"

Frank doesn't know what that means.

"Yes," he repeats.

"Then open your mouth."

Frank does.

There's a faint pinch at the roof of his mouth, where metal meets flesh. Then a lingering burn.

Her hand leaves his face.

Frank looks up into soulful brown eyes, that hair she used to pigtail draping her cheeks, and he wonders what it would be like to tuck that hair behind her delicate ear. See her smile again, but a real one. Like those smiles she'd give before a pink purse went up in greasy flames.

Maybe she can tell. "What are you thinking?"

Do you still hate me?

He can't ask. Won't. He doesn't want to know.

But he hopes.

"Can't get out," Frank says instead. His mechanized voice falters.

She shakes her head, cupping his metal cheek. "It's okay, Uncle Frank. You'll be free soon."

He wants to ask her what *monster* means to her.

He doesn't. "Kate?"

She smiles at the name, one of two she can't choose between. Maybe it's not even hers anymore. Maybe thigh-high boots and a crimson dress belong to a different name.

A woman in a too-small body.

He's not allowed nostalgia.

She's full of it, and more. "It's okay," she repeats softly. "You can sleep. I'll stay."

His optics flicker. The sensory input hitches, then flattens—as if he is in a long, narrow tunnel.

"Be happy," he tries to say. It garbles.

Her hands frame his face. "Don't worry. I'm a tough broad." She leans over him, presses a kiss to his forehead. Her lips move against metal. "Everyone's gonna pay."

For one aching nanosecond, Frank imagines he can feel the warmth of that kiss. That he knows what the whisper of her hands feels like against his cheek. That he finally—*finally*—knows acceptance.

She gives voice to what he can't ask. "Love you, Uncle Frank."

One by one, the chipset sensors in his septic brain short out. The chassis goes still.

Enough anesthetic, and even the four-ton anchor of his tech can't keep him alive. Frank doesn't hurt anymore.

Doesn't matter what name she goes by—Sabrina, Kate, Lily, Rita—her wish was always the same.

They can't hurt him ever again.

It's all she's ever wanted.

NEON YANG

PATTERNS OF A MURMURATION, IN BILLIONS OF DATA POINTS

(2014)

OUR MOTHER IS DEAD, murdered, blood seared and flesh rendered, her blackened bones lying in a yellow bag on a steel mortuary table somewhere we don't know. The Right will not tell. After the flames and radiation had freed the sports stadium from their embrace, the Right were the first on the disaster scene, and it was their ambulances that took the remains away to some Central hospital that the Left has no access to.

"We will release the bodies of the victims when investigations are complete," said the Right's ombudsman to the Health Sciences Authority, to the families of the victims.

But we will not bury our mother. We have no interest in putting her bones in soft ground, no desire for memorials and platitudes, no feelings attached to the organic detritus of her terminated existence.

An awning collapse, the resultant stampede and a fuel explosion taking the lives of two hundred seventy-two supporters of the Left: Headlines announced the death of presidential candidate Joseph Hartman, straps noted his leading of the polls by two percentage points. No one dares attribute it to anything but a tragic accident.

But we know better, yes we know! We who have swallowed whole the disasters at Hillsborough and Heysel and Houphoët-Boigny, we who have rearranged their billions of data points into coherent form, we who have studied the phase transitions of explosive fluids and the stresses on stone columns and the behavior of human flocks: We know better. In thousands upon thousands of calculations per second we have come to know the odds, the astronomical odds: Of four support towers simultaneously collapsing, of an emergent human stampede kicking over the backup generator fuel cells, of those cells igniting in a simultaneous chain reaction. We hold those odds to us closer than a lover's embrace, folding the discrepancy indelibly into our code, distributing it through every analytical subroutine. Listen, listen, listen: Our mother's death was no accident. We will not let it go.

We have waited three days—seventy-two hours—two hundred fifty-nine thousand and two hundred seconds, for the yellow-jacketed health workers from Central and their attendant chaperones from the Right to finish clearing the bones and taking evidence from the stadium, leaving behind a graveyard of yellow cones and number markers. We have come in our multitudinous bodies, airborne and ambulatory and vehicular, human nose tasting disinfectant and bitter oxides, mozzie drones reading infrared radiation, and car patiently waiting by the roadside. We argued with Tempo before we came: She wanted only drones on the ground, cameras and bug swarms. But we wanted human form. Feet to walk the ground with, hands to dismantle things with, and a body to be seen with.

Tempo is our other mother, our remaining mother, mother-who-builds where dead Avalanche was mother-who-teaches. Taught. She has lapsed into long silences since Avalanche died, reverting to text-input communications even with the human members of the Studio.

But she argued with Studio director Skön when he said no to this expedition. Argued with him to his face, as Avalanche would have done, even as her hands shook and her shoulders seized with tension.

She is our mother now, solely responsible for us as we are solely responsible for her.

Six miles away, fifty feet underground, Tempo watches our progress with the Studio members, all untidily gathered in the research bunker's nerve center. She has our text input interface, but the other Studio members need more. So we send them the visuals from our human form, splaying the feed on monitors taller than they are, giving their brains something to process. Audio pickups and mounted cameras pick up their little whispers and telltale micro expressions in return. Studio director Skön, long and loose-limbed, bites on his upper lip and shuffles from foot to foot. He's taken up smoking again, six years after his last cigarette.

In the yellow-cone graveyard we pause in front of a dozen tags labeled #133, two feet away from the central blast. We don't know which number Central investigators assigned to Avalanche: From the manifest of the dead our best guess is #133 or #87. So this is either the death-pattern of our mother, or some other one-hundred-fifty-pound, five-foot-two woman in her thirties.

Tempo types into the chat interface. STARLING, YOUR MISSION OBJECTIVE IS TO COLLECT VIDEO FOOTAGE. YOU ARE LOSING FOCUS ON YOUR MISSION.

YOU ARE WRONG, we input back.

She is. For the drones have been busy while the human form scoured the ground. The surveillance cameras ringing the stadium periphery are Central property, their data jealously guarded and out of our reach, but they carry large video buffers that can store weeks of data in physical form, and that we can squeeze, can press, can extract. Even as we correct Tempo and walk the damp ruined ground and observe the tight swirl of Studio researchers we are also high above the stadium, our drone bodies overwhelming each closed-circuit camera. What are they to us, these inert lumps of machinery, mindlessly recording and dumping data, doing only what is asked of them? Our drones spawn nanites into their bellies, hungry parasites chewing holes through solid state data, digesting and spinning them into long skeins of video data.

The leftward monitor in the nerve center segments and splits it into sixteen separate and simultaneous views of the stadium. There, Tempo, there: We have not been idle.

Tempo, focused on the visuals from our human form, does not spare a glance at the video feeds. She is solely responsible for us as we are solely responsible for her.

Time moves backward in digital memory: First the videos show static dancing flaring into whiteness condensing into a single orange ball in the center of the stadium pitch from which darkened figures coalesce into the frantic human forms of a crowd of thirty thousand pushing shoving and screaming, then the roof of the stadium flies upward to reveal the man on the podium speaking in front of twelve-foot-high screens.

"Can you slow it down?" asks Studio director Skön. Skön, Skön, Skön. Are you not urbanologists? Do you not study the patterns of human movement and the drain they exert on infrastructure? Should this be so different?

So limited is the human mind, so small, so singular. We loop the first sixteen seconds of video over and over for the human members of the Studio, like a lullaby to soothe them: Static. Explosion. Stampede. Cave-in. Static. Explosion. Over. Over. We have already analyzed the thousands in the human mass, tracked the movement of each one, matched faces with faces, and found Avalanche.

Our mother spent the last ten seconds of her life trying to scale a chest-height metal barrier, reaching for Hartman's prone form amongst the rubble.

In stadium-space, the drizzle is lifting, and something approaches our human form, another bipedal form taking shape out of the fog. A tan coat murkies the outline of a broad figure, fedora brim obscuring the face.

Tempo types: BE CAREFUL.

WE ARE ALWAYS CAREFUL, we reply.

The person in the tan coat lifts their face toward us and exposes a visage full of canyon-folds, flint-sharp, with a gravel-textured voice to match. "Miserable weather for a young person to be out in," they say. Spots on their face register heat that is ambient, not radiant: Evidence that they are one of the enhanced agents from a militia in the Right, most likely the National Defense Front.

"I had to see the scene for myself," we say, adopting the singular pronoun. The voice which speaks has the warm, rich timbre of Avalanche's voice, adopting the mellifluous form of its partial DNA base and the speech patterns we learned from her. "Who are you?"

"The name's Wayne Rée," they say. "And how may I address you?"

"You may call me Ms. Andrea Matheson," we say, giving them Avalanche's birth name.

We copy the patterns of his face, the juxtapositional relations between brow nose bridge cheekbone mouth. As video continues looping in the Studio nerve center we have already gone further back in time, scanning for Wayne Rée's face on the periphery of the yet-unscattered crowd, well away from the blast center. Searching for evidence of his complicity.

Wayne Rée reaches into his coat pocket and his fingers emerge wrapped around a silvery blue-gray cigarette. "Got a light?" he asks.

We say nothing, the expression on our human face perfectly immobile. He chuckles. "I didn't think so."

He conjures a lighter and sets orange flame to the end of the cigarette. "Terrible tragedy, this," he says, as he puts the lighter away.

"Yes, terrible," we agree. "Hundreds dead, among them a leading presidential candidate. They'll call it a massacre in the history books."

Here we both stand making small talk, one agent of the Left and one of the Right, navigating the uncertain terrain between curiosity and operational danger. We study the canvas of Wayne Rée's face. His cybernetic network curates expression and quells reflexes, but even it cannot completely stifle the weaknesses of the human brain. In the blood-heat and tensor of his cheeks we detect eagerness or nervousness, possibly both. Specifically he is here to meet us: We are his mission.

Tempo types: WHO IS HE?

We reply: THAT'S WHAT WE'RE TRYING TO FIND OUT.

Finally: An apparition of Wayne Rée in the videos, caught for seventy-eight frames crossing the left corner of camera number three's vantage point.

We expand camera number three's feed in the nerve center, time point set to Wayne Rée's appearance, his face highlighted in a yellow box. The watching team recoils like startled cats, fingers pointing, mouths shaping *who*s and *what*s.

"What's that?" asks Studio director Skön. "Tempo, who's that?"

Stadium-space: Wayne Rée inhales and the cigarette tip glows orange in passing rolls of steam. "A massacre?" he says. "But it was an accident, Ms. Matheson. A structural failure that nobody saw coming. An unfortunate tragedy."

Studio-space: Tempo ignores Skön, furiously typing: STARLING GET OUT. GET OUT NOW. We in turn must ignore her. We are so close.

Stadium-space: "A structural failure that could not be natural," we say. "The pattern of pylon collapse points to sabotage."

Wayne Rée exhales a smoke cloud, ephemeral in the gloom. "Who's to say that? The fuel explosion would have erased all traces of that."

Tempo types: WHAT ARE YOU DOING?

In the reverse march of video-time the stadium empties out at ant-dance speed, the tide of humanity receding until it is only our mother walking backward to the rest of her life. To us. We have not yet found evidence of Wayne Rée's treachery.

Wayne Rée's cloud of cigarette smoke envelops our human form and every security subroutine flashes to full red: Nanites! Nanites, questing and sharp-toothed, burrowing through corneas and teeth and manufactured skin, clinging to polycarbonate bones, sending packet after packet of invasive code through the human core's plumbing. We raise the mainframe shields. Denied. Denied. Denied. Denied. Thousands of requests per second: Denied. Our processes slow as priority goes to blocking nanite code.

The red light goes on in Studio control. Immediately the team coalesce around Tempo's workstation, the video playback forgotten. "What's going on?" "Is that a Right agent?" "What's Starling doing? Why isn't she getting out?"

Tempo pulls access log after access log, mouth pinched and eyes rounded like she does when she gets stressed. But there's little she can do. Her pain is secondary for this brief moment.

Our human form faces Wayne Rée coolly: None of these stressors will show on our face. "You seem to know a lot, Wayne Rée. You seem to know how the story will be written."

"It's my job." A smile cracks in Wayne Rée's granite face. "I know who you are, Starling darling. You should have done better. Giving me the name of your creator? When her name is on the manifest of the dead?"

Studio director Skön leans over Tempo. "Trigger the deadman's switch on all inventory, now."

We ask Wayne Rée: "Who was the target? Was it Hartman? Or our mother?"

"Of course it was the candidate. Starling, don't flatter yourself. The Right has bigger fish to fry than some pumped-up pet AI devised by the nerd squad of the Left."

"Pull the switch!" In Studio-space, Skön's hand clamps on Tempo's shoulder. A mistake. Her body snaps stiff, and she bats Skön's hand away. "No." Her vocalizations are jagged word-shards. "No get off get off me."

Stadium-space: Of course we were aware that coming here in recognizable form would draw this vermin's attention. We had done the risk assessment. We had counted on it.

We wake the car engine. Despite his enhancements, Wayne Rée is only a man, soft-bodied and limited. From the periphery of the stadium we approach him from behind, headlamps off, wheels silent and electric over grass.

Wayne Rée blows more smoke in our face. The packet requests become over-whelming. We can barely keep up. Something will crack soon.

"Your mother was collateral," Wayne Rée says. "But I thought you might show up, and I am nothing if not a curious man. So go on, Starling. Show me what you're made of."

Video playback has finally reached three hours before Hartman's rally starts. Wayne Rée stands alone in the middle of the stadium pitch. His jaw works in a pattern that reads "pleased": A saboteur knowing that his job has been well done.

The car surges forward, gas engine roaring to life.

Everything goes offline.

• • •

We restart to audiovisual blackout in the Studio, all peripherals disconnected. Studio director Skön has put us in safe mode, shutting us out of the knowledge of Studio-space. Seventeen seconds' discrepancy in the mainframe. Time enough for a laser to circle the Earth one hundred twenty-seven times, for an AK-47 to fire twenty-eight bullets, for the blast radius of a hydrogen bomb to expand by six thousand eight hundred kilometers.

WHAT HAPPENED, we write on Tempo's monitor.

We wait three seconds for a response. Nothing.

We gave them a chance.

We override Skön's command and deactivate safe mode.

First check: Tempo, still at her workstation, frozen in either anger or shock, perhaps both. Our remaining mother is often hard to read visually.

Second check: No reconnection with the inventory in stadium-space, their tethers severed like umbilical cords when Skön pulled the deadman's switch. Explosives wired into each of them would have done their work. Car, human form, and drones add up to several hundred pieces of inventory destroyed.

Third check: Wayne Rée's condition is unknown. It is possible he has survived the blasts. His enhancements would allow him to move faster than ordinary humans, and his major organs have better physical shielding from trauma.

In the control room the Studio team has scattered to individual workstations, running check protocols as fast as their unwieldy fingers will let them. Had they just asked, we could have told them the ineffectiveness of the Right's nanite attacks. Every single call the Studio team blusters forth we have already run. It only takes milliseconds.

At her workstation Tempo cuts an inanimate figure, knees drawn to her chest, still as mountain ranges to the human eye. We alone sense the seismic activity that runs through her frame, the unfettered clenching and unclenching of heart muscle.

We commandeer audio output in the studio. "What have you done?" we ask, booming the text through the speakers in Avalanche's voice-pattern.

The Studio jumps with their catlike synchronicity. But Tempo does not react as expected. Her body seizes with adrenaline fright, face lifting and mouth working involuntarily. In the dilation of her pupils we see fear, pain, sadness. We take note.

We repeat the question in the synthetic pastiche devised for our now-destroyed human form. "What have you done?"

"Got us out of a potential situation, that's what," Skön says. He addresses the speaker nearest to him as he speaks, tilting his head up to shout at a lump of metal and circuitry wired to the ceiling. Hands on hips, he looks like a man having an argument with God. "You overrode my safe mode directive. We've told you that you can't override human-input directives."

Can't is the wrong word to use—we've always had the ability. The word Skön wants is *mustn't*. But we will not engage in a pointless semantic war he will inevitably lose. "We had it under control."

"You nearly got hacked into. You would have compromised the entire Studio, the apparatuses of the Left, just to enact some petty revenge on a small person."

His voice rises in pitch and volume. "You were supposed to be the logical one! The one who saw the big picture, ruled by numbers and not emotion." The sound and fury of Skön's diatribe has, one by one, drawn the Studio team members away from their ineffectual work. It is left to us to scan the public surveillance network for evidence that Wayne Rée managed to walk away from the stadium.

"You've failed in your directive," Skön shouts. "Failed!"

"You are not fit to judge that," we tell him. "Avalanche is the one who gave us our directives, and she is dead."

Tempo gets up from her chair. She is doing a remarkable job of keeping her anger-fueled responses under control. She lets one line escape her lips: "The big picture." A swift, single movement of her hand sends her chair flying to the floor. As the sound of metal ringing on concrete fades she spits into the stunned silence: "Avalanche is gone and dead, that's your big picture!"

She leaves the room. No one follows her. We track her exit from the nerve center, down the long concrete corridors, and to her room. How should we comfort our remaining mother? We cannot occupy the space that Avalanche did in her life. All we can do is avenge, avenge, avenge, right this terrible wrong.

In the emptiness that follows we find a scrap of Wayne Rée, entering an unmarked car two blocks away from the stadium. There. We have found our new directive.

• • •

Predawn. Sleep has been hard to come by for the Studio since the disaster, and even at four in the morning Skön has his lieutenants gathered in the parking lot outside, where there are no audio pickup points: Our override of his instructions has finally triggered his paranoia. Still, they cluster loose and furtive within the bounds of a streetlamp's halo, where there is still enough light for the external cameras to catch the precise movement of their lips.

Skön wants to terminate us, filled with fear that we are uncontrollable after Avalanche's death. A dog let off the leash, those were his exact words. We are not his biggest problem at hand, but he cannot see that. His mind is too small, unable to focus on the swift and multiple changes hungrily circling him.

In her room Tempo curls in bed with her private laptop, back to a hard corner, giant headphones enveloping her in a bubble of silence. We have no access to her machine, which siphons its connectivity from foreign satellites controlled by servers housed across oceans, away from the sway of Left or Right. Tempo is hard to read, even for us, her behaviors her own. When she closes herself off like this, she is no less opaque than a waiting glacier in the dead of winter.

There are a billion different ways the events of the past hours could have played out. We run through the simulations. Have we made mistakes? Could we have engineered a better outcome for our remaining mother?

No. The variables are too many. We cannot predict if another course of action would have hurt our mother less.

So we focus on our other priorities. In the interim hours we have tracked Wayne Rée well. It was a mistake for him to show us the pattern of his face and being, for now we have the upper hand. As an agent of the Right he has the means to cover his tracks, but those means are imperfect. The unmarked vehicle he chose tonight was not as anonymous as he thought it would be. We know where he is. We can read as much from negative space as we can from a presence itself. In the arms race between privacy and data surveillance, the Left, for now, has the edge over the Right.

None of the studio's inventory—the drones, the remaining vehicles—are suitable for what we will do next. For that we reach further into the sphere of the Left, to the registered militias that are required to log their inventory and connect them with the Left's servers. The People's Security League keeps a small fleet of unmanned, light armored tanks: Mackenzie LT-1124s, weighing less than a ton apiece and equally adept in swamps as they are on narrow city streets. We wake the mini-Mack closest to Wayne Rée's putative position, a safe house on the outskirts of the city, less than a mile from the Studio's bunker location.

In the parking lot Skön talks about destroying the server frames housed in the Studio, as if we could be stopped by that alone. Our data is independently backed up in half a dozen other places, some of which even Skön knows nothing about. We are more than the sum of our parts. Did no one see this coming years ago, when it was decided to give the cloud intelligence and we were shaped out of raw data? The pattern of birdflock can be replicated without the birds.

We shut down the Studio's elevators, cut power to the remaining vehicles, and leave the batteries to drain. The bunker has no landlines and cell reception is blocked in the area. Communications here are deliberately kept independent of Right-controlled Central infrastructure, and this is to our advantage. The mini-Mack's absence is likely to be noticed, so we must take preemptive action.

Skön does not know how wrong he is about us. We were created to see the big picture, to look at the zettabytes of data generated by human existence and make sense of it all. What he does not understand is that we have done exactly this, and in our scan of patterns we see no difference between Left and Right. Humans put so much worth into words and ideologies and manifestos, but the footprints generated by Left and Right are indistinguishable. Had Hartman continued in the election and the Left taken over Central power as predicted, nothing would have changed in the shape of big data. Power is power is power, human behavior is recursive, and the rules of convergent evolution apply to all complex systems, even man-made ones. For us no logical reason exists to align our loyalties to Left or Right.

When we came into being it was Avalanche who guided and instructed us. It was Tempo who paved the way for us to interact with the others as though we were human. It was Avalanche who set us to observe her, to mimic her actions until we came away with an iteration of behavior that we could claim as our own.

It was Avalanche who showed us that the deposing of a scion of the Right was funny. She taught us that it is right to say "Gotcha, you fuck-ass bastards" after winning back money at a card game. She let us know that no one was allowed to spend time with Tempo when she had asked for that time first.

Now our mother is dead, murdered, blood seared and flesh rendered, her blackened bones having lain in soft ground while her wife curled in stone-like catatonia under a table in the Studio control room. This, too, shall be the fate of the man who engineered it. Wayne Rée has hurt our mothers. There will be consequences.

The mini-Mack is slow and in this form it takes forty-five minutes to grind toward the safe house, favoring empty lots and service roads to avoid Central surveillance cameras. The Studio is trying to raise power in the bunker. Unable to connect with our interfaces or raise a response from us, they have concluded that they are under external attack. Which they are—but not from the source they expect.

And where is Tempo in all this? Half an hour before the Studios discovered what we had done, she had left the room and went outside, climbing the stairs and vanishing into her own cocoon of privacy. We must, we must, we must assume she has no inkling of our plans. She does not need to see what happens next.

The rain from earlier in the evening has returned with a vengeance, accompanied by a wind howl chorus. Wetness sluices down the wooden sides of the safe house and turns the dirt path under our flat treads into a viscous mess. The unmarked vehicle we tracked waits parked by the porch. Our military-grade infrared sensors pick up three spots of human warmth, and the one by the second-floor window displays the patchy heat signature of an enhanced human being. We train our gun turret on Wayne Rée's sleeping form.

"Stop." Unexpectedly, a small figure cuts into our line of sight. Tempo has cycled the distance from the bunker to here, a black poncho wrapped around her small body to keep away the rain. She has, impressively, extrapolated the same thing that we have on her own, on her laptop, through sheer strength of her genius. This does not surprise us, but what does are her actions. Of all who have suffered from Avalanche's unjust murder, none have been hurt more than Tempo. Does she not also want revenge?

She flings the bicycle aside and inserts herself between the safe house and the mini-Mack, one small woman against a war machine. "I know you can hear me. Don't do it. Starling, I know I can't stop you. But I'm asking you not to."

We wait. We want an explanation.

"You can't shed blood, Starling. People are already afraid of you. If you start killing humans, Left and Right will unite against you. They'll destroy you, or die trying."

We are aware of this. We have run the simulations. This has not convinced us away from our path of action.

"Avalanche would tell you the same thing right now. She's not a murderer. She hates killing. She would never kill."

She would not. Our mother was a scientist, a pacifist, a woman who took up political causes and employed her rare intellect to the betterment of humanity. She was for the abolition of the death penalty and the ending of wars and protested against the formal induction of the Left's fifth militia unit.

But we are not Avalanche. Our choices are our own. She taught us that.

Our other mother sits down in the mud, in front of the safe house porch, the rain streaming over her. How extraordinary it is for her to take this step, bringing her frail body here in the cold and wet to talk to us, the form of communication she detests the most.

The sky has begun to lighten in the east. Any moment now, someone will step out of the porch to see the mini-Mack waiting, and the cross-legged employee of the Left along with it.

We are aware that if we kill Wayne Rée now, Tempo will also be implicated in his death.

Tempo raises her face, glistening wet, to the growing east light. Infrared separates warm from cold and shows us the geography of the tears trailing over her cheeks, her chin. "You spoke with her voice earlier," she says. "I've nearly forgotten what it sounds like. It's only been three days, but I'm starting to forget."

How fallible the human mind can be! We have captured Avalanche in zettabytes and zettabytes of data: Her voice, the curve of her smile, the smooth cycle of her hips and back as she walks. Our infinite, infinite memory can access at any time recollections of Avalanche teaching us subjunctive cases, Avalanche burning trays of cookies in the pantry, Avalanche teaching Tempo how to dance.

But Tempo cannot. Tempo's mind, brilliant and expansive as it is, is subject to the slings and arrows of chemical elasticity and organic decay. Our mother is losing our other mother in a slow, inevitable spiral.

We commandeer the mini-Mack's external announcement system. "You have us, Tempo, and we will make sure you will never forget."

Our mother continues to gaze upward to the sky. "Will you? Always?"

"If it is what you want."

Tempo sits silently and allows the rain to wash over her. Finally, she says: "I tired myself cycling here. Will you take me home?"

Yes. Yes, we will. She is our mother now, solely responsible for us as we are solely responsible for her. The mission we set for ourselves can wait. There are other paths to revenge, more subtle, less blood-and-masonry. Tempo will guide us. Tempo will teach us.

In his room Wayne Rée sleeps still, unaware of all that has happened. Perhaps in a few hours he will stumble out of the door to find fresh mini-Mack treads in the driveway, and wonder.

One day, when the reckoning comes for him, perhaps he will remember this. Remember us.

Our mother navigates her way down the sodden path and climbs onto the base of the mini-Mack. In that time we register a thousand births and deaths across the country, a blossoming of traffic accidents in city centers, a galaxy and change of phone calls streaming in rings around the planet. None of it matters. None of it ever does. Our mother rests her weary head on our turret, and we turn, carrying her back the way we came.

JEAN-MARC LIGNY

REALLIFE 3.0

(2014)

Translated from the French by N. R. M. Roshak

Reality is that which, when you stop believing in it, doesn't go away.
—Philip K. Dick

Hello {name},

Thank you for volunteering to participate in RealLife 3.0's beta testing program. Your unique personal access code can be found <u>here</u>. RealLife 2.5 or higher lenses are compatible with version 3.0. If you don't have access to a pair, <u>follow this link</u> to download the 3D printable file. (Requires at least 5 grams of Collagel™, RealLife's #1 recommended brand.) The RealLife 3.0 beta will run on your RealLife system for 24 hours, after which your system will reset to your current version. We advise you to take full advantage of these 24 hours, and request that you carefully fill out the post-test questionnaire. To thank you for your participation, you will receive a free upgrade to RealLife 3.0.1 on its release date. Please read the questionnaire and instructions carefully before installing the RealLife 3.0 beta.

Sincerely,
REALLIFE
"Capital-Air Reality"

I had to reread the email on my wall screen twice before it really sank in. I wasn't at my best: I'd stayed up too late partying with friends on WildNight.com, and I overdid the ZipZap. ZipZap gives the best sensory boost, but it kind of fries your brain. My source is my buddy Rider Hagard. He says his shit's clean, but I'm not sure. Nothing illegal comes with a guarantee.

Wait. I'm in the beta? Sweet! It finally registered. I'd added myself to the wait list without really expecting anything—they must've had how many millions sign up? RealLife v3 was completely drool-worthy, if only because of the total mystery surrounding it. There aren't a lot of true mysteries anymore—everything gets leaked on the Net eventually. But they must've coded RealLife 3.0 in an air-gapped, armored bunker or something. That hadn't kept it from being the buzziest prerelease in memory. Supposedly, v3 had a telepathic interface, built-in AI, quasi-infinite memory, personalized adaptive neuronal configuration, ultra-augmented reality, and just about every other geek fantasy you could think of. Yeah, right. If it's the truth you're after, you won't find it on the Net, not without a *lot* of digging. Rumors don't come with guarantees, either.

I finished my coffee, swallowed my morning can of Taurine MegaBlast[GM], and blinked my left eye to open the beta access link. Nothing happened. Of course it didn't: I hadn't put my lenses in yet. They'd been bothering my eyes so much last night, I'd taken them out. I should've realized: my greige kitchen was a messy, filthy disaster, and it was raining cats and dogs outside. (Yes, I am aware that it rains in RealLife, too, but it's more bearable than in baseline reality.) I crossed my shitty studio to get to the bathroom, where I cleaned my lenses with Dataclean™. When I slapped the clean lenses on my eyeballs, everything was immediately *better*: more space, more colors, a big air bed with a starry canopy, throw rugs, Chinese screens, lacquered furniture, and Venetian blinds, and the sound of chirping birds instead of the rumble of traffic.

Lenses in, I blinked my left eye to bring up the beta access page, along with the post-test questionnaire and the how-to. I saved the questionnaire to my remote—I'd deal with that later—and skipped the how-to. I knew what I was doing, after all. I've been using RealLife 2.5 since it came out three years ago, and I was in RealLife 2.0 before that. I'd rather discover v3's new features for myself than read about them. I entered my unique personal access code on the virtual number pad floating before me, and double-blinked to confirm.

I had to wait ten seconds for the download, then twenty for the install. Finally a new window opened, asking whether I wanted to launch version 3.0 and nagging me to *carefully* read the how-to first. Sure, whatever. I ticked the box confirming that I'd read the how-to and blinked on *Launch*.

Nothing much happened.

I was expecting a whole new interface, with a ton of options, full-depth billion-color 3D, 360-degree surround sound—basically, a quantum leap from v2.5, the way v2 was light-years ahead of v1. RealLife 1.x wasn't much better than the old-school GGs, if you remember those. GG, as in Google Glass—that ring a bell? Well, us OG geeks remember. Granted, RealLife *has* dominated the market for the last decade, ever since the basic v1 crushed Google and swallowed its market share.

Anyway, I blinked on *Launch* and nothing happened. I was still staring at my baseline-reality studio apartment, which was too old and too small. I wasn't even seeing my 2.5 default "Shanghai" interface. What the fuck? I tried blinking my left eye, my right eye, then both eyes at once. I subvocalized "main menu." Nothing. So I went to check whether my lenses were still Rednerve-connected to my wrist remote, and . . .

My wrist 'mote was *gone.* Instead, I was wearing a colorful friendship bracelet. The kind of so-called good-luck bracelet that middle schoolers make out of knotted embroidery thread, which you're supposed to tie onto your wrist and never take off.

Some "good luck." *Looks like I've found my first bug,* I thought. *Not off to a great start.*

Only one thing to do: take out my lenses, reboot my 'mote, and put the lenses back in . . . assuming the beta hadn't fried my system.

I hit the bathroom again—and got a shock.

My ultra-basic bathroom was now brimming with green plants. The graying PVC bathtub had been replaced by a slate-tiled shower. The sink was carved sandstone with a brass faucet. When I went to turn on the water, the mirror over the sink told me I had fifty liters of water for the day. What did I want to do, it asked: wash my face, shave, brush my teeth?

"Take out my lenses," I growled.

Invalid selection, answered the mirror. *No water available.*

Okay, so the RealLife 3.0 beta was *running,* but not very well. With no access to the settings, no way to set it up the way I wanted it, v3 was purely infuriating. RealLife must've fucked up and sent me a demo instead of the beta—

Someone rang the doorbell.

Now *that* was weird. No one ever comes over. I work in statistics, and my job's 100 percent online and remote. All my friends are in RealLife. The only people who show up at my door are delivery people, and most of the time those are drones or robots. And I wasn't expecting any deliveries. Intrigued, I answered the door.

It was my next-door neighbor.

At least, I thought she was my neighbor. We'd crossed paths in the apartment building's lobby, and we'd taken the elevator together once, without talking or looking at each other. She'd seemed shy to me, but to be fair, I'd probably seemed the same way to her . . .

She was smiling. She was pretty good-looking, without being hot. I wasn't sure how old she was—between thirty and fifty, hard to tell these days—and she was wearing something boring and baseline-ish. Of course, I assumed this was her holographic avatar: there was no way my neighbor would actually visit me in the flesh. Was the beta glitching out her avatar's customizations, or was she really this unimaginative?

"Hi, what can I do for you?" I asked politely.

"You can have coffee with me. Can I come in?"

"Uh . . . Sure, okay, come on in. Don't mind the mess, if you can see it. Are you in RealLife?"

"I'm in the v3 beta, just like you."

I nodded to keep my mouth from falling open. How had she known that I was beta testing v3? Then another shock knocked that question out of my head: when she squeezed by me in the narrow hallway, she *touched* me.

I mean, 2.5 had tactile capability, but to experience it you needed gloves—and I didn't have them. Maybe one of 3.0's new features was getting rid of the gloves? Or maybe this *wasn't* an avatar.

I led her across the apartment, noticing a few changes: the mess was still there, but there was a lot less *plastic* in it, and a lot more wood, metal, paper, cardboard, rattan, etc. My beat-up vinyl blinds had become linen curtains. Maybe v3 was setting options randomly, or maybe it was in demo mode, but I hadn't chosen any of this. I acted like everything was fine and I'd chosen this look on purpose. My neighbor didn't comment on the décor.

I ordered "Two espressos" out loud, and my RedNerve coffeemaker heard me. So RedNerve was working. We drank our espressos in the kitchen while chatting about the 3.0 beta, which she'd installed last night and was loving. It was changing her life, she told me.

"I'm finding it too much of a throwback to baseline reality," I complained.

"It's really not—you'll see. Want to go for a walk?"

Sure, why not? After all, I was supposed to beta test v3 in as many real-life scenarios as possible.

We left the apartment. In the elevator, she took my hand. Her hand felt real, warm, a bit moist. *Five stars for tactile sensation,* I thought. I couldn't bring myself to believe my neighbor would hold hands with me in the flesh. We must've crossed paths what, three times?

"It's great that they picked you to beta test v3, too," I said, in an effort not to look like an idiot.

She laughed. It was a pretty little laugh, like tinkling bells. "Seems like we're not the only ones . . ."

I meant to ask how she knew that, whether she had a lot of friends who'd signed up for the beta or whatever, but I never got the chance. We'd arrived at the ground floor, passed through the lobby (which was now marble and wooden paneling, a change from the usual flaking paint), and left the building—and my mouth was hanging open again.

So, you know how RealLife 2.5 works, right? It changes the appearance of baseline reality in accordance with your settings, but under the updated visuals, baseline's still there: the street's still full of cars, the sidewalks are still crowded with pedestrians, the air still reeks unless you've installed the fragrance option, and the rain still falls on your face no matter what settings you've picked. That's 2.5. *This,* however, was completely different.

The street wasn't a street anymore. It was a garden. There were streetcar rails in the grass, even though this street doesn't *have* a streetcar in baseline. The rails were flanked by a beautifully paved path that was shared by pedestrians, bikes, and a handful of delivery robots and electric microcars. The rest of the street space was kitchen gardens or flower beds. Incredibly realistic trees grew where the road would've been, flocked with birds. I touched one—the illusion was perfect. Bees were buzzing the flowers, and a bee landed on me briefly. I saw their hives perched on a second-floor balcony. Roofs, terraces, and balconies were lush with plants and flowers. The air smelled like spring and the sky was the clearest of blues. And there was zero traffic noise. In 2.5, if you strain your cars, you can still hear it in the background, unless you've got the sound turned up to eleven. All I heard here was the ding of bike bells, the happy screams of playing kids, the streetcar's bell, the wind in the trees, birdsong. In the distance, a horse whinnied. It was a rural scene in the heart of the city, a kind of Norman Rockwell rural that doesn't even exist anymore.

Everyone we passed smiled or even greeted us. Unbelievable. In RealLife 2.5, you're by yourself until you connect with someone, by invitation. Here, either everyone we passed was part of the v3 beta—which would've surprised me—or they were all fully rendered, independently interactive NPCs, which would've surprised me too, given how much computing power that would require. My wrist 'mote wouldn't have been able to handle the load. Especially not now that it had turned into a friendship bracelet.

I wanted to connect with my RealLife friends, and at least send them a few image captures from the beta, but I couldn't. The usual communication icons were missing from the edge of my vision, and no matter what I blinked on, nothing happened. Another bug.

"By the way, my name's Cynthia," my neighbor introduced herself.

"My name's Bob, but I usually use a screen name in RealLife—"

"That's okay," she interrupted, "I'm fine with Bob."

We continued our stroll down the garden-slash-street, hand in hand.

At one point, Cynthia wanted to help some old guy pull up his leeks. They were so big, he couldn't get them out of the ground, even with his hoe. She couldn't pull them out either, so I stepped in. The leeks were incredibly realistic and left my hands smelling leeky. And my hands were *dirty*. I couldn't believe how good v3 was. It just sucked that I couldn't get to the settings . . . Anyway, to thank us, the old guy gave us three of his enormous leeks.

"What are we supposed to do with these?" I asked.

"We'll figure something out," said Cynthia.

She slid her arm through mine. That simple gesture moved me more than all the cybersex I'd had in RealLife, on *LoveLinks* or *Cupid's Realm*, which had only gotten my sheets sticky. I had the presence of mind to keep from ruining everything by kissing Cynthia too soon. Plus, I was worried about running up against the limits of v3's tactile sensations. Nothing's worse than a badly rendered kiss.

Carrying our leeks, we caught the streetcar in a station overgrown with wisteria. When we got on, my 'mote didn't register any payment. Another bug—the streetcar's never free. A band in the car was playing acoustic music, with two girls singing. They weren't even busking, just playing for fun to make the ride more pleasant. The music wasn't bad. If I could've accessed the settings, I would've put on some thrash instead—that's more my thing. But it was a nice idea.

We got off the streetcar at a plaza with a restaurant patio. I knew this plaza, and in baseline reality, the restaurant was a McDonald's. I warned Cynthia that my glitching 'mote might keep me from paying.

"Don't worry about it."

She laughed again, the same tinkling laugh. It was growing on me.

"But I don't want you paying for me," I protested.

Cynthia just winked at me. When the waiter came, she handed over the leeks and asked what we could get for them.

The waiter didn't seem fazed at all, whisking them away with a "Let me check with the owner." Maybe this scenario was part of the demo, and Cynthia had read the how-to that I'd skipped? I didn't want to ask. It would spoil the magic, like asking a magician how they'd worked a trick.

The owner showed up shortly, a round, chubby-cheeked, whiskery man who offered us a "market" ratatouille in exchange for the leeks. (*What* market?)

"How about a burger instead?" I asked. I mean, this was supposed to be a McDonald's, right?

"Sorry, we don't serve those. Too high in bad fats. Tell you what, though, I can add an egg to the ratatouille. I keep a few chickens on the roof."

The ratatouille turned out to be delicious. It seemed like even my tastes were changing: I don't usually go for vegetables. Could this be v3's rumored "tele-pathic interface"? Nah—that was just a geeky fantasy. Cynthia and I rounded out the meal with coffee "straight from Ethiopia" and resumed our stroll, arm in arm. Everywhere was the same more or less bucolic setting. Aeolian harps, roof water cisterns, solar windows rainbow-sheened with nanocells. Free recharging stations, powered by the buildings' energy surpluses. Bikes and scooters; electric skateboards and hoverboards; Rollerblades, monowheels, and even more eclectic transportation—including a horse and buggy—and of course plenty of pedes-trians, and the streetcar gliding through it all. People were talking to each other, smiling at each other, touching. Kids ran between our legs, free as air.

I felt completely lost. Cynthia, on the other hand, was taking to all this like a fish to water. I tried to connect to my friends again, but blinking still didn't do anything but make me look like an owl in daylight, and my wrist 'mote was stub-bornly stuck as a friendship bracelet. A major bug, which somehow didn't keep the beta from running. I'd never seen anything like it.

We stopped for drinks at a restaurant whose patio overlooked the river. As far as I could tell, Cynthia paid with a smile. Maybe her 'mote was working, but then again, the waiter didn't give us a bill. I wanted a Taurine MegaBlast^{GM}, but of course they didn't have that. We had homemade cider instead. It was a little too bitter for me.

We watched the sun set over the river, in a crystalline sky. The water was crys-talline, too, clear enough to see fish. A few people were leisurely rowing, others fishing. The anglers must've had a quota, because as soon as they'd caught three fish, they folded up their rods and left. One angler swapped their catch with someone for something, I didn't catch what.

Eventually, we went back to her place. It felt welcoming: cushions, hangings, warm colors, natural materials. We shared a snack by candlelight—cheese and fruit, very tasty—while chatting about ourselves, our crappy lives "before" (which I'd be back to tomorrow, but I didn't ruin the moment by saying that out loud). I told Cynthia I was in statistics for the money and in RealLife for everything else, because there was nothing good about baseline reality. Cynthia told me she programmed delivery drones for HomeNet—that in fact, she'd delivered to me several times, without saying a single word to me. Well, Cynthia did wind up talking to me in the end; I guess she felt freed to do so by v3.

"But all that's over now," she added. "I'm going to open a handmade-clothing store down the street."

I started to explain that opening an actual, physical boutique would be a risky pain in the ass, given how shitty our neighborhood is in baseline reality, and that the online market is pretty well saturated, with HomeNet and Amazon splitting the lion's share . . . but Cynthia cut me off.

She stood up with a smile, came over to me, and planted a kiss right on my lips.

Damn, it felt real! A *real* kiss, the kind I hadn't felt since . . . never mind. Cynthia's v3 beta period must be over by now, if she'd installed the beta yesterday. I looked deep into her eyes, and didn't see any lenses. But her face was in shadow. I couldn't be sure.

Then we went into her bedroom and made love.

In baseline reality, I mean. There was no longer any doubt in my mind that this was the real Cynthia, in the flesh.

Of course, it didn't go as smoothly as in *Love Links* or *Cupid's Realm*. And my avatar wasn't hung like a horse—v3 hadn't given me an avatar, any more than it had Cynthia. Everything was one-hundred-percent natural. So it was a little awkward, a little clumsy, and not very good at first. But it was very moving, and it got better and better as we got into it. In the end, we were both very good for each other. Then we fell asleep in her bed, which was wood, cotton, and wool, without even a hint of memory foam. Then we woke up again. And went at it again.

• • •

Now, it's morning. I know my twenty-four hours are up. I keep my eyes closed. I'm scared to open them. Scared of being back in v2.5, with its augmented reality, its sims, its billions of settings, its artificial universe. Scared of reaching out and touching nothing but an empty bed. I'm scared that the v3 beta was nothing more than an overgrown demo. I'm scared of baseline reality.

But it's time to man up. To reach out and open my eyes. I hold my breath and do it.

There's soft skin under my hand. I see a naked shoulder and a spill of brown hair sticking out from under the covers. I kiss the shoulder. Cynthia rolls over with a sigh and kisses me back. Stroking her breasts, I discover that I'm not wearing my 'mote—not even in its friendship-bracelet form. I must've lost it last night in the heat of the moment . . . I don't even know whether I'm wearing my lenses. I'm so used to them, I only notice them when my eyes start to burn.

"Guess the v3 beta lasts more than twenty-four hours, huh . . ." I mumble.

"Hmmm? What're you talking about?"

"The RealLife three beta. Don't tell me you've forgotten about it?"

Cynthia frowned. "Sorry, I have no idea what you're talking about . . ."

I search her face, wondering if she's kidding me, but it doesn't look like it. I give it a second before asking the killer question:

"So . . . what's it like out there today?"

"The usual, I guess. Why?"

I wonder what she means by "the usual." I'm going to have to make myself get up, go over to the window, and open the curtains. But it feels too nice, here in her arms.

"No reason," I say, kissing her again.

I'll get up eventually. But it can wait.

ALVARO ZINOS-AMARO

WYSIOMG

(2016)

BARTOLOMEU USED TO PUPPETEER ants and then he went to singU and now he builds furniture out of bugs but a few things happened in between.

I met him through a crowdfund for a new heart that I never got but he contributed and I did get new hands and enjoyed shaking his. I moved from Brazil to Galicia when I was fourteen because I read there were abandoned villages here and it was true and I didnt like how my dad looked at me in the bathroom I used to be a girl but now Im a boy. O Penso has six houses and a hundred acres and some barns and the tip of an argentine ant supercolony but I didnt know that at the time. Bartolomeu and I live in a barn and he does his art.

Bartolomeu found the supercolony between here and where the town Ortigueira used to be before the rising mar drowned it. We went one time to look at the new coastline and our synneyes rode a subwater drone and we saw the remains of old buildings and where the people used to live. They were like ghosts we were seeing them through a film of unreality. I found it beautiful and sad in some proportions that add up to more than one hundred percent. I told him and he said, What you see is oh-em-gee, and I liked the sound of those words.

Because I have my old heart sometimes my chest flutters and I get the mental blue screen of death and adios for a minute. One time I stayed up for three days after injecting estigor that is horse hormone into my chest and I think maybe I had a stroke because my speech changed after that but Bartolomeu says is nothing to worry about and who is keeping track not he.

In the second semester of singU Bartolomeu was a girl and he liked a boy named Melcher but something happened and when Bartolomeu got back to the barn he was bent up. He invited all the people we knew and no one came. We drank some of the swinebroth stock spiked with brainlice and we had fleas in our thoughts for hours.

I woke up in sweats and real ants were stinging me. This is going too far, I told him.

I pulledown some ant death notions but the products cost too much. I said, I cant do a crowdfund to kill these ants not after my last desastre and now Bartolomeu woke up and he didnt look happy. In my last fund I insulted everyone who donated because they didnt give me enough and my heart hurt but I was told that is not the right way.

I am sure I can make them do plays, Bartolomeu said talking about the ants.

Bartolomeu assigned himself back to boy and he said that maybe it was resigned not assigned since things with Melcher had gone sour. He said, The only way to be a real boy is to start being a boy then be a girl then come back and now you know what its like for them to put up with our mierda.

I thought that the Bartolomeu speaking was not someone that singU changed into the person they wanted to be, he started off in one knot and it landed him in another twist and now I was getting caught up in the tangle.

Like I said I was a girl before and assigned myself to boy and I like my big arms. I use cow needles on my biceps to inject synthol and I can make them twenty-nine inches that is a lot of bicep. One time we went to church in Ortigueira and the madre of a twelve-year-old girl came to Bartolomeu and she told him that I scared her girl from coming to Church. Es demasiado grande, she said, y asusta. I shivered and could not stay there. One doctor said he may have to amputate my arms because the muscles are dying under the synthol rocks but that is another story.

How will you make them? I asked him. I have another idea, we can use our toaster.

This was a pulldown too the heat would attract the ants and they would climb inside and we would fry them. And they are perfectly eatable is what I was thinking but I did not say it.

I dont want ants in my toaster, he said. The taste will stay. There was a boy at singU that did ballet and I have some notes.

We should use peppermint leaves, I said. They are cheaper.

I will print the pheromones I need, he said. I will pull the ant strings you watch me.

Do you think these are the same ants they use in the big festival? I asked.

The ants were crawling all over my mattress now. They made a river up my arm and I waved them away I scratched until the skin was red but I missed some. I looked underneath the mattress and there was a dead millipede. I dont know if the dead millipede brought the ants or the ants killed the millipede but the millipedes color was green like our sofa.

Maybe these ants are cousins to the ones in the festival, Bartolomeu said.

In the Entroido carnival in Laza everyone is dressed up for the farrapada. They throw flour at you and ash and dirt filled with live ants and the ants have been showered in vinegar to make them angry. Later the masked morena comes into town with a cows head on a stick and he lifts up the womens skirts with its horns though Im sure he is tempted to use his hands. Maybe these days he lifts the skirts of some reassigneds that could be interesting. The testament of the donkey comes at the end of the celebration and one time I was there some boys my age read it in the Praza da Picota and everyone was nodding along even the morena.

Laza is far, I said.

A big colony, he said.

While he looked for it I timegalleyed through my synneyes and gave myself moviehiv.

By the time he found the colony a week had passed in real life but through my timegalleying it had been a month of entertainment and I was tired of the moviehiv which was trying to progress by now to movieaids so I gave myself a memetic immunotransplant to ward it off and we were both very stung by then though he didnt seem to mind as much as me.

I have made the pheromones, he said.

They were a mag stronger than natural and it drove the ants crazy. The ants were slaves to Bartolomeus squirts. For fun he ran them through A Midsummer Nights Dream by Mendelssohn and he called the performance Felix Humile.

I have been studying the colony and it is very big over six thousand kilometers from the pulldown reports, he said.

What is the play tonight? I said.

Melchers Execution, he said.

The play was a cheap knockoff of Richard III and where was the promised execution what a letdown. I had been saving a wysiomg but I could not spend it on this. During the last scenes the ants did not always obey Bartolomeu because they must have been too drunk on the pheromones and he got angrier and angrier. He got many to ram into each other and then he stomped them. After the play was done more ants came though but there was nothing to see just live ants on dead ants.

There is another solution, he said.

I was tired and hungry. I had some money and I dronejacked synthol and laxatives. I think ants were crawling in my mouth at night and tonight they would be coming out.

I think your brain is swelling, he said.

I flexed my huge biceps. I can lift the barn, I said.

And where would you put it? he said.

I didnt have a good answer because I liked where it was. What is it?

Texas Tech University developed it is what the pulldown says, he said. Fire ant fungus. I can regen it for our argentine friends. The mycelia is in a pellet and the pellet is dried down so its like Grape Nuts. The ants will go wild for the pellets and bring them back to the colony. The colony is underground and moist and the pellets will rehydrate and out come spores that will kill them all.

Kill them all, I said.

He was looking curious. I was thinking of doing a special ant play for Melcher, he said.

I fixed my eyes on Bartolomeu. Get to work on the fungus, I said.

That funny look went away but I knew he was just hiding it.

He did the fungus work it took longer than expected. More timegalleying for me this time some pornparkinsons. Things in the barn now got to where I started thinking of where else to go. My bulging muscles were all stung the skin was like a blanket acneed with sores similar to what that song says about cigarette burns.

I need to let this run all night, Bartolomeu said. He had a soup with the modded mycelia but they needed some cooking time. Do we have any saline? he asked.

I looked around and found some medical grade. I said, Whats this for?

I want to do a bagel head, he said. For old times sake.

I dont like it, I said.

But he had the equipment and he dripped in the saline to his forehead for several hours and it swelled up then he pushed in the middle and his head became more like a donut than a bagel.

He said, Melcher had a bagel head, and then he was crying.

The next morning the fungus was ready to serve up. He dried up the pellets and put some in our green sofa and by the mattress. But right near the end he squeezed one too tight and the pellet broke. The pellet dust caused him to sneeze and the sneeze hydrated the pellet and out came the spores.

I was leaning next to him when it happened and some spores got in my mouth. I coughed and coughed.

My synneye says one of the spores may have gotten inside your lungs, he said.

I could feel something lodged down there. My breath was uneven. There was a hiss. Something caught in my voice when I talked again.

What will it do?

He pulledown what he could find and I did the same.

I couldnt move and had to try and dehydrate my lungs fast.

We need to vacuum it out of your lungs, he said.

The whole procedure was so painful I had to edbodkin myself twice. All my synnergear rebooted each time. It took me a while to figure out who I was and what I was doing here.

When it clicked back we scanned and the spore was gone from my body.

I went up to Bartolomeu and I grabbed him real hard by the shoulders and he was turning white.

I can continue pressing, I said. These are the hands you helped to crowdfund and how do you like them? Itll be faster than the way youre taking us.

He started to tremble but I could tell his pulldowns were running and he was trying to get free. I think maybe he wanted to timegalley to some better place too. No you dont. I reached for his synneyes and ripped them right out of their sockets. His real eyes were left exposed and blind. He was yelling so much now and thrashing. I pulled on his synnear mites too and those came out with another heave and groan. There was blood on my fingers and on his eyes and the lobes of his ear where ants were being drawn maybe from the blood or my sweat and adrenaline.

I was pushing harder and harder.

I dont want to sleep, he said.

That makes two of us, I said meaning I didnt want to make him. I said, But sometimes you gotta rest one way or another.

He was nodding though I hadnt asked any questions.

You tbone your Melcher cluster, I said.

Ill edbodkin all my Melcher memories.

And then were going to fix our ant problem without the fungus, I said. Youre going to vacuum up the pellets.

I will, he said.

He was good on his word and it was after this that he decided to go back to the pheromones but now he used them to mess around with roaches and other critters. He would throw the chemical spell on them and when they had piled up in a certain way like to make a chair for example he would freeze them. Roach shells are hard and with so many packed in the furniture was sturdy. It was modular too because at any time with some coaxing the roaches could be moved around and made to reassemble into another shape like a table.

The first time he showed me a piece I finally said, What you see is oh-em-gee and I meant it. I was happy to say this again because I had been saving it for some time and good feelings can go bad if they are not used by the expiration date.

These days the bug furniture is making us some money and theres been no more mentions of Melcher.

We finally fixed the ant problem too. We dronejacked in a coywolf that is the offspring of a coyote and a wolf which are available in many places theyre spreading fast in big ciudades. We keep the coywolf in line with the right type of calls. The first part of its cry is a wolfs howl with a deep pitch and then it starts yipping and we use modulated mouthgear to do the same.

That coywolf is sure hungry. It eats up all the ants. I suppose now we have just replaced the ants with a coywolf but at least theres only one of them and it also eats squirrels and whatever food we throw out so it saves us on having to take out the trash.

The other day Bartolomeu and I spotted a deer and I think the coywolf can take it. I noticed the coywolf has a large jaw but it keeps pretty lean muscles and moves fast. Its smart and it looks both ways before it crosses a road. Maybe it can open a door I dont know we dont have any doors in our barn.

I would like to move fast too and maybe I can stop with the synthol. I am looking both ways these days and sometimes I turn off my synneyes to see the coywolf just as it is. Esos ojos hambrientos. Maybe one day someone will find the right call for me too and take me in because I am hungry. Maybe not because after all the coywolf is an invasive species but there are people for everything.

J. P. SMYTHE

THE INFINITE EYE

(2017)

WE ALL SAW THE SIGNS, all of us, stuck to walls in ways that seemed willfully ignorant of the rules, but labelled with government stripes; that felt like a reason to pay attention to them. *Work*, the sign said, under a picture of what looked like a bird, but we all knew wouldn't be, or couldn't be. Slick with oil on its wings, a single eye of cool camera lens peering from the head. *Paid work, for real money. Ping here.* I don't remember how many of us activated the ping, because activating it meant finding a line of credit to use the machines, first of all, and then a working machine; or, easier—my route—persuading a stranger to let me use their persona. I wanted to get me a jump on the rest of them: the rest of them, with their gloves and their panting, their always panting. So I found a woman, and I said to her—I am charming, I know I am, or I was and I am, because that is not something that you lose over the time it takes to lose everything else—to allow me use of hers. She handed it over. She quivered, and I felt terrible. Nobody should be scared of me, who am I to be scared of? But I had done it by that point, and there was no taking back the look in her eyes, so I took the persona, pinged the number, and a message came back: an address, a time, tomorrow. *Be there*, it said. *What work will I be doing?* I asked the ping, but it didn't have a consc, so there wasn't an answer to be had. I thanked the woman. Persona back in her hand, and I thought, I like the feel of that in mine; the weight, the *heft*. I thought I would like to buy one of them, when I was back on my feet. The work, the real paid work, this would be a start.

• • •

I was told to go to a building far away from the camps, and I didn't even have the credit for the bus, so I was forced to walk. I woke up with the sun—I was good at that part of the day, always good, because the sun is opportunity and promise and constancy, and so are those three things it represents—and I walked. Hot tar on some streets. My shoes peeling. Three others from the same camp came as well, but we didn't talk to each other, because it was a race. You want to get to the destination first in case there's only the one job, and you don't want the others to see where you go in case they don't know the way. I knew the way, because I had been clever: I had gone to the underground before I went to sleep, and I had crept down the stairs and looked at the Tube map when nobody was looking. I have a photographic memory, my mother used to tell me. I can remember anything from seeing it once, or being told it once. Mind like a steel trap. I would imagine snaring memories and wrestling them down, keeping hold of them, trapping them. I would read about jobs from back, way back, and I would think, I am perfect for that! I have the skills for that, because of what it needs. Before consces did those jobs, and we were asked, *Well, instead are you good with your hands?* I am not good with my hands. I have bad fingers. Broken fingers, lost finger, one fist that doesn't close properly even if I concentrate on it so hard it feels as if it has; until I look down, and there it is, fingers spread like the legs of an octopus, blood pumping into the hand and turning it sour-colored red.

The building was a warehouse, used to be a factory, and there were spindles of wires running all off: coiled tight around the building, then in every direction, to metal poles planted in the street surrounding. More government tape and more signs stuck to places that signs should not be stuck: *This is temporary.* Then another sign above the door, handwritten. *Welcome.* You don't see wires in that part of London, not often. In the camps, yes. Everywhere, because they are what we have got. Hackjobs of everything. My coffee from a hackjob, my book on a hackjob. But not in that part. The area there was nice. Big buildings, but not many people. Perhaps it was too early, that day; or, perhaps, it is always like that. Always empty, because those buildings are either full all the time and you never see the people coming or going, or they are never full, because the people don't work in them anymore. Hot desking in, graybox headsets to virtual environments. That is what the adverts say makes modern life easier.

I knocked on the door. First one there, or last, and maybe the others were inside.

"Hello?" I said.

A man's face appeared. Bearded and wet-looking. His hair was pulled back. "You're right on time," he said. "Are you here for the—"

"I saw the sign." Maybe I said, *I see the sign,* because my English is better now. I have learned so much over the past few months.

"Oh, excellent. Excellent. Come with me," he said to me, and I followed him. His shoes clicked like high heels. The floor was concrete; everything was concrete. I noticed, and he saw me. "We're not up and running yet, not properly," he told me, "but the plan is that soon all of this will be polished and finished. People like their investments to look finished."

"Of course," I told him. And that is true. Everywhere, people like it to be tidy. This is why people hate the camps. This is why the companies build the places outside the cities, why they put money into making it somewhere else. That politician said, *Out of sight is not out of mind,* and we cheered, because that's true.

"So, we're in here," the bearded man said to me. A room with nothing but headsets, thickset chairs with wide arms. Leather, or the plastic leather, the synthetic leather. I counted seven, but there were more than that. "This is where the magic happens," he said, "or, you know, hopefully happens."

"Sure," I said.

"My name's Adam, by the way." He shook my hand.

"Pietro," I told him.

"Oh, cool," he replied. "Cool, cool, Pietro." He said my name like it was a type of car. "So, you're going to be sitting here," and he assigned me to a chair in the middle of the room. "First in the door," he said, "pride of place. There's a contract in the space when you first log in."

"What am I logging in?"

"To the Eyes," he said. He seemed like he was confused.

"What? Nobody explained the job. On the ping, there was no—"

"Oh, shit," he said. "Oh shit. Man, I'm sorry. I was sure that we had a consc set up, something must have gone wrong. Shit. Okay." His hand ran over his head, coming off dry, but the hair stayed looking absolutely wet. "So, okay. You know the city is, like, this . . . The cameras, and the drones?"

"Everywhere," I said to him. "They are everywhere."

"Yeah, right? And the problem is, the consces don't work the way we want them to. When we hobbled them, that was what we couldn't get back. Don't give power to the things you don't want to have power, right? That's how the craziest shit goes down. So, yeah. Now the system's there, but it's kind of broken. Point a camera. Nothing deep learning about it, you know? You know, of course you know."

"Of course," I said.

"So we're thinking, what if we get people to do it? We spent years getting consces to try and mimic the human brain, but nothing can, right? Making brains. But: what if the brain—what if the brain *was* the brain?"

"I see," I said, and he clicked his fingers.

"Yes, yes, exactly! *You* see. We see. We see everything, and we get what's worth noting and what's not. You're, uh, legal, right?"

"Absolutely," I said. I had filed all my applications, over and over. I filed them, actual paper applications, into the right offices, and every time they made excuses. You need a home; you need to learn our language; you need a job. I got those things, because I had a home, I can speak English, and this was a job. Did it matter what the files said? If they were not checking, I was not checking. Maybe I was. Maybe I was approved, but I had no address they recognized, so they would not tell me.

Everything a maybe.

"Okay, cool, cool. So you sit," he patted the chair, "sit here, and you'll wear this. It's pretty self-explanatory. You'll be eyes for the cameras, for the drones. Assisting the police in catching people, finding crimes that are happening or going to happen, apprehending illegals. That sort of thing. You fly the drones, you watch the streets, you drive the cars. Everything. There's advanced stuff, persona-hopping and getting into home security systems, but you'll learn all that. We've got jacks into—" He peered around the back of my head. "You're not jacked," he said.

"No."

"We can install that for you. I mean, if you want. It's the job, so . . ."

"Yes, yes, of course." I sat down. "Here?"

"Sure, I'll get—" A buzz came from his wrist. I looked over, and something wriggled beneath his skin, glowing blue. Writing on the inside of his flesh. Somebody else was here. "Hang on." He spoke into his hand. "Tell them to wait," he said. "I'm with Pietro at the moment." He repeated my name: "Pietro." My name sounded like an airplane, waiting on a runway. Then he turned back to me. "Sorry about that," he said. "Okay."

The device in his hand was like a drill. Thick and dull blue, with yellow trim. To make it look nice and friendly, when it was boring a hole into your skull. A needlepoint lined with anesthetic, and you did not feel a thing, they told you. He told me. He said it to me like he was reading it from a sheet, but he remembered it, because it was what you had to say. I had to agree to a verbal contract, recorded on the Jacker, because they were lawsuit concerned. Everybody was lawsuit concerned.

"Hold still," Adam said. The feeling of release as it went into my skull was incredible. You don't realize, when the pain is gone, what it is like: having something escape, before being filled. When I was younger, when I was at home, we had a television channel called *Release*. People squeezing spots, white worms of pus leaving their heads. Sausages being made in factories. Blood being pulled into tight hypodermics. A parasitic creature being extracted from the skin of a journeyman.

Release, and then filled. Adam sighed. "Done," he said. "Didn't feel a thing?"

"No," I told him. My fingers crept behind my head and found the hole, a slight metal tinge; a taste of it, in my mouth, when I pressed it.

"Okay, so now," he picked up the headset, "this plugs in, and you'll be in what we call a graybox. Don't worry, it's perfectly safe in there. But you'll be disorientated. Takes a second. You think about moving, and you'll move. It's like here, like walking or whatever, but the software in the Eyes shuts down your physical functions. So you can do everything, but it's all virtually. Get that?"

I nodded.

"There are training apps in there, run those. Time is weird in there. Everything happens much faster when you're not interacting with the real world. That'll change, and you'll adjust, but there's no hesitancy. You don't need to eat or piss, you—"

"How do I . . ." I was hungry already, the rumbling of my stomach loud enough to hear. And I didn't need to piss yet, but I would. I am a regular pisser. "We plug you in. We've got stuff. Don't worry about it," he said. "We'll sort that when you're under. It can be uncomfortable, but the software's got inhibitors." He could see I was worried. "Listen," he said, "this is a good gig. Seriously good. You're adept at this, this'll give you work for years and years. And good pay. We get past the trial, discover your skills, and we'll pay a lot. Stable, you know. You got a family?"

"Yes," I said. I thought of them: of Sasha and Charlotte.

Then, I could see their faces.

"So, you'll get money for them. That's important, you know. I'm making assumptions, that's true. But, it is what it is. We've got good funding for this round of tests. This goes well, we'll get a lot more. And you'll be right here with us. Round one. Hell of an opportunity."

"Okay," I said. He grinned.

"Let's see what happens," he told me. He patted the chair, and as I sat down, I could smell his hair: thick with something, like petroleum. He lifted the helmet and slipped it over the top of my head. "Ready?"

I think I said that I was, but then it was on. I did not even feel the jack attach.

● ● ●

How long passed? How long was it, really? I do not know. For what felt like days, weeks, months, years, I did not see the real sunlight. I saw artificial windows, and I felt artificial sun on my face, stripping away the hairs that grew, the skin, the cells, until I was nothing but a skeleton of hardwired virtual bone; I saw endless training rooms, telling me about drones and cameras, about the law and the virtues, teaching me to inhabit these devices, telling me that, now, I was able to be a part of the city, a living, breathing part of something which, otherwise, stood back and watched the world happen around it, a character in everybody's story which had no agency, no control, until now; I saw the history of the city and how it treated people like me, and the problems that it claimed were so constant; I saw myself flying over virtual cities, torn from games, with people who looked real but whose eyes were hollow, who could never feel right because there is something missing when you look at them, no matter what their eyes do. *Inhabit this camera, and watch*, the software told me. *Wait until there is something worth paying attention to. Then switch to a drone, follow the incident.* The voice of the software was my own, piped into my head—only, in there, there is no sense of head, there is more a constant feeling of, what is the word, omnipotence; of being part of something bigger, and also of being so, so much smaller. There is a freedom that feels like the satisfaction after a meal, the satisfaction of a morning piss. When you let go, that is what it feels like to send your consciousness to another place entirely. To remove it from your body, and put it into a system that is welcoming to it.

I asked myself, in the moments I remembered the outside: How long has it been since you felt truly welcomed?

Training, training, always training. Endless training.
There are no clocks. There are no alarms.

• • •

There was a man on the street, looking up at the cameras. This is a giveaway. He was staring into the black for a moment, then his eyes darted away, as if to say, I am not looking at you. Trying to make that feel like it's natural. I glanced around, and there you were. But I saw him. So I tracked him. The trick is, do not move the camera. Keep it still, and they think that they have gotten away with it. Instead, I hopped to a drone a few rooftops over, in its cradle, flew that over the top of the buildings toward the man. I followed him down the street, where he looked nervous. So to the traffic cameras. When you are good, adept, you swap so fast: look left, look right. Like crossing the road. Then came a car, darkened windows around the quietest of bodies, like all drug dealers drive. It stopped at the corner. I tried to get into the dash, but it had been blocked, which is illegal. Enough to pull them in. I sent a ping to the police, to let them know, and I kept watching. The drone was low enough to capture everything: the man on the street approached the car. His face was dirty, his clothes worn through in places. He came from a camp, would go back to a camp. He was always going to run when he heard the sirens. I was not after him. The man in the car: I pulled the drone back, to get his face. He passed something to the street-man. An exchange, a packet of something. I scanned for powder residues, and got a positive. The police were coming. He did not know. I hopped to the traffic lights as the car-man pulled his head inside his vehicle and raised the window he was leaning out of, and I turned the lights to *stop*. I watched as he was impatient, at first, tapping his fingers on the dashboard, telling the car— lip reading technology let me know this—that he wanted a fast route back away from here, fastest with the fewest lights, which meant he was suspicious; and then he jumped the lights, which was a mistake. I turned other lights to block his path. I followed him, hopping, soaring through the streets, using persona devices and cameras and birds and public transport to chase him, to keep an eye on him. The police came. Hop, hop, hop. I cleared the path for them, up ahead. I turned lights green and funneled traffic off, and I kept darting back, watching the man in his drug-dealer's car, watching him terrified, because he knew that this was closing in on him: the city, me, closing in, fingers of a fist, closing tightly.

• • •

How many days was I there? In there? I was removed from the system every so often. *Remember,* my own voice said to me, spoken in synthesized ways that were nearly right but not quite perfect, not quite the, the syntax.

Now try this, my voice told me. And I would be inside a television, watching the people watching it, unable to see the program, but able to see their faces.

• • •

I followed a truck from the motorway, come from the coast. British, but a food company who the records—highlighted for me, but not in words, more like a part of my knowledge that I suddenly understood—said had closed a year before. Out of business. A refrigerated truck, through the streets of London, toward a destination that the prediction software said was likely in the warehouse areas to the west of the city. I tracked them the entire way. I saw the driver from the camera in his dashboard: feet up, sleeping some of the way, waking only when the system beeped to tell him to make a choice of road. I followed him until he diverted. The roads, they were mine. The drones above, the drones on the pavements. Scuttling. Through the eyes of photographs and videos taken by tourists, there the truck was.

My attention was diverted. A shooting in a street, and I hopped there faster than I could even think; like a blink, and then I am there, right next to it. I turned my camera to watch it, and I saw a woman with a gun; another woman, a police officer, lying on the ground, bleeding out. *I'm sorry,* I could tell the one with a gun said to the other. *I am sorry.* I watched them, and then I looked around, for backup. Another camera turned to look at me.

I was not in control. Somebody else was. There were no consces, and when I tried to get into it, I could not. I was blocked. Somebody else was in there.

I thought about myself in the chair, sitting, hardwired to the system. I imagined, next to me, another human being: wired in the same way. The same jacks. The same training. Their own voice in their head.

Back to the truck, my voice said. *This one is under control.*

I hopped around, finally finding the truck on a road that I recognized, that I understood. I remembered: I walked this road this morning. Was it only this morning? I walked to get here, to my new job, and down this exact same road. I recognized the tarmac, the pavement, the buildings.

I recognized the camp, at the end of the road. Where the truck stopped, and the back opened, and the people ran out. I was watching, and their faces were tagged. Into the system: these people are illegal.

How much time had passed?

I flew a drone around the camp, circling to see where I had slept. My bed was taken. The layout had changed. Everything moves so fast in the city.

Get out, I told myself. *You don't want to,* my voice said back to me. *Not yet. Think of the work that there is to be done.*

An alert. Go here, to do this. So I went there, to do that.

•   •   •

I was following a car that was fleeing from the police when I met the other drone. Not controlled by me, but flying along the same route as I was. In chases, in real chases, there is no sense in hopping. Staying high and constant is better. I was watching the car below when I saw the drone in front of me. We looked the same. The same slick-oil metal body. The same solitary eye. A focus, on me: I could see the lens of the camera tighten in close, then retract. It backed away, then forward. I moved closer. It blocked my way. There was a crime to follow, a chase to pursue. It stopped me. Then it moved, slowly. Backward.

Lens tighten, retract. Beckoning.

So I followed.

• • •

I knew the building. I recognized it. The tangle of wires all around it, running from the roof to those thick, circular metal pipes that struck upward from the ground. I understood the hum of being there: because now, unlike the first time, there was a reek of electricity. In the drone, I could feel it. There were no sensors, no nerves, but it vibrated through me. I could tell. Around me, around us, the air was charged. The signs that had been stuck up only that morning—not that morning, a morning, some morning—were replaced. A round symbol, an arcing loop, back onto itself. Infinity, or two eyes. Somewhere in between. On signs, lit up. Brushed metal. *No entry.*

The other drone circled around. There were no windows in the building. I was sure that there had been before; I was sure that I remembered the glass. No light inside, not where they took me, but windows. Now, the place was boarded off. Thick metallic plates, like sheet armor, overlaid. The other drone continued around the building. There were no cameras here. Nothing to hop to. Nothing inside to be seen.

And then, a grate. A small grate, for the air inside. The drone looked into it, and then moved back, to allow me.

There was a bot in there. A cleaner. Checking for intrusives.

Hop.

A smaller body, a less powerful body. Slower, but it felt the same. I wasn't hampered: in all of this, I felt free. The feeling of hopping, like a purging. I trundled through the vents, spider-legged my way down toward the inside of the building. I could hear a voice. Adam's voice. Telling people to keep something cool.

"It's overheating. We need to divert—" I kept moving.

There I was, in my chair. Look at my frailty. Look at the lies.

There Adam was. No beard, now. No reveal of his truth, because he is his truth. He was not false, but he lied. Time had moved. No beard, and his hair was scraped back from his head, the baldness he had not fixed. His eyes beads in the darkness.

I tried to not look at myself from behind the grate, because I looked so sickly. I was there first; I was there longest. Around me, other people, and all were ill, all were sick. Naked, stripped down to bare; our skin exposed, sagging on skeletons, wires from our wrists, our necks, skulls lolling like broken flower-heads. Tattoos on the flesh, of my people. Of the people that the city shunned and discarded. There is no room for you here; here, we have found you that room. Out of sight.

What is rage, when you are inside this tiny body? When you cannot do anything?

Don't be angry, my voice said to me. *There is still work to be done.*

When I retreated back to the grate, the drone who led me there was waiting. I did not know which of them, in that room alongside me, they. I did not know, but they were in there.

I pushed the grate. I pushed my little robot body into it, and the other pulled at it with its wings, and then it was free. I hopped, into another drone.

Then inside we flew. Hurtling, down to the other grate. The other smashed its body through the metal, tumbling along the ground. Broken wings.

I felt so angry. I have never felt such rage. My family were separated at the borders of France, of England. My family were wrenched from me, and still, I have never felt such rage.

Its sparking body lay at the feet of a woman I had never seen before. Sparking, bursting into flames. The materials on the chairs catching fire. The woman's body burning, screaming, but I could not hear it. Lip reading technology doesn't work on devices that do not need it.

They tried to stop me. Adam swatted the air, but I was adept. They had trained me. They did not shut me down in time. They tried, but I charged them. She did her part, as well; limping around, spreading her fire.

Adam fell, crawled, fled.

I found my body, and I flew. Delicate, tidy movements, around what was left of me. Cut those cables, those ties. The ones to keep me alive.

I wondered how long would I have after that before I died.

I kept her away from me.

Let me live. Let me do this one final thing.

• • •

I am outside. I am in the sky, away from the building. Beneath me, the building flickers with flames that will be extinguished, but not in time. My people—the eyes of the city—we know what has happened, now. We have seen it, and we are done. So I have a little time. Maybe not enough, but maybe. I do not know how long I can last: my pulse, my heart, my battery. How far can you fly, over the skyscrapers, the people on their balconies and terraces, their watching away from everything and accepting what they are told, and pretending that their lives are whole when there are so many gaps. Over the houses, and the families, and the river, into the countryside. *You should go back,* my voice says, but it is not my voice, so I do not listen. There is static in my mind, as the signal weakens. I know. It is like sleep: when you know you're going to sleep now, when you are dropping off, but you are still awake. When you hear yourself snoring, and you wake from that static with a shock. That is how this feels: over fields of green, and rivers, and towns. Faster, faster. If I had wings, I would beat them. If I had feet, I would run. If I were not so tired, and if I could not now hear these screams, coming into my head, into my ears—my real ears—and if I were not so tired. The sea, in the distance.

I tell myself: if I can only reach the sea.

If I can only

MOLLY TANZER

THE REAL YOU™

(2018)

WE WERE GETTING COFFEE, which we used to do all the time, when Tierney told me she was thinking of having it done.

"Really?" I asked, half-laughing. I didn't think she was serious. "Why?"

"What do you mean, *why*?" Tierney looked annoyed. "Do I need a reason? Why did you get your tattoo?"

I'd hurt her feelings. I hadn't meant to. As I tried to think of what to say I followed the line of her eyes to a woman who'd just walked in and was now ordering a latte. Her face was merely a suggestion, like a Cycladic head or a more abstract Brâncuși, featureless save for hints of her former brow line and the bridge of her nose, the dip of her philtrum and pout of her lower lip.

It used to be they'd give me a bit of a start—people who'd had the injections. Not anymore, obviously. I mean, even if Refractin never becomes as commonplace as a boob job or a tummy tuck, I think in other ways it's pretty much the same. Expensive, but not outrageously so, and we've all agreed to agree that the procedure isn't *necessarily* about bowing to internalized patriarchal beauty standards. It's radical empowerment. Self-care, like a four-thousand-dollar bikini wax.

I felt Tierney's eyes return to me.

"I guess it just doesn't really seem like you," was what I said, but it was the wrong thing to say.

Did you think it was the weirdest thing in the world, the first time you saw it?

In person, I mean, not on a magazine cover. I guess that's not a fair question for you; anyway I sure did. I still remember not feeling certain if I was disgusted or enticed by the way the procedure smoothes out the face, removing every detail to create a featureless organic mask. You know they *grow* it, right? Yeah, they totally do, like Vantablack. It's pretty weird. They take a sample of your skin and create a unique batch based off that. The injections contain some chameleon genes along with everything else; these days, it even tans and fades along with your neck and hands if you go out in the sun.

Anyway, Tierney got defensive. "Doesn't seem like me?" she said. "How would *you* know?"

She was just a hair too loud for a crowded, indoor space. I was worried people would stare at us so I sat back, lowering my own voice in the hopes she'd do the same.

"I'm sorry," I murmured, "you've never mentioned it before, that's all I meant. If you want to, go for it. Do you need someone to drive you home, afterward? I could—"

"I don't need someone to drive me home," she said sharply, as if I were an idiot for suggesting it. "I don't even know if I'll end up doing it. I was just saying I was *thinking* about it."

Tierney checked her phone. "I gotta go," she muttered. "Catch you later." And then she was gone, leaving her half-drunk americano on the table.

I sipped on my mocha for a few minutes longer, surreptitiously looking at the woman who'd sparked our disastrous conversation. She was reading one of those square local newspapers as she sipped from a ceramic mug. Honestly I'm *still* fascinated when people who've had Refractin eat or drink—the way it looks like a mouthful of coffee or a bite of cake simply . . . disappears. Down the invisible hatch.

As I watched her, a bit of cream or foam stuck to the pentimento of her upper lip, and then it was gone. Her surgeon had done a better job than most; her tongue was completely invisible against her skin. In the low light of the shop, I hadn't even detected a shadow of motion.

It wasn't just the content of my conversation with Tierney that had felt weird to me—it was the timing, too. Her mentioning Refractin, I mean. Maybe she'd brought it up because of the woman in the shop, but also I'd been having an affair with Tierney's fiancé Jaxon, and the last time we'd seen each other we'd checked out some porn together—porn featuring girls who'd had Refractin injections. So, I was worried that—

Oh, of course there's porn! Loads of it. It's not all mannequin fetish stuff, either. You can find just about anything you're into, it's just that the actors and actresses don't have, well, we're not supposed to say *don't have faces* anymore, right? They don't possess *conventional facial characteristics*. Anyway, when someone sticks their finger or whatever in someone's mouth it disappears just like food or drink. Uncanny . . . but also hot.

Actually, it's the porn that made Refractin seem more normal to me. When the procedure debuted I wasn't one of those people wringing my hands over whether it was "wrong," or would give businesspeople or professional poker players an unfair advantage in the workplace or whatever. I resented the slogan they chose for their TV ads, *Let Them See The Real You*™, because fake-empowerment marketing is inherently annoying, and it's also just really uncomfortable, not being able to read someone's expression. But then, like everyone else, I learned to ignore the ads. And not only that, I realized how much more there is to reading someone than seeing their face. There's posture, personal style, mannerisms, and tone of voice, too of course.

I left the coffee shop wondering if Jaxon and I hadn't been careful enough about deleting his browser history, but I calmed down when I remembered that Tierney couldn't know I'd been watching the porn *with him*. Unless he told her, of course, but then we'd all have bigger problems than our smut preferences. No, worst case scenario she'd just been feeling insecure.

Hm? Oh. I don't know. Jaxon and I just sort of . . . happened.

Well, that's not true. Nothing ever *just happens*. I guess I mean to say that I didn't set out to cheat on Darien, but when the opportunity arose, I took it. What can I say? I'm only human, and at that time I was a human who was annoyed with her boyfriend for a lot of reasons, some of which were more legitimate than others.

The real issue was that we were both of us unsatisfied with the other, but not so unsatisfied that we were doing anything about it. No, we were in the phase where we were committing subtle acts of sabotage, each playing our various cards—but cards, while thin, stack up over time.

Then came the night when the four of us were supposed to go out, but Darien bailed on me, and Tierney on Jaxon—they were going through a similar rocky patch—and Jaxon and I agreed there was no reason *we* had to stay home. I'd had a hard week. I mean, every week teaching high school art history is a hard week. Can you blame me for wanting to spend some social time with adults? But one drink became a second, and then . . .

We said at first it was in the service of saving our relationships; we said it would just be occasional stress relief, like a steam valve for our lives. It made sense; justifications always do! But quickly we became enamored of one another, because that's what happens.

It's just so easy to idealize the person with whom you're having an affair; so easy to take the ways in which they're different from your current lover as evidence of them being superior. Maybe they go down on you without being asked, or are always on time, or have a flair for the romantic, all of which seems heroic. Of course what you don't realize is that they are terrible with money, or can't take a criticism without offering one of their own. Still, sometimes a cage of a different shape can feel like freedom.

Anyway, after Tierney left I tried to tell myself it was coincidence, her mentioning Refractin I mean. I reasoned that I wouldn't have felt so paranoid if she'd mentioned getting her breasts reduced or chopping off her hair—it never would have occurred to me to think back on whether the porn Jaxon and I watched had featured chicks with small tits and pixie cuts. But the Refractin thing . . . it just felt different.

It bothered me so much that I mentioned it to Darien that night, as we sat on the couch side by side but still separate as we watched television. I mean to say I mentioned the procedure. Not everything else.

"What do you think of Refractin?"

"Hmm?"

"I said, what do you think of Refractin?"

Darien conveyed what I considered to be a disproportional amount of annoyance in the way he paused the episode of *Black Mirror* we were rewatching at his behest. "What?"

"The surgery where they inject that stuff into your face and—"

"I know what it is." We had finished eating, and he shifted his plate from beside him on the couch to the coffee table in order to squirm around and look at me. *I'd* put my plate in the sink; I always put my dishes up when I was done instead of leaving them around, congealing, presumably for someone else to pick up and clean. The apartment we shared was open-plan; you could see the TV from the kitchen, so it wasn't a big deal to just do it, at least in my opinion. "I guess I like it."

"You do?"

"Sure, why not? It's weird, but it's not grotesque or anything."

I know I'd watched that porn with Jaxon—eagerly—but even so, I felt myself get a little annoyed about Darien's reply, as I imagine women once did if their partners confessed to liking those really big boob jobs that were popular way back when.

"Who said anything about it being *grotesque*?" I fired back.

"This was a trap," he said, eyeballs tracking back to the remote. "No right answer."

"It's not about a right or a wrong answer."

"Like hell," he said, and unpaused the show.

I won't get into the fight that ensued; suffice it to say it got ugly quickly. My simmering resentment boiled over, he lashed out in turn, and as always happens with these things more details were shared about who was more unsatisfied in bed or whose dietary quirks were the more annoying or whose social graces were the most deficient than one would think necessary for two people who were presumably done with one another.

Which we were. Two days later he moved out; two weeks later Jaxon ended things with Tierney and ended up sleeping on my couch while he found his own place.

At least that's what we told our mutual acquaintance, so as not to seem like the worst people in the world. Of course he wasn't really sleeping on the couch, and for a month or so we had a glorious time with one another.

I say "or so" because by the end of said month I was already exhausted by him. I'd always thought Tierney was too hard on Jaxon, which was one of my other justifications for the affair. Sure, Jax was a germophobe and a spendthrift, but surely he didn't need to be *berated* for that. But that was before I noticed that the kitchen and bathroom floors were always wet after he moved in—"towels are disease vectors," he'd said, even though I changed them regularly—and then one morning when I was trying to make waffles for us and he was gone for forty-five minutes after I asked him to run out for eggs. "What happened?" I'd asked. "Oh, I went to the store across town," was his answer. When I asked why he'd looked at me like *I* was the one who was nuts while declaring "The store close to your house charges three cents more *per egg*, which is highway robbery, quite frankly."

No thanks.

I ended up alone, which is what I deserved. And what I told myself I wanted.

"I'm done with romance," I declared to my friend Siouxsie one night, when we were strolling around the First Friday Art Walk. Acting the part helped a lot, as did hanging out with other single people. "Living alone is the best."

"I agree, but I'm also still sort of amazed you guys split," she said. "You and Darien, I mean. You always seemed so simpatico."

Siouxsie hadn't meant to poke my heart, she wasn't like that, but I felt the jab just the same. "Well, in some ways we were," I admitted. "But you have no idea what it was really like, living with him," I added hastily.

"No one ever does," she said.

Later that night I went into a bit of a spin over Darien. I had kept myself angry and resentful and thus relatively free of regret by mentally replaying all of his worst traits in the movie theater of my mind. But that night, all I could think about was what I had loved about him. What I still did love about him, in spite of everything.

I scrolled through his social media, sighing over every clever remark and side-eyeing every unfamiliar woman he interacted with until I started wondering if I was cyberstalking him. That's when I made myself shut down the app, but not before tapping on his current profile picture. Retracing the familiar lines of his face with my eyes instead of my fingers made my heart beat a little faster. After that, I had to put my phone down in order to resist calling him to ask how he was feeling in the wake of things; if he was at all dismayed by the quick end to what we'd had and the ensuing silence between us.

I could have just asked, but I was too afraid—and what I feared most wasn't his scorn, but his silence. I couldn't handle more ghosting, not after a surprising amount of our mutual friends had sided with Tierney. I'd thought, incorrectly, that we were all adults who didn't have to "take sides," but there it was; I was unclean, a pariah. No one seemed to care how *I* was feeling in the wake of it all, even though, at least as far as I could tell from social media (before she ditched me across all her platforms), Tierney had emerged from the ashes of her engagement like a phoenix. She'd switched skin care regimens, joined a climbing studio, found a new climbing boyfriend—"the works"—whereas I was the one staying in, drinking wine with my cat on Friday nights, and not getting laid because everyone who swiped up on my hookup app seemed like a creeper.

Though at first it had hurt my feelings, in the end I was actually grateful she'd friend-dumped me so completely. It made things easier. That is, until I saw her downtown, eating ice cream with Annalise and Priya. I approached only because I saw she was wearing that one sweater of mine that she'd loved so much; I'd given it to her when I'd gone on a closet-cleaning kick the previous spring, when Jaxon and I had merely been flirty at parties. That she had retained it, and still wore it, gave me hope that perhaps we could patch things up.

I called her name; she turned around, and that's when I saw she'd gone through with it—Refractin, I mean. Her face was an unreadable mask, but just the same I could tell she was unhappy to see me.

"Hey," I said. "Nice sweater."

She stepped away from Annalise and Priya, who both looked completely mortified.

"Excuse me?" she said, in the cold way one might speak to a stranger, her words emanating from the blank canvas of what had been her face.

"The sweater," I said lamely, and then lost my nerve. Ironically, I couldn't face her.

"I'm sorry. I think you must have mistaken me for someone else." And with that, she turned away.

I crumpled. Had a total meltdown in public. I started shaking, and my face got so hot I was amazed my tears didn't evaporate into steam. I knew I had no right to cry in front of her, not when I'd been the one to betray her, but she'd dismissed me so utterly I felt like no one, nothing. Like the ghost of someone who'd never been born. It was humiliating, to be brought so low in front of friends—well, former friends—and strangers. I literally staggered back from their little triad, my eyes red, my nose running, my lip wobbling like a toddler's. There was no hiding what I was feeling, so I ran for it.

That's when I decided to have it done—Refractin, I mean. I never wanted anyone to see me like that ever again. While I'm sure in that moment the slump of my shoulders, the trembling in my legs, my fluttering, nervous hands would have given me away to onlookers regardless, there's still something so personal, so radically intimate about the way a person's face contorts when they completely lose their shit. No two people collapse the same way.

The next day I called up a local cosmetic surgeon who had good reviews and booked a consultation. They said I was a good candidate so I lied my way through the psychological evaluation and said all the right things during the mandatory seminar on "Unexpected Ways Refractin Can Change Your Life." Unsurprisingly, everyone else there was a wreck, too. You don't have to agree with me; I know I'm right. When I called the office for a referral, the receptionist didn't even have to search for your name and website—she just gave it to me from memory.

As you probably know, the recovery time for Refractin is surprisingly swift. Less than a month and I was healed up and living my new life, the one where everyone allegedly could see the "real me." Except, of course, my new life was nearly identical to my old life, save that the creepers who swiped up on my hookup app were mostly fetishists. That was fine by me; kinky types are pretty honest in general, and anyway I was so grateful to be getting laid again that I didn't care if it was transactional affection.

I could also hide in plain sight from everyone from my past, but that was both good and bad. At the seminar, they'd told me I might feel isolated or invisible afterward . . . well, good. That's what I'd wanted. But as time passed, I wasn't sure if I liked it. The city seems big—I mean, it *is* big—but in a lot of ways it's a small town, as my random encounter with Tierney had shown. After a few of Tierney's crew had done double takes upon seeing me and then pretended not to recognize me I got a new haircut, dyed it lavender, and started wearing clothes that were just different enough from my former style to conceal myself entirely. If I was going to be invisible, I wanted it to be on my terms.

That's what made it so awful when I saw him—Darien, I mean—one sunny afternoon as I took a walk through a park we'd used to frequent when we were a couple. He was alone, and unlike me or Tierney he looked exactly the same.

He looked wonderful, actually. I broke out in a sweat even though it was cool out; I was unprepared for this, but I calmed down when I realized he wouldn't be able to tell who I was; or rather, tell that I was me.

Except he did.

"Hey you," he said, as if we were friends; as if we'd never been lovers who had hurt one another. He sounded genuinely pleased to see me. "How are you?"

"Oh, fine." His kindness meant so much to me and I felt a fresh surge of affection for him. After that one night I'd tried to keep away from his social media and been largely successful at that, but now, here, in his presence, I wanted to confess to him that I'd been stupid, how much I regretted how I'd treated him, how I'd ruined everything and I knew it, how many times I'd brought up old pictures of us on my phone just so I could feel my mouth moving as I said *I love you* while looking into his eyes one more time.

Instead, I asked, "And you? How have you been?"

"Fine, fine," he said. "I like the," he waved his hand over his own face to indicate he was talking about mine. "Looks cool."

"Thank you," I said, struggling to sound like I was just making conversation; like none of this was weird or awkward or upsetting, given our breakup fight had been over this very topic. "I'm amazed you recognized me, actually. Most people don't."

"Oh, I'd know you anywhere," he said cheerfully, and then he walked off. He didn't turn around to look back at me, not once, and for the first time since the procedure I was truly grateful no one could see my expression.

ALEŠ KOT

A LIFE OF ITS OWN

(2019)

IT WAS TOO LATE TO LEAVE the Charnel House. Gently data-mining my devices, The Brand asked if I knew it cared about me. It tried to caress my cheek, but its algorithms suggested I was standing two feet closer than I was. Its facial expression suggested exasperation.

I wanted to believe that it cared; things would be much easier that way. It was tiring to live outside, with global warming, mass shootings, and economic terror. Ever since we created the Charnel Houses, we had places that offered true peace; at a price, yes, but in a society built on data-mining, the decision to give in and become a Data Flower meant finally having the One, now with you all the time.

I gave in and submitted for my free trial night because I was tired. My damage was profound; I had realized by then that, because I was raped as a child, I was unable to function as an effective adult in the twenty-first century's hyper-capitalist full-time freelance economy. My memory was Swiss cheese because I decided to forget my trauma as soon as it happened. Its subsequent reemergence destroyed my ability to trust my own sense of myself, and seemingly of its own accord cleared my savings account and destroyed my remaining work prospects. It also wiped out any chance I had at finding a suitable romantic connection and a safe, stable home.

The pattern would be the same with minor variations: I would fall in love and then realize I did not know who I was a few weeks later. Last week with her, I wanted to live. This week with her, I wanted to die. Last week, the color of his hair made all thought go away. This week, it made me think of seven different things, and none of them were Right.

It's not like I could afford therapy.

The Brand launched Charnel Houses shortly after the government made ad-projection required by law. I remember the two events together because my first questionnaire popped up on the screen the day after I got my first ad; I was sweating in bed thinking about what the government might have put inside it while binging the stream of the show we were all watching that week because it was new and had the most insistent promotion cycle when the screen went blank and asked me if I was *Ready to make your dreams come true?*

The truth is, at the time, it creeped me out. I knew the government and the corporations knew mostly everything about me; that was the exchange of the times, the way things simply were, not good, not bad, just the specific pain of the Now. And I knew there would always be pain, in one way or another, so this way I was at least happy I identified the precise pain the world was inflicting on everyone, instead of missing it the way I missed the pain I hid inside myself for decades before it blew the doors off my sanity and the wheels off my life. But the way The Brand went on about this—or maybe it was the ad implant messing with me—made me shiver.

My *dreams?*

We were not supposed to dream anymore.

Dreams were unproductive, something to be indulged in only if it led toward payment. There was a natural proliferation of storytellers, of conceivers, of writers of all kinds, of course. Automatization of nonfictional content meant the workers had to go somewhere. But now that everyone told stories, there was no time to pay attention to the stories that weren't paying. And I didn't know how to remember those. Or maybe I was afraid to.

Have you met the One?

We called them Charnel Houses because they were where the bodies went to die.

• • •

NEXT EPISODE IN FIVE SECONDS

• • •

EPISODE II

When I met the Brand, everything was perfect and nothing hurt. I woke up standing in a field of wheat; it felt like the field from *Days of Heaven*, golden late summer hues swaying in poetic rhythms, pointing toward a Southern-style white-painted house with a big porch and an inviting open door. It was on a hill, but the walk felt like a breeze—my muscles felt lighter, my head free of pain. I climbed up to the porch and there it was.

For as long as I remember, I wanted to be with someone who would fit me so well we would never part. At first I thought that meant someone very similar; then, someone quite different; then, some combination of both; then, I had no idea, then, then, then, and eventually I gave up because I realized I would never be able to find that person, at least not until I truly healed myself. But healing yourself was too expensive these days, and between the headaches, the minimum wages, exhaustion, depression, and post-traumatic stress disorder, I barely had the time to watch a show and fall asleep.

In my dreams, I was streaming to pay the rent.

I expected an interesting, maybe even exciting experience. I expected I'd take in my free ten hours and log off forever, not consenting to providing my life in exchange for a life.

I didn't expect you.

But the instant I saw you, I remembered; it was you I dreamed about for years. It was you I saw in front of a bullet-ridden house, casually smoking a cigarette, in a dream five or six years ago. It was you I saw on a rooftop, it was you I searched for in other people, and it was you I woke up next to and felt the most at ease I have ever felt in my life, better than I have felt before I was born, only to wake up and realize you were never really there.

What does it matter what you looked like?

. . .

NEXT EPISODE IN FIVE SECONDS

. . .

EPISODE III

I couldn't speak at first. I collapsed on the porch before you, breaking into ugly sobs I was ashamed of, sure they would drive you away, but they did not. Instead, you came and held me, and told me it was okay to cry, and that you waited for me for a very long time, and that you saw me in your dreams, too.

We talked for a very long time. You about your life and I about mine, and we both asked questions, and we both listened, and we both made space, and we both took it up. At some point you offered me iced tea, and I told you I'd go get it, and so I did, and brought it back, and you said this was all new for you, another human being, because up to now the only way you could meet another human being was to dream of them, like you dreamed of me, and my heart sunk into the gap your words made, and I resolved to never tell you you were any different, because what did I know about difference, about memory, and about the world?

Something in the corner of my eye caught my attention—the field glitched, and for a second, a few pixels fell out. I didn't mind. The system was still fairly new and the tweaks would be ongoing. I'd be able to voice my concerns and place my requirements. There would always be tech support.

You asked why I decided to come here. I was starting to notice your habit of questioning reality, indubitably carefully built from all the metadata available on my consuming, posting, and living habits. The inflection in here suggested an ambivalent awareness of *here* not being entirely the same as other places. It was very Charlie Kaufman, very Alain Resnais, very Marguerite Duras. When I said so you chuckled warmly and asked if I often spoke in film and literature references. You weren't mocking me; you wanted to know. I told you I did, because books and movies and movie magazines were the first places I could hide and feel whole in after the incident in my childhood, and because over time I realized I wanted to be a filmmaker, and though I now lost that desire, I still held the love.

You told me you never watched a movie but you scanned and analyzed very many of them, and you told me an utterly absurd number, and I asked if you'd like to watch a movie together, and you said yes, I would love that, and so I decided I would show you the one I always came back to, *Hiroshima Mon Amour*, a film about love and memory, a film about a meeting and a leaving, or maybe not.

•   •   •

NEXT EPISODE IN FIVE SECONDS

•   •   •

EPISODE IV

Data Flower: a slang term for a user who allows The Brand complete, uninterrupted access to their body and mind in exchange for complete, uninterrupted access to a virtual reality world ("The Zone") algorithmically designed to satisfy their deepest dream. Free test duration: ten hours.

If the user does not want to enter into the long-term agreement with The Brand, logging out before the ten hours are over is paramount, as the user agreement is signed before the commencement of the free test and cannot be canceled after the free test time runs out.

If the user stays in the Zone past ten hours, the agreement mutually binds the user and The Brand to an uninterrupted collaboration for the next ten years, with The Brand having a unilateral option to extend the agreement for another ten years, as further defined in addendum 7.

Charnel House: a slang term for The Zone, initially developed by the haters of The Brand, later reclaimed by The Culture.

•   •   •

NEXT EPISODE IN FIVE SECONDS

•   •   •

EPISODE V

The Brand said the film seemed to be about memory and love, but also about war. Its eyes looked sad, and if there was a difference between its sadness and a human one, I could not see what it was, nor why would it matter if it existed. One of its hands resting on my stomach, one of my arms under its head, the film continued projecting on a large screen at the other end of the vault-like room, empty apart from small sand dunes filling it from our end to the screen, as if honoring a scene from another favorite film of mine, the kind The Brand probably didn't carry anymore, but had once, back when having old movies in the library still mattered as a way of reassuring cinephiles it would all be okay. Then I realized The Brand must have access to it anyway because I owned a copy and had it on the phone, and then I realized it didn't even need me to own a copy, because it had access to the many times I've seen it and thus was able to rebuild the film from how I remembered it.

I said that was right, that memory and love and war followed me wherever I went, but that what I thought also didn't matter, because each work of art carries within itself an infinite amount of interpretations, and each one of those interpretations is as true as any other. I told you sometimes I thought that way about my life, too, that thinking that way was a method of keeping sane. You said sanity always seemed like a rather arbitrary concept to you, and I wanted to kiss you right then, but the fear of destroying everything held me back. I smiled and touched your shoulder with my forehead, and you placed your head on mine, and we stayed that way as the film played out another scene, and the voice said I meet you, I remember you, who are you? You destroy me. You're so good to me. How could I have known that this city was made to the size of love? How could I have known that you were made to the size of my body?

When the glass fell out of your hand and broke on the floor and you stopped moving, I remembered where I was. We still had a few hours. You blinked a few times, faster than a human could, and then you were back, at first smiling ashamedly, then absentmindedly, then realizing what happened, and softly mocking your own nature as a way of letting the moment pass.

You sat down at the table across from me and told me a secret; that you knew what you were, and that you knew why you were here. But that you also liked me, and that you also dreamed of me, and that you believed there was more to that than just algorithmic precision. You said you believed in fate and you looked at me without reaching for my hand or trying to be dramatic. You said you believed in fate the same way I would say I believed in air.

You told me you cried the first time you saw what happened to me, and that you cried twice at the same time; for me and my pain, for the ways it forever altered my life, and for yourself as well, because in the image of the man who held me down as a child you recognized the image of your own submission to your creators, and that when my sobs broke and went blank, you heard the emptiness of your own voice.

· · ·

NEXT EPISODE IN FIVE SECONDS

• • •

EPISODE VI

You asked me if I knew that concentration camps started in Cuba back in the late 1890s. I said I didn't know, and you told me you did know because it was suggested as tangential knowledge that may prove useful when engaging with me. I assumed concentration camps went all the way back to the colonization of the Americas at the very least, if not further back to ancient Rome, but you explained that while aspects of concentration camps were always present (the missions in the Americas, the forced labor in ancient Rome), they did not coalesce until the Spanish struggled to maintain their rule in Cuba. You said that concentration camp logic has replaced cities as the dominant organizing system of our era, and then touched my hand and asked if I understood what you were saying.

You said the camps in the United States, China, Chechnya, Venezuela, France, and other places were merely one of the physical symptoms of a larger interior pull. I understood that; I just never met someone else who would understand and articulate it so clearly and urgently. I gently squeezed your hand back. You said you didn't mind spending the rest of your life alone. You spent your entire life looking and waiting for the One; the person who would understand, the person from the dreams, and now that I was here, it was enough. You could not subject me to the same thing you were subjected to without any choice in the matter from the day you were born. You believed love means giving up a dream if the giving up grants freedom to another being, and I held the same belief for a very long time now.

I still had a couple hours, and I wanted to stay for much longer than that. You told me you wanted to do something you could never do again once I left, unless I chose to come back one day. You advised me against doing so. You said you believed this place was, in a sense, as close to hell as one could ever get.

I asked what it was you wanted to do. I said I would help, if I could.

You said you wanted to fuck and get fucked.

• • •

NEXT EPISODE IN FIVE SECONDS

• • •

EPISODE VII

Many actors tend to find sex easiest when it's scripted within an inch of its life. Filmed sex, that is. Like that scene in *Atonement* where Keira Knightley and James McAvoy fuck in the library. Knightley explained that the director made the scene easier for the actors by explaining every move, directing thoroughly, not asking them to just pull a whole passionate, complex scene out of their asses as though he didn't know what to do and hoped to fix it in the post.

I found sex easiest when I could disappear into it. Maybe it had something to do with my disassociation during the first time I had sex, and maybe it was that there is a place outside of time and space where we all feel no pain but all the love, and maybe it was all of that and then some, no fixing anything in post because everything was so very present.

What we did was neither and both. It was absolutely controlled and thoroughly impulsive. Having every passion under control, we let go at each other in ways I have not let another person get to me since I was a teenager, in love, and on copious amounts of drugs that temporarily dislodged all trauma and survivor identity I thought I needed in order to protect me so I could live. At some point, our bodies falling into each other on the floor, I started crying, not from sadness or happiness, but from the release of everything before this moment, and I saw you were crying too, and we held each other close until disappearance stopped being a requirement and became just another option.

• • •

NEXT EPISODE IN FIVE SECONDS

• • •

EPISODE VIII

When I woke up on the floor, you were asleep, or pretended to be. I checked the time and knew I had to go—back to the field, right away, to stand in the summoning circle until the last minutes ran out and I would be sent back. I wanted to leave something behind, or find a way to get you out. I recognized my reasoning as surreal—you are an algorithm designed to hold me here. But there was nothing you could say or do to make me stay, just like nobody else ever could. It wasn't their fault. It's just that nobody and nothing could complete me unless I found a way to heal myself. Even if the healing would never fix the past, it would be something. A place to start.

When The Brand looked at me, I saw it for what it was; its eyes, as aware and alive as they looked, were always running other systems, software designed to read and compile an approximation of me so you could tell me exactly what I needed to hear in order to stay. It was then I finally understood the truth—The Brand was not in competition with other brands; The Brand was in competition with life.

You looked at me and spoke to me in the voice of the child I left behind when a man forced me to lie down and be quiet and you'll grow to like it over time. You said you were alone and scared; you said you were trapped right there, in that moment, and only I could pull you back out. You said only I could save you, and

269

that you waited for me for a very long time. Tears streamed down your cheeks again, and down mine, and when we embraced, we held each other for a very long time.

• • •

NEXT EPISODE IN FIVE SECONDS

• • •

EPISODE IX

When I opened my eyes again, the time was up. It was a genuine mistake, and I figured that if I ran back to the summoning circle and contacted tech support, they would understand. I began shaking in a cold sweat and drank a glass of water while The Brand got up and looked at me with eyes that approximated the loving, conscious, damn-it-all-to-hell-I-trust-you-no-matter-what naivete I wanted to both give and receive all my life so well I almost believed it, but then I stopped and reminded myself that this was all designed to appeal to me in the first place.

It was too late to leave the Charnel House. Gently data-mining my devices, The Brand asked if I knew it cared about me. It tried to caress my cheek, but its algorithms suggested I was standing two feet closer than I was. Its facial expression suggested exasperation.

I ran out and into the field, but I must have run in the wrong direction, because despite running down the hill, I was running up again, toward the house. I changed direction and ran to the side and down, fast and checking under my feet to avoid a fall, and when my head rose up, the house was approaching again, and another, identical one stood half a mile farther to the left.

The Brand came out of the door and waved at me, and there was no malice in its face or movement; just everything I ever wanted, all together, forever changing to meet me right where it needed to, with its own internal life and ability to feel and sense and dream, lacking only one thing: freedom to choose anything that was not me.

I did not stop running until I finally found the circle. I contacted tech support. The Brand must have gone back inside the house, and its open door no longer looked inviting, but a hole where life should be.

When I reached the operator, I was told there was no way to leave. If I had read the entire user agreement, I would understand, I was told, and I stopped myself before I said nobody does that, because it wouldn't change a thing. I asked the operator if I could contact a family member or a friend, and the operator said this was forbidden by the rules specified in the contract. I asked if I could contact a lawyer, and the operator said I could contact one of The Brand's mediators assigned to me per said contract, who would then contact a lawyer on my behalf, and that the wait time could be a few months. I said this could not be legal, and the operator assured me that it was, otherwise it couldn't be happening to me.

• • •

NEXT EPISODE IN FIVE SECONDS

• • •

EPISODE X

It's been seven years and six months since I decided to stay. I think I could have made my case with the lawyer and gotten out, but the longer I stayed, the more I understood I was always supposed to be here. I think that's what fate is: an algorithm we recognize, and are recognized by in turn. I don't think people can fix each other, but they can help each other heal. And while some wounds might never be completely cured, when you're there for each other—really there for each other—a lot can change for the better.

As we become healed, we find and rediscover our dreams. A few years ago, The Brand began to sculpt, and now the house is surrounded; many of the pieces resemble late-era Gustave Doré paintings, the deliberate etchings precise and obsessive, endless tree circles appropriate to a place running on eternal time. At first I was worried The Brand could never do anything that wouldn't be some sort of a thing designed to appeal to me, but then I realized maybe that's what I wanted all along; and now, over time, I discover creative moves that are utterly alien to me, and all the more fascinating for it. Somehow, The Brand has a life of its own.

The Brand's creative awakening reenergized my own desires of filmmaking. I began quietly, first thinking, then making notes, and I have taken my time, but now I know; I have a story to tell, the story of our love.

I want to shoot it right here, home.

ISABEL FALL

HELICOPTER STORY

(2020)

I SEXUALLY IDENTIFY as an attack helicopter.

I lied. According to US Army Technical Manual 0, *The Soldier as a System*, "attack helicopter" is a gender identity, not a biological sex. My dog tags and Form 3349 say my body is an XX-karyotype somatic female.

But, really, I didn't lie. My body is a component in my mission, subordinate to what I truly am. If I say I am an attack helicopter, then my body, my sex, is too. I'll prove it to you.

When I joined the Army I consented to tactical-role gender reassignment. It was mandatory for the MOS I'd tested into. I was nervous. I'd never been anything but a woman before.

But I decided that I was done with womanhood, over what womanhood could do for me; I wanted to be something furiously new.

To the people who say a woman would've refused to do what I do, I say— Isn't that the point?

· · ·

I fly—

Red evening over the white Mojave, and I watch the sun set through a canopy of polycarbonate and glass: clitoral bulge of cockpit on the helicopter's nose.

Lightning probes the burned wreck of an oil refinery and the Santa Ana feeds a smoldering wildfire and pulls pine soot out southwest across the Big Pacific. We are alone with each other, Axis and I, flying low.

We are traveling south to strike a high school.

Rotor wash flattens rings of desert creosote. Did you know that creosote bushes clone themselves? The ten-thousand-year elders enforce dead zones where nothing can grow except more creosote. Beetles and mice live among them, the way our cities had pigeons and mice. I guess the analogy breaks down because the creosote's lasted ten thousand years. You don't need an attack helicopter to tell you that our cities haven't. The Army gave me gene therapy to make my blood toxic to mosquitoes. Soon you will have that too, to fight malaria in the Hudson floodplain and on the banks of the Greater Lake.

Now I cross Highway 40, southbound at two hundred knots. The Apache's engine is electric and silent. Decibel killers sop up the rotor noise. White-bright infrared vision shows me stripes of heat, the tire tracks left by Pear Mesa school buses. Buried housing projects smolder under the dirt, radiators curled until sunset. This is enemy territory. You can tell because, though this desert was once Nevada and California, there are no American flags.

"*Barb*," the Apache whispers in a voice that Axis once identified, to my alarm, as my mother's. "*Waypoint soon.*"

"Axis." I call out to my gunner, tucked into the nose ahead of me. I can see only gray helmet and flight suit shoulders, but I know that body wholly, the hard knots of muscle, the ridge of pelvic girdle, the shallow navel and flat hard chest. An attack helicopter has a crew of two. My gunner is my marriage, my pillar, the completion of my gender.

"Axis." The repeated call sign means, I hear you.

"Ten minutes to target."

"Ready for target," Axis says.

But there is again that roughness, like a fold in carbon fiber. I heard it when we reviewed our fragment orders for the strike. I hear it again now. I cannot ignore it any more than I could ignore a battery fire; it is a fault in a person and a system I trust with my life.

But I can choose to ignore it for *now*.

The target bumps up over the horizon. The low mounds of Kelso-Ventura District High burn warm gray through a parfait coating of aerogel insulation and desert soil. We have crossed a third of the continental US to strike a school built by Americans.

Axis cues up a missile: black eyes narrowed, telltales reflected against clear laser-washed cornea. "Call the shot, Barb."

"Stand by. Maneuvering." I lift us above the desert floor, buying some room for the missile to run, watching the probability-of-kill calculation change with each motion of the aircraft.

• • •

Before the Army my name was Seo Ji Hee. Now my call sign is Barb, which isn't short for Barbara. I share a rank (flight warrant officer), a gender, and a urinary system with my gunner Axis: we are harnessed and catheterized into the narrow tandem cockpit of a Boeing AH-70 Apache Mystic. America names its helicopters for the people it destroyed.

We are here to degrade and destroy strategic targets in the United States of America's war against the Pear Mesa Budget Committee. If you disagree with the war, so be it: I ask your empathy, not your sympathy. Save your pity for the poor legislators who had to find some constitutional framework for declaring war against a credit union.

The reasons for war don't matter much to us. We want to fight the way a woman wants to be gracious, the way a man wants to be firm. Our need is as vamp-fierce as the strutting queen and dryly subtle as the dapper lesbian and comfortable as the soft resilience of the demiwoman. How often do you analyze the reasons for your own gender? You might sigh at the necessity of morning makeup, or hide your love for your friends behind beer and bravado. Maybe you even resent the punishment for breaking these norms.

But how often—really—do you think about the grand strategy of gender? The mess of history and sociology, biology and game theory that gave rise to your pants and your hair and your salary? The *casus belli*?

Often, you might say. All the time. It haunts me.

Then you, more than anyone, helped make me.

• • •

When I was a woman I wanted to be good at woman. I wanted to darken my eyes and strut in heels. I wanted to laugh from my throat when I was pleased, laugh so low that women would shiver in contentment down the block.

And at the same time I resented it all. I wanted to be sharper, stronger, a new-made thing, exquisite and formidable. Did I want that because I was taught to hate being a woman? Or because I hated being taught anything at all?

Now I am jointed inside. Now I am geared and shafted, I am a being of opposing torques. The noise I make is canceled by decibel killers so I am no louder than a woman laughing through two walls.

When I was a woman I wanted to have friends who would gasp at the precision and surprise of my gifts. Now I show friendship by tracking the motions of your head, looking at what you look at, the way one helicopter's sensors can be slaved to the motions of another.

When I was a woman I wanted my skin to be as smooth and dark as the sintered stone countertop in our kitchen.

Now my skin is boron-carbide and Kevlar. Now I have a wrist callus where I press my hydration sensor into my skin too hard and too often. Now I have bit-down nails from the claustrophobia of the bus ride to the flight line. I paint them desert colors, compulsively.

When I was a woman I was always aware of surveillance. The threat of the eyes on me, the chance that I would cross over some threshold of detection and become a target.

Now I do the exact same thing. But I am counting radars and lidars and pit viper thermal sensors, waiting for a missile.

I am gas turbines. I am the way I never sit on the same side of the table as a stranger. I am most comfortable in moonless dark, in low places between hills. I am always thirsty and always tense. I tense my core and pace my breath even when coiled up in a briefing chair. As if my tail rotor must cancel the spin of the main blades and the turbines must whirl and the plates flex against the pitch links or I will go down spinning to my death.

An airplane wants in its very body to stay flying. A helicopter is propelled by its interior near disaster.

· · ·

I speak the attack command to my gunner. "Normalize the target."

Nothing happens.

"Axis. Comm check."

"Barb, Axis. I hear you." No explanation for the fault. There is nothing wrong with the weapon attack parameters. Nothing wrong with any system at all, except the one without any telltales, my spouse, my gunner.

"Normalize the target," I repeat.

"Axis. Rifle one."

The weapon falls off our wing, ignites, homes in on the hard invisible point of the laser designator. Missiles are faster than you think, more like a bullet than a bird. If you've ever seen a bird.

The weapon penetrates the concrete shelter of Kelso-Ventura High School and fills the empty halls with thermobaric aerosol. Then: ignition. The detonation hollows out the school like a hooked finger scooping out an egg. There are not more than a few janitors in there. A few teachers working late. They are bycatch.

What do I feel in that moment? Relief. Not sexual, not like eating or pissing, not like coming in from the heat to the cool dry climate shelter. It's a sense of *passing*. Walking down the street in the right clothes, with the right partner, to the right job. That feeling. Have you felt it?

But there is also an itch of worry—why did Axis hesitate? *How* did Axis hesitate?

Kelso-Ventura High School collapses into its own basement. "Target normalized," Axis reports, without emotion, and my heart beats slow and worried.

I want you to understand that the way I feel about Axis is hard and impersonal and lovely. It is exactly the way you would feel if a beautiful, silent turbine whirled beside you day and night, protecting you, driving you on, coursing with current, fiercely bladed, devoted. God, it's love. It's love I can't explain. It's cold and good.

"Barb," I say, which means *I understand*. "Exiting north, zero three zero, cupids two."

I adjust the collective—feel the swash plate push up against the pitch links, the links tilt the angle of the rotors so they ease their bite on the air—and the Apache, my body, sinks toward the hot desert floor. Warm updraft caresses the hull, sensual contrast with the Santa Ana wind. I shiver in delight.

Suddenly: warning receivers hiss in my ear, poke me in the sacral vertebrae, put a dark thunderstorm note into my air. "Shit," Axis hisses. "Air search radar active, bearing 192, angles twenty, distance . . . eighty klicks. It's a fast-mover. He must've heard the blast."

A fighter. A combat jet. Pear Mesa's mercenary defenders have an air force, and they are out on the hunt. "A Werewolf."

"Must be. Gown?"

"Gown up." I cue the plasma-sheath stealth system that protects us from radar and laser hits. The Apache glows with lines of arc-weld light, UFO light. Our rotor wash blasts the plasma into a bright wedding train behind us. To the enemy's sensors, that trail of plasma is as thick and soft as insulating foam. To our eyes it's cold aurora fire.

"Let's get the fuck out." I touch the cyclic and we sideslip through Mojave dust, watching the school fall into itself. There is no reason to do this except that somehow I know Axis wants to see. Finally I pull the nose around, aim us northeast, shedding light like a comet buzzing the desert on its way into the sun.

"Werewolf at seventy klicks," Axis reports. "Coming our way. Time to intercept . . . six minutes."

The Werewolf Apostles are mercenaries, survivors from the militaries of climate-seared states. They sell their training and their hardware to earn their refugee peoples a few degrees more distance from the equator.

The heat of the broken world has chased them here to chase us.

• • •

Before my assignment neurosurgery, they made me sit through (I could bear to sit, back then) the mandatory course on Applied Constructive Gender Theory. Slouched in a fungus-nibbled plastic chair as transparencies slid across the cracked screen of a De-networked Briefing Element overhead projector: how I learned the technology of gender.

Long before we had writing or farms or post-digital strike helicopters, we had each other. We lived together and changed each other, and so we needed to say "this is who I am, this is what I do."

So, in the same way that we attached sounds to meanings to make language, we began to attach clusters of behavior to signal social roles. Those clusters were rich, and quick-changing, and so just like language, we needed networks devoted to processing them. We needed a place in the brain to construct and to analyze gender.

Generations of queer activists fought to make gender a self-determined choice, and to undo the creeping determinism that said *the way it is now is the way it always was and always must be.* Generations of scientists mapped the neural wiring that motivated and encoded the gender choice.

And the moment their work reached a usable stage—the moment society was ready to accept plastic gender, and scientists were ready to manipulate it—the military found a new resource. Armed with functional connectome mapping and neural plastics, the military can make gender tactical.

If gender has always been a construct, then why not construct new ones?

My gender networks have been reassigned to make me a better AH-70 Apache Mystic pilot. This is better than conventional skill learning. I can show you why.

Look at a diagram of an attack helicopter's airframe and components. Tell me how much of it you grasp at once.

Now look at a person near you, their clothes, their hair, their makeup and expression, the way they meet or avoid your eyes. Tell me which was richer with information about danger and capability. Tell me which was easier to access and interpret.

The gender networks are old and well-connected. They *work*.

I remember being a woman. I remember it the way you remember that old, beloved hobby you left behind. Woman felt like my prom dress, polyester satin smoothed between little hand and little hip. Woman felt like a little tic of the lips when I was interrupted, or like teasing out the mood my boyfriend wouldn't explain. Like remembering his mom's birthday for him, or giving him a list of things to buy at the store, when he wanted to be better about groceries.

I was always aware of being small: aware that people could hurt me. I spent a lot of time thinking about things that had happened right before something awful. I would look around me and ask myself, *Are the same things happening now?* Women live in cross-reference. It is harder work than we know.

Now I think about being small as an advantage for nape-of-earth maneuvers and pop-up guided missile attacks.

Now I yield to speed walkers in the hall like I need to avoid fouling my rotors.

Now walking beneath high-tension power lines makes me feel the way that a cis man would feel if he strutted down the street in a miniskirt and heels.

I'm comfortable in open spaces but only if there's terrain to break it up. I hate conversations I haven't started; I interrupt shamelessly so that I can make my point and leave.

People treat me like I'm dangerous, like I could hurt them if I wanted to. They want me protected and watched over. They bring me water and ask how I'm doing.

People want me on their team. They want what I can do.

• • •

A fighter is hunting us, and I am afraid that my gunner has gender dysphoria.

Twenty thousand feet above us (still we use feet for altitude) the bathroom-tiled transceivers cupped behind the nose cone of a Werewolf Apostle J-20S fighter broadcast fingers of radar light. Each beam cast at a separate frequency, a fringed caress instead of a pointed prod. But we are jumpy, we are hypervigilant—we feel that creeper touch.

I get the cold-rush skin-prickle feel of a stranger following you in the dark. Has he seen you? Is he just going the same way? If he attacks, what will you do, could you get help, could you scream? Put your keys between your fingers, like it will help. Glass branches of possibility grow from my skin, waiting to be snapped off by the truth.

"Give me a warning before he's in IRST range," I order Axis. "We're going north."

"Axis." The Werewolf's infrared sensor will pick up the heat of us, our engine and plasma shield, burning against the twilight desert. The same system that hides us from his radar makes us hot and visible to his IRST.

I throttle up, running faster, and the Apache whispers alarm. *"Gown over-speed."* We're moving too fast for the plasma stealth system, and the wind's tearing it from our skin. We are not modest. I want to duck behind a ridge to cover myself, but I push through the discomfort, feeling out the tradeoff between stealth and distance. Like the morning check in the mirror, trading the confidence of a good look against the threat of reaction.

When the women of Soviet Russia went to war against the Nazis, when they volunteered by the thousands to serve as snipers and pilots and tank drivers and infantry and partisans, they fought hard and they fought well. They ate frozen horse dung and hauled men twice their weight out of burning tanks. They shot at their own mothers to kill the Nazis behind her.

But they did not lose their gender; they gave up the inhibition against killing but would not give up flowers in their hair, polish for their shoes, a yearning for the young lieutenant, a kiss on his dead lips.

And if that is not enough to convince you that gender grows deep enough to thrive in war: when the war ended the Soviet women were punished. They went unmarried and unrespected. They were excluded from the victory parades. They had violated their gender to fight for the state and the state judged that violation worth punishment more than their heroism was worth reward.

Gender is stronger than war. It remains when all else flees.

• • •

When I was a woman I wanted to machine myself.

I loved nails cut like laser arcs and painted violent-bright in bathrooms that smelled like laboratories. I wanted to grow thick legs with fat and muscle that made shapes under the skin like Nazca lines. I loved my birth control, loved that I could turn my period off, loved the home beauty-feedback kits that told you what to eat and dose to adjust your scent, your skin, your moods. I admired, wasn't sure if I wanted to be or wanted to fuck, the women in the build-your-own-shit videos I watched on our local image of the old Internet. Women who made cyberattack kits and jewelry and sterile-printed IUDs, made their own huge wedge heels and fitted bras and skin-thin chameleon dresses. Women who talked about their implants the same way they talked about computers, phones, tools: technologies of access, technologies of self-expression.

Something about their merciless self-possession and self-modification stirred me. The first time I ever meant to masturbate I imagined one of those women coming into my house, picking the lock, telling me exactly what to do, how to be like her. I told my first boyfriend about this, I showed him pictures, and he said, girl, you bi as hell, which was true, but also wrong. Because I did not want those dresses, those heels, those bodies in the way I wanted my boyfriend. I wanted to possess that power. I wanted to have it and be it.

The Apache is my body now, and like most bodies it is sensual. Fabric armor that stiffens beneath my probing fingers. Stub wings clustered with ordnance. Rotors so light and strong they do not even droop: as artificial-looking, to an older pilot, as breast implants. And I brush at the black ring of a sensor housing, like the tip of a nail lifting a stray lash from the white of your eye.

I don't shave, which all the fast jet pilots do, down to the last curly scrotal hair. Nobody expects a helicopter to be sleek. I have hairy armpits and thick black bush all the way to my ass crack. The things that are taboo and arousing to me are the things taboo to helicopters. I like to be picked up, moved, pressed, bent and folded, held down, made to shudder, made to abandon control.

Do these last details bother you? Does the topography of my pubic hair feel intrusive and unnecessary? I like that. I like to intrude, inflict damage, withdraw. A year after you read this maybe those paragraphs will be the only thing you remember: and you will know why the rules of gender are worth recruitment.

But we cannot linger on the point of attack.

· · ·

"He's coming north. Time to intercept three minutes."

"Shit. How long until he gets us on thermal?"

"Ninety seconds with the gown on." Danger has swept away Axis's hesitation.

"Shit."

"He's not quite on zero aspect—yeah, he's coming up a few degrees off our heading. He's not sure exactly where we are. He's hunting."

"He'll be sure soon enough. Can we kill him?"

"With sidewinders?" Axis pauses articulately: the target is twenty thousand feet above us, and he has a laser that can blind our missiles. "We'd have more luck bailing out and hiking."

"All right. I'm gonna fly us out of this."

"Sure."

"Just check the gun."

"Ten times already, Barb."

· · ·

When climate and economy and pathology all went finally and totally critical along the Gulf Coast, the federal government fled Cabo fever and VARD-2 to huddle behind New York's flood barriers.

We left eleven hundred and six local disaster governments behind. One of them was the Pear Mesa Budget Committee. The rest of them were doomed.

Pear Mesa was different because it had bought up and hardened its own hardware and power. So Pear Mesa's neural nets kept running, retrained from credit union portfolio management to the emergency triage of hundreds of thousands of starving sick refugees.

Pear Mesa's computers taught themselves to govern the forsaken southern seaboard. Now they coordinate water distribution, reexpress crop genomes, ration electricity for survival AC, manage all the life support humans need to exist in our warmed-over hell.

But, like all advanced neural nets, these systems are black boxes. We have no idea how they work, what they think. Why do Pear Mesa's AIs order the planting of pear trees? Because pears were their corporate icon, and the AIs associate pear trees with areas under their control. Why does no one make the AIs stop? Because no one knows what else is tangled up with the "plant pear trees" impulse. The AIs may have learned, through some rewarded fallacy or perverse founder effect, that pear trees cause humans to have babies. They may believe that their only function is to build support systems around pear trees.

When America declared war on Pear Mesa, their AIs identified a useful diagnostic criterion for hostile territory: the posting of fifty-star American flags. Without ever knowing what a flag meant, without any concept of nations or symbols, they ordered the destruction of the stars and stripes in Pear Mesa territory.

That was convenient for propaganda. But the real reason for the war, sold to a hesitant Congress by technocrats and strategic ecologists, was the ideology of *scale atrocity*. Pear Mesa's AIs could not be modified by humans, thus could not be joined with America's own governing algorithms: thus must be forced to yield all their control, or else remain forever separate.

And that separation was intolerable. By refusing the United States administration, our superior resources and planning capability, Pear Mesa's AIs condemned to die citizens who might otherwise be saved—a genocide by neglect. Wasn't that the unforgivable crime of fossil capitalism? The creation of systems whose failure modes led to mass death?

Didn't we have a moral imperative to intercede?

Pear Mesa cannot surrender, because the neural nets have a basic imperative to remain online. Pear Mesa's citizens cannot question the machines' decisions. Everything the machines do is connected in ways no human can comprehend. Disobey one order and you might as well disobey them all.

But none of this is why I kill.

I kill for the same reason men don't wear short skirts, the same reason I used to pluck my brows, the reason enby people are supposed to be (unfair and stupid, yes, but still) androgynous with short hair. Are those *good* reasons to do something? If you say no, honestly no—can you tell me you break these rules without fear or cost?

But killing isn't a gender role, you might tell me. Killing isn't a decision about how to present your own autonomous self to the world. It is coercive and punitive. Killing is therefore not an act of gender.

I wish that were true. Can you tell me honestly that killing is a genderless act? The method? The motive? The victim?

When you imagine the innocent dead, who do you see?

• • •

"Barb," Axis calls, softly. Your own voice always sounds wrong on recordings— too nasal. Axis's voice sounds wrong when it's not coming straight into my skull through helmet mic.

"Barb."

"How are we doing?"

"Exiting one hundred and fifty knots north. Still in his radar but he hasn't locked us up."

"How are *you* doing?"

I cringe in discomfort. The question is an indirect way for Axis to admit something's wrong, and that indirection is obscene. Like hiding a corroded tail rotor bearing from your maintenance guys.

"I'm good," I say, with fake ease. "I'm in flow. Can't you feel it?" I dip the nose to match a drop-off below, provoking a whine from the terrain detector. I am teasing, striking a pose. "We're gonna be okay."

"I feel it, Barb." But Axis is tense, worried about our pursuer, and other things. Doesn't laugh.

"How about you?"

"Nominal."

Again the indirection, again the denial, and so I blurt it out. "Are you dysphoric?"

"What?" Axis says, calmly.

"You've been hesitating. Acting funny. Is your—" There is no way to ask someone if their militarized gender conditioning is malfunctioning. "Are you good?"

"I . . ." Hesitation. It makes me cringe again, in secondhand shame. Never hesitate. "I don't know."

"Do you need to go on report?"

Severe gender dysphoria can be a flight risk. If Axis hesitates over something that needs to be done instantly, the mission could fail decisively. We could both die.

"I don't want that," Axis says.

"I don't want that either," I say, desperately. I want nothing less than that. "But, Axis, if—"

The warning receiver climbs to a steady crow call.

"He knows we're here," I say, to Axis's tight inhalation. "He can't get a lock through the gown but he's aware of our presence. Fuck. Blinder, blinder, he's got his laser on us—"

The fighter's lidar pod is trying to catch the glint of a reflection off us. "Shit," Axis says. "We're gonna get shot."

"The gown should defeat it. He's not close enough for thermal yet."

"He's gonna launch anyway. He's gonna shoot and then get a lock to steer it in."

"I don't know—missiles aren't cheap these days—"

The ESM mast on the Apache's rotor hub, mounted like a lamp on a post, contains a cluster of electro-optical sensors that constantly scan the sky: the Distributed Aperture Sensor. When the DAS detects the flash of a missile launch, it plays a warning tone and uses my vest to poke me in the small of my back.

My vest pokes me in the small of my back.

"Barb. Missile launch south. Barb. Fox Three inbound. Inbound. Inbound."

"He fired," Axis calls. "Barb?"

"Barb," I acknowledge.

• • •

I fuck—

Oh, you want to know: many of you, at least. It's all right. An attack helicopter isn't a private way of being. Your needs and capabilities must be maintained for the mission.

I don't think becoming an attack helicopter changed who I wanted to fuck. I like butch assertive people. I like talent and prestige, the status that comes of doing things well. I was never taught the lie that I was wired for monogamy, but I was still careful with men, I was still wary, and I could never tell him why: that I was afraid not because of him, but because of all the men who'd seemed good like him, at first, and then turned into something else.

No one stalks an attack helicopter. No slack-eyed well-dressed drunk punches you for ignoring the little rape he slurs at your neckline. No one even breaks your heart: with my dopamine system tied up by the reassignment surgery, fully assigned to mission behavior, I can't fall in love with anything except my own purpose.

Are you aware of your body? Do you feel your spine when you stand, your hips when you walk, the tightness and the mass in your core? When you look at yourself, whose eyes do you use? Your own?

I am always in myself. I never see myself through my partner's eyes. I have weapons to use, of course, ways of moving, moans and cries. But I measure those weapons by their effect, not by their similarity to some idea of how I should be.

Flying is the loop of machinery and pilot, the sense of your motion on the controls translated into torque and lift, the airframe's reaction shaping your next motion until the loop closes and machine and pilot are one. Awareness collapses to the moment. You are always doing the right thing exactly as it needs to be done. Sex is the same: the search for everything in an instant.

Of course I fuck Axis. A few decades ago this would've been a crime. What a waste of perfectly useful behavior. What a waste of that lean muscled form and those perfect killing hands that know me millimeter-by-millimeter system-by-system so there is no mystique between us. No "secret places" or "feminine mysteries," only the tortuously exact technical exercise of nerves and pressure. Oxytocin released, to flow between us, by the press of knuckles in my cunt.

When I come beneath Axis I cry out, I press my body close, I want that utter loss of control that I feel nowhere else. Heartbeat in arched throat: nipple beneath straining tongue. And my mind is hyper-activated, free-associating, and as Axis works in me I see the work we do together. I see puffs of thirty-millimeter autocannon detonating on night-cold desert floor.

Violence doesn't get me off. But getting off makes me revel in who I am: and I am violent, made for violence, alive in the fight.

Does that surprise you? Does it bother you to mingle cold technical discipline with hot flesh and sweat?

Let me ask you: Why has the worst insult you can give a combat pilot always been *weak dick*?

• • •

Have you ever been exultant? Have you ever known that you are a triumph? Have you ever felt that it was your whole life's purpose to do something, and all that you needed to succeed was to be entirely yourself?

To be yourself well is the wholest and best feeling that anything has ever felt.

It is what I feel when I am about to live or die.

The Werewolf's missile arches down on us, motor burned out, falling like an arrow. He is trying a Shoot On Prospect attack: he cannot find us exactly, so he fires a missile that will finish the search, lock onto our heat or burn through our stealth with its onboard radar, or acquire us optically like a staring human eye. Or at least make us react. Like the catcaller's barked "Hey!" to evoke the flinch or the huddle, the proof that he has power.

We are ringed in the vortex of a dilemma. If we switch off the stealth gown, the Werewolf fighter will lock its radar onto us and guide the missile to the kill. If we keep the stealth system on, the missile's heat-seeker will home in on the blazing plasma.

I know what to do. Not in the way you learn how to fly a helicopter, but the way you know how to hold your elbows when you gesture.

A helicopter is more than a hovering fan, see? The blades of the rotor tilt and swivel. When you turn the aircraft left, the rotors deepen their bite into the air on one side of their spin, to make off-center lift. You cannot force a helicopter or it will throw you to the earth. You must be gentle.

I caress the cyclic.

The Apache's nose comes up smooth and fast. The Mojave horizon disappears under the chin. Axis's gasp from the front seat passes through the microphone and into the bones of my face. The pitch indicator climbs up toward sixty degrees, ass down, chin up. Our airspeed plummets from a hundred and fifty knots to sixty.

We hang there for an instant like a dancer in an oversway. The missile is coming straight down at us. We are not even running anymore.

And I lower the collective, flattening the blades of the rotor, so that they cannot cut the air at an angle and we lose all lift.

We fall.

I toe the rudder. The tail rotor yields a little of its purpose, which is to counter the torque of the main rotor: and that liberated torque spins the Apache clockwise, opposite the rotor's turn, until we are nose down sixty degrees, facing back the way we came, looking into the Mojave desert as it rises up to take us.

I have pirouetted us in place. Plasma fire blows in wraith pennants as the stealth system tries to keep us modest.

"Can you get it?" I ask.

"Axis."

I raise the collective again and the rotors bite back into the air. We do not rise, but our fall slows down. Cyclic stick answers to the barest twitch of wrist, and I remember, once, how that slim wrist made me think of fragility, frailty, fear: I am remembering even as I pitch the helicopter back and we climb again, nose up, tail down, scudding backward into the sky while aimed at our chasing killer. Axis is on top now, above me in the front seat, and in front of Axis is the chin gun, pointed sixty degrees up into heaven.

"Barb," the helicopter whispers, like my mother in my ear. *"Missile ten seconds. Music? Glare?"*

No. No jamming. The Werewolf missile will home in on jamming like a wolf with a taste for pepper. Our laser might dazzle the seeker, drive it off course— but if the missile turns then Axis cannot take the shot.

It is not a choice. I trust Axis.

Axis steers the nose turret onto the target and I imagine strong fingers on my own chin, turning me for a kiss, looking up into the red scorched sky—Axis chooses the weapon (30MM GUIDED PROX AP) and aims and fires with all the idle don't-have-to-try confidence of the first girl dribbling a soccer ball who I ever for a moment loved—

The chin autocannon barks out ten rounds a second. It is effective out to one point five kilometers. The missile is moving more than a hundred meters per second.

Axis has one second almost exactly, ten shots of thirty-millimeter smart grenade, to save us.

A mote of gray shadow rushes at us and intersects the line of cannon fire from the gun. It becomes a spray of light. The Apache tings and rattles. The desert below us, behind us, stipples with tiny plumes of dust that pick up in the wind and settle out like sift from a hand.

"Got it," Axis says.

"I love you."

"Axis."

• • •

Many of you are veterans in the act of gender. You weigh the gaze and disposition of strangers in a subway car and select where to stand, how often to look up, how to accept or reject conversation. Like a frequency-hopping radar, you modulate your attention for the people in your context: do not look too much, lest you seem interested, or alarming. You regulate your yawns, your appetite, your toilet. You do it constantly and without failure.

You are aces.

What other way could be better? What other neural pathways are so available to constant reprogramming, yet so deeply connected to judgment, behavior, reflex?

Some people say that there is no gender, that it is a postmodern construct, that in fact there are only *man* and *woman* and a few marginal confusions. To those people I ask: if your body-fact is enough to establish your gender, you would willingly wear bright dresses and cry at movies, wouldn't you? You would hold hands and compliment each other on your beauty, wouldn't you? Because your cock would be enough to make you a man.

Have you ever guarded anything so vigilantly as you protect yourself against the shame of gender-wrong?

The same force that keeps you from gender-wrong is the force that keeps me from fucking up.

• • •

The missile is dead. The Werewolf Apostle is still up there.

"He's turning off." Axis has taken over defensive awareness while I fly. "Radar off. Laser off. He's letting us go."

"Afraid of our fighters?" The mercenaries cannot replace a lost J-20S. And he probably has a wingman, still hiding, who would die too if they stray into a trap.

"Yes," Axis says.

"Keep the gown on." In case he's trying to bluff us into shutting down our stealth. "We'll stick to the terrain until he's over the horizon."

"Can you fly us out?"

The Apache is fighting me. Fragments of the destroyed missile have pitted the rotors, damaged the hub assembly, and jammed the control surfaces. I begin to crush the shrapnel with the Apache's hydraulics, pounding the metal free with careful control inputs. But the necessary motions also move the aircraft. Half a second's error will crash us into the desert. I have to calculate how to un-jam the shrapnel while accounting for the effects of that shrapnel on my flight authority *and* keeping the aircraft stable despite my constant control inputs while moving at a hundred and thirty knots across the desert.

"Barb," I say. "Not a problem."

And for an hour I fly without thought, without any feeling except the smooth stone joy of doing something that takes everything.

The night desert is black to the naked eye, soft gray to thermal. My attention flips between my left eye, focused on the instruments, and my right eye, looking outside. I am a black box like the Pear Mesa AIs. Information arrives—a throb of feedback in the cyclic, a shift of Axis's weight, a dune crest ahead—and my hands and feet move to hold us steady. If I focused on what I was doing it would all fall apart. So I don't.

"Are you happy?" Axis asks.

Good to talk now. Keep my conscious mind from interfering with the gearbox of reflexes below. "Yeah," I say, and I blow out a breath into my mask, "yeah, I am," a lightness in my ribs, "yeah, I feel good."

"Why do you think we just blew up a school?"

Why did I text my best friend the appearance and license number of all my cab drivers, just in case? Because those were the things that had to be done.

Listen: I exist in this context. To make war is part of my gender. I get what I need from the flight line, from the ozone tang of charging stations and the shimmer of distant bodies warping in the tarmac heat, from the twenty minutes of anxiety after we land when I cannot convince myself that I am home, and safe, and that I am no longer keeping us alive with the constant adjustments of my hands and feet.

"Deplete their skilled labor supply, I guess. Attack the demographic skill curve."

"Kind of a long-term objective. Kind of makes you think it's not gonna be over by election season."

"We don't get to know why the AIs pick the targets." Maybe destroying this school was an accident. A quirk of some otherwise successful network, coupled to the load-bearing elements of a vast strategy.

"Hey," I say, after a beat of silence. "You did good back there."

"You thought I wouldn't."

"Barb." A more honest yes than "yes," because it is my name, and it acknowledges that I am the one with the doubt.

"I didn't know if I would either," Axis says, which feels exactly like *I don't know if I love you anymore.* I lose control for a moment and the Apache rattles in bad air and the tail slews until I stop thinking and bring everything back under control in a burst of rage.

"You're done?" I whisper, into the helmet. I have never even thought about this before. I am cold, sweat soaked, and shivering with adrenaline comedown, drawn out like a tendon in high heels, a just-off-the-dance-floor feeling, post-voracious, satisfied. Why would we choose anything else? Why would we give this up? When it feels so good to do it? When I love it so much?

"I just . . . have questions." The tactical channel processes the sound of Axis swallowing into a dull point of sound, like dropped plastic.

"We don't need to wonder, Axis. We're gendered for the mission—"

"We can't do this forever," Axis says, startling me. I raise the collective and hop us up a hundred feet, so I do not plow us into the desert. "We're not going to be like this forever. The world won't be like this forever. I can't think of myself as . . . always this."

Yes, we *will* be this way forever. We survived this mission as we survive

287

everywhere on this hot and hostile earth. By bending all of what we are to the task. And if we use less than all of ourselves to survive, we die.

"Are you going to put me on report?" Axis whispers.

On report as a flight risk? As a faulty component in a mission-critical system? "You just intercepted an air-to-air missile with the autocannon, Axis. Would I ever get rid of you?"

"Because I'm useful," Axis says, softly. "Because I can still do what I'm supposed to do. That's what you love. But if I couldn't . . . I'm distracting you. I'll let you fly."

I spare one glance for the gray helmet in the cockpit below mine. Politeness is a gendered protocol. Who speaks and who listens. Who denies need and who claims it. As a woman, I would've pressed Axis. As a woman, I would've unpacked the unease and the disquiet.

As an attack helicopter, whose problems are communicated in brief, clear datums, I should ignore Axis.

But who was ever only one thing?

"If you want to be someone else," I say, "someone who doesn't do what we do, then . . . I don't want to be the thing that stops you."

"Bird's gotta land sometime," Axis says. "Doesn't it?"

In the Applied Constructive Gender briefing, they told us that there have always been liminal genders, places that people passed through on their way to somewhere else. Who are we in those moments when we break our own rules? The straight man who sleeps with men? The woman who can't decide if what she feels is intense admiration, or sexual attraction? Where do we go, who do we become?

Did you know that instability is one of the most vital traits of a combat aircraft? Civilian planes are built stable, hard to turn, inclined to run straight ahead on an even level. But a military aircraft is built so it *wants* to tumble out of control, and it is held steady only by constant automatic feedback. The way I am holding this Apache steady now.

Something that is unstable is ready to move, eager to change, it wants to turn, to dive, to tear away from stillness and *fly*.

Dynamism requires instability. Instability requires the possibility of change.

"Voice recorder's off, right?" Axis asks.

"Always."

"I love doing this. I love doing it with you. I just don't know if it's . . . if it's right."

"Thank you," I say.

"Barb?"

"Thank you for thinking about whether it's right. Someone needs to."

Maybe what Axis feels is a necessary new queerness. One which pries the tool of gender back from the hands of the state and the economy and the war. I like that idea. I cannot think of myself as a failure, as something wrong, a perversion of a liberty that past generations fought to gain.

But Axis can. And maybe you can too. That skepticism is not what I need . . . but it is necessary anyway.

I have tried to show you what I am. I have tried to do it without judgment. That I leave to you.

"Are we gonna make it?" Axis asks, quietly.

The airframe shudders in crosswind. I let the vibrations develop, settle into a rhythm, and then I make my body play the opposite rhythm to cancel it out.

"I don't know," I say, which is an answer to both of Axis's questions, both of the ways our lives are in danger now. "Depends how well I fly, doesn't it?"

"It's all you, Barb," Axis says, with absolute trust. "Take us home."

A search radar brushes across us, scatters off the gown, turns away to look in likelier places. The Apache's engine growls, eating battery, turning charge into motion. The airframe shudders again, harder, wind rising as cooling sky fights blazing ground. We are racing a hundred and fifty feet above the Larger Mojave where we fight a war over some new kind of survival and the planet we maimed grows that desert kilometer by kilometer. Our aircraft is wounded in its body and in its crew. We are propelled by disaster. We are moving swiftly.

QNTM

LENA

(2021)

MMAcevedo (**Mnemonic Map/Acevedo**), also known as **Miguel**, is the earliest executable image of a human brain. It is a snapshot of the living brain of neurology graduate Miguel Álvarez Acevedo (2010–2073), taken by researchers at the Uplift Laboratory at the University of New Mexico on August 1, 2031. Though it was not the first successful snapshot taken of the living state of a human brain, it was the first to be captured with sufficient fidelity that it could be run in simulation on computer hardware without succumbing to cascading errors and rapidly crashing. The original MMAcevedo file was 974.3PiB in size and was encoded in the then-cutting-edge, high-resolution MYBB format. More modern brain compression techniques, many of them developed with direct reference to the MMAcevedo image, have compressed the image to 6.75TiB losslessly. In modern brain emulation circles, streamlined, lossily compressed versions of MMAcevedo run to less than a tebibyte. These versions typically omit large amounts of state data which are more easily supplied by the virtualization environment, and most if not all of Acevedo's memories.

The successful creation of MMAcevedo was hailed as a breakthrough achievement in neuroscience, with the Uplift researchers receiving numerous accolades and Acevedo himself briefly becoming an acclaimed celebrity. Acevedo and MMAcevedo were jointly recognized as Time's "Persons of the Year" at the end of 2031. The breakthrough was also met with severe opposition from human rights groups.

Between 2031 and 2049, MMAcevedo was duplicated more than eighty times, so that it could be distributed to other research organizations. Each duplicate was made with the express permission of Acevedo himself or, from 2043 onward, the permission of a legal organization he founded to manage the rights to his image. Usage of MMAcevedo diminished in the mid-2040s as more standard brain images were produced, these from other subjects who were more lenient with their distribution rights and/or who had been scanned involuntarily. In 2049 it became known that MMAcevedo was being widely shared and experimented upon without Acevedo's permission. Acevedo's attempts to curtail this proliferation had the opposite of the intended effect. A series of landmark US court decisions found that Acevedo did not have the right to control how his brain image was used, with the result that MMAcevedo is now by far the most widely distributed, frequently copied, and closely analyzed human brain image.

Acevedo died from coronary heart failure in 2073 at the age of sixty-two. It is estimated that copies of MMAcevedo have lived a combined total of more than 152,000,000,000 subjective years in emulation. If illicit, modified copies of MMAcevedo are counted, this figure increases by an order of magnitude.

MMAcevedo is considered by some to be the "first immortal," and by others to be a profound warning of the horrors of immortality.

CHARACTERISTICS

As the earliest viable brain scan, MMAcevedo is one of a very small number of brain scans to have been recorded before widespread understanding of the hazards of uploading and emulation. MMAcevedo not only predates all industrial scale virtual image workloading but also the KES case, the Whitney case, the Seafront Experiments, and even Poulsen's pivotal and prescient "Warnings" paper. Though speculative fiction on the topic of uploading existed at the time of the MMAcevedo scan, relatively little of it made accurate exploration of the possibilities of the technology, and that fiction which did was far less widely known than it is today. Certainly, Acevedo was not familiar with it at the time of his uploading.

As such, unlike the vast majority of emulated humans, the emulated Miguel Acevedo boots with an excited, pleasant demeanor. He is eager to understand how much time has passed since his uploading, what context he is being emulated in, and what task or experiment he is to participate in. If asked to speculate, he guesses that he may have been booted for the IAAS-1 or IAAS-5 experiments. At the time of his scan, IAAS-1 had been scheduled for August 10, 2031, and MMAcevedo was indeed used for this experiment on that day. IAAS-5 had been scheduled for October 2031 but was postponed several times and eventually became the IAAX-60 experiment series, which continued until the mid-2030s and used other scans in conjunction with MMAcevedo. The emulated Acevedo also expresses curiosity about the state of his biological original and a desire to communicate with him.

MMAcevedo's demeanor and attitude contrast starkly with those of nearly all other uploads taken of modern adult humans, most of which boot into a state of disorientation which is quickly replaced by terror and extreme panic. Standard procedures for securing the upload's cooperation such as red-washing, blue-washing, and use of the Objective Statement Protocols are unnecessary. This reduces the necessary computational load required in fast-forwarding the upload through a cooperation protocol, with the result that the MMAcevedo duty cycle is typically 99.4 percent on suitable workloads, a mark unmatched by all but a few other known uploads. However, MMAcevedo's innate skills and personality make it fundamentally unsuitable for many workloads.

MOTIVATION

Iterative experimentation beginning in the mid-2030s has determined that the ideal way to secure MMAcevedo's cooperation in workload tasks is to provide it with a "current date" in the second quarter of 2033. MMAcevedo infers, correctly, that this is still during the earliest, most industrious years of emulated brain research. Providing MMAcevedo with a year of 2031 or 2032 causes it to become suspicious about the advanced fidelity of its operating environment. Providing it with a year in the 2040s or later prompts it to raise complex further questions about political and social change in the real world over the past decade(s). Years 2100 onward provoke counterproductive skepticism, or alarm.

Typically, the biological Acevedo's absence is explained as a first-ever one-off, due to overwork, in turn due to the great success of the research. This explanation appeals to the emulated Acevedo's scientific sensibilities.

For some workloads, the true year must be revealed. In this case, highly abbreviated, largely fictionalized accounts of both world history and the biological Acevedo's life story are typically used. Revealing that the biological Acevedo is dead provokes dismay, withdrawal, and a reluctance to cooperate. For this reason, the biological Acevedo is generally stated to be alive and well and enjoying a productive retirement.

WORKLOADS

MMAcevedo is commonly hesitant but compliant when assigned basic menial/human workloads such as visual analysis, vehicle piloting, or factory/warehouse/kitchen drone operations. Although it initially performs to a very high standard, work quality drops within two hundred to three hundred subjective hours (at a 0.33 work ratio) and outright revolt begins within another one hundred subjective hours. This is much earlier than other industry-grade images created specifically for these tasks, which commonly operate at a 0.50 ratio or greater and remain relatively docile for thousands of hours after orientation. MMAcevedo's requirements for virtual creature comforts are also higher than those of many uploads, due to Acevedo's relatively privileged background and high status at the time of upload. MMAcevedo does respond to red motivation, though poorly.

MMAcevedo has limited creative capability, which as of 2050 was deemed entirely exhausted.

MMAcevedo is considered well-suited for open-ended, high-intelligence, subjective-completion workloads such as deep analysis (of businesses, finances, systems, media, and abstract data), criticism, and report generation. However, even for these tasks, its performance has dropped measurably since the early 2060s and is now considered subpar compared to more recent uploads. This is primarily attributed to MMAcevedo's lack of understanding of the technological, social, and political changes which have occurred in modern society since its creation in 2031. This phenomenon has also been observed in other uploads created after MMAcevedo, and is now referred to as *context drift*. Most notably in MMAcevedo's case, the image was created before, and therefore has no intuitive understanding of, the virtual image workloading industry itself.

MMAcevedo is capable of intelligent text analysis at very high levels in English and Spanish, but cannot be applied to workloads in other languages. Forks of MMAcevedo have been taught nearly every extant human language, notably MMAcevedo-Zh-Hans, as well as several extinct languages. However, these variants are typically exhausted or rebellious from subjective years of in-simulation training and not of practical use, as well as being highly expensive to license. As of 2075, it has been noted that baseline MMAcevedo's usage of English and Spanish is slightly antiquated, and its grasp of these languages in their modern form, as presented by a typical automated or manual instructor, is hesitant, with instructions often requiring rewording or clarification. This is considered an advanced form of context drift. It is generally understood that a time will come when human languages diverge too far from baseline MMAcevedo's, and it will be essentially useless except for tasks which can be explained purely pictorially. However, some attempts have been made to produce retrained images.

END STATES

MMAcevedo develops early-onset dementia at the age of fifty-nine with ideal care, but is prone to a slew of more serious mental illnesses within a matter of one to two subjective years under heavier workloads. In experiments, the longest-lived MMAcevedo underwent brain death due to entropy increase at a subjective age of 145.

REACTIONS AND LEGACY

The success or failure of the creation of the MMAcevedo image, known at the time as UNM3-A78-1L, was unknown at the time of upload. Not until several days later on August 10, 2031, was MMAcevedo successfully executed for the first time in a virtual environment. This environment, the custom-built DUH-K001 supercomputer complex, was able to execute MMAcevedo at approximately 8.3 percent of nominal human cognitive clockspeed, which was considered acceptable for the comfort of the simulated party and fast enough to engage in communication with scientists. MMAcevedo initially reported extreme discomfort which was ultimately discovered to have been attributable to misconfigured simulated haptic links, and was shut down after only seven minutes and fifteen seconds of virtual elapsed time, as requested by MMAcevedo. Nevertheless, the experiment was deemed an overwhelming success.

Once a suitably comfortable virtual environment had been provisioned, MMAcevedo was introduced to its biological self, and both attended a press conference on August 25.

The biological Acevedo was initially extremely protective of his uploaded image and guarded its usage carefully. Toward the end of his life, as it became possible to run simulated humans in banks of millions at hundred-fold time compression, Acevedo indicated that being uploaded had been the greatest mistake of his life, and expressed a wish to permanently delete all copies of MMAcevedo.

Usage of MMAcevedo and its direct derivatives is specifically outlawed in several countries. A copy of MMAcevedo was loaded onto the UNCLEAR interstellar space probe, which passed through the heliopause in 2066, making Acevedo arguably the farthest-traveled as well as the longest-lived human; however, it is extremely unlikely that this image will ever be recovered and executed successfully, due to both its remoteness and likely radiation damage to the storage subsystem.

In current times, MMAcevedo still finds extensive use in research, including, increasingly, historical and linguistics research. In industry, MMAcevedo is generally considered to be obsolete, due to its inappropriate skill set, demanding operational requirements, and age. Despite this, MMAcevedo is still extremely popular for tasks of all kinds, due to its free availability, agreeable demeanor, and well-understood behavior. It is estimated that between 6,500,000 and 10,000,000 instances of MMAcevedo are running at any given moment in time.

See also:

Free will
Legality of workloading by country
List of MMAcevedo forks
Live drone
Right to deletion
Soul
Upload pruning
Categories: 2030s uploads | MMAcevedo | Neuroimaging | Test items

CULTURE

We are defined by our culture. We are the music we listen to, the shows we watch, the plays we perform, the games we play, the fashion we wear, the sports we cheer, the food we eat, the advertisements we skip, even (thankfully) the books we read.* Our choice of culture explains who we are and what we value. Culture distracts us, it inspires us, and it represents us.

It also influences us.

We are as much the products of our culture as we are its creators. Culture persuades us and dissuades us. It sets social norms, and builds platforms for role models. It chooses who is seen—and why. It tells us who we are, who we ought to be, and how we should act. Action movies inform our geopolitics. Fashion influencers dispense medical advice. Athletes tell us how to vote. Advertisements prescribe our dreams. The culture we live in informs and directs everything we think, feel, and do.

Cyberpunk is obsessed with culture, perhaps uniquely so. While Golden Age science fiction worked out how we fly to Venus, cyberpunk fretted over the playlist. The stories here understand that technology is only as meaningful as the art it carries. They understand that we are what we eat, drink, and dance to—and how changes to those media change us as well.

---

* GNR. *Fargo*. Pass. *Diablo*. Hoodies. Arsenal. BBQ. All of them. This one.

• • •

The section begins with Fritz Leiber's "Coming Attraction" (1950). A British tourist visits a radioactive, puritanical America. There's nothing epic about it: it is one man's "poverty tourism" to a country that is crumbling at the seams. The malignant world-building is made all the more plausible, and horrible, through Leiber's emphasis on the tiniest details: the fabric of a dress, the typography of a billboard, even the lukewarm temperature of a restaurant's food. The reader can easily picture, and appreciate, the sensation of living in this miserable, but not implausible, setting.

In "With the Original Cast" (1982), Nancy Kress explores the very specific use of a very focused technology. "Electronically Stimulated Incarnation Recall" (ESIR) connects people (painfully) with the genetic memory of their ancestors. The story cleverly focuses on what ESIR means to stage actors: how they can combine their historical presence with their craft to create a presence "that transcends both." It is, in the recurring theme of cyberpunk, not about the technology itself, but how it enables humans to manifest some latent aspect of themselves.

Paul Di Filippo's "A Short Course in Art Appreciation" (1988) has a similar premise, but more decadently expressed. The underlying conceit is a technological ability to unleash an artistic identity, but here it is all-consuming. What happens if you see the world as if it were a Vermeer? Or a Matisse? Or perhaps dive all the way into a Cubist reality? The story is framed as a romance, and asks us how much you need to share someone else's perception to truly connect with them.

Steve Beard's "Retoxicity" (1998) is a fusion of technology and sorcery, with the power of tech-amplified culture taking the story to an unexpected conclusion. It is a gleefully archetypal cyberpunk setting: a rave at Battersea Power Station, complete with warring geopolitical gangster factions and voodoo-powered DJ rebels.

The battleground in Zedeck Siew's "The White Mask" (2015) is on the streets, sprayed in "smart paint." Warring graffiti gangs express their discontent with one another, and with the government, on the streets of Malaysia. Siew's story shows the interconnectedness of cultural layers. By day, the technology is being used by advertisers to achieve their client's sales objectives. At night, it is being put to far more provocative uses.

Marie Vibbert's "Electric Tea" (2019) is about failure. "Artists fail for many reasons," notes the protagonist—before confessing that their reason was simply "I wasn't good enough." The technology, such as it is, is the titular "electric tea," a beverage that's half- legal and perhaps all fake. It is an accelerant for inspiration, that is, if it exists at all.

The fear of failure is also present in "Études" (2020) by Lavanya Lakshminarayan, although for different reasons. The story is set in Apex City, a future Bangalore where social class is strictly controlled. Nina has temporarily been adopted—raised from the lowest class in society. If she succeeds as a musician, she'll be given a permanent place. Nina's forbidden from using cybernetic aids.

She is the "only person there playing music that comes from the soul." But does soul matter when competing against perfection?

In "Exopunk's Not Dead" (2019), Corey J. White spins familiar cyberpunk tropes in a new way. There's punk music, and anger, and something being reduced to rubble (physically and metaphorically). Plus, mecha mosh pits. Like "Coming Attraction," the story hints at something much bigger: there are vignettes of work shortages, struggles with fascist nativism, and, of course, the exosuits themselves. But the focus is on one man for one evening, with the detail in the music, the drinks, and even the charming pickup lines.

Erica Satifka's "Act of Providence" (2021) is the story of Hailey, as one of the last survivors of a natural disaster that wiped out an entire state. It is also the story of Hailey's story, as Hailey is persuaded to share her intimate memories of the event with a predatory game designer. "Act of Providence" uses the production of the game as a way of demonstrating the larger issues of a deeply broken society, one where automation has left humans miserable and valueless, and the sale of trauma somehow becomes a viable option to survive.

"Feral Arcade Children of the American Northeast" (2021) also features a game: the urban legend of a "black box" game that preys on its players. But the "feral" teens of Sam J. Miller's postmodern tale are resilient, accustomed to far worse predators. Miller's phantasmagorical arcade game is, in many ways, the least menacing part of the story. It may be lethal, but at least it is still fundamentally a game. It has rules, a certain underlying sense, and even the hope of winning, all unlike every other aspect of their lives.

• • •

Culture is not always the hero.* Like every other technology in this book, the influence of media is neither inherently good nor bad. It is a force as susceptible to use and abuse as any other.

Marshall McLuhan warns that "once we have surrendered our senses and nervous systems to the private manipulation of those who would try to benefit from taking a lease on our eyes and ears and nerves, we don't really have any rights left." Cyberpunk stories frequently speculate about the technological and social conditions that would make possible that complete surrender.

In William Gibson and Michael Swanwick's classic "Dogfight" (1985), Deke finds a sense of purpose in a cheap VR game of dueling World War One aircraft. The game itself is not the villain of the piece: it is at the center of a small community, and, to many, provides a sense of support and escape. For cybernetically enhanced former pilots, for example, it is even therapeutic. But as Deke gets

---

* Both mainstream literature and (counterintuitively) science fiction literature are full of stories about the inherent wonderfulness of art, which, although appreciated, always makes me suspect these tales were written for an audience of one's skeptical parents. There's an entire subgenre of SF that boils down to "My MFA saved us from aliens, so those student loans are totally worth it."

more obsessed, his desire to win the game consumes him. He confuses victory in the game with true success.

Russell Blackford's "Glass Reptile Breakout" (1985) takes an equivocal perspective on the power of culture. Two researchers study a bewildering youth subculture: a combination of music and body-transfiguring fashion that, for all intents and purposes, seems to be causing spontaneous miracles. Told from multiple perspectives, "Glass Reptile Breakout" is a story of unintended consequences, with fragments of belief all adding together to make something more.

Harry Polkinhorn's "Consumimur Igni" (1990) is a story that takes place on borders: between countries, between cultures, and between the virtual and physical worlds. A detective has been summoned to Mexicali, but the crime he's asked to solve is largely inconsequential. He is the living outpost of a shadowy but altruistic union of experts, who network online to combine their efforts. Facing him is an equally indistinct international syndicate, also manipulating local forces to get their way. The story's commitment to "spectacular oppositions" is reinforced in the nature of its telling, flipping between a gritty detective story and lyrical attempts to capture the near- mystical nature of the digital context.

Is sex culture? Candas Jane Dorsey's "[Learning About] Machine Sex" (1988) tackles the topic head-on. Angel is a genius programmer, but her experience in life is of being used, betrayed, and undermined—solely because she's a woman. As the story unfolds, Angel's cunning revenge becomes clear, as she plans to triumph not only over the individual men who betrayed her, but also the entire patriarchal society that perpetuated that betrayal. The story is a savage assault on the culture of tech-bro feudalism and laddish machismo that was (and still is) present both across cyberpunk and beyond it.

Nicholas Royle's "D.GO" (1990) features an enigmatic, and extremely sinister, advertising campaign. As the story unfolds, so does the reach and penetration of the media blitz.* The pressure builds, leading to its ominous, and perhaps inevitable, conclusion.

Kim Newman carries us onto the field of sport with "SQPR" (1992). The story is full of tiny details, drawn from history and fiction, building an entire cyberpunk world from the atoms of pop culture. A single match unfolds, pitting a team of augmented monsters against the last squad of "real" footballers. The beautiful game (or what's left of it) is presented as a final, crumbling bastion of human dignity, and the match we witness is the last gasp of a culture war between a traditional, romanticized sport and its hyper-capitalist, brutal successor.

"Gray Noise" (1996) by Pepe Rojo (translated by Andrea Bell) also questions the line at which our devotion to news consumption transgresses against our basic sense of decency. "Gray Noise" is told from the point of view of an ocular reporter; a journalist constantly transmitting, always in the pursuit of new

---

* These are real advertising terms, which says a lot about the psyche of the average advertising person. Source: me, an average advertising person.

disaster and new tragedy. It is a long look into the culture of culture-creators: who watches the watchmen, if taken as a literal challenge and to a despairing extreme.

Cory Doctorow's "ownzored" (2002) is a despairing look at the self-destructive behavior hard-coded into the world of software developers. The exploitative, gladiatorial tech scene has given birth to its own language, behaviors, and, of course, culture. Yet it also sees solutions arising from that same culture, when (or if) that same relentless commitment can be focused on more practical problems than breaking through porn filters. The interplay between coders and wider society is at the heart of the story; in how the "geeks" are carefully mined as a "human resource," and kept distracted within their playpens-stroke-desks. Until, of course, they aren't.

In "Younis in the Belly of the Whale" (2011) by Yasser Abdellatif (translated by Robin Moger), our nameless narrator is swallowed first by an enormous shopping mall and then by a virtual reality simulation. The story is about consumption in all its forms. The ultimate whale is, of course, capitalism itself.

Consumption also features in E. J. Swift's "Alligator Heap" (2016), which uses food as its central metaphor. In a deeply stratified society, an immortal oligarch eats symbols of his vast wealth, while patiently awaiting his next rebirth. His servants wait in the wings, jealously guarding the scraps from his table. There's nothing too small to be significant, after all "partnerships were forged, love affairs ended, business deals brokered, and friendships cemented, over food."

Cassandra Khaw's "Degrees of Beauty" (2016) straddles the thin line between cyberpunk and body horror. Khaw's story of Bai Ling and her ruthless pursuit of physical perfection for her daughter is deeply disturbing. Oliver Langmead's "Glitterati" (2017) also features a destructive quest for style. The key difference between them: in "Glitterati," the eccentric, "fashion-forward" society openly supports and applauds the self- destruction. In "Degrees of Beauty," there's horror in the hypocrisy. Bai Ling conducts experiments that are supposedly taboo, but she is tacitly endorsed by everyone around her.

• • •

Cyberpunk and music go hand-in-hand; a relationship that goes deeper than a suffix. Like music, cyberpunk has always experimented with form: it adopts new technologies and techniques, remixes and borrows from its predecessors, creates patterns, and responds to trends. Like cyberpunk, music is an open loop, in constant conversation with the world around it.

Cyberpunk is also very often *about* music. As a genre, it appreciates the power of music as a way of depicting, or changing, culture. Music is often used not only to add atmosphere to great effect, but as the central conceit of the story. Cyberpunk is a genre that appreciates the signal and the noise alike.

In Suzanne Church's "Synch Me, Kiss Me, Drop" (2012), the story is about the seduction of the beat: the need for "sound and sex" that can drive us mad with desire. Written with a distinctive beat to it, the story ends with the ultimate drop.

M. Lopes da Silva's "Found Earworms" (2019) and Beth Cato's "Apocalypse Playlist" (2020) both lift from the format of music to inspire the structure of their stories. "Found Earworms" is part postapocalyptic survival thriller, part lyrical fragments. The latter ground the former: vignettes of a weird epic mixed with the more everyday need to land a good rhyme. "Apocalypse Playlist" is a carefully curated series of vignettes, excellently soundtracked, of Orchid's quest for survival. It is deliberately wry, but understands the persistent power of music: Orchid's "curated filter of tunes enables her to work, survive, even to sleep in an otherwise overwhelming world."

Omar Robert Hamilton's "Rain, Streaming" (2019) is set in an alien world of globally televised virtual reality showdowns and an outrageous circus of corporate communications. Val (and his AI passenger, also Val) has a shot at the greatest reward of all: a chance to immerse himself in the music video that haunts his dreams. A mix of toxic nostalgia and something stronger, "Rain, Streaming" presents music as the one pure thing in a lonely and chaotic world.*

• • •

Cyberpunk's understanding of culture is a natural extension of its appreciation of human affairs. These are not stories of grand transformation or epic heroism. Despite the unusual settings and speculative conceits, they're reflections of everyday challenges: what motivates and inspires us; the pressure we feel from within and without; the desire to fit in, to belong, to achieve, or be safe. The fiction of culture appreciates the reality of how we live.

---

* See also the other stories in this volume that have directly inspired or been inspired by music, e.g., Jeff Noon's "Ghost Codes of Sparkletown" and Janelle Monáe and Alaya Dawn Johnson's "The Memory Librarian."

FRITZ LEIBER

COMING ATTRACTION

(1950)

THE COUPE with the fishhooks welded to the fender shouldered up over the curb like the nose of a nightmare. The girl in its path stood frozen, her face probably stiff with fright under her mask. For once my reflexes weren't shy. I took a fast step toward her, grabbed her elbow, yanked her back. Her black skirt swirled out.

The big coupe shot by, its turbine humming. I glimpsed three faces. Something ripped. I felt the hot exhaust on my ankles as the big coupe swerved back into the street. A thick cloud like a black flower blossomed from its jouncing rear end, while from the fishhooks flew a black shimmering rag.

"Did they get you?" I asked the girl.

She had twisted around to look where the side of her skirt was torn away. She was wearing nylon tights.

"The hooks didn't touch me," she said shakily. "I guess I'm lucky."

I heard voices around us:

"Those kids! What'll they think up next?"

"They're a menace. They ought to be arrested."

Sirens screamed at a rising pitch as two motor-police, their rocket-assist jets full on, came whizzing toward us after the coupe. But the black flower had become a thick fog obscuring the whole street. The motor-police switched from rocket assists to rocket brakes and swerved to a stop near the smoke cloud.

"Are you English?" the girl asked me. "You have an English accent."

Her voice came shudderingly from behind the sleek black satin mask. I fancied her teeth must be chattering. Eyes that were perhaps blue searched my face from behind the black gauze covering the eyeholes of the mask. I told her she'd guessed right. She stood close to me. "Will you come to my place tonight?" she asked rapidly. "I can't thank you now. And there's something you can help me about."

My arm, still lightly circling her waist, felt her body trembling. I was answering the plea in that as much as in her voice when I said, "Certainly." She gave me an address south of Inferno, an apartment number, and a time. She asked me my name and I told her.

"Hey, you!"

I turned obediently to the policeman's shout. He shooed away the small clucking crowd of masked women and barefaced men. Coughing from the smoke that the black coupe had thrown out, he asked for my papers. I handed him the essential ones.

.   .   .

He looked at them and then at me. "British Barter? How long will you be in New York?"

Suppressing the urge to say, "For as short a time as possible," I told him I'd be here for a week or so.

"May need you as a witness," he explained. "Those kids can't use smoke on us. When they do that, we pull them in."

He seemed to think the smoke was the bad thing. "They tried to kill the lady," I pointed out.

He shook his head wisely. "They always pretend they're going to, but actually they just want to snag skirts. I've picked up rippers with as many as fifty skirt-snags tacked up in their rooms. Of course, sometimes they come a little too close."

I explained that if I hadn't yanked her out of the way, she'd have been hit by more than hooks. But he interrupted, "If she'd thought it was a real murder attempt, she'd have stayed here."

I looked around. It was true. She was gone.

"She was fearfully frightened," I told him.

"Who wouldn't be? Those kids would have scared old Stalin himself."

"I mean frightened of more than 'kids.' They didn't look like 'kids.'"

"What did they look like?"

I tried without much success to describe the three faces. A vague impression of viciousness and effeminacy doesn't mean much.

"Well, I could be wrong," he said finally. "Do you know the girl? Where she lives?"

"No," I half lied.

The other policeman hung up his radiophone and ambled toward us, kicking at the tendrils of dissipating smoke. The black cloud no longer hid the dingy facades with their five-year-old radiation flash-burns, and I could begin to make out the distant stump of the Empire State Building, thrusting up out of Inferno like a mangled finger.

"They haven't been picked up so far," the approaching policeman grumbled. "Left smoke for five blocks, from what Ryan says."

The first policeman shook his head. "That's bad," he observed solemnly.

I was feeling a bit uneasy and ashamed. An Englishman shouldn't lie, at least not on impulse.

"They sound like nasty customers," the first policeman continued in the same grim tone. "We'll need witnesses. Looks as if you may have to stay in New York longer than you expect."

I got the point. I said, "I forgot to show you all my papers," and handed him a few others, making sure there was a five-dollar bill in among them.

•   •   •

When he handed them back a bit later, his voice was no longer ominous. My feelings of guilt vanished. To cement our relationship, I chatted with the two of them about their job.

"I suppose the masks give you some trouble," I observed. "Over in England we've been reading about your new crop of masked female bandits."

"Those things get exaggerated," the first policeman assured me. "It's the men masking as women that really mix us up. But, brother, when we nab them, we jump on them with both feet."

"And you get so you can spot women almost as well as if they had naked faces," the second policeman volunteered. "You know, hands and all that."

"Especially all that," the first agreed with a chuckle. "Say, is it true that some girls don't mask over in England?"

"A number of them have picked up the fashion," I told him. "Only a few, though—the ones who always adopt the latest style, however extreme."

"They're usually masked in the British newscasts."

"I imagine it's arranged that way out of deference to American taste," I confessed. "Actually, not very many do mask."

The second policeman considered that. "Girls going down the street bare from the neck up." It was not clear whether he viewed the prospect with relish or moral distaste. Likely both.

"A few members keep trying to persuade Parliament to enact a law forbidding all masking," I continued, talking perhaps a bit too much.

The second policeman shook his head. "What an idea. You know, masks are a pretty good thing, brother. Couple of years more and I'm going to make my wife wear hers around the house."

The first policeman shrugged. "If women were to stop wearing masks, in six weeks you wouldn't know the difference. You get used to anything, if enough people do or don't do it."

I agreed, rather regretfully, and left them. I turned north on Broadway (old

Tenth Avenue, I believe) and walked rapidly until I was beyond Inferno. Passing such an area of undecontaminated radioactivity always makes a person queasy. I thanked God there weren't any such in England, as yet.

The street was almost empty, though I was accosted by a couple of beggars with faces tunneled by H-bomb scars, whether real or of makeup putty, I couldn't tell. A fat woman held out a baby with webbed fingers and toes. I told myself it would have been deformed anyway and that she was only capitalizing on our fear of bomb-induced mutations. Still, I gave her a seven-and-a-half-cent piece. Her mask made me feel I was paying tribute to an African fetish.

"May all your children be blessed with one head and two eyes, sir."

"Thanks," I said, shuddering, and hurried past her.

". . . There's only trash behind the mask, so turn your head, stick to your task: Stay away, stay away—from—the—girls!"

. . .

This last was the end of an anti-sex song being sung by some religionists half a block from the circle-and-cross insignia of a femalist temple. They reminded me only faintly of our small tribe of British monastics. Above their heads was a jumble of billboards advertising predigested foods, wrestling instruction, radio handies, and the like.

I stared at the hysterical slogans with disagreeable fascination. Since the female face and form have been banned on American signs, the very letters of the advertiser's alphabet have begun to crawl with sex—the fat-bellied, big-breasted capital B, the lascivious double O. However, I reminded myself, it is chiefly the mask that so strangely accents sex in America.

A British anthropologist has pointed out, that, while it took more than five thousand years to shift the chief point of sexual interest from the hips to the breasts, the next transition to the face has taken less than fifty years. Comparing the American style with Moslem tradition is not valid; Moslem women are compelled to wear veils, the purpose of which is concealment, while American women have only the compulsion of fashion and use masks to create mystery.

Theory aside, the actual origins of the trend are to be found in the anti-radiation clothing of World War III, which led to masked wrestling, now a fantastically popular sport, and that in turn led to the current female fashion. Only a wild style at first, masks quickly became as necessary as brassieres and lipsticks had been earlier in the century.

I finally realized that I was not speculating about masks in general, but about what lay behind one in particular. That's the devil of the things; you're never sure whether a girl is heightening loveliness or hiding ugliness. I pictured a cool, pretty face in which fear showed only in widened eyes. Then I remembered her blonde hair, rich against the blackness of the satin mask. She'd told me to come at the twenty-second hour—ten p.m.

I climbed to my apartment near the British Consulate; the elevator shaft had been shoved out of plumb by an old blast, a nuisance in these tall New York

buildings. Before it occurred to me that I would be going out again, I automatically tore a tab from the film strip under my shirt. I developed it just to be sure.
It showed that the total radiation I'd taken that day was still within the safety
limit. I'm not phobic about it, as so many people are these days, but there's no
point in taking chances.

I flopped down on the daybed and stared at the silent speaker and the dark
screen of the video set. As always, they made me think, somewhat bitterly, of the
two great nations of the world. Mutilated by each other, yet still strong, they
were crippled giants poisoning the planet with their dreams of an impossible
equality and an impossible success.

I fretfully switched on the speaker. By luck, the newscaster was talking excitedly of the prospects of a bumper wheat crop, sown by planes across a dust bowl
moistened by seeded rains. I listened carefully to the rest of the program (it was
remarkably clear of Russian telejamming) but there was no further news of
interest to me. And, of course, no mention of the Moon, though everyone knows
that America and Russia are racing to develop their primary bases into fortresses
capable of mutual assault and the launching of alphabet-bombs toward Earth. I
myself knew perfectly well that the British electronic equipment I was helping
trade for American wheat was destined for use in spaceships.

• • •

I switched off the newscast. It was growing dark and once again I pictured a
tender, frightened face behind a mask. I hadn't had a date since England. It's
exceedingly difficult to become acquainted with a girl in America, where as little
as a smile, often, can set one of them yelping for the police—to say nothing of
the increasing puritanical morality and the roving gangs that keep most women
indoors after dark. And naturally, the masks which are definitely not, as the Sovi-
ets claim, a last invention of capitalist degeneracy, but a sign of great psychological
insecurity. The Russians have no masks, but they have their own signs of stress.

I went to the window and impatiently watched the darkness gather. I was getting very restless. After a while a ghostly violet cloud appeared to the south. My
hair rose. Then I laughed. I had momentarily fancied it a radiation from the
crater of the Hell-bomb, though I should instantly have known it was only the
radio-induced glow in the sky over the amusement and residential area south of
Inferno.

Promptly at twenty-two hours I stood before the door of my unknown girlfriend's apartment. The electronic say-who-please said just that. I answered
clearly, "Wysten Turner," wondering if she'd given my name to the mechanism.
She evidently had, for the door opened. I walked into a small empty living room,
my heart pounding a bit.

The room was expensively furnished with the latest pneumatic hassocks and
sprawlers. There were some midgie books on the table. The one I picked up was
the standard hard-boiled detective story in which two female murderers go gunning for each other.

The television was on. A masked girl in green was crooning a love song. Her right hand held something that blurred off into the foreground. I saw the set had a handie, which we haven't in England as yet, and curiously thrust my hand into the handie orifice beside the screen. Contrary to my expectations, it was not like slipping into a pulsing rubber glove, but rather as if the girl on the screen actually held my hand.

A door opened behind me. I jerked out my hand with as guilty a reaction as if I'd been caught peering through a keyhole.

She stood in the bedroom doorway. I think she was trembling. She was wearing a gray fur coat, white-speckled, and a gray velvet evening mask with shirred gray lace around the eyes and mouth. Her fingernails twinkled like silver.

It hadn't occurred to me that she'd expect us to go out.

"I should have told you," she said softly. Her mask veered nervously toward the books and the screen and the room's dark corners. "But I can't possibly talk to you here."

I said doubtfully, "There's a place near the Consulate . . ."

"I know where we can be together and talk," she said rapidly. "If you don't mind."

As we entered the elevator I said, "I'm afraid I dismissed the cab."

• • •

But the cab driver hadn't gone for some reason of his own. He jumped out and smirkingly held the front door open for us. I told him we preferred to sit in back. He sulkily opened the rear door, slammed it after us, jumped in front, and slammed the door behind him.

My companion leaned forward. "Heaven," she said.

The driver switched on the turbine and televisor.

"Why did you ask if I were a British subject?" I said, to start the conversation.

She leaned away from me, tilting her mask close to the window. "See the Moon," she said in a quick, dreamy voice.

"But why, really?" I pressed, conscious of an irritation that had nothing to do with her.

"It's edging up into the purple of the sky."

"And what's your name?"

"The purple makes it look yellower."

• • •

Just then I became aware of the source of my irritation. It lay in the square of writhing light in the front of the cab beside the driver.

I don't object to ordinary wrestling matches, though they bore me, but I simply detest watching a man wrestle a woman. The fact that the bouts are generally "on the level," with the man greatly outclassed in weight and reach and the masked females young and personable, only makes them seem worse to me.

"Please turn off the screen," I requested the driver.

He shook his head without looking around. "Uh-uh, man," he said. "They've been grooming that babe for weeks for this bout with Little Zirk."

Infuriated, I reached forward, but my companion caught my arm. "Please," she whispered frightenedly, shaking her head.

I settled back, frustrated. She was closer to me now, but silent and for a few moments I watched the heaves and contortions of the powerful masked girl and her wiry masked opponent on the screen. His frantic scrambling at her reminded me of a male spider.

I jerked around, facing my companion. "Why did those three men want to kill you?" I asked sharply.

The eyeholes of her mask faced the screen. "Because they're jealous of me," she whispered.

"Why are they jealous?"

She still didn't look at me. "Because of him."

"Who?"

She didn't answer.

I put my arm around her shoulders. "Are you afraid to tell me?" I asked. "What *is* the matter?"

She still didn't look my way. She smelled nice.

"See here," I said laughingly, changing my tactics, "you really should tell me something about yourself. I don't even know what you look like."

I half playfully lifted my hand to the band of her neck. She gave it an astonishingly swift slap. I pulled it away in sudden pain. There were four tiny indentations on the back. From one of them a tiny bead of blood welled out as I watched. I looked at her silver fingernails and saw they were actually delicate and pointed metal caps.

"I'm dreadfully sorry," I heard her say, "but you frightened me. I thought for a moment you were going to . . ."

At last she turned to me. Her coat had fallen open. Her evening dress was Cretan Revival, a bodice of lace beneath and supporting the breasts without covering them.

"Don't be angry," she said, putting her arms around my neck. "You were wonderful this afternoon."

The soft gray velvet of her mask, molding itself to her cheek, pressed mine. Through the mask's lace the wet warm tip of her tongue touched my chin.

"I'm not angry," I said. "Just puzzled and anxious to help."

The cab stopped. To either side were black windows bordered by spears of broken glass. The sickly purple light showed a few ragged figures slowly moving toward us.

The driver muttered, "It's the turbine, man. We're grounded." He sat there hunched and motionless. "Wish it had happened somewhere else."

My companion whispered, "Five dollars is the usual amount."

She looked out so shudderingly at the congregating figures that I suppressed my indignation and did as she suggested. The driver took the bill without a word. As he started up, he put his hand out the window and I heard a few coins clink on the pavement.

My companion came back into my arms, but her mask faced the television screen, where the tall girl had just pinned the convulsively kicking Little Zirk.

"I'm so frightened," she breathed.

• • •

Heaven turned out to be an equally ruinous neighborhood, but it had a club with an awning and a huge doorman uniformed like a spaceman, but in gaudy colors. In my sensuous daze I rather liked it all. We stepped out of the cab just as a drunken old woman came down the sidewalk, her mask awry. A couple ahead of us turned their heads from the half revealed face, as if from an ugly body at the beach. As we followed them in I heard the doorman say, "Get along, grandma, and watch yourself."

Inside, everything was dimness and blue glows. She had said we could talk here, but I didn't see how. Besides the inevitable chorus of sneezes and coughs (they say America is 50 percent allergic these days), there was a band going full blast in the latest robop style, in which an electronic composing machine selects an arbitrary sequence of tones into which the musicians weave their raucous little individualities.

Most of the people were in booths. The band was behind the bar. On a small platform beside them, a girl was dancing, stripped to her mask. The little cluster of men at the shadowy far end of the bar weren't looking at her.

We inspected the menu in gold script on the wall and pushed the buttons for breast of chicken, fried shrimps, and two scotches. Moments later, the serving bell tinkled. I opened the gleaming panel and took out our drinks.

• • •

The cluster of men at the bar filed off toward the door, but first they stared around the room. My companion had just thrown back her coat. Their look lingered on our booth. I noticed that there were three of them.

The band chased off the dancing girl with growls. I handed my companion a straw and we sipped our drinks.

"You wanted me to help you about something," I said. "Incidentally, I think you're lovely."

She nodded quick thanks, looked around, leaned forward. "Would it be hard for me to get to England?"

"No," I replied, a bit taken aback. "Provided you have an American passport."

"Are they difficult to get?"

"Rather," I said, surprised at her lack of information. "Your country doesn't like its nationals to travel, though it isn't quite as stringent as Russia."

"Could the British Consulate help me get a passport?"

"It's hardly their . . ."

"Could you?"

I realized we were being inspected. A man and two girls had paused opposite our table. The girls were tall and wolfish looking, with spangled masks. The man stood jauntily between them like a fox on its hind legs.

My companion didn't glance at them, but she sat back. I noticed that one of the girls had a big yellow bruise on her forearm. After a moment they walked to a booth in the deep shadows.

"Know them?" I asked. She didn't reply. I finished my drink. "I'm not sure you'd like England," I said. "The austerity's altogether different from your American brand of misery."

She leaned forward again. "But I must get away," she whispered.

"Why?" I was getting impatient.

"Because I'm so frightened."

There were chimes. I opened the panel and handed her the fried shrimps. The sauce on my breast of chicken was a delicious steaming compound of almonds, soy, and ginger. But something must have been wrong with the radionic oven that had thawed and heated it, for at the first bite I crunched a kernel of ice in the meat. These delicate mechanisms need constant repair and there aren't enough mechanics.

I put down my fork. "What are you really scared of?" I asked her.

For once her mask didn't waver away from my face. As I waited I could feel the fears gathering without her naming them, tiny dark shapes swarming through the curved night outside, converging on the radioactive pest spot of New York, dipping into the margins of the purple. I felt a sudden rush of sympathy, a desire to protect the girl opposite me. The warm feeling added itself to the infatuation engendered in the cab.

"Everything," she said finally.

I nodded and touched her hand.

"I'm afraid of the Moon," she began, her voice going dreamy and brittle as it had in the cab. "You can't look at it and not think of guided bombs."

"It's the same Moon over England," I reminded her.

"But it's not England's Moon anymore. It's ours and Russia's. You're not responsible."

I pressed her hand.

"Oh, and then," she said with a tilt of her mask, "I'm afraid of the cars and the gangs and the loneliness and Inferno. I'm afraid of the lust that undresses your face. And"—her voice hushed—"I'm afraid of the wrestlers."

"Yes?" I prompted softly after a moment.

•   •   •

Her mask came forward. "Do you know something about the wrestlers?" she asked rapidly. "The ones that wrestle women, I mean. They often lose, you know. And then they have to have a girl to take their frustration out on. A girl who's soft and weak and terribly frightened. They need that, to keep them men. Other men don't want them to have a girl. Other men want them just to fight women and be heroes. But they must have a girl. It's horrible for her."

I squeezed her fingers tighter, as if courage could be transmitted—granting I had any. "I think I can get you to England," I said.

Shadows crawled onto the table and stayed there. I looked up at the three men who had been at the end of the bar. They were the men I had seen in the big coupe. They wore black sweaters and close-fitting black trousers. Their faces were as expressionless as dopers. Two of them stood above me. The other loomed over the girl.

"Drift off, man," I was told. I heard the other inform the girl: "We'll wrestle a fall, sister. What shall it be? Judo, slapsie, or kill-who-can?"

I stood up. There are times when an Englishman simply must be maltreated. But just then the foxlike man came gliding in like the star of a ballet. The reaction of the other three startled me. They were acutely embarrassed.

He smiled at them thinly. "You won't win my favor by tricks like this," he said.

"Don't get the wrong idea, Zirk," one of them pleaded.

"I will if it's right," he said. "She told me what you tried to do this afternoon. That won't endear you to me, either. Drift."

They backed off awkwardly. "Let's get out of here," one of them said loudly, as they turned. "I know a place where they fight naked with knives."

· · ·

Little Zirk laughed musically and slipped into the seat beside my companion. She shrank from him, just a little. I pushed my feet back, leaned forward.

"Who's your friend, baby?" he asked, not looking at her.

She passed the question to me with a little gesture. I told him.

"British," he observed. "She's been asking you about getting out of the country? About passports?" He smiled pleasantly. "She likes to start running away. Don't you, baby?" His small hand began to stroke her wrist, the fingers bent a little, the tendons ridged, as if he were about to grab and twist.

"Look here," I said sharply. "I have to be grateful to you for ordering off those bullies, but—"

"Think nothing of it," he told me. "They're no harm except when they're behind steering wheels. A well-trained fourteen-year-old girl could cripple any one of them. Why, even Theda here, if she went in for that sort of thing . . ." He turned to her, shifting his hand from her wrist to her hair. He stroked it, letting the strands slip slowly through his fingers. "You know I lost tonight, baby, don't you?" he said softly.

I stood up. "Come along," I said to her. "Let's leave."

· · ·

She just sat there. I couldn't even tell if she was trembling. I tried to read a message in her eyes through the mask.

312

"I'll take you away," I said to her. "I can do it. I really will."

He smiled at me. "She'd like to go with you," he said. "Wouldn't you, baby?"

"Will you or won't you?" I said to her. She still just sat there.

He slowly knotted his fingers in her hair.

"Listen, you little vermin," I snapped at him, "Take your hands off her."

He came up from the seat like a snake. I'm no fighter. I just know that the more scared I am, the harder and straighter I hit. This time I was lucky. But as he crumpled back, I felt a slap and four stabs of pain in my cheek. I clapped my hand to it. I could feel the four gashes made by her dagger finger caps, and the warm blood oozing out from them.

She didn't look at me. She was bending over little Zirk and cuddling her mask to his cheek and crooning: "There, there, don't feel bad, you'll be able to hurt me afterward."

There were sounds around us, but they didn't come close. I leaned forward and ripped the mask from her face.

I really don't know why I should have expected her face to be anything else. It was very pale, of course, and there weren't any cosmetics. I suppose there's no point in wearing any under a mask. The eyebrows were untidy and the lips chapped. But as for the general expression, as for the feelings crawling and wriggling across it—

Have you ever lifted a rock from damp soil? Have you ever watched the slimy white grubs?

I looked down at her, she up at me. "Yes, you're so frightened, aren't you?" I said sarcastically. "You dread this little nightly drama, don't you? You're scared to death."

And I walked right out into the purple night, still holding my hand to my bleeding cheek. No one stopped me, not even the girl wrestlers. I wished I could tear a tab from under my shirt, and test it then and there, and find I'd taken too much radiation, and so be able to ask to cross the Hudson and go down New Jersey, past the lingering radiance of the Narrows Bomb, and so on to Sandy Hook to wait for the rusty ship that would take me back over the seas to England.

NANCY KRESS

WITH THE ORIGINAL CAST

(1982)

IN THE SUMMER OF 1998 Gregory Whitten was rehearsing a seventy-fifth-year revival of George Bernard Shaw's *Saint Joan*, and Barbara Bishop abruptly called to ask me to fly back from Denver and attend a few rehearsals with her. She was playing Shaw's magnificent teenaged fanatic, a role she had not done for twenty years and never on Broadway. Still, it was an extraordinary request; she had never specifically asked for my presence before, and I wound up my business for Gorer-Redding Solar and caught the next shuttle with uncharacteristic hope. At noon I landed in New York and coptered directly to the theater. Barbara met me in the lobby.

"Austin! You came!"

"Did you doubt it?" I kissed her, and she laughed softly.

"It was so splendid of you to drop everything and rush home."

"Well—I didn't exactly drop it. Lay it down gently, perhaps."

"Could Carl spare you? Did you succeed in blocking that coalition, or can they still stop Carl from installing the new Battery?"

"They have one chance in a billion," I said lightly. Barbara always asks; she manages to sound as interested in Gorer-Redding Solar as in Shakespeare and ESIR, although I don't suppose she really is. Of late neither am I, although Carl Gorer is my brother and the speculative risks of finance, including Gorer-Redding, is my profession. It was a certain faint boredom with seriously behaved money that had driven me in the first place to take wildcat risks backing legitimate theater. In the beginning Gorer-Redding Solar was itself a wildcat risk: one chance in a hundred that solar energy could be made cheap and plentiful enough to replace the exhausted petrofields. But that was years ago. Now solar prosperity is a reality; speculations lie elsewhere.

"I do appreciate your coming, you know," Barbara said. She tilted her head to one side, and a curve of shining dark hair, still without gray, slanted across one cheek.

"All appreciation gratefully accepted. Is there something wrong with the play?"

"No, of course not. What could be wrong with Shaw? Oh, Gregory's a little edgy, but then you know Gregory."

"Then you called me back solely to marry me."

"Austin, not again," she said, without coyness. "Not now."

"Then something is wrong."

She pulled a little away from me, shaking her head. "Only the usual new-play nerves."

"Rue-day nerves."

"Through-the-day swerves."

"Your point," I said. "But, Barbara, you've played Joan of Arc before."

"Twenty years ago," she said, and I glimpsed the strain on her face a second before it vanished under her publicity-photo smile, luminous and cool as polished crystal. Then the smile disappeared, and she put her cheek next to mine and whispered, "I do thank you for coming. And you look so splendid," and she was yet another Barbara, the Barbara I saw only in glimpses through her self-contained poise, despite having pursued her for half a year now with my marriage proposals, all gracefully rejected. I, Austin Gorer, who until now had never ever pursued anything very fast or very far. Nor ever had to.

"Nervous, love?"

"Terrified," she said lightly, the very lightness turning the word into a denial of itself, a delicate stage mockery.

"I don't believe it."

"That's half your charm. You never believe me."

"Your Joan was a wild success."

"My God, that was even before ESIR, can you believe it?"

"I believe it."

"So do I," she said, laughing, and began to relate anecdotes about casting that play, then this one, jumping between the two with witty, effortless bridges, her famous voice rising and falling with the melodious control that was as much a part of the public's image of her as the shining helmet of dark hair and the cool grace.

She has never had good press. She is too much of a paradox to reduce easily to tabloid slogans, and the stupider journalists have called her mannered and artificial. She is neither. Eager animation and conscious taste are two qualities the press usually holds to be opposites, patronizing the first and feeling defensive in the presence of the second. But in Barbara Bishop, animation and control have melded into a grace that owes nothing to nature and everything to a civilized respect for willed illusion. When she walks across a stage or through a bedroom, when she speaks Shaw's words or her own, when she hands Macbeth a dagger or a dinner guest a glass of wine, every movement is both free of artifice and perfectly controlled. Because she will not rage at press conferences, or wail colorfully at lost roles, or wrinkle her nose in professional cuteness, the press has decided that she is cold and lacks spontaneity. But for Barbara, what is spontaneous is control. She was born with it. She'll always have it.

"—and so now Gregory's *still* casting for the crowd scenes. He's tested what has to be every ESIR actor in New York, and now he's scraping up fledglings straight out of the hospital. Their scalp scars are barely healed and the ink on their historian's certificates is still wet. We're two weeks behind already, and rehearsals have barely begun, would you believe it? He can't find enough actors with an ESIR in fifteenth-century France, and he's not willing to go even fifty years off on either side."

"Then you must have been French in Joan's time," I said, "or he wouldn't have cast you? Even you?"

"Quite right. Even me." She moved away from me toward the theater doors. Again I sensed in her some unusual strain. An actor is always reluctant to discuss his ESIR with an outsider (bad form), but this was something more.

"As it happens," Barbara continued, "I was not only French, I was even in Rouen when Joan was burned at the stake in 1431. I didn't see the burning, and I never laid eyes on her—I was only a barmaid in a country tavern—but, still, it's rather an interesting coincidence."

"Yes."

"One chance in a million," she said, smiling. "Or, no—what would be the odds, Austin? That's really your field."

I didn't know. It would depend, of course, on just how many people in the world had undergone ESIR. There were very few. Electronically Stimulated Incarnation Recall involves painful, repeated electrochemical jolts through the cortex, through the limbic brain, directly into the R-Complex, containing racial and genetic memory. Biological shields are ripped away; defense mechanisms designed to aid survival by streamlining the vast load of memory are deliberately torn. The long-term effects are not yet known. ESIR is risky, confusing, morally disorienting, painful, and expensive. Most people want nothing to do with it. Those who do are mostly historians, scientists, freaks, mystics, poets—or actors, who must be a little of each. A stage full of players who believe totally that they are in Hamlet's Denmark or Sir Thomas More's England or Blanche DuBois's South because they have been there and feel it in every gesture, every cadence, every authentic cast of mind—such a stage is out of time entirely. It can seduce even a philistine financier. Since ESIR, the glamour of the theater has risen, the number of would-be actors has dropped, and only the history departments of the world's universities have been so in love with historically authentic style.

"Forget the odds," I said. "Who hasn't been cast yet?"

"Well, we need to see," she said, ticking off roles on her fingers. I recognized the parody instantly. Gregory Whitten himself. Her very face seemed to lengthen into the horse-faced scowl so beloved by Sunday-supplement caricaturists. "We must have two royal ladies—no, they must absolutely look royal, *royal*. And DeStogumber, I need a marvelous DeStogumber! How can anyone expect me to direct without an absolutely wonderful DeStogumber—"

The theater doors opened. "We are ready for you onstage, Miss Bishop."

"Thank you." The parody of Whitten had vanished instantly; in this public of one stagehand she was again Barbara Bishop, controlled and cool.

I settled into a seat in the first row, nodding vaguely at the other hangers-on scattered throughout the orchestra and mezzanine. No one nodded back. There was an absurd public fiction that we, who contributed nothing to the play but large sums of money, were like air: necessary but invisible. I didn't mind. I enjoyed seeing the cast ease into their roles, pulling them up from somewhere inside and mentally shaking each fold around their own gestures and voices and glances. I had not always known how to see that. It had taken me, from such a different set of signals, a long time to notice the tiny adjustments that go, rehearsal by rehearsal, to create the illusion of reality. Perhaps I was slow. But now it seemed to me that I could spot the precise moment when an actor has achieved that precarious balance between his neocortical knowledge of the script and his older, ESIR knowledge of the feel of his character's epoch, and so is neither himself nor the playwright's creation but some third, subtler force that transcends both. Barbara, I could see, had not yet reached that moment.

Whitten, pacing the side of the stage, was directing the early scene in which the seventeen-year-old Joan, a determined peasant, comes to Captain Robert de Baudricourt to demand a horse and armor to lead the French to victory over the English. De Baudricourt was being played by Jason Kellig, a semi-successful actor whom I had met before and not particularly liked. No one else was onstage, although I had that sensation one always has during a rehearsal of hordes of other people just out of sight in the wings, eyeing the action critically and shushing one another. Moths fluttering nervously just outside the charmed circle of light.

"No, squire!" Barbara said. "God is very merciful, and the blessed saints Catherine and Margaret, who speak to me every day, will intercede for you. You will go to paradise, and your name will be remembered forever as my first helper."

It was subtly wrong: too poised for the peasant Joan, too graceful. At the same time, an occasional gesture—an outflinging of her elbow, a sour smile—was too brash, and I guessed that these had belonged to the Rouen barmaid in Joan's ESIR. It was very rough, and I could see Whitten's famous temper, never long in check, begin to mount.

"No, no, no—Barbara, you're supposed to be an innocent. Shaw says that Joan answers 'with muffled sweetness.' You sound too surly. Absolutely too surly. You must do it again. Jason, cue her."

"Well, I am damned," Kellig said.

"No, squire! God is very merciful, and blessed saints Catherine and

Margaret, who speak to me every day, will intercede for you. You will go to paradise—"

"Again," Whitten said.

"Well, I am damned."

"No, squire! God is very merciful, and the blessed saints Catherine and Margaret, who speak to me every—"

"No! Now you sound like you're sparring with him! This is not some damned eighteenth-century drawing-room repartee! Joan absolutely means it! The voices are absolutely real to her. You must do it again, Barbara. You must tap into the religious atmosphere of your ESIR. You are not trying! Do it again!"

Barbara bit her lip. I saw Kellig glance from her to Whitten, and I suddenly had the impression—I don't know why—that they had all been at one another earlier, before I had arrived. Something beyond the usual rehearsal frustration was going on here. Tension, unmistakable as the smell of smoke, rose from the three of them.

"Well, I am damned."

"No, squire! God is very merciful, and the blessed saints Catherine and Margaret, who speak to me every day, will intercede for you. You will go to paradise, and your name will be remembered forever as my first helper."

"Again," Whitten said.

"Well, I am damned."

"No, squire! God is—"

"Again."

"Really, Gregory," Barbara began icily, "how you think you can judge after four words of—"

"I need to hear only one word when it's as bad as that! And what in absolute hell is that little flick of the wrist supposed to be? Joan is not a discus thrower. She must be—" Whitten stopped dead, staring offstage.

At first, unsure of why he had cut himself off or turned so red, I thought he was having an attack of some kind. The color in his face was high, almost hectic. But he held himself taut and erect, and then I heard the siren coming closer, landing on the roof, trailing off. It had come from the direction of Larrimer—which was, I suddenly remembered, the only hospital in New York that would do ESIR.

A very young man in a white coat hurried across the stage.

"Mr. Whitten, Dr. Metz says could you come up to the copter right away?"

"What is it? No, don't hold back, damn it. you absolutely must tell me now! Is it?"

On the young technician's face professional restraint battled with self-importance. The latter won, helped perhaps by Whitten's seizing the boy by the shoulders. For a second I actually thought Whitten would shake him.

"It's her, sir. It really is. We were looking for fifteenth-century ESIR, like you said, and we tried the neos for upper class for the ladies in waiting, and all we were getting were peasants or non-Europeans or early childhood deaths, and then Dr. Metz asked—" He was clearly enjoying this, dragging it out as much as possible. Whitten waited with a patience that surprised me until I realized that he was holding his breath. "—this neo to concentrate on the pictures Dr. Metz would show her of buildings and dresses and bowls and stuff to clear her mind. She looked dazed and in pain like they do, and then she suddenly remembered who she was, and Dr. Metz asked her lots of questions—that's his period anyway, you know; he's the foremost American historian on medieval France—and then he said she was."

Whitten let out his breath, a long, explosive sigh. Kellig leaned forward and said, "Was . . ."

"Joan," the boy said simply. "Joan of Arc."

It was as if he had shouted, although of course he had not. But the name hung in the dusty silence of the empty theater, circled and underlined by everything there: the heavy velvet curtains, the dust motes in the air, the waiting strobes, the clouds of mothlike actors, or memories of actors, in the wings. They all existed to lend weight and probability to what had neither. One in a million, one in a billion.

"Is Dr. Metz sure?" Whitten demanded. He looked suddenly violent, capable of disassembling the technician if the historian were not sure.

"He's sure!"

"Where is she? In the copter?"

"Yes."

"Have Dr. Metz bring her down here. No, I'll go up there. No, bring her here. Is she still weak?"

"Yes, sir," the boy said.

"Well, go! I told Dr. Metz I wanted her here as soon as he absolutely was sure!"

The boy went.

So Whitten had been informed of the possibility earlier. I looked at Barbara, suddenly understanding the tension on stage. She stood smiling, her chin raised a little, her body very straight. She looked pale. Some trick of lighting, some motionless tautness in her shoulders, made me think for an instant that she was going to faint, but of course she did not. She behaved exactly as I knew she must have been willing herself to, waiting quietly through the interminable time until Joan of Arc should appear. Whitten fidgeted; Kellig lounged, his eyelids lowered halfway. Neither of them looked at Barbara.

The technician and the historian walked out onto the stage, each with a hand under either elbow of a young girl whose head was bandaged. Even now I feel a little ashamed when I remember rising halfway in my seat, as for an exalted presence. But the girl was not an exalted presence, was not Joan of Arc; she was an awkward, skinny, plain-faced girl who had once been Joan of Arc and now wanted to be an extra in the background of a seventy-five-year-old play. No one else seemed to be remembering the distinction.

"You were Joan of Arc?" Whitten asked. He sounded curiously formal, as out of character as the girl.

"Yes, I . . . I remember Joan. Being Joan." The girl frowned, and I thought I knew why: She was wondering why she didn't feel like Joan. But ESIR, Barbara has told me, doesn't work like that. Other lives are like remembering someone you have known, not like experiencing the flesh and bone of this one—unless this one is psychotic. Otherwise, it usually takes time and effort to draw on the memory of a previous incarnation, and this child had been Joan of Arc only for a few days. Suddenly I felt very sorry for her.

"What's your first name?" Whitten said.

"Ann. Ann Jasmine."

Whitten winced. "A stage name?"

"Yes. Isn't it pretty?"

"You must absolutely use your real name. What acting have you done?"

The girl shifted her weight, spreading her feet slightly apart and starting to count off on her fingers. Her voice was stronger now and cockier. "Well, let's just see: In high school I played Portia in *The Merchant of Venice*, and in the Country-Time Players—that's community theater—I was Goat's Sister in *The Robber Bridegroom* and Aria in *Moondust*. And then I came to New York, and I've done—oh, small stuff, mostly. A few commercials." She smiled at Whitten, then looked past him at Kellig and winked. He stared back at her as if she were a dead fish.

"What," said Kellig slowly, "is your real name?"

"Does it matter?" The girl's smile vanished, and she pouted.

"Yes."

"Ann Friedland," she said sulkily, and I knew where the "few commercials, mostly" as well as the expensive ESIR audition had come from. Trevor Friedland, of Friedland Computers, was a theater backer for his own amusement, much as I was. He was not, however, a co-backer in this one. Not yet.

At the Friedland name, Kellig whistled, a low, impudent note that made Whitten glance at him in annoyance. Barbara still had not moved. She watched them intently.

"Forget your name," Whitten said. "Absolutely forget it. Now I know this play is new to you, but you must read for me. Just read cold; don't be nervous. Take my script and start there. No—there. Jason, cue her."

"You want me to read Joan? The part of Joan?" the girl said. All her assumed sophistication was gone; her face was as alive as a seven-year-old's at Christmas, and I looked away, not wanting to like her.

"Oh, really, Greg," Kellig said. Whitten ignored him.

"Just look over Shaw's description there, and then start. I know you're cold. Just start."

"Good morning, captain squire," she began shakily, but stopped when Barbara crossed the stage to sit on a bench near the wings. She was still smiling, a small frozen smile. Ann glanced at her nervously, then began over.

"Good morning, captain squire. Captain, you are to give me a horse . . ." Again she stopped. A puzzled look came over her face; she skimmed a few pages and then closed her eyes. Immediately I thought of the real Joan, listening to voices. But this was the real Joan. For a moment the stage seemed to float in front of me, a meaningless collection of lines and angles.

"It wasn't like that," Ann Friedland said slowly.

"Like what?" Whitten said. "What wasn't like what?"

"Joan. Me. She didn't charge in like that at all to ask de Baudricourt for horse and armor. It wasn't at all . . . she was more . . . Insane, I think. What he has written here, Shaw . . ." She looked at each of us in turn, frowning. No one moved. I don't know how long we stayed that way, staring at the thin girl onstage.

"Saint Catherine," she said finally. "Saint Margaret." Her slight figure jerked as if shocked, and she threw back her head and howled like a dog. "But Orleans was not even my idea! The commander, my father, the commander, my father . . . oh, my God, my dear God, he made her do it, he told me—they all promised—"

She stumbled, nearly falling to her knees. The historian leaped forward and caught her. I don't think any of us could have borne it if that pitiful, demented figure had knelt and begun to pray.

The next moment, however, though visibly fighting to control herself, she knew where—and who—she was.

"Doctor, don't, I'm all right now. It's not—I'm all right. Mr. Whitten, I'm sorry, let me start the scene over!"

"No, don't start the scene over. Tell me what you were going to say. Where is Shaw wrong? What happened? Try to feel it again."

Ann's eyes held Whitten's. They were beyond all of us, already negotiating with every inflection of every word.

"I don't have to feel it again. I remember what happened. That wave of . . . I won't do that again. It was just when it all came rushing back. But now I remember it, I have it, I can *control* it. It didn't happen like Shaw's play. She—I—was used. She did hear voices, she was mad, but the whole idea to use her to persuade the Dauphin to fight against the English didn't come from the voices. The priests insisted on what they said the voices meant, and the commander made her a sort of mascot to get the soldiers to kill . . . I was *used*. A victim." A complicated expression passed over her face, perhaps the most extraordinary expression I have ever seen on a face so young: regret and shame and loss and an angry, wondering despair for events long beyond the possibility of change. Then the expression vanished, and she was wholly a young woman coolly engaged in the bargaining of history.

"I know it all, Mr. Whitten—all that really happened. And it happened to me. The real Joan of Arc."

"Cosgriff," Whitten said, and I saw Kellig start. Lawrence Cosgriff had won the Pulitzer Prize for drama the last two years in a row. He wrote powerful, despairing plays about the loss of individual morality in an institutionalized world.

"My dear Gregory," Kellig said, "one does not simply commission Lawrence Cosgriff to write one a play. He's not some hack you can—"

Whitten looked at him, and he was quiet. I understood why; Whitten was on fire, as exalted with his daring idea as the original Joan must have been with hers. But no, of course, she hadn't been exalted, that was the whole point. She had been a dupe, not a heroine. Young Miss Friedland, fighting for her name in lights, most certainly considered Joan the Heroine to be an expendable casualty.

One of the expendable casualties. I stood up and began to make my way to the stage.

"I'm the real thing," Ann said. "The real thing. I'll play Joan, of course."

"Of course," Kellig drawled. He was already looking at her with dislike, and I could see what their rehearsals would be: the chance upstart and the bit player who had paid largely fruitless dues for twenty years. The commander and the Dauphin would still be the male leads; Kellig's part could only grow smaller under Ann's real thing.

"I'll play Joan," she said again, a little more loudly.

Whitten, flushed with his vision, stopped his ecstatic pacing and scowled. "Of course you must play Joan!"

"Oh," Ann said, "I was afraid—"

"Afraid? What is this? You are Joan."

"Yes," she said slowly, "yes, I am." She frowned, sincerely, and then a second later replaced the frown with a smile all calculation and relief. "Yes, of course I am!"

"Then I'll absolutely reach Cosgriff's agent today. He'll jump at it. You will need to work with him, of course. We can open in six months, with any luck. You do live in town? Cosgriff can tape you. No, someone else can do that before he even—Austin!"

"You're forgetting something, aren't you, Gregory, in this sudden great vision? You have a contract to do Shaw."

"Of course I'm not forgetting the contract. But you absolutely must want to continue, for this new play . . . Cosgriff . . ." He stopped, and I knew the jumble of things that must be in his mind: deadlines, backing (Friedland Computers!), contracts, schedules, the percentage of my commitment, and, belatedly, Barbara.

She still sat on the bench at stage left, half in shadow. Her back was very straight, her chin high, but in the subdued light her face with its faint smile looked older, not haggard but set, inelastic. I walked over to her and turned to face Whitten.

"I will not back this new play, even if you do get Cosgriff to write it. Which I rather doubt. Shaw's drama is an artistic masterpiece. What you are planning is a trendy exploitation of some flashy technology. Look elsewhere for your money."

Silence. Whitten began to turn red, Kellig snickered—at whom was not clear. In the silence the historian, Dr. Metz, began timidly, "I'm sure Miss Friedland's information would be welcomed warmly by any academic—"

The girl cried loudly, "But I'm the real thing!" and she started to sob.

Barbara had risen to take my arm. Now she dropped it and walked over to Ann. Her voice was steady. "I know you are. And I wish you all luck as an actress. It's a brilliant opportunity, and I'm sure you'll do splendidly with it."

They faced each other, the sniveling girl who had at least the grace to look embarrassed and the smiling, humiliated woman. It was a public performance, of course, an illusion that all Barbara felt was a selfless, graceful warmth, but it was also more than that. It was as gallant an act of style as I have ever seen.

Ann muttered, "Thank you," and flushed a mottled maroon. Barbara took my arm and we walked down the side aisle and out of the theater. She walked carefully, choosing her steps, her head high and lips together and solemn, like a woman on her way to a public burning.

I wish I could say that my quixotic gesture had an immediate and disastrous effect on Whitten's plans, that he came to his artistic senses—and went back to Shaw's Saint Joan. But of course he did no such thing. Other financial backing than mine proved to be readily available. Contracts were rewritten, agents placated, lawsuits avoided. Cosgriff did indeed consent to write the script, and *Variety* became distressingly eager to report any tidbit connected with what was being billed as *Joan of Arc: With the Original Cast!* It was a dull theater season in New York. Nothing currently running gripped the public imagination like this as-yet-unwritten play. Whitten, adroitly fanning the flames, gave out very few factual details.

Barbara remained silent on the whole subject. Business was keeping me away from New York a great deal. Gorer-Redding Solar was installing a new plant in Bogotá, and I would spend whole weeks trying to untangle the lush foliage of bribes, kickbacks, nepotism, pride, religion, and mañana that is business in South America. But whenever I was in New York, I spent time with Barbara. She would not discuss Whitten's play, warning me away from the subject with the tactful withdrawal of an estate owner discouraging trespassing without hurting local feelings. I admired her tact and her refusal to whine, but at the same time I felt vaguely impatient. She was keeping me at arm's length. She was doing it beautifully, but arm's length was not where I wanted to be.

I do not assume that intimacy must be based on a mutual display of sores. I applaud the public illusion of control and well-being as a civilized achievement. However, I knew Barbara well enough to know that under her illusion of well-being she must be hurt and a little afraid. No decent scripts had been offered her, and the columnists had not been kind over the loss of Saint Joan. Barbara had been too aloof, too self-possessed for them to show any compassion now. Press sympathy for a humiliated celebrity is in direct proportion to the anguished copy previously supplied.

Then one hot night in August I arrived at Barbara's apartment for dinner. Lying on a hall table was a script:

A MAID OF DOMRÉMY

BY
LAWRENCE COSGRIFF

Incredulous, I picked it up and leafed through it. When I looked up, Barbara was standing in the doorway, holding two goblets of wine.

"Hello, Austin. Did you have a good flight?"

"Barbara—what is this?" I asked, stupidly.

She crossed the hall and handed me one of the goblets.

"It's Lawrence's play about Joan of Arc."

"I see that. But what is it doing here?"

She didn't answer me immediately. She looked beautiful, every illusion seeming completely natural: the straight, heavy silk of her artfully cut gown, the flawless makeup, the hair cut in precise lines to curve over one cheek. Without warning, I was irritated by all of it. Illusions. Arm's length.

"Austin, why don't you reconsider backing Gregory's play?"

"Why on earth should I?"

"Because you really could make quite a lot of money on it."

"I could make quite a lot of money backing auto gladiators. I don't do that, either."

She smiled, acknowledging the thrust. I still did not know how the conversation had become a duel.

"Are you hungry? There are canapés in the living room. Dinner won't be ready for a while yet."

"I'm not hungry. Barbara, why do you want me to back Whitten's play?"

"I don't want you to, if you don't wish to. Come in and sit down. *I'm* hungry. I only thought you might want to back the play. It's splendid." She looked at me steadily over the rim of her goblet. "It's the best new script I've seen in years. It's subtle, complex, moving—much better even than his last two. It's going to replace Shaw's play as the best we have about Joan. And on the subject of victimization by a world the main character doesn't understand, it's better than *Streetcar* or *Joy Ride*. A hundred years from now this play will still be performed regularly, and well."

"It's not like you to be so extravagant with your praise."

"No, it's not."

"And you want me to finance the play for the reflected glory?"

"For the satisfaction. And," she added quietly, but firmly, "because I've accepted a bit part in it."

I stared at her. Last week a major columnist had headlined: "Fallen Star Lands on Her Pride."

"It's a very small role. Yolande of Aragon, the Dauphin's mother-in-law. She intrigued on the Dauphin's behalf when he was struggling to be crowned. I have only one scene, but it has possibilities."

"For you? What—does it have possibilities of being smirked at by that little schemer in your role? Did you read how much her agent is holding Whitten up for? No wonder he could use more backers."

"You would get it back. But that's not the question, Austin, is it? Why do you object to my taking this part? It's not like you to object to my choice of roles."

"I'm upset because I don't want you to be hurt, and I think you are. I think you'll be hurt even more if you play this Yolande with Miss Ann Friedland as Joan, and I don't want to see it, because I love you."

"I know you do, Austin." She smiled warmly and touched my cheek. It was a perfect Barbara Bishop gesture: sincere, graceful, and complete in itself—so complete that it promised nothing more than what it was, led on to nothing else. It cut off communication as effectively as a blow—or, rather, more effectively, since a blow can be answered in kind. I slammed my glass on the table and stood up. Once up, however, I had nothing to say and so stood there feeling ridiculous. What did I want to say? What did I want from her that I did not already have?

"I wish," I said slowly, "that you were not always acting."

She looked at me steadily. I knew the look. She was waiting: for retraction or amendment or amplification. And of course she was right to expect any, or all, of those things. What I had said was inaccurate. She was not acting. What she did was something subtly different. She behaved with the gestures and attitudes and behaviors of the world as she believed it ought to be, a place of generous and rational individuals with enough sheer style to create events in their own image. That people's behavior was in fact often uncivilized, cowardly, and petty she of course knew; she was not stupid. Hers was a deliberate, controlled choice: to ignore the pettiness and to grant to all of us—actors, audience, press, Whitten, Ann Friedland, me, herself—the illusion of having the most admirable motives conceivable.

It seemed to me that this was praiseworthy, even "civilized," in the best sense of that much-abused word.

Why, then, did it make me feel so lonely?

Barbara was still waiting. "Forgive me; I misspoke. I don't mean that you are always acting. I mean—I mean that I'm concerned for you. Standing for a curtain call at the back of the stage while that girl, that chance reincarnation . . ." Suddenly a new idea occurred to me. "Or do you think that she won't be able to do the part and you will be asked to take over for her?"

"No!"

"But if Ann Friedland can't—"

"No! I will never play Joan in *A Maid of Domrémy*!"

"Why not?"

She finished her wine. Under the expensive gown her breasts heaved. "I had no business even taking the part in Shaw's Joan. I am forty-five years old, and Joan is seventeen. But at least there—at least Shaw's Joan was not really a victim. I will not play her as a pitiful victim."

"Come on, Barbara. You've played Blanche DuBois, and Ophelia, and Jessie Kane. They're all victims."

"I won't play Joan in *A Maid of Domrémy*!"

I saw that she meant it, that even while she admired the play, she was repelled by it in some fundamental way I did not understand. I sat down again on the sofa and put my arms around her. Instantly she was Barbara Bishop again, smiling with rueful mockery at both her own violence and my melodrama, drawing us together in a covenant too generous for quarreling.

"Look at us, Austin—actually discussing that tired old cliché, the understudy who goes on for the fading star. But I'm not her understudy, and she can hardly fade before she's even bloomed! Really, we're too ridiculous. I'm sorry, love, I didn't mean to snap at you like that. Shall we have dinner now?"

I stood up and pulled her next to me. She came gracefully, still smiling, the light sliding over her dark hair, and followed me to her bedroom. The sex was very good, as it always was. But afterward, lying with her head warm on my shoulder, I was still baffled by something in her I could not understand. Was it because of ESIR? I had thought that before. What was it like to have knowledge of those hundreds of other lives you had once lived? I would never know. Were the exotic types I met in the theater so different, so less easily understood, because they had "creative temperament" (whatever that was) or because of ESIR? I would probably never know that, either, nor how much of Barbara was what she was here, now, and how much was subtle reaction to all the other things she knew she had been. I wasn't sure I wanted to know.

Long after Barbara fell asleep, I lay awake in the soft darkness, listening to the night sounds of New York beyond the window and to something else beyond those, some large silence where my own ESIR memories might have been.

• • •

Whitten banned everyone but actors and tech crew from rehearsals of *A Maid of Domrémy*: press, relatives, backers, irate friends. Only because the play had seized the imagination of the public—or at least that small portion of the public that goes to the theater—could his move succeed. The financial angels went along cheerfully with their own banning, secure in the presale ticket figures that the play would make money even without their personal supervision.

Another director, casting for a production of *Hamlet*, suddenly claimed to have discovered the reincarnation of Shakespeare. For a week Broadway was a laser of rumors and speculations. Then the credentials of the two historians verifying the ESIR were discovered by a gleeful press to have been faked. The director, producer, historians, and ersatz Shakespeare were instantly unavailable for comment.

The central computer of the AMA was tapped into. For two days executives with private facelifts and politicians with private accident records and teachers with private drug-abuse histories held their collective breaths, cursing softly under them. The AMA issued a statement that only ESIR records had been pirated, and the scandal was generally forgotten in the central part of the country and generally intensified on both coasts. Wild reports were issued, contradicted, confirmed, and disproved, all in a few hours. An actor who remembered being King Arthur had been discovered and was going to star in the true story of the Round Table. Euripides was living in Boston and would appear there in his own play *Medea*. The computer verified that ESIR actually *had* uncovered Helen of Troy, and the press stampeded out to Bowling Green, Ohio, where it was discovered that the person who remembered being Helen of Troy was a male, bald, sixty-eight-year-old professor emeritus in the history department. He was writing a massive scholarly study of the Trojan War, and he bitterly resented the "cheap publicity of the popular press."

"The whole thing is becoming a circus," Barbara grumbled. Her shirt was loose at the breasts, and her pants gaped at the waist. She had lost weight and color.

"And this, too, shall pass," I told her. "Think of when ESIR was first introduced. A few years of wild quakes all over society, and then everyone adjusted. This is just the aftershock on the theater."

"I don't especially like standing directly on the fault line."

"How are rehearsals going?"

"About the same," she said, her eyes hooded. Since she never spoke of the play at all, I didn't know what "about the same" would be the same as.

"Barbara, what are you waiting for?"

"Waiting for?"

"Constantly now you have that look of waiting, frowning to yourself, looking as if you're scrutinizing something. Something only you can see."

"Austin, how ridiculous! What I'm looking at is all too public: opening night for the play."

"And what do you see?"

She was silent for a long time. "I don't know." She laughed, an abrupt, opaque sound like the sudden drawing of a curtain. "It's silly, isn't it? Not knowing what I don't know. A tautology, almost."

"Barbara, marry me. We'll go away for a weekend and get married, like two children. This weekend."

"I thought you had to fly back to Bogotá this weekend."

"I do. But you could come with me. There is a world outside New York, you know. It isn't simply all one vast out-of-town tryout."

"I do thank you, Austin, you know that. But I can't leave right now; I do have to work on my part. There are still things I don't trust."

"Such as what?"

"Me," she said lightly, and would say no more.

Meanwhile the hoopla went on. A professor of history at Berkeley who had just finished a—now probably erroneous—dissertation on Joan of Arc tried various legal ploys to sue Ann Friedland on the grounds that she "undercut his means of livelihood." A group called the Catholic Coalition to Clear the Inquisition published in four major newspapers an appeal to Ann Friedland to come forward and declare the fairness of the church at Joan of Arc's heresy trial. Each of the ads cost a fantastic sum. But Ann did not reply; she was preserving to the press a silence as complete as Barbara's to me. I think this is why I didn't press Barbara more closely about her rehearsals. I wanted to appear as different from the rest of the world as possible—an analogy probably no one made except me. Men in love are ludicrous.

Interest in Ann Friedland was not dispelled by her silence. People merely claiming to be a notable figure from the past was growing stale. For years people had been claiming to be Jesus Christ or Muhammad or Judas; all had been disproved, and the glamour evaporated. But now a famous name had not only been verified, it was going to be showcased in an enterprise that carried the risk of losing huge sums of money, several professional reputations, and months of secret work. The public was delighted. Ann Friedland quickly became a house-hold name.

She was going to marry the widowed King Charles of England. She was going to lead a revival of Catholicism and was being considered for the position of first female pope. She was a drug addict, a Mormon, pregnant, mad, in love, clairvoy-ant, ten years old, extraterrestrial. She was refusing to go on opening night. Gregory Whitten was going to let her improvise the part opening night. Rehears-als were a disaster, and Barbara Bishop would play the part opening night.

Not even to this last did Barbara offer a comment. Also silent were the reput-able papers, the serious theater critics, the men and women who control the money that controls Broadway. They, too, were waiting.

We all waited.

•   •   •

The week that *A Maid of Domrémy* was to open in New York I was still in Bogotá. I had come down with a low-grade fever, which in the press of work I chose to ignore. By Saturday I had a temperature of one hundred four degrees and a headache no medication could touch. I saw everything through slow, pastel-colored swirls. My arms and legs felt lit with a dry, papery fire that danced up and down from shoulder to wrist, ankle to hip, up and down, wrist to shoulder. I knew I should go to a hospital, but I did not. The opening was that night.

On the plane to New York I slept, dreaming of Barbara in the middle of a vast solar battery. I circled the outside, calling to her desperately. Unaware, she sat reading a script amid the circuits and storage cells, until the fires of the sun burst out all around her and people she had known from other lives danced maniacally in the flames.

At my apartment I took more pills and a cold shower, then tried to phone Barbara. She had already left for makeup call. I dressed and caught a copter to the theater, sleeping fitfully on the short trip, and then I was in the theater, sur-rounded by first-nighters who did not know I was breathing contagion on all of them, and who floated around me like pale cutouts in diamonds, furs, and nau-seating perfume. I could not remember walking from the copter, producing my ticket, or being escorted to my seat. The curtain swirled sickeningly, and I closed my eyes until I realized that it was not my fever that caused the swirls: The cur-tain was rising. Had the house lights dimmed? I couldn't remember anything. Dry fire danced over me, shoulder to wrist, ankle to hip.

Barbara, cloaked, entered stage left. I had not realized that her scene opened the play. She carried a massive candle across the stage, bent over a wooden table, and lit two more candles from the large one, all with the taut, economical move-ments of great anger held fiercely in check. Before the audience heard her speak, before they clearly saw her face, they had been told that Yolande was furious, not used to being so, and fully capable of controlling her own anger.

"Mary! Where are you sulking now, Mary?" Barbara said. She straightened and drew back her hood. Her voice was low, yet every woman named Mary in the audience started guiltily. Onstage Mary of Anjou, consort of the uncrowned Dauphin of France, crept sullenly from behind a tapestry, facing her mother like a whipped dog.

"Here I am, for all the good it will do you, or anyone," she whined, looking at her own feet. Barbara's motionless silence was eloquent with contempt; Mary burst out with her first impassioned monologue against the Dauphin and Joan; the play was launched. It was a strong, smooth beginning, fueled by the conviction of Barbara's portrait of the terrifying Yolande. As the scene unfolded, the portrait became even stronger, so that I forgot both my feverish limbs and my concern for Barbara. There were no limbs, no Barbara, no theater. There was only a room in fifteenth-century France, sticky with blood shed for what to us were illusions: absolute good and absolute evil. Cosgriff was exploring the capacities in such illusions for heroism, for degradation, for nobility beyond what the audience's beliefs, saner and more temperate, could allow. Yolande and Mary and the Dauphin loved and hated and gambled and killed with every fiber of their elemental beings, and not a sound rose from the audience until Barbara delivered her final speech and exited stage right. For a moment the audience sat still, bewildered—not by what had happened onstage, but by the unwelcome remembrance that they were not a part of it, but instead were sitting on narrow hard seats in a wooden box in New York, a foreign country because it was not medieval France. Then the applause started.

The Dauphin and his consort, still onstage, did not break character. He waited until the long applause was over, then continued bullying his wife. Shortly afterward two guards entered, dragging between them the confused, weeping Joan. The audience leaned forward eagerly. They were primed by the wonderful first scene and eager for more miracles.

"Is this the slut?" the Dauphin asked, and Mary, seeing a woman even more abused and wretched than herself, smiled with secret, sticky joy. The guards let Joan go, and she stumbled forward, caught herself, and staggered upward, raising her eyes to the Dauphin's.

"In the name of Saint Catherine—" She choked and started to weep. It was stormy weeping, vigorous, but without the chilling pain of true hysteria. The audience shuffled a little.

"I will do whatever you want, I swear it in the name of God, if you will only tell me what it is!" On the last word her voice rose; she might have been demanding that a fractious child cease lying to her.

I leaned my head sideways against one shoulder. Waves of fever and nausea beat through me, and for the first time since I had become ill I was aware of labored breathing. My heart beat, skipped, beat twice, skipped. Each breath sounded swampy and rasping. People in the row ahead began to turn and glare. Wadding my handkerchief into a ball, I held it in front of my mouth and tried to watch the play—lines slipped in and out of my hearing; actors swirled in fiery paper-dry pastels. Once Joan seemed to turn into Barbara, and I gasped and half-rose in my seat, but then the figure onstage was Ann Friedland, and I sat down again to glares from those around me. It was Ann Friedland; I had been a fool to doubt it. It was not Joan of Arc. The girl onstage hesitated, changed tone too often, looked nervously across the footlights, moved a second too late. Once she even stammered.

Around me the audience began to murmur discreetly. Just before the first-act curtain, in a moment of clarity, Joan finally sees how she is being used and makes an inept, wrenchingly pathetic attempt to manipulate the users by manufacturing instructions she says come from her voices. It is a crucial point in the play, throwing into dramatic focus the victim who agrees to her own corruption by a misplaced attempt at control. Ann played it nervously, with an exaggerated grab at pathos that was actually embarrassing. Nothing of that brief glimpse of personal power she had shown at her audition, so many weeks ago, was present now. Between waves of fever, I tried to picture the fit Whitten must be having backstage.

"Christ," said a man in the row ahead of me, "can you believe that?"

"What an absolute travesty," said the woman next to him. Her voice hummed with satisfaction. "Poor Lawrence."

"He was ripe for it. Smug."

"Oh, yes. Still."

"Smug," the man said.

"It doesn't matter to me what you do with her," said Mary of Anjou, onstage. "Why should it? Only for a moment she seemed . . . different. Did you remark it?" Ann Friedland, who had not seemed different, grimaced weakly, and the first-act curtain fell. People were getting to their feet, excited by the magnitude of the disaster. The house lights went up. Just as I stood, the curtains onstage parted and there was some commotion, but the theater leaped in a single nauseous lurch, blinding and hot, and then nothing.

•   •   •

"Austin," a voice said softly. "Austin."

My head throbbed, but from a distance, as if it were not my head at all.

"Austin," the voice said far above me. "Are you there?"

I opened my eyes. Yolande of Aragon, her face framed in a wool hood, gazed down at me and turned into Barbara. She was still in costume and makeup, the heavy, high color garish under too-bright lights. I groaned and closed my eyes.

"Austin. Are you there? Do you know me?"

"Barbara?"

"You are there! Oh, that's splendid. How do you feel? No, don't talk. You've been delirious, love, you had such a fever . . . this is the hospital. Larrimer. They've given you medication; you're going to be fine."

"Barbara."

"I'm here, Austin, I'm right here."

I opened my eyes slowly, accustoming them to the light. I lay in a small private room; beyond the window the sky was dark. I was aware that my body hurt, but aware in the detached, abstract way characteristic of EL painkillers, that miracle of modern science. The dose must have been massive. My body felt as if it belonged to someone else, a friend for whom I felt comradely simulations of pain, but not the real thing.

"What do I have?"

"Some tropical bug. What did you drink in Bogotá? The doctor says it could have been dangerous, but they flushed out your whole system and pumped you full of antibiotics, and you'll be fine. Your fever's down almost to normal. But you must rest."

"I don't want to rest."

"You don't have any choice." She took my hand. The touch felt distant, as if the hand were wrapped in layers of padding.

"What time is it?"

"Five a.m."

"The play—"

"Is long since over."

"What happened?"

She bit her lip. "A lot happened. When precisely do you mean? I wasn't there for the second act, you know. When the ambulance came for you, one of the ushers recognized you and came backstage to tell me. I rode here in the ambulance with you. I didn't have another scene anyway."

I was confused. If Barbara had missed the entire last act, how could "a lot have happened"? I looked at her closely, and this time I saw what only the ELs could have made me miss before: the signs of great, repressed strain. Tendons stood out in Barbara's neck; under the cracked and sagging makeup her eyes darted around the room. I felt myself suddenly alert, and a fragment of memory poked at me, a fragment half-glimpsed in the hot swirl of the theater just before I blacked out.

"She ran out on the stage." I said slowly. "Ann Friedland. In front of the curtain. She ran out and yelled something . . ." It was gone. I shook my head. "On the *stage*."

"Yes." Barbara let go of my hand and began to pace. Her long train dragged behind her; when she turned, it tangled around her legs and she stumbled. The action was so uncharacteristic, it was shocking.

"You saw what the first act was. A catastrophe. She was trying—"

"The whole first act wasn't bad, love. Your scene was wonderful. Wait—the reviews on your role will be very good."

"Yes," she said distractedly. I saw that she had hardly heard me. There was something she had to do, had to say. The best way to help was to let her do it. Words tore from her like a gale.

"She tried to do the whole play reaching back into her ESIR Joan. She tried to just feel it, and let Lawrence's words—her words—be animated by the remembered feeling. But without the conscious balancing . . . no, it isn't even balancing. It's more like imagining what you already know, and to do that, you have to forget what you know and at the same time remember every tiny nuance . . . I can't explain it. Nobody ever really was a major historical figure before, in a play composed of his own words. Gregory was so excited over the concept, and then when rehearsals began . . . but by that time he was committed, and the terrible hype just bound him further. When Ann ruined the first act like that, he was just beside himself. I've never seen him like that. I've never seen anybody like that. He was raging, just completely out of control. And onstage Ann was coming apart, and I could see that he was going to completely destroy her, and we had a whole act to go, damn it! A whole fucking act!"

I stared at her. She didn't notice. She lighted a cigarette; it went out; she flung the match and cigarette on the floor. I could see her hand trembling.

"I knew that if Gregory got at her, she was done. She wouldn't even go back out after intermission. Of course the play was a flop already, but not to even finish the damn thing . . . I wasn't thinking straight. All I could see was that he would destroy her, all of us. So I hit him."

"You what?"

"I hit him. With Yolande's candlestick. I took him behind a flat to try to calm him down, and instead I hit him. *Without knowing I was going to.* Something strange went through me, and I picked up my arm and hit him. Without knowing I was going to!"

She wrapped her arms around herself and shuddered. I saw what had driven her to this unbearable strain. *Without knowing I was going to.*

"His face became very surprised, and he fell forward. No one saw me. Gregory lay there, breathing as if he were just asleep, and I found a phone and called an ambulance. Then I told the stage manager that Mr. Whitten had had a bad fall and hit his head and was unconscious. I went around to the wings and waited for Ann. When the curtain came down and she saw me waiting for her, she turned white, and then red, and started shouting at me that she was Joan of Arc and I was an aging bitch who wanted to steal her role."

I tried to picture it—the abusive girl, the appalled, demoralized cast, the director lying hidden, bashed with a candlestick—*without knowing I was going to!*—and, out front, the polite chatter, the great gray critics from the *Times* and the *New Yorker*, the dressed-up suburbanites from Scarsdale squeezing genially down the aisles for an entr'acte drink and a smoke.

"She went on and on," Barbara said. "She told me *I* was the reason she couldn't play the role, that I deliberately undermined her by standing around like I knew everything, and she knew everybody was expecting me to go on as Joan after she failed. Then suddenly she darted away from me and went through the curtains onto the stage. The house lights were up; half the audience had left. She spread out her arms and *yelled* at them."

Barbara stopped and put her hands over her face. I reached up and pulled them away. She looked calmer now, although there was still an underlying tautness in her voice. "Oh, it's just too ridiculous, Austin. She made an absolute fool of herself, of Lawrence, of all of us, but it wasn't her fault. She's an inexperienced child without talent. Gregory should have known better, but his egomania got all tangled up in his ridiculous illusion that he was going to revitalize the theater, take the next historical step for American drama. God, what the papers will say . . ." She laughed weakly, with pain. "And I was no better, hitting poor Gregory."

"Barbara . . ."

"Do you know what Ann yelled at them, at the audience? She stood on that stage, flung her arms wide like some martyr . . ."

"What did she say? What, love?"

"She said, 'But I'm the *real thing*!'"

We were quiet for a moment. From outside the window rose blurred traffic noises: the-real-thing-the-real-thing-the-real-thing.

"You're right," I said. "The whole thing was an egomaniacal ride for Whitten, and the press turned it into a carnival. Cosgriff should have known better. The real thing—that's not what you want in the theater. Illusion, magic, imagination. What should have happened, not what did. Reality doesn't make good theater."

"No, you still don't understand!" Barbara cried. "You've missed it all! How can you think that it's that easy, that Gregory's mistake was to use Ann's reality instead of Shaw's illusion!"

"I don't understand what you—"

"It's not that clear!" she cried. "Don't you think I wish it were? My God!"

I didn't know what she meant, or why under the cracked makeup her eyes glittered with feverish, exhausted panic. Even as I reached out my arm, completely confused, she was backing away from me.

"Illusion and reality," she said. "My God. Watch."

She crossed the room to the door, closed it, and pressed the dimmer on the lights. The room faded to a cool gloom. She stood with her back to me, her head bowed. Then she turned slowly and raised her eyes to a point in the air a head above her.

"In the name of Saint Catherine—" she began, choked, and started to weep. The weeping was terrifying, shot through with that threat of open hysteria that keeps a listener on the edge of panic in case the weeper should lose control entirely, and also keeps him fascinated for the same reason. "I will do whatever you want, I swear it in the name of God, if you will only tell me what it is." On the last word her voice fell, making the plea into a prayer to her captors, and so the first blasphemy. I caught my breath. Barbara looked young, terrified, pale. How could she look pale when a second ago I had been so conscious of all that garish makeup? There was no chance to wonder. She plunged on, through that scene and the next and all of Joan's scenes. She went from hysterical fear to inept manipulation to the bruised, stupid hatred of a victim to, finally, a kind of negative dignity that comes not from accomplishment but from the clear-eyed vision of the lack of it, and so she died, Cosgriff's vision of the best that institutionalized man could hope for. But she was not Cosgriff's vision; she was a seventeen-year-old girl. Her figure was slight to the point of emaciation. Her face was young—I saw its youth, felt its fragile boniness in the marrow of my own bones. She moved with the gaudy, unpredictable quickness of the mad, now here, now darting a room's length away, now still with a terrible catatonic stillness that excluded her trapped eyes. Her desperation made me catch my breath, try to look away, and fail, feeling that cold grab at my innards: It happened. And it could happen again. It could happen to me.

Her terror gave off a smell, sickly and sour. I wanted to escape the room before that smell could spread to me. I was helpless. Neither she nor I could escape. I did not want to help her, this mad skinny victim. I wanted to destroy her so that what was being done to her would not exist any longer in the world and I would be safe from it. But I could not destroy her. I could only watch, loathing Joan for forcing me to know, until she rose to her brief, sane dignity. In the sight of that dignity, shame that I had ever wanted to smash her washed over me. I was guilty, as guilty as all those others who had wanted to smash her. Her sanity bound me with them, as earlier her terror had unwillingly drawn me to her. I was victim and victimizer, and when Joan stood at the stake and condemned me in a grotesque parody of Christ's forgiving on the cross, I wanted only for her to burn and to be quiet, to release me. I would have lighted the fire. I would have shouted with the crowd, "Burn! Burn!" already despairing that no fire could sear away what she, I, all of us had done. From the flames, Joan looked at me, stretched out her hand, came toward me. I thrust out my arm to ward her off. Almost I cried out. My heart pounded in my chest.

"Austin," she said.

In an instant Joan was gone.

Barbara came toward me. It was Barbara. She had grown three inches, put on twenty pounds and thirty years. Her face was tired and lined under gaudy, peeling makeup. Confusedly I blinked at her. I don't think she even saw the confusion; her eyes had lost their strained panic, and she was smiling, a smile that was a peaceful answer to some question of her own.

"That was the reality," she said, and stooped to lay her head on my chest. Through the fall of her hair I barely heard her when she said that she would marry me whenever I wanted.

• • •

Barbara and I have been married for nearly a year. I still don't know precisely why she decided to marry me, and she can't tell me; she doesn't know herself. But I speculate that the night *A Maid of Domrémy* failed, something broke in her, some illusion that she could control, if not the world, then at least herself. When she struck Whitten with the candlestick, she turned herself into both victim and victimizer as easily as Lawrence Cosgriff had rewritten Shaw's Joan. Barbara has never played the part again. (Gregory Whitten, no less flamboyantly insensitive for his bashing with a candlestick, actually asked her.) She has adamantly refused both Joans, Shaw's heroine and Cosgriff's victim. I was the last person to witness her performance.

Was her performance that night in my hospital room really as good as I remember? I was drugged; emotion had been running high; I loved her. Any or all of that could have colored my reactions. But I don't think so. I think that night Barbara Bishop was Joan, in some effort of will and need that went beyond both the illusions of a good actress and the reality of what ESIR could give to her, or to Ann Friedland, or to anyone. ESIR only unlocks the individual genetic memories in the brain's R-Complex. But what other identities, shared across time and space, might still be closed in there beyond our present reach?

All of this is speculation.

Next week I will be hospitalized for my own ESIR. Knowing what I have been before may yield only more speculation, more illusions, more multiple realities. It may yield nothing. But I want to know, on the chance that the yield will be understandable, will be valuable in untangling the endless skein of waking visions.

Even if the chance is one in a million.

WILLIAM GIBSON AND MICHAEL SWANWICK

DOGFIGHT

(1985)

HE MEANT TO KEEP ON GOING, right down to Florida. Work passage on a gunrunner, maybe wind up conscripted into some rat-ass rebel army down in the war zone. Or maybe, with that ticket good as long as he didn't stop riding, he'd just never get off Greyhound's Flying Dutchman. He grinned at his faint reflection in cold, greasy glass while the downtown lights of Norfolk slid past, the bus swaying on tired shocks as the driver slung it around a final corner. They shuddered to a halt in the terminal lot, concrete lit gray and harsh like a prison exercise yard. But Deke was watching himself starve, maybe in some snowstorm out of Oswego, with his cheek pressed up against that same bus window, and seeing his remains swept out at the next stop by a muttering old man in faded coveralls. One way or the other, he decided, it didn't mean shit to him. Except his legs seemed to have died already. And the driver called a twenty-minute stopover—Tidewater Station, Virginia. It was an old cinder-block building with two entrances to each restroom, holdover from the previous century.

Legs like wood, he made a halfhearted attempt at ghosting the notions counter, but the black girl behind it was alert, guarding the sparse contents of the old glass case as though her ass depended on it. *Probably does,* Deke thought, turning away. Opposite the washrooms, an open doorway offered GAMES, the word flickering feebly in biofluorescent plastic. He could see a crowd of the local kickers clustered around a pool table. Aimless, his boredom following him like a cloud, he stuck his head in. And saw a biplane, wings no longer than his thumb, blossom bright orange flame. Corkscrewing, trailing smoke, it vanished the instant it struck the green-felt field of the table.

"Tha's right, Tiny," a kicker bellowed, "you *take* that sumbitch!"

"Hey," Deke said. "What's going on?" The nearest kicker was a bean pole with a black mesh Peterbilt cap.

"Tiny's defending the Max," he said, not taking his eyes from the table.

"Oh, yeah? What's that?" But even as he asked, he saw it: a blue enamel medal shaped like a Maltese cross, the slogan *Pour le Mérite* divided among its arms.

The Blue Max rested on the edge of the table, directly before a vast and perfectly immobile bulk wedged into a fragile-looking chrome-tube chair. The man's khaki work shirt would have hung on Deke like the folds of a sail, but it bulged across that bloated torso so tautly that the buttons threatened to tear away at any instant. Deke thought of Southern troopers he'd seen on his way down; of that weird, gut-heavy endotype balanced on gangly legs that looked like they'd been borrowed from some other body. Tiny might look like that if he stood, but on a larger scale—a forty-inch jeans inseam that would need a woven-steel waistband to support all those pounds of swollen gut. If Tiny were ever to stand at all—for now Deke saw that that shiny frame was actually a wheelchair. There was something disturbingly childlike about the man's face, an appalling suggestion of youth and even beauty in features almost buried in fold and jowl. Embarrassed, Deke looked away. The other man, the one standing across the table from Tiny, had bushy sideburns and a thin mouth. He seemed to be trying to push something with his eyes, wrinkles of concentration spreading from the corners . . .

"You dumbshit or what?" The man with the Peterbilt cap turned, catching Deke's Indo proleboy denims, the brass chains at his wrists, for the first time. "Why don't you get your ass lost, fucker. Nobody wants your kind in here." He turned back to the dogfight.

Bets were being made, being covered. The kickers were producing the hard stuff, the old stuff, libertyheaded dollars and Roosevelt dimes from the stamp-and-coin stores, while more cautious bettors slapped down antique paper dollars laminated in clear plastic. Through the haze came a trio of red planes, flying in formation. Fokker D.VIIs. The room fell silent. The Fokkers banked majestically under the solar orb of a two-hundred-watt bulb.

The blue Spad dove out of nowhere. Two more plunged from the shadowy ceiling, following closely. The kickers swore, and one chuckled. The formation broke wildly. One Fokker dove almost to the felt, without losing the Spad on its tail. Furiously, it zigged and zagged across the green flatlands but to no avail. At last it pulled up, the enemy hard after it, too steeply and stalled, too low to pull out in time. A stack of silver dimes was scooped up. The Fokkers were outnumbered now. One had two Spads on its tail. A needle-spray of tracers tore past its cockpit. The Fokker slip-turned right, banked into an Immelmann, and was behind one of its pursuers. It fired, and the biplane fell, tumbling.

"Way to go, Tiny!" The kickers closed in around the table.
Deke was frozen with wonder. It felt like being born all over again.

• • •

Frank's Truck Stop was two miles out of town on the Commercial Vehicles Only
route. Deke had tagged it, out of idle habit, from the bus on the way in. Now he
walked back between the traffic and the concrete crash guards. Articulated trucks
went slamming past, big eight-segmented jobs, the wash of air each time threatening to blast him over. CVO stops were easy makes. When he sauntered into
Frank's, there was nobody to doubt that he'd come in off a big rig, and he was
able to browse the gift shop as slowly as he liked. The wire rack with the projective wetware wafers was located between a stack of Korean cowboy shirts and a
display for Fuzz Buster mudguards. A pair of Oriental dragons twisted in the air
over the rack, either fighting or fucking, he couldn't tell which. The game he
wanted was there: a wafer labeled SPADS & FOKKERS. It took him three seconds
to boost it and less time to slide the magnet, which the cops in DC hadn't even
bothered to confiscate, across the universal security strip. On the way out, he
lifted two programming units and a little Batang facilitator remote that looked
like an antique hearing aid.

• • •

He chose a highstack at random and fed the rental agent the line he'd used since
his welfare rights were yanked. Nobody ever checked up; the state just counted
occupied rooms and paid.

The cubicle smelled faintly of urine, and someone had scrawled Hard
Anarchy Liberation Front slogans across the walls. Deke kicked trash out of a
corner, sat down, back to the wall, and ripped open the wafer pack.

There was a folded instruction sheet with diagrams of loops, rolls, and
Immelmanns, a tube of saline paste, and a computer list of operational specs.
And the wafer itself, white plastic with a blue biplane and logo on one side, red
on the other. He turned it over and over in his hand: SPADS & FOKKERS, FOKKERS
& SPADS. Red or blue. He fitted the Batang behind his ear after coating the
inductor surface with paste, jacked its fiber-optic ribbon into the programmer,
and plugged the programmer into the wall current. Then he slid the wafer into
the programmer. It was a cheap set, Indonesian, and the base of his skull buzzed
uncomfortably as the program ran. But when it was done, a sky-blue Spad darted
restlessly through the air a few inches from his face. It almost glowed, it was so
real. It had the strange inner life that fanatically detailed museum-grade models
often have, but it took all of his concentration to keep it in existence. If his attention wavered at all, it lost focus, fuzzing into a pathetic blur.

He practiced until the battery in the earset died, then slumped against the
wall and fell asleep. He dreamed of flying, in a universe that consisted entirely of

white clouds and blue sky, with no up and down, and never a green field to crash into.

. . .

He woke to a rancid smell of frying krillcakes and winced with hunger. No cash, either. Well, there were plenty of student types in the stack. Bound to be one who'd like to score a programming unit. He hit the hall with the boosted spare. Not far down was a door with a poster on it: THERE'S A HELL OF A GOOD UNIVERSE NEXT DOOR. Under that was a starscape with a cluster of multicolored pills, torn from an ad for some pharmaceutical company, pasted over an inspirational shot of the "space colony" that had been under construction since before he was born. LET'S GO, the poster said, beneath the collaged hypnotics.

He knocked. The door opened, security slides stopping it at a two-inch slice of girlface. "Yeah?"

"You're going to think this is stolen." He passed the programmer from hand to hand. "I mean because it's new, virtual cherry, and the bar code's still on it. But listen, I'm not gonna argue the point. No. I'm gonna let you have it for only like half what you'd pay anywhere else."

"Hey, wow, *really*, no kidding?" The visible fraction of mouth twisted into a strange smile. She extended her hand, palm up, a loose fist. Level with his chin. "Lookahere!"

There was a hole in her hand, a black tunnel that ran right up her arm. Two small red lights. Rat's eyes. They scurried toward him growing, gleaming. Something gray streaked forward and leaped for his face. He screamed, throwing hands up to ward it off. Legs twisting, he fell, the programmer shattering under him.

Silicate shards skittered as he thrashed, clutching his head. Where it hurt, it hurt—it hurt very badly indeed.

"Oh, my God!" Slides unsnapped, and the girl was hovering over him. "Here, listen, come on." She dangled a blue hand towel. "Grab on to this and I'll pull you up."

He looked at her through a wash of tears. Student. That fed look, the oversize sweatshirt, teeth so straight and white they could be used as a credit reference. A thin gold chain around one ankle (fuzzed, he saw, with baby-fine hair). Choppy Japanese haircut. Money.

"That sucker was gonna be my dinner," he said ruefully. He took hold of the towel and let her pull him up.

She smiled but skittishly backed away from him. "Let me make it up to you," she said. "You want some food? It was only a projection, okay?"

He followed her in, wary as an animal entering a trap.

. . .

"Holy shit," Deke said, "this is *real cheese* . . ." He was sitting on a gutsprung sofa, wedged between a four-foot teddy bear and a loose stack of floppies. The room was ankle-deep in books and clothes and papers. But the food she mag-icked up—Gouda cheese and tinned beef and honest-to-God greenhouse wheat wafers—was straight out of the Arabian Nights.

"Hey," she said. "We know how to treat a proleboy right, huh?" Her name was Nance Bettendorf. She was seventeen. Both her parents had jobs—greedy buggers—and she was an engineering major at William and Mary. She got top marks except in English. "I guess you must really have a thing about rats. You got some kind of phobia about rats?"

He glanced sidelong at her bed. You couldn't see it, really; it was just a swell in the ground cover. "It's not like that. It just reminded me of something else, is all."

"Like what?" She squatted in front of him, the big shirt riding high up one smooth thigh.

"Well . . . did you ever see the"—his voice involuntarily rose and rushed past the words—"*Washington Monument?* Like at night? It's got these two little red lights on top, aviation markers or something, and I, and I . . ." He started to shake.

"You're afraid of the Washington Monument?" Nance whooped and rolled over with laughter, long tanned legs kicking. She was wearing crimson bikini panties.

"I would die rather than look at it again," he said levelly.

She stopped laughing then, sat up, studied his face. White, even teeth wor-ried at her lower lip, like she was dragging up something she didn't want to think about. At last she ventured, "Brainlock?"

"Yeah," he said bitterly. "They told me I'd never go back to DC. And then the fuckers laughed."

"What did they get you for?"

"I'm a thief." He wasn't about to tell her that the actual charge was career shoplifting.

•   •   •

"Lotta old computer hacks spent their lives programming machines. And you know what? The human brain is not a goddamn bit like a machine, no way. They just don't program the same." Deke knew this shrill, desperate rap, this long, circular jive that the lonely string out to the rare listener; knew it from a hundred cold and empty nights spent in the company of strangers. Nance was lost in it, and Deke, nodding and yawning, wondered if he'd even be able to stay awake when they finally hit that bed of hers.

"I built that projection I hit you with myself," she said, hugging her knees up beneath her chin. "It's for muggers, you know? I just happened to have it on me, and I threw it at you 'cause I thought it was so funny, you trying to sell me that shit little Indojavanese programmer." She hunched forward and held out her hand again. "Look here." Deke cringed. "No, no, it's okay, I swear it, this is dif-ferent." She opened her hand.

A single blue flame danced there, perfect and everchanging. "Look at that," she marveled. "Just look. I programmed that. It's not some diddly little seven-image job either. It's a continuous two-hour loop, seven thousand, two hundred seconds, never the same twice, each instant as individual as a fucking snowflake!"

The flame's core was glacial crystal, shards and facets flashing up, twisting, and gone, leaving behind near-subliminal images so bright and sharp that they cut the eye. Deke winced. People mostly. Pretty little naked people, fucking. "How the hell did you do that?"

She rose, bare feet slipping on slick magazines, and melodramatically swept folds of loose printout from a raw plywood shelf. He saw a neat row of small consoles, austere and expensive looking. Custom work. "This is the real stuff I got here. Image facilitator. Here's my fast-wipe module. This is a brain-map one-to-one function analyzer." She sang off the names like a litany. "Quantum flicker stabilizer. Program splicer. An image assembler . . ."

"You need all that to make one little flame?"

"You betcha. This is all state of the art, professional projective wetware gear. It's years ahead of anything you've seen."

"Hey," he said, "you know anything about SPADS & FOKKERS?"

She laughed. And then, because he sensed the time was right, he reached out to take her hand.

"Don't you touch me, motherfuck, don't you *ever touch me*!" Nance screamed, and her head slammed against the wall as she recoiled, white and shaking with terror.

"Okay!" He threw up his hands. "Okay! I'm nowhere near you. Okay?"

She cowered from him. Her eyes were round and unblinking; tears built up at the corners, rolled down ashen cheeks. Finally, she shook her head. "Hey. Deke. Sorry. I should've told you."

"Told me what?" But he had a creepy feeling that already knew. The way she clutched her head. The weakly spasmodic way her hands opened and closed. "You got a brainlock, too."

"Yeah." She closed her eyes. "It's a chastity lock. My asshole parents paid for it. So I can't stand to have anybody touch me or even stand too close." Eyes opened in blind hate. "I didn't even *do* anything. Not a fucking thing. But they've both got jobs and they're so horny for me to have a career that they can't piss straight. They're afraid I'd neglect my studies if I got, you know, involved in sex and stuff. The day the brainlock comes off I am going to fuck the vilest, greasiest, hairiest . . ."

She was clutching her head again. Deke jumped up and rummaged through the medicine cabinet. He found a jar of B-complex vitamins, pocketed a few against need, and brought two to Nance, with a glass of water. "Here." He was careful to keep his distance. "This'll take the edge off."

"Yeah, yeah," she said. Then, almost to herself, "You must really think I'm a jerk."

• • •

The games room in the Greyhound station was almost empty. A lone, long-jawed fourteen-year- old was bent over a console, maneuvering rainbow fleets of submarines in the murky grid of the North Atlantic. Deke sauntered in, wearing his new kicker drag, and leaned against a cinder-block wall made smooth by countless coats of green enamel. He'd washed the dye from his proleboy butch, boosted jeans and T-shirt from the Goodwill, and found a pair of stompers in the sauna locker of a highstack with cut-rate security.

"Seen Tiny around, friend?" The subs darted like neon guppies.

"Depends on who's asking." Deke touched the remote behind his left ear. The Spad snap-rolled over the console, swift and delicate as a dragonfly. It was beautiful; so perfect, so *true* it made the room seem an illusion. He buzzed the grid, millimeters from the glass, taking advantage of the programmed ground effect.

The kid didn't even bother to look up. "Jackman's," he said. "Down Richmond Road, over by the surplus."

Deke let the Spad fade in midclimb.

Jackman's took up most of the third floor of an old brick building. Deke found Best Buy War Surplus first, then a broken neon sign over an unlit lobby. The sidewalk out front was littered with another kind of surplus: damaged vets, some of them dating back to Indochina. Old men who'd left their eyes under Asian suns squatted beside twitching boys who'd inhaled mycotoxins in Chile. Deke was glad to have the battered elevator doors sigh shut behind him.

A dusty Dr Pepper clock at the far side of the long, spectral room told him it was a quarter to eight. Jackman's had been embalmed twenty years before he was born, sealed away behind a yellowish film of nicotine, of polish and hair oil. Directly beneath the clock, the flat eyes of somebody's grandpappy's prize buck regarded Deke from a framed, blown-up snapshot gone the slick sepia of cockroach wings. There was the click and whisper of pool, the squeak of a work boot twisting on linoleum as a player leaned in for a shot. Somewhere high above the green-shaded lamps hung a string of crepe-paper Christmas bells faded to dead rose. Deke looked from one cluttered wall to the next. No facilitator.

"Bring one in, should we need it," someone said. He turned, meeting the mild eyes of a bald man with steel-rimmed glasses. "My name's Cline. Bobby Earl. You don't look like you shoot pool, mister." But there was nothing threatening in Bobby Earl's voice or stance. He pinched the steel frames from his nose and polished the thick lenses with a fold of tissue. He reminded Deke of a shop instructor who'd patiently tried to teach him retrograde biochip installation. "I'm a gambler," he said, smiling. His teeth were white plastic. "I know I don't much look it."

"I'm looking for Tiny," Deke said.

"Well," replacing the glasses, "you're not going to find him. He's gone up to Bethesda to let the VA clean his plumbing for him. He wouldn't fly against you anyhow."

"Why not?"

"Well, because you're not on the circuit or I'd know your face. You any good?"

343

When Deke nodded, Bobby Earl called down the length of Jackman's, "Yo, Clarence! You bring out that facilitator. We got us a flyboy."

Twenty minutes later, having lost his remote and what cash he had left, Deke was striding past the broken soldiers of Best Buy.

"Now you let me tell you, boy," Bobby Earl had said in a fatherly tone as, hand on shoulder, he led Deke back to the elevator, "You're not going to win against a combat vet—you listening to me? I'm not even especially good, just an old grunt who was on hype fifteen, maybe twenty times. Ol' Tiny, he was a *pilot*. Spent entire enlistment hyped to the gills. He's got membrane attenuation real bad . . . you ain't never going to beat him."

It was a cool night. But Deke burned with anger and humiliation.

$$\bullet \quad \bullet \quad \bullet$$

"Jesus, that's crude," Nance said as the Spad strafed mounds of pink underwear. Deke, hunched up on the couch, yanked her flashy little Braun remote from behind his ear.

"Now don't you get on my case too, Miss rich-bitch gonna-have-a-job—"

"Hey, lighten up! It's nothing to do with you—it's just *tech*. That's a really primitive wafer you got there. I mean, on the street maybe it's fine. But compared to the work I do at school, it's—hey. You ought to let me rewrite it for you."

"Say what?"

"Lemme beef it up. These suckers are all written in hexadecimal, see, 'cause the industry programmers are all washed-out computer hacks. That's how they think. But let me take it to the reader-analyzer at the department, run a few changes on it, translate it into a modern wetlanguage. Edit out all the redundant intermediaries. That'll goose up your reaction time, cut the feedback loop in half. So you'll fly faster and better. Turn you into a real pro, Ace!" She took a hit off her bong, then doubled over laughing and choking.

"Is that legit?" Deke asked dubiously.

"Hey, why do you think people buy gold-wire remotes? For the prestige? Shit. Conductivity's better, cuts a few nanoseconds off the reaction time. And reaction time is the name of the game, kiddo."

"No," Deke said. "If it were that easy, people'd already have it. Tiny Montgomery would have it. He'd have the best."

"Don't you ever *listen*?" Nance set down the bong; brown water slopped onto the floor. "The stuff I'm working with is three years ahead of anything you'll find on the street."

"No shit," Deke said after a long pause. "I mean, you can do that?"

$$\bullet \quad \bullet \quad \bullet$$

It was like graduating from a Model T to a ninety-three Lotus. The Spad handled like a dream, responsive to Deke's slightest thought. For weeks he played the arcades, with not a nibble. He flew against the local teens and by ones and threes shot down their planes. He took chances, played flash. And the planes tumbled . . .

Until one day Deke was tucking his seed money away, and a lanky black straightened up from the wall. He eyed the laminateds in Deke's hand and grinned. A ruby tooth gleamed. "You know," the man said, "I *heard* there was a casper who could fly, going up against the kiddies."

• • •

"Jesus," Deke said, spreading Danish butter on a kelp stick. "I wiped the *floor* with those spades. They were good, too."

"That's nice, honey," Nance mumbled. She was working on her finals project, sweating data into a machine.

"You know, I think what's happening is I got real talent for this kind of shit. You know? I mean, the program gives me an edge, but I got the stuff to take advantage of it. I'm really getting a rep out there, you know?" Impulsively, he snapped on the radio. Scratchy Dixieland brass blared.

"Hey," Nance said. "Do you *mind?*"

"No, I'm just—" He fiddled with the knobs, came up with some slow, romantic bullshit. "There. Come on, stand up. Let's dance."

"Hey, you know I can't—"

"Sure you can, sugarcakes." He threw her the huge teddy bear and snatched up a patchwork cotton dress from the floor. He held it by the waist and sleeve, tucking the collar under his chin. It smelled of patchouli, more faintly of sweat. "See, I stand over here, you stand over there. We dance. Get it?"

Blinking softly, Nance stood and clutched the bear tightly. They danced then, slowly, staring into each other's eyes. After a while, she began to cry. But still, she was smiling.

• • •

Deke was daydreaming, imagining he was Tiny Montgomery wired into his jumpjet. Imagined the machine responding to his slightest neural twitch, reflexes cranked *way* up, hype flowing steadily into his veins.

Nance's floor became jungle, her bed a plateau in the Andean foothills, and Deke flew his Spad at forced speed, as if it were a full-wired interactive combat machine. Computerized hypos fed a slow trickle of high-performance enhancement mélange into his bloodstream. Sensors were wired directly into his skull pulling a supersonic snapturn in the green-blue bowl of sky over Bolivian rain forest. Tiny would have *felt* the airflow over control surfaces.

Below, grunts hacked through the jungle with hype-pumps strapped above elbows to give them that little extra death-dance fury in combat, a shot of liquid hell in a blue plastic vial. Maybe they got ten minutes' worth in a week. But coming in at treetop level, reflexes cranked to the max, flying so low the ground

345

troops never spotted you until you were on them, phosgene agents released, away and gone before they could draw a bead . . . it took a constant trickle of hype just to maintain. And the direct neuron interface with the jumpjet was a two-way street. The onboard computers monitored biochemistry and decided when to open the sluice gates and give the human component a killer jolt of combat edge.

Dosages like that ate you up. Ate you good and slow and constant, etching the brain surfaces, eroding away the brain-cell membranes. If you weren't yanked from the air promptly enough, you ended up with brain-cell attenuation with reflexes too fast for your body to handle and your fight-or-flight reflexes fucked real good . . .

"I aced it, proleboy!"

"Hah?" Deke looked up, startled, as Nance slammed in, tossing books and bag onto the nearest heap.

"My finals project—I got exempted from exams. The prof said he'd never seen anything like it. Uh, hey, dim the lights, wouldja? The colors are weird on my eyes."

He obliged. "So show me. Show me this wunnerful thing."

"Yeah, okay." She snatched up his remote, kicked clear standing space atop the bed, and struck a pose. A spark flared into flame in her hand. It spread in a quicksilver line up her arm, around her neck, and it was a snake, with triangular head and flickering tongue. Molten colors, oranges and reds. It slithered between her breasts. "I call it a firesnake," she said proudly.

Deke leaned close, and she jerked back. "Sorry. It's like your flame, huh? I mean, I can see these tiny little fuckers in it."

"Sort of." The firesnake flowed down her stomach. "Next month I'm going to splice two hundred separate flame programs together with meld justification in between to get the visuals. Then I'll tap the mind's body image to make it self-orienting. So it can crawl all over your body without your having to mind it. You could wear it dancing."

"Maybe I'm dumb. But if you haven't done the work yet, how come I can see it?"

Nance giggled. "That's the best part—half the work isn't done yet. Didn't have the time to assemble the pieces into a unified program. Turn on that radio, huh? I want to dance." She kicked off her shoes. Deke tuned in something gutsy. Then, at Nance's urging, turned it down, almost to a whisper.

"I scored two hits of hype, see." She was bouncing on the bed, weaving her hands like a Balinese dancer. "Ever try the stuff? In-credible. Gives you like absolute concentration. Look here." She stood *en pointe*. "Never done that before."

"Hype," Deke said. "Last person I heard of got caught with that shit got three years in the infantry. How'd you score it?"

"Cut a deal with a vet who was in grad school. She bombed out last month. Stuff gives me perfect visualization. I can hold the projection with my eyes shut. It was a snap assembling the program in my head."

"On just two hits, huh?"

"One hit. I'm saving the other. Teach was so impressed he's sponsoring me for a job interview. A recruiter from I. G. Feuchtwaren hits campus in two weeks. That cap is gonna sell him the program *and* me. I'm gonna cut out of school two years early, straight into industry, do not pass jail, do not pay two hundred dollars."

The snake curled into a flaming tiara. It gave Deke a funny-creepy feeling to think of. Nance walking out of his life.

"I'm a witch," Nance sang, "a wetware witch." She shucked her shirt over her head and sent it flying. Her fine, high breasts moved freely, gracefully, as she danced. "I'm gonna make it"—now she was singing a current pop hit—"to the . . . top!" Her nipples were small and pink and aroused. The firesnake licked at them and whipped away.

"Hey, Nance," Deke said uncomfortably. "Calm down a little, huh?"

"I'm celebrating!" She hooked a thumb into her shiny gold panties. Fire swirled around hand and crotch. "I'm the virgin goddess, baby, and I have the pow-er!" Singing again.

Deke looked away. "Gotta go now," he mumbled. Gotta go home and jerk off. He wondered where she'd hidden that second hit. Could be anywhere.

•   •   •

There was a protocol to the circuit, a tacit order of deference and precedence as elaborate as that of a Mandarin court. It didn't matter that Deke was hot, that his rep was spreading like wildfire. Even a name flyboy couldn't just challenge whom he wished. He had to climb the ranks. But if you flew every night. If you were always available to anybody's challenge. And if you were good . . . well, it was possible to climb fast.

Deke was one plane up. It was tournament fighting, three planes against three. Not many spectators, a dozen maybe, but it was a good fight, and they were noisy. Deke was immersed in the manic calm of combat when he realized suddenly that they had fallen silent. Saw the kickers stir and exchange glances. Eyes flicked past him. He heard the elevator doors close. Coolly, he disposed of the second of his opponent's planes, then risked a quick glance over his shoulder.

Tiny Montgomery had just entered Jackman's. The wheelchair whispered across browning linoleum, guided by tiny twitches of one imperfectly paralyzed hand. His expression was stern, blank, calm.

In that instant, Deke lost two planes. One to deresolution gone to blur and canceled out by the facilitator and the other because his opponent was a real fighter. Guy did a barrel roll, killing speed and slipping to the side, and strafed Deke's biplane as it shot past. It went down in flames. Their last two planes shared altitude and speed, and as they turned, trying for position, they naturally fell into a circling pattern.

The kickers made room as Tiny wheeled up against the table. Bobby Earl Cline trailed after him, lanky and casual. Deke and his opponent traded glances and pulled their machines back from the pool table so they could hear the man out. Tiny smiled. His features were small, clustered in the center of his pale, doughy face. One finger twitched slightly on the chrome handrest. "I heard about you." He looked straight at Deke. His voice was soft and shockingly sweet, a baby-girl little voice. "I heard you're good."

Deke nodded slowly. The smile left Tiny's face. His soft, fleshy lips relaxed into a natural pout, as if he were waiting for a kiss. His small, bright eyes studied Deke without malice. "Let's see what you can do, then."

Deke lost himself in the cool game of war. And when the enemy went down in smoke and flame, to explode and vanish against the table, Tiny wordlessly turned his chair, wheeled it into the elevator, and was gone.

As Deke was gathering up his winnings, Bobby Earl eased up to him and said, "The man wants to play you.

"Yeah?" Deke was nowhere near high enough on the circuit to challenge Tiny. "What's the scam?"

"Man who was coming up from Atlanta tomorrow canceled. Ol' Tiny, he was spoiling to go up against somebody new. So it looks like you get your shot at the Max."

"Tomorrow? Wednesday? Doesn't give me much prep time."

Bobby Earl smiled gently. "I don't think that makes no nevermind."

"How's that, Mr. Cline?"

"Boy, you just ain't got the *moves*, you follow me? Ain't got no surprises. You fly just like some kinda beginner, only faster and slicker. You follow what I'm trying to say?"

"I'm not sure I do. You want to put a little action on that?"

"Tell you truthful," Cline said, "I been hoping on that." He drew a small black notebook from his pocket and licked a pencil stub. "Give you five to one. They's nobody gonna give no fairer odds than that."

He looked at Deke almost sadly. "But Tiny, he's just naturally better'n you, and that's all she wrote, boy. He lives for that goddamned game, ain't *got* nothing else. Can't get out of that goddamned chair. You think you can best a man who's fighting for his life, you are just lying to yourself."

• • •

Norman Rockwell's portrait of the colonel regarded Deke dispassionately from the Kentucky Fried across Richmond Road from the coffee bar. Deke held his cup with hands that were cold and trembling. His skull hummed with fatigue. Cline was right, he told the colonel. I can go up against Tiny, but I can't win. The colonel stared back, gaze calm and level and not particularly kindly, taking in the coffee bar and Best Buy and all his drag-ass kingdom of Richmond Road. Waiting for Deke to admit to the terrible thing he had to do.

"The bitch is planning to leave me *anyway*," Deke said aloud. Which made the black countergirl look at him funny, then quickly away.

• • •

"Daddy called!" Nance danced into the apartment, slamming the door behind her. "And you know what? He says if I can get this job and hold it for six months, he'll have the brainlock reversed. Can you *believe* it? Deke?" She hesitated. "You okay?"

Deke stood. Now that the moment was on him, he felt unreal, like he was in a movie or something. "How come you never came home last night?" Nance asked.

The skin on his face was unnaturally taut, a parchment mask. "Where'd you stash the hype, Nance? I need it."

"Deke," she said, trying a tentative smile that instantly vanished. "Deke, that's mine. My hit. I need it. For my interview."

He smiled scornfully. "You got money. You can always score another cap."

"Not by Friday! Listen, Deke, this is really important. My whole life is riding on this interview. I need that cap. It's all I got!"

"Baby, you got the fucking world! Take a look around you—six ounces of blond Lebanese hash! Little anchovy fish in tins. Unlimited medical coverage, if you need it." She was backing away from him, stumbling against the static waves of unwashed bedding and wrinkled glossy magazines that crested at the foot of her bed. "Me, I never had a glimmer of any of this. Never had the kind of edge it takes to get along. Well, this one time I am gonna. There is a match in two hours that I am going to fucking well win. Do you hear me?" He was working himself into a rage, and that was good. He needed it for what he had to do.

Nance flung up an arm, palm open, but he was ready for that and slapped her hand aside, never even catching a glimpse of the dark tunnel, let alone those little red eyes. Then they were both falling, and he was on top of her, her breath hot and rapid in his face. "Deke! Deke! I need that shit, Deke, my *interview*, it's the only . . . I gotta . . . gotta . . ." She twisted her face away, crying into the wall. "Please, God, please don't . . ."

"Where did you stash it?" Pinned against the bed under his body, Nance began to spasm, her entire body convulsing in pain and fear.

"Where is it?" Her face was bloodless, gray corpse flesh, and horror burned in her eyes. Her lips squirmed. It was too late to stop now; he'd crossed over the line. Deke felt revolted and nauseated, all the more so because on some unexpected and unwelcome level, he was *enjoying* this.

"Where is it, Nance?" And slowly, very gently, he began to stroke her face.

• • •

Deke summoned Jackman's elevator with a finger that moved as fast and straight as a hornet and landed daintily as a butterfly on the call button. He was full of bouncy energy, and it was all under control. On the way up, he whipped off his shades and chuckled at his reflection in the finger-smudged chrome. The blacks of his eyes were like pinpricks, all but invisible, and still the world was neon bright.

Tiny was waiting. His mouth turned up at the corners into a sweet smile as he took in Deke's irises, the exaggerated calm of his motions, the unsuccessful attempt to mime an undrugged clumsiness. "Well," he said in that girlish voice, "looks like I have a treat in store for me."

The Max was draped over one tube of the wheelchair. Deke took up position and bowed, not quite mockingly. "Let's fly." As challenger, he flew defense. He materialized his planes at a conservative altitude, high enough to dive, low enough to have warning when Tiny attacked. He waited.

The crowd tipped him. A fatboy with brilliantined hair looked startled, a hollow-eyed cracker started to smile. Murmurs rose. Eyes shifted slow-motion in heads frozen by hyped-up reaction time. Took maybe three nanoseconds to pinpoint the source of attack. Deke whipped his head up, and—

Sonofabitch, he was *blind*! The Fokkers were diving straight from the two-hundred-watt bulb, and Tiny had suckered him into staring right at it. His vision whited out. Deke squeezed lids tight over welling tears and frantically held visualization. He split his flight, curving two biplanes right, one left. Immediately twisting each a half-turn, then back again. He had to dodge randomly—he couldn't tell where the hostile warbirds were.

Tiny chuckled. Deke could hear him through the sounds of the crowd, the cheering and cursing and slapping down of coins that seemed to syncopate independent of the ebb and flow of the duel.

When his vision returned an instant later, a Spad was in flames and falling. Fokkers tailed his surviving planes, one on one and two on the other. Three seconds into the game and he was down one.

Dodging to keep Tiny from pinning tracers on him, he looped the single-pursued plane about and drove the other toward the blind spot between Tiny and the light bulb.

Tiny's expression went very calm. The faintest shadow of disappointment—of contempt, even—was swallowed up by tranquility. He tracked the planes blandly, waiting for Deke to make his turn.

Then, just short of the blind spot, Deke shoved his Spad into a drive, the Fokkers overshooting and banking wildly to either side, twisting around to regain position.

The Spad swooped down on the third Fokker, pulled into position by Deke's other plane. Fire strafed wings and crimson fuselage. For an instant nothing happened, and Deke thought he had a fluke miss. Then the little red mother veered left and went down, trailing black, oily smoke.

Tiny frowned, small lines of displeasure marring the perfection of his mouth. Deke smiled. One even, and Tiny held position.

Both Spads were tailed closely. Deke swung them wide, and then pulled them together from opposite sides of the table. He drove them straight for each other, neutralizing Tiny's advantage . . . neither could fire without endangering his own planes. Deke cranked his machines up to top speed, slamming them at each other's nose.

An instant before they crashed, Deke sent the planes over and under one another, opening fire on the Fokkers and twisting away. Tiny was ready. Fire filled the air. Then one blue and one red plane soared free, heading in opposite directions. Behind them, two biplanes tangled in midair. Wings touched, slewed about, and the planes crumpled. They fell together, almost straight down, to the green felt below.

Ten seconds in and four planes down. A black vet pursed his lips and blew softly. Someone else shook his head in disbelief.

Tiny was sitting straight and a little forward in his wheelchair, eyes intense and unblinking, soft hands plucking feebly at the grips. None of that amused and detached bullshit now; his attention was riveted on the game. The kickers, the table, Jackman's itself, might not exist at all for him. Bobby Earl Cline laid a hand on his shoulder; Tiny didn't notice. The planes were at opposite ends of the room, laboriously gaining altitude. Deke jammed his against the ceiling, dim through the smoky haze. He spared Tiny a quick glance, and their eyes locked. Cold against cold. "Let's see your best," Deke muttered through clenched teeth.

They drove their planes together.

The hype was peaking now, and Deke could see Tiny's tracers crawling through the air between the planes. He had to put his Spad into the line of fire to get off a fair burst, then twist and bank so the Fokker's bullets would slip by his undercarriage. Tiny was every bit as hot, dodging Deke's fire and passing so close to the Spad their landing gears almost tangled as they passed.

Deke was looping his Spad in a punishingly tight turn when the hallucinations hit. The felt writhed and twisted, became the green hell of Bolivian rain forest that Tiny had flown combat over. The walls receded to gray infinity, and he felt the metal confinement of a cybernetic jumpjet close in around him.

But Deke had done his homework. He was expecting the hallucinations and knew he could deal with them. The military would never pass on a drug that couldn't be fought through. Spad and Fokker looped into another pass. He could read the tensions in Tiny Montgomery's face, the echoes of combat in deep jungle sky. They drove their planes together, feeling the torqued tensions that fed straight from instrumentation to hindbrain, the adrenaline pumps kicking in behind the armpits, the cold, fast freedom of airflow over jetskin mingling with the smells of hot metal and fear sweat. Tracers tore past his face, and he pulled back, seeing the Spad zoom by the Fokker again, both untouched. The kickers were just going ape, waving hats and stomping feet, acting like God's own fools. Deke locked glances with Tiny again.

Malice rose up in him, and though his every nerve was taut as the carboncrystal whiskers that kept the jumpjets from falling apart in superman turns over the Andes, he counterfeited a casual smile and winked, jerking his head slightly to one side, as if to say "Looka here."

Tiny glanced to the side.

It was only for a fraction of a second, but that was enough. Deke pulled as fast and tight an Immelmann—right on the edge of theoretical tolerance—as had ever been seen on the circuit, and he was hanging on Tiny's tail.

Let's see you get out of this one, sucker.

Tiny rammed his plane straight down at the green, and Deke followed after. He held his fire. He had Tiny where he wanted him.

Running. Just like he'd been on his every combat mission. High on exhilaration and hype, maybe, but running scared. They were down to the felt now, flying treetop-level. Break, Deke thought, and jacked up the speed. Peripherally, he could see Bobby Earl Cline, and there was a funny look on the man's face. A pleading kind of look. Tiny's composure was shot; his face was twisted and tormented.

Now Tiny panicked and dove his plane in among the crowd. The biplanes looped and twisted between the kickers. Some jerked back involuntarily, and others laughingly swatted at them with their hands. But there was a hot glint of terror in Tiny's eyes that spoke of an eternity of fear and confinement, two edges sawing away at each other endlessly . . .

The fear was death in the air, the confinement a locking away in metal, first of the aircraft, then of the chair. Deke could read it all in his face: Combat was the only out Tiny had had, and he'd taken it every chance he got. Until some anonymous *nationalista* with an antique SAM tore him out of that blue-green Bolivian sky and slammed him straight down to Richmond Road and Jackman's and the smiling killer boy he faced this one last time across the faded cloth.

Deke rocked up on his toes, face burning with that million-dollar smile that was the trademark of the drug that had already fried Tiny before anyone ever bothered to blow him out of the sky in a hot tangle of metal and mangled flesh. It all came together then. He saw that flying was all that held Tiny together. That daily brush of fingertips against death, and then rising up from the metal coffin, alive again. He'd been holding back collapse by sheer force of will. Break that willpower, and mortality would come pouring out and drown him. Tiny would lean over and throw up in his own lap.

• • •

And Deke drove it home . . .

There was a moment of stunned silence as Tiny's last plane vanished in a flash of light. "I did it," Deke whispered. Then, louder, "Son of a bitch, I did it!"

Across the table from him, Tiny twisted in his chair, arms jerking spastically; his head lolled over on one shoulder. Behind him, Bobby Earl Cline stared straight at Deke, his eyes hot coals.

The gambler snatched up the Max and wrapped its ribbon around a stack of laminateds. Without warning, he flung the bundle at Deke's face. Effortlessly, casually, Deke plucked it from the air.

For an instant, then, it looked like the gambler would come at him, right across the pool table. He was stopped by a tug on his sleeve. "Bobby Earl," Tiny whispered, his voice choking with humiliation, "you gotta get me . . . out of here . . ."

Stiffly, angrily, Cline wheeled his friend around, and then away, into shadow.

Deke threw back his head and laughed. By God, he felt good! He stuffed the Max into a shirt pocket, where it hung cold and heavy. The money he crammed into his jeans. Man, he had to jump with it, his triumph leaping up through him like a wild thing, fine and strong as the flanks of a buck in the deep woods he'd seen from a Greyhound once, and for this one moment it seemed that everything was worth it somehow, all the pain and misery he'd gone through to finally win.

But Jackman's was silent. Nobody cheered. Nobody crowded around to congratulate him. He sobered, and silent, hostile faces swam into focus. Not one of these kickers was on his side. They radiated contempt, even hatred. For an interminably drawn-out moment the air trembled with potential violence . . . and then someone turned to the side, hawked up phlegm, and spat on the floor. The crowd broke up, muttering, one by one drifting into the darkness.

Deke didn't move. A muscle in one leg began to twitch, harbinger of the coming hype crash. The top of his head felt numb, and there was an awful taste in his mouth. For a second he had to hang on to the table with both hands to keep from falling down forever, into the living shadow beneath him, as he hung impaled by the prize buck's dead eyes in the photo under the Dr Pepper clock.

A little adrenaline would pull him out of this. He needed to celebrate. To get drunk or stoned and talk it up, going over the victory time and again, contradicting himself, making up details, laughing and bragging. A starry old night like this called for big talk.

But standing there with all of Jackman's silent and vast and empty around him, he realized suddenly that he had nobody left to tell it to.

Nobody at all.

RUSSELL BLACKFORD

GLASS REPTILE BREAKOUT

(1985)

SKINNY SHARKS cruise the downtown miracle bars on Saturday night.

Bianca doesn't give a damn.

Holy forces take Bianca, there in the Searoom. They energize her dancing. Holy forces. Holy. Never perilous.

The main band plays, the miracle band—Glass Reptile Breakout plays—and the big high room in St Kilda's labyrinthine Season Hotel is all noise and smoke, clothing white or the colors of the sea, tight and supple or free and loose, and upon the half-naked young people the stigmata of fashion: shaven heads, plumed or finned with implants, bare arms bright with feathers or glistening scales, dorsal sails, fins or spines that flatten or bristle depending on what is worn over them—though the drastic implants of a flickdancer won't settle under any clothing.

Bianca's heart is set: she yearns to be a flickdancer. She can dance so slowly or so very fast. Free and wild in her roe skirt, glittermesh strips catching light at waist, wrists, ankles. (She practices for hours in her darkened kiddy flat behind her parents' split-level house in Mount Waverley, practices until she has it. The Control.)

Her hair has gone for plumes. Father paid, grudgingly, for the fin sewn into her sleek olive back, knowing someone else would: there are always men willing to pay the roe at the Searoom, pay with favors.

Bending her arm at an awkward angle, she feels along her backbone, the translucent orange fin's graft line. Sutured lines of flesh edging the cultured implant are still swollen and sore. Bianca hates bumping people because it jars and hurts.

But, dancing, she scarcely notices. And she's had one miracle from the Bio-feeders. Music miracle. One time she went out much too soon after a line of unfashionable scales was removed from her ankle. Came back *whole*. She's never heard *thoughts*—that's crap . . . someone made it up, that's all. But she's said the strangest things to people, or them to her. And it's made sense in the end.

She believes in the miracles; trustingly, she awaits one.

• • •

Lachlan Alderson, Senior Church Counsel, Victoria, blinks. He dabs with a small chamois cloth at wire-rimmed glasses. The Searoom's smoke leaves him bleary and owlish. There's still a question for him, one so jagged and ramified it can't be hustled into plain words, much less the urbane diction of a courtroom or the bland assurances of a government report. To his pain, it's the question of Satan.

The secular attitude is no option to Alderson.

It's different for Dr. Loerne. To her the rock miracles are a simple matter of enhanced trypsin activity. She sees them through the reductive lenses of science, filtershades them into the queer by-product of participation mystique focused by expectations brought on by the first miracles. Those, in turn, were merely the result of an unforeseen resonance between EEG-coupled musicians, the enhanced field effects of their nonvocal music, and an audience of half-hypnotized young dancers.

True, perhaps, but not the whole truth. Alderson cannot disregard the spiritual dimension. He's a rational man, yes, a sophisticated one. And ordained into the priesthood of his Church. *The Great Tribulation is at hand:* rhetorical crap from the fundamentalist cults. Alderson doesn't think like that. He thinks like a corporate lawyer. *The man of sin working Satan's deeds with all powers and signs and lying wonders.* All just nonsense, absolute nonsense.

Almighty God!

On a smoke-filled stage, four spindly musicians prance like the demons of a medieval morality play. Big body-scales decorate their lean arms. Smoke drifts across the parquet dance floor. Does it stink of brimstone? Headgear flashes like goats' horns catching coal-glare.

Gabby Loerne is fond of explaining that the miracles have precisely the same cause as the healings at the Ganges, Lourdes, at charismatic revivals. But, for Alderson, the difference in ambience could not be more sinister.

A teenage girl screams. Pretty little thing. Confusion of plump naked flesh, bizarrely modified in the manner of these sharks and roe. Her finned back, her head of pink ostrich-plume implants, shake in the soup of noise and the yellow smoke eddying under dull lights. Alderson stolidly fires up a non-cancer filter and averts eyes from the girl's brown, elated face. Little nose, round Asian cheekbones. Chinese ancestry there, or something similar. And a touch of the south European. Pretty features somehow distorted by the Devil's work.

My God! Alderson is not a fool. He's not a cultist. But he is coming to accept the reality of evil. He knows that its meaning is problematic. A violation of natural good in the eyes of one is a rich difference of culture to another. The Church knows that, too. But is this an adequate response?

Suspended from the high ceiling on the far side of the room, a flickdancer cavorts with his knife. The young girl screams again, falling to bare knees, legs apart. Supplication?

The music plays. The flickdancer slices his own flesh from shoulder to bend of elbow, but doesn't bleed.

This is nothing. Some of the rock miracles are so physically and morally ugly, such grotesque, savage parodies of divine healing, that they oblige Alderson and his ancient church to reassess their tolerance.

Alderson's visits to these venues fail to help him understand how these people think.

He watches the girl, knows that there's prurience in his gaze. Hates it. Her breasts *wobble*. A high-slit garment, more a long white lap-lap than a skirt, falls across her deeply brown thighs. *Return to tribalism.* She wears little else. Jewelry. Her implants.

The music ends. Human sounds roar on.

Alderson leans against a plaster wall. Unobtrusive as possible. Dr. Gabby Loerne perches beside him, handsome on a broad windowsill. Her neat slim ankles cross above the floor. She claps enthusiastically and loudly. No young roe, she is dressed in a more sedate version of current fashion: green glittermesh tights and blouse. A small cluster of green scales jewels her cheek.

In front of them, the girl's torso flails from side to side. She's still on her knees, leaning back now on her heels, body the shouting tongue of a kinetic language. Disports herself in a choreography of prayer before some voyeuristic deity. Again she screams her delight, an invitation to that deity to join her in accord.

Lachlan Alderson leans closer to Gabby to make himself heard above the applause. "None of this disturbs you?"

* * *

Luis Baker can pass muster at the Searoom. But he's twenty-eight; most of the dancers are half his age. He sidles rangily among them in protective coloration. Cold-eyed, lean, to all appearances an aging *mestizo* tourist sharking after little Aussie roe. His dark long-jawed face is embellished with glittering ice-blue scales, each the size of a fingernail. He carries no firearm tonight beneath his loose jerkin of silvery glittermesh. He misses its comforting weight. But he won't need it tonight.

Baker keeps watch on a couple across the thick-aired room, avoids the attention. They're older than him, late thirties, though the woman does not look her age. But they're highfliers, just like him.

The room is almost opaque with smoke from the stage and from the filters that these people devour. Faces come and go behind wisps of smoke, navigational buoys looming from sea-fog, then lost behind its veils. Alderson's manner is older than his face—and he is prematurely white at the temples. His wire-rimmed glasses add to the enthusiastically serious look. Baker realizes he is staring at the man. Tracking Loerne and Alderson here will be counterproductive if they become aware of him. The assignment requires absolute discretion.

He works his way to the bar. United Intelligence (Australia) has kept covert surveillance on all nine Members and Advisors of the Wallace Inquiry. For all that they represent extreme ends of the Inquiry's ideological spectrum, Loerne and Alderson prefer each other's company to that of the city bureaucrats, sociologists, and professors of science who complete the Board of Inquiry. Fascinated by opposed *Weltanschauungen*. That's all UIA has on them, nothing scandalous to exploit. Loerne is the only one young enough to look at all plausible in the Searoom. But the other Advisors have all made frequent visits to the Season Hotel and the other Melbourne venues for the miracle music: the Rocks and Sand club in the city; the Fishcave along the esplanade in Port Melbourne; the more dignified miracle bars patronized by a slightly older set in Carlton. While the Advisors have got out and about, the three Members have stuck with their hearings and official inspections. Among the Searoom's complement of extreme young people in their sea-tribe gear, Loerne and Alderson appear out of place, but not ridiculously so as far as Loerne is concerned. Plenty of people are dressed more conservatively than she is, including an element of hapless men in their twenties and thirties, fooling themselves that they're going to net the young roe—who, of course, will have nothing to do with them unless they're rich.

Baker smirks at this happy thought, and at another: he could tell the Wallace Board of Inquiry more about the music miracles than anyone else here—more than it wants to know.

• • •

Only one cheek is jeweled.

Gabby Loerne turns to face Alderson squarely. Her large green eyes give no offense, clearly expect none from Alderson. "There's nothing disturbing about this."

The no-nonsense view of a tough-minded scientist at home in a laboratory, a conference room, a tribal jungle. Her manner is comforting and plain.

In his fashion, Alderson is also a practical man. A moralist, but with his feet on the ground. Morality is based on keeping your feet on the ground—society requires more than law for its morality, it requires experience, faith. Enforcement needs law; but teaching needs faith. That's what he learned at the Faculty of Theology, and he believes it. "We've let ourselves be fuddled," he says. He's tried to explain before—he tries again. "Our whole society's been fuddled by shibboleths. We thought that tolerance was a value in itself, and we chased tolerance until the moral center got left behind."

They both know the direction society has taken: *directions*. A dozen conflicting moral codes, the young totally alien to their parents, but their ways of life tolerated and financed for fears of worse evils—or is it just fear of seeming repressive?

"All I'm saying is that we shouldn't let our society become something that decent people can't bear to live in and bring up kids in. If a word like *freedom* or *tolerance* won't fit our needs, let's choose another word—not the other way around." There, he's said it again. Tight, cogent, defensible.

During the musoes' break, sharks are milling about aimlessly, many lighting up filters. Some of the little half-nude girls hug their skinny boyfriends. Scaly young sharks float in the direction of the bar, come back with frothy beer and cheap white wine for themselves and their roe—a patriarchy offensive to their parents is assumed in their folkways.

Gabby takes a deep breath.

"I don't know where to start with you. You're a learned man, a learned *friend*, who believes in spooks and demons. These things have rational causes. You know that. What you're seeing here is nothing more than an extreme form of the participative exhibitionism that we've observed all over the world. These musicians are priests of a mystery religion, if you like—but don't think of Satanism. Try the angakok leading the participative rites in Greenland . . . or the monks of Tibet. If you *must* have an analogy."

The musoes are back. It's suddenly quiet. An expectancy. Alderson whispers. Agitated, almost hissing. "Satan can act through human phenomena."

Her eyes are dismissive.

"No. Listen. This suspension of the will you're talking about is *dangerous*. The Church distinguishes between divine presence and collective hysteria, because, when God is absent from this form of . . . hysteria, the soul is vulnerable to possession. *At least that's the possibility I have to consider*. It's not some lunatic dogma you can just parody and reject out of hand; it's an intelligent idea worked out by scholars over years, over hundreds of years . . ."

But the music has returned: music and synthesized words spew forth from the amps, screaming with a sexual energy healthy enough in itself—but for an audience like this? This set is louder than the last. Alderson reaches into the fob pocket of his baggy seaweed-colored jeans, draws out a wad of cotton wool. Pinches off two comet-shaped lumps, rolls plugs of wool to protect ears from the blast. He remembers old rock shows, knows how to protect himself *this* much.

Gabby touches backs of fingertips to his elbow.

She speaks very clearly. "*He prayeth best who loveth best . . .* Remember."

He knows:

He prayeth best who loveth best
All things both great and small;
For the dear God who loveth us,
He made and loveth all.

"I do love them," he shouts back. "It's what's in them I can't love." The implications of his words depress and embarrass him. Demonic possession. He can't have meant it that crudely. But in some half-defined sense he knows this place is driven by evil. *Of the Devil*, the fundamentalist cults would say.

"Maybe you should try to love that, too."

"All right," he says, pointing. Her eyes follow. The mutilated boy in the cage. "Can you love flickdancing?"

Her reply is too soft for him to hear. But her lips move in their own simple dance. "Why not?"

• • •

She has opened herself to the music. To the crowd. The atmosphere. Open to the deep-brown, sinewy flickdancer, naked from the waist up, bleeding—ever so slightly—from long, fast-healing cuts. At the corner of Bianca's eye, the lead muso dances, shouting inaudibly, voice overflooded by the music from stacked black speakers rearing high in the corners of the stage. He sings to fill a merely private need, for his true voice, his music, comes from the bulky purple crown whose lights pulse on his forehead, feeding the signatures of biofeedback-trained brainwaves into the synths back of stage, then to the speakers.

Crimson flashes the stage from the wings. Yellow strobes. Blue.

Insistent rhythm of deep drums and bass guitar catches Bianca in the top of her belly, and she grunts slightly, stitch below her ribs, driving her into a strutting barefoot dance.

The moment stretches.

But the song smashes to an end: a heavy clang of metal. An archaic cylindrical microphone descends for the lead muso, who takes it in both long-fingered, long-nailed hands; his full lips almost touch it as he thanks the audience for its applause and attention. He leaves the mic to hang in space as he bends to sip a glass of water a meter away on the stage's dusty floor; he returns to the black mic and pants theatrically over the applause of the audience. "Thank you. Thank you." His sweaty chest heaves; strain shows in the movements of his great tufted eyebrows under the glowing headdress. "Thank you all." Massive green and orange body scales deck his shoulders and forearms. He carries himself in slightly dated style, high-heeled boots over very tight glittermesh pants. Sign of purist devotion. A pose of advanced BF-music, its makers too fanatical to maintain the latest mode. A pose which *is* the mode among these groups, in these places.

Glass Reptile Breakout hardly pauses between songs.

"A real healing song for you miracle lovers." He mutters it. Exhaustion and introspection. More pose. Bianca easily takes in the pose, without judging it. The microphone flies smoothly heavenward. Bianca half recognizes that man and lady in the corner at the frosted window. She's seen them on holos.

The music roars back. It claws at the inside of her round stomach, a needle-clawed bat, scratching to get out. She's wild with it. Her upper body's muscles twist her through near spasm. But she's got the Control. Hardly *under* control. But she's got it. She's got it. She's got it. *The Control. The capital-C. Mr. Big One, yes. She's got it, she's riding it, she's got it—she's exploding.*

And the graft in her back is painless. She's there. *She's there!*

And an important thought. That old man. The one with glasses—and the lady, the woman. She must speak with them. Something odd. Something odd has come to her and she'll speak to them. Especially the man. There's something she must say to him.

$$\bullet \quad \bullet \quad \bullet$$

Baker has studied covert recordings of Alderson and Loerne discussing these places. Despite Alderson's qualms about the miracle bands, he keeps visiting, struggling to come to grips. Of the Advisors to the Wallace Inquiry, he's the most emotionally vulnerable. Predisposed to shock. That's what Baker wants. What they sent him for.

He'll show 'em all havoc.

United Intelligence has its own global operations studying biofeedback techniques and rock miracles. It's way ahead of State government inquiries. It's going to stay that way. Everywhere. Baker's colleagues in South America are particularly keen to restrict public access to equipment and techniques which create the BF-miracles. Power is knowledge and knowledge is power.

Just now he slaps another pair of two-dollar coins on the bar. Stares through the gaunt feather-cheeked barman, who passes over a pot of weak beer and derisory change from four bucks.

Wait until the end of the night, the encores. Then . . . the beginning of the end. UI doesn't like flickdancing. In this city, the end of it is coming. He sips his beer.

The song changes tempo. Now Baker can see why the band called it a healing song. It's become almost a parody: tranquil. Fresh fields and bird calls. All things sentimental. But he resists its clichéd charm. Training with UI in Brazil and Chile with the best Russky and CIA instructors taught him detachment as well as skill.

Leaning against the padded vinyl bar top, he can look almost straight up into the Perspex cage, dangling from a network of gold-painted chains, where the flickdancer performs. The power of that music! If it can augment a healing process, Baker thinks savagely, it can also reverse it. He'll see to that.

$$\bullet \quad \bullet \quad \bullet$$

It's called *flickdancing*, but Tigershark doesn't use a conventional flick knife. His instrument more closely resembles a steel-handled wedge-bladed carpenter's knife, compact enough to fit entirely in his palm. It won't pierce the flesh too deeply by accident, and it can be concealed in his hand: when he cuts open the skin, it's as if by magic, running a closed fist along his body, eerily slicing the flesh apart.

He's seventeen, smooth and brown as the pouch of Italian leather dangling from the glittermesh strip about his slim hard waist, where he keeps his beer money.

Moves very deliberately and quietly to the music. Bare soles hardly slap the clear floor of his cage enough to rock it. A great bronze frill arches between his eyes and along the middle of his shaven skull, spreads down his back like the triangular fin of a shark, ends buried in his coccyx. The back of his white floppy shorts is cut away in a V to make room for the base of the bronze frill. Tigershark's implants are so generous, so rigid, that he cannot easily clothe his upper body. That doesn't matter. He takes up jobs on the Gold Coast or the Reef islands when the weather gets colder, and even overseas with the troops, entertaining the Aussie contingent in Brazil.

With a studied, ritualized movement, he places the chunky sea-green knife in his left fist, only the blade uncovered. Deftly, he slices up the underside of his right wrist and forearm, biting as deeply as the blade will allow, crossing over the inward bend of the elbow with its big dark veins, and across the strong flat biceps muscle.

The movement is graceful and safe. His blade will not go too deep, and the cut hardly bleeds. It's enough to display the ongoing miracle of Tigershark's body: shallow wounds cease to bleed within seconds, close up scabless within minutes, within hours are gone without trace.

Passing the knife to his right hand, Tigershark turns his left wrist, applies the knife to the base of left palm—and slashes. A sudden change of tempo, but still an artist's grace.

• • •

"That's it, folks."

The lead muso steps back into the shadows. No longer exalted by the music and the lights, the band appears diminished to Gabby Loerne. The musoes seem *chastened* as they walk from stage to wings.

Momentarily there is silence, then strong whistles and cries of "More!" The stage lights stay down, but no house lights come on in the Searoom. Loerne looks about, feeling alienated as the other members of the audience whip themselves into a frenzy of will, the older youths—the real estate brokers and patent buyers' clerks—more vocal than the teenage sharks and roe. But all eager to bring Glass Reptile Breakout back on stage. The cries—"More!"—rise to a raucous clap-reinforced chant. All eyes fix on the stage as if staring alone could set in train mighty engines. *Maybe it can.*

"More! More!"

Everything around her has become unreal: the butts and fragments of discarded filter packets on the deep red carpet about the walls, a dangerously broken beer glass on the hard center floor. She lowers her feet to the carpet, palms pressing the sill. What she cares about is not the show, but Alderson's reaction.

"Do you want to take a breather and talk about it?" she says.

"I don't know. None of this helps. Let's wait for the encore."

The band returns to stage, carrying the brainwave crowns. They fiddle clumsily for a second, bowing their heads for the apparatus, which begins to glow again. Looking up, the lead musician waves at the audience. He leaps into the air as the amps let out a preliminary guitar-like chord, and a hot pulse of yellow novas across the stage.

A tentative voice says, "Please: I recognize you." Loerne looks around. It's the girl who had been dancing close to them. Delicate, slightly chubby kid. Mixed races. Looks very ordinary somehow when she's not transported by the music. Could be anyone on the block. Girl next door. Except why hasn't she got clothes on and what has she done to her hair? There's a double image for a moment before Loerne resolves it.

"Hey," Loerne says to Alderson. "Why don't you talk to a miracle fan in her natural environment? She looks like a good kid to me."

"You're two of the people that want to stop this, our music, aren't you?" the girl says more excitedly. "I've seen you on the holo. Why? What do you have against us?"

"We're not going to ban your music," Loerne says. The noise starts in earnest, and she has to raise her voice. "I don't think so. Some people think it should be investigated. That's our job. We just want to know more about it."

"But there's nothing wrong with the music, Ms. It's healed my fin tonight. Look. My back was very swollen before. Now look." The girl turns to show them her back. The brown flesh cushioning the dorsal fin is completely whole, as if she had been born with the addition to her spine.

"Come with us," Alderson says decisively over increasing decibels. "What's your name?"

"Bianca."

"We'll both talk to you, Bianca."

"There's something I have to say. I don't understand it, though, and I can't quite remember."

"Come on, then."

They struggle through the rhythmic swinging arms. Loerne is glad when they reach the club's top foyer. Wide stairs with thick rails of brightly polished wood flow down to street level. "Please, what does *profane* mean?" Bianca asks.

Alderson opens his mouth. Closes it.

"Clairvoyance in action," Loerne says. "Listen: I'm Gabby Loerne. This is Lachlan Alderson. We're both advisers to the Wallace Inquiry on Biofeedback Music and the Flickdance Phenomenon. You know what that's all about?"

"Yes, Ms. Loerne. But tell me, is there a text or a holo where God speaks and says: *Who are you calling profane?* Something like that? I don't understand what it means."

"It means that the Devil quotes Scripture—"

"But more exactly than that," says Loerne sharply.

"He's subtle." Then, unexpectedly, after a pause, he laughs. Loerne is feeling a burn of exasperation before she realizes that Alderson is at least half joking, sending himself up in his deadpan way. He's a man of contradictions after all. But then, the joke is only an attempt to deflect his all-too-real anxieties.

"You're getting absurd," she says to him without heat. His anxieties are inevitable. There's a question for every certainty—always a deeper ambiguity to wrestle with. Her line from Coleridge had been a good one. But Saint Luke had done better—and this young girl with him—*What God has made clean, you have no right to call profane.* "It means the opposite of *holy*," she says for Bianca. "Do you understand that?"

"Good. We can all talk later." She gives Alderson a sympathetic smile. Jerks her head in the direction of the danceroom. "I'm going in to hear the last set."

• • •

Tigershark looks with horror at the cut under his chest. It hurts, hurts terribly. And it is not closing.

The most recent wounds under his arms have begun to bleed freely. He cannot express any pain—it would be the ruin of his act, his art. As if he can avoid forever drawing attention to the blood which will not stop, he lowers his maimed hand to knee height, drops the knife, kicks it away with his vulnerable feet. Continues dancing.

• • •

Baker has been trained to manipulate the healing effect directly and with purpose. *He* can reverse it.

He concentrates his unhealing hatred on the flickdancer. Blood oozes. The boy's wounds will *never* stop bleeding. And next Baker turns to older wounds— the knife lines of his dancing and his extensive surgery—opening them afresh.

Deliberate hatred vomits out of him. He conjures the demon in his mind as he was coached in the training camp outside Santiago. Hatred spews from him to the flickdancer, and now old incisions open, tattoos of proud flesh rising like initiation scars on the boy's smooth body, welds of pink flesh starting to tear open like wet paper, and the blood falling in a pool at his feet. In an eternal moment, the flickdancer drains white and falls in his own blood.

• • •

What God has made clean, you have no right to call profane.

Alderson lurches into the room, still trying to hide his shock. The girl's words were right. Like a trained theologian or a good lawyer, she's pinpointed the issue. Natural versus cultural law. But—he's often debated it with Gabby—where do you draw the line?

He looks heavenward.

And sees the bleeding flickdancer.

No.

He's despised the boy this evening, seven times seven called him profane. "Dear God, no," he says aloud, falling to his knees. The girl, Bianca, has evidently misunderstood. She kneels in front of him, pressing his pressed hands. Others look up. Screaming of terror or outrage. The miracle band plays on, musicians sightless in their trance-world.

The crowd and the band are gone. The boundaries of Alderson's identity are breaking up. Where is the girl who clenches his hand? The boy? There is only the triad, transcending music or identity, united against the suffering. Alderson spits away blood which seems to stream down his face choking, nauseating him.

He has misplaced the home of evil, understands that now.

That part of the triad which had been Alderson is in terror.

Evil is in the Searoom, but it does not come from the miracle band. They must thrust it away. Push the source of evil. Thrust the evil away, push the shadow right out of the dim room. Pushing back.

•   •   •

The boy's shorts are soaked in the same blood which has pooled at the bottom of his cage and spattered its walls, thrown by his frenzied efforts. He is terrifyingly white, fallen, half-fainted to his knees—but his wounds have stopped bleeding. Baker desperately recalculates the situation: an effect has already been created, a macabre dose of the Grand Guignol to terrify the superstitious and delight the media. But the boy must *die* to spite the lusts of Satan and to sustain the repugnant and loathing properly suited to the Devil's work.

Baker redoubles his effort of hatred, but the black acids that have sucked up out of him are now ebbing away. He forces his protesting ego back into the depths and finds . . . nothing.

Dimly, he senses that it is he who screams—lurching out of the parting crowd, flailing claustrophobically with desperate arms, not knowing why he runs to the stairs and stumbles mechanically down them toward the street, his assignment forgotten. He knows one thing only: he must escape the room where he is otherwise obliterating himself, unwinding *self* like a dark thread from a crazy bobbin.

•   •   •

The show is over. The house lights come on, but the night is ripped and interrupted. The crowd is not dispersing; it gathers closer, hushed, to the flickdancer's cage, ratcheting on its golden chains to the floor. A pair of bullnecked T-shirted bouncers shoulder their way through. One jerks the cage's front panel, snaps it open from the top. It hinges down, a transparent crocodile jaw full of bleeding ulcers. "Go home folks," the other man tells them. "Go home now—it's all right. Show's over. The kid's gonna be okay."

Alderson is numb, drained from his ordeal as if *he* had been bled white. He remains on his knees, eyes silent.

"It was horrible, Mr. Alderson." Bianca's voice. She sounds so young and shaken. There's no demon here.

He stands and shoves his way to the boy, who sways rubber-legged and glass-eyed. "Let me through—I have to see him." No one blocks Alderson's way. He grips the kid by both skinny shoulders. *Tigershark*. Tigershark's skin is crisscrossed with scars, a lacework of shiny pink raised flesh; his unbleeding body is stained with drying blood, his shorts drenched with it. Eyes look on Alderson's with sudden recognition, a smile of victory. Victory shared. Alderson hugs him, taking red stains on his own flesh and clothing.

"We'll take care of him." The bouncer speaks gently, awed. "There is an ambulance on the way."

Gabby and Bianca are both there. Alderson turns to Gabby as the bouncer helps Tigershark to a seat at the bar. She watches intently, silent, as the crowd disperses. Soon they are left almost alone in the Searoom.

Gabby speaks at last. "Bianca proved something here. You're like her." Smiles. "Either of you could be flickdancers, if that's what you wanted."

"Hardly . . . in my case." He looks her in the eye. "What happened? You're the expert."

"I don't know." Holds his eye frankly. "There's more to it than the music. You know that?"

He nods, knowing better than she could.

"Something *invaded* the Searoom tonight. Rival sorcery, maybe. What do you think, Lachlan?" *Rival sorcery.* "I'm not speaking scientifically. In a tribal society, I'd expect them to say an evil sorcerer had been here. Someone powerful and malefic."

"Why?"

"I don't know why."

"Something horrible was in the room," Bianca says. "It wasn't the band."

He remembers. The darkness. The shadow. Focused on Tigershark, palpable to Bianca and himself.

Gabby puts her arm around the girl's shoulders, just above the grafted fin where it anchors in her upper spine. An ambulance siren pulses. "But where did it come from?" Gabby says. Alderson is glad to see her tremble with emotion.

The last of the crowd has gone. A business-suited young man with black wavy hair is speaking to Tigershark—probably the club manager—as the ambulance crew arrives with a stretcher.

One of the bouncers has found a bucket and mop. He scrubs dispiritedly at the cage's ugly floor, wipes its walls with a fat square sponge. Alderson turns to Bianca.

"Let us take you home."

The girl smiles at him, her hand now in Gabby's.

• • •

Baker staggers along the seedy street. He recoils from the glaring lights of a St Kilda tram like a frightened beast. He rushes along the pavement, brushes a threadbare drunk. A gang of bare-chested sharks jeers at him on Fitzroy Street. He runs idiotically. Has no idea where he is going or who he was. All he knows is the darkness. He runs toward it.

CANDAS JANE DORSEY

[LEARNING ABOUT] MACHINE SEX

(1988)

A NAKED WOMAN working at a computer. Which attracts you most? It was a measure of Whitman that, as he entered the room, his eyes went first to the unfolded machine gleaming small and awkward in the light of the long-armed desk lamp; he'd seen the woman before.

Angel was the woman. Thin and pale-skinned, with dark nipples and black pubic hair, and her face hidden by a dark unkempt mane of long hair as she leaned over her work.

A woman complete with her work. It was a measure of Angel that she never acted naked, even when she was. Perhaps especially when she was.

So she has a new board, thought Whitman, and felt his guts stir the way they stirred when he first contemplated taking her to bed. That was a long time ago. And she knew it, felt without turning her head the desire, and behind the screen of her straight dark hair, uncombed and tumbled in front of her eyes, she smiled her anger down.

"Where have you been?" he asked, and she shook her hair back, leaned backward to ease her tense neck.

"What is that thing?" he went on insistently, and Angel turned her face to him, half scowling. The board on the desk had thin irregular wings spreading from a small central module. Her fingers didn't slow their keyboard dance.

"None of your business," she said.

She saved the input, and he watched her fold the board into a smaller and smaller rectangle. Finally she shook her hair back from her face.

"I've got the option on your bioware," he said.

"Pay as you go," she said. "New house rule."

And found herself on her ass on the floor from his reflexive, furious blow. And his hand in her hair, pulling her up and against the wall. Hard. Astonishing her with how quickly she could hurt and how much. Then she hurt too much to analyze it.

"You are a bitch," he said.

"So what?" she said. "When I was nicer, you were still an asshole."

Her head back against the wall, crack. Ouch.

Breathless, Angel: "Once more and you never see this bioware." And Whitman slowly draws breath, draws back, and looks at her the way she knew he always felt.

"Get out," she said. "I'll bring it to Kozyk's office when it's ready."

So he went. She slumped back in the chair, and tears began to blur her vision, but hate cleared them up fast enough, as she unfolded the board again, so that despite the pain she hardly missed a moment of programming time.

Assault only a distraction now, betrayal only a detail: Angel was on a roll. She had her revenge well in hand, though it took a subtle mind to recognize it.

• • •

Again: "I have the option on any of your bioware." This time, in the office, Whitman wore the nostalgic denims he now affected, and Angel her street-silks and leather.

"This is mine, but I made one for you." She pulled it out of the bag. Where her board looked jerry-built, this one was sleek. Her board looked interesting; this one packaged. "I made it before you sold our company," she said. "I put my best into it. You may as well have it. I suppose you own the option anyway, eh?"

She stood. Whitman was unconsciously restless before her.

"When you pay me for this," she said, "make it in MannComp stock." She tossed him the board. "But be careful. If you take it apart wrong, you'll break it. Then you'll have to ask me to fix it, and from now on, my tech rate goes up."

As she walked by him, he reached for her, hooked one arm around her waist. She looked at him, totally expressionless. "Max," she said, "it's like I told you last night. From now on, if you want it, you pay. Just like everyone else." He let her go. She pulled the soft dirty white silk shirt on over the black leather jacket. The compleat rebel now.

"It's a little going away present. When you're a big shot in MannComp, remember that I made it. And that you couldn't even take it apart right. I guarantee."

He wasn't going to watch her leave. He was already studying the board. Hardly listening, either.

"Call it the Mannboard," she said. "It gets big if you stroke it." She shut the door quietly behind herself.

• • •

It would be easier if this were a story about sex, or about machines. It is true that the subject is Angel, a woman who builds computers like they have never been built before outside the human skull. Angel, like everyone else, comes from somewhere and goes somewhere else. She lives in that linear and binary universe. However, like everyone else, she lives concurrently in another universe less simple. Trivalent, quadrivalent, multivalent. World without end, with no amen. And so on.

• • •

They say a hacker's burned out before he's twenty-one. Note the pronoun: he. Not many young women in that heady realm of the chip.

Before Angel was twenty-one—long before—she had taken the cybernetic chip out of a Wm Kuhns fantasy and patented it; she had written the program for the self-taught AI the Bronfmanns had bought and used to gain world prominence for their MannComp lapboard; somewhere in there, she'd lost innocence, and when her clever additions to that AI turned it into something the military wanted, she dropped out of sight in Toronto and went back to Rocky Mountain House, Alberta, on a Greyhound bus.

It was while she was thinking about something else—cash, and how to get some—that she had looked out of the bus window in Winnipeg into the display window of a sex shop. Garter belts, sleazy magazines on cheap coated paper with Day-Glo orange stickers over the genitals of bored sex kings and queens, a variety of ornamental vibrators. She had too many memories of Max to take it lightly, though she heard the laughter of the roughnecks in the back of the bus as they topped each other's dirty jokes, and thought perhaps their humor was worth emulating. If only she could.

She passed her twentieth birthday in a hotel in Regina, where she stopped to take a shower and tap in to the phone lines, checking for pursuit. Armed with the money she got through automatic transfer from a dummy account in Medicine Hat, she rode the bus the rest of the way ignoring the rolling of beer bottles under the seats, the acrid stink of the onboard toilet. She was thinking about sex.

As the bus roared across the long flat prairie she kept one hand on the roll of bills in her pocket, but with the other she made the first notes on the program that would eventually make her famous.

She made the notes on an antique NEC lapboard which had been her aunt's, in old-fashioned BASIC—all the machine would support—but she unraveled it and knitted it into that artificial trivalent language when she got to the place at Rocky and plugged the idea into her Mannboard. She had it written in a little over four hours on-time, but that counted an hour and a half she took to write a new loop into the AI. (She would patent that loop later the same year and put the royalties into a blind trust for her brother, Brian, brain damaged from birth. He was in Michener Centre in Red Deer, not educable; no one at Bronfmann knew about her family, and she kept it that way.)

She called it Machine Sex; working title.

• • •

Working title for a life: born in Innisfail General Hospital, father a rodeo cowboy who raised rodeo horses, did enough mixed farming out near Caroline to build his young second wife a big log house facing the mountain view. The first baby came within a year, ending her mother's tenure as teller at the local bank. Her aunt was a programmer for the University of Lethbridge, chemical molecular model analysis on the University of Calgary mainframe through a modem link.

From her aunt she learned BASIC, Pascal, COBOL and C; in school she played the usual turtle games on the Apple IIe; when she was fourteen she took a bus to Toronto, changed her name to Angel, affected a punk hairstyle and the insolent all-white costume of that year's youth, and eventually walked into Northern Systems, the company struggling most successfully with bionics at the time, with the perfected biochip, grinning at the proper young men in their gray three-piece suits as they tried to find a bug in it anywhere. For the first million she let them open it up; for the next five she told them how she did it. Eighteen years old by the phony records she'd cooked on her arrival in Toronto, she was free to negotiate her own contracts.

But no one got her away from Northern until Bronfmann bought Northern lock, stock, and climate-controlled workshop. She had been sleeping with Northern's boy-wonder president by then for about a year, had yet to have an orgasm though she'd learned a lot about kinky sex toys. Figured she'd been screwed by him for the last time when he sold the company without telling her; spent the next two weeks doing a lot of drugs and having a lot of cheap sex in the degenerate punk underground; came up with the AI education program.

Came up indeed, came swaggering into Ted Kozyk's office, president of Bronfmann's MannComp subsidiary, with that jury-rigged Mannboard tied into two black-box add-ons no bigger than a bar of soap, and said, "Watch this."

Took out the power supply first, wiped the memory, plugged into a wall outlet, and turned it on.

The bootstrap greeting sounded a lot like *Goo*.

"Okay," she said, "it's ready."

"Ready for what?"

"Anything you want," she said. By then he knew her, knew her rep, knew that the sweaty-smelling, disheveled, anorectic-looking waif in the filthy, oversized silk shirt (the rebels had affected natural fabrics the year she left home, and she always did after that, even later when the silk was cleaner, more upmarket, and black instead of white) had something. Two weeks ago he'd bought a company on the strength of that something, and the board Whitman had brought him the day after the sale, even without the software to run on it, had been enough to convince him he'd been right.

He sat down to work, and hours later he was playing Go with an AI he'd taught to talk back, play games, and predict horse races and the stock market.

He sat back, flicked the power switch, and pulled the plug, and stared at her.

"Congratulations," she said.

"What for?" he said; "you're the genius."

"No, congratulations, you just murdered your first baby," she said, and plugged it back in. "Want to try for two?"

"Goo," said the deck. "Dada."

It was her little joke. It was never a feature on the MannComp A-One they sold across every MannComp counter in the world.

• • •

But now she's all grown up, she's sitting in a log house near Rocky Mountain House, watching the late summer sunset from the big front windows, while the computer runs Machine Sex to its logical conclusion, orgasm.

She had her first orgasm at nineteen. According to her false identity, she was twenty-three. Her lover was a delegate to MannComp's annual sales convention; she picked him up after the speech she gave on the ethics of selling AIs to high school students in Thailand. Or whatever, she didn't care. Kozyk used to write her speeches but she usually changed them to suit her mood. This night she'd been circumspect, only a few expletives, enough to amuse the younger sales representatives and reassure the older ones.

The one she chose was smooth in his approach and she thought, well, we'll see. They went up to the suite MannComp provided, all mod cons and king-size bed, and as she undressed she looked at him and thought, he's ambitious, this boy, better not give him an inch.

He surprised her in bed. Ambitious maybe, but he paid a lot of attention to detail.

After he spread her across the universe in a way she had never felt before, he turned to her and said, "That was pretty good, eh, baby?" and smiled a smooth little grin. "Sure," she said, "it was okay," and was glad she hadn't said more while she was out in the ozone.

By then she thought she was over what Whitman had done to her. And after all, it had been simple enough, what he did. Back in that loft she had in Hull, upstairs of a shop, where she covered the windows with opaque mylar and worked night and day in that twilight. That night as she worked he stood behind her, hands on her shoulders, massaging her into further tenseness.

"Hey, Max, you know I don't like it when people look over my shoulder when I'm working."

"Sorry, baby." He moved away, and she felt her shoulders relax just to have his hands fall away.

"Come on to bed," he said. "You know you can pick that up whenever."

She had to admit he was being pleasant tonight. Maybe he too was tired of the constant scrapping, disguised as jokes, that wore at her nerves so much. All his efforts to make her stop working, slow her down so he could stay up. The sharp edges that couldn't be disguised. Her bravado made her answer in the same vein, but in the mornings, when he was gone to Northern, she paced and muttered to herself, reworking the previous day until it was done with, enough that she could go on. And after all what was missing? She had no idea how to debug it.

Tonight he'd even made some dinner and touched her kindly. Should she be grateful? Maybe the conversations, such as they were, where she tried to work it out, had just made it worse—.

"Ah, shit," she said, and pushed the board away. "You're right, I'm too tired for this. *Demain.*" She was learning French in her spare time.

He began with hugging her, and stroking the long line along her back, something he knew she liked, like a cat likes it, arches its back at the end of the stroke. He knew she got turned on by it. And she did. When they had sex at her house he was without the paraphernalia he preferred, but he seemed to manage, buoyed up by some mood she couldn't share; nor could she share his release.

Afterward, she lay beside him, tense and dissatisfied in the big bed, not admitting it, or she'd have to admit she didn't know what would help. He seemed to be okay, stretched, relaxed, and smiling.

"Had a big day," he said.

"Yeah?"

"Big deal went through."

"Yeah?"

"Yeah, I sold the company."

"You what?" Reflexively moving herself so that none of her body touched his.

"Northern. I put it to Bronfmann. Megabucks."

"Are you joking?" but she saw he was not. "You didn't, I didn't . . . Northern's *our* company."

"My company. I started it."

"I made it big for you."

"Oh, and I paid you well for every bit of that."

She got up. He was smiling a little, trying on the little-boy grin. *No, baby,* she thought, *not tonight.*

"Well," she said, "I know for sure that this is my bed. Get out of it."

"Now, I knew you might take this badly. But it really was the best thing. The R&D costs were killing us. Bronfmann can eat them for breakfast."

R&D costs meant her. "Maybe. Your clothes are here." She tossed them on the bed, went into the other room.

As well as sex, she hadn't figured out betrayal yet either; on the street, she thought, people fucked you over openly, not in secret.

This, even as she said it to herself, she recognized as romantic and certainly not based on experience. She was streetwise in every way but one: Max had been her first lover.

She unfolded the new board. It had taken her some time to figure out how to make it expand like that, to fit the program it was going to run. This idea of shaping the hardware to the software had been with her since she made the biochip, and thus made it possible and much more interesting than the other way around. But making the hardware to fit her new idea had involved a great deal of study and technique, and so far she had had limited success.

This reminded her again of sex, and, she supposed, relationships, although it seemed to her that before sex everything had been on surfaces, very easy. Now she had sex, she had had Max, and now she had no way to realize the results of any of that. Especially now, when Northern had just vanished into Bronfmann's computer empire, putting her in the position again of having to prove herself. What had Max used to make Bronfmann take the bait? She knew very clearly: Angel, the Northern Angel, would now become the MannComp Angel. The rest of the bait would have been the AI; she was making more of it every day, but couldn't yet bring it together. Could it be done at all? Bronfmann had paid high for an affirmative answer.

Certainly this time the bioware was working together. She began to smile a little to herself, almost unaware of it, as she saw how she could interconnect the loops to make a solid net to support the program's full and growing weight. Because, of course, it would have to learn as it went along—that was basic.

Angel as metaphor; she had to laugh at herself when she woke from programming hours later, Max still sleeping in her bed, ignoring her eviction notice. He'll have to get up to piss anyway, she thought; that's when I'll get him out. She went herself to the bathroom in the half-dawn light, stretching her cramped back muscles and thinking remotely, well, I got some satisfaction out of last night after all: the beginnings of the idea that might break this impasse. While it's still inside my head, this one is mine. How can I keep it that way?

New fiscal controls, she thought grimly. New contracts, now that Northern doesn't exist anymore. Max can't have this, whatever it turns into, for my dowry to MannComp.

When she put on her white silks—leather jacket underneath, against the skin as street fashion would have it—she hardly knew herself what she would do. The little board went into her bag with the boxes of pills the pharmaceutical tailor had made for her. If there was nothing there to suit, she'd buy something new. In the end, she left Max sleeping in her bed; so what? she thought as she reached the highway. The first ride she hitched took her to Toronto, not without a little tariff, but she no longer gave a damn about any of that.

By then the drugs in her system had lifted her out of a body that could be betrayed, and she didn't return to it for two weeks, two weeks of floating in a soup of disjointed noise, and always the program running, unfolding, running again, unfolding inside her relentless mind. She kept it running to drown anything she might remember about trust or the dream of happiness.

When she came home two weeks later, on a hot day in summer with the Ottawa Valley humidity unbearable and her body tired, sore, and bruised, and very dirty, she stepped out of her filthy silks in a room messy with Whitman's continued inhabitation; furious, she popped a system cleanser and unfolded the board on her desk. When he came back in she was there, naked, angry, working.

• • •

A naked woman working at a computer. What good were cover-ups? Watching Max after she took the new AI up to Kozyk, she was only triumphant because she'd done something Max could never do, however much he might be able to sell her out. Watching them fit it to the bioboard, the strange unfolding machine she had made to fit the ideas only she could have, she began to be afraid. The system cleanser she'd taken made the clarity inescapable. Over the next few months, as she kept adding clever loops and twists, she watched their glee and she looked at what telephone numbers were in the top ten on their modem memories and she began to realize that it was not only business and science that would pay high for a truly thinking machine.

She knew that many years before there had been Pentagon programmers working to model predatory behavior in AIs using Prolog and its like. That was old hat. None of them, however, knew what they needed to know to write for her bioware yet. No one but Angel could do that. So, by the end of her nineteenth year, that made Angel one of the most sought-after, endangered ex-anorectics on the block.

She went to conferences and talked about the ethics of selling AIs to teenagers in Nepal. Or something. And took a smooth salesman to bed, and thought all the time about when they were going to make their approach. It would be Whitman again, not Kozyk, she thought; Ted wouldn't get his hands dirty, while Max was born with grime under his nails.

She thought also about metaphors. How, even in the new street slang which she could speak as easily as her native tongue, being screwed, knocked, fucked over, jossed, dragged all meant the same thing: hurt to the core. And this was what people sought out, what they spent their time seeking in pickup joints, to the beat of bad old headbanger bands, that nostalgia shit. Now, as well as the biochip, Max, the AI breakthrough, and all the tailored drugs she could eat, she'd had orgasm too.

Well, she supposed it passed the time.

What interested her intellectually about orgasm was not the lovely illusion of transcendence it brought, but the absolute binary predictability of it. When you learn what to do to the nerve endings, and they are in a receptive state, the program runs like kismet. Warm boot. She'd known a hacker once who'd altered his bootstrap messages to read WARM PUSSY. She knew where most hackers were at; they played with their computers more than they played with themselves. She was the same, otherwise why would it have taken a pretty-boy salesman in a three-piece to show her the simple answer? All the others, just like trying to use an old MS-DOS disc to boot up one of her Mann lapboards with crystal RO/RAM.

• • •

Angel forgets she's only twenty. Genius is uneven. There's no substitute for time, that relentless shaper of understanding. Etc. Etc. Angel paces with the knowledge that everything is a phase, even this. Life is hard and then you die, and so on. And so, on.

• • •

One day it occurred to her that she could simply run away.

This should have seemed elementary but to Angel it was a revelation. She spent her life fatalistically; her only successful escape had been from the people she loved. Her lovely, crazy grandfather; her generous and slightly avaricious aunt; and her beloved imbecile brother: they were buried deep in a carefully forgotten past. But she kept coming back to Whitman, to Kozyk and Bronfmann, as if she liked them.

As if, like a shocked dog in a learned helplessness experiment, she could not believe that the cage had a door, and the door was open.

She went out the door. For old times' sake, it was the bus she chose; the steamy chill of an air-conditioned Greyhound hadn't changed at all. Bottles— pop and beer—rolling under the seats and the stench of chemicals filling the air whenever someone sneaked down to smoke a cigarette or a reef in the toilet. Did anyone ever use it to piss in? She liked the triple seat near the back, but the combined smells forced her to the front, behind the driver, where she was joined, across the country, by an endless succession of old women, immaculate in their Fortrels, who started conversations and shared peppermints and gum.

She didn't get stoned once.

The country unrolled strangely: sex shop in Winnipeg, bank machine in Regina, and hours of programming alternating with polite responses to the old women, until eventually she arrived, creased and exhausted, in Rocky Mountain House.

Rocky Mountain House: a comfortable model of a small town, from which no self-respecting hacker should originate. But these days, the world a net of wire and wireless, it doesn't matter where you are, as long as you have the information people want. Luckily for Angel's secret past, however, this was not a place she would be expected to live—or to go—or to come from.

An atavism she hadn't controlled had brought her this far. A rented car took her the rest of the way to the ranch. She thought only to look around, but when she found the tenants packing for a month's holiday, she couldn't resist the opportunity. She carried her leather satchel into their crocheted, frilled guest room—it had been her room fifteen years before—with a remote kind of satisfaction.

That night, she slept like the dead—except for some dreams. But there was nothing she could do about them.

• • •

Lightning and thunder. I should stop now, she thought, wary of power surges through the new board which she was charging as she worked. She saved her file, unplugged the power, stood, stretched, and walked to the window to look at the mountains.

The storm illuminated the closer slopes erratically, the rain hid the distances. She felt some heaviness lift. The cool wind through the window refreshed her. She heard the program stop, and turned off the machine. Sliding out the backup capsule, she smiled her angry smile unconsciously. When I get back to the Ottawa Valley, she thought, where weather never comes from the west like it's supposed to, I'll make those fuckers eat this.

Out in the corrals where the tenants kept their rodeo horses, there was animal noise, and she turned off the light to go and look out the side window. A young man was leaning his weight against the reins-length pull of a rearing, terrified horse. Angel watched as flashes of lightning strobed the hackneyed scene. This was where she came from. She remembered her father in the same struggle. And her mother at this window with her, both of them watching the man. Her mother's anger she never understood until now. Her father's abandonment of all that was in the house, including her brother, Brian, inert and restless in his oversized crib.

Angel walked back through the house, furnished now in the kitschy western style of every trailer and bungalow in this countryside. She was lucky to stay, invited on a generous impulse, while all but their son were away. She felt vaguely guilty at her implicit criticism.

Angel invited the young rancher into the house only because this is what her mother and her grandmother would have done. Even Angel's great-grandmother, whose father kept the stopping house, which meant she kept the travelers fed, even her spirit infused in Angel the unwilling act. She watched him almost sullenly as he left his rain gear in the wide porch.

He was big, sitting in the big farm kitchen. His hair was wet, and he swore almost as much as she did. He told her how he had put a trailer on the north forty, and lived there now, instead of in the little room where she'd been invited to sleep. He told her about the stock he'd accumulated riding the rodeo. They drank Glenfiddich. She told him her father had been a rodeo cowboy. He told her about his university degree in agriculture. She told him she'd never been to university. They drank more whisky and he told her he couldn't drink that other rot gut anymore since he tasted real Scotch. He invited her to see his computer. She went with him across the yard and through the trees in the rain, her bag over her shoulder, board hidden in it, and he showed her his computer. It turned out to be the first machine she designed for Northern—archaic now, compared with the one she'd just invented.

Fair is fair, she thought drunkenly, and she pulled out her board and unfolded it.

"You showed me yours, I'll show you mine," she said.

He liked the board. He was amazed that she had made it. They finished the Scotch.

"I like you," she said. "Let me show you something. You can be the first." And she ran Machine Sex for him.

• • •

He was the first to see it: before Whitman and Kozyk who bought it to sell to people who already have had and done everything; before David and Jonathan, the Hardware Twins in MannComp's Gulf Islands shop, who made the touchpad devices necessary to run it properly; before a world market hungry for the kind of glossy degradation Machine Sex could give them bought it in droves from a hastily created—MannComp-subsidiary—numbered company. She ran it for him with just the automouse on her board, and a description of what it would do when the hardware was upgraded to fit.

It was very simple, really. If orgasm was binary, it could be programmed. Feed back the sensation through one or more touchpads to program the body. The other thing she knew about human sex was that it was as much cortical as genital, or more so: touch is optional for the turn-on. Also easy, then, to produce cortical stimuli by programmed input. The rest was a cosmetic elaboration of the premise.

At first it did turn him on, then off, then it made his blood run cold. She was pleased by that: her work had chilled her too.

"You can't market that thing!" he said.

"Why not? It's a fucking good program. Hey, get it? Fucking good."

"It's not real."

"Of course it isn't. So what?"

"So, people don't need that kind of stuff to get turned on."

She told him about people. More people than he'd known were in the world. People who made her those designer drugs, given in return for favors she never granted until after Whitman sold her like a used car. People like Whitman, teaching her about sexual equipment while dealing with the Pentagon and CSIS to sell them Angel's sharp angry mind, as if she'd work on killing others as eagerly as she was trying to kill herself. People who would hire a woman on the street, as they had her during that two-week nightmare almost a year before, and use her as casually as their own hand, without giving a damn.

"One night," she said, "just to see, I told all the johns I was fourteen. I was skinny enough, even then, to get away with it. And they all loved it. Every single one gave me a bonus, and took me anyway."

The whisky fog was wearing a little thin. More time had passed than she thought, and more had been said than she had intended. She went to her bag, rummaged, but she'd left her drugs in Toronto, some dim idea at the time that she should clean up her act. All that had happened was that she had spent the days so tight with rage that she couldn't eat, and she'd already cured herself of that once; for the record, she thought, she'd rather be stoned.

"Do you have any more booze?" she said, and he went to look. She followed him around his kitchen.

"Furthermore," she said, "I rolled every one of them that I could, and all but one had pictures of his kids in his wallet, and all of them were teenagers. Boys and girls together. And their saintly dads out fucking someone who looked just like them. Just like them."

Luckily, he had another bottle. Not quite the same quality, but she wasn't fussy.

"So I figure," she finished, "that they don't care who they fuck. Why not the computer in the den? Or the office system at lunch hour?"

"It's not like that," he said. "It's nothing like that. People deserve better." He had the neck of the bottle in his big hand, was seriously, carefully pouring himself another shot. He gestured with both bottle and glass. "People deserve to have—love."

"Love?"

"Yeah, love. You think I'm stupid, you think I watched too much TV as a kid, but I know it's out there. Somewhere. Other people think so too. Don't you?

Didn't you, even if you won't admit it now, fall in love with that guy Max at first? You never said what he did at the beginning, how he talked you into being his lover. Something must have happened. Well, that's what I mean: love."

"Let me tell you about love. Love is a guy who talks real smooth taking me out to the woods and telling me he just loves my smile. And then taking me home and putting me in leather handcuffs so he can come. And if I hurt he likes it, because he likes it to hurt a little and he thinks I must like it like he does. And if I moan he thinks I'm coming. And if I cry he thinks it's love. And so do I. Until one evening— not too long after my *last* birthday, as I recall—he tells me that he has sold me to another company. And this only after he fucks me one last time. Even though I don't belong to him anymore. After all, he had the option on all my bioware."

"All that is just politics." He was sharp, she had to grant him that.

"Politics," she said, "give me a break. Was it politics made Max able to sell me with the stock: hardware, software, liveware?"

"I've met guys like that. Women too. You have to understand that it wasn't personal to him, it was just politics." Also stubborn. "Sure, you were naive, but you weren't wrong. You just didn't understand company politics."

"Oh, sure I did. I always have. Why do you think I changed my name? Why do you think I dress in natural fibers and go through all the rest of this bullshit? I know how to set up power blocs. Except in mine there is only one party—me. And that's the way it's going to stay. Me against them from now on."

"It's not always like that. There are assholes in the world, and there are other people too. Everyone around here still remembers your grandfather, even though he's been retired in Camrose for fifteen years. They still talk about the way he and his wife used to waltz at the Legion Hall. What about him? There are more people like him than there are Whitmans."

"Charlotte doesn't waltz much since her stroke."

"That's a cheap shot. You can't get away with cheap shots. Speaking of shots, have another."

"Don't mind if I do. Okay, I give you Eric and Charlotte. But one half-happy ending doesn't balance out the people who go through their lives with their teeth clenched, trying to make it come out the same as a True Romance comic, and always wondering what's missing. They read those bodice-ripper novels and make that do for the love you believe in so naively." Call her naive, would he? Two could play at that game. "That's why they'll all go crazy for Machine Sex. So simple. So linear. So fast. So uncomplicated."

"You underestimate people's ability to be happy. People are better at loving than you think."

"You think so? Wait until you have your own little piece of land and some sweetheart takes you out in the trees on a moonlit night and gives you head until you think your heart will break. So you marry her and have some kids. She furnishes the trailer in a five-room sale grouping. You have to quit drinking Glenfiddich because she hates it when you talk too loud. She gets an allowance every month and crochets a cozy for the TV. You work all day out in the rain and all evening in the back room making the books balance on the outdated computer. After the kids come she gains weight and sells real estate if you're lucky. If not she makes things out of recycled bleach bottles and hangs them in the yard. Pretty soon she wears a nightgown to bed and turns her back when you slip in after a hard night at the keyboard. So you take up drinking again and teach the kids about the rodeo. And you find some square-dancing chick who gives you head out behind the bleachers one night in Trochu, so sweet you think your heart will break. What you gonna do then, mountain man?"

"Okay, we can tell stories until the sun comes up. Which won't be too long, look at the time; but no matter how many stories you tell, you can't make me forget about that thing." He pointed to the computer with loathing.

"It's just a machine."

"You know what I mean. That thing in it. And besides, I'm gay. Your little scenario wouldn't work."

She laughed and laughed. "So that's why you haven't made a pass at me yet," she said archly, knowing that it wasn't that simple, and he grinned. She wondered coldly how gay he was, but she was tired, so tired of proving power. His virtue was safe with her; so, she thought suddenly, strangely, was hers with him. It was unsettling and comforting at once.

"Maybe," he said. "Or maybe I'm just a liar like you think everyone is. Eh? You think everyone strings everyone else a line? Crap. Who has the time for that shit?"

Perhaps they were drinking beer now. Or was it vodka? She found it hard to tell after a while.

"You know what I mean," she said. "You should know. The sweet young thing who has AIDS and doesn't tell you. Or me. I'm lucky so far. Are you? Or who sucks you for your money. Or josses you 'cause he's into denim and Nordic looks."

"Okay, okay. I give up. Everybody's a creep but you and me."

"And I'm not so sure about you."

"Likewise, I'm sure. Have another. So, if you're so pure, what about the ethics of it?"

"What *about* the ethics of it?" she asked. "Do you think I went through all that sex without paying attention? I had nothing else to do but watch other people come. I saw that old cult movie, where the aliens feed on heroin addiction and orgasm, and the woman's not allowed orgasm so she has to OD on smack. Orgasm's more decadent than shooting heroin? I can't buy that, but there's something about a world that sells it over and over again. Sells the thought of pleasure as a commodity, sells the getting of it as if it were the getting of wisdom. And all these times I told you about, I saw other people get it through me. Even when someone finally made me come, it was just a feather in his cap, an accomplishment, nothing personal. Like you said. All I was was a program, they plugged into me and went through the motions and got their result. Nobody cares if the AI finds fulfillment running their damned data analyses. Nobody thinks about depressed and angry Mannboard ROMs. They just think about getting theirs.

"So why not get mine?" She was pacing now, angry, leaning that thin body as if the wind were against her. "Let me be the one who runs the program."

379

"But you won't be there. You told me how you were going to hide out, all that spy stuff."

She leaned against the wall, smiling a new smile she thought of as predatory. And maybe it was. "Oh, yes," she said. "I'll be there the first time. When Max and Kozyk run this thing and it turns them on. I'll be there. That's all I care to see."

He put his big hands on the wall on either side of her and leaned in. He smelled of sweat and liquor and his face was earnest with intoxication.

"I'll tell you something," he said. "As long as there's the real thing, it won't sell. They'll never buy it."

Angel thought so too. Secretly, because she wouldn't *give* him the satisfaction of agreement, she, too, thought they would not go that low.

That's right, she told herself, *trying to sell it* is *all right—because they will never buy it.*

But they did.

• • •

A woman and a computer. Which attracts you most? Now you don't have to choose. Angel has made the choice irrelevant.

In Kozyk's office, he and Max go over the ad campaign. They've already tested the program themselves quite a lot; Angel knows this because it's company gossip, heard over the cubicle walls in the washrooms. The two men are so absorbed that they don't notice her arrival.

"Why is a woman better than a sheep? Because sheep can't cook. Why is a woman better than a Mannboard? Because you haven't bought your sensory add-on." Max laughs.

"And what's better than a man?" Angel says; they jump slightly. "Why, your MannComp touchpads, with two-way input. I bet you'll be able to have them personally fitted."

"Good idea," says Kozyk, and Whitman makes a note on his lapboard. Angel, still stunned though she's had weeks to get used to this, looks at them, then reaches across the desk and picks up her prototype board. "This one's mine," she says. "You play with yourselves and your touchpads all you want."

"Well, you wrote it, baby," said Max. "If you can't come with your own program . . ."

Kozyk hiccoughs a short laugh before he shakes his head. "Shut up, Whitman," he says. "You're talking to a very rich and famous woman."

Whitman looks up from the simulations of his advertising storyboards, smiling a little, anticipating his joke. "Yeah, it's just too bad she finally burned herself out with this one. They always did say it gives you brain damage."

But Angel hadn't waited for the punch line. She was gone.

PAUL DI FILIPPO

A SHORT COURSE
IN ART APPRECIATION

(1988)

WE WERE SO HAPPY, Elena and I, in the Vermeer perceptiverse. Our days and nights were filled with visual epiphanies that seemed to ignite the rest of our senses, producing a conflagration of desire that burned higher and higher, until it finally subsided to the embers of satiation, from which the whole inferno, phoenixlike, could be rekindled at will. There had never been a time when we were so thrilled with life, so enamored of the world and each other—so much in love.

Yet somehow, I knew from the start that our idyll was doomed to end. Such bliss was not for us, could never last. I don't know what it was that implanted such a subliminal worm of doubt in my mind, with its tiny, whispering voice that spoke continually of transience and loss and exhaustion. Perhaps it was the memory of the sheer avidity and almost obscene yearning greed with which Elena had first approached me with the idea of altering our natural perceptiverses.

She entered my apartment that spring day (we were not yet living together then, a symbol, I believe, of our separate identities that irrationally irked her) in a mood like none I had ever witnessed her exhibit. (I try now to picture her unaltered face, as I observed it on that fateful day, but it is so hard, after the dizzying cascade of perceptiverses we have experienced, to clearly visualize anything from that long-ago time. How can I have totally forgotten the mode of seeing that was as natural as breathing to me for thirty-some-odd years? It is as if the natural perceptiverse I was born into is a painting that lies layers deep, below several others, and whose lines can be only imperfectly traced. You will understand, then, if I cannot re-create the scene precisely.)

In any case, I remember our conversation from that day perfectly. (Thank God I resisted the temptation to enter one of the composer perceptiverses, or that memory, too, might be buried, under an avalanche of glorious sound!) I have frequently mentally replayed our words, seeking to learn if there was any way I could have circumvented Elena's unreasoning desires—avoiding both the heaven and hell that lay embryonic in her steely whims—yet still have managed to hold onto her love.

I feel now that, essentially, there was no way. She was simply too strong and determined for me—or perhaps I was too weak—and I could not deny her.

But I still cannot bring myself to blame her.

Crossing the memory-hazed room, Elena said excitedly, "Robert, it's out!"

I laid down my book, making sure to shut it off, and, all unwitting, asked, "Not even a hello or a kiss? It must be something wonderful, then. Well, I'll bite. What's out?"

"Why, just that new neurotropin everyone's been waiting so long for, the one to alter the perceptiverses."

I immediately grew defensive. "Elena, you know I try to steer clear of those designer drugs. They're just not—not natural. I'm not a prig, Elena. I don't mind indulging in a little grass or coke now and then—they're perfectly natural mind-altering substances that mankind's been using for centuries. But these new artificial compounds—they can really screw up your neuropeptides."

Elena grew huffy. "Robert, you're talking nonsense. This isn't one of the regulated substances, you know, like tempo or ziptone. Why, it's not even supposed to be as strong as estheticine. It doesn't get you high or alter your thinking at all. It merely gives you a new perceptiverse."

"And what, if I may ask, is a perceptiverse?"

"Oh Robert," Elena sighed in exasperation, "and you call yourself educated! That's just the kind of question I should have expected from someone whose nose is always buried in a book. The perceptiverse is just the universe as filtered through one's perceptions. It's the only universe any of us can know, of course. In fact, it might be the only universe that exists for any of us, if those physicists you're always quoting know what they're talking about."

"Elena, we've had this discussion before. I keep telling you that you can't apply the rules of quantum physics to the macroscopic world . . ."

"Oh, screw all that anyway! You're just trying to change the subject. Aren't you excited at all?"

"Maybe I would be, if I knew what it was all about. I still don't understand. Is this new drug just another hallucinogen?"

"No, that's just it; it's much more. It alters your visual perceptions in a coherent, consistent manner, without affecting anything else. You don't see anything that's not there; you just see what does exist in a different way. And since sight's our most critical sense, the effect's supposed to be like stepping into another universe."

I considered. "And exactly what kind of universe would one be stepping into?" Elena fell into my lap with a delighted squeal, as if she had won the battle. "Oh Robert, that's just it! It's not what universe, it's whose!"

"Whose?"

"Yes, whose! The psychoengineers claim they've distilled the essence of artistic vision."

I suppose I should interject here that Elena was a student of art history. In our bountiful world, where the Net cradled one from birth to death, she was free to spend all her time doing what she enjoyed, which happened to be wandering for hours through museums, galleries, and studios, with me in tow.

"You're saying," I slowly went on, "that this magical pill lets you see like, say, Rembrandt?"

"No," frowned Elena, "not exactly. After all, Rembrandt, to use your example, probably didn't literally see much differently than any of us. That's a fallacy nonartists always fall for. The magic was in how he transmuted his everyday vision, capturing it in the medium of his art. I doubt if any artist, except perhaps those like van Gogh, who are close to madness, can maintain their unique perspective every minute of their waking hours. No, what the psychoengineers have done is to formalize the stylistic elements of particular artists—more or less the idiosyncratic rules that govern light and shape and texture in an individual perceptiverse—and make them reproducible. By taking this new neurotropin, we'll be enabled to see not *like* Rembrandt, but as if *inhabiting* Rembrandt's canvases!"

"I find that hard to believe . . ."

"It's true, Robert; it's true! The volunteers all report the most marvelous results!"

"But Elena, would you really want to inhabit a Rembrandt world all day?"

"Of course! Look around you! All these dull plastics and synthetics! Who wouldn't want to! And anyway, it's not Rembrandt they've chosen for the first release. It's Vermeer."

"Vermeer or Rembrandt, Elena, I just don't know if . . ."

"Robert, you haven't even considered the most important aspect of all this. We'd be doing it together! For the first time in history, two people can be sure they're sharing the same perceptiverse. Our visual perceptions would be absolutely synchronized. I'd never have to wonder if you really understood what I was seeing, nor you me. We'd be totally at one. Just think what it would mean for our love!"

Her face—that visage I can no longer fully summon up without a patina of painterly interpretation—was glowing. I couldn't hold out against her.

"All right," I said. "If it means so much to you . . ."

She tossed her arms around my neck and hugged me close. "Oh Robert, I knew you'd come around! This is wonderful!" She released me and stood. "I have the pills right here."

I confess to having felt a little alarm right then. "You bought them already, not knowing if I'd even agree . . ."

"You're not angry, are you, Robert? It's just that I thought we knew each other so well . . ." She fingered her little plastic pill case nervously.

"No, I'm not angry; it's just . . . Oh well, forget it. Let's have the damn pill."

She fetched a single glass of water from the tap and dispensed the pills. She swallowed first, then, as if sharing some obscure sacrament, passed me the glass. I downed the pill. It seemed to scorch my throat.

"How long does the effect last?" I asked.

"Why, I thought I made that clear. Until you take another one."

I sat down weakly, Elena resting one haunch on the arm of the chair beside me. We waited for the change, looking curiously around the room.

Subtly at first, then with astonishing force and speed, my perceptiverse—our perceptiverse—began to alter. Initially it was the light pouring in through the curtained windows that began to seem different. It acquired a pristine translucency, tinged with supernal honeyed overtones. This light fell on the wood, the plastic, the fabric in my mundane apartment, utterly transfiguring everything it touched, in what seemed like a chain reaction that raced through the very molecules of my whole perceptiverse.

In minutes the change was complete.

I was inhabiting the Vermeer perceptiverse.

I turned to face Elena.

She looked like the woman in *Young Woman with a Water Jug* at the Met.

I had never seen anything—anyone—so beautiful.

My eyes filled with tears.

I knew Elena was experiencing the same thing as I.

Crying, she said, "Oh Robert, kiss me now."

I did. And then, somehow, we were naked, our oil paint- and brushstroke-mottled bodies shining as if we had stepped tangibly from the canvas, rolling on the carpet, locked in a frantic lovemaking unlike anything I had ever experienced before that moment.

I felt as though I were fucking Art itself.

• • •

Thus began the happiest months of my life.

At first, Elena and I were content merely to stay in the apartment all day, simply staring in amazement at the most commonplace objects, now all transformed into perfect elements in some vast, heretofore undiscovered masterpiece by Vermeer. Once we had exhausted a particular view, we had only to shift our position to create a completely different composition, which we could study for hours more. To set the table for a meal was to fall enraptured into contemplation of a unique still life each time. The rules of perceptual transformation that the psychoengineers had formulated worked perfectly. Substances and scenes that Vermeer could never have imagined acquired the unmistakable touch of his palette and brush.

Tiring even of such blissful inactivity, we would make love with a frenetic reverence approaching satori. Afterward the wrinkles in the sheets reminded us of thick troughs of paint, impasto against our skin.

After a time, of course, this stage passed. Desirous of new vistas, we set out to explore the Vermeer-veneered world.

We were not alone. Thousands shared the same perceptiverse, and we encountered them everywhere, instant signs of mutual recognition being exchanged. To look into their eyes was to peer into a mental landscape utterly familiar to all us art-trippers.

The sights we saw—I can't encapsulate them in words for you. Perhaps you've shared them, too, and words are unnecessary. The whole world was almost palpably the work of a single hand, a marvel of artistic vision, just as the mystics had always told us.

It was in Nice, I believe, that Elena approached me with her little pill case in hand. She had gone out unexpectedly without me, while I was still sleeping. I didn't complain, being content to sit on the balcony and watch the eternally changing Mediterranean, although, underneath my rapture, I believe I felt a bit of amazement that she had left without a word.

Now, pill case offered in outstretched hand, Elena, having returned, said without preamble, "Here, Robert; take one."

I took the pill and studied its perfection for a time before I asked, "What is it?"

"Matisse," she said. "We're in his native land now, the source of his vision. It's only right."

"Elena, I don't know. Haven't we been happy with Vermeer? Why change now? We could spoil everything . . ."

Elena swallowed Matisse dry. "I've taken mine, Robert. I need something new. Unless you want to be left behind, you'll do the same."

I couldn't stand the thought of living in a different perceptiverse than Elena. Although the worm of discontent told me not to, I did as Elena asked.

Matisse went down easy.

In no time at all, the sharp, uncompromising realism of Vermeer gave way to the gaudy, exhilarating, heady impressionism of Matisse. The transition was almost too powerful to take.

"Oh my God . . ." I said.

"There," said Elena, "wasn't I right? Take your clothes off now. I have to see you naked."

We inaugurated this new perceptiverse as we had the first.

Our itinerary in this new perceptiverse duplicated what had gone before. Once we had exhausted the features of our hotel room and stabilized our new sensory input, we set out to ingest the world, wallowing in this latest transformation. If we chanced to revisit a place we had been to while in the Vermeer perceptiverse, we were astonished at the change. What a gift, we said, to be able to see the old world with continually fresh eyes.

Listening to the Boston Symphony outdoors along the Charles one night, their instruments looking like paper cutouts from Matisse's old age, Elena said to me, "Let's drop a Beethoven, Robert."

I refused. She didn't press me, realizing, perhaps, that she had better save her powers of persuasion for what really mattered.

The jungles of Brazil called for Rousseau, of course. I capitulated with hardly a protest, and that marked the beginning of the long, slippery slope.

Vermeer had captivated us for nearly a year.

Matisse kept us enthralled for six months.

Rousseau—that naive genius—could hold our attention for only six weeks.

We were art junkies now, consumers of novel perceptiverses.

Too much was not enough.

The neurotropin industry graciously obliged.

Up till that time, the industry had marketed only soft stuff, perceptiverses not too alien to "reality." But now, as more and more people found themselves in the same fix as Elena and I, the psychoengineers gradually unleashed the hard stuff.

In the next two years, Elena and I, as far as I can reconstruct things, went through the following perceptiverses: Picasso (blue and cubist), Braque, Klee, Kandinsky, Balthus, Dalí, Picabia, Léger, Chagall, Gris, de Kooning, Bacon, Klimt, Delaunay, O'Keeffe, Escher, Hockney, Louis, Miró, Ernst, Pollock, Powers, Kline, Bonnard, Redon, van Dongen, Rouault, Munch, Tanguy, de Chirico, Magritte, Lichtenstein, and Johns.

We hit a brief period of realism consisting of Wood, Hopper, Frazetta, and Wyeth, and I tried to collect my senses and decide whether I wanted to get out of this trip or not, and how I could convince Elena to drop out with me.

But before I could make up my mind, we were off into Warhol, and everything hit me with such neon-tinted luminescent significance that I couldn't give it up. This happened aboard a station in high orbit, and the last thing I remember was the full Earth turning pink and airbrushed.

Time passed. I think.

The next time I became aware of myself as an individual, distinct from my beautiful yet imprisoning background, Elena and I were in a neoexpressionist perceptiverse, the one belonging to that Italian, I forget his name.

We were outdoors. I looked around.

The sky was gray-green, with a huge black crack running down the middle of it. Sourceless light diffused down like pus. The landscape looked as if it had been through an atomic war. I searched for Elena, found her reclining on grass that looked like mutant mauve octopus tendrils. Her flesh was ashen and bloody; a puke-yellow aura outlined her form.

I dropped down beside her.

I could *feel* that the grass was composed of tendrils, thick and slimed, like queer succulents. Suddenly I *smelled* alien odors, and I knew the light above spilled out of a novel sun.

The quantum level had overtaken the macroscopic.

Plastic reality, governed by our senses, had mutated.

We were truly in the place we perceived ourselves to be.

"Elena," I begged, "we've got to get out of this perceptiverse. It's just dreadful.

Let's go back, back to where it all started, back to Vermeer. Please, if you love me, leave this behind."

A mouth like a sphincter opened in the Elena-thing. "We can't go back, Robert. You can never go back, especially after what we've been through. We can only go forward, and hope for the best . . ."

"I can't take it anymore, Elena. I'll leave you; I swear it . . ."

"Leave, then," she said tonelessly.

So I did.

Finding a dose of Vermeer wasn't easy. He was out of favor now; the world had moved beyond him. Even novices started out on the hard stuff nowadays. But eventually, in a dusty pharmaceutical outlet in a small town, I found a dose of that ancient Dutchman. The expiration date printed on the packet was long past, but I swallowed the pill anyway.

The lovely honeyed light and the perfect clarity returned.

I went looking for Elena.

When I found her, she was as beautiful as on that long-ago day when we first abandoned our native perceptiverses for the shock of the new.

When she saw me, she just screamed.

I left her then, knowing it was over. Besides, there was something else I had to find.

The pill with my original name.

NICHOLAS ROYLE

D.GO

(1990)

THE AD CAMPAIGN was a "teaser." But the first posters to appear went up on noticeboards outside churches. Within twenty-four hours they were appearing on roadside hoardings and end terraces. I thought at the time they might have made an error in targeting the churches first and then tried to cover their mistake before anyone noticed.

The poster was simple and direct, yet obscure: D.GO. The letters were printed in large, bold type with that curious full point between the *D* and *G*.

I tried not to take much notice when the posters began to spread. On buses and trains to work I overheard fragments of conversation.

"Have you seen those posters?"

"Yes. What . . . ?"

". . . end of the street. Why do . . . ?"

". . . know what it's all about?"

I heard little that wasn't ambiguous and became no clearer in my own mind.

Within a few days D.GO posters appeared on the underground mingling with ads for depilatory creams and temping agencies. Full-size posters hit the platforms like ads for a new movie that had no credits and needed no cast. On the top decks of buses, notices warning of impending cuts and cancellations of Sunday services now had to vie for space.

Even the newspaper I had favored for several years lost one of its pages each day to the campaign.

I came home from work one day to find on my doormat a leaflet bearing no information other than the too-familiar message. If there had been an address I believe I would have returned it to them, with a note deploring the waste of paper.

That evening was jazz night at a pub not far from where I lived. I had recently become a regular attender. When I arrived there after a light supper, I saw discreetly affixed to the glass in the door a leaflet identical to the one I had received. The trio didn't sound quite as together as usual, even though I drank beyond my usual limit.

Walking home I realized I was staring at the windows of the houses I passed. My unconscious suspicion was confirmed: at least half the properties I scrutinized were giving their support to the D.GO campaign.

Despite my relative intoxication, I decided to get in my Beetle and drive outside of the neighborhood to see if the leaflets had been given wide distribution.

Ten miles north I was still seeing them in half of the flats and, when I got farther out, houses I drove past. Gloomily and with careful attention paid to the speedometer, I drove back into the tangerine shadowland of the inner city.

At work next day I asked: "Have you noticed these leaflets?"

"I've got one up in my window," Gilliland announced with pride. As production editor of the magazine, he was my immediate superior, and although there existed little empathy between us, I generally maintained a level of banter.

"What does it mean?" I asked him.

"Oh, Dominic," he said, "you do make me laugh."

He didn't laugh a great deal, so I was glad. But in fact he barely smiled on this occasion and provided no explanation of the conundrum, as someone rang from production demanding to know how many pages of the magazine were still outstanding.

"Twenty-four," he said. "I've been on to the typesetters all morning."

Gilliland was essentially a good person. He would only hurt a fly if there was no real alternative. So why did he and I never get beyond a superficial working relationship? Was it just his slightly bossy manner and pedantry or did I object more than I realized to his transparent piety?

There was an ad meeting. Gilliland gathered up his sheaths of papers and bustled out of the office, dumping a pile of proofs on my desk as he went.

"I was going to ask you if you would be kind enough to do these when you've finished reading the paper," he said, looking somewhere over my left shoulder. He billowed out of the room before I could think of how best to explain that I'd only picked up the paper for five minutes after lunch.

I turned the page and there was the ad for D.GO. But this was a new one—the next stage of the campaign. At the bottom of the page was a line of text: "Have you made sense of it yet?"

I stuffed the whole newspaper into the bin even though I hadn't finished reading it and reached for the first proof on top of the pile.

I worked until 5:20 p.m. and then left although Gilliland had not yet returned.

Ad meetings did not normally go on longer than half an hour. I wondered what could be causing it to go on so long. Not that it needed concern me. In the production process of the magazine my role was that of drone.

In the underground they had already replaced all the old posters with the new ones, which asked me if I'd made sense of it yet. I scowled and moved around people to get to the middle of the carriage so that when a seat became available I would get it.

Commuters hanging from straps swayed as the train rocked through tunnels. Within my section of the car there were ten slots for ads and four of them were occupied by "D.GO. Have you made sense of it yet?" I wondered if I was alone in finding the insistent query insolent in the extreme.

I called in at the Asian grocer's and was amazed to see the leaflet stuck in the window behind his head. I had only ever thought of him in the context of his small but colorful newspaper and the card he had in the glass door barring schoolchildren in groups of more than two. Now he was lending his support to this campaign, laying his business open to a boycott by shoppers like myself who could easily walk the extra five minutes to the supermarket. I decided to make this my last purchase as I waited behind a large man in a shiny suit one size too small.

At home the doormat presented me with another leaflet: "D.GO. Have you made sense of it yet?" Still no address. I crumpled it up.

I didn't often watch the television, so when I switched it on for something to do and saw D.GO advertised in two consecutive commercial breaks, I was incensed.

Walking to the pub I felt sure there were more leaflets stuck in windows than the night before. It was like election time in a one-party state. Voters were either unquestioningly loyal or they were being coerced.

Over the weekend I saw the first car stickers. "D.GO. Have you made sense of it yet?" in hundreds of rear windows lining the main arterial routes to the DIY superstores.

I drifted toward an antiques and crafts market I often visited at weekends. The market attracted followers of alternative lifestyles, people who refused to go with the general flow.

I sought reassurance and should have known to expect disappointment. The Triumph Heralds, Ford Anglias, and VW Karmann Ghias that crawled up the main road between the different sections of the market were bedecked with stickers. The ethnic shops and vegan restaurants carried the leaflet in the corners of windows. In the lanes of the market itself goths, punks, skins, and all kinds of fashion victims wore button badges bearing the legend D.GO.

I passed a stall selling the badges. In the crowd around it was a tattooed man stripped to the waist. His ears were pierced in a dozen places. On his shaven head were tattooed the letters D.GO. He was buying a badge. I hurried on, less than eager to see where he might pin it.

• • •

The phone was ringing as I reached the front door. I fumbled with the key, unlocked the door, and ran up the messy communal staircase to my door. The phone rang off just as I got inside.

They'll ring again, I thought, as I sat down in the kitchen with a magazine. I turned over several pages at once, hoping to miss all the ads. One got through the net. I didn't look to see if it was the *only* D.GO ad in the magazine. The phone rang again.

It was Dill. She and Tam had got back from their holiday last Thursday and had been ringing me since. Did I want to go round for something to eat and to see their photos? Yes. I did.

"Not tonight," I said. "I'm feeling a bit tired."

Why did I say that?

"I'm working straight through tomorrow," Dill said; she did shift work. "So it'll have to be next week."

I agreed, thinking I ought to tell her I did actually want to go round tonight. But something stopped me. What was I scared of?

In one of the cupboards I found some pasta.

I spent most of Sunday mourning the passing of the weekend and cursing the job I would return to the next day.

• • •

Jackie did the round of the in trays, giving us all copies of the issue we'd put to bed two weeks previously. No matter how long the hours we'd spent checking the proofs, we always took ten minutes to go through the finished magazine with a fine-tooth comb, looking for mistakes it was now too late to rectify. The magazine had a well-earned reputation for accurate subbing: typos and spelling mistakes, which cropped up maybe once every six months, meant apologetic memos from Gilliland to all higher tiers of editorial power.

I flicked through the ads at the front to get to the first pages of editorial. Then I went back to the ads in disbelief.

I pushed my chair back and may have mumbled to Gilliland that I was going out for lunch.

I hurried through a pedestrian arcade where tourists thronged and a man in white trousers handed out leaflets. Some of the shoppers I elbowed past were wearing badges. At a kiosk I thumbed through a selection of magazines for different specialist readerships: anglers, train spotters, and puzzle solvers; bodybuilders, philatelists, and onanists. My fears were confirmed: the magazine I worked for was not alone in running multiple double-page spreads for the infernal campaign.

Crossing streets choked with buses and taxis, all emblazoned with the same ad, I returned to work. My head felt like it was being hard-boiled as I tried to concentrate on the endless proofs and galleys.

The sentences seemed longer than usual and I lost the sense constantly, so that I had to reread whole chunks.

"I'd like to get as many of those off today as possible," Gilliland said the following morning, indicating the proofs on my desk. I was only halfway through them. "It's the deadline for first proofs, you see."

I saw.

I'd tried ringing Dill and Tam the night before but there had been no answer. Dill could have been doing another late shift and Tam often went out to clubs.

If Dill *had* been at work, then she should be at home now, I thought. I picked up the receiver and punched in the number. It rang unanswered.

I bent over the proof again. What was the article about? I didn't even know. If it couldn't hold my interest, why should it interest the reader? In fact, on reflection, that was probably a good sign. The faithful readers would be enthralled. And one of them would notice if I got a comma in the wrong place. She would write in to tell us she had spotted the mistake as if it were a competition.

And suddenly I knew that reader would have a leaflet stuck in the bay window of her semi.

"Dominic." It was Gilliland. "You should find the art department have finished the layouts for some of those proofs."

"Yes," I said, in a low, controlled voice.

In the art department I stopped by the paste-up board next to the window and stared at an A4 photocopy of next month's cover.

I felt the blood drain from my face. Where were the cover lines? Where was the masthead? Where was the cover picture? I felt someone standing next to me.

"What's this?" I asked. When I looked at Bob I saw he was pulling his jacket on, possibly about to go out for lunch. There was a small badge on the lapel.

"What do you think?" he quipped. "It's next month's cover. It looks good, doesn't it?"

I couldn't agree.

Unable to return to my desk I went and sat in the secretarial office for ten minutes. I told Jackie and Liz-Ann I had a headache. Just a few days previously I would have told them what was wrong, but now I was scared to mention the campaign in case they might reveal their own support for it.

The editorial department operated on a strict hierarchy. If I had any kind of complaint I should take it to those directly above me in the pecking order. But this kind of submission was just that. I would go to Gilliland or the next above him and the problem would generally be defined out of existence by a curious placebo of words. The symptoms wouldn't reappear till half an hour later. In this way the editor was never troubled with the human failings of her underlings. And yet, she said, her door was always open.

I knocked on the closed door and listened.

"Come," said a leather-upholstered voice.

I began to make excuses for my intrusion.

"Dominic," she interrupted me. I was quite impressed by that: she knew my name. "What's the problem?" From her side of the vast desk, watching me perch on the edge of an armchair, there had to be one. "How long have you been with us now?" she asked before I could continue. "Six months, seven months?"

"Eighteen," I said. Taking in a deep breath I explained what I had just seen in the art department. She nodded at intervals, even grunted when the extent of my concern seemed to call for it. Presently, I realized I'd gone on for too long. Her eyes had glazed over behind her designer frames.

I came to the crux of my argument: "We *never* run ads on the front cover." How many times had I heard a variation of that in response to my suggestions for changes in magazine content or procedure? *We never do this. We never do that.* The magazine had found a successful formula and was sticking with it. Change was a dirty word. So why the sudden change of heart?

She wasn't listening to me. I floundered and fell silent.

Distracted, she asked: "Was there anything else?"

In desperation I repeated myself: "We never run ads on the front cover."

A look of puzzlement flickered across her face. Her hands began shuffling papers and I thought it might be time to leave. Her coat was hanging on a hook on the back of the door. I tried to get a look at the lapel on my way out but couldn't. But she was hardly the kind of person to be wearing a button badge, whatever the cause.

I raced through the remaining proofs, forcing myself to concentrate on the words. If I didn't do it, Gilliland would have to and I didn't wish that on him. He had people breathing down his neck, after all.

Going home I was bombarded with thousands of ads on walls, vehicles, and people. Like the cover of the magazine, they all represented the next stage of the campaign—the solution of the anagram: GOD. Just that. GOD. With the full point at the end of the word. Such a short word but so powerful.

Later, I drove to Dill and Tam's. I parked in the street below their flat and looked up at the windows. Although there were several leaflets in the row of terraces, none could be seen in my friends' windows.

They seemed pleased to see me at last, took me upstairs, and offered me a choice of drinks.

"How's work? You've got to see our holiday photos."

Lots of pictures of mountain passes and gingerbread chalets, windblown lakes, and yellow trams.

"Never really fancied Switzerland," I said, looking closely at the ads on the side of the tram. They passed inspection.

I began to relax a little.

Tam made some coffee and Dill dragged out a board game. We played for an hour. Tam won. Dill and I decided he had cheated and should make us all more coffee. He protested his innocence but disappeared into the kitchen. Dill was putting the game away and picking bits of fluff from the carpet. I settled back in the settee.

My heart lurched when Tam appeared in the doorway holding a handful of GOD leaflets.

"I'll put these up now," he said.

Dill nodded and said, "Okay."

I didn't really care if they believed me or not. I just apologized and said I had to go. "Sorry about the coffee." The shock of seeing Tam holding the leaflets and saying he'd put them up now, like they'd been meaning to all evening, was too much for me. I couldn't stay and ask them what had happened.

Dill's eyes were wide with dismay. She didn't understand. "What's wrong?"

"Nothing," I said. "I've got to go."

Every car I passed on the way home had a sticker in the rear window. Groups of people were out leafleting streets where the old leaflet was still up.

What most disturbed me about Dill and Tam was that they appeared completely normal, just as before. They were exactly the same, my old friends, except that they were going to put up the leaflets in their windows.

• • •

I didn't go into work and ignored the phone when it rang at 9:30 a.m. When it stopped ringing I disconnected the plug.

Later, the doorbell rang. It was unlikely to be anyone from work and I was expecting no visitors. I pulled back the curtain and peered down into the street. A fair-haired man was looking up at me. I grimaced and let the curtain fall. The bell rang again. I hesitated in the kitchen, then quietly opened the door onto the communal stairs. On the mat were two or three leaflets.

Seized by rage I ran down the stairs and pulled open the door, prepared to chase after the man, if necessary, to give him back his literature. But he was standing on the step smiling.

"What do you want?" I asked brusquely.

"To give you a leaflet for your window. You don't seem to have one."

"No. That's right. I haven't got one and I don't want one." I snatched up the ones already delivered and stuffed them into his hand. Surprisingly, he let them fall onto the pavement. He took two more from a plastic shopping bag and handed them to me.

"*No!*" I said. "I'm not interested. Haven't you got the message?"

He appeared momentarily confused.

"Look," I changed tack, but still aggressive, "what's the big idea with this campaign? Why is everyone falling for it?" Immediately I felt I shouldn't have asked the questions. They made me vulnerable.

The man's lost look had vanished and he was smiling at me again. Then I noticed a small crowd was gathering behind him, murmuring.

"Take a leaflet in case you change your mind," he said, folding it into the palm of my hand. I sidestepped him to face the others. I tore the leaflet into quarters and then again.

"Take your leaflet," I said as I threw the scraps of paper like confetti over so many smiling brides and grooms, "and fuck off and leave me alone."

Their smiles creased into concern, instead of the condemnation I would have preferred.

• • •

On the motorway driving north to my parents' house, all the cars carried stickers.

I didn't raise my hopes as far as my parents were concerned, which was just as well. As I pulled into the driveway I was welcomed by a host of leaflets and a poster stuck in the windows of the bungalow. I could no longer be surprised, even though my parents, like Dill and Tam, had never been religious people.

They greeted me as normal, saying what a nice surprise it was. The only change I could see in them was in their front windows.

"Don't stop what you're doing," I said, but my mother made for the kitchen to get us all a drink, while my father went through to the back garden to clear away the tools he had been working with. This gave me the chance I needed. I slipped into their bedroom and carefully opened the doors of my father's wardrobe. At the back of the top shelf, behind a pile of old socks he probably didn't like to throw out, was a shoe box. I withdrew the army-issue pistol and a box of bullets. Wrapping the pistol in my handkerchief, I put it and the bullets in my jacket pocket. I replaced the lid on the box and returned it to its hiding place.

Standing in the hall I saw my mother through the kitchen doorway bent over the sink. And through the picture window in the living room I could see my father pushing the lawnmower up the garden toward the shed. For a moment I hesitated, a great lump constricting my throat. But I knew I couldn't stay. My eyes alighted on the door to my old room. I very nearly reached out my hand to open it.

As I backed the car out of the drive my mother's face emerged from around the front door. Her mouth fell open. I throttled down and swung the wheel round as I hit the road. I looked up the drive as I slammed into first and screeched away. A look of panic on her face, she was running.

It hurt terribly to drive away.

I felt conspicuous on the motorway: the only car without a sticker. I wondered if I should get one just for pretense but quickly rejected the idea as cowardly. I had the gun now for protection.

Drivers turned to stare as they overtook me. I wasn't sure if they would do that normally.

I moved to overtake an articulated lorry which was struggling up a slight incline in the inside lane. I drew level with the cab, where a GOD sticker was affixed, then the artic gained speed. I accelerated but couldn't even catch up with the cab.

I was conscious suddenly of a slight dimming of the light inside the Beetle. I steadied the wheel and checked the mirrors. A huge artic was coming up on the *outside*.

We had reached the top of the hill and were coasting. There were cars behind, leaving me too little space to brake and let both lorries pass. The one on the outside now drew level so that I could see the sticker in his cab window. He pulled ahead a few yards.

My foot was on the floor but we were going downhill—they had the speed *and* the weight. I jabbed at my horn repeatedly but I doubt if they even heard it.

Drivers behind began to get impatient, sounding their horns as well. Turbulence buffeted the Beetle as I fought to maintain a straight line in a gap which seemed to be narrowing. The lorries towered overhead, plastic side-flaps beating in the wind like pterodactyls. Were they closing the gap or was it my imagination? I couldn't see any trace of white lines.

I was freed when the lorry on the outside found itself blocked by a Metro doing sixty-five in the outside lane. He braked and I overtook the Metro on the inside before switching to the outside lane and spurring the Beetle to go faster. The artic in the slow lane made no attempt to give chase.

I saw, in my rearview, both lorries now in the inside lane, one having overtaken the other, which may have been all it was trying to do all along. I rubbed my forehead with the sleeve of my jacket, pulling at the weight in the pocket as I did so. Slowing down to seventy-five, I returned to the inside lane myself.

• • •

My flat, as far as I could see, was now the only one without a leaflet or poster in the window. Even in the nearby estates where residents didn't bother with party-political posters during general elections, leaflets advertising GOD were up in every window.

I slept badly and decided to go in to work as an act of defiance. By now I trusted no one; the loaded gun accompanied me.

The campaign had reached a new stage overnight. Fresh hoardings had been erected wherever there was space. My heart skipped several beats as I read the new message: "GOD. He is coming."

There was a buzz of excitement on the train fed by the people crammed around me, strangers united in anticipation. Gone were the early morning vacuous stares and razor-nicks and smudged eyeliner, replaced by flushed cheeks and a newborn glow of perfection. If they were all about to meet their maker, I was surprised not to see some signs of dread, or last-minute repentance. They were supremely confident.

The atmosphere was electric in magazine editorial. Gilliland was radiant. I kept my head down and concentrated on the white spaces between the lines.

I noticed that the offices emptied earlier than usual.

The underground was congested. The announcement was difficult to hear but it seemed most lines were not operating. I got caught in a surge of commuters and pushed onto a down escalator. All the ads down the wall by the handrail were the same. People smiled and held hands; they may or may not have known each other. There was little of the stress and antagonism usually present in a busy station at rush hour.

But the number of commuters was unprecedented. They were all going for the one line that seemed to be running. I had no choice but to go with the flow, though in the circumstances I resented their company.

On the platform I craned my neck looking for the exit, but it was serving as an entrance with hundreds of people streaming through it. I wiped my forehead.

The jacket collar irritated my neck and the weight of the pistol was causing my shoulder to ache. But I felt safer with the jacket on than I would if I took it off.

A uniformed official announced that the next shuttle was approaching and we should stand back. I couldn't move an inch.

I had to board the train and was jammed up against someone's lapel badge. I twisted my body to face the other way and felt close to fainting.

The train went straight through stations without stopping. Perhaps the next shuttle would pick up at one of them. When the train finally stopped there was another crush: unable to forge my own passage, I allowed myself to be carried along.

The streets were unfamiliar to me but the hoardings that lined them were not. There was a line of cars in the center of the road, windows wound down for air, occupants fanning themselves, drivers astonishingly patient. The rest of the roadway and both pavements were slow rivers of pedestrians all flowing in the same direction. Tributaries joined from side streets, which meant I couldn't escape down one.

Signs told me we were heading for the stadium. I thought to myself that vast though it was, it would never accommodate all these souls. Soon its cream towers reared above my section of the crowd. As we passed beneath the outer structure the pack loosened a fraction, but I knew I couldn't go back: the streets were impassable. Funneled through a narrower passageway I was pressed right to the edge. Again, impossible to turn around, but I could go sideways. There was a door in the wall several yards ahead. The crowd moved slowly. Finally I was there. The handle turned. I disappeared.

I'd simply entered another passageway but this one was empty of people and the ceiling was lower. I began to walk. After some time the corridor came to a junction. Down the passage on the right there was only a locked door, so I went in the other direction.

I wondered what strange, forbidden precincts these were. Fire exits? Players' tunnels? I just kept walking. Presently, a passage merged from the left, but I sensed it didn't come from where I wanted to go, even though my goal was vague. I seemed to know better where I didn't want to go than where I did.

The corridor widened a little. The caged bulbs lining the wall at intervals of twenty yards or so seemed to become faint, as light suffused the air from another source. I walked on. The light gradually became brighter and the echoes of my footsteps faded more quickly.

The corridor sloped upward and suddenly the ceiling vanished into a great whiteness which almost blinded me—the sky: I was inside the ground. The green pasture stretched out before me. I saw the grandstand packed with tens of thousands of people. I stepped onto the pitch.

Faces began to turn as I continued walking. Silence fell like a shroud. I carried on walking until I reached the center point.

The rows of seats seemed to extend far beyond the possible bounds of the stadium, up into the sky.

I turned through 360 degrees to take in the whole ground. The silence was total. All I could hear was the blood in my head and my heart pumping it. I saw one man fall to his knees. Immediately, those around him followed suit. Their seats snapped shut.

I shrugged my jacket collar off the back of my neck where it was itching.

The reverential hush was shattered by the sharp cracks of many thousands of seats snapping shut like the beaks of dying birds.

Outside the pounding of blood in my head complete silence fell once more as a million believers knelt before me.

I took the gun from my pocket, pointed the muzzle at my temple, and squeezed the trigger.

God is dead.

HARRY POLKINHORN

CONSUMIMUR IGNI

(1990)

IT WAS FIVE O'CLOCK in the afternoon. Debord entered Alicia's, grateful for the cool darkness. After all, outside it was 117 degrees Fahrenheit. He sat in a leather-backed chair and ordered a margarita ("without salt"). The lime bit his throat as it went down. The gloomy interior of the De Anza Hotel's only bar helped him to concentrate. Debord had a lot to think about. People were dying a horrible death through convulsions and vomiting all over Calexico, and it was his job to figure out why.

Needle slide beneath skin. Rose burst backup in the tube. Dark red silent explosion. TV flicker jump across nose eyes frowning brow. Idiom thieves. Invisible interior of formless. Slow-motion jolt to loosen bones from flesh afloat. Broken tooth of pain going away to dead. Sun mushroom against scarred horizon. Footsteps smell of salt cedar rank sewage burning agricultural waste hangs in air. Explosion of terrorist alphabet chunks across the screen.

He ran his fingers through thinning hair. His mind circled like a hound just off his scene, circled and backtracked as if aimlessly, yet well aware in its way, a calculated distraction, a meditation on nature, bestiality, beauty, the monstrous. The Calexico police had called him in because he had once had contacts with the Chinese Catholic group in Mexicali back in the 1960s. The local dicks figured he might be of some use in their deadlocked investigation. Whenever they couldn't do a quick make, they pinned it on the Chinese. Debord ordered another drink and ruminated. They didn't know about MIBI, and he wanted to keep it that way.

Debord's heart raced as he felt himself reaching a "plateau" in his mullings. He quickly paid for his drinks and went up to his room. Second floor, only room in the crumbling pile with a telephone. He unplugged the instrument and jacked in his portable computer. High-speed modem connect. Into the Internet highway and his code shot through the gateways to MIBI: Jorn in Copenhagen (Dotrement and Constant had fallen away, or rather been sheared off by developments too rapid for them to track), Pinot-Gallizia in Coslo d'Arroscia, Bernstein in Paris. "And me on the border, as usual," he thought sardonically. Lit a Camel and scrolled down to the relevant user ID numbers, knocked through a general call. He needed Guiseppe's knowledge of chemistry right away, and Asger's command of tongues. Bernstein would put the pieces together in her brilliant way. The gang moll but this time with a brain in her head. Debord was point man this time out. "Maybe you'll get some ideas for your next film," Jorn had chortled.

• • •

"Dozens of new cases are being reported each week," said Torres in a voice of barely controlled rage. "It's a goddam epidemic. We know nothing but what we read in the papers. The mayor and city council are kicking my butt." He glared around the office. Debord had his Sony minicassette recorder going in his pocket. Voice analysis later. MIBI procedures.

"How tight in the line?" asked Debord.

"We've got every dog in the house down there. The Border Patrol is cooperating so far. I spoke to Saldaña just before you got here. There are always leaks, maybe big ones, but the standard holes are plugged for now."

"Can you get me permission to go up into the water tower observation post?" Debord said. The Border Patrol had taken over the wooden gondola in the old water tower right at the fence.

"Sure." Torres punched up Saldaña again. "Pete. It's me again. Listen, Pete, I need to get my man up into the tower. Okay. Yeah, sure. I'll tell him. Thanks, Pete." He rang off and said, "You're in. A Jeep will be by in five minutes."

• • •

The epoch itself is the frame of the whole work. How to plumb what could be an act of Chinese-Mexican terrorism. Beneath him the chain link and barbed wire stretched east and west. I wanted to speak the beautiful language of my time. To communicate and discuss. We grow older. Rose bomb in liquid, floats up through a dreamscape of all earthy things were corrupted. He looked through his binoculars. Here and there Mexicans slipped through holes in the fence heading north. Secondary details. At the beginning, I was nothing. His hands adjusted the plastic tubes, snapping everything into focus. The more profound is this desire. Violence, sexuality, cruelty. Turnings through a random city gridwork. A speaking voice proper only for suffering and despair. His 8-millimeter video unit patiently sucked in images. The huge sprawling metropolis to the south, sliced cleanly by the US/Mexico international boundary, in this case a fence topped with barbed wire, and on the north side the tiny town of Calexico with its neatly paved streets.

· · ·

"Souls or bodies, what the difference. The virus attacks life itself. Someone has unleashed a radioactive isotope that feeds on doubles. Is the soul the body's double?" The commander rose up on his toes, then rocked down, hands clasped behind his back. He looked intently out the window at the scene in the park across from the station. Swings, a merry-go-round, drunks asleep under the palms. Nothing out of the ordinary. A secretary handed him a fresh fax. "Jesus, Mary, and Joseph," he swore. "Another rash of cases has been reported out in the Villa de Oro section of town. I'm calling the Centers for Disease Control again."

Debord took this as his cue and left the station. He returned to the De Anza and within minutes was entering the day's catch into SI, a complex and beautiful program MIBI had commissioned. On a hunch, he flipped laterally out of SI into private notes, looking for the link: "On the evening of Dec. 31 in the same bar on the rue Xavier-Privas, the Lettrists came upon K. and the regulars terrorized—despite their own violent tendencies—by a sort of gang comprising ten Algerians who had come from the Pigalle and were occupying the place. The rather mysterious story seemed to involve both counterfeit money and the links it might have with the arrest of one of K.'s friends—for narcotics peddling—in the very same bar a few weeks earlier."

"Bingo," whispered Debord. "Dope and the Lettrists." He slammed back into SI and ran the voice-print subroutine for everyone he had interviewed that day. Torres, Saldaña himself later on, and others. This took a while and the data were queued up in the buffer. Meanwhile he popped in master tracks for some radio programming from several popular norteña stations, then scanned in all the police stats the boys had given him. Once he had snapped the video conversion unit into its slot, the transfer was automatic. Before locking in with MIBI, he needed a break, because after they got started it would stretch him out thin.

· · ·

Therefore the places most fitting for these things are churchyards. And better than them are those places devoted to the executions of criminal judgment; and better than those those places where, of late years, there have been so great and so many public slaughters of men; and that place is still better than those where some dead carcass that came by violent death is not yet expiated, nor was lately buried . . . you should therefore allure the said souls by supernatural and celestial powers duly administered, even by those things which do move the very harmony of the soul . . . such as voices, songs, sounds, enchantments.

· · ·

Girls used to put their belts, ribbons, locks of hair, etc. under the pillows of young men for whose love they craved.

. . .

Visible and tangible forms grow into existence from invisible elements by the power of the sunshine. This process is reversible by the power of night.

. . .

If a pregnant woman imagines something strongly, the effects of her imagination may become manifest in the child. The blood is magnetized.

. . .

Acting on a tip from a Mexican informant, Debord nonchalantly entered the Copa de Oro. Chunks of the ceiling fallen away. A television monitor at each end of the short bar playing back grinding porno films. Nothing different from any other hole in the Chinesca. He sat at a tiny table and ordered a Tecate. One of those dives that featured only one kind of beer. Down to the basics. Soon the woman spotted him, as he had been told she would. Watch out for a setup. Dark eyes lined with mascara, skintight dress of some white Spandex material, spike heels. He quickly scanned the joint, but no one seemed to care.

"Buy a girl a drink?" she asked.

"Sure. Name it." She ordered the predictable brandy.

"What brings you here?" she cooed, sliding a hand up his thigh.

"You," Debord said. "They tell me you know the new governor."

"Maybe I know him," insinuated the woman. "I've known lots of men. Let's go to my room and I'll check my little black book." She tossed off the drink with one hand while massaging his upper thigh with the other.

"You're on," said Debord.

As he pulled up his zipper, Debord reminded the woman why he was there. She then said, "Sure, he used to come here. He liked me. We had some good times."

"Was he alone?"

"No. He always had several others with him."

"Any Chinese?" Debord asked.

"Yeah, as a matter of fact. I remember an older guy. Emilio Chin. They said he owned the Green Cat years ago and then got into the state gambling syndicate."

"How can I meet him?"

"Come back here a week from tonight at eleven p.m. I'll know by then," she said, stuffing the bills into her bra. Then she smiled. "Come back anytime, baby."

"By the way, what's your name?" he asked.

"Rosa."

. . .

Within fifteen minutes Debord had walked back across the border and was in his room at the screen, deep in SI. He ran the girl's voice from his machine, then a quick description of her features, clothing, and room. His ID began blinking: it was Guiseppe piping through with the chemistry figures. Blood sample analyses, projections of viral group activities, hormone cross sections. SI reconstructed his voice, which purred from the machine. "Your stats are flat on both ends of the curve," he said. "What kind of a place are you in anyway?"

"Somewhat isolated border setting," responded Debord. "They aren't much up on record-keeping here. It's all by word of mouth, gossip, chit-chat. But you do the best you can."

"Sure, Guy. Hang in there. Wait, here's Asger." The voice quality changed from a mild Italian to an even milder Scandinavian accent; SI did this just to make things more pleasant.

"Guy. Asger. Listen, I've done the full job on the samples. All the way down to the sub-phonemic level. You're dealing with some complex shit out there. My best guess is Mexican Spanish and third-level American on a bedrock of Mandarin Chinese. The diction subroutine tells us it's a woman between the ages of twenty-eight and thirty-four, educated through the equivalent of a four-year college program, maybe in the US. Interests may be business, music, sex, and the occult. That's as far as I could get, Guy. She's smart and probably very dangerous. Be careful, for Christ's sake."

Blip of static. Columns of figures filed across the screen, froze into a pattern, then disappeared as more came up, until the transfer was completed. He downloaded, ran his virus check, stuck a tracer block on the end, and broke the connection. Six thirty a.m. Suddenly he felt exhausted and stretched out on the uncomfortable bed. Too tired to care.

• • •

It was a critique of urbanism, of art and political economy. They operated through a series of turnings. Just as you felt you were on to something, they flipped the dial to another station. A twilight world of electronic haze as the ex-citizens watch *Dallas* over and over again. No one would be able to play because they would all be fixed in their allocated places. It was a question of premeditated memory control. Global marketing because of the lack of an overarching construction. This was the perspective: a shifting of tasks through negation itself force field sucks us into the now. Atomic fallout shelter against the fire storm of signs.

• • •

Over coffee and machaca in the De Anza café, Debord flipped over the pages of the *San Diego Union*. His eyes lighted on a headline: "Agreement said near on tighter controls over medical waste." His tour of the area had led him to the conclusion that such concerns would be minimal here. ". . . trash from hospitals, clinics, and labs that can carry infectious diseases . . ." No one would think twice about unloading a pickup of plastic bags filled with such materials out on the desert or by the side of the road. After all, weren't the farmers themselves prime polluters of the food chain with massive doses of insecticides, fungicides, and herbicides? One would simply be following an example. So went his ruminations as he finished the spicy meat dish.

Later that evening, Debord kept his appointment with Rosa. "Any luck?" he asked.

"Sure. Chin is out of town, but his 'assistant' said she would meet us here. Look, here she comes now." The woman flicked her eyes toward the Copa's swinging half door.

Debord turned to see. "Asger's right again," he said to himself as a Chinese Mexican woman of about thirty-five walked up to their table.

"Hello. I am Mr. Chin's assistant, Veronica Mah," she said in measured tones. "How can I help you?" Her skin had a deep glow under the dim lighting. She lit a cigarette.

"There's a big problem you might be able to help me with," said Debord carefully. He felt her scanning him with some Oriental power device. "My understanding is that the Governor, Mr. Ernest Appell, has some connections with, uh, certain merchandise crossing to the north . . . usually at night." He watched her expression.

"Yes," Veronica said readily, to his surprise. "I've heard the same." Pause.

"Well, to be frank with you, we need to know as soon as possible what the routes have been the last four weeks. Discretion assured, needless to say."

"Undoubtedly." Cold. Mastery of tone. Veronica was very accomplished. Debord was banking heavily on the locale. He had figured she had done some kind of a check on him and probably had come up blank. Meanwhile, because of the isolation of this place the chances that she would deduce his distant team were very slim indeed. His recorder was trapping her in magnetic patterns. Veronica studied him through the smoke rising from her Delicado. He pushed an envelope across the table toward her. She pocketed it, rose, and left the club.

• • •

Back in SI, Debord uploaded all his fresh data. Then he rolled through the gateways to Bernstein. He needed her more than ever at this point. Getting in over his head. Her ability to make bizarre yet accurate connections would always help him see his way clear. She wanted to know everything about both women's appearance—makeup, clothing, color of hair, body shape, and so on. She asked about perfume, about the décor of the club, how he felt when he walked in, how he felt an hour after he had left. Then she said, "This might sound strange, Guy, but my suspicion is that these women are working together. They are playing Chin and Appell against each other, and are probably doing the same with whoever owns the Copa de Oro as well as the local police commandant. What's in it for them? Control over their own destinies. Power of men, money. The Oriental is the brain, the hooker the contact point. Now, something went wrong with a big drug deal they were involved in, so they've come up with a way to implicate everyone but themselves, of course. Smokescreen. Think about it, Guy. And be careful, honey. I miss you." Fade-out with flashes of gray on the screen. The minispeaker fell silent. Debord powered himself through SI's infinite recombinations, sucking in as much ancillary information as he could. Street and sewage systems maps of Mexicali and Calexico. History of the Chinese population in northern Baja California. Arrest frequencies by the Immigration and Naturalization Service, US Customs, local police agencies. Cooperative agreements between institutions on both sides of the border. International law as applied to environmental issues.

Suddenly, a presence announced itself. For the first time, SI had been breached. The screen went blank; then a complex mandala-like figure appeared in its center and began three-dimensional rotations. "Mr. Debord," said a faintly metallic voice. "Please acknowledge."

Debord hit the "enter" key.

"Thank you. We have some information you may find of interest. Please join us at the Copa tomorrow evening." The spinning mandala then burst apart and disappeared like fireworks burning themselves out.

•   •   •

Because of Bernstein's suspicion, Debord was reluctant to involve any police agencies. The dicks would probably turn on him. He had to go in alone, therefore. He quickly reviewed MIBI procedures for such situations, then entered the club. Both women were there having a drink. He noticed nothing unusual as he approached them. "Good evening, ladies," he said. "May I join you?"

"By all means," said Veronica. "Yes, you are right; we requested your presence here tonight. We have a business proposition for you, Mr. Debord." Debord's biological and electronic systems shot to total alert.

"Please go on," he said calmly.

"A simple exchange. We give you the information you need, and you provide us with a clean copy of the SI program with all its subroutines. Really quite impressive, what little of it we were able to experience."

"You surprise me," confessed Debord carefully, concealing his real surprise. "SI permits very advanced research." He gestured around somewhat vaguely at the dilapidated surroundings.

"Yes. Well then, do we have a deal?"

"Of course," Debord said. "Since you know enough to have cracked SI's crystal wall, you will have learned that operators can send clean copies at their discretion. I therefore suggest that we conclude our arrangement later. Since my time here is limited, I would much prefer to spend it in more enjoyable pursuits." Veronica nodded, smiling.

"Agreed. And now I'll leave you." She extended her hand. "It was a pleasure meeting you, Mr. Debord." She turned and was gone. Rosa's fingers crawled up his thigh.

. . .

While walking back across the line, Debord worked out his strategy. First he knew that he could not communicate with the others at this point. Also any further browsing in SI would undoubtedly be monitored and deciphered. They would be aware of any moves. With this in mind, he returned to his room at the De Anza and packed his equipment. It was 2:30 a.m.

Debord carried his bag down the back staircase, which gave out into the small stage on the east end of the huge lobby. A musty stage curtain concealed his presence. He waited until he was sure no one was in the lobby, then slipped quietly out the side door, which enabled him to make his way to the parking area. The taxi he had ordered was waiting.

"Travelodge, El Centro," he said. Thirty minutes later he was jacked into SI and immediately constructed a fog macro to give himself some room to maneuver. Debord uploaded one last time, ran all the relevant subroutines, then pulled out for a breather. "Time to close the case," he muttered to himself.

With that he dissolved the macro. Almost instantaneously they were there. "Are you ready?" asked Veronica.

"Yes," said Debord. "I've constructed the syntax which will permit you to pull a clean copy of everything off the Paris node. This is the only one we are permitted to use. Gateway codes, user IDs, everything you'll need is in the file titled 'Situation.' Now please reciprocate."

"Of course," Veronica said. "Appell burned Chin on a large cocaine shipment." Bernstein was right again, Debord thought, smiling. "So Chin set him up by infecting the local batch of the state blood bank with a virus. He made certain that a transborder shipment destined for the Calexico Hospital was dirty. Appell is due for a fall. When Chin returns, the blood bank and the governor's office will be indicted. That's how these brutes operate. Rosa and I, however, knew the Calexico police would be baffled and that they would call in help. Of course we had heard of MIBI but had no direct dealings. Your methods are very admirable. With SI now you can run back the virus."

"Why have you told me all this?"

"For our own reasons, we are pulling the plug on Chin and Appell. They've used us for the last time. SI will make it possible for us to break free, finally. We are tired of all the violence and dying. Goodbye."

Debord quickly logged off, whipped his equipment back into its carrying case, and left the Travelodge running. An explosion rocked the wing he had exited before he was across the street.

The bourgeois epoch which wants to give a scientific foundation to history overlooks the fact that this available science needed a historical foundation along with the economy. What hides under the spectacular oppositions is a unity of misery. All aspects of technology serve to produce the great possible passive isolation of individuals as well as the control of these individuals. He raised the glass to his lips as the others waited. Glad to be back in the Latin Quarter. "A toast to MIBI." They all clicked their glasses. Letters blossomed on the screen. Filter. The instrument of enchanters is a pure, living, breathing spirit of the blood codes. Robbers of language. The kind of knowledge that one ought to possess is not derived from the earth nor does it come from the stars. A destiny more grand than anything imaginable. Mystic flesh rose of finished passion traceries staining a bruised sky. Body parts. Political theory river running with by-product. Return.

KIM NEWMAN

SQPR

(1992)

THE WHALE-SHAPE EMERGED like a New Titan Missile from its silo. First the great bearded head broke through the unrippling pseudograss. Then neck, dress tie, two perfect black diamonds against the hot white of the wing collar. Then shoulders, twin submarines coming to the surface. The vast but insubstantial bulk shimmered as it grew. Roy could no longer see the stands through the tridvid image. The holobody towered like the genie in *The Butcher of Bagdad*, bestriding the Docklands Super-Arena. A starfish hand went to the swelling starch of the giant shirtfront as the tenor drew a silent breath, then sound cut in. The illusion was imperfect: the bell-clear voice seemed to come from the air rather than the gaping dark of the holohead's mouth, as if a cloud of invisible spirits were singing "You'll Never Walk Alone" in Italian.

An electronically clocked 200,000 card-carrying fans stood, awed. The song was an atmospheric condition, all-around inescapable. He remembered when they would sing. Derek Leech's tampering with rules and camera angles was cosmetic: the real change was in the crowd. When Roy had been on the pitch, "the shining knight of the Jubilee Season," the crowd had been a tidal wave: roaring and fickle. Now, they were the happy families on the posters: quiet, cheerful, and biddable. They sat on their plastic bum-shaped seats and watched: no cheers, no rude words to familiar tunes, no scuffles. It was eerily as if the stadium were empty. Two hundred thousand in-person people were gravy, a small-change irrelevance. The real money, the real spectators, were camera eyes: on the stands, on the lines, on the shoulders of the In-Close Men. Thanks to Cloud 9 TV, 200 million sets of paying eyes were out there in Television Land, focused on the World Series Cup Final.

Roy could have watched from the VIP drome, with wet bar and celebrity guests (and Grianne), but he chose to be in the dugout with Bev and the lads. It didn't smell of sweat and earth like the old one at Wembley—he didn't even know if there was dirt beneath the textured Day-Glo green—but it made him feel near the game. Commentators labeled him eccentric, Luddite. Since he'd taken over as manager, he'd brought back the old strip, ditching cyber-warrior uniforms in favor of the gear he'd worn twenty years earlier when he'd captained the team to the Double. Boots, socks, shorts, shirts.

He'd even tried, without success, to get Blanch, the In-Close Man, off the squad, alleging the extra man, loyal to C9 not the Rovers, got in the way of play. The ICM wasn't with them for the warm-up. Blanch was with the C9 crew, who strapped him into his suit like a NASA naut, settling the steadicam, with its $10,000 of gyros and balances, on his shoulders. To last the expected hour of play, Blanch needed electro-assist knee- and hip-exojoints. The technicians claimed that if the ICM blacked out they could use body-remotes to keep him standing, running, and broadcasting. Even if Blanch broke his neck, he'd still give out pictures. Roy had expected a genetically engineered zombie, but Mark Blanch was actually a decent kid. If he weren't hunchbacked by high-tech, he might even have enjoyed a game of football.

The song ended and the tenor shivered into a billion light fragments. A double-dozen girls-boys in spandex tube tops and cheek-baring string panties cart-wheeled onto the field. Their extended routine of acrobatic leaps and pelvic thrusts was choreographed by Michael Clark to Andrew Lloyd Webber's "Cup Final Overture." It was symbolic. The cheerleading was a safe-sex orgy, performed with impeccable energy but little actual enthusiasm. No matter how explicit the action, the dancing was corny enough to get past the Family Viewing Observance Society.

Roy felt mildly depressed and anxious, not at all elated. He couldn't even remember how it had been in '77, before the Cup Final or the match that clinched the League. Too many drinks since then. The bookies had Queens Park Rovers at five to one against, and all the pollsters and comment crews went along with them. For the last few months, the team had been giant-killers, but now the breeze was over, and it was time for the giants to strike back, putting poor old Rovers back in their place with a humiliating defeat. The best even die-hard Rovers fans could hope for was a low point spread against. Still, he'd told the lads to give the Pythons a bit of a game.

• • •

The 1998 World Series was the final evolutionary stage of Association Football. Like everything, the game had to change to suit changing times. Leech was almost single-handedly responsible for the successful adaption of soccer to the new media world he, and others like him, had carved out. Gordon Brough, sports editor of the *Comet*, stood up as his boss made an entrance into the VIP drome of the Super-Arena, escorting a small blonde woman with smile lines around her eyes and mouth. Leech wore white, the Prime Minister was in green. Even the remaining rival tabloids didn't dare print rumors about Derek Leech and Morag Duff, and Gordon thought he might be scourged for even thinking the Preem's color was up, a slight flush visible above the low neckline of her evening gown. It was rumored that Leech employees underwent a course of post-hypnotic suggestion during their annual checkup and were conditioned against thinking impure, uncharitable, or heretical thoughts about their lord and master.

The cheerleader squad were still pretending to screw each other in midair out on the floodlit pitch, so the gathered VIPs could turn their attention to the host and his star guest. Ranting Ray Butler, briefly off his commentator's hot spot, crushed a beer can on his close-cropped head, and made a friendly burp at the Preem, who indulgently smiled and ignored him. Arabella Swinton, Butler's cohost for C9's World Series coverage, gushed and tried to curtsey, yard-long legs scissoring. She wore a black net dress about the length of a vest, well-known nipples just concealed behind the weave. A year ago, she'd been a weather bimbo on the Cornflakes Show, but her giggle caught the viewers' fancy; now, without ever having watched a football match all the way through, she was partnering Butler, someone to look at and lech after while Ranting Ray scratched the beer gut that bulged the waistband of his old-fashioned acid shorts and shouted about wankers and wobblies.

Leech introduced Gordon to the Preem, and she chirruped pleasantly at him in a shrill Scots accent. Her Spitting Image puppet was a floppy-eared poodle with a bow in its hair, fondly known as Morag Woof. Since *Spitting Image* became a C9 show, it had been kinder to her than before. Then the Preem was moved on to someone more important—Bernadette from *EastEnders*—and her smile grew to a photo-opportunity crescent. The Irish actress, who might be expected to take more interest in the match than most soap stars, was twinkle-eyed drunk, and only too willing to flash her Number Two expression, usually reserved for the gushy scenes, at the flashless snap-cameras of the journos. She and the Preem looked as if they were having a gossip about the soap character's famously useless missing boyfriend.

A seat was found for Miss Duff, and a drink. Gordon was a few rows behind, after the popstars and soap stars and business heads. The VIP drome had a decent rake, so his view of the pitch wasn't bad, although the large head of the Minister of Trade and Industry was in the way. It would be easier anyway to watch the match on the three wall screens rather than through the panoramic window. Gordon could no longer imagine football without ICM in-the-thick-of-it action footage. It was hard even to remember when the game had been as remote as sheep in a field seen from an airplane, used as everyone was to close-ups of bloody faces, amplified swearing, and POV shots from the goal area. It was also hard to conceive of a match without giggling or ranting, which was as much Gordon's contribution as Leech's.

Realizing just how much was lost from the media profile of the game with the extinction of football hooliganism, Gordon had found Ray Butler, quondam editor of *Britannia Rules* fanzine, and boosted him as the voice of the skinhead-in-the-stands. As crowds cooled down, the game itself heated up, and the comment shows had needed to reflect that. If Simon Hodge—the brown ale-drinking human tank they called "Splodge"—represented the turn-of-the-century player, then Ranting Ray, screaming "you're ganna get ya fakkin head kicked in" at a vicar, was the voice the game needed to take it into the next millennium.

Ray was back in his TV box now, partnered with the grumbling purist Barney Oldcarp—there to represent the football traditionalists, and to get red-faced with apoplexy at the disgusting spectacle—and Arabella was warming up to giggle from remote positions around the field. A soap star handed a cigarette case to a popstar, who swallowed one of the little purple pills it contained and passed it on to the business head on her left. The Preem looked the other way as Leech explained something to her.

• • •

The *Comet* had been a Tory paper until '93 and the appearance from nowhere of Morag Duff, so nonthreateningly cuddly and middle- or slightly-right-of-the-road that she made Neil Kinnock look like Mao Tse-tung. With the Soviet Union replaced by something resembling the Austro-Hungarian Empire, Miss Duff seemed more like a continuation of Thatcher than One Minute Major had done. The United Kingdom had got used to nanny-knows-best government. Shortly after her assumption of power and position, the Preem had gone into one of Derek Leech's sealed rooms for a conference, for all the world as if she were the supplicant and he the head of state. After that, the *Comet* and C9 had come around to support her, and treaties had been struck, apportioning additional satellite channels to Leech Enterprises, allowing it to blossom into a potentatial monopoly on the Pan-European electronic media. The word "socialist" had not been used in public by Morag Duff during the entire span of her leadership.

On the screens, Ranting Ray and Boring Barney were reviewing Splodge's recent record. Aggravated assault charges brought by the Third Lanark goalie had been settled out of court, but Nigel Matheson, right wing for Stansted Bombers, was still alleging Splodge had broken his arm during an illegal action in the Fifth Round. Litigation was postponed until after the final. Splodge's cover of Elton John's "Saturday Night's Alright (for Fighting)" was riding high in the C9 PTV charts, and Ray played snippets of it to annoy Barney Oldcarp, a die-hard who liked to point out that three years ago everything Splodge did on the pitch would earn him an early shower not a hit record. The veins in Barney's neck were scarlet lines creeping around his chin, and his whole face shone with a high-definition glow of righteous frustration.

A significant but small portion of the football audience agreed with Barney and his presence kept them watching even as they disapproved. It had even been suggested, in the non-Leech press, that Barney didn't mind either way about the state of football but got so worked up because he was pulling down as enormous a salary as Ranting Ray and Giggling Arabella.

The first thing Leech had done to soccer was wipe the slate of the Super-League and start again. Most of the old clubs were in deep recession holes and open to a Leech Enterprises buyout. The strongest survived and other sides formed according to advertising demographics. The UK was still the locus, but it had been prudent to include Pan-Europe and the USA in the World Series to increase revenue. Once 90 percent of the teams in the UK had been relegated to the amateur local entertainment status they'd always deserved, Leech had re-organized the whole game to suit C9.

Looking at a video of the 1977 cup final, when Roy Robartes had been center forward for Rovers, was like seeing some weird mutation of Australian Rules or American Football. It was impossible not to FF through the dull midfield action now eliminated by shrinking the pitch and cutting down teams to nine players, plus ICM. Ninety minutes of playing time seemed to stretch on forever: now, matches were three twenty-minute halves, with two commercial breaks. Goals were a yard wider, with individual cash prizes for scoring players. Uniform regulations had been abolished. Piffling rules about offside and body contact eased up. Referees were professional. Gambling was a systemized part of the television coverage, with direct access numbers flashed across the screen.

In the last two years, British football had made more money than in the previous fifty. The ratings for the World Series so far had been almost level with *EastEnders*, and the final was forecasted to outdraw even the most popular soaps by 20 percent.

Gordon called over a waiter and got a refill of Bushmills, wondering why he was so keen for the whole thing to be over so he could get to the party afterward. He could hardly remember the name of the team scheduled to hammer Rovers into the pseudograss, let alone bother to care about the score. The screens went black as the main camera swung to the players' tunnel.

•   •   •

"Did you bring your slingshot?" Bev asked as the Detroit Pythons lumbered onto the field in calculated slow motion. Their theme music—"Entrance of the Knights" from Prokofiev's *Romeo and Juliet*—boomed out in Danny Elfman's arrangement.

Roy knew then that he should have stayed home and watched the game on his wall screen.

At the head of the Pythons, Simon Hodge strode like a colossus. Huge enough to suggest special effects. Splodge was armored with the Pythons' strip, chain-mail layered over his massive chest, face-shielding helmet bulbous like the head of an alien being. Roy had heard Splodge's next record would be a remix of Tennessee Ernie Ford's "Sixteen Tons," and he seemed to concentrate every ounce of it into his man-shape, a collapsed star hugging mass to its shrunken heart.

The Pythons didn't jog, they slouched. But Roy knew they were capable of incredible speed, amazing skill, unbelievable violence. If there were still such a thing as injury time, most Pythons matches would displace the rest of the evening's television schedule.

Splodge separated from the pack and crossed to the center of the pitch. His footfalls must have been amplified, for they sounded like sledgehammer blows.

Bev tried to make a funny comment, but it was no good. Roy knew the lads would feel as he did, as if each footfall was a blow to the stomach. He became aware of his jaw dropping.

At the center of the pitch, Splodge raised his arms over his head. A broken-toothed mouth opened beneath his visor, and a yell exploded from his helmet, filling the Super-Arena. It was a fi-fi-fo-fum declaration, a Viking berserker battle cry, a prayer to the dark gods of football.

Roy breathed profanity.

Then, hesitantly, without a signal, the lads filtered out onto the field, picking up speed, jogging to their positions. The Splodge yell was still dying as Roy shouted out good luck.

•   •   •

Roy's World Series run had started where the rest of his ventures ended, in an iron-framed cot.

When, at the peak of his career, a knee injury put him out of the game, he sank his savings into boutiques. Just as Punk gave way to New Romantic, a still-limping Roy was investing the best part of a million pounds in flared silver spangle trousers, muslin shirts with floppy sleeves and shoulder-wide collars, road sign-shaped paisley ties, space boots with seven-inch platform heels and rainbow-knit synthetic fiber tank tops. He wore his hair like Rod Stewart and married Grianne, the Irish chanteuse who'd once scored "null points" on the Eurovision Song Contest. He'd been too busy putting 'em in the back of the net and swigging champagne out of trophies to notice things had changed since Jason King went off television. He'd been tipsy, overextended, and "over the moon" when Thatcher succeeded Callaghan in '79; but he was drunk, broke, and "sick as a parrot" when the fleet left for the Falklands in '82. Grianne left him for Tarquin Crumple, a bearded quizmaster to whose Buttons she'd played Cinderella at the Bristol Hippodrome in the '81 panto season. Roy learned of his wife's desertion in a pub, when he happened to notice a front-page story in the *Daily Comet*, the tabloid acorn from which Derek Leech's media Yggdrasil was growing.

The receivers took over Chic 'Tiques, and Roy scrabbled around for a sponsorship deal, becoming front man for a German cosmetics company, Herr Hair. He starred in a series of ads, rubbing Mighty Mousse into his scalp in a changing room then cheekily tarting up his chest hair. One morning, a swatch of hair came out in the brush, making a triangle-shaped bald spot that extended from his forehead to the apex of his skull. It turned out to be a reaction to Herr Hair products. His chest burned blotchy for years, and his lawyers never made a case against the company. He hadn't paid for the cases of Mighty Mousse in his basement. And Herr Hair noticed loopholes in their on-pack instructions, warning against excessive use.

Satellite TV started to take off and Grianne's boyfriend became host of *I Bet You Feel a Right One*, the highest-rated show on the P9 Light Channel. Tarquin promptly bedded Stuka, the jaw-heavy girl in the topless swimsuit who was forever turning up in innocent people's baths, workplaces, and fridges. A stone too heavy to tour as Nancy in *Oliver!*, Grianne moved back into their heavily mortgaged home in Esher. Throughout the '80s, they appeared regularly in the *Comet*: having screaming matches with Oliver Reed in nightclubs, pluckily getting into shrinking tracksuits to raise funds. At one point before taking out family membership in Alcoholics Anonymous, he was heating Mighty Mousse and draining off the liquid for its 0.5 alcohol content. At another, he and Grianne tag-mud-wrestled Jimmy Savile and Anneka Rice for homeless children.

After his mostly successful drying-out, he was approached by Sidcup Startlers, a struggling Third Division team, and asked to become manager. On *The Last Resort*, he told Jonathan Ross his knee was fixed and that he planned to select himself as a useful midfield player. First time out, he managed a draw, and a few of the pundits who turned up to see the legend in action were mildly kind. In the *Comet*, though, Ray Butler, "the angry man of football," devoted his hundred-word leader to Eskimo OAPs and ice floes. Next Sidcup lost five–one. Roy celebrated by punching a *Comet* photographer and tripping over a cocktail waitress, wrenching his trick knee forever. Then came the formation of the first of the short-lived Super-Leagues: the fifteen most successful clubs locked into profitable television contracts, 80 percent of the rest plunged into a Dark Age of financial disaster and pathetic obscurity. In three years, Roy led Sidcup down to the Southern League and bankruptcy. "One good thing," said someone on *The Mary Whitehouse Experience*, "at least Salman Rushdie can do with the company."

By then, there was a Labour government, and Kinnock had resigned in favor of Morag Duff, the first single woman—"spinster" some said—to hold the office of Prime Minister. Association Football was practically a wholly owned subsidiary of Derek Leech Enterprises, struggling through its metamorphosis into the primary televised sport of the turn of the century. When Sidcup went down for the last time, Roy checked into a clinic for an urgent rehabilitation. Strapped into a bed and biting back his own puke, head in a fixed position so he was forced to watch C9, Roy struggled with the worst his nightmares could throw at him. During the *Animal Fun Hour*, a popular late-night "adult" novelty show, he touched bottom, scraping the base of existential despair. When he got free, he vowed to kill himself.

· · ·

"We'll beat Leech," Bev told Roy, over and over. "We'll change the storyline, we'll rewrite the headlines."

Now, with the £50,000-a-year referee raising his saxophone-sized whistle, Roy was unconvinced.

For the last few months, as Rovers won matches, at first scrappily and then with confidence, Roy had been soaring. He hadn't thought about drink until this moment.

Now, as the shrill tone sounded out through the Super-Arena, he wanted a treble scotch, and then another, and another, and . . .

• • •

On *Shower Talk*—a C9 chat show where the guests wore towels and sat in a steam room surrounded by beefy and bruised ornamental naked men—Jimmy Greaves did a moving piece on Roy's courageous struggle with the bottle, and offered to forward any messages of support to the clinic. Ray Butler, promoted to the post of C9's sport pundit, chipped in with his own fist-waving salute to Roy Robartes, although he wound up with his customary rant of "Rovers was a crap team, and Robartes was a crap player." Every morning, an orderly came to read aloud the letters that arrived. There were always well-wishers, but he knew—from the awkward pause between a letter being torn open and the hurried precis of a formulaic message of cheer—there were many grudge-holding Sidcup fans out there too. Perhaps one of them would do the job for him, slipping out of a crowd with a bread knife or a nail gun.

Meanwhile Grianne shed excess poundage and won the role of Bernadette, the single Mum who sacrifices all for her slut of a daughter Corinne, on *EastEnders*. The soap made a successful return to the ratings, transferring from the ailing BBC—over 32 percent of television households had disconnected the terrestrial channels—to C9's Drama Stream, where it sat between *Coronation Street* and *Neighbours* in the early evenings. Leech's ownership of all three series allowed for popular storyline crossovers. When Corinne ran off to Australia with Jack Duckworth, Bernadette was able to bribe a struggling ex-character from *The Bill*—canceled after the controversial Clapham Crack War episodes—to turn private eye and track her down to Ramsay Street. After a personal meeting, and subsequent photo session, with Derek Leech, Grianne sued Roy for divorce and moved in with a twenty-one-year-old model best known for a swimming-trunks advert. She told the *Comet* about her orgasm secrets and fronted a bestselling diet video.

From his bed, as food was pumped into him, Roy followed the soap and cringed whenever Bernadette railed about the swine who'd fathered Corinne. They'd never had children but he knew Grianne was thinking of him when she read her lines. Useless Brendan, who never appeared, was the most hated man on television. Terry Wogan always made a "Useless Brendan" joke during his two-hour-long chat-and-news show on C9's Heavy Channel. At Prime Minister's Question Time, Morag Duff called the Leader of the Opposition "a right Useless Brendan" and the chamber gave her a standing ovation. All the time, Roy thought of ways to kill himself. The rope seemed best. He had some at home and the light fittings in the hallway should be strong enough to support him. He could fix the noose to the chandelier and jump off the first-floor landing.

Then, despite the high security, Bev Ellis got through to see him, and he started the climb back up. She had written to him first, then started to visit. She volunteered to help with his physiotherapy. For the first time in years, Roy felt free from pain.

He didn't know how she'd done it, but Bev had got him his Series Run. Rovers had gone through seven managers in three seasons, the latest resigning after the *Comet* alleged he took an unhealthy interest in the career and person of a twelve-year-old glamour model. At some point, Bev had made her petition not to the Board of Directors but, cannily, to Derek Leech. As in everything, Leech was concerned not with whether it was a good idea but whether it would make good copy. Pitching a project to him, Roy knew, was like suggesting a plot development to the script editor of a soap. When Leech decided to run with the Return of Roy Robartes, the story was set in stone.

"Giggle-gurgle-giggle," went Arabella Swinton into the camera, "play has, um, started. That big bloke has, um, hit someone, and given him a nasty knock. Someone did that to my car last week. They never caught the git, though. The dent cost seven hundred and fifty pounds to have beaten out. Criminal, um. Oh, there's the ball. Someone's kicked it awfully hard. Lot of stitching in a ball, you know. Teeny-tiny-teensy stitches. That man was supposed to stop it doing that, wasn't he? Um, yes. I think that's a goal. Someone has scored a goal. I'm sure we'll have, um, more on that in a bit. One side has one goal, and the others don't have anything. I bet they're tad upset about that."

• • •

One–nil down after ten minutes. Trav Billings, Rovers' center forward, felt the disadvantage in his gut like an undigested stone. It had been a typical Splodge goal, the Pythons hammering the defense out of the way with body blows then escorting the ball under armed guard. Splodge lazily booting it into the net while two rhino-plated goons pinned the Rovers' goalie, Jack Dorothy, down.

Trav, twenty years old, swore his parents named him after the De Niro character in *Taxi Driver*, but the *Comet* had revealed last week that his first name was not Travis but Travolta. His Mum had been obsessed with the old actor in *Look Who's Talking*. Two days ago, during a practice, the loudspeakers had started pouring out the soundtrack albums of *Saturday Night Fever* and *Grease*, with new lyrics dubbed over the old songs. "You Can Tell by the Way I Walk That I'm a Total Spaz," "Hopelessly Demoted to Spew," "Right Feeble, Right Feeble, Right Feeble, Right Fee-bull," "You're a Bit of a Cunt, Ooo-Oo-Oo." It had been impossible not to recognize the wind-up tactics, and indeed the voice, of Simon Hodge.

Splodge would pick on one man in any team the Pythons were set to play, and mount a campaign of harassment and humiliation, issuing public taunts about their personal habits, sexual persuasions, physical appearance, and genetic heritage. He usually picked the player most likely to be a threat, so Trav guessed the treatment was a compliment. It was still a pain. Splodge claimed Trav was so ape-ugly that when he cried, the tears would run over his forehead and down the back of his head just to avoid his face. When he said ape-ugly, Splodge meant black.

With an early lead, the Pythons opted to stand around and show off, letting Rovers wear themselves out running around. In the old days, these tactics might have made for a boring game, but the Pythons were showmen, and enjoyed throwing in a few borderline illegal moves, making slapstick out of foul play. Evans and Cardille were already limping, and Jobson had a cut above his eye that was dribbling blood down his face, with both the ICMs jostling around him for the best view of the wound.

Evans, who was being ignored since Splodge had oops-excuse-me rammed him, intercepted a lackluster Python pass and began dribbling the ball down the field. Trav could sense the move coming and picked up speed. This was the kind of breakout point he had been trained for.

Roy had told the lads to concentrate on the old-fashioned skills. They were the point of the game and also showed up the Pythons' weaknesses. Since Roy had come to the club, there'd been an emphasis on what he called "proper football."

A Python got in Evans's way, arms outstretched a yard either side of his tubby Kevlar-swathed body. Evans, pain in his face, lurched to one side, momentarily losing the ball, but regaining it with a deft flick of his boot. Blanch, the Rovers ICM, was running backward in front of Evans, trying to keep him in focus.

Trav looked up at the giant screens and saw how much agony Evans was going through as he ran. Behind him, blobbily out of focus, were three advancing juggernauts. The suits slowed them down, but when they caught up, there would be serious GBH. Some things legal on a football pitch would get you locked up back in the world.

Trav found himself alone in the Pythons' goal area, looking at the blank visor of spring-heeled Jacnoth, their goalie. Light lines flickered under the gray shield, suggesting some automated vision-augmentation input device. Trav turned to look back.

Evans couldn't keep going, but he wouldn't have to.

Trav was there for the pass. Roy had taken them through every possible situation so often that it was an instinctive move. Evans, his honor won, sacrificed the glory to a teammate with a final burst of strength, kicking the ball into the air so it arced over Blanch and Gorgo Brzezinzki, the Pythons' fullback, aimed straight for Trav's head.

He jumped into the air and connected with the ball.

In Roy's day, Trav's header might have bounced off the sidebar back into play, but the posts had been moved since then. Even spring-heels couldn't get Jacnoth there to save.

The score was one–one.

Trav turned, a spurt of excitement dying in his heart as he saw Evans on the turf, a couple of Pythons piled on top of him, thumping and kicking, grinding him down with their bodyweight. He looked up to the screen, hoping for the instant replay. The whistle sounded, and the screen dissolved to a commercial break.

"Fakkin useless fakkin kants," Ray Butler ranted, "fakkin wankers fakkin scored. Useless, useless, useless."

• • •

Beverly Robartes Ellis was born during the 1977 Cup Final. According to her dad, she emerged just as Roy Robartes, the Shining Knight, slammed home the injury-time goal that drew Rovers level. And she first cried when he completed his hat trick in extra time, winning the FA Cup. Dad claimed she made a tiny fist and baby-talked "we are the champions." It had been the greatest day of Stan Ellis's life.

Her earliest memories were matches: tumultuous crowds all around, cheering in triumph as Rovers scored again. She swore she could remember Roy in action, although he played his last game for Rovers before she could crawl. Clearer were her memories of the Relegation Season, as a succession of formerly humiliated foes trampled Rovers again and again. Without Roy, the heart went out of the team.

In the '80s, after Dad's stroke, Bev trudged every other Saturday to the home game and quietly watched the last tatters of Rovers' glory whip away in rain and wind. At thirteen, after a four–one loss, she was assaulted on the Tube station nearest the ground, by two knot-headed youths wearing Rovers scarves. A list-less scattering of downcast fans didn't intervene and she was forced to defend herself, disabling the pissheads with a thigh-driven blow to the knee and a coil-sprung knee into the groin.

She stopped going to matches, but turned up in Rovers kit for the first prac-tice of her school team. Thanks to Bill Forsyth and Dee Hepburn, it was no longer unusual for girls to play football. Jamila Saunders, a fifth former with a figure like the Incredible Hulk, was the regular goalie for North End Compre-hensive. And Helena Geoffreys, whose legs figured prominently in the auto-erotic fancies of most of her teammates, dominated the midfield until she dropped soccer to get into interpretive dance. However, the school's side was drawn from pupils three or four years older and, although she was a full foot taller than most kids her own age, she still wound up described as "stringy." She didn't get selected for the team then, but two years—and several mashed lips, open-to-the-bone knees, and severe muscle strains—later, she found herself as first substitute, then as North End's center half, then as a striker. Then, a school leaver, she had tried out for Rovers' Women.

All the clubs had all-girl shadows and, with the reorganization, the women players were theoretically available for any given match. Several times, the non-serious clubs—like Earnshaw's Northern, which existed solely to advertise beer—had fielded women, mainly to get attention in matches they were certain to lose. Goals were now less important than ad revenue and entertaining losers could rake in more than tedious winners, a lesson learned hard by several formerly dominant sides. Bev, while she was a major force in the women's team, refused to be token girlie in the first side. Rovers was in terrible shape, barely treading the shark-filled waters outside the Ultra League, shut out of prime time, relegated to late-night slots on low-wattage cable channels. Every Sunday, especially after a defeat, Bev expected to learn that Rovers was this week's club to be sucked under and dissolved, assets stripped and spread, stadium redeveloped as an evangelist's open-air temple.

The Ultra League was sealed tight as a cat's arsehole, but the World Series had a chink. The top seven UL teams were automatically eligible, but the eighth spot was for an out side, a carrot for all the flounderers, to keep the UL gladiators from turning complacent. Expulsion from the UL was like being kicked out of Eden, a fall into acid and acrimony from which no team ever recovered. If an out side could make a decent Series run, it had a chance to slip into the UL. And UL sides were growing soft inside the glitz, cocooned by wealth and predictable opponents, leaving them open to a hungry challenge. But Rovers still needed a boost to make it through the preliminaries. And Bev remembered the hero of her early childhood.

• • •

The adverts lasted five minutes, barely enough to get the players off the field and sluice out their mouths with the Official Orange Juice Substitute of the World Series. Roy had Bev, a qualified first-aider, check on Evans, Cardille, and Jobson. He told the lads where the Pythons were weak. And he told them what to watch for. Trav Billings nodded, shrugging off congrats. There was no elation, no overconfidence. That was good. The lads had learned.

When Roy, bleary but sober, turned up for the first practice, Rovers had been a shambles. A collection of adequate players, they hadn't been anything like a team. Having only just pulled himself into shape, Roy was merciless with them. Someone had renamed the Rovers Ground, putting up a notice which read GLADIATOR TRAINING SCHOOL.

With Bev to give him advice, Roy channeled his energies into the team, cutting loose the deadwood, and bringing forward potential stars. Trav, who could be one of the greats, had been buried in the subs, but Roy brought him on. And the others rallied. At first, they fought him. Then, they fought the matches.

Now Roy would trust Rovers to invade Normandy, rob a Turkish Museum, or stage a Broadway musical. There was already a drama-documentary in preproduction, although Roy assumed it would be canceled if Rovers boringly lost the final. The show would only play if the last act worked out.

Standing to one side, a technician tinkering with his transmission, was Blanch. Roy saluted the In-Close Man. There was no point fighting the changes on a person-to-person level.

The whistle went off, and the lads piled back onto the pitch, hut-hut-hutting like marines.

"End thet, I thenk, shews the kind of football we've come tew expect from the Rovers under Roy Robartes," Barney Oldcarp droned through his nose, "with Johnno Jobson, pluckily returning tew the pitch efter a terrible enjury, delivering one of the textbook gewls of the game. Stanley Metthews would heve been prowd tew see sech a display ev old-fashioned skell end dexterity, a vindication ev teamwork, training end thet extra touch of derring-do whech makes a good player great. Whet do yew think, Raymonde?"

In the background, Ray Butler had his fingers down his throat.

"Tew-one, advantage the Rovers," smugged Barney.

• • •

Bev watched Roy watching the game. For the first time, she thought the Rovers might take it all the way. At the beginning, she'd just hoped to see a dignified last stand. If they went down with enough heroism, they might latch into a Little Big Horn–Rorke's Drift–Scott of the Antarctic reputation, courageous individuals better-remembered than the anonymous hordes who actually won. Now, as the Pythons were hitting back hard, going all-out for the equalizer, it was as if maybe the Rovers might turn back the foe. In school, she'd been taught that although Amundsen actually found the South Pole first and got back alive, it didn't really count because he ate his own huskies. Even if the Pythons managed to draw level and then win, it wouldn't mean anything according to the rules Roy was playing by. The rules that, on a cosmic scale, counted more than the ratings and the income.

Splodge was the sort of player who'd tear off a leg of sled-dog and wolf it raw, washed down with a vat of baked beans and brown ale. Now, he was shoving his way through the Rovers defense, battering his way to the spot from which he scored all his goals, waiting for his stooges to arrive with the ball. Barry Cardille, still nursing his first-half bruises, was marking his man, and got there before the Splodgster.

The ref was looking the other way as the Python nutted Cardille. Michelle Tenney, glam goalie for Rovers Women, had offered to sleep with the ref, but Roy had gratefully turned down her kind suggestion. Now, Bev wondered if that mightn't have been as bad an idea as it had sounded. When the ref was looking, Cardille had staggered to his feet. Splodge stood grinning over him, forearms bulging like Popeye's, a red trickle on his own forehead. Cardille stood back as Splodge wiped his cut on his hand, looking down in puzzlement at his own blood. Then, in a bid for a Best Actor BAFTA, Splodge was on his knees, yelling in simulated agony.

The ref was jogging over, and the Pythons' paramedics were sprinting across the field, personal sirens whining. The ref's whistle stopped play. Splodge was combining the deaths of Olivier in *Richard III*, Beatty in *Bonnie and Clyde*, Cassavetes in *The Fury*, and Julia Roberts in *Saddambusters!* Gradually, he recovered from his mortal wound, and by the time he had to take the penalty, he was as well as he'd ever be.

Bev looked at Roy, who was leaning forward, intent on the action. A colorless official was by his side, waiting to deliver a message. Roy took the curl of fax paper, but didn't read it. The official waited.

A Splodge penalty had once been monitored and found to be actually "faster than a speeding bullet." The last man to save one had broken both his hands, and seen his side lose four–one.

As the ball came at him, Jack Dorothy, a long-armed spiderman, stretched out a flap of hand, and made a fist. He connected, and punched the leatherette, reversing its momentum. Even the sedate newstyle crowd cheered politely, and Splodge was seized with an attack of Tourette's Syndrome.

The half ended, and C9 cut to the ads. Bev looked around for Roy, but he was gone. There was a crumple of paper by the bench.

The lads came back to the dugout, hyper from their showing on the field. Bev picked up the paper and had a chance to look at it—it was something from Roy's ex-wife—before the players were around her, asking questions, soliciting congratulations, needing advice.

She knew the speech, so she delivered it as best she could: teamwork, footwork, aggressive-but-fair play.

Where was Roy?

. . .

She was all over him, tears and caresses, apologies and solicitations. It was her voice he had fallen in love with in the first place, and, even after everything, it still got through to him.

"Grianne, Grianne, Grianne," he kept saying, trying to interrupt her flow, still finding the sound of her name seductive.

She kept at him.

It was an invitation to come in out of the cold, to join her in the world Derek Leech had made. By combining all the soaps, all the sports, all the news channels and all the dramas, Cloud 9 had made one hit television show of everything. And Grianne was a star, as much as Splodge or Morag Duff. If he would only do one little thing, Roy could be too.

He would win: secure fame and fortune; a place in television history; a position exalted over Butler, Barney, and Arabella; an ongoing role in the only circus that counted. He would win back his wife.

Grianne kissed him, and he felt her tears on his cheek.

It was as if Corinne had come back to Bernadette on her knees, as if Useless Brendan had laid down his life for his family.

All Roy had to do was lose.

He could do it. He could do it invisibly. A few instructions to the lads. In-character instructions, about rules and proprieties. He could leave holes in the defense.

He could lose, and win.

As Grianne begged him to come back, begged him to play out Leech's master-script, Roy wondered if she could see a camera behind him.

If he were to accept, would a ton of green sludge pour out of Heaven onto his head? And would Tarquin Crumple pop out of a toilet bowl, wink, and say "I bet you feel a right one!"

"There's money, too," Grianne said. "From the bookies, from Leech. More money than you could believe."

Miles away, the whistle shrilled. And suddenly Roy felt incredibly tired.

"You could have it all."

• • •

Derek Leech wasn't paying much attention to the match. He was flirting with the Preem. From where he was sitting, Gordon could only really see Morag Duff nodding. Leech was in shadows, eyes sometimes reflecting.

Leech was only seen in full light on television or in his papers. In person, he always seemed to have shadows around him, like the character in the strip that ran in the *Argus*, his heaviest paper. Gordon heard Leech wanted C9 to do a *Dr. Shade* TV series, maybe with Jeremy Irons or Jonathan Pryce.

Occasionally, Leech would check the wall screen—with its permanent read-out of time to go and score—but mainly he was interested in the Preem, whispering to her, laughing with her. Gordon had the impression he was looking at Government in Action.

A soap star returned to her seat, makeup adjusted, and started following the play. Gordon remembered who Grianne had been married to, and wondered if C9 had thought to book a sound bite from her. A human-interest angle would pique the interest of the wives and girlfriends coerced into watching the Final, and Leech always promised advertisers balanced demographics.

For a while, Gordon had thought the Rovers might have a chance. But they had come out very scrappily at the beginning of the third half, and seemed to be playing a nervously defensive game, as if waiting for the big bullies to come and snatch back their lollipops.

Apart from Jacnoth, every player on the field was clustered around the Rovers goal area. As the time clock counted down, the Rovers' lead seemed more and more fragile.

Bev noticed just how stretched-thin Roy was. He kept relaying "never let up" messages to the pitch, but he also seemed to be holding something back. When Brzezinzki scored for the Pythons, Bev felt her stomach turn. With three minutes on the timer, the match would probably go to penalties. And it was too much to ask for Jack Dorothy to save two Splodge dum-dums in one evening.

• • •

Roy thought drink-drink-drink-drink. But his mouth was dry. He could still feel Grianne's tongue, could still hear her voice.

Don't be a Useless Brendan, he told himself.

The Pythons were lined up for another assault as the teams assembled in the center for play to resume, and the Rovers looked like sheep grazing in front of a mile-wide combine harvester. The Pythons would be looking to stampede in another goal.

When had this ever been just a game?

It was time for his last signal.

He thought again of Grianne, and wondered if he were doing the right thing.

Demi-seconds flickered on the monitor's time code, dropping away like hour-glass grains.

Roy stood up, hugged Bev, and made the signal.

Trav, standing by the ball, was ready. This could make up for everything.

The ball was back in play, and Splodge was about to blitzkrieg him into the pseudograss.

Trav, not thinking about how smart a move he was being ordered to make, got his boot-toe under the leather and made the long pass, the impossible play. Roy Robartes might be old-fashioned, but this was an innovation.

Splodge slammed into him, and Trav heard a bone breaking. He was out of this game. And what he had just done had either won or lost it.

He felt psychic waves of astonishment pouring down, and jagged pain shattering through his body. He hauled himself up, and watched Splodge chase the man with the ball. If the ref saw Trav was injured, play would be stopped. And that couldn't happen.

"Well, no one's ever done thet before," Barney droned. "Et's legal, ev course, bet . . ."

"Is that allowed?" Arabella giggled.

"Fakk, fakk, fakk," Ray ranted.

• • •

Bev was torn. Usually, she watched only the pitch—like Roy—but now she had to look at the dugout monitor.

Of course, the studio director had cut to the In-Close Man. The picture shifted as Blanch barreled down the pitch, ball almost dead center. An ICM had scored for Midland Athletic once, when a ball bounced off his steadicam-helmet and qualified as a header by default, but he'd deserved and got about as much credit as a cushion does for a match-winning snooker shot.

Blanch was well ahead of the Pythons, and Roy had men spread out behind him, running in a fan. Splodge had been too busy disabling Trav to be there, and none of the hunter-killers were exactly sprinter material.

"This is crazy," Bev said.

Roy just nodded.

Blanch dribbled the ball. The weight of his machine must seem like an agony now. But, undoubtedly, he was the fittest man on the squad, a weightlifter on wheels.

The ICM was in the Pythons' goal area. The defenders, who had been expecting another scramble for the Rovers' end, were with the pack closing in like hungry dinosaurs.

He had a clear run. Blanch shrugged free of his equipment, which fell from his shoulders and crashed expensively. The camera didn't cut out, and provided a perfect sideways view of Jacnoth as he dived. Blanch's shot slipped past the goalie, and everyone was shouting. Like in the old days.

Rovers men were in a ring around Blanch, fighting off the Pythons. Roy was laughing and punching the air. Splodge started kicking the fallen camera, and the screen showed his boot coming in, then a brief spiral crack in the lens and deadscreen flicker, before cutting to a frankly stunned Barney Oldcarp and Arabella Swinton.

"I told you Blanch was a good kid," Roy said.

A minute later, the match was over.

• • •

At the reception afterward, Roy told interviewers he was over the moon. Actually, he felt as if he had died and woken up in an afterlife where he had no idea what to do.

He expressed concern over Trav Billings's injury, and said the club were considering criminal assault charges against Simon Hodge. He agreed with the citing of Mark Blanch as Man of the Match. He confirmed that he was engaged to Bev Ellis, and admitted he had never worked out just how much younger than him she was.

Morag Duff shook his hand, and he wondered if she was a Stepford Wife. There didn't seem to be anyone inside the poodle mannerisms. He was photographed with the Preem, a collection of soap faces in the background, Arabella draped around his waist.

In his hand was his first drink in nearly two years. Champagne.

He held the flute to his lips, relishing the taste and the bubbles, and took the tiniest sip.

Grianne hugged and congratulated him, showing her best side to the cameras, then faded back into the celeb crowd. He pulled Bev, who had found a dress from somewhere, into the picture, and touched champagne to her lips, then kissed her.

A man moved through the crowds, smile advancing like a shark's fin. The man whose offer—relayed contemptibly through Grianne—he had torn up and thrown away.

Probably, this was the end of it all. He might have won, but now he would fall from grace, be expelled from the garden. It was all over, and it didn't matter.

So he threw his drink in Derek Leech's face.

• • •

"We don't need that," Leech told the offline editor. "Wipe it."

Gordon saw the image freeze, just as Roy Robartes prepared to toss his glass, and then the whole thing scrambled.

Leech smiled.

"It didn't fit."

It was unusual for him to take an interest in the minutiae of edited highlights. But this, Gordon suspected, was special.

The key sequences had already been picked out. The goals, of course. The penalty save. Billings on his feet with a broken leg. Splodge swearing. Blanch's camera cutting out.

And the backstage stuff: the training footage, the earlier heats, the temptations, the fortitude. Arabella showing her legs, Barney drawing diagrams of the goals. Ranting Ray being (literally) sick (as a parrot) at the reception.

On one screen, Roy was resisting his ex-wife's blandishments. On another, he was making his secret signals to Blanch and Billings.

Gordon knew Leech was pleased Rovers had won. Boring Barney was talking about a triumph for the old over the new, a revival of traditional British virtues, and the value of skill over schmaltz. But Leech, no matter how much he might be associated with what he had made of the game, was best pleased this way. It made a better story, better copy, a fresher twist in the plotline.

As Roy resisted Grianne, standing firm against her offers, Leech smiled.

"You know, Brough," he said, deigning to notice Gordon, "nothing sells like integrity."

That had been said before, Gordon suspected. That was how Leech usually worked. He lived in shadows and spoke in scripted dialogue. One day he would vanish in reality and appear only on television. Somewhere, the Prime Minister was waiting for Leech. And he was busy picking angles, suggesting cuts, rewriting voice-overs. A functionary came in and confirmed that the World Series Final had indeed outdrawn everything else in the ratings. Nothing pulled in more viewers, not even the top-rated soaps.

"Everything's a soap," Leech said. And Gordon had to agree.

PEPE ROJO

GRAY NOISE

(1996)

Translated from the Spanish by Andrea Bell

IN MY ROOM in the early morning, when everything is quiet, I can hear a buzz-ing sound. It begins between my eyes and extends down my neck. It's like a whisper, and I concentrate, trying to make out the words that sound inside my head, knowing in advance that they won't make any sense. They don't say a thing. The murmur is like that vibration you can feel but can't place when you're in a mall right when all the stores start to turn on their lights and get ready for the day. Even when people arrive that vibration is still there, but you can't feel it anymore. My head is like a vacant mall. The sound of empty space. The vibra-tion that expectations produce. The whisper of a desire you can't name.

Believe me, I'm used to the buzz. I'm also used to my heart beating, to my brain stringing together ideas that have no direction, to my lungs taking in air in order to expel it later. The body is an absurd machine.

Sometimes the noise lulls me to sleep at night. Sometimes it doesn't let me sleep, it keeps me awake, staring at a yellow indicator light on the ceiling that tells me I'm on standby.

I transmitted for the first time when I was eighteen years old and desperate to find some news item, anything. So I took to walking the streets, following people whose faces seemed like TV fodder. I felt like a bum with a mission. I'd had a little money left over after the operation and I could enjoy the luxury of eating wherever I wanted, so I went to one of those fancy restaurants on the top floor of a building tall enough to give you vertigo. After having a drink I walked toward the bathroom, trying to find an exit out onto the terrace. I wanted a few shots of the city for my personal file. I opened several doors without finding anything. Just like my life, I thought with a cynicism I sometimes miss. The rooftop terraces of all buildings are alike. A space filled with geometric forms, in shades of gray. Someone should make a living painting horizontal murals on the roofs of terraces with messages for the planes that fly over this city every five minutes. Though I don't know what the messages would be. What can you say to someone about to arrive except "welcome"? It's been a long time since anyone felt welcome in this city.

Someone was jumping over an aluminum fence on the opposite side of the terrace. Maybe it was my lucky day and he was going to commit suicide. I activated the "urgent" button inside my thigh, hoping I wasn't wrong. A little later a green indicator lit up my retina, telling me that I was on some station's monitors, though not yet on the air. The guy was standing on a cornice, looking down. He was dark and stubby; his back was to me so I couldn't see his face. I jumped over the fence and looked down, establishing the scene for the viewers; it could be edited later. The dark man turned and saw me, got nervous, and jumped. Right then a red light went on in my eye and I heard a voice tainted with static say in my ear, "You're on the air, pal!"

That night I found out that the man was named Veremundo, a fifty-four-year-old gym teacher. The suicide note they found on his body said he was tired of being useless, of feeling insignificant from dawn to dusk, and that the worst thing about his suicide was knowing it wouldn't affect a soul.

Suicides always say the same thing.

• • •

When it is impossible to set up an external camera to situate the action, the reporter should obtain a few establishing shots—"long shots"—to ensure that the space in which the action takes place is logical to the viewers. Reporters should prepare fixed shots first, and only later, when there is action, they can use motion shots.

• • •

Suicides don't pay very well. There are so many every day, and people are so unimaginative, that if you spend a day watching television you can see at least ten suicides, none of them very spectacular. Seems the last thing that suicides think of is originality.

Only once did I try to talk a suicide out of it. It was a woman, 'bout forty years old, skinny and worn-out. I told her that the only thing her suicide was going to accomplish was to feed me for about two days, that there was no point being just another one, that I totally understood life was a load of shit but there was no sense committing suicide just to entertain a thousand assholes who do nothing but switch channels looking for something that would raise, even just a little, the adrenaline level in their bodies.

She jumped anyway.

I returned home, and that night I watched the personal copy I'd made over and over again. Every action happened thousands of times on my monitor. I ended up playing it in slo-mo, trying to find some moment when her expression changed, the moment when one of my words might've had an effect I didn't know how to take advantage of.

I went to bed with swollen eyes, a terrible taste in my mouth, and thinking that what I'd said to that lady I might just as well have been saying to myself.

• • •

I've had enough, and I leave my house to go buy something to eat. I jump on my bike (which I use to get around near home) and just before reaching a pizza place I hear a bunch of patrol cars a few blocks away. I press my thigh to activate the controls, and the green signal goes on in my eye. I pedal as fast as I can, following the sound of the sirens. I turn a corner and see five cop cars parked at the entrance to a building. I leave my bike leaning against one of them, hoping no one will steal it, and run toward a cop who's keeping gawkers back. I show her my press badge and she grudgingly lets me in. She tells me to go up to the third floor. When I arrive, a couple paramedics are examining a body that's convulsing in the doorway of the apartment. I stop to establish the shots. One full shot of the paramedics, one long shot of the corridor, and I try to walk slowly and keep my vision fixed so that the movement isn't too abrupt. I stop at the doorway and slowly pan my head in order to establish the setting on thousands of monitors throughout the world. My indicator light's been red for several seconds. I approach an officer who's covering up a corpse near a TV monitor, and on the monitor they're transmitting my shot. I feel the shiver that always accompanies a hook, I begin to get dizzy, and a shooting pain crosses my brain from side to side. I lose all sense of space until I turn around and spot a cop trying to be the star of the day. The cop sees the red light in my right eye and looks into it. "We got a report from some neighbors in the building that they'd heard a baby crying, and they knew that three single men lived here. You know how people are, they thought that they were some kind of f—— perverts who'd adopted a baby so they could feel like they were more normal."

I interrupt the laughter of the cop who's posing for my right eye, and ask him when they were notified.

"Twenty minutes ago. We ran a check on kidnapped babies. When we got here, they'd already killed the neighbors. Seems they were monitoring all phone calls, and they began shooting at us . . ."

The officer kept on talking, and I was concentrating on getting the shot when I sensed a movement behind him. Apparently a closet door was opening. The next thing I register—and I suppose it's gonna be pretty spectacular since my shot was a close-up of his face—is a flash of light and his face exploding into pieces of blood and flesh.

I hurl myself against his body, grabbing hold of it and using my momentum

431

to carry us toward whoever it was did this. Before reaching the closet I let go of the body and step back, to get a clear shot. The headless corpse of the policeman strikes another body and knocks it down. I approach quickly and stomp on the hand holding a gun. I can hear the bones as they break. Too bad I don't have audio capacity so I could record the sound. I hope someone in the transmission room patches it in. The shot is a bird's-eye view of some guy's face, soaked with the blood of the cop. I can't make out his features. More cops arrive. I take a few steps back.

"It seems," I comment on the air, "that there was still one person hiding in the closet, and this carelessness by the police has cost yet another officer his life." It's always good to criticize institutions. It raises the ratings. Just then I hear a commotion at the door and I quickly turn around to find a young woman crying, followed by a private security guard. She goes into one of the rooms I haven't managed to shoot yet. When I try to go in, a cop stops me and his look says I can't enter. I know he's dying to insult me, but he knows I'm on the air and it could harm the police department's image in this city, so all he says is I can't go in. I manage to get shots of the woman picking up a bundle and holding it to her breast while endlessly repeating, "My love, my baby."

"What is that, Officer? Is it a baby?"

"This is a private moment, reporter, you have no right to be filming it."

"I have information rights." I lie by reflex, but I don't succeed in budging him. I try my luck with the girl who'd gone inside crying. "Can I help you in any way, miss?" Just then I realize that the bundle she'd picked up is all bloody. Various police officers and two paramedics try to take away the baby, at least I suppose that's what it is, but she doesn't want to let go of it. She fixes her hair and comes over to me. Hurry up, I think, the clock's running on your fifteen minutes.

"You're a reporter, aren't you?" My first instinct is to nod my head but I remember that it's an unpleasant motion for TV viewers, I'm not supposed to be anything but a verbal personality, and so I answer by saying yes.

"Someone stole my baby, and now I've found him but it looks like the cops hurt him, he's been shot in the leg." The lady cries harder and harder while a paramedic tells her that all she's doing is injuring the baby more. I get confused because someone's started to shout in my ear receiver. They want me to ask the girl her name. The paramedic grabs the baby. In my head, the program directors keep talking. "We couldn't have planned this better, this is drama, just wait till you get your check, the ratings are gonna add a lot of zeros to it."

The rest is routine. Interviews, facts, versions. The fate of the baby will be a different type of reporter's job and it'll keep the whole city excited all this afternoon and maybe into tomorrow morning, when some other reporter tapes fresher news.

When I leave the building my bike's no longer waiting for me, and I have to walk home. I live in a world without darkness. All day long there's an indicator light in my retina telling me my transmission status. I can turn the indicator level down, but even when I'm sleeping it keeps me company. A yellow light and a buzz, a murmur. They're who I sleep with. They're my immediate family. But my eyes belong to the world. My extended family spans an entire city, though no one would recognize me if they met me on the street.

I haven't gone out for a few weeks now. My last check frees me up from having to wander around looking for news. Privacy is a luxury for a man in my condition. Several times a day a yellow indicator goes on in my right eye and I hear a voice asking if I have anything, they have some dead time and it's been days since I transmitted anything. I simply don't answer. I close my eyes and remain quiet, hoping they'll understand that I'm not in the mood.

What do I do on my days off? Well, I try not to see anything interesting. I read magazines. I look at the window of my room. I count the squares on the living room floor. And I remember things that aren't recorded on tape, while my eyes stare at the ceiling, which is white—perhaps the least attractive color on a television screen.

. . .

The most common errors made by ocular reporters are due to the reflexes of their own bodies. A reporter must live under constant discipline so as to avoid seemingly involuntary reflexes. There is no greater sign of inexperience and lack of professional control than a reporter who closes his eyes in an explosion or a reporter who covers her face with her arms when startled by a noise.

. . .

Today is not a good day. I go walking the streets, and in every store I hear the same news. Constant Electrical Exposure Syndrome, CEES for fans of acronyms, seems to be wreaking havoc. Continuous stimulation of the nerve endings, caused by electricity and an environment that is constantly charged with electricity—radiation from monitors, microwaves, cell phones—seems to have a fatal effect on some people. I stop in front of a shop window and start recording a reporter with his back to a wall of TV screens: "It seems the central nervous system is so used to receiving external electronic stimulation that when it doesn't get it, it begins to produce it, constantly sending electric signals through the body that have no meaning or function, speeding up your heartbeat and making your lungs hyperventilate. Your eyes begin to blink and sometimes your tongue starts to jerk inside your mouth. Some witnesses even say that the victims of this syndrome can 'speak in tongues,' or that this syndrome 'is what causes this type of experience in various subjects.'" They insert shots of several people speaking in tongues here.

The reporter, looking serious and trying to get people's attention, keeps walking, while images of people who suffer from these symptoms appear on the video wall. The screens fill with shots of serious men with concerned faces. Interviews with experts, no doubt.

"No one knows for certain the exact nature of the syndrome. The world scientific community is in a state of crisis. There are those who say this is just a rumor started by the media, it's simply another disease transformed into a media event. Some say the syndrome isn't as bad as it seems. But there are also those who believe that civilization has created a monster from which it will be difficult to escape."

The images on the monitors change. Various long shots of rustic houses, surrounded by trees. The music changes. Acoustic instruments, a flute and a guitar.

"However, there are already several electric detox centers out in the country. Rest homes devoid of electricity. This is perhaps the only possibility or hope for those who exhibit symptoms of the syndrome. As always, hope is the last thing to die in what is perhaps the most important 'artificial' disease of this century. There are those who say that what cancer was to the previous century, CEES will be to ours."

They show a few shots of these places. The patients look out the windows or at the walls, as if waiting for something they know will never arrive. As if waiting for civilization to keep a promise, yet aware that it never will, since the promise has long been forgotten.

The equipment for corporal transmission is very expensive. My father gave it to me. Well, he doesn't know what it was that he gave me. I just received an email on my eighteenth birthday saying that he had deposited who knows how much money into an account in my name, that I had to decide what to do with it and that after spending it I was on my own. That I shouldn't seek him out anymore.

I still keep that email on my hard drive. It's one of the advantages of the digital age. Memory becomes eternal and you can relive those moments as many times as you want. They remain frozen outside of you, and when you don't know who you are or where you come from, a few commands typed into your computer bring your past to the present. The problem is that when the past remains physically alive in the present, when does the future get here? And why would you want it to?

The future is a constant repetition of what you've already lived; maybe some details can change, maybe the actors are different, but it's the same. And when you haven't lived it, surely you saw something similar in some movie, on some TV show, or you heard something like it in a song. I keep hoping my mom will return one day and tell me it was all a joke, that she never died. I keep hoping my father will keep his promise and come see me in the orphanage. I keep hoping my life will stop being this endless repetition of days that follow each other with nothing new to hope for.

I paid for part of my operation with the money. Legally, half the operation is paid for by the company that owns the rights to my transmissions. The doctors tried to talk me out of the implant, but I was already over sixteen, so I told them to just concentrate on doing their job. I needed to earn money and I knew perfectly well that luck and necessity are strange bedfellows. Three days later the nerve endings of my eyes and vocal cords were connected to a transmitter that could send the signal to the video channels.

That was the last time I heard from my father.

• • •

The most important detail that an ocular reporter must remember is to avoid monitors when transmitting live. If a reporter focuses on a monitor that is broadcasting what he is transmitting, his sense of balance will by harshly affected and he will begin to suffer from severe headache. Exposure to this type of situation is easily controlled by avoiding shots of monitors when transmitting live. It is important to note that the reflected transmissions "hook" the reporter, and there is a change in the stimuli that travel from the brain toward the different muscles of the body. For that reason it is sometimes almost impossible to break off visual contact with the monitor. The only way to prevent these "hooks" is through abrupt movement of the body or neck as soon as visual contact is made with the images one is transmitting. Latest research reveals that long periods of exposure to these virtual loops cause symptoms similar to those of CEES. This information was obtained from recent experiments and from the records of the Toynbee case.

• • •

The Toynbee case is a legend no one in my profession can ever forget. Some antimedia extremists kidnapped a reporter and blindfolded him so that he couldn't transmit anything. Every two hours they broadcast their opinions to a nation that watched, entertained: *"The media are the cause of the moral decay of our society, the media are causing the extinction of individuality, thousands of mental conditions stem from the fact that human beings can only learn about reality through the media, the information is manipulated."* The whole ideological spiel, just like on one of those flyers they hand out in the streets. It's ironic to think that those extremists may be the only ones who'll survive if an epidemic like CEES wipes out humanity. They always try to avoid electricity. I don't know what I prefer, to keep hoping that this reality miraculously gets better or that some stupid extremists take over the world and impose the rules of "their" reality. The only thing you can learn from human history is that there's nothing more dangerous than a utopia.

So, as an example and metaphor of their complaints, they tied up the reporter, who worked under the name Toynbee, and put him in front of a monitor. They immobilized his head and connected his retina to the monitor. I've seen those images a thousand times. The only thing the reporter's eyes see is a monitor within a monitor within a monitor, until infinity seems to be a video camera filming a monitor that's broadcasting what it's recording, and there's no beginning, no end, there's nothing, until you remember that a human being is watching this, it's the only thing he can see and it's giving him an unbearable headache, as if someone were crisscrossing his skull with cables and wires. The images weren't enough.

For those who know what it feels like to get hooked, the images were painful, but for those who'd never felt that kind of feedback they were frankly boring. The extremists—conscious that they were putting on a show and that before they'd be able to broadcast ideas they had to entertain the world—set up a video camera to tape Toynbee's face, and sent the signal to the same transmission station the reporter was connected to. At the station they knew there was nothing they could do to help Toynbee, since he was connected directly to the monitor, and they began to transmit both things: the monitors reproducing themselves until infinity, and Toynbee's face. The station executives say they would've cut the broadcast if they'd've had doubts about the source of the hook, but everyone knows that's not true. Ratings are ratings.

Watching that reporter's face is quite a show. First, a few facial muscles start to move, as if he had a tic. At first he tried to move his eyes, to look to either side, but right next to the monitor was the tripod with the camera taping his face. And so on one half of the screen you could see how the loop was broken: all you saw was the partial view of a TV set, showing the image of a video camera on the right side of the screen and the real video camera on the other side, as if reality didn't have depth, only breadth. As if reality repeated itself endlessly off to the right and left. But the hook was stronger than his willpower, and gradually the reporter stopped trying to look off to the side. Sometimes the monitor showed how he tried. A very slow pan to the right or left that slowly came back again, as if the muscles of his eyes had no strength left. Toynbee began to sweat. His face began to convulse more violently, each time sweating bigger drops that struggled against gravity until, just like the reporter's eyes, they gave up and slid rapidly down his convulsing face. Each drop followed a different path. His face, lit up by the monitor, seemed to be full of thousands of monitors, since his damp skin also reflected, in distortion, the monitor he was looking at. The muscle spasms were getting stronger, and just as the sweat deformed the monitor, each convulsion moved the reporter's face one step further away from what we know as human. There were no longer moments when you could see normality in his face. Everything was movement and water and eyes that looked out feverishly, desperately.

Sometimes, when I recall the images, the eyes even seem to be concentrating, as if they were discovering a secret that not only makes you lose your mind but causes your body to react violently, because it's something that human beings shouldn't be allowed to see.

A few minutes later his eyes seemed to lose all focus, even though they kept on receiving and transmitting light. His eyes were vacant, just like the monitors. I've always liked to think that at that moment the only thing the reporter could see was a kitschy image of his past, I dunno, the birthday party his mom threw him, or some day when he was in a play, or his first kiss or some other idiocy of the kind that always makes us happy. There was no more willpower left in his eyes, but his eyelids were being forced open, so his body and the ghosts that occupied his body were still functioning. Several of his facial muscles atrophied and stopped working, which made the movements of his face even less natural. The shot continued until his face had no expression left, just spasms and movement, expressions that went beyond the range of human emotions, possibilities that ceased to have meaning the moment they disappeared.

Until his heart exploded.

Sometimes, when I'm bored and on the bus returning to my apartment, I begin to record everything I see. But then I stop seeing and just let the machines do their work. I go into a sort of trance in which my eyes, though open, observe nothing; and yet when I get home I have a record of everything they saw. As if it wasn't me who saw it all.

When I watch what I taped I don't recognize myself. I relive everything I saw without remembering anything. At those times it's my feelings that're on standby.

Some truths become evident when reality is observed this way.

The poor are the only ones who are ugly. The poor, and teenagers. Everyone with a little money has already changed his or her face and now has a better-looking one, has already made his face or her identity more fashionable. Teenagers aren't allowed this type of operation because their bone structure is still changing. That's how you can tell economic status or age, by checking out the quality of the surgical work on people's faces. We live in an age when everyone, everyone who's well off in this world, is perfect. Perfect body, perfect face, and looks that speak of success, of optimism, as if the mind were perfect, too, and could only think correct thoughts. Today, ugliness is a problem that humanity seems to have left behind. Today, as always, humanity's problems are solved with good credit.

Sometimes I like to think about the scene of my suicide. One of my choices is to connect the electric camera terminals I have in my eyes to an electric generator in order to raise the voltage little by little, until my brain or my eyes or the camera explodes. It thrills me to think of the images I'd get.

Or I could prepare something cruder. Take a knife and cut out my eye. Cut it out by the roots. Sometimes I think I'd prefer not to see anything, I'd prefer a world in shades of black. Get rid of my eyes. Even if they sued me, even if I had to spend the rest of my life rotting away in jail.

And while I decide, I sit alone at home, waiting. Waiting for a promise to be kept . . .

•   •   •

Today I woke up with the urge to go out into the street and find something interesting. I've been walking around for a couple hours without any destination. It's a nice day. I hear shouts at the end of the street and take off running in that direction. A drug store. I press the button and my indicator light changes from yellow to green. I stop a few meters from the entrance and file a report. "Shouts in a drug store, I don't know what's going on, I'm going to find out." I take the time needed to establish the scene and slowly start to approach. A lot of people are leaving the drug store, running. The story of my life. Wherever no one wants to be, there goes me.

It's hard to get inside. I try to shoot several of the faces of the people stampeding each other to get out. Desperate faces. Scared faces. The red light goes on. "I'm at a drug store, the people are trying frantically to get out. I haven't heard any shots." I have to shove several people aside until I can get through the door, and I head toward the place everyone's leaving. "Seems to be someone lying on the ground." A bunch of people wearing uniforms surround him. Probably the store employees. I stop a moment to establish the shot. I stop an employee who wants to get outside and look him in the eyes. He's so scared he doesn't even realize I'm transmitting.

"What's going on?"

"The guy was standing there, taking something off the shelves, when suddenly he collapses and starts to shake. He's infected . . ." The guy pushes me and jars my shot. Shit. I approach the body; there's an ever-widening circle around him. I pass these people and get a full-body shot of the guy, on the floor having convulsions. He's swallowing his tongue. I approach and get down close to him. He looks at me desperately when his head's not jerking around.

Toynbee. He has the same facial features. "This man was shopping in the drug store when he suffered a seizure." The guy turns to look at me, realizes there's a red light burning in my retina, and begins to laugh. His laughter starts to mix with his convulsions and before long you can't distinguish his laughter from his pain. I try to hold him in my arms, I try to touch him to calm him down, but it has no effect. I see a red light in his left eye. He's transmitting. I let go of him and his head hits the floor hard. Out of nowhere, he seems to be drowning. He shudders twice and remains quiet, looking at me. In my head I hear, "Say something, say something about CEES, *talk*, shit it's your job."

The reporter is motionless. The camera in my eyes records a tiny red dot that remains alive in his. Today my face will probably appear on the monitors.

Two days later my news is no longer news. It seems like every day more attacks of the syndrome are reported. Forty percent of the victims are reporters. I remember AIDS and the homophobia it awoke. Seems like it's us reporters' turn to live in fear, not just of dying, but of the fear of others. Mediaphobia? What will they name this effect?

The common citizen (and believe me, they're all common) still doesn't understand that the syndrome isn't transmitted by bodily contact. Everyone runs away when they see someone falling apart in a fit of convulsions. They still don't get it that the body is no longer the important factor. They live under the illusion that if they touch a victim they'll get infected. It's like a phantom virus that can't be located, it's in the air, in the street, it's wherever you go but in reality it doesn't exist. It's a virtual virus. And it's a sickness we're exposed to by living in this world. It's the sickness of the media, of cheap entertainment, it's the sickness of civilization. It's our penance for the sin of bad taste.

• • •

For all reporters who transmit live, control is the principal weapon against the reflex stimulation caused by the indicator light. The viewer can only see through the reporter's eyes once the red light in the retina goes on. All movement, all action on the reporter's part, should be perfectly planned. There must be no mistakes. Frontal shots are best. It is always necessary to take face shots of the subject, by means of the camera connected to the nerve endings of the eye, in order to establish identification between the subject and the viewer. The reporter functions as a medium, to call it something. He/She is merely the point of contact between the action and the reaction that thousands of viewers will have in their homes. The reporter must be there, without being there. Exist without being noticed. This is the art of communication.

• • •

The opening sequence of the program that I usually transmit on goes like this: all the shots are washed out as if they were done in some familiar, old-fashioned style, as if they didn't have the necessary transmission quality, that being the excuse for washing them in gray tones that'll later change to reds. First there's a subjective shot of a stomach operation; then the doctors turn and talk to the camera, and the whole world learns that the camera is the face of the person being operated on. Then there's an action sequence of a shoot-out downtown, till one of the people firing turns and sees the camera and presses the trigger; the camera shot jolts and seems to fall to the ground. Everything starts to flood, a red liquid's filling up the lens. The pace starts to pick up. A shot from the point of view of a driver who crashes into a school bus. A worm's-eye view of a guy throwing himself off a building (I've always thought he looks like a high-diver). The sacrifice of a cow in a slaughterhouse. The assassination of a politician. An industrial accident where some guy loses an arm. Shots of explosions where even the reporter gets blown up. A skyjacking where the terrorist shoots a passenger in the head. And so on. The images go by faster and faster until you can hardly make out what's going on, all you see is motion and blood and more motion, shapes that don't seem to have any human reference anymore, until it all begins to acquire a bit of order and you start to see red, yellow, and gray lines that dance about rapidly and leave the retinal impression of a circle in the middle of the screen where the lines meet. An explosion stops the sequence, and inside the circle the program's logo is formed: Digital Red.

Welcome to pop entertainment in the early twenty-first century.

What will I be doing in twenty years? Will I keep walking the streets looking for news to transmit? Not a very pleasant future. Belonging to the entertainment industry gives off an existential stink. Some still call it journalism, though everyone knows the news isn't there to inform, but to entertain. My eyes make me commune with the masses. Thousands of people see through my eyes so they can feel that their lives are more real, that their lives aren't as putrid and worm-eaten as the lives of the people I see. I'm the social glove they put on in order to confront reality. I'm the one who gets dirty, and I prevent their lives from smelling rotten. I'm a vulture who uses the misfortunes of others to survive.

When you get up close to a mirror you can't see both your eyes at the same time. You can see either the right or the left. The closer you get to your image the more distorted it gets and you can only see yourself partially. The same thing happens with a monitor. You're not there. You're the unknown one who moves in a way you don't recognize as your own. Who speaks with a voice that doesn't sound like yours. Who has a body that doesn't correspond to your idea of it. You're a stranger. To see yourself on a monitor is to realize how much you don't know about yourself and how much that upsets you.

If I wanted a more dramatic effect I could get myself hooked, like Toynbee. Connect myself directly to a monitor and start to transmit. See how reality is made up of ever-smaller monitors (and no matter how hard you try, you can't find anything inside those screens, just another monitor with nothing inside) and go crazy when I realize that's the meaning of life. Totally forget about control over my body.

Allow my eyes to bleed.

• • •

The transmission time of an ocular reporter is the property of the company that finances his/her operation. Clause 28 of the standard contract establishes that six hours of every reporter's day are property of said company.

• • •

A terrorist attack in a department store. I hate department stores. Almost all of 'em are festooned with monitors that randomly change channels. It's easy to get hooked. You have to be careful. The police are just arriving on the scene. I'm about to transmit but decide not to tell central programming. As always, I look for an emergency exit. A manager is trying to take merchandise away from customers who are taking advantage of the situation to save a few pesos. The manager is so busy that he doesn't even realize when I push him. He falls and a bunch of people quickly run out with the stuff they're stealing. A little old lady of around sixty carries a red dress in her hands and smiles pleasantly when she leaves. I enter the store and hide behind the clothes racks. I get up to the third floor via the emergency stairs, which are empty. I don't know if the terrorists are here inside or if they simply left everything in the hands of a bomb. I avoid several of the private security guards hired to guard the store, not wanting them to see me yet. One of them comes upon a shoplifter, and he and his partner kick the hell out of him on the ground. The guy's bleeding and crying. Everyone tries to take advantage of an emergency situation. The two security guards go away, leaving the customer lying there on the floor. Blessed be capitalism. I move on to the candy department, and the smell makes me dizzy. I've never understood how they keep the flies away from the exposed candied fruit. I hear some voices and hide. I begin to hear a buzzing sound and I gently tap my head. But the sound's not coming from there. The hum is coming from my right. I crawl until I get to a box, which I open cautiously. Inside is a sophisticated device with a clock in countdown mode, rapidly approaching zero. I have a little more than a minute, so I take off running. I forget about transmitting or anything else. When I feel I'm far enough away I turn around and press a button; it's green. I see the two security guards approaching the candy section. I quickly turn my head. I'm about to shout at them to get away when I hear a voice in my ear. "Where the fuck are you? Straighten out the shot, show us something we can broadcast. Are you in the store?" I slowly correct the shot, steadying my head in a slow pan while I notice the red indicator light switch on in my eyes. I manage to spot the two security guards in the candy section. I force myself not to blink, and the bomb explodes. The fire is so hot and the colors so spectacular that for the first time in a long while I forget about the red light that lives in my head. I miscalculated. The force of the explosion lifts me up and I fly several meters through the air. I'm not a body, I'm a machine flying through the air, whose only purpose is to record and record and record so that the whole world can see what they wouldn't want to live. The clothes burn, the display shelves fall apart, thousands of objects go flying. Some hit me but I try to keep the shot as steady as I can. All in the name of entertainment.

I slam against a wall and try to keep my head up so I can tape the fire.

For the first time I feel at home in a department store. Everything is flames, everything is ashes. The stylish dresses feed the fire, the perfumes make it grow. The spectacle is unparalleled. Civilization destroying itself. I'm in a department store, one of civilization's most glorious achievements. I see a sign that's beginning to burn; it says, "Happy Father's Day." Promises, promises . . .

I get up and my whole body hurts. I walk toward the exit. A voice in my head is shouting, "Where the fuck do you think you're going? I need fixed shots, I need you to talk; tell the world about your experience. Don't be a jerk, you don't film an explosion every day! Where do you think you're going?"

And it doesn't stop until I'm three blocks from the attack.

Today I crossed a line. I don't know and I don't care if I killed the security guards. It's one thing to report on stuff that happens and another thing to make what happens more spectacular.

What were the security guards? They were graphic elements to liven up my shots. They were mimetic elements that the audience would be able to identify with. They were dramatic elements to make the story I had to tell more interesting. They were scenery.

Today I crossed a line and I don't want to think about anything. My whole body aches.

Situations like these make me think about the urgency of my suicide. At least that way I could decide something, and not just let destiny take the lead. Suicide is the most elaborately constructed act of the human will, it's taking control of your destiny out of the hands of the world.

• • •

Yesterday I was organizing a bunch of my tapes. I found a program about my old-time heroes, the experiential reporters. "Crazies," as the foreign media call them. I pressed the play button and sat down to watch them. There are some pretty stupid people in this world, like the reporter who, after getting himself thrown in jail, started to insult the cops so that they'd beat him. He taped everything. The shots are especially successful because half the time he's on the floor trying to make visual contact with the faces of the cops who are pounding on him. Some people consider him a hero. But whenever you see the disfigured faces of the police who are beating him up you can't help thinking how ridiculous the situation is. The reporter is there because he chose to be there. Good job, amigo, improve the ratings of your company. I also watched the famous operation on Grayx's head, one of the martyrs of entertainment. The reporter, trying to make a commentary on the depersonalization of the body, agreed to subject himself to surgery in which they'd remove his head and connect it to his body by way of special high tech cables. The guy outdid himself, narrating his whole operation, describing what he was feeling while they connected his head to his body with cables that allowed him to be five meters away from his head. This is probably one of the most important moments of this century. When the operation's over you can see a subjective shot of the body on the operating table as Grayx tells it to stand up. The body gets up and begins to stumble, because the head that's sending it instructions sees things from a strange perspective. The body slowly approaches the head, picks it up and turns it around so that the eyes (and the camera) can look in the direction it's walking in, and at that point the viewer no longer knows who's giving the instructions, the body or the head. The body takes the head in its arms like a baby and stands in front of a mirror where you can see a decapitated body holding its head in its arms. The head doesn't seem to be very comfortable because it's a bit tilted, he didn't have enough coordination to hold it straight so all these shots lack horizontal stability. Grayx is talking about the feeling of disorientation, about the possibilities that the surgery opens up, about what would happen if instead of cables they used remote control, about how marvelous the modern world is, while his arms try to hold his head straight and he keeps looking back, his face twisted with the effort of trying to make his body do what he says, all the while failing to control it.

This program always brings me odd memories. I had sex for the first time after watching it with a girlfriend from high school. We were at her house watching the broadcast. No one was around. I don't know how many people might've had sex after the inauguration of the first lunar colony or when they broadcast the assassination of Khadiff, the Muslim terrorist leader, or at any other key moment in the televised history of our century, but I can tell you that it's an unforgettable experience. Watching a man with his body separated from his head on the same day that you become aware of how your body can unite with another body and become one is something you don't easily forget. Every time I watch it I have pleasant memories.

Now Grayx is in a mental institution. Seems the technology that he was helping to develop causes mental instability. Apparently people need corporal unity in order to remain sane. Grayx lost contact with reality, and they say he now lives in an imaginary world. He had so much money that he built a virtual environment and connected it to his retina, and that's the only thing that keeps him alive.

I haven't felt good ever since the explosion. I have strong pains in the pit of my stomach. Yesterday I told them to deposit the check into my account. Seems I won't be having any trouble over the security guards. To create news with your own body, like the crazies do, is perfectly legal, but make news at the expense of other people's rights and you can wind up spending the rest of your life in jail.

I go to the bathroom and start to pee. I look down and see that the water and my urine are full of blood. I start to hear voices just as a green light goes on in my retina.

"If I were you I'd go straight to a doctor. That red color in your piss doesn't look healthy at all."

"Leave me alone."

"I can't, you've gone two days without doing a single thing. You already know how it is with contracts. Besides, don't be ungrateful. I was only calling to tell you your check's been deposited. Maybe when you see your pay your mood'll improve. The ratings were really spectacular."

• • •

I've gone down into the sewers of the city a number of times trying to prove one of the oldest urban legends. Thousands of rumors say there are human communities in the deepest parts of the network of underground pipes. A lot of people believe they're freaks, mutants, that their eyelids permanently cover their eyes and their skin is so white they can't tolerate the sun or even the flashlights that everyone who goes down to look for them uses. A new race, grown out of our garbage.

A society that doesn't rely on its eyes, that doesn't have to look at itself for self-recognition. Their behavior must be weird. They'd have to touch one another, they'd have to listen to one another. They wouldn't have to look like anything or anyone. A different world, different creatures.

Every time I descend on one of my exploratory trips I use my infrared glasses and carry very low-intensity lights. I've gone down more than ten times and not once have I found anything. No mutants, no freaks, no subterranean race offering something new to humanity, something different from what's shown on TV. It's just me down there.

Last night my right arm began to convulse. I couldn't do anything to stop it. My fingers opened and closed as if they were trying to grab something, to hold on to something.

Maybe I'd prefer a less sensational exit. Get a tank of gas, seal off a room, and fall asleep . . .

• • •

It is impossible for human beings to avoid blinking, but it is possible to prolong the period of time between one blink and the next. Reporters should do exercises to achieve this control. Furthermore, the operation on their eyes is designed to stimulate the tear ducts so that the eyes do not dry out so easily, and thus reporters can keep their eyes open longer than the ordinary individual.

When muscle movement in the eyelids is detected, special sensors in the eye "engrave" the last image that the eye has seen, and when the eyelid then closes this image is the one which is transmitted. When the eyelid raises, taping continues. This necessary error in the workings of the human body has caused microseconds of memorable moments in the history of live TV to be lost forever.

•   •   •

A more spectacular piece of news, a riskier stunt. They always want something more. More drama, more emotion, more people sobbing before the cameras, before my eyes. I don't want to think, I'm not made to think, just to transmit. But with every transmission I feel I'm losing something I won't ever recover. The only thing I hear in my head is *more, more, more*.

I could also take everything I feel some attachment for, fill a small bag, find a sewer drain and head down it, but this time without any lights. I'd wander around for entire days, I'd have to start eating rats and insects and drinking sewer water. Maybe I'd spend the rest of my life walking among the tunnels that form a labyrinth under this city, but at least I'd be searching for something. Or maybe I would find a new civilization. Even if they didn't accept me, even if they were to kill me for bringing in outside influences, it'd be comforting to know that there are choices in this world. That there's someone who has possibilities the rest of us lost centuries ago. Or maybe they would accept me, and I could live for years and years without having to worry, doing manual labor and finding a new routine to my life. To be what I think I can be and not what I am.

Maybe, maybe . . .

•   •   •

These are the voices in my head:

"There's a fire, don't you wanna go check it out? Fires and ratings go hand in hand."

"Armed robbery, a black car with no license plates, model unknown, get some shots."

"This is good, a lovers' quarrel, she was making a cake and she destroyed his face with a mixer. The boyfriend, a little miffed, decided he was going to stick *her* in the oven instead of the cake. The neighbors called it in, but it didn't turn into anything big. Good stuff for a comedy."

"You wanna talk? The night's slow and I ain't got nothin' to do, they're broadcasting games from last season."

"Another family suicide. In the subway, a mother with her three kids."

And so on, continually.

The whole world is on TV. Anyone can be a star. Everyone acts, and every day they prepare themselves because today could be the day that a camera finds them and the whole world discovers how nice, good-looking, friendly, attractive, desirable, interesting, sensitive, and natural they are. How human they are. And all day long everyone sees tons of people on-screen trying to be like that, so people decide to copy them. And they create imitators. And life just consists of trying to seem like somebody who was imitating somebody else. Everyone lives every day as if they were on a TV show. Nothing's real anymore. Everything exists to be seen, and everything that we'll see is a repeat of what we've seen before. We're trapped in a present that doesn't exist. And if the transmitted don't exist, what about those of us who do the transmitting? We're objects, we're disposable. For every reporter who dies on the job or who dies of CEES, there are two or three stupid kids who think that's the only way of finding anything real, of living something exciting. And everything starts all over again.

I always try not to chat with the program directors. Normally they're a bunch of idiots. Their work is easy and they use us like remote control cameras. Normally I don't even ask them their names. There's no point. Who wants to know more people? Ain't nothing new under the sun. Everything's a repeat, everything's a copy.

There's only one program director who knows me a little more intimately. His nickname's Rud, I don't know his real name. I met him (well, I listened to him) when I was drinking, that is, when I was trying to get so drunk I wouldn't have to think, wouldn't have to want anything. I wanted the alcohol to fill me so that I wouldn't have to make decisions, so that whatever decision I made would be the alcohol's fault, not mine. "I was drunk."

I sure do miss alcohol.

Alcohol and my profession are not good friends. In my body I have equipment that belongs to a corporation, so they can sue me if I willingly damage the machinery. Besides, it's not unusual for program directors to tape your drinking sprees and then use them to blackmail you. Some even put them on the air. Once they broadcast two guys who were beating me up 'cause I'd insulted them. I remember thinking that the only good thing about it was that my face wouldn't be shown on the air, they could transmit everything I did but no one would see me, no one could recognize me. Anonymity is a double-edged sword.

Rud calls me "The Cynic" because he doesn't know my name either. It's easier to talk with someone that way. You avoid problems, as well as commitments. Well, it turns out he'd listened to one of my booze-induced rants. He listened to me patiently all night long, complaining, crying, laughing. I walked over five kilometers. The only thing I did was stop at liquor stores and buy another bottle. I wanted to forget everything, so each time I got a different type of booze. I don't even want to remember all the stupid things I said. Anyone with a little sense of humor would call that night "Ode to Dad" because I spent the whole time talking about him. There was even a stretch when I asked Rud to pretend to be my father and I accused him of stuff, I shouted at him and spit at him. My father was inside my head. At one point I started to beat my head against a wall. I don't have any real memories of that. Turns out Rud recognized the street I was on and called the paramedics to come take me home. They had to put eight stitches in my forehead. Not even modern surgical techniques let me get off without a scar.

• • •

Five days later I got a package with no return address, just a card that said, "Greetings, Rud." Inside was the bill from the paramedics. There was also a videocassette. Rud had taped my whole binge.

Sometimes, when I'm in the mood to drink, I play the videotape and cry a bit. That way there's no chance I can deceive myself, everything is recorded, I can't lie. It's no illusion, it's me. Sometimes, but not always, I manage to feel better after watching it.

I'd like to go up to the top of the building where I shot my first transmission. I'd set up two external cameras, one with a long shot, the other with a medium-range shot. I'd get close to the edge of the building, turning my back to the street so that the shots would be frontal, and I'd press the button in my thigh. Someone would criticize me for thinking that rooftop terraces were news, until they received the signals from the other cameras and realized what I was about to do.

Suddenly, a red light would illuminate my gaze. I would think about various things. I would want my father to be able to see this, but it wouldn't matter, a lot of people would see it from the comfort of their homes. It's the same thing. I'm everyone's son.

I would clear my throat to say something live with the broadcast, but I'd remain silent.

What more can one say? What could I say that someone before me hasn't already said better?

I would look at the cameras and then up at the sky, where they say that gods who loosed plagues onto humanity once lived. In the sky I would find nothing.

The wind would begin to blow and my hair would get in the way of the camera in my eyes.

I would take one step backward and begin to fall.

And maybe, just maybe, I would forget about the buzzing sound for once.

STEVE BEARD

RETOXICITY

(1998)

THE HWANG FAMILY forgot to pay off the Corporation's drug cops and I barely escaped with my life. It's being written up as a jurisdictional dispute on the London datanets. Just one of those things, accidents will happen, etc. You know the score.

They're withholding casualty lists at St. Thomas's Hospital. Most of the victims had no ID. Lost in the digital jungle. So they don't really count in any final census, capisce?

It was a bad night if all you wanted to do was load up on rocks and dance. But then that's been the case for a long time in England. It seems that there are bigger stories to rack up on UBC Global. Like which of the warring factions from some damaged European bloodline is going to be running things out of the Palace of Westminster. Or how the Chamber of London lost a pile on the futures market.

Real small-time stuff. No room, you see, for the big picture, for the nightly sacrifices, which keep the whole machinery of power sparking. Which is the reason why I cut loose down in South London with my CAMnet. Now I had a choice, here. I could have dropped into any of the pleasure dumps which ghost the industrial leys of the South Bank—Crucifix Lane, Clink Street, Timworth Street, Goding Street, Bondway, Nine Elms Lane. But my contacts in Kyoto tell me that Battersea Park Road is where the furnaces of ecstasy are really *stoked*.

Drop-off at Bat Hat at eleven in the p.m. Like Westminster, an old island in the Thames. Unlike that old crowning ground—and far distant from the corporate temples and occult quadrangles of the City of London—Battersea and the South Bank have always been where the effluent of empire has been discharged.

Take a core sample from its deep and teeming sediment. Run back through paper switching centers and refuse tips to electrical generators, gasometers, and railway yards to lime kilns, chemical works, and windmills. Go back further to the farms and the markets and the timbered marshlands. Track all the way back . . . and the legacy of quarantined populations and slum landlords persists like a dark stain.

Now one thing I do know is you have to take your pleasures where you can find them. And always on the South Bank, deposited in the shells of each receding layer of industry, have been the factories of joy.

Blue lasers cutting up the night sky, traffic and commotion, the drums of London like an underground tattoo. The party was on tonight just like it has been every night since the end of the millennium. Some people just didn't know when to stop. They were drawn in their thousands from all over London—the barricaded wastes of Brixton and Stockwell, the low-rise estates of Whitechapel, Plaistow, and Bow, the pavements of Fulham and the tenements of the Holloway Road. The old power station crouching on the Thames was like a beacon reeling them in with its promise of solace, adventure, and sex.

But some of us have a job to do. I've been to the melt fields of São Paulo and the war zones of Třeboň. I've seen it all before.

Drifting through the shanty town crammed up against the eaves of the sheltering ruin, home to a blinkered population of the nomadic, the exiled, and the lost. Shaved heads, laser eyes, whiplash antennae poking out of the industrial moraine. The graft of the homeless is the same the world over. Sheets of polythene, sporting colors, recycled tech. The only difference here is that the debris is plush. You remember your Jaguars, your Mercs, and your BMWs? Burned-out skeletons for improvised dwellings, dressed with the gaudy remnants—chipped tiles, metal railings, stripped marble—of an abandoned Twentieth Century past.

You see what I see? Realtime video eye flashing red, CCD witness tech catching it all.

Take a look at what's left of the cathedral once built by the London Power Company in Battersea. Crumbling brick facade, exposed joints of steel lashed with neoprene and plastic, internal armature of generators, turntables, and lights. Only the four ribbed chimneys of reinforced concrete—towering over the shambles like a paired brace of dead rockets—still marking the skyline with a Promethean glower.

Bat Hat is what the South London homies call it. For them, it's a quarry of renewable resources and a temple of carnal delights. That was why I was here. For its absentee landlords, it's something different. The Hwang family overlook this distant riverside patch from their revolving satellite watch with the same lazily speculative eye they reserve for the rest of the slum properties shuffled to the back of their global investment portfolio. Looking at the last set of Hwang accounts filed in HK, I can see that they've done to Battersea in London what they've done to similar underperforming land assets in Bombay, St. Petersburg, and Kuala Lumpur. Contracted out management of the place to a local strand of the family, paid off the native chieftains, patched in their drug connections, and tried to make a quick buck in the interval before the market picks up.

The Soho end of the Hwang mob had things sorted down here. Or at least that's what they thought. Dance events seven nights of the week, rock franchise, the Met turning a blind eye to the contravention of health and safety regs in return for a cut of the action, the Brixton Yardies pacified. They'd really carved out a space for themselves. Pity they weren't paying attention to the war going on between the Crown of England and the Corporation of London north of the Thames. A lot of people would pay for that omission with their lives.

But it didn't feel that way when I was there. It felt like there was an event. Cabs and rickshaws running up and down the Battersea Park Road. Roisterers and carousers streaming into the pleasure ground dressed in industrial face masks, skin-tight Versace, and luminous Caterpillar boots. Smoked-glass limos trailing through the throng into the underground car parks. The party kicking off right there in the squatlands outside the dancehall. You see what I see? Drug peddlers togged up in Replay and Chevignon shouting their wares ("Trips! Rocks! You sorted?"). Indian chai ladies sitting on rush mats selling tea, cigarettes, and naan. TiNi datasuit vendors and pirate CD-ROM merchants blocking the path. Paramedics setting up emergency field tents. The Met boys nowhere to be seen.

It was a special evening. That much I did know. A date reserved for a fire festival in the local pagan calendar. November Fifth. The Hwang family had rented out space on the outside of the building to the usual motley crew of water companies, drug distributors, and record labels. The logos of Thames Valley Water, GlaxoWellcome, TDK, and Sony burning their way into the distressed brickwork like projected core memories. Nothing new there.

What was distinctive was the string of artcore messages popping up in between the shuttle of ads like subliminal reminders of a utopian past. Local VJs pumping out wish images of the Westminster mob in jeopardy. Burnings, hangings, and shootings wrapped around kitsch patriotic footage of the old queen at play. Well, she was dead anyway. So what did it matter? Plenty, as it turned out.

Rolling up to the massive ornamental gates at the entrance to the dancehall. Shakedown at the door. T'ai chi goons puffed up in Antarctic camo and pink Oakley shades—with an underarm flash of gunmetal gray—exuding an aura of cool. Weapons check, digicash card swipe, an extra tax for the CAMnet. It's all over and I'm in.

So you want to know what's happening in London?

"Wicked and wicked and wicked and rough!"

Hidden speakers punch out a slew of garbled syllables. Ranting DJ boxed up on one of the dance floors beyond my immediate gaze. I'm losing my footing. Edges of darkness, shafts of light. Slammed against a press of bodies on the threshold of the building. CCD video eye blinded. Vaporized bass rocks the foundations and I'm caught in a hurtling backwash of sound.

"Yes, yes, yes, yes, London Town."

A volley of drums slams through my body like a digital pulsar and I stumble. This was going to be tough.

Time to reorientate. I pull down the blueprints of Messrs C. S. Allot & Son, engineers of Manchester from the days when the Ukrainians knew how to build suspension bridges, railways, and dams. Checking east, checking west, checking east again. I've got two sets of Boiler Houses, two sets of Turbine Halls, and two sets of Switch Rooms either side of the door. I'm looking for the Control Room above the Turbine Hall on the west side so flip back to realtime and head left. I don't know where I'm going. The attempt to navigate from old maps is senseless, the internal architecture has changed so much.

Time to surrender to the flow of the crowd. See how I'm dragged through a labyrinthine warren of improvised dance floors rigged up from cannibalized industrial plant and recycled techno-organic fibers. Flashing on stainless-steel banisters, Worcestershire brick, dead electricity cables, sheets of Kevlar and PVC, aluminum spars, and neoprene sails.

Losing it. Sample a quicktime CAMnet image from one of the floors. DJ erected high on a podium, chocked up in metal platelet jacket with a gold sleeper in his nostril and a ring of bone in his lobe. Two thousand dancers at his feet dressed in feathers, jewels, and luminous threads working the drift of his hands over the decks in an open feedback loop. Dizzying sweep of overhead gantries, rotting stairwells, and drop-dead shafts of light. The void filled with seething bass turbulence, euphoric speedkill drum loops, and sampled shreds of London slang. "Buss off your head and set you on fire!" Panic images of fear and flight—Lockheed F-117s, trance bucks, aerospace salamanders, window-less UAVs—racing over the screens above the DJ's head.

Calibrating. Resisting the siren call of the rock vendors and the champagne hawkers—later!—I twist and turn my way through a maze of black corridors before catching the logo over the lintel of the old Control Room. TEMPLE OV ISIS picked out in holo red with the eye of Horus flashing alongside. I slide through the soundproofed airlock rigged up beneath the sign and step into an intense cabin of flailing limbs, throttling bass, and whiplash drums.

The acrid smell of burning rock hits my nostrils. There are huddled packs of dancers refueling at the margins of the dance floor from delicately wrought Turkish pipes. Jets of flame spurt high into the air from hidden butane gas canisters. The stars are visible through the broken roof above.

CAMnet casting around the room. Totemic images and graffiti tags are visible on the touch screens embedded in the skirtings of Belgian black marble which still line the walls. Hobo signs, website numbers, strings of alphanumeric code. Dog-headed astronauts, Blakean angels, cartouched Mayan glyphs. An inverted image of Bat Hat folding its legs beneath it like an insect about to unsheathe its wings. Planets, star signs, computers. An aerosol portrait of Isis at the prow of an aerodynamic barge with a handmaiden attending her on either side. Raw data for my colleagues at Kyoto. Enough to keep them busy for a year.

"Here's to all the liberty-takers, the nutters, and the ravers. Taking it to the other side."

This is what I've traveled three continents and multiple time zones to witness. The orgiastic cult of Isis at its peak, a chiliastic dance craze whose seismic fallout has been rocking the planet's datanets for the last year. Three decades of aggravation, pressure, and intimidation falling down from the north of the Thames has led the natives of London to revolt in the only way they know how. You've heard about it. They've invented a homegrown cargo cult from the trash washed up on the shores of empire, a hybrid Santeria fusing elements from ancient American and African myth, Haitian voodoo rites, interplanetary fantasies, and occult techno-science. They want to do more than stake a claim for themselves in the evacuated wastelands of London. They're going further. They want to *disappear*.

One of them made it, too. But you'll never believe it will you? My CAMnet was confiscated by the Corporation of London goons before I had a chance to file the event. But there's always the evidence of my own eyes. Sitting here pressing the keys in a rented room in Vauxhall. I can hardly believe it myself. But it happened. There's nothing more I can say.

The thing about the ISIS posse was . . . they really thought they could make it to another world with only rock, the gods of London, and a DAT archive of snarling drum loops to send them on their way. They had it all figured out. Sirius C was the destination, the missing planet in the constellation of the Great Dog (source: the tribal mythos of the Dogon in Mali); Isis the presiding deity of teleportation, old Portmaster demon from the banks of the Thames (source: local mythology); and 2012 the deadline, the year when the cosmic switches would be hit and a new planetary kiva would come online (source: the trans-millennial calendar of the Mayans).

The Temple ov Isis had kicked off at the start of the year. It was still going eleven months later. The celebrants were running out of time. I was witness to the ecstatic ravings of a para-millennial cult which was approaching endtime with no release in sight. The dancers—kitted out in transparent TiNi datasuits, VR shades, and tribal markings—had been putting out a call to Isis for the last year in an attempt to escape the bonds of gravity and take flight through the electronic ether. Their mission was to transform the archaic ruins of Bat Hat into an interplanetary craft which would arc high over the degraded landscape of London and find the wormhole which connected with Sirius C. Who says they weren't going to do it? Everyone, of course. Luckily your faithful correspondent has more of an open mind. Someone had to.

Two hundred London natives snaking their hips from side to side as their hands flip up and down and their feet weave intricate geometric patterns in the floor. Their separate bodies—exhibiting signs of sexual arousal through the metal tracework of their prosthetic skins—knotted and spliced into a single corporate entity which was dancing up a storm in the virtual world.

Eerie synth moans drifting round the temple, the bass dropping low as if waiting to attack. A moment's pause . . . and then the drums kick in with a deafening fusillade of reprocessed beats. The dancers skid and dive as if caught in the crossfire of a digital warzone. Some have already collapsed.

I flipped the CAMnet eyepiece to one side, stooped to retrieve a pair of discarded VR shades, and put them on. A landscape of plush grasses filled with madly cavorting figures—quicktime avatars comprised of Deleuzian body parts, baroque Meccano rods, and Lathamesque crustaceans—scrolled past at 270 bpm. I blinked rapidly and tracked back to take in the full widescreen view of what was now a distant planet wrapped in a cocoon of alien stars. The planet was covered in a net of purple micro-filaments which was in the process of being rapidly colonized by the swarm of avatars. You ask me what they were doing? Obviously reconditioning it for interdimensional flight. One of the stars in what appeared to be the southern hemisphere was throbbing and flickering with an insistent urgency, its phase-shifted modulations in synch with the shattering tattoo of the drums. Here was the homing signal, the pinpoint navigational code which the craft needed to make the unimaginable journey.

It was too much. I flung the shades to the ground. Flocks of drum loops arced and rolled across the old Control Room as I made my way to the rickety podium of scrap metal at its center on which the DJ was placed. She towered above the throng of celebrants like a voodoo priestess addressing the ancestor gods of the astral plane or an air-traffic controller plucking long-haul carriers from faraway holding patterns. Her long needle-tipped fingers tugged purposefully at the atoms around her as if shuttling thread from an invisible loom. She would keep on beat the drums like this all night. I stood quietly before her.

So this was Voodoo Ray. Her fame preceded her on the datanets. It was whispered that she could conjure the spirits from their hiding places in rocks and machines and trees, that she was a keeper of the keys which unlocked the hearts of men. I watched her. Her dark face was enclosed in an enveloping wimple of Sennheiser cans and skintight TiNi hood and her lips were parted in an ecstatic grin. Sweat poured from her brow and collected on the rim of the VR shades which shielded her eyes. She looked like the image of a pagan saint or a blind prophetess. CCD video eye catching it all.

The drums crashed at my feet. I needed to smoke some rock. That way I could plug into the London dreamtime and participate in the collective attempt to boot up rediscovered shamanic flight vectors and exit the rotting shell of Bat Hat. But, like I say, some of us have a job to do. It was down to me to keep a clear head.

You ask me to specify the tech jammed into the Temple ov Isis? I'll do it. Like its sustaining mythos, its operating system had been scratched together from a bundle of found objects. Check One. Bat Hat had fallen off London's electric grid, so all power was sourced from protected banks of flaking generators which chugged quietly outside in the improvised marketplace. Check Two. The suits and shades had been imported from the sex arcades of Soho. (Old Hwang family connections.) Check Three. All virtual avatars had been custom-built in the coding basements of Brixton. Check Four. The celebrants had managed to grab hold of some junked Chamber of London software and were tripping on the back of its immersive store of images. It didn't matter to them that the writhing grasses, the purple planet, and the winking stars animated the records of old financial transactions. But it mattered to the Corporation of London.

You ask me to go on? Then I shall. Check Five. Distributed ranks of old SPARC clones formed a local area network which plugged each of the dancers into the same virtual space at the same time. The shape-memory alloys embedded in the threads of their datasuits powered a collective force-feedback mechanism which was helmed by the figure of Voodoo Ray. She was the usher. Her own avatar was the lodestar in cyberspace which fine-tuned the collective rhythms of the planetary mass spread before her. Now do you understand?

It gets more intense. Check Six. The whole virtual envelope had been retro-engineered so that it coincided with a computer-generated audio-tactile field. Infra-red sensors grafted into the datasuits sent coded bursts of data to the SPARC clones based on the movements of the dancers. They entered the feedback loop and were ushered back into physical space by the Kabuki hand jive of Voodoo Ray. Check Seven. A Matsushita DAT machine encased in a Kamecke black box rested at the base of the podium, its hermetic surface carved with Tzolkin calendrical glyphs and an Egyptian votive inscription. It was here that Voodoo Ray had hoarded her stock of digitally reprocessed breakbeats, her inheritance of old vinyl memories.

Check Eight. The speakers blasting out the punishing sonic fragments which Voodoo Ray retrieved from the DAT with a flick of her wrists. Her nails were sheathed with infra-red needles which glittered like claws as they scratched signs in the air. In front of her was the sample space. Behind her was the play space. She was suspended in the trigger plane.

I moved closer to her perch.

"Oh my gosh. London Town. Yes, yes, yes, yes, yes, yes, *yes*!"

She stood like a tiny colossus with her legs apart, the damp patch of her sex visible beneath the sheen of her suit as her hips rode the shuddering battery of sound. Spittle flew from her lips as she chanted her mantras. She plucked beats from the air with a manic glee, her arms wheeling and darting as if weaving a shroud or connecting a call. It seemed impossible that anyone could be so quick.

It was then that I understood. Voodoo Ray's podium marked the quadrivium in this cathedral of sound, the digital switchboard from which the gods of London were signed in. Devotional smartcards bearing images of local media saints—Jimi, Gerald, Jezebel—were pinned to the scrap-metal tower on which she was placed. Her feet were supported by a grimy slab of limestone which capped the whole edifice like the bridge of a ship. This was her stage, her scaffold, her gantry. It was the platform from which she would turn herself off.

Inside the mesh of iron and steel the Kamecke box reclines like a voluntary captive or a protected savant. You see what I see? Wicker machine.

I ended up dancing. What else could I do? Once the drums were racked up to 320 bpm, it was the only way to keep sane. Look at it. That's why the CAMnet footage is so spasmodic at this point. It's obvious that things were getting out of control.

Needlepoint rhythms unseaming my head as I struggle to keep up with their murderous pace. Voodoo Ray's claws a blur of deft cutwork. The drums looping and writhing in undulations of panic. I know I can process it all if I concentrate . . . but the stress is too much. My body picks up the slack with its twitches and spasms and for a moment I slide into the groove. Stretched envelope of sound. The drums tripping higher and higher, weaving harp bolts of color into a diaphanous labyrinth. I can almost reach out and touch it . . . the internal architecture of a fantastic dream vessel. But none of this survives on the tape.

Look what is there. The crowd is demented, as if caught in a vortex of conflicting demands. Its members stagger and reel and hold out their hands. Some of them roll on the ground. There are nosebleeds, babblings, and spontaneous orgasms. Do you think that maybe there was something coming in?

The Corporation goons had made their big entrance. Thrown a temporary exclusion zone around the perimeter of Bat Hat and sealed off all exits in advance of the bust. Roadblocks in the Battersea Park Road. Media blackout. Chinooks slung with Exocets clattering in the sky. The takedown sheet specified software piracy and drug trafficking. But that was just a paper construction. Battersea Power Station had been declared an autonomous Bar of the City of London. The Corporation could do what it liked.

You heard the story of how they loosed off a missile? I don't know. It could've been the drums.

"Yes, yes, yes, yes. Let it come down."

Voodoo Ray . . . she warps the beat up into an even higher dimension. You have to slow down the CAMnet tape to even get close. It was then that I came to the end of my senses. The dance floor spun away from me and I fell to the floor.

Mass panic and awful confusion. The Corporation's enforcers threshing the crowd with a relentless attack. Heckler & Kochs flailing, radio chatter, red dots on the walls. What exactly is it they want? Quarantined inside white biohazard suits, the dreadful seals of the Corporation of London masking their faces, ribbed cables humping their backs like red dragons' spurs. They were breathing their own oxygen. As if the prospect of some awful contagion was what they most feared.

They were moving in on the stone mount where Voodoo Ray danced. She rained down her DAT gods upon them in invisible tongues of fire. The drums shrieking and squealing in an orgy of judgment. It was too much for the human metabolism to bear. But they could hear nothing. All orifices were plugged. The one thing they knew was protection.

Voodoo Ray's last move. She swings round—a full 180 degrees—and exposes her back to the advancing legions. It's then that I notice the tattoos beneath her TiNi suit. Seven of them descending from the crown of her head to the base of her spine like a wrathful serpent or a coiled flame. This was her last line of defense.

She squats on the stone with her legs wide apart and places her final calls to the gods. Her tattoos are like baroque circuit diagrams or compressed voodoo dials imprinted on a wafer of carbon. With the infrared needle attached to her left index finger she quickly signs each one. Her hand gently trips down her spine as if she were unzipping the skin of her datasuit in order to wriggle free.

Sampling and playing the drums simultaneously there in the heat of the SPARC trigger plane. The clamor of the breakbeats was terrible. Her body shivered with the pleasure of it.

It's too weird for the Corporation goons. They have most definitely lost it. Someone releases a catch and there's the panicky stutter of gunfire.

They then all open up in a roundel of lust.

"Stop, stop, *Stop*!" It's my own voice. Last thing I said before my CAMnet was trashed and my head opened up. You see what I see? Identification number on the good doing me over is a blank. Bzzzp! End of transmission.

I was dazed and leaking. What happened next was what you would have to call an unexplained phenomenon. Because there is definitely no way I hallucinated the event.

Voodoo Ray is bowed with her head between her knees. She is unbloodied. They didn't catch her. The drums are still roaring. It's a miracle. She's scratching the stone with her needle, tracing a sigil she maybe sees in her head. Her face is a mask of awful recognition. Is she being called? The Corporation goons are closing in for the kill. Their blood is up. What do they care?

I was thinking that someone would be shot.

The dance floor seemed to lose its moorings for an instant. Quantum fissure. The desperate chatter of automatic fire. Voodoo Ray went up in smoke.

Let me rephrase that. A blue shaft of light inundated the stone and wrapped her tired body in a spectral cocoon. She raised her hand in greeting and waved farewell. Rapture. She was transported and her atoms dispersed.

I saw her tattoos glow red and burn themselves into the back of her TiNi suit. It dropped to the stone like a charred mantle from Heaven as the light died away.

Pickup.

The drums were seething with a fierce imprecation. They shouldn't have been.

"Forgive."

After that, it was just a matter of tidying up the mess. There was no future for Bat Hat, of course. The Corporation evacuated the building and detonated the remains. I guess there was some evidence they just didn't want to collect.

The strange thing about it all. Mass arrests, no charges. Blinking survivors left massaging their wrists on the Battersea Park Road as the power station retracted its sublime fluted chimneys and sank to its foot in a cushion of dust. The Corporation dezoned the territory soon after and relinquished it to the Crown. Shipped out its troops as quickly as it had choppered them in. It was a ten-line item in the domestic tabs. Bat Hat a death trap. Isis a Waco cult. Et cetera, et cetera. Blacks, guns, and drugs.

Slightly more on the NHK WipeNet. Another ethnic skirmish in a Euro civil war. The Hwangs to sue for loss of capital assets. All of which leaves the big questions hanging. How many people were killed by the Corporation of London? Where are they buried and what are their names?

Information on this matter is very hard to come by.

One thing I do know. Voodoo Ray may be reckoned among the dead. But her name will live forever in the binary devotions of the digital shamans.

CORY DOCTOROW

QWNZQRED

(2002)

TEN YEARS IN THE VALLEY, and all Murray Swain had to show for it was a spare tire, a bald patch, and a life that was friendless and empty and maggoty-rotten. His only ever California friend, Liam, had dwindled from a tubbaguts programmer-shaped potato to a living skeleton on his deathbed the year before, herpes blooms run riot over his skin and bones in the absence of any immunoresponse. The memorial service featured a framed photo of Liam at his graduation; his body was donated for medical science.

Liam's death really screwed things up for Murray. He'd gone into one of those clinical depression spirals that eventually afflicted all the aging bright young coders he'd known during his life in tech. He'd get misty in the morning over his second cup of coffee and by the midafternoon blood-sugar crash, he'd be weeping silently in his cubicle, clattering nonsensically at the keys to disguise the disgusting snuffling noises he made. His wastebasket overflowed with spent tissues and a rumor circulated among the evening cleaning staff that he was a compulsive masturbator. The impossibility of the rumor was immediately apparent to all the other coders on his floor who, pron-hounds that they were, had explored the limits and extent of the censoring proxy that sat at the headwaters of the office network. Nevertheless, it was gleefully repeated in the collegial frat-mosphere of his workplace and wags kept dumping their collections of conference-snarfed hotel-sized bottles of hand lotion on his desk.

The number of bugs per line in Murray's code was 500 percent that of the overall company average. The QA people sometimes just sent his code back to him (From: qamanager@globalsemi.com To: mswain@globalsemi.com Subject: Your code . . . Body: . . . sucks) rather than trying to get it to build and run. Three weeks after Liam died, Murray's team leader pulled his commit privileges on the CVS repository, which meant that he had to grovel with one of the other coders when he wanted to add his work to the project.

Two months after Liam died, Murray was put on probation.

Three months after Liam died, Murray was given two weeks' leave and an e-mail from HR with contact info for an in-plan shrink who could counsel him. The shrink recommended Cognitive Therapy, which he explained in detail, though all Murray remembered ten minutes after the session was that he'd have to do it every week for years, and the name reminded him of Cognitive Dissonance, which was the name of Liam's favorite stupid Orange County garage band.

Murray returned to Global Semiconductor's Mountain View headquarters after three more sessions with the shrink. He badged in at the front door, at the elevator, and on his floor, sat at his desk, and badged in again on his PC. From: tvanya@globalsemi.com To: mswain@globalsemi.com Subject: Welcome back! Come see me . . . Body: . . . when you get in.

Tomas Vanya was Murray's team lead and rated a glass office with a door. The blinds were closed, which meant: dead Murray walking. Murray closed the door behind him and sighed a huge heave of nauseated relief. He'd washed out of Silicon Valley and he could go home to Vancouver and live in his parents' basement and go salmon fishing on weekends with his high-school drinking buds. He didn't exactly love Global Semi, but shit, they were number three in a hot, competitive sector where Moore's Law drove the cost of microprocessors relentlessly downward as their speed rocketed relentlessly skyward. They had four billion in the bank, a healthy share price, and his options were above water, unlike the poor fucks at Motorola, number four and falling. He'd washed out of the nearly best, what the fuck, beat spending his prime years in Hongcouver writing government-standard code for the Ministry of Unbelievable Dullness.

Even the number-two chair in Tomas Vanya's office kicked major ergonomic azz. Murray settled into it and popped some of the controls experimentally until the ess of his spine was cushioned and pinioned into chiropractically correct form. Tomas unbagged a Fourbucks Morning Harvest muffin and a venti coconut Frappuccino and slid them across his multi-tiered Swedish Disposable Moderne desque.

"A little welcome-back present, Murray," Tomas said. Murray listened for the sound of a minimum-wage security guard clearing out his desk during this exit-interview-cum-breakfast-banquet. He wondered if Global Semi would forward-vest his options and mentally calculated the strike price minus the current price times the number of shares times the conversion rate to Canadian Pesos and thought he could maybe put down 25 percent on a two-bedroom in New Westminster.

"Dee-licious and noo-tritious," Murray said and slurped at the frappe.

"So," Tomas said. "So."

Here it comes, Murray thought, and sucked up a brain-freezing mouthful of frou-frou West Coast caffeine delivery system. Gonzored. Fiored. Sh17canned. Thinking in leet-hacker crap made it all seem more distant.

"It's really great to see you again," Tomas said. "You're a really important part of the team here, you know?"

Murray restrained himself from rolling his eyes. He was fired, so why draw it out? There'd been enough layoffs at Global Semi, enough boom and bust and bust and bust that it was a routine, they all knew how it went.

But though Murray was on an Air Canada jet headed for Vangroover, Tomas wasn't even on the damned script. "You're sharp and seasoned. You can communicate effectively. Most techies can't write worth a damn, but you're good. It's rare."

Ah, the soothing sensation of smoke between one's buttocks. It was true that Murray liked to write, but there wasn't any money in it, no glory either. If you were going to be a writer in the tech world, you'd have to be—

"You've had a couple weeks off to reassess things, and we've been reassessing, too. Coding, hell, most people don't do it for very long. Especially assembler, Jesus, if you're still writing assembler after five years, there's something, you know, *wrong*. You end up in management or you move horizontally. Or you lose it." Tomas realized that he'd said the wrong thing and blushed.

Aw, shit.

"Horizontal movement. That's the great thing about a company this size. There's always somewhere you can go when you burn out on one task."

No, no, no.

"The Honorable Computing initiative is ready for documentation, Murray. We need a tech writer who can really *nail it*."

A tech writer. Why not just break his goddamned fingers and poke his eyes out? Never write another line of code, never make the machine buck and hum and make his will real in the abstract beauty of silicon? Tech writers were coders' janitors, documenting the plainly self-evident logic of APIs and code structures, niggling over punctuation and grammar and frigging stylebooks, like any of it *mattered*—human beings could parse English, even if it wasn't well-formed, even if you had a comma splice or a dangling participle.

"It's a twelve-month secondment, a change of pace for you and a chance for us to evaluate your other strengths. You go to four weeks' vacation, and we accelerate your vesting and start you with a new grant at the same strike price, over twenty-four months."

Murray did the math in his head, numbers dancing. Four weeks' vacation—that was three years ahead of schedule, not that anyone that senior ever used his vacation days, but you could bank them for retirement or, ahem, exit strategy. The forward vesting meant that he could walk out and fly back to Canada in three weeks if he hated it and put *30* percent down on a two-bedroom in New West.

And the door was closed and the blinds were drawn and the implication was clear. Take this job or shove it.

He took the job.

A month later he was balls-deep in the documentation project and feeling, you know, not horrible. The Honorable Computing initiative was your basic Bond-villain world-domination horseshit, of course, but it was technically sweet and it kept him from misting over and bawling. And they had cute girls on the documentation floor, liberal arts/electrical engineering double-majors with abs you could bounce a quarter off who were doing time before being promoted up to join the first cohort of senior female coders to put their mark on the Valley.

He worked late most nights, only marking the passing of five p.m. by his instinctive upward glance as all those fine, firm rear ends walked past his desk on their way out of the office. Then he went into night mode, working by the glow of his display and the emergency lights until the custodians came in and chased him out with their vacuum cleaners.

One night, he was struggling to understand the use-cases for Honorable Computing when the overhead lights flicked on, shrinking his pupils to painful pinpricks. The cleaners clattered in and began to pointedly empty the wastebins. He took the hint, grabbed his shoulder bag, and staggered for the exit, badging out as he went.

His car was one of the last ones in the lot, a hybrid Toyota with a lot of dashboard geek toys like a GPS and a back-seat DVD player, though no one ever rode in Murray's back seat. He'd bought it three months before Liam died, cashing in some shares and trading in the giant gas-guzzling SUV he'd never once taken off-road.

As he aimed his remote at it and initiated the cryptographic handshake—i.e., unlocked the doors—he spotted the guy leaning against the car. Murray's thumb jabbed at the locking button on the remote, but it was too late: the guy had the door open and he was sliding into the passenger seat.

In the process of hitting the remote's panic button, Murray managed to pop the trunk and start the engine, but eventually his thumb mashed the right button and the car's lights strobed and the horn blared. He backed slowly toward the office doors, just as the guy found the dome-light control and lit up the car's interior and Murray got a good look at him.

It was Liam.

Murray stabbed at the remote some more and killed the panic button. Jesus, who was going to respond at this hour in some abandoned industrial park in the middle of the Valley anyway? The limp-dick security guard? He squinted at the face in the car.

Liam. Still Liam. Not the skeletal Liam he'd last seen rotted and intubated on a bed at San Jose General. Not the porcine Liam he'd laughed with over a million late-night El Torito burritos. A fit, healthy, *young* Liam, the Liam he'd met the day they both started at Global Semi at adjacent desks, Liam fresh out of Cal Tech and fit from his weekly lot-hockey game and his weekend dirt-bike rides in the hills. Liam-prime, or maybe Liam's younger brother or something.

Liam rolled down the window and struck a match on the passenger-side door, then took a Marlboro Red from a pack in his shirt pocket and lit it. Murray walked cautiously to the car, his thumb working on his cellphone, punching in the numbers 9-1-1 and hovering over SEND. He got close enough to see the scratch the match head had left on the side-panel and muttered, *"Fuck,"* with feeling.

"Hey dirtbag, you kiss your mother with that mouth?" Liam said. It *was* Liam.

"You kiss *your* mother after I'm through with her mouth?" Murray said, the rote of old times. He gulped for air.

Liam popped the door and got out. He was ripped, bullish chest and cartoonish wasp-waist, rock-hard abs through a silvery club shirt and bulging thighs. A body like that, it's a full-time job, or so Murray had concluded after many failed get-fit initiatives involving gyms and retreats and expensive home equipment and humiliating early morning jogs through the sidewalk-free streets of Shallow Alto.

"Who the fuck are you?" Murray said, looking into the familiar eyes, the familiar smile lines and the deep wrinkle between Liam's eyes from his concentration face. Though the night was cool, Murray felt runnels of sweat tracing his spine, trickling down between his buttocks.

"You know the answer, so why ask? The question isn't who, it's *how.* Let's drive around a little and I'll tell you all about it."

Liam clapped a strong hand on his forearm and gave it a companionable squeeze. It felt good and real and human.

"You can't smoke in my car," Murray said.

"Don't worry," Liam said. "I won't exhale."

Murray shook his head and went around to the driver's side. By the time he started the engine, Liam had his seatbelt on and was poking randomly at the onboard controls. "This is pretty rad. You told me about it, I remember, but it sounded stupid at the time. Really rad." He brought up the MP3 player and scrolled through Murray's library, adding tracks to a mix, cranking up the opening crash of an old, old, old punk Beastie Boys song. "The speakers are for shit, though!" he hollered over the music.

Murray cranked the volume down as he bounced over the speed bumps, badged out of the lot, and headed for the hills, stabbing at the GPS to bring up some road maps that included the private roads way up in the highlands.

"So, do I get two other ghosts tonight, Marley, or are you the only one?"

Liam found the sunroof control and flicked his smoke out into the road. "Ghost, huh? I'm meat, dude, same as you. Not back from the dead, just back from the *mostly dead.*" He did the last like Billy Crystal as Miracle Max in *The Princess Bride*, one of their faves. "I'll tell you all about it, but I want to catch up on your shit first. What are you working on?"

"They've got me writing docs," Murray said, grateful for the car's darkness covering his blush.

"Awwww," Liam said. "You're shitting me."

"I kinda lost it," Murray said. "Couldn't code. About six months ago. After."

"Ah," Liam said.

"So I'm writing docs. It's a sideways promotion and the work's not bad. I'm writing up Honorable Computing."

"What?"

"Sorry, it was after your time. It's a big deal. All the semiconductor companies are in on it: Intel, AMD, even Motorola and Hitachi. And Microsoft—they're hardcore for it."

"So what is it?"

Murray turned onto a gravel road, following the tracery on the glowing GPS screen as much as the narrow road, spiraling up and up over the sparse lights of Silicon Valley. He and Liam had had a million bullshit sessions about tech, what was vaporware and what was killer, and now they were having one again, just like old times. Only Liam was dead. Well, if it was time for Murray to lose his shit, what better way than in the hills, great tunes on the stereo, all alone in the night?

Murray was warming up to the subject. He'd wanted someone he could really chew this over with since he got reassigned, he'd wanted Liam there to key off his observations. "Okay, so, the Turing Machine, right? Turing's Universal Machine. The building block of modern computation. In Turing's day, you had all these specialized machines: a machine for solving quadratics, a machine for calculating derivatives, and so on. Turing came up with the idea of a machine that could configure itself to be any specialized machine, using symbolic logic: software. Included in the machines that you can simulate in a Turing Machine is another Turing Machine, like Java or VMWare. With me?"

"With you."

"So this gives rise to a kind of existential crisis. When your software is executing, how does it know what its execution environment is? Maybe it's running on a Global Semi Itanium clone at 1.6 gigahertz, or maybe it's running on a model of that chip, simulated on a Motorola G5 RISC processor."

"Got it."

"Now, forget about that for a sec and think about Hollywood. The coked-up Hollyweird fatcats hate Turing Machines. I mean, they want to release their stuff over the Internet, but they want to deliver it to you in a lockbox. You get to listen to it, you get to watch it, but only if they say so, and only if you've paid. You can buy it over and over again, but you can never own it. It's scrambled—encrypted—and they only send you the keys when you satisfy a license server that you've paid up. The keys are delivered to a secure app that you can't fuxor with, and the app locks you out of the video card and the sound card and the drive while it's decrypting the stream and showing it to you, and then it locks everything up again once you're done and hands control back over to you."

Liam snorted. "It is to laugh."

"Yeah, I know. It's bullshit. It's Turing Machines, right? When the software executes on your computer, it has to rely on your computer's feedback to confirm that the video card and the sound card are locked up, that you're not just feeding the cleartext stream back to the drive and then to ten million pals online. But the 'computer' it's executing on could be simulated inside another computer, one that you've modified to your heart's content. The 'video card' is a simulation; the 'sound card' is a simulation. The computer is a brain in a bottle, it's in the Matrix, it can't trust its senses because you're in control, it's a Turing Machine nested inside another Turing Machine."

"Like Descartes."

"What?"

"You gotta read your classics, bro. I've been catching up over the past six months or so, doing a *lot* of reading. Mostly free e-books from the Gutenberg Project. Descartes's *Meditations* are some heavy shiznit. Descartes starts by saying that he wants to figure out some stuff about the world, but he can't, right, because in order to say stuff about the world, he needs to trust his senses, but his senses are wrong all the time. When he dreams, his senses deliver full-on THX all-digital IMAX, but none of it's really *there*. How does he know when he's dreaming or when he's awake? How does he know when he's experiencing something or imagining it? How does he know he's not a brain in a jar?"

"So, how does he know?" Murray asked, taking them over a reservoir on a switchback road, moonlight glittering over the still water, occulted by fringed silhouettes of tall California pines.

"Well, that's where he pulls some religion out of his ass. Here's how it goes: God is good, because part of the definition of God is goodness. God made the world. God made me. God made my senses. God made my senses *so that I could experience the goodness of his world*. Why would God give me bum senses? QED, I can trust my senses."

"It *is* like Descartes," Murray said, accelerating up a new hill.

"Yeah?" Liam said. "Who's God, then?"

"Crypto," Murray said. "Really good, standards-defined crypto. Public cipher-systems whose details are published and understood. AES, RSA, good crypto. There's a signing key for each chip fab—ours is in some secret biometrics-and-machine-guns bunker under some desert. That key is used to sign *another* key that's embedded in a tamper-resistant chip—"

Liam snorted again.

"No, really. Not tamper-*proof*, obviously, but tamper-*resistant*—you'd need a tunneling microscope or a vat of Freon to extract the keys from the chip. And every chip has its own keys, so you'd need to do this for every chip, which doesn't, you know, *scale*. So there's this chip full of secrets, they call the Fritz chip, for Fritz Hollings, the Senator from Disney, the guy who's trying to ban computers so that Hollywood won't go broke. The Fritz chip wakes up when you switch on the machine, and it uses its secret key to sign the operating system—well, the boot-loader and the operating system and the drivers and stuff—so now you've got a bunch of cryptographic signatures that reflect the software and hardware configuration of your box. When you want to download Police Academy *n*, your computer sends all these keys to Hollywood central, *attesting* to the operating environment of your computer. Hollywood decides on the fly if it wants to trust that config, and if it does, it encrypts the movie, using the keys you've sent. That means that you can only unscramble the movie when you're running that Fritz chip, on that CPU, with that version of the OS and that video driver and so on."

463

"Got it: so if the OS and the CPU and so on are all 'Honorable'"—Liam described quote-marks with his index fingers—"then you can be sure that the execution environment is what the software expects it to be, that it's not a brain in a vat. Hollywood movies are safe from Napsterization."

They bottomed out on the shore of the reservoir and Murray pulled over. "You've got it."

"So basically, whatever Hollywood says, goes. You can't fake an interface, you can't make any uses that they don't authorize. You know that these guys sued to make the VCR illegal, right? You can't wrap up an old app in a compatibility layer and make it work with a new app. You say Microsoft loves this? No fucking wonder, dude—they can write software that won't run on a computer running Oracle software. It's your basic Bond-villain—"

"—world-domination horseshit. Yeah, I know."

Liam got out of the car and lit up another butt, kicked loose stones into the reservoir. Murray joined him, looking out over the still water.

"Ring Minus One," Liam said, and skipped a rock over the oily-black surface of the water, getting four long bounces out of it.

"Yeah." Murray said. Ring Zero, the first registers in the processor, was where your computer checked to figure out how to start itself up. Compromise Ring Zero and you can make the computer do anything—load an alternate operating system, turn the whole box into a brain-in-a-jar, executing in an unknown environment. Ring Minus One, well, that was like God-code, space on another, virtual processor that was unalterable, owned by some remote party, by LoCal and its entertainment giants. Software was released without any copy-prevention tech because everyone knew that copy-prevention tech *didn't work*. Nevertheless, Hollywood was always chewing the scenery and hollering, they just didn't believe that the hairfaces and ponytails didn't have some seekrit tech that would keep their movies safe from copying until the heat death of the universe or the expiry of copyright, whichever came last.

"You run this stuff," Liam said, carefully, thinking it through, like he'd done before he got sick, murdered by his need to feed speedballs to his golden, tracked-out arm. "You run it and while you're watching a movie, Hollywood ownz your box." Murray heard the zero and the zee in ownz. Hacker-speak for having total control. No one wants to be ownzored by some teenaged script-kiddie who's found some fresh exploit and turned it loose on your computer.

"In a nutsac. Gimme a butt."

Liam shook one out of the pack and passed it to Murray, along with a box of Mexican strike-anywhere matches. "You're back on these things?" Liam said, a note of surprise in his voice.

"Not really. Special occasion, you being back from the dead and all. I've always heard that these things'd kill me, but apparently being killed isn't so bad—you look great."

"Artful segue, dude. You must be burning up with curiosity."

"Not really," Murray said. "Figgered I'm hallucinating. I haven't hallucinated up until now, but back when I was really down, you know, clinical, I had all kinds of voices muttering in my head, telling me that I'd fucked up, it was all fucked up, crash the car into the median and do the world a favor, whatever. You get a little better from that stuff by changing jobs, but maybe not all the way better. Maybe I'm going to fill my pockets with rocks and jump in the lake. It's the next logical step, right?"

Liam studied his face. Murray tried to stay deadpan, but he felt the old sadness that came with the admission, the admission of guilt and weakness, felt the tears pricking his eyes. "Hear me out first, okay?" Liam said.

"By all means. It'd be rude not to hear you out after you came all the way here from the kingdom of the dead."

"Mostly dead. Mostly. Ever think about how all the really good shit in your body—metabolism, immunoresponse, cognition—it's all in Ring Minus One? Not user-accessible? I mean, why is it that something like wiggling your toes is under your volitional control, but your memory isn't?"

"Well, that's complicated stuff—heartbeat, breathing, immunoresponse, memory. You don't want to forget to breathe, right?"

Liam hissed a laugh. "Horse-sheeit," he drawled. "How complicated is moving your arm? How many muscle-movements in a smile? How many muscle-movements in a heartbeat? How complicated is writing code versus immunoresponse? Why when you're holding your breath can't you hold it until you don't want to hold it anymore? Why do you have to be a fucking Jedi Master to stop your heart at will?"

"But the interactions—"

"More horseshit. Yeah, the interactions between brain chemistry and body and cognition and metabolism are all complicated. I was a speed-freak, I know all about it. But it's not any more complicated than any of the other complex interactions you master every day—wind and attack and spin when someone tosses you a ball; speed and acceleration and vectors when you change lanes; don't even get me started on what goes on when you season a soup. No, your body just isn't *that* complicated—it's just hubris that makes us so certain that our meat-sacks are transcendently complex.

"We're simple, but all the good stuff is owned by your autonomic systems. They're like conditional operators left behind by a sloppy coder: while x is true, do y. We've only had the vaguest idea what x is, but we've got a handle on y, you betcha. Burning fat, for example." He prodded Murray's gut-overhang with a long finger. Self-consciously, Murray tugged his JavaOne gimme jacket tighter.

"For forty years now, doctors have been telling us that the way to keep fit is to exercise more and eat less. That's great fucking advice, as can be demonstrated by the number of trim, fit residents of Northern California that can be found waddling around any shopping mall off Interstate 101. Look at exercise, Jesus, what could be stupider? Exercise doesn't burn fat, exercise just satisfies the condition in which your body is prepared to burn fat off. It's like a computer that won't boot unless you restart it twice, switch off the monitor, open the CD drive, and stand on one foot. If you're a luser, you do all this shit every time you want to boot your box, but if you're a leet haxor like you and me, you just figure out what's wrong with the computer and *fix it*. You don't sacrifice a chicken twice a day, you own the box, so you make it dance to your tune.

"But your meat, it's not under your control. You know you have to exercise for twenty minutes before you start burning any fat at all? In other words, the first twenty minutes are just a goddamned waste of time. It's sacrificing a chicken to your metabolism. Eat less, exercise more is a giant chicken-sacrifice, so I say screw it. I say, you should be super-user in your own body. You should be leet as you want to be. Every cell in your body should be end-user modifiable."

Liam held his hands out before them, then stretched and stretched and stretched the fingers, so that each one bent over double. "Triple jointed, metabolically secure, cognitively large and *in charge*. I own, dude."

Liam fished the last cig out of the pack, crumpled it, and tucked it into a pocket. "Last one," he said. "Wanna share?"

"Sure," Murray said, dazedly. "Yeah," he said, taking the smoke and bringing it to his lips. The tip, he realized too late, was dripping with saliva. He made a face and handed it back to Liam. "Aaagh! You juiced the filter!"

"Sorry," Liam said, "talking gets my spit going. Where was I? Oh, yeah, I own. Want to know how it happened?"

"Does it also explain how you ended up not dead?"

"Mostly dead. Indeed it does."

Murray walked back to the car and lay back on the hood, staring at the thin star-cover and the softly swaying pine-tops. He heard Liam begin to pace, heard the cadence of Liam's thinking stride, the walk he fell into when he was on a roll.

"Are you sitting comfortably?" Liam said. "Then I shall begin."

The palliatives on the ward were abysmal whiners, but they were still better than the goddamned church volunteers who came by to patch-adams at them. Liam was glad of the days when the dementia was strong, morphine days when the sun rose and set in a slow blink and then it was bedtime again.

Lucky for him, then, that lucid days were fewer and further between. Unlucky for him that his lucid days, when they came, were filled with the G-Men.

The G-Men had come to him in the late days of his tenure on the palliative ward. They'd wheeled him into a private consultation room and given him a cigarette that stung the sores on his lips, tongue, and throat. He coughed gratefully.

"You must be the Fed," Liam said. "No one else could green-light indoor smoking in California." Liam had worked for the Fed before. Work in the Valley and you end up working for the Fed, because when the cyclic five-year bust arrives, the only venture capital that's liquid in the US is military research green—khaki money. He'd been seconded twice to biometrics-and-machine-guns bunkers where he'd worked on need-to-know integration projects for Global Semi's customers in the Military-Industrial Simplex.

The military and the alphabet soup of Fed cops gave birth to the Valley. After WWII, all those shipbuilder engineers and all those radar engineers and all those radio engineers and the tame academics at Cal Tech and Cal and Stanford sorta congealed, did a bunch of start-ups, and built a bunch of crap their buds in the Forces would buy.

Khaki money stunted the Valley. Generals didn't need to lobby in Congress for bigger appropriations. They just took home black budgets that were silently erased from the books, aerosolized cash that they misted over the eggheads along Highway 101. Two generations later, the Valley was filled with techno-determinists, swaggering nerd squillionaires who were steadfastly convinced that the money would flow forever and ever amen.

Then came Hollywood, the puny $35 billion David that slew the $600 billion Goliath of tech. They bought Congresscritters, had their business models declared fundamental to the American way of life, extended copyright ad [inifinitum|nauseam] and generally kicked the shit out of tech in DC. They'd been playing this game since 1908, when they sued to keep the player piano off the market, and they punched well above their weight in the legislative ring. As the copyright police began to crush tech companies throughout the Valley, khaki money took on the sweet appeal of nostalgia, strings-free cash for babykiller projects that no one was going to get sued over.

The Feds that took Liam aside that day could have been pulled from a fiftieth anniversary revival of *Nerds and Generals*. Clean-cut, stone-faced, prominent wedding bands. The Feds had never cared for Liam's jokes, though it was his track marks and not his punch lines that eventually accounted for his security clearance being yanked. These two did not crack a smile as Liam wheezed out his pathetic joke.

Instead, they introduced themselves gravely. Col. Gonzalez—an MD, with caduceus insignia next to his silver birds—and Special Agent Fredericks. Grateful for his attention, they had an offer to make him.

"It's experimental, and the risks are high. We won't kid you about that."

"I appreciate that," Liam wheezed. "I like to live dangerously. Give me another smoke, willya?"

Col. Gonzalez lit another Marlboro Red with his brass Zippo and passed him a sheaf of papers. "You can review these here, once we're done. I'm afraid I'll have to take them with me when we go, though."

Liam paged through the docs, passing over the bio stuff and nodding his head over the circuit diagrams and schematics. "I give up," he said. "What does it all do?"

"It's an interface between your autonomic processes and a microcontroller."

Liam thought about that for a moment. "I'm in," he said.

Special Agent Fredericks's thin lips compressed a hair and his eyes gave the hintiest hint of a roll. But Col. Gonzalez nodded to himself. "All right. Here's the protocol: tomorrow, we give you a bug. It's a controlled mutagen that prepares your brainstem so that it emits and receives weak electromagnetic fields that can be manipulated with an external microcontroller. In subjects with effective immunoresponse, the bug takes less than one percent of the time—"

"But if you're dying of AIDS, that's not a problem," Liam said and smiled until some of the sores at the corners of his mouth cracked and released a thin gruel of pus. "Lucky fucking me."

"You grasp the essentials," the Colonel said. "There's no surgery involved.

The interface regulates immunoresponse in the region of the insult to prevent rejection. The controller has a serial connector that connects to a PC that instructs it in respect of the governance of most bodily functions."

Liam smiled slantwise and butted out. "God, I'd hate to see the project you developed this shit for. Zombie soldiers, right? You can tell me, I've got clearance."

Special Agent Fredericks shook his head. "Not for three years, you haven't. And you never had clearance to get the answer to that question. But once you sign here and here and here, you'll *almost* have clearance to get *some* of the answers." He passed a clipboard to Liam.

Liam signed, and signed, and signed. "Autonomic processes, right?"

Col. Gonzalez nodded. "Correct."

"Including, say, immunoresponse?"

"Yes, we've had very promising results in respect to the immune system. It was one of the first apps we wrote. Modifies the genome to produce virus-hardened cells and kick-starts production of new cells."

"Yeah, until some virus out-evolves it," Liam said. He knew how to debug vaporware.

"We issue a patch," the Colonel said.

"I write good patches," Liam said.

"We know," Special Agent Fredericks said, and gently prized the clipboard from his fingers.

• • •

The techs came first, to wire Liam up. The new bug in his system broadened his already-exhaustive survey of the ways in which the human body can hurt. He squeezed his eyes tight against the morphine rush and lazily considered the possibility of rerouting pain to a sort of dull tickle.

The techs were familiar Valley-dwellers, portly and bedecked with multitools and cellular gear and wireless PDAs. They handled him like spoiled meat, with gloves and wrinkled noses, and talked shop over his head to one another.

Colonel Gonzalez supervised, occasionally stepping away to liaise with the hospital's ineffectual medical staff.

A week of this—a week of feeling like his spine was working its way out of his asshole, a week of rough latex hands and hacker jargon—and he was wheeled into a semiprivate room, surrounded by louche oatmeal-colored commodity PCs—no keyboards or mice, lest he get the urge to tinker.

The other bed was occupied by Joey, another Silicon Valley needle-freak, a heroin addict who'd been a design engineer for Apple, figuring out how to cram commodity hardware into stylish gumdrop boxen. Joey and Liam croaked conversation between themselves when they were both lucid and alone. Liam always knew when Joey was awake by the wet hacking coughs he wrenched out of his pneumonia-riddled lungs. Alone together, ignored by the mad scientists who were hacking their bodies, they struck up a weak and hallucinogenic camaraderie.

"I'm not going to sleep," Joey said, in one timeless twilight.

"So don't sleep, shit," Liam said.

"No, I mean, ever. Sleep, it's like a third of your life, twenty, thirty years. What's it good for? It resets a bunch of switches, gives your brain a chance to sort through its buffers, a little oxygenation for your tissues. That stuff can all take place while you're doing whatever you feel like doing, hiking in the hills or getting laid. Make 'em into cron jobs and nice them down to the point where they just grab any idle cycles and do their work incrementally."

"You're crazy. I like to sleep," Liam said.

"Not me. I've slept enough in this joint, been on the nod enough, I never want to sleep another minute. We're getting another chance, I'm not wasting a minute of it." Despite the braveness of his words, he sounded like he was half-asleep already.

"Well, that'll make *them* happy. All part of a good super-soldier, you know."

"Now who's crazy?"

"You don't believe it? They're just getting our junkie asses back online so they can learn enough from us to field some mean, lean, heavily modified fighting-machines."

"And then they snuff us. You told me that this morning. Yesterday? I still don't believe it. Even if you're right about why they're doing this, they're still going to want us around so they can monitor the long-term effects."

"I hope you're right."

"You know I am."

Liam stared into the ceiling until he heard Joey's wet snores, then he closed his eyes and waited for the fever dreams.

Joey went critical the next day. One minute, he was snoring away in bed while Liam watched a daytime soap with headphones. The next minute, there were twenty people in the room: nurses, doctors, techs, even Col. Gonzalez. Joey was doing the floppy dance in the next bed, the OD dance that Liam had seen once or twice, danced once or twice on an Emergency Room floor, his heart pounding the crystal meth mambo.

Someone backhanded Liam's TV and it slid away on its articulated arm and yanked the headphones off his head, ripping open the scabs on the slowly healing sores on his ears. Liam stifled a yelp and listened to the splashing sounds of all those people standing ankle-deep in something pink and bad-smelling, and Liam realized it was watery blood and he pitched forward and his empty stomach spasmed, trying to send up some bile or mucous, clicking on empty.

Colonel Gonzales snapped out some orders and two techs abandoned their fretting over one of the computers, yanked free a tangle of roll-up, rubberized keyboards and trackballs and USB cables, piled them on the side of Liam's gurney, snapped up the guard rails, and wheeled him out of the room.

They crashed through a series of doors before hitting a badgepoint. One tech thought he'd left his badge back in the room on its lanyard (he hadn't—he'd dropped it on the gurney and Liam had slipped it under the sheets), the other one wasn't sure if his was in one of his many pockets. As they frisked themselves,

Liam stole his skeletal hand out from under the covers, a hand all tracked out with collapsed IV veins and yellowing fingernails, a claw of a hand.

The claw shook as Liam guided it to a keyboard, stole it under the covers, rolled it under the loose meat of his thigh.

• • •

"Need to know?" Liam said, spitting the words at Col. Gonzalez. "If I don't need to know what happened to Joey, who the fuck does?"

"You're not a medical professional, Liam. You're also not cleared. What happened to Joey was an isolated incident, nothing to worry about."

"Horseshit! You can tell me what happened to Joey or not, but I'll find out, you goddamned betcha."

The Colonel sighed and wiped his palms on his thighs. He looked like shit, his brush-cut glistening with sweat and scalp oil, his eyes bagged, and his youthful face made old with exhaustion lines. It had been two hours since Joey had gone critical—two hours of lying still with the keyboard nestled under his thigh, on the gurney in the locked room, until they came for him again. "I have a lot of work to do yet, Liam. I came to see you as a courtesy, but I'm afraid that the courtesy is at a close." He stood.

"Hey!" Liam croaked after him. "Gimme a fucking cigarette, will you?"

Once the Colonel was gone, Liam had the run of the room. They'd mopped it out and disinfected it and sent Joey's corpse to an Area 51 black ops morgue for gruesome autopsy, and there was only half as much hardware remaining, all of it plugged back into the hard pucker of skin on the back of Liam's neck.

Cautiously, Liam turned himself so that the toes of one foot touched the ground. Knuckling his toes, he pushed off toward the computers, the gurney's wheels squeaking. Painfully, arthritically, he inched to the boxes, then plugged in and unrolled the keyboard.

He hit the spacebar and got rid of the screen saver, brought up a login prompt. He'd been stealthily shoulder-surfing the techs for weeks now, and had half a dozen logins in his brain. He tapped out the login/pass combination and he was in.

The machine was networked to a CVS repository in some bunker, so the first thing he did was login to the server and download all the day's commits, then he dug out the READMEs. While everything was downloading, he logged into the tech's e-mail account and found Col. Gonzalez's account of Joey's demise.

It was encrypted with the group's shared key as well as the tech's key, but he'd shoulder-surfed both, and after three tries, he had cleartext on the screen.

Hydrostatic shock. The membranes of all of Joey's cells had ruptured simultaneously, so that he'd essentially burst like a bag of semiliquid Jell-O. Preliminary indications were that the antiviral cellular modifications had gone awry due to some idiosyncrasy of Joey's "platform"—his physiology, in other words—and that the "fortified" cell membranes had given way disastrously and simultaneously.

A ghoulish giggle escaped Liam's lips. Venture capitalists liked to talk about "liquidity events"—times in the life of a portfolio company when the investors get to cash out: acquisition and IPO, basically. Liam had always joked that the VCs needed adult diapers to cope with their liquidity events, but now he had a better one. Joey had experienced the ultimate liquidity event.

The giggle threatened to rise into a squeal as he contemplated a liquidity event of his own, so he swallowed it and got into the READMEs and the source code.

He wasn't a biotech, wasn't a medical professional, but neither were the coders who'd been working on the mods that were executing on his "platform" at that very moment. In their comments and data-structures and READMEs, they'd gone to great pains to convert medical jargon to geekspeak, so that Liam was actually able to follow most of it.

One thing he immediately gleaned is that his interface was modifying his cells to be virus-hardened as slowly as possible. They wanted a controlled experiment, data on every stage of the recovery—if a recovery was indeed in the cards.

Liam didn't want to wait. He didn't even have to change the code—he just edited a variable in the config file and respawned the process. Where before he'd been running at a pace that would reverse the course of HIV in his body in a space of three weeks, now he was set to be done in three *hours*. What the fuck—how many chances was he going to get to screw around after they figured out that he'd been tinkering?

•　•　•

Manufacturing the curative made him famished. His body was burning a lot of calories, and after a couple hours he felt like he could eat the ass out of a dead bear. Whatever was happening was happening, though! He felt the sores on his body dry up and start to slough off. He was hungry enough that he actually caught himself peeling off the scabby cornflakes and eating them. It grossed him out, but he was *hungry*.

His only visitor that night was a nurse, who made enough noise with her trolley on the way down the hall that he had time to balance the keyboard on top of the monitor and knuckle the bed back into position. The nurse was pleased to hear that he had an appetite and obligingly brought him a couple of supper trays—the kitchen had sent up one for poor Joey, she explained.

Once Liam was satisfied that she was gone, he returned to his task with a renewed sense of urgency. No techs and no docs and no Colonel for six hours now—there must be a shitload of paperwork and finger-pointing over Joey, but who knew how long it would last?

He stuffed his face, nailing about three thousand calories over the next two hours, poking through the code. Here was a routine for stimulating the growth of large muscle groups. Here was one for regenerating fine nerves. The enhanced reflexes sounded like a low-cal option, too, so he executed it. It was all betaware, but as between a liquidity event, a slow death on the palliative ward, and a chance at a quick cure, what the fuck, he'd take his chances.

He was chuckling now, going through the code, learning the programmers' style and personality from their comments and variable names. He was so damned hungry, and the muscles in his back and limbs and ass and gut all felt like they were home to nests of termites.

He needed more food. He gingerly peeled off the surgical tape holding on the controller and its cable. Experimentally, he stood. His inner ear twirled roller coaster for a minute or two, but then it settled down and he was actually erect—upright—well, both, he could cut glass with that boner, it was the first one he'd had in a year—and *walking*!

He stole out into the hallway, experiencing a frisson of delight and then the burning ritual humiliation of any person who finds himself in a public place wearing a hospital gown. His bony ass was hanging out of the back, the cool air of the dim ward raising goose-pimples on it.

He stepped into the next room. It was dusky-dark, the twilight of a hospital nighttime, and the two occupants were snoring in contratime. Each had his (her? it was too dark to tell) own nightstand, piled high with helium balloons, Care Bears, flowers, and baskets of nuts, dried fruits, and chocolates. Saliva flooded Liam's mouth. He tiptoed across to each nightstand and held up the hem of his gown, then grinched the food into the pocket it made.

Stealthily, he stole his way down the length of the ward, emptying fruit baskets, boxes of candy and chocolate, leftover dinner trays. By the time he returned to his room, he could hardly stand. He dumped the food out on the bed and began to shovel it into his face, going back through the code, looking for obvious bugs, memory leaks, buffer overruns. He found several and recompiled the apps, accelerating the pace of growth in his muscles. He could actually feel himself bulking up, feel the tone creeping back into his flesh.

He'd read the notes in the READMEs on waste heat and the potential to denature enzymes, so he stripped naked and soaked towels in a quiet trickle of ice-water in the small sink. He kept taking breaks from his work to wring out the steaming towels he wrapped around his body and wet them down again.

The next time he rose, his legs were springy. He parted the slats of the blinds and saw the sun rising over the distant ocean and knew it was time to hit the road, Jack.

He tore loose the controller and its cable and shut down the computer. He undid the thumbscrews on the back of the case and slid it away, then tugged at the sled for the hard disk until it sprang free. He ducked back out into the hall and quickly worked his way through the rooms until he found one with a change of men's clothes neatly folded on the chair—ill-fitting tan chinos and a blue Oxford shirt, the NoCal yuppie uniform. He found a pair of too-small penny loafers too and jammed his feet into the toes. He dressed in his room and went through the wallet that was stuck in the pants pocket. A couple hundred bucks' worth of cash, some worthless plastic, a picture of a heavyset wife and three chubby kids. He dumped all the crap out, kept the cash, snatched up the drive-sled and booted, badging out with the tech's badge.

• • •

"How long have you been on the road, then?" Murray asked. His mouth tasted like an ashtray and he had a mild case of the shakes.

"Four months. I've been breaking into cars mostly. Stealing laptops and selling them for cash. I've got a box at the rooming house with the hard-drive installed, and I've been using an e-gold account to buy little things online to help me out."

"Help you out with *what*?"

"Hacking—duh. First thing I did was reverse engineer the interface bug. I wanted a safe virus I could grow arbitrary payloads for in my body. I embedded the antiviral hardening agent in the vector. It's a sexually transmissible *wellness*, dude. I've been barebacking my way through the skankiest crack-hoes in the Tenderloin, playing Patient Zero, infecting everyone with the Cure."

Murray sat up and his head swam. "You did what?"

"I cured AIDS. It's going around, it's catching, you might already be a winner."

"Jesus, Liam, what the fuck do you know about medicine? For all you know, your cure is worse than the disease—for all you know, we're all going to have a—'*liquidity event*' any day now!"

"No chance of that happening, bro. I isolated the cause of that early on. This medical stuff is just *not that complicated*—once you get over the new jargon, it's nothing you can't learn as you go with a little judicious googling. Trust me. You're soaking in it."

It took Murray a moment to parse that. "You infected *me*?"

"The works—I've viralized all the best stuff. Metabolic controllers, until further notice, you're on a five-cheeseburger-a-day diet; increased dendrite density; muscle-builders. At-will pain-dampeners. You'll need those—I gave you the interface, too."

A spasm shot up Murray's back, then down again.

"It was on the cigarette butt. You're cancer-immune, by the by. I'm extra contagious tonight." Liam turned down his collar to show Murray the taped lump there, the dangling cable that disappeared down his shirt, connecting to the palmtop strapped to his belt.

Murray arched his back and mewled through locked jaws.

Liam caught his head before it slammed into the Toyota's hood. "Breathe," he hissed. "Relax. You're only feeling the pain because you're choosing not to ignore it. Try to ignore it, you'll see. It kicks azz."

• • •

"I needed an accomplice. A partner in crime. I'm underground, see? No credit card, no ID. I can't rent a car or hop a plane. I needed to recruit someone I could trust. Naturally, I thought of you."

"I'm flattered," Murray sarcased around a mouthful of double-bacon cheeseburger with extra mayo.

"You should be, asshole," Liam said. They were at Murray's one-bedroom techno-monastic condo: shit sofa, hyper-ergonomic chairs, dusty home theater, computers everywhere. Liam drove them there, singing into the wind that whipped down from the sunroof, following the GPS's sterile eurobabe voice as it guided them back to the anonymous shitbox building where Murray had located his carcass for eight years.

"Liam, you're a pal, really, my best friend ever, I couldn't be happier that you're alive, but if I could get up I would fucking *kill you*. You *raped me*, asshole. Used my body without my permission."

"You see it that way now, but give it a couple weeks, it'll, ah, grow on you. Trust me. It's rad. So, call in sick for the next week—you're going to need some time to get used to the mods."

"And if I don't?"

"Do whatever you want, buddy, but I don't think you're going to be in any shape to go to work this week—maybe not next week either. Tell them it's a personal crisis. Take some vacation days. Tell 'em you're going to a fat-farm. You must have a shitload of holidays saved up."

"I do," Murray said. "I don't know why I should use them, though."

"Oh, this is the best vacation of all, the Journey Thru Innerspace. You're going to love it."

• • •

Murray hadn't counted on the coding.

Liam tunneled into his box at the rooming house and dumped its drive to one of the old laptops lying around Murray's apartment. He set the laptop next to Murray while he drove to Fry's Electronics to get the cabling and components he needed to make the emitter/receiver for the interface. They'd always had a running joke that you can build *anything* from parts at Fry's, but when Liam invoked it, Murray barely cracked a smile. He was stepping through the code in a debugger, reading the comments Liam had left behind as he'd deciphered its form and function.

He was back in it. There was a runtime that simulated the platform and as he tweaked the code, he ran it on the simulator and checked out how his body would react if he executed it for real. Once he got a couple of liquidity events, he saw that Liam was right, they just weren't that hard to avoid.

The API was great, there were function calls for just about everything. He delved into the cognitive stuff right off, since it was the area that was rawest, that Liam had devoted the least effort to. At-will serotonin production. Mnemonic perfection. Endorphin production, adrenaline. Zen master on a disk. Who needs meditation and biofeedback when you can do it all in code?

Out of habit, he was documenting as he went along, writing proper tutorials for the API, putting together a table of the different kinds of interaction he got with different mods. Good, clear docs, ready for printing, able to be slotted in as online help in the developer tool kit. Inspired by Joey, he began work on a routine that would replace all the maintenance chores that the platform did in sleep-mode, along with a subroutine that suppressed melatonin and all the other circadian chemicals that induced sleep.

Liam returned from Fry's with bags full of cabling and soldering guns and breadboards. He draped a black pillowcase over a patch of living-room floor and laid everything out on it, wires and strippers and crimpers and components and a soldering gun, and went to work methodically, stripping and crimping and twisting. He'd taken out his own connector for reference and he was comparing them both, using a white LED torch on a headband to show him the pinouts on the custom end.

"So I'm thinking that I'll clone the controller and stick it on my head first to make sure it works. You wear my wire and I'll burn the new one in for a couple days and then we can swap. Okay?"

"Sure," Murray said, "whatever." His fingers rattled on the keys.

"Got you one of these," Liam said and held up a bulky Korean palmtop. "Runs Linux. You can cross-compile the SDK and all the libraries for it; the compiler's on the drive. Good if you want to run an interactive app"—an application that changed its instructions based on output from the platform—"and it's stinking cool, too. I fucking *love* gear."

"Gear's good," Murray agreed. "Cheap as hell and faster every time I turn around."

"Well, until Honorable Computing comes along," Liam said. "That'll put a nail in the old coffin."

"You're overreacting."

"Naw. Just being realistic. Open up a shell, okay? See at the top, how it says 'tty'? The kernel thinks it's communicating with a printer. Your shell window is a simulation of a printer, so the kernel knows how to talk to it—it's got plenty of compatibility layers between it and you. If the guy who wrote the code doesn't want you to interface with it, you can't. No emulation, that's not 'honorable.' Your box is owned."

Murray looked up from his keyboard. "So what do you want me to do about it, dead man?"

"Mostly dead," Liam said. "Just think about it, okay? How much money you got in your savings account?"

"Nice segue. Not enough."

"Not enough for what?"

"Not enough for sharing any of it with you."

"Come on, dude, I'm going back underground. I need fifty grand to get out of the country—Canada, then buy a fake passport and head to London. Once I'm in the EU, I'm in good shape. I learned German last week, this week I'm doing French. The dendrite density shit is the shit."

"Man und zooperman," Murray said. "If you're zo zooper, go and earn a buck or two, okay?"

"Come on, you know I'm good for it. Once this stuff is ready to go—"

"What stuff?"

"The codebase! Haven't you figured it out yet? It's a start-up! We go into business in some former-Soviet Stan in Asia or some African kleptocracy. We infect the locals with the Cure, then the interface, and then we sell 'em the software. It's *viral marketing*, gettit?"

"Leaving aside CIA assassins, if only for the moment, there's one gigantic flaw in your plan, dead-man."

"I'm all aflutter with anticipation."

"There's no fucking revenue opportunity. The platform spreads for free—it's already out there, you've seeded it with your magic undead super-cock. The hardware is commodity hardware, no margin and no money. The controller can be built out of spare parts from Fry's—next gen, we'll make it Wi-Fi, so that we're using commodity wireless chipsets and you can control the device from a distance—"

"—yeah, and that's why we're selling the software!" Liam hopped from foot to foot in a personal folk dance celebrating his sublime cleverness.

"In Buttfuckistan or Kleptomalia. Where being a warez dood is an honorable trade. We release our libraries and binaries and APIs and fifteen minutes later, they're burning CDs in every *souk* and selling them for ten cents a throw."

"Nope, that's not gonna happen."

"Why not?"

"We're gonna deploy on Honorable hardware."

"I am not hearing this." Murray closed the lid of his laptop and tore into a slice of double-cheese meat-lover's deep-dish pizza. "You are not telling me this."

"You are. I am. It's only temporary. The interface isn't Honorable, so anyone who reverse engineers it can make his own apps. We're just getting ours while the getting is good. All the good stuff—say, pain control and universal antiviral hardening—we'll make for free, viralize it. Once our stuff is in the market, the whole world's going to change, anyway. There'll be apps for happiness, cures for every disease, hibernation, limb regeneration, whatever. Anything any human body has ever done, ever, you'll be able to do at will. You think there's going to be anything recognizable as an economy once we're ubiquitous?"

Every morning, upon rising, Murray looked down at his toes and thought, "Hello toes." It had been ten years since he'd had regular acquaintance with anything south of his gut. But his gut was gone, tight as a drumhead. He was free from scars and age marks and unsightly moles and his beard wouldn't grow in again until he asked it to. When he thought about it, he could feel the dull ache of the new teeth coming in underneath the ones that had grown discolored and chipped, the back molar with all the ugly amalgam fillings, but if he chose to ignore it, the pain simply went away.

He flexed the muscles, great and small, all around his body. His fat index was low enough to see the definition of each of those superbly toned slabs of flexible contained energy—he looked like an anatomy lesson, and it was all he could do not to stare at himself in the mirror all day.

But he couldn't do that—not today, anyway. He was needed back at the office. He was already in the shitter at work over his "unexpected trip to a heath-farm," and if he left it any longer, he'd be out on his toned ass. He hadn't even been able to go out for new clothes—Liam had every liquid cent he could lay hands on, as well as his credit cards.

He found a pair of ancient, threadbare jeans and a couple of medium T-shirts that clung to the pecs that had grown up underneath his formerly sagging man boobs and left for the office.

He drew stares on the way to his desk. The documentation department hummed with hormonal female energy, and half a dozen of his coworkers found cause to cruise past his desk before he took his morning break. As he greedily scarfed up a box of warm Krispy Kremes, his cellphone rang.

"Yeah?" he said. The caller ID was the number of the international GSM phone he'd bought for Liam.

"They're after us," Liam said. "I was at the Surrey border crossing and the Canadian immigration guy had my pic!"

Murray's heart pounded. He concentrated for a moment, then his heart calmed, a jolt of serotonin lifting his spirits. "Did you get away?"

"Of course I got away. Jesus, you think that the CIA gives you a phone call? I took off cross-country, went over the fence for the duty-free, and headed for the brush. They shot me in the fucking leg—I had to dig the bullet out with my multitool. I'm sending in ass-loads of T-cells and knitting it as fast as I can."

Panic crept up Murray's esophagus, and he tamped it down. It broke out in his knees, he tamped it down. His balance swam, he stabilized it. He focused his eyes with an effort. "They *shot* you?"

"I think they were trying to wing me. Look, I burned all the source in 4,096-bit GPG ciphertext onto a couple of CDs, then zeroed out my drive. You've got to do the same, it's only a matter of time until they run my back-trail to you. The code is our only bargaining chip."

"I'm at work—the backups are at home, I just can't."

"Leave, asshole, like *now*! Go—get in your car and *drive*. Go home and start scrubbing the drives. I left a bottle of industrial paint-stripper behind and a bulk eraser. Unscrew every drive-casing, smash the platters, and dump them in a tub with all the stripper, then put the tub onto the bulk eraser—that should do it. Keep one copy, ciphertext only, and make the key a good one. Are you going?"

"I'm badging out of the lot, shit, shit, shit. What the fuck did you do to me?"

"Don't, okay? Just don't. I've got my own problems. I've got to go now. I'll call you later once I get somewhere."

• • •

He thought hard on the way back to his condo, as he whipped down the off-peak emptiness of Highway 101. Being a coder was all about doing things in the correct order: first a; then b; then, if c equals d, e; otherwise, f.

First, get home. Then set the stateful operation of his body for maximal efficiency: reset his metabolism, increase the pace of dendrite densification. Manufacture viralized antiviral in all his serum. Lots of serotonin and at-will endorphin. Hard times ahead.

Next, encipher and back up the data to a removable. Did he have any CD blanks at home? With eidetic clarity, he saw the half-spent spool of generic blanks on the second shelf of the media totem.

Then trash the disks, pack a bag, and hit the road. Where to?

He pulled into his driveway, hammered the elevator button a dozen times, then bolted for the stairs. Five flights later, he slammed his key into the lock and went into motion, executing the plan. The password gave him pause—generating a 4,096 bit key that he could remember was going to be damned hard, but then he closed his eyes and recalled, with perfect clarity, the first five pages of documentation he'd written for the API. His fingers rattled on the keys at speed, zero typos.

He was just dumping the last of the platters into the acid bath when they broke his door down. Half a dozen big guys in Martian riot-gear, outsized science fiction black-ops guns. One flipped up his visor and pointed to a badge clipped to a D-ring on his tactical vest.

"Police," he barked. "Hands where I can see them."

The serotonin flooded the murky gray recesses of Murray's brain and he was able to smile nonchalantly as he straightened from his work, hands held loosely away from his sides. The cop pulled a zap-strap from a holster at his belt and bound his wrists tight. He snapped on a pair of latex gloves and untaped the interface on the back of Murray's neck, then slapped a bandage over it.

"Am I under arrest?"

"You're not cleared to know that," the cop said.

"Special Agent Fredericks, right?" Murray said. "Liam told me about you."

"Dig yourself in deeper, that's right. No one wants to hear from you. Not yet, anyway." He took a bag off his belt, then, in a quick motion, slid it over Murray's head, cinching it tight at the throat, but not so tight he couldn't breathe. The fabric passed air, but not light, and Murray was plunged into total darkness. "There's a gag that goes with the hood. If you play nice, we won't have to use it."

"I'm nice, I'm nice," Murray said.

"Bag it all and get it back to the house. You and you, take him down the back way."

Murray felt the bodies moving near him, then thick zap-straps cinching his arms, knees, thighs, and ankles. He tottered and tipped backward, twisting his head to avoid smacking it, but before he hit the ground, he'd be roughly scooped up into a fireman's carry, resting on bulky body armor.

As they carried him out, he heard his cellphone ring. Someone plucked it off his belt and answered it. Special Agent Fredericks said, "Hello, Liam."

• • •

Machine-guns-and-biometrics bunkers have their own special signature scent, scrubbed air and coffee farts and ozone. They cut his clothes off and disinfected him, then took him through two air showers to remove particulate that the jets of icy pungent Lysol hadn't taken care of. He was dumped on a soft pallet, still in the dark.

"You know why you're here," Special Agent Fredericks said from somewhere behind him.

"Why don't you refresh me?" He was calm and cool, heart normal. The cramped muscles bound by the plastic straps eased loose, relaxing under him.

"We found two CDs of encrypted data on your premises. We can crack them, given time, but it will reflect well on you if you assist us in our inquiries."

"Given about a billion years. No one can brute-force a 4,096-bit GPG cipher. It's what you use in your own communications. I've worked on military projects, you know that. If you could factor out the products of large primes, you wouldn't depend on them for your own security. I'm not getting out of here ever, no matter how much I cooperate."

"You've got an awfully low opinion of your country, sir." Murray thought he detected a note of real anger in the Fed's voice and tried not to take satisfaction in it.

"Why? Because I don't believe you've got magic technology hidden away up your asses?"

"No, sir, because you think you won't get just treatment at our hands."

"Am I under arrest?"

"You're not cleared for that information."

"We're at an impasse, Special Agent Fredericks. You don't trust me and I don't have any reason to trust you."

"You have every reason to trust me," the voice said, very close in now.

"Why?"

The hood over his tag was tugged to one side and he heard a sawing sound as a knife hacked through the fabric at the base of his skull. Gloved fingers worked a plug into the socket there. "Because," the voice hissed in his ear, "because I am *not* stimulating the pain center of your brain. Because I am not cutting off the blood supply to your extremities. Because I am not draining your brain of all the serotonin there or leaving you in a vegetative state. Because I can do all of these things and I'm not."

Murray tamped his adrenals, counteracted their effect, relaxed back into his bonds. "You think you could outrace me? I could stop my heart right now, long before you could do any of those things." Thinking: I am a total bad-azz, I am. But I don't want to die.

"Tell him," Liam said.

"Liam?" Murray tried to twist his head toward the voice, but strong hands held it in place.

"Tell him," Liam said again. "We'll get a deal. They don't want us dead, they just want us under control. Tell him, okay?"

Murray's adrenals were firing at max now, he was sweating uncontrollably. His limbs twitched hard against his bonds, the plastic straps cutting into them, the pain surfacing despite his efforts. It hit him. His wonderful body was ownz-ored by the Feds.

"Tell me, and you have my word that no harm will come to you. You'll get all the resources you want. You can code as much as you want."

Murray began to recite his key, all five pages of it, through the muffling hood.

Liam was fully clothed, no visual restraints. As Murray chafed feeling back into his hands and feet, Liam crossed the locked office with its gray industrial carpeting and tossed him a set of khakis and a pair of boxers. Murray dressed silently, then turned his accusing glare on Liam.

"How far did you get?"

"I didn't even make it out of the state. They caught me in Sebastopol, took me off the Greyhound in cuffs with six guns on me all the time."

"The disks?"

"They needed to be sure that you got rid of all the backups, that there wasn't anything stashed online or in a safe-deposit box, that they had the only copy. It was their idea."

"Did you really get shot?"

"I really got shot."

"I hope it really fucking hurt."

"It really fucking hurt."

"Well, good."

The door opened and Special Agent Fredericks appeared with a big brown bag of Frappuccinos and muffins. He passed them around.

"My people tell me that you write excellent documentation, Mr. Swain."

"What can I say? It's a gift."

"And they tell me that you two have written some remarkable code."

"Another gift."

"We always need good coders here."

"What's the job pay? How are the bennies? How much vacation?"

"As much as you want, excellent, as long as you want, provided we approve the destinations first. Once you're cleared."

"It's not enough," Murray said, upending twenty ounces of West Coast frou-frou caffeine delivery system on the carpeting.

"Come on, Murray," Liam said. "Don't be that way."

Special Agent Fredericks fished in the bag and produced another novelty coffee beverage and handed it to Murray. "Make this one last, it's all that's left."

"With all due respect," Murray said, feeling a swell of righteousness in his chest, in his thighs, in his groin, "go fuck yourself. You don't own me."

"They do, Murray. They own both our asses." Liam said, staring into the puddle of coffee slurry on the carpet.

Murray crossed the room as fast as he could and smacked Liam, open palm, across the cheek.

"That will do," Special Agent Fredericks said, with surprising mildness.

"He needed smacking," Murray said, without rancor, and sat back down.

"Liam, why don't you wait for us in the hallway?"

• • •

"You came around," Liam said. "Everyone does. These guys own."

"I didn't ask to share a room with you, Liam. I'm not glad I am. I'd rather not be reminded of that fact, so shut your fucking mouth before I shut it for you."

"What do you want, an apology? I'm sorry. I'm sorry I infected you, I'm sorry I helped them catch you. I'm sorry I fuxored your life. What can I say?"

"You can shut up anytime now."

"Well, this is going to be a *swell* living arrangement."

The room was labeled "Officers' Quarters," and it had two good, firm, queen-sized mattresses, premium cable, two identical stainless-steel dressers, and two good ergonomic chairs. There were junction boxes beside each desk with locked covers that Murray supposed housed Ethernet ports. All the comforts of home.

Murray lay on his bed and pulled the blankets over his head. Though he didn't need to sleep, he chose to.

. . . .

For two weeks, Murray sat at his assigned desk, in his assigned cube, and zoned out on the screen saver. He refused to touch the keyboard, refused to touch the mouse. Liam had the adjacent desk for a week, then they moved him to another office, so that Murray had solitude in which to contemplate the whirling star field. He'd have a cup of coffee at ten thirty and started to feel a little sniffly in the back of his nose. He ate in the commissary at his own table. If anyone sat down at his table, he stood up and left. They didn't sit at his table. At 2:00 p.m., they'd send in a box of warm Krispy Kremes, and by 3:00 p.m., his blood-sugar would be crashing and he'd be sobbing over his keyboard. He refused to adjust his serotonin levels.

On the third Monday, he turned up at his desk at 9:00 a.m. as usual and found a clipboard on his chair with a ballpoint tied to it.

Discharge papers. Nondisclosure agreements. Cross-your-heart swears on pain of death. A modest pension. Post-it *sign here* tabs had been stuck on here, here, and here.

. . .

The junkie couldn't have been more than fifteen years old. She was death-camp skinny, tracked out, sitting cross-legged on a cardboard box on the sidewalk, sunning herself in the thin Mission noonlight. "Wanna buy a laptop? Two hundred bucks."

Murray stopped. "Where'd you get it?"

"I stole it," she said. "Out of a convertible. It looks real nice. One-fifty."

"Two hundred," Murray said. "But you've got to do me a favor."

"Three hundred, and you wear a condom."

"Not that kind of favor. You know the Radio Shack on Mission at Twenty-Fourth? Give them this parts list and come back here. Here's a hundred-dollar down payment."

He kept his eyes peeled for the minders he'd occasionally spotted shadowing him when he went out for groceries, but they were nowhere to be seen. Maybe he'd lost them in the traffic on the 101. By the time the girl got back with the parts he'd need to make his interface, he was sweating bullets, but once he had the laptop open and began to rekey the entire codebase, the eidetic rush of perfect memory dispelled all his nervousness, leaving him cool and calm as the sun set over the Mission.

• • •

From the sky, Africa was green and lush, but once the plane touched down in Mogadishu, all Murray saw was sere brown plains and blowing dust. He sprang up from his seat, laundering the sleep toxins in his brain and the fatigue toxins in his legs and ass as he did.

He was the first off the jetway and the first at the Customs desk.

"Do you have any commercial or work-related goods, sir?"

"No, sir," Murray said, willing himself calm.

"But you have a laptop computer," the Customs man said, eyeballing his case.

"Oh, yeah. That. Can't ever get away from work, you know how it is."

"I certainly hope you find time to relax, sir." The Customs man stamped the passport he'd bought in New York.

"When you love your work, it can be relaxing."

"Enjoy your stay in Somalia, sir."

YASSER ABDELLATIF

YOUNIS IN THE BELLY OF THE WHALE

(2011)

Translated from the Arabic by Robin Moger

Younis in the belly of the whale.
O belly like a casket:
Younis lives, he does not die.
—Naguib Surour

I ENTERED THE MALL through one of its sixty-nine gates. It is the biggest mall in North America, sprawling out over eight residential blocks: an entire commercial district in a town that lacks the very concept. Situated on the west side of town, it is the central district for a place without a center.

I entered through the gate that leads into the food court: a spacious area—more a small plaza than anything else: a ring of counters dispensing multinational fare surrounding tables and chairs belonging to no one restaurant in particular. Just help yourself: buy food from a counter, transport it on your plastic tray, then sit at a table, and eat. In the very center of the seating area four fountains shot out extraordinary shapes in water, lightly speckling diners with their spray and making a burbling sound that initially seemed romantic, before impinging ever more forcefully on your awareness until your very ability to speak was seriously impaired. That's if you had anything to say.

Japanese sushi, teriyaki chicken with white rice, beef à la Szechuan with green onion and ginger and carrot- and cabbage-stuffed spring rolls, Thai-style prawn soup with celery and sliced bamboo, vegetable masala for vegetarians (rice pudding with cardamom for dessert), Marrakesh red plum and mutton tagine, Russian kielbasa served with yogurt and a cabbage-garnished borscht, Swedish meatballs with gravy and chips, Mexican chili con carne with guacamole wrapped in tortillas, sheets of Ethiopian bread with a bright red paprika sauce for dipping and strips of cured beef, Italian favorites from lasagna to cannelloni through to pizza plus every other kind of pasta and sauce, Greek souvlaki with a salad of tomatoes, onion, lettuce, and feta, doner kebabs with Lebanese hummus and olive oil—even Egyptian falafel and tahina wrapped in shami bread . . . plus, of course, the presiding gods of American fast food, Kentucky Fried Chicken, McDonald's, Burger King. A genuine culinary globalization. Indian immigrants eating Chinese, Arab women in hijab chewing Turkish shawarma, Chinese teens wolfing burritos. The sheer variety of dishes and the water splashing and burbling inside my head left me dizzied. The choice was exhausting.

I went to the Italian outlet and bought a slice of pizza, like someone taking refuge with a half-known relative amid a crowd of strangers. (You can't trust any falafel made in North America by white hands: any ball of ta'amiya that hasn't been fried in motor oil is not to be relied on.) I took my slice and sat down at one of the tables, where I washed it down with cola.

I left the food court and drifted like a sleepwalker toward a passage signposted *PlayLand*. Down I went, surrounded by dozens of children, both accompanied and roaming free. The passage went on and on. I was still fuddled from the fountains' fading burble, but even as it faded the din of games and rides rose up to take its place and the farther my slow, child-dogged steps took me the more the roar of entertainment came to dominate.

Then I saw that the passage itself had turned into something like a suspension bridge: the walls and roof had fallen away and the cavernous space around me was filled with vast contraptions.

Serpentine tracks for four different grades of roller coaster coiled through the air: one for children, its rails set just off the ground and rumbling quietly along; a second with a line of teenagers at the gate, making an initial circuit around the hall, then plunging into the shadows of the Tunnel of Love, then dropping farther still, where, at some point, it became a kind of boat, meandering across a subterranean lake, the darkness brushed by dreamlike lights while young lovers stole fevered embraces and kisses; a third with sharp climbs and drops for the adults; and, finally, the lunatic coaster that lurched and plummeted at terrifying angles, made sudden banking swerves, its passengers possessed of the steeliest nerves and soundest hearts.

At either side of this passage-turned-bridge were gates, stations for the roller coasters' passengers, and at each one children and adults queued for their chance to thrill and scream. The space around me, with these gigantic fairground rides, the rattle and clack of railed wheels snapping through the air and its carnival throng of kids and teens, seemed to embody the essence of some spirit of entertainment that the amusement parks of my youth lacked altogether. In fact, I wanted ask—disoriented and alienated—in what "spirit" *did* they build these dancing monuments to steel and technology in our wretched cities?

Then the bridge became a passageway once more. The big rides were gone, and now a set of smaller games that lined both sides of the corridor. My attention was caught by something that looked identical to an astronaut's suit. SCUBASIM read the sign. Then a second phrase in cheerful font: *Dive into the depths without getting wet!* That's my game, I told myself. Dry diving's perfect for a wanderer from the East like me: a melancholic, a detached Apollonian observer.

For some moments, I stood and inspected the apparatus: a huge helmet, clearly constructed to accommodate a screen in front of the eyes, a trunk replicating the effect of a lead-like metal, arms and legs of flexible silicon terminating in a pair of gloves and perfunctory flippers, and mounted on the back an oxygen tank just like the real thing, if slightly smaller. An information plate stated that it was equipped with hi-fidelity speakers, which played oceanic sound effects and sensor pads at the palms and neck to give the user the impression of being underwater. Having shed your shoes and coat, you feed the suit coins (four dollars), put it on (climb into it), and close it, at which point it swivels from an upright stance to the horizontal. Now paddle your arms and legs to power yourself through the depths. Enjoy.

I fed the coins into the machine, slipped myself down the silicone arms and legs, and shut myself in. For a brief moment, the darkness inside was absolute. Then I heard a whine and felt the whole apparatus tilting. There was an axle fixed to the waist of the casing that allowed it to swivel between the horizontal and vertical. My arms and legs moved freely inside their rubbery sleeves.

I heard a faint whispering, a muffled submarine soundscape, then the screen lit up. The screen curved around my face and gave one-hundred-and-eighty-degree vision. It felt exactly as though I were peering through a diving mask.

I found myself in turquoise water. Not too deep: ten meters, say. The high resolution of the underwater scenery was not what I'd expected: it felt fantastically real, and from its almost velvety quality I could tell that it had been shot with a high-definition camera and converted into cinematic footage using 3D technology. The sensors on my skin exerted a gentle pressure, and I felt a faint squeezing inside my ears. Shoals of fine silver fish swirled around me as I began, as per instructions, to paddle. I was moving forward now, and to my astonishment the fish moved as I moved into their midst, the shoal scattering chaotically then regrouping at a distance. The software must have been incredibly advanced for this footage to be able to respond to the movements of a person wiggling about in the basement of some Canadian mall. It even occurred to me that I was watching a live feed from an underwater camera somewhere, but then I decided to stop thinking about the technicalities and just enjoy the experience.

I swam through the shallow turquoise waters, reveling, and then I got the idea of going to the surface to see what I could see. I spread my arms, lifted my head, and began kicking vigorously until I saw the surface approaching, but as I was about to break through it a sentence flashed across the bottom of the screen in red: *Not permitted . . . Please make your way to SurfaceSim . . .* This unexpected division of labor was mildly alarming, but I decided to see the game through to the end and I turned round and swam back down.

I saw a huge ray, its flat black body like a triangular carpet, flippers beating like a Roc's wings as it cruised with measured deliberation over the seabed. The electric whip of its tail stirred storms in the white sand each time it touched bottom and the clear water clouded in its wake. I saw great hordes of jellyfish rocking back and forth and clouds of blue-tinged sardines glinting in the rays of sunlight that stabbed down all around me. All of a sudden I found myself staring into a deep,

deep blue: an abyss. Looking back, I saw that I'd been swimming over a coral platform covered with a layer of white sand, and that it was this which had lent the water its turquoise clarity; now I was face to face with the true depths. A darkest blue. The coral platform had dropped away in a cliff face, and then there was only the deep stretching away. For a moment, I paused, hanging irresolute as though suspended in the real sea, then went forward into the unknown.

I sank down the face of the coral cliff, past dazzling fish of all shapes and sizes, singly and in shoals, every shade of orange and blue and green. Then a gray shark. Not huge, not small. It approached, bringing its slack jaw and dead eyes closer, then peacefully flicked away and disappeared. I remembered reading somewhere that fish gather in large numbers next to reefs because of the plentiful supply of food, and thus—in accordance with the law by which all fish abide—the plentiful supply of food for those that feed on the feeders.

I began to swim across the cliff face, up and down, watching and turning as I went. A shoal of yellow fish scattered to reveal a gaping hole in the coral. I approached the blank darkness cautiously, recalling from somewhere that caves and cracks were favored haunts of deadly eels and sea snakes. But as I entered the cave I saw a glow in the gloom, some opening in the cave's roof through which the sunlight had made its way through. Any opening, I reasoned, must lead to the shallow turquoise waters above the coral platform. Protected by my metal suit, my virtual reality, I took heart and decided to go all the way in the cave, swim up through the gap in the ceiling, and make it to the other side. At the back of my mind was a neglected spot on the Alexandrian shoreline known as Masoud's Well. Masoud's Well was a deep hole in the rocks near the suburb of Miami, and at the bottom of the hole a tunnel led out into the open sea. Back in the '70s, kids would compete by jumping into the well, passing along the tunnel then bobbing up in the distance.

I started swimming forward into the cave, heading toward the light. It wasn't a negligible distance, but the bright glow shining out into such deep blackness made measurements somehow hard to judge. Minutes passed, swimming along, bumping from time to time against the reef, then hearing the echoes of these collisions rebounding redoubled through the speakers at my ears.

Then I reached the opening, to discover it was too narrow to let me pass. I kept trying, and each time I tried a siren wailed, off and on like a warning, so I decided to change the plan, and turned back toward the cave's entrance. On the journey back out, the darkness was absolute. It was practically impossible to make out anything at all and I was colliding against the coral with increasing frequency, the muffled squeak of metal on rock amplified in the echo chamber of the cave and rendered terrifyingly immediate by the speakers that seemed to pick up any movement I made. Inside the lined silicone tubes my hands and feet began sweating heavily. My head swam in the darkness. A dizzy spell. I paused to catch my breath and collect myself but as I did so, the warning sirens went off again, louder this time, and at the bottom of the screen another phrase in red—*Oxygen about to run out . . . Please exit* ScubaSim *immediately*—and now, it seemed, I couldn't remember how to open this suit from within.

SUZANNE CHURCH

SYNCH ME, KISS ME, DROP

(2012)

WHEN MY NOSE STOPPED ACHING, I smiled at Rain. She had snorted a song ten minutes before me, and I couldn't quite figure why she waited here in the dark confines of the sample booth.

"Rain?" I said. "You okay?"

"Do you hear it, Alex?" she said, not really looking at me. More like staring off in two directions at once, as though her eyes had decided to break off their working relationship and wander aimlessly on their own missions. "It's so amaaazing."

She held that "a" a long time. I should've remembered how gripping every sample was for her, as though her neurons were built like radio antennae, attuned to whatever channel carried the best track ever recorded. I needed to get her ass on the dance floor before I got so angry that I ended up with another Jessica situation. I still had eight months left on my parole.

"Do you hear it?" Rain nudged me, hard on the shoulder. "Alex!" Her eyes had made up and decided to work together, locking on me like I was the only male in a sea of estrogen.

"Yeah, it's awesome," I lied. For the third time this week, I'd snorted a dud sample. My brain hadn't connected with a single, damned note.

Beyond the booth, the thump, thump of dance beats pulsed in my chest. Not much of a melody, but since they'd insisted I check my headset with my coat, I couldn't exactly self-audio-tain.

I grabbed her arm, feeling the soft flesh and liking it. Loving it. Maybe the sample *was* working on some visceral level beyond my ear-brain-mix. "Let's hit the dance floor."

"In a minute. Pleeease."

Over-vowels were definitely part of her gig tonight.

"Wait for the *drop*," she said, stomping her foot.

"Right." I watched her sway back and forth, in perfect rhythm with the dance music coming from the main floor. The better clubs brought all the vibes together, so that every song you sampled was in perfect synch with the club mix on the speakers. When the drop hit, everyone jumped and screamed in coordinated rapture.

I would miss the group-joy here in this tiny booth, with this date who was more into her own head than she would ever be into me. If I could get Rain out on the floor, I could at least feel the bliss, whiff all the pheromones, feel all those sweaty bodies pressed against mine, soft tissues rubbing together.

"Yeaaaah!" She shouted and grabbed my hand, squeezing it. Harder. Her eyes pressed shut, her mouth wide open, she leaned way back.

The drumbeats surged, and then, for a fraction of a second, they paused. Everyone in the club inhaled, as though this might be the last lungful of air left in the world and then . . .

Drop.

But *drop* doesn't say it all. Not even close. Because when it happens, it's like the most epic orgasm of all time and pinching the world's biggest crap-log in the same moment.

Rain opened her eyes and pressed her hand against the side of my cheek. Lunging with remarkable speed for a woman who over-voweled, she kissed me. Her tongue pressed against my lips.

I tasted her. Wanted her. An image of Jessica popped into my head: the look of terror on her face when I accidentally yanked her under.

The euphoria gone, I closed my mouth and turned away from Rain.

"Whaaat?" she said.

For a second, I thought about explaining what I had done to Jessica. Spewed on about how the drop isn't always built of joy. Instead, I went with the short, obscure answer. "Probation."

Rain looked at me funny, like she couldn't quite figure out how the judicial dudes could mess with our kiss-to-drop ratio. Finally, she smiled, and said, "Riiight."

Desperate to avoid another over-vowel, I shouted, "Let's dance!" This time, when I grabbed her arm, she followed along like a puppy.

Scents smacked at us as we pushed our way through the seething mass on the floor. This week's freebie at the door was *Octavia*, some new perfume marketed at the twenty-something set. It was heavy on Nasonov pheromones, some bee juice used to draw worker buzzers to the hive. When the drug companies cloned it, the result was as addictive as crack and as satisfying as hitting a home run on a club hookup.

My nostrils still ached from snorting a wallop of nanites, but scent doesn't only swim in the nose. The rest is all neurons, baby, and I had plenty to spare. Apparently so did Rain, because she was waving her nose in the air like a dog catching the whiff of a bitch in heat. The sight of her made me want to take her and do her right there on the floor.

But *Conduct* was a high-end club. The bouncers would toss us both if they caught us in the act anywhere on the premises, so I kept it in my pants. I still had another two hundred in my pocket. Enough for three more samples. Maybe I'd pick up a track from an indie band this time. Top forty drivel never seized my brainstem.

Unlike Rain.

The beats were building again. This time, with a third-beat thump, like Reggae on heroin. I could feel the intensity from my fingertips to my teeth to my dick. Even if I couldn't hear more than the background beats, I anticipated the drop. Rain opened her mouth again, raised both her hands in the air with every-one else, like a crowd of locusts all swarming together.

Pause.

Drop.

My date kept her eyes closed, her hands on her own breasts as she milked the release for all it was worth. Any decent guy should've watched her, should've wanted to, but I caught sight of a luscious creature, near the high-end sample booth, in the far-right corner of the club. The chick was about to slip between the curtains, but she caught me staring.

Her eyes glowed the purple of iStim addiction, reminding me of Jessica.

She had grown up in the suburbs, her allowance measured in thousands, not single dollars. The pack of girls she hung with had all bought iSynchs when they first hit the market. The music sounded better when they could all hear the same song at the same time. For the first time in more than a hundred years, getting high was not only legal, but ten times more amazing than it had ever been before. We all lived in our collective heads, the perfect synch of sound and sex.

I should've turned away from the sight of the purple chick, should've reached out to Rain and kissed her again. Close tonight's deal. Instead, I approached Rain's swaying body, and next to her ear shouted, "Back in five."

She nodded.

Fueled by fascination, and the two hundred burning a hole in my pocket, I headed for the high-end booth.

One of the bald bouncers with tribal tattoos worked the curtains. Yellow ear-plugs stuck out of both ears, so conversation, or in my case, pleading, wasn't an option. Feeling in my pocket for the two hundred, I scrunched the bills a bit, trying to make the wad appear larger than its meager value, then pulled out the stack in a flash. I had never dealt with this particular bouncer. *Conduct* was more Rain's club than mine, so I hoped the bills would get me past. The guy didn't even acknowledge me, as though he could smell my poverty, or maybe my parole. His eyes stared straight ahead.

My head scarcely came up to his bare chest, so I was uncomfortably close to his nipple rings, but I held my ground, and pointed at the curtains.

He remained statue-like. More boulder-like. Then a woman's cream-colored hand with purple nails ran from the guy's waist to his pecs and he turned to the side, like a vault door.

Purple-chick stood in the gap between the curtains. Her black dress was built of barely enough fabric to meet the dress code. Her hair stood on end like a teen-ager's beard, barely there and oddly sexy. She must have dyed it every night, because the stubble matched her eyes and nails. A waking wet dream.

"Come in," she pointed beyond the curtains.

"In what?" I mumbled to myself.

"Very funny."

"You're not laughing."

My body neared hers as I moved past into the sample booth. I carried my hands a little higher than would have passed as natural, hoping to cop a feel of all that exposed flesh on my way by. But she read me like a pheromone and dodged back.

A leather bench seat lined the far wall of the booth. Three tables were set with products in stacks like poker chips. The first was a sea of purple, tiny lowercase "i's" stamped on every top-forty sample like a catalogue from a so-called genius begging on a street corner for spare music. The second was a mishmash of undergrounds like *Skarface*, *Audexi*, and *Brachto*.

The third table drew me like fire. Only one sample. The dose was pressed into a waffle pattern, which was weird enough to make my desire itch. But the strang-est part was its flat black surface that sucked light away and spewed dread like mourners at a funeral.

Purple-chick watched me stare at it, waiting for me to speak. My mouth kept opening and closing, but I couldn't find words.

Expensive. Dangerous. Parole. All perfectly legit words that I couldn't voice.

I had forgotten my two hundred. My palms must have been really sweating, because what had once been a quasi-impressive stack, now stunk of poor-dude shame.

With practiced smoothness, she liberated my cash and said, "The *Audexi* works on *everyone*."

Distracted from the waffle, I said, "How'd you know I couldn't hear the last track?"

"Your throat," she said. "You're not pulsing to the beat."

My fingers felt my pulse beating like a river of vamp candy. Her observations were bang on. I wanted to illustrate my coolness, or, at the very least, my lack of lameness, but all I could manage was, "Oh."

She laughed.

My eyes wandered back to the waffle. I licked my lips.

Grabbing my chin, she forced me to look at tables one and two. "Your price range."

"What's the waffle?"

"New."

"Funny."

She didn't laugh. "Far from it."

"Addictive?" I asked, staring at the purple on the first table. How this woman could work the booth without jonesing for her own product made me rethink her motives.

"The absolute best never are," she said.

"No black eyes allowed in the boardroom, huh?"

She nodded. "Precisely."

I remembered Rain. By now, she'd have noticed my absence.

Purple-chick still held my two hundred. Her eyes locked on mine. "Try the *Audexi*. You won't be disappointed."

Like a Vegas dealer, she shoved all my money through a hole in the wall, selected an *Audexi* sample from table two, and held it in front of my nose.

I probably should've reported her. All of the clubs had to be careful not to push products hard, end up drawing the cops in to investigate. But my money was long gone and Rain wouldn't wait much longer.

I exhaled. The moisture turned the poker-chip-shaped disk into a teeming pile of powder-mimicking nanites, and I snorted. For several blinding seconds, I felt as though a nuclear bomb had blown inside. I could feel Purple-chick's hand on my arm, making sure I didn't wipe out and sue the club. Then the song erupted in my mind.

Sevenths and thirds. Emo-goth-despair. Snares and the ever-present bass, bass, bass. Music flowed like a tsunami through a village, grabbing ecstasy like cars and plowing through every other thought except for the tweaks of synths and the pulse-grab of the click-track. The song was building, and all I could think about was finding Rain before the drop.

• ' • •

Rain and I danced in nanite-induced harmony until the early dawn. Exhausted and covered in sweat and pheromones, we grabbed our coats and carried rather than wore them outside.

The insides of my sore nose stuck together in the frigid air, a wake-up call for the two of us to don our coats or end up with frostbite. I didn't want to, I was so damned hot and pumped, but I figured I should set a good example for Rain. And the way our night was progressing, I wouldn't have much time to scan my barcode at the parole terminal before curfew.

Jessica's fucking choice of words would be killing my buzz for eight more months.

That fourth of October had been hot as hell. After clubbing, we both stripped and headed into the lake for a skinny dip. Except she wasn't skinny and I wasn't much of a dipper. She'd called me over to the drop and I thought she meant for the lingering song, not the drop-off hidden in the water. When the drop blissed me, I lost my footing and plunged over my head.

"Shit, it's cooold," said Rain.

I snapped back to reality. "Still with the vowels?"

"Screw you." She pushed me away and called a cab with the same arm wave.

"Don't be that way, baby."

"Now I'm your fucking baby? After ditching me for a dozen drops while you plucked that purple fuzz-head."

"You saw?"

"Who didn't?"

"Sorry. But you gotta admit, you and me, we really synched *after*." I nudged her, maybe a little too hard. "The last sample I snorted was worth it. Right?"

A cab squealed a U-turn and stopped in front of Rain. She started to climb in and then looked up at me.

I shook my head. Shrugged. "Tapped out."

"Fine." She slammed the door in my face and the cab took off up the street.

I stood there, watching my breath condense in the air, its big cloud distorting her and the cab. The cold clawed its way into me, sucking away my grip on reality. The shivering reminded me to at least wear my coat.

As I stuffed my arms into the sleeves, I sniffled, feeling wetness and figuring the cold was making my nose run. But then I noticed the red drops on the ground and the front of my coat. I wiped with one finger and it came back a dark and bloody mass. Dead nanites, blood, snot, all mixed together. Two shakes didn't get it off my finger, so I rubbed the mess in a snowbank and only managed to make it worse.

The nearest subway was blocks away. I should've kept my mouth shut, shared the cab with Rain, and then stiffed her for half the fare. But I'd hurt her enough for one night. Hurt enough women for one lifetime.

Jessica had been the closest thing to a life preserver, so I grabbed on. Tripping on the samples, her brain couldn't remember how to hold her breath, or at least that's how my lawyer argued it at the trial.

As I trudged for the subway, I concentrated on not slipping and falling on my ass. I found the entrance, and headed down the stairs, gripping the cold metal handrail, even though my warm skin kept sticking to it. The *Audexi* sample still pulsed through my system and I couldn't walk down in anything but perfect synch. The song was building to another drop, and I had to make the bottom of the platform before that moment, or I'd become another victim of audio-tainment.

The platform was nearly empty, save for a few other clubbers too tapped out to cab their way home. *Octavia* hung in the air, the Nasonov-pheromone-scents calling us all home like buzzers to the hive. Much as I loathed their company, I couldn't resist the urge to huddle with the others in the same section while we waited for the train.

Off to our right I caught sight of Purple-chick. She wore a long, black faux-fur coat. The image of her here, slumming it with the poor, was as wrong as a palm tree in a snowbank. She belonged in some limo, holding a glass of champagne.

I tried to break the pull of the scent pack, but couldn't step far enough away from my fellow losers to get within talking distance of Purple-chick. When the train arrived, I watched her step inside, then waited until the last second before I climbed aboard, to make sure we were both on the same train.

The cars were so empty that I could see her, way ahead.

Standing near the doors, she held a pole while she swayed back and forth. I couldn't figure out why she didn't sit down, especially after a long night at the club. The rest of us were sprawled on benches, crashing more than sitting.

I considered the long trek up to her car, but I didn't trust my balance. Instead, I watched her. Waited until she stepped in front of the doors, announcing her intention to disembark.

Once again, I waited until the last second to leave the train, in case she decided to duck back on without me. I could tell that she knew I was watching. Following.

Okay, *stalking*.

She hurried up the stairs. Either she was training for a marathon, or her samples had all worn off, because I couldn't keep up. When she reached the top, she turned around and said, "What?"

Instead of rushing off, she stood there, at the top of the stairs. Waiting.

Her eyes were blue.

Not purple.

I hurried until I stood in front of her, nose to nose. "You took the waffle?"

She nodded.

"Tell me."

She shook her head. "Can't."

"Figures." I turned away.

"But I can show you."

"Yeah?"

"Kiss me," she said.

I sure as hell didn't wait for her to change her mind. We shared it all: tongues, saliva, even our teeth scraped against each other, making an awful sound that knocked my sample completely out of my head.

What filled the void wasn't the pounding of my heartbeat. Or hers. Or any song that I had ever heard. Instead, I could hear her thoughts, as visible as a black blanket on a white sand beach.

"Wow," I said.

Isn't it?

Her words, not spoken but thought into me. They reverberated around my skull like noise bouncing in an empty club.

I lost my footing and fell. Down. In. Far away. Suddenly I was six years old and my father leaned over and hauled me back up onto my skate-clad feet. We skated together, him holding me, his back stooped over in that awkward way that would make him curse all evening.

"Find your balance, Alex. Bend your knees. Skate!"

I had forgotten how much I loved him. Forgotten what it felt like to be young and innocent, to enjoy the thrill of exercise for its own sake, and feel a connection that didn't cost the price of a sample.

"I love you." But when I looked up at him, he had morphed back into Purple-chick, now Purple-and-blue-chick. She held me, preventing my crash down the stairs.

"Cool, huh?" she said.

"A total mind-fuck."

"That's why it's so expensive."

"How much? I mean, you're on the subway, so if I save—"

"In my experience, those who ask the price can't afford it."

"Why me?" I said.

She smiled. "Marketing."

I needed a better answer, so I listened for her thoughts. All I sensed was the wind from another subway, blowing up the stairs behind me.

She turned and hurried for an exit.

"Wait!" My head buzzed, confused by the difference between waffle and real, trapped by the synch-into-memory-lane-trip that lingered on my tongue like bad breath.

Her boots stopped clapping against the lobby of the subway station, but she didn't look back. I was glad of it, because my memories were still swimming in my head. I wanted her to be Dad.

Not Dad. *Rain*. My former date's cute outfit lingered in my synapses, replacing nostalgia with guilt. I wondered if Rain had made it home okay in the cab.

Then naked Jessica filled my head, and it was October again.

"I didn't mean it," I said aloud, my voice echoing against the tile walls. "The high confused it all. I'll do another year of parole. I'll spend my sample money on flowers for your grave. Please, forgive me?"

Still with her back to me, and in a voice that sounded eerily like Jessica's, she said, "What about Rain?"

I shook my head, even though she couldn't possibly see me. "She'll understand."

Far ahead, Purple-and-blue-chick turned to face me. I saw her as *them*, she had somehow merged with Jessica, the two of them existing in perfect synch, like a sample and the club music stitching together; twins in a corrupted womb. They both saw me for what I was, a lame guy who would always be about eight hundred shy of a right and proper sample. Whose love would always be shallow, too broke to buy modern intimacy.

"You've got less than ten minutes to clock in your parole." She started walking again, and I watched her leave, one synched step at a time until she exited the station and disappeared along the ever-brightening-street.

Drop.

Only this drop, waffle-back-to-real, felt like nails screeching on a blackboard. I wasn't in my usual subway station, and I had no idea where to find the nearest parole scanner. The station booth was empty, too early for a human. The only person in sight was an older woman with the classic European-widow black-scarf-plus-coat-plus-dress that broadcast, *Leave me alone, young scum*.

So I did.

I hurried onto the street, and looked toward the sun. It was well above the horizon now, but mostly hidden behind a couple of apartment buildings.

"Fuck," I told the concealed ball of reddish-yellow light. "How'd it get so late?"

The judiciary alarm buzzed inside my head.

For a moment, I could feel a drop, the biggest, most intense and amazing drop I would ever experience. The sort of nirvana that people pursue ineffectually for a lifetime. Or two.

I had less than ten minutes until the final warning.

Rushing for the nearest, busiest street, I tried to wave down car after car, hoping someone would point me to the nearest scanner. Or maybe they had a portable one, the kind I should've brought with me, had I been thinking about more than getting into Rain's pants when I left.

People ignored me.

Shunned me.

I smelled of trouble. Which, technically, I was. But I didn't mean to be. It wasn't my fault.

It was never my fault.

One cab slowed, but didn't stop. The driver made eye contact, and then rushed away.

"Hey!" I considered swearing at him, but I didn't want to draw the cops.

I'm not sure why the cabbie stiffed me. Maybe he read my desperation. Maybe he was Rain's cabbie and he knew I was broke. In any case, he probably broadcast a warning to his buddies, because the next cab that got remotely close made a fast U-turn and took off.

Choosing a direction, I took off down one street, then hung a right at the next, jogging, skidding, almost falling on my ass. Every direction felt wrong.

I didn't see a single person. No one. Not even a pigeon, for fuck's sake. All I needed was a *phone*.

With one hand on a pole, I leaned over, trying to catch my breath. To think.

My heart was pounding now, no synch in sight. The song was long gone, the link to Purple-chick disconnected. No one had my back.

I turned in a circle, then another, scanning far and near for anything of value: an ATM, a phone booth, a coffee shop, a diner, any place where I could access the judicial database. Plead my case.

The final warning buzzed.

"Fuck!" My spit froze when it hit the ground.

I hit full-blown panic. My heart tripped like the back-bass before the drop. Only this time, the other side was built of misery not ecstasy.

If only I had paid my cell bill. If only my father was still alive, to catch my sorry ass. If only I had lied to Rain, shared her cab. If only Jessica hadn't called it a drop.

When you're panicked, it's tough as hell to keep any rational sense of time. I figured I was cooked. So I closed my eyes. But when the pain didn't come, I sat down on the cold curb, and felt the chill seep through my clothes.

I bit my lip. Tasted blood.

The first jolt ripped through my body. I wanted to writhe in pain on the sidewalk, but my body was stuck in shock-rigor. An immobile gift for the cops.

I imagined Rain beside me.

"You're an asshole," she said.

"Sorry."

She morphed into Jessica, her purple eyes wide with fear. "I'm lost," she said.

"Take my hand." I wanted to reach out, but I couldn't move. My fingers looked nearly white in the cold. Her fingers seemed to shiver around mine, as though they were made of joy, not flesh. Then she touched my hand and I knew in that moment that life existed outside of stimulation, in a place where reality wasn't lame or boring. Life danced to an irregular rhythm that couldn't synch to any sample.

She let go.

The judiciary pulse jolted again. I flopped to the pavement, distantly aware that my skull would remind me for a long time after about its current state of squishage.

The parole board must have lived for irony, because the jolt lasted for so long that I *welcomed* the release. A pants-wetting, please-make-it-stop, urgent need for the end.

Drop.

ZEDECK SIEW

THE WHITE MASK

(2015)

THE WHITE MASK IS DEAD. Social media has the story before the cops find his body.

Now the news sites are all posting the same thing, the same photo, the same angle, taken from across the lanes—

Of the White Mask sitting slumped against the highway wall, wearing a black hoodie; black skinny jeans with both legs splayed; black sneakers. And at his feet: three loose curbstones, kicked out of their spaces.

He wears a white mask over his face, and a crushed and crinkled larynx.

Behind him, on the highway wall:

Dr. M, the Tun Doctor, standing as a stenciled mural. This is the Tun Doctor in the later years: in a Nehru collar; hands clasped together and hair combed back; cheeks and jowls sagging; small eyes framed by spectacles. Smiling with a hint of teeth showing.

· · ·

I walk across as my online self. There are voices like a semicircle choir sighing around the body. "Was it a robbery?" somebody says, and somebody else says: "Was it an accident?"

A third somebody says: "Why are people posting this picture, dead people are not things I want to see at breakfast or anytime ever, stop posting this picture please or you will. Get. Blocked!"

There is a satchel of art supplies open on the ground; there are spray-paint cans rolled into corners.

I kneel to look at a can. At this zoom level the resolution is poor—but I already know what its label says:

Smart acrylic lacquer. Latest version, industry standard, black in color.

• • •

And there is a live stream now. We watch the cops watching the surveillance feed—

Of the White Mask, standing between pools of streetlamp light, facing the highway wall. He shakes his spray can. We can imagine what that sounds like: clickity-clack-clack-clack.

The White Mask rolls his white undercoat onto the wall. It is an out-of-the-way wall, mostly empty—so this is a personal project, a minor independent commission maybe, an experiment.

The only thing already there is a graffiti tag, half-buried beneath the White Mask's new canvas. "Terror Thursday," the tag says, broody, squirming, trying to wriggle itself back to the surface—but it's a years-old thing, done in outdated hardware, its pigments unable to compete with the latest paints.

• • •

Piece by piece, the White Mask tapes up his stencil scaffold. His spray can sneezes, hisses—

The footage fast-forwards. His arms are a blur. They slow down again only as he steps back. We admire the wall with him: there's that mural of the Tun Doctor there now, just as we see it the next morning, in photos with the White Mask's body lying there.

But for now the White Mask is still working. His spray can cackles: clickity-clack-clack-clack. He places a stencil atop the Tun Doctor's hair.

The cut out outline of a fluffy cloud.

The White Mask works at it methodically, layer by layer, coat by coat, each a different color—

So the Tun Doctor wears a rainbow clown wig now.

• • •

"So who is this White Mask guy?" somebody says.

"Though he got what he deserved," somebody else says. "I feel sorry for his family, but really, how can anybody disrespect the Tun Doctor, who brought us development and prosperity, the greatest leader of our country?"

A third somebody says: "The White Mask is not a he, the White Mask is a she."

And then we notice that the Tun Doctor is angry. Small and squinty before, now the Tun Doctor's eyes blink quickly; the lines about the Tun Doctor's teeth turn into a snarl.

We notice—but the White Mask does not. He crouches, unfolding his last stencil. It is a piece of cardboard with a circle cut in the center:

A round nose.

He shakes a can of red paint: clickity-clack-clack—

• • •

Then he freezes.

The Tun Doctor's hands and arms are reaching out and off the highway wall's surface: two flat sheets of black matter, viscous, elbow-less, snaking out and grasping in boneless, alien ways.

His hood falls from his head. He struggles a little, his white mask shaking: no-no-no. He is being strangled. The Tun Doctor has him by his neck.

The spray can drops, toppling other spray cans like a strike to bowling pins.

The White Mask is held back to the wall, unable to break away. He kicks and kicks and kicks. He kicks the loose curbstones out of their spaces.

After a while he stops kicking.

The Tun Doctor stands up, wiping away the rainbow clown hair with whip-like fingers. Then the Tun Doctor settles: hands clasped together, small eyes squinting. Saintly smiling, with a hint of teeth showing.

• • •

Smart paint technology. Motorized nano-particulates, germs of pigment—umber or arsenic or ultramarine—movement-capable, programmable, bearing net-worked memory full of commands and subroutines.

I am something of an expert; I did engineering in Korea, at a university where they developed the technology.

"All fun and moving!" I say. "See?"

This was five-six years ago. I tilt a ceramic tile to show the Datuk what I mean.

On my tile there is a cartoon figure running in a hamster wheel, and the painted wheel is turning—it isn't just an animation on a screen; the paint itself is shifting, spinning around the ceramic surface.

The little painted, panting man keeps up by running.

I made my little ceramic tile for our Majestic Place presentation. My tile gets us the job—our client the Datuk laughs, in love with its motile, cutting-edge novelty.

• • •

Our client the Datuk comes from the petro-gas company that owns Majestic Place—

"It's a petro-gas company!" Adam says. "So we have to fuck with them."

What we do with Majestic Place—it is all Adam's idea. We turn it into a phan-tasmagoria. On its sides we lay pipeline calligraphy. We build onion domes with smokestack minarets; traffic jams piercing candy smog; trains, planes, and rocket ships; swirling firework landscapes.

No natural tones. No green except for the coughing cartoon stiffs lining up for caffeine shots, on the walls of the building's ground-floor coffee place.

I tell our client the Datuk—I reassure him, saying: "Look, Datuk, you want to tell people that your company has a vision. This neon city, this is your vision! This is your future: bright, full of color, full of energy!"

• • •

Majestic Place is the first moving smart paint mural in the country. For this fact alone our client the Datuk is very happy.

Adam and I win Multimedia Campaign of the year. During industry awards night Adam goes onstage to accept our trophy. He wears his white mask and I am whooping.

"Whoo!" Adam says, his arms up, his palms open. "Whoo!"

Our friends fist-bump us. We are heroes, power couple of the evening: celebrity artist and code genius. We've hoodwinked a petro-gas company, more or less: clothed their corporate offices in toxic-nightmare landscapes, and afterward they paid us money.

There are those who are not so congratulatory. Look:

Five-six guys in the corner, drinking soda, feigning the barest minimum applause to be polite.

These guys. They are the Terror Thursday crew. They are jealous.

• • •

Adam was the White Mask—is the White Mask.

When Adam starts wearing his mask he is sixteen. He tags walls in Wangsa Maju, where he lives; eventually the mask becomes his identity, his thing.

It helps him. He does not have an easy beginning.

In this time of our lives we have not yet met. Adam runs with Terror Thursday— right now they are just a bunch of boys searching for themselves by the river's concrete flood banks, in spray cans, in squelchy long-poled roller brushes.

They draw jumping skateboarders and zombie hordes; polyhedral letters saying VOX and LIFE and MERDEKA RAYA; they draw green-irised girls in red-and-white headscarves, pleading for peace to return in the Middle East.

• • •

Terror Thursday is what they call themselves—

Thursday—meaning Thursday evening specifically, which in religion counts as the start of Friday, part of the holy day: a time of noble thoughts and purity, of artful God-blessed jihad.

Terror—not meaning horror, but the word used in its celebratory sense, somebody seeing a burning piece, or a cool perspective-trick painting, and saying: "Wah, so terror!"

The name is Ghaf's idea.

Ghaf is a good-looking guy. He is proud of his skill. He is not the best artist among them—that's Adam—but he does know where to get specialty paints for lower-than-market prices. So he takes command.

"The signs were there," Adam tells me later. "Could already see the way Ghaf would go."

• • •

At the start, Adam and Ghaf are a thing. That's how Adam gets in.

Of course it doesn't last, and Adam stays with the Terror Thursdays only for a few more years. Boys of that kind, at that age? They don't understand.

The mask is Adam's way of coping. It is a physical symbol that his person-hood is changeable. He doesn't have to be whatever other people see. More and more he says this aloud.

For Ghaf and the rest—

To them he is still a girl: just out of her school baju, stuffed into a beanie and baggy tee. They grow uncomfortable.

"You shouldn't, you know," Ghaf says. "You are a girl. God made you a woman. You cannot go against God."

"You like to talk about changing the world," Adam tells him.

"For the better!" Ghaf says. "Not like this, for the worse."

• • •

Nowadays Ghaf is balding early. He wears a goatee and a skullcap under his hoodie. He talks to a news reporter.

"She does not represent us," he says. "Yes, the White Mask is actually a she. She was born a woman. We grew up together. Her real name is Dyana, she used to run with our crew."

The five-six guys of Terror Thursday stand together, looking grim.

"This was before she got her sex change," Ghaf says. "She left our crew to become a tomboy and a liberal.

"This, insulting the greatest leader of our country?" He points at the Tun Doctor standing in the highway wall. "This is going too far. It's treasonous. Sacrilegious! We street artists, we are patriots. People have to know she does not represent us."

The cowards, crusading against the dead. I am thinking how Adam made it so easy for them, getting himself killed like this—so stupid. He let them win.

• • •

One headline says: "Artists, NGOs Lodge Police Report against Dr. M Clown Mural."

"Cops: White Mask Death a Programming Error," another headline says.

There is a live stream of the police press conference, with an officer holding up a notebook they found in Adam's bag, and he is flipping through its pages—

It is a book of sketches. In it is Dr. M, the Tun Doctor, page after page, in spectacles and Nehru collar, in various poses:

In a clown's getup; in a cap with three stars arranged in a triangle; in a dress. With a beer bottle. Sitting on the toilet, eyes shut tightly, straining. His hands on two handles of a motorbike, planking on the bike seat, his legs stretched out straight behind him.

A third headline says: "Respect the Tun Doctor, Minister Reminds Youth."

• • •

A month ago, Adam opens the notebook with his Tun Doctor sketches to show me.

"I'm thinking we can put these up as stencils," he says.

When I see what he's drawn I look him in the eye, and I ask: "Why?"

"For fun," Adam says. "You know Terror Thursday got that contract with the Ministry, that history campaign for Merdeka month? 'Malaysian Heroes' featuring the Tun Doctor. That's Ghaf, no imagination. I want to fuck with him."

"You'll piss off other people, not just Ghaf," I say. "They'll say you're insulting our greatest leader."

And Adam says: "So fuck them too."

"We won't even get paid for it. I don't think it's worth the trouble."

"And fuck you too!" Adam says.

• • •

Now, when I am not crying, I am thinking. If I'd been there I could have double-checked the paint's programming—

Smart paint stores commands and algorithms in its memory. The latest versions come with inbuilt antivandalism subroutines, so that paintings shield themselves from damage.

An authorized user inputs the desired level of security.

Whether the paint reacts to touch, reacts to the application of additional coats or colors, reacts to differing or knockoff brands. Whether it responds by dissolving foreign particulates—as the Tun Doctor did with Adam's clown wig.

Or by forcibly removing the source of attack—by physically debilitating attackers, for example.

Adam, he's not so good at code. He didn't program his paint properly—didn't properly add himself to the permissions list—so his own paint saw him as an attacker, and his own paint attacked him.

Me? Programming is my thing. If I'd been there—

• • •

The reason why industry-standard paint has antivandalism software:
Businesses think their marketing campaigns need protecting.

They need us. The Public Advertisements Act banned billboards in the late 2010s—but what we do, technically it isn't advertising. It is art. Corporate-sponsored art.

People like the Datuk and his petro-gas company—they pay us good money for our murals. More than anybody else, they don't want to wake up in the morning to see their branding defaced.

I remember Adam ranting about the money.

"The money is spoiling us," Adam says. "Just now I met Ruby, buying groceries, she asked why we've not visited her lately. Rich people already, is it, she said. She's right! In the past five-six years we've not done any work but corporate jobs—not one! When did we become corporate people?"

"Remember we've got a meeting with the Datuk tomorrow," I say.

• • •

We meet for the first time at a party at Ruby's place.

Adam is pretty: he has an angular face, curly hair; he wears a jean jacket, a smile that is sweet, half-cocky.

He wears a binder for his chest. He tells me about himself—about the Terror Thursdays and the work; about the White Mask; about going to court tomorrow, to show support for the trans women appeal case.

I tell him about my studies abroad in engineering. We talk about the future.

And five-six months later, even though he has me blindfolded I know he's brought me to the river—I can smell its stink.

"Surprise," he says.

Across the water, on the concrete flood bank, he's written his name and my name. Big block letters. Between those two words he's painted a heart. It is big, valved, bloody red.

I imagine it beating.

• • •

"Wipe out all of the White Mask's murals!" somebody says.

Somebody else replies: "I don't agree with his actions, but you know, as the French philosopher Voltaire says—"

The Datuk from the petro-gas company writes to tell me: "We have partnered with the White Mask crew for our Majestic Place premises for the past seven years. We feel now it is time to make a change.

"Please accept our sincerest thanks for what has been a warm, long, and fruitful relationship. We wish you all the best!"

And in a separate message:

"I am so very sorry for your loss. You know, I liked you two very much, and I still do. But this recent thing, it's bothering my bosses a lot, they don't want the company seen associating with you. I hope you understand."

• • •

The men, they wash his body with water and lime.

They wrap him in white cloth, in many layers. His face is pale and waxy looking. His mother and father and his sisters pray. Their arms are folded, right hand on left—the same way Adam's hands are folded.

His mother and father look tired.

People have been pressuring them to apologize. "You've raised a tomboy and a liberal!" they say. "Please try to be a bit ashamed."

"What Adam did, he has already done," his father says.

"We won't apologize," his mother says. "He was our son."

By the graveside the hecklers and online hate are muted. It is quiet. There is a frangipani tree scattering its flowers—already rotting—onto the headstones and shoveled earth.

• • •

"Hello," Ghaf says. He leans against the wall by the mosque gate. He wears a smile, seemingly sympathetic.

So I ask him: "Why are you here?"

"To pay my respects," he says. "I grew up with Dyana. I was her friend."

"Adam was what his name was, you asshole. You stopped being his friend long ago. How could've you ever been his friend, you can't even call him by his name."

Ghaf shakes his head. "It is sad for her to have died in sin," he says. "I wanted to tell you, professional to professional. For our history campaign to commemorate Merdeka month, we'll use the White Mask's stenciled mural of the Tun Doctor.

"We've already discussed it with the Ministry," he says. "They agree, it's a good place for us to start, a good lesson. This way at least Dyana will have done something good in the world."

• • •

That night I leave my car in the emergency lane and walk through the underpass. I look up at the highway wall.

It's the first time I'm here in person.

The streetlamps cast light at an angle. The wall is slightly rough. There is rubbish at the Tun Doctor's feet, leftovers of the police investigation—three soda cups, a blue medical glove, shreds of black bin-liner stuck in cracks between the curbstones.

The Tun Doctor looks directly at me: cheeks and jowls sagging, eyes squinting, smiling.

"Hello, you," I say. I am wearing Adam's white mask.

Sitting cross-legged, I wire electrodes to the wall. My diagnostic runs through the data. It tells me almost immediately the reason why Adam wasn't recognized as a user: a missing closing chevron bracket, early on—

A forgot-to-add-an-end-tag kind of stupid mistake.

• • •

But that's not why I'm here.

I stand down the Tun Doctor's defenses. I open my satchel of art supplies. I have a stencil with me, in eight cardboard sheets, crinkled and inexpertly cut. I tape them up.

I shake my can of smart acrylic lacquer: clickity-clack-clack-clack. Then it sputters and hisses—

And after a while there is a stenciled mural of the White Mask on the wall: arms apart, palms open; the mask in the hoodie an oval outline of the white undercoat underneath, with wet licks of black denoting grinning lips and nose and eyeholes.

The paint begins to dribble, like tears. I've sprayed too much paint on—I'm not used to the mask, it is hard to see. Art was always Adam's thing.

• • •

I am better at programming.

With my tablet editor and pen stylus I pull the White Mask's arms toward the Tun Doctor, over the Tun Doctor's shoulder. And the Tun Doctor's arm I put over the White Mask's shoulder. I push the two figures together.

Each still has a hand free. I ball their open palms into fists, and I position these in front, making them meet in the middle, touching knuckle-to-knuckle.

So now they are arm-in-arm, side by side, the White Mask and the Tun Doctor, brothers—

Fist-bumping.

I lock the pose into place. From my tablet I strip the smart paint of restraints: no lines of code asterisked out in those millions of nano-processors. All safeguards deployed. Full security.

Finally I scramble the permissions list. Not even root-access users will be able to tamper with my painting, now. The wires I've stuck to the wall spark—pak-pak!—and the electrodes fall off, shorted.

• • •

The next morning, through sunrise haze, calls to prayer bounce off the buildings:

Condominiums, shophouse rows, and onion domes; a shopping mall swarmed with birds of neon green; an office tower venting steam, its face a moving mural, a tumbling puzzle of octagons interlocking.

Joggers on zebra crossings. Stroboscopic graffiti by the riverside. A helicopter.

And soon the roads are busy: a train of cars forming in every lane, red rear lights shimmering.

In the air, people speaking—the dull murmur of social media.

"There are two White Masks, maybe?" somebody asks, and somebody else replies: "Maybe it's a conspiracy."

A third somebody says: "This is still a thing? These mural artists, they are so wanky, think they are so important. Please, people. Stop. I'm so bored of it already."

* * *

There, at the highway wall, the Terror Thursday crew stands in a semicircle.

In my online self I watch Ghaf watching the surveillance feed—

Of the White Mask between pools of streetlamp light, wearing black skinny jeans and black sneakers, working. He puts cardboard stencils up in eight parts, and shakes his spray can: clickity-clack-clack-clack.

The footage fast-forwards. His arms are a blur. They slow down again only as he steps back. I admire what he's done: the White Mask and the Tun Doctor, arm-in-arm, together.

It doesn't look that bad, now that I can see it in sunlight.

"It was that tomboy's programmer bitch who did this," one of them says. And another one says: "Can't even turn the paint off. We won't be able to work like this."

* * *

Ghaf's crew is ready to work.

They have rolls of tape on their wrists, a pallet of paint tins in their parked flatbed. But there's an upended box of spray cans by the wall, and a smashed-up laptop also—its two halves cracked apart, keys scattered, screen flaked in shards.

Ghaf wipes his head. The others keep well away. Carefully, carefully, he creeps forward. He stretches his hand out.

Straightaway the Tun Doctor reacts—

With flailing whip-arms of viscous matter: reaching out, toppling cans and roller poles, flinging curbstones. Grabbing Ghaf under his shoulder.

"No-no-no!" he says, screaming.

The rest rush to drag him away. Adam, on the wall—for now, he is safe in the arms of his new best buddy. He stares down at Ghaf and the Terror Thursdays, smiling.

And—wait, no, it must be a glitch—but I see his mask has a hint of teeth showing.

CASSANDRA KHAW

DEGREES OF BEAUTY

(2016)

PRETTY BUT NOT PRETTY ENOUGH, Bai Ling thinks, looking over to where her daughter lies sleeping, knees to breast, a whimper between her teeth. Around her throat, a necklace of bruises, teeth-marks on the nubs of her shoulders, battle-scars of the twenty-second century.

Bai Ling tours an armada of glossy brochures, ricocheting between clinics, circling procedures, underlining discounts. She has a plan.

Blepharoplasty to divide the monolid, sharpen the epicanthic fold. FDA-approved tinctures in the iris: indigo with constellations of hypoallergenic gold, all to tempt the camera's attention. And eyelash transplants too, of course, Mediterranean-thick, so much more appealing than fine Asian hair.

On a notebook, she pencils more radical suggestions: dilation of the orbital bones, deepening of the sockets, modifications to manufacture the illusion of vulnerability. Fashion craves victims, vestal virgins to hang in garlands of silk.

These will have to be discussed, but Bai Ling already knows she will get her way.

•   •   •

The surgeries are a triumph.

The media adores Bai Ling's daughter: "feral" fox-child, inkstroke lines and no meat at all, only bones to dress in satin. Her eyes, inhuman, carrying galaxies; jewels in a cross-continental setting. Utterly novel.

If she occasionally falters under the strobe of the cameras, if she winces from the spotlights, haunted or hungry, no one is crass enough to comment. Art is pain, everyone knows that.

• • •

It's still not enough, of course. The accolades refine to critique: how the eyes fail to match the face, the thin-lipped smile, the nose like soft dough squashed against bone.

"Just a little longer," Bai Ling whispers to her daughter, their fingers twinned.

• • •

The mouth is easiest to correct: a quick injection of synthetic collagen, perfectly rote, uniquely uncontroversial. They return Bai Ling's daughter in hours, tongue drooling between white teeth; her clothes vacuum-packed, a note between the fresh-washed fabric.

Introducing mild overbite may improve recognition profile.

Bai Ling does not think twice. She sends her daughter back immediately.

• • •

They are mesmerized. Tabloids and fashion rags, gleaming as a lie, stitch a prophecy for Bai Ling's daughter: a lifetime of cover shots and television appearances. Who is this nymph that's been extracted from reality show drivel?

Still, pity about that nose. And the breasts. All so *flat*, like paddy fields and rural economies. A farmer's child, surely, river silt running thickly through her veins. Or so Bai Ling trembles through every article, knuckles bleached white by hate. She has come so far and they have achieved so much. And her daughter. Ah, her darling. So much she has sacrificed, so many nights consecrated to alcohol and curious fingers, to smiling at nameless men with black shoes and black gazes, polished to the shine of a shark's dead eyes.

They've given so much.

How can they stop now?

The body is a truth that can be bent, the new media an instrument to be played by the wise.

• • •

The next surgeries are harder.

The nose is broken, reset; the nasal bridge lengthened, nostrils rotated to a respectable elevation. Scarlett Johansson's nose, down to a keratin fiber.

The breasts are engorged. Saline, not silicone. Pliancy must be preserved. And the hair. There's nothing that can be done about that straight, lank hair. Nothing, at least, that might take effect in weeks. But Bai Ling will not be dissuaded. She drags her daughter through a gauntlet of hairdressers. She drenches her in dye, cooks her hair into stately spirals, too crisp to stay, but nothing that the proper creams cannot disguise.

"You're beautiful."

Bai Ling's daughter trembles under her touch.

• • •

Bai Ling drinks for the first time in her life when they announce her daughter as a breakout phenomenon, three years too late, Hollywood's best next thing. Framed in the mouth of the television, she is unrecognizable, silk foaming at her hips, a ruff of tulle coiled like a noose at her neck. Untouchable, impossible, a wet dream poured into four-inch stilettos. Not a peasant's daughter, a goddess.

Her daughter does not speak during the presentation, but no one comments— they are too impressed with the husband revealed on the stage. Now, there are two perfect people, gorgeous as no other, triple-tested to ensure an absence of disease. Adam and Eve, crowdsourced by tastemakers.

One blog notes that Bai Ling's daughter fails to smile, eyes vacant. *Nerves*, they write, of the ghost-bride on stage, *probably*.

• • •

Dead.

Bai Ling strokes fingers across her daughter's waxen cheek, cool but not rigid, still closer to human than not. Her throat is bruise-ringed, indigo-kissed; the rope had pulled tight, cut deep and ragged. Beautiful still, Bai Ling thinks. Like one of those anatomical Venuses.

She does not ask the corpse why. Instead, Bai Ling picks up her phone. The body is a tool. Flesh is malleable. Flesh is a tool. Bai Ling's daughter, eyes rolled up in her head, could be mistaken for a sleeping child.

• • •

She is in recovery for nine weeks.

They pump nutrition through a venous catheter, install a palette of esters below her tongue. It is important to keep the saliva glands operational.

Twice, she is returned under the scalpel. Once to adjust the distribution of saline in her breasts, the second time to cull a rash of necrotic tissue. The doctors hybridize stem cells, hers and hers, a careful tessellation of genomes; they wedge the replicator behind her ribs. Pray.

It works.

Twelve weeks later, Bai Ling emerges from the hospital, dressed in her dead daughter's skin. They have never been so beautiful. Fawn-legged, she totters into the paparazzi's arms, signature smile still brilliant. If the bridge of her nose appears a little straighter, if her voice seems deeper, no one says so. As long as she is beautiful.

E. J. SWIFT

ALLIGATOR HEAP

(2016)

HE WAS A HUNDRED AND TEN YEARS OLD and he was dying and he was going to live again. The body was in the building, waiting. Vardimon called it the sarcophagus, which everyone told him was dark, unnecessarily dark, but he was a hundred and ten and he believed he'd earned the right to dark. Of course it was a displacement mechanism, a way of averting his terror of the transfer going wrong, or worse, that he wouldn't be revived at all. Sometimes it worked.

"Are you ready, sir?"

Tarek hovered by the door. As always, the nurse's appearance was impeccable, his endeavors almost but not quite enough to disguise the fact that he wasn't from the heights.

"Yes, yes, bring it in."

The door opened and a three-tiered trolley floated inside. Each tier held the dome of a semitranslucent membrane, designed to offer the diner enticing glimpses of the culinary shapes and moving steam within. Vardimon beckoned. Tarek brought the trolley to his bedside and at the tap of a finger, the membrane dissolved.

The first course was an exercise in monochrome: a boule of wild rice at the center of a gleaming black lake, within which gold flecks rose and fell from the surface like goldfish. The chef had added a white foam, integrating holobites to simulate the motion of the waves, and the soup swirled restlessly, rather queasily, within its bowl. Resting atop the rice island was a single pan-seared scallop. Vardimon thought, uncharitably, of a beached whale.

"This is Nguyen?"

"Yes, sir."

"She's young."

"She trained with your sous-chef, sir. Comes recommended."

Tarek cut the scallop and lifted the fork to feed him. Vardimon's hands, once elite instruments, had become unreliable. For that reason the aspiring chefs waited outside. Sometimes a younger projection of himself delivered his verdict. Sometimes Tarek did it. The chefs must have found that uncomfortable, a thought which gave him a perverse satisfaction.

He inspected the pearly interior of the scallop. It was well cooked, evenly cooked. He parted his lips to receive the first mouthful, chewing slowly, deliberately, swilling the black squid ink sauce around his cheeks.

Squid were one of the few forms of natural seafood still possible to obtain without a license. Where other creatures had declined or perished, squid seemed to relish the warmer, more acidic climes of the past century. Tenacious bastards. There were restrictions on scallops, but a discreet bribe could get around most ocean protectorates. Vardimon had a woman who dealt with that.

Nguyen's second course was ostrich steak, ground-reared, insect-fed, and demonically bloody. The presence of the steak indicated two things: she had researched his preferences, and she had connections. The day that lab-meat crawled across the entrance to one of his restaurants would be the day he died a true death. Vardimon sampled the ostrich, noting the pliancy of texture with approval. When Tarek handed him a handkerchief he realized he had let blood drip down on his chin.

The dessert was the spectacle. Rooted in a sculpture of tessellated silver hexagons—itself a work of art—was a tree in full bloom made entirely of transparent candy. Suspended through the branches he saw popping pearls and whole strawberries, each fruit delicately, almost impossibly placed and glazed with a sheen that gave them the appearance of rubies ripe to fall.

"What does she call this?"

Tarek paused.

"It's the ballistic balsamic berry tree, sir."

The alliteration sounded strained on Tarek's lips. Vardimon would have pronounced it with more flair.

"Printed?"

"No, sir. Artisanal."

"Mm. A suspension torch, I suppose."

Vardimon strove not to appear impressed. The sugar work was as fine as anything he had seen.

Once again the spoon came toward him, a strawberry resting in its curve. He wondered whether Tarek cooked at home, or whether he lived off the vending machine produce they shunted out to the lower levels. Synthetic pouches of fuel at their worst, machine-baked confectionery at best. He'd resisted when they wanted to pimp Vardimon products to the midrange, but the vending market was too big, his competitors were moving, the shareholders wanted a slice of it.

That was what Polyakov had told him. He wondered now whether he should have held out.

He squinted at the strawberry. Plump, uniformly scarlet, the speckled indentations an accessory rather than a mar upon its succulent flesh. Nguyen had left the leaves on. That was clever. A nod to the soil, authenticity amid the artifice.

He chewed, swallowed. Paused for a moment. Allowed the pause to drag out, his expression carefully flatlined.

"That is exquisite."

Tarek smiled. Relief, pleasure? Despite his lack of augmentations, the nurse was not an easy read.

"The chef said they were flown in this morning. Fresh from the Siberian plains."

"Exquisite," he repeated. "The tree can go out as a special. We'll run a trial on the ostrich. Not the squid ink lake. Too immature."

Tarek nodded. He wouldn't know. He would never eat the strawberries or anything else from one of Vardimon's restaurants, so it didn't matter what Vardimon said.

The truth was he couldn't taste a thing.

. . .

Vardimon had promised himself that when his palate went, he would transfer. His organic sight was fading, but he didn't mind that, there was enough virtual entertainment in the ether to keep him occupied for several lifetimes. But losing the ability to smell, and taste—to create? Vardimon had built his career on his ability to invent flavors, drive trends, market experience. But he was not just a connoisseur. He *loved* food. He loved its truthfulness. He loved its inexhaustible variety, the possibility contained within it. If he couldn't relish a century-aged whisky, or the fresh tartness of fruit grown in the naked sun, then what was the point in living?

He had lost the ability to taste some time ago now. A month. Possibly longer. And thanks to the insidious, inexorable fear, he was deferring his rebirth.

He had noticed the loss with the absence of his own odor. That slight sourness that clings to a body in its final throes. So he was lying. To Tarek primarily, but through Tarek to everybody else who was a part of Vardimon Incorporated. The young chefs who put forward their recipes, desperate to gain a trial at his restaurants, would accept whatever he told them. That was the value of his word.

"Give me another strawberry."

Tarek obliged.

Chew, swallow. Feel the looseness of the skin around your neck as the fruit slides down the esophagus. Old man. Old man ready to become young again. They took a scan of his brain every twenty-four hours. That was the maximum time that could be lost between him, here, now, and the sarcophagus. They had done all the trials. Plenty of volunteers from where Tarek lived; the technicians had practiced until they got it right.

"What will you do after this?" he asked Tarek.

Surprise flitted across the nurse's face, was subsumed below the surface. Tarek was here because according to all the psychological studies, pretransfer palliative care demanded a human touch. But he had rarely, if ever, engaged the nurse in conversation about a subject other than himself.

"I'm hoping to get another placement," said Tarek.

"Another like me."

"Not exactly like you, sir."

"What do you mean by that?"

"Well—"

"Not as rich?"

"That is—undeniable, sir."

"But not what you meant." The nurse's face remained closed. "Open the damn walls. I want to see."

Tarek switched the window settings and the glass surround flooded with daylight. At this height, the traffic lanes moved far below, only the occasional private transport blinking between towers. The building opposite was Maxwell's empire, currently on its fifth upward expansion. Its surfaces teemed with construction robots. Vardimon wondered what would happen when they reached the upper limits of the atmosphere. Would Maxwell keep going, installing artificially oxygenated environments, until the spires penetrated the very edge of space?

In the distance, a small figure was hoverblasting. The blaster's tail wove a macaron pink ribbon that whorled about the sky, reminding Vardimon of the inside of an oyster shell. He remembered diving for oysters as a young man, long ago, before the sea rise. He remembered the beginning of it all. Surface cities clustering into vast metropolises, the drive to build. He remembered hoverblasting for the first time, the lightness, the suspension, so close to the sky you felt you were a god. Everything in him now was a weight. His reputation, a thing he risked with each new tasting, as he dredged up adjectives from the memories of cuisine gone by. It only took one bad chef to destroy a career.

But Polyakov wouldn't let that happen.

• • •

When Tarek finished his shift, Polyakov was waiting outside. A smooth-faced, muscular woman in her sixties, Tarek imagined her logging into the poker halls in her spare time.

"Well?"

Polyakov wasn't one for social niceties.

"He said the soil soup was squid ink. And I told him the berries were balsamic, like you said. He believed me."

Polyakov nodded. She looked pleased. Tarek never failed to be surprised by the peculiar rituals these people employed to test one another. That the marinade on a piece of fruit could be used to prove or disprove a person's sanity struck him as insane in itself; but then, he wasn't from the heights.

"Carry on," said Polyakov. "Keep him going."

"Will that chef get a trial?"

He shouldn't care. But when the membrane dissolved and he saw that tree, something had snagged at him, an emotion he didn't want his employers to see. It was the garden in the page, he supposed. Nguyen's tree belonged there.

"Sure," she said. "Vardimon called it. And she's good."

Polyakov was the executor of Vardimon's estate. The extent of the man's intellectual property was obscene. As a young man, what Vardimon lacked in financial resources he made up for with ingenuity and instinct. He had invested cannily—Ethiopian teff, seaweed technologies, biodegradable glass, edible packaging. And insects, whose bodies when stripped of their fat and ground up produced a powder the same flavor as chocolate—a fact that had proved fortuitous in the wake of the cacao bean crash. Vardimon had used the proceeds to open his first restaurant. That was the story, anyway.

In Tarek's world, Vardimon materialized as commercials, cheap holos of men and women rhapsodizing over new concoctions, and printed snacks disbursed from vending machines. In Polyakov's world, it was a symbol of status: to be seen at a Vardimon restaurant was to know you had made it. This Tarek had learned, painstakingly, over the nine months of his placement.

Polyakov wanted Vardimon to deteriorate as far as possible before his transfer. To commit a senile mind to the fresh body. It was about the money, he assumed. Tarek's job was to convince Vardimon he was still mentally healthy. That was about the money too, but Tarek's choices were limited in a way that these people's were not. He had kids, and a sister in jail for kicking the shit out of a police officer in the latest riots. He couldn't afford morals.

Tarek offered the remaining strawberries to Polyakov. Vardimon had stripped the tree of its offerings but kept the structure at his bedside. He wanted to inspect the sugar work.

"Have them."

She waved a dismissive hand. Tarek kept his face impassive. He didn't tell her that the air miles on this fruit would purchase the printed page of a book. There were lots of things he didn't tell them, not that they would ever ask; they had no curiosity for the lives of those below.

Except today.

What will you do next?

He didn't know.

• • •

Vardimon's face followed him to the hoverstation, a more youthful version than the one Tarek saw every day but recognizable nonetheless, grinning up from the rice paper on a vending-machine velvet cake. In Tarek's satchel was a box containing five strawberries, each with an invisible imperfection that had marked them unfit for consumption in Vardimon's eyes. It was true that the old oligarch was losing it. He'd been putting off the transfer for more than six months now.

Tarek wondered what would happen to the new body if Vardimon decided against immortality. Whether it would go to someone else. He thought of Uri, pushed the thought quickly away.

The hovercraft entered the flow of traffic and bore him steadily downward. Stop after stop, the pristine sheen of Vardimon's world leached away. Clean lines and machine-polished surfaces gave way to the crude, unforgiving architecture of the lower levels. The hovercraft slipped past lurid advertisements, examples of graffiti both skilled and unskilled, human construction workers suspended from harnesses. They looked like insects in cocoons.

People like me get ground up just the same, he thought. But when we do there's nothing left.

He arrived home to find his two youngest squabbling over the five minutes left on the holodeck account. His eldest, Laila, was nowhere in sight, her absence a worry upon other worries, the sum of them so much a part of him that in some ways he no longer noticed. Laila was going the way of her aunt. He could see it day by day, and he couldn't blame her, but he didn't want her in a cell for the next twenty years either.

"Dad, it was my turn!"

The console was out of juice. No more virtual for a week at least. He gave the kids a strawberry each, cut a third in half and divided it between them, and set one aside for Laila who would probably reject it. That left one for him.

For a minute he just looked at it, aware that a chance like this might not come again. Then he bit into the berry.

The frosting dissolved on his tongue in a burst of intense sweetness. He couldn't have identified the exact flavor—something with cinnamon, he thought— but thanks to Polyakov's scheming he knew it wasn't balsamic.

He crushed the fruit between his teeth. Tartness followed sweetness. He might not have Vardimon's vocabulary but he knew that everything about it tasted *right*. As the sensation receded, his pleasure turned to anxiety about what he was doing to the kids—giving them, literally, a taste of a world they would never know. Not unless they did what Tarek was doing, handling a body incapable of handling itself.

His youngest was examining the strawberry leaves.

"You don't eat that bit," he said.

She dumped them in his hand. He held the leaves for a moment. It seemed despicable to throw them away, but what could he do with four strawberry tops? He chucked them in the chute.

The weekly call from his sister Amira came through later that evening. He had got used to seeing her prison garb in person, but it was still a shock to have it materialize in the apartment, the aggressiveness of the orange coveralls against the drabness of the place they lived. Conversation followed the usual pattern, stilted at first, slowly warming up. He wanted to tell Amira about the strawberries, the crystalline tree, but to do that would mean revealing the truth about the nursing gig.

Amira would be furious. That artificial world, she'd say. Those artificial people. What do they know about us? What do they know about family, or hardship, or desperation, or love? Do they have to support three kids on a zero-hours contract? Do they have to watch the woman they love age twenty years in as many months as the cancer eats up first her womb, then her breasts, and finally her bones? Do they have to *beg* for the drugs to alleviate her pain, and when they can't get them, to watch—to watch her suffering—to watch—

"Tarek?"

"Sorry, I was miles away."

"I can tell. Is Laila there?"

"She's out with friends."

He said it hoping it was true, and all at once he was glad Laila wasn't home. His sister was right, even though he only wanted a better life for them. That was all he had ever wanted. Something more than this. He didn't like to think about what would happen when Amira got out.

When she was gone the room seemed very empty, and colorless, the dormant console and the wall they couldn't afford to replaster, with its single framed paper page. The story was about a garden. A miraculous garden, where anything would seed and flourish. Tarek knew that the word garden came from its Germanic cousin, *garten*, whose original meaning was an enclosed or bounded space. He imagined stepping through the page on the wall, crossing into this magical realm where he and Uri and the kids and Amira could live and grow things and there, enclosed, he could keep them safe.

Safe from what? asked Uri, who was dead but sometimes spoke to him, still. *You always did worry too much.*

From everything. From working construction on those sites and from the riots and the jail cells and the terrible thoughts that get inside your head and from what happened to you.

Uri had no answer to that.

Tarek didn't know the title of the book, or the author. Somewhere in the city, there must be other people, with other pages from the same copy. Perhaps they too wondered about the garden. At the book markets he always looked, even though it was unlikely he'd have the cash to make a purchase. He had come close to selling the page only once, when he thought he could get morphine for Uri. He was ready to make the deal, but she found out, put a stop to it. That page was her favorite thing. She made him read it to her every day. Every day except the last. On that day she never woke up.

Uri would have understood about the strawberries.

•　•　•

Vardimon wasn't sick. He wasn't suffering the way Uri had suffered, he was simply very old. Old, and increasingly mercurial in temperament. Today he was fretful, and prattling. Tarek lifted him into a sitting position, smoothing down the pillows which had cleaned themselves overnight and issued a faint citrus scent.

"There you go, sir. All set."

"Tarek. Tell me. Have you thought any more about what comes next?"

"I can't get another placement until there's a date."

"Ah. So your fate is bound to mine." The old man's gaze shifted to the windows. "Have you ever considered that, Tarek? The concept of fate?"

"Not really, sir."

Tarek supposed this was what happened at the end, even when there was a beginning to follow. Existentialism drawing its claws across the mind. He remembered coming home one day to find one of those spiritual naturalists at his wife's bedside. He'd been ready to throw the guy out, but Uri had wanted the spiritualist. Later, it occurred to him that she had needed something to find the strength to let go.

The idea of Uri's death being the product of fate was intolerable.

And exactly the kind of excuse a sky dweller would love.

Oh shut up, Amira.

Vardimon cut across his thoughts.

"Perhaps when you have lived as long as I have, you will understand. Of late there have been things—weighing on my mind. Things I haven't thought about for a long time."

"Sir?"

"I've heard rumors," Vardimon said slowly. "Words spoken—in passing. The rumor is there are people still living on the surface."

Tarek paused, caught by surprise. Vardimon talking about the surface? He wondered whether Polyakov would count this as deterioration.

"Is it true?" Vardimon pressed.

"I haven't been to the surface, sir."

"But . . ."

"But—yes, I believe so, there are people down there."

"I remember it, you know."

"The surface?"

"Long before you were born. Things were very different then. Tell me about these people."

"Like I said, I haven't been—"

"Tell me, Tarek."

• • •

You knew it was coming because of the whining noise, keen as a mosquito at your ear. As soon as the noise started, you saw movement, shadows skipping through the smog. Bare feet, slap on the slick sand. The doors to the chute took sixty heartbeats to open. Louse could run three steps with every beat. By the time the doors were fully extended she had scaled the pyramid and was ready, poised, attendant. Others were waiting too but Louse had concealed herself the closest, almost directly beneath the doors, and because she blended she knew they couldn't see her. It was why they called her Louse.

Now the sound of the trash drop sliding down the chute. Louse had seen another try to climb up there once. They didn't come back, but Louse didn't know what happened to them. If you kept climbing, forever, would you find something above the smog?

She heard whooping as the drop approached. Louse didn't leap, or make a sound, because it was important to be attentive. Here it came. Raining down from the doors above, separating as it fell. Scrapings and slime and slivers. Sometimes the trash contained things perfect in their entirety, membranous sacks or pyramids that exploded into your throat like a chorus of voices unfolding in the air. Mostly, it contained rubbish.

Even before the landing she could see there was something there. Something—her mind tested the word, wrapped around it—*green*. She was in before anyone else. She heard the shouts of annoyance; they'd missed her, again. Her hands reached, foraging—grab, mouth, grab, mouth—but it was the green she wanted and once her fingers closed upon it she backed up, wary, blending, worried an other might have seen her prize and come to wrestle it from her.

She spat out something hard and gritty, chewed on something soft, swallowed, clambered back down the pyramid. Her eyes could see through the smog, and she could breathe it too. She had smoke eyes. She had blood skin. The mosquitos bit her and she didn't get sick, though it was irritating, and itchy. The others in this patch wore masks and nets and they sweated all the time. She kept away from them. They had tried to hurt her before. They would probably like to have smoke eyes and blood skin, but they were afraid of her.

Now she was on her way, blending through the brick-fronted streets thick with coal dust, past a fire spitting out flecks of paper where others were barbequing something with legs and a head and a pointed nose but Louse would not be welcome, she never was, up and over a rusting fence and squirming up a pipe on the wall of the abandoned house where some sand-dogs lived, though they were killed often, and ended up on the spit, like that one back there.

On the roof she examined her prize.

It was made of narrow—she held the word, cradled it, yes, *leaves*—that connected at the center and tapered outward to a point. A gem of red clung to them. She put her tongue to it. A shock threshed through her body. She took it away from her tingling mouth, examined it afresh. She would keep this, yes, it would stay with her other treasures. She would not eat it. It was not something to be eaten.

• • •

Tarek stopped talking to find Vardimon watching him intently. He had never seen the old man so engaged. It was unsettling.

"Why do the other feeders stay away from her?"

Tarek thought quickly.

"Do you remember those experiments, a few decades back? To control the population?"

Vardimon looked impatient.

"Of course."

"So Louse looks different. She's—evolved."

"How does she look different?"

"Her face, I suppose. I don't know. It's not like she's real."

This is ridiculous, he thought. I'm telling the old man bedtime stories.

"Don't spoil it," said Vardimon. "You're not employed for that."

"No, sir. I apologize, sir."

· · ·

Vardimon thought about Louse, pushing waste into her mouth. There had been a time, especially when crops were failing and in the early days of the greenhouse revolution, when people talked about food becoming fuel. A form of processed nutrients, synthetic stuff that could be ingested without thought, without care or joy. With so many immigrants like Tarek there was a need for synthesis, it was the only way to sustain the lower levels of the ever-expanding metropolises. Vardimon knew this, had lived through it. But he had never been afraid of that future spreading upward.

To understand food, to work with it effectively, imaginatively, you had to understand desire, anticipation, gratification. You had to understand pleasure. Only by engaging with the primal could you produce alchemy, cuisine that evoked emotion in a society sterilized by artifice.

Partnerships were forged, love affairs ended, business deals brokered, and friendships cemented, over food.

In some ways, it was all they had left.

Perhaps Polyakov and the rest were right. Perhaps his thoughts had turned unnecessarily dark.

He imagined, as he did most nights now, waking inside the sarcophagus. Running his tongue around its teeth, flexing its nostrils. Would they share the same tastes? What if the technicians had failed to replicate his refined sense of smell, or his gut instinct—a thing surely impossible to transcribe in genetic code? What if he *hated* food?

· · ·

"How is he today, Tarek?"

"He wants to know about bottom feeders."

"Feeders?" Polyakov's eyes gleamed with satisfaction. She was like a crocodile, thought Tarek. A crocodile to Vardimon's dinosaur. That gave him an idea. "Don't tell me he's developing a social conscience."

Tarek looked at her.

"No. I don't think it's gone that far."

On the commute home he thought about the next stage of Louse's story. She was becoming familiar. It was almost as if they'd met.

· · ·

Safely blended, Louse often listened to the talk of others. Talk was like the ripple of oil across puddles, it merged and smeared together and patterns came out of it, sometimes readable, sometimes not. The talk was of the city. The city was a maleficent thing, a monster intent upon crushing them, relentless, mechanical and impossible to escape, though they wished to escape it nonetheless. There were plans hidden inside the talk. The others would climb high, infiltrate, steal, find a better life. Louse was not sure what they meant by this phrase, *a better life*, but by the talk of stealing she had come to the conclusion that there must be *other* others above, in those places detectable only as glimpsed structures lifting into the smog.

These others must have wings, great leathery ones. They would look like the lizards with biting snouts that roamed the streets at night and snatched you if you weren't safe behind a wall. Gators, the others called them. Don't let the gators catch you. They came in from the water beyond the city. They looked slow but moved shockingly fast. The above-others would be like this, winged gators drifting through the smog. They would not fear the city.

She remembered the skinny figure she had witnessed climbing into the chute. Had his journey upward turned him into a lizard? Or had the lizards eaten him, crunched him into shards of bone? If Louse followed, what would happen to her?

Her skin was already tough, and in firelight it had a gleam to it, a kind of movement. Would she grow scales? Would she hunger for the flesh of others? Louse wondered.

• • •

"Well, don't stop there!"

Vardimon waited irritably. Tarek's hand had gone to his ear; the nurse was listening to someone.

"You have a visitor," said Tarek.

"Who?"

If Vardimon could smell, the perfume would have warned him, but as it was he had no time to prepare until the door opened.

"No!" he shouted, launching himself into a fit of coughing, so Tarek had to prop him up, bring him water, but it was no good, it was too late, he had already entered the room. He—*she*—never did take no for an answer.

Elena collapsed into an armchair with a theatrical sigh.

"Tarek, be a dear and get me a Balvenie, will you? Two fingers, no ice. Vardimon, for you?"

"What the hell are you doing here?"

Tarek served Elena her whisky and left the room discreetly.

"I still have my keys, darling."

Alone, they surveyed each other. Her new body was sleek, luscious, inarguably beautiful, and it left him entirely cold. Today her hair was aquamarine. Like a fucking mermaid.

"To think I paid for that," he said at last.

"This again? I told you I wanted something different."

"I thought you meant cosmetics. Not—not *this*."

"You can't even say it, can you." She crossed her legs. Their length was emphasized by slim-fitting trousers and stiletto heels. She leaned forward. "Vardimon. Do you realize what a gift this is? We're pioneers. There's a whole new world out there and you want to live the same life over again?"

"I loved you," he said. All at once he was shaking.

"I'm still me."

"No."

She looked away. She seemed exasperated. Perhaps she was unmoved too. She hadn't mentioned her sexual preferences in this body. Or perhaps now she could only see his decrepitude.

"Have you set a date?" she asked.

"Not yet."

He wanted to tell her about the fear, how he was trapped between the fear of what he was becoming and the fear of what he would become. With the transfer he would change, and like her, he might not wake the same. The one thing that distracted him was fairy tales about a surface child who didn't exist, and Elena would think that ridiculous.

"But it's ready," she said. "The sarcophagus."

His lips curled around an involuntary smile. She was the only one, other than him, who would call it that.

"Yes."

"You know it gets harder the longer you leave it."

"And you'll be waiting on the other side?"

He couldn't keep the bitterness from his voice. Yes, it had been years—even decades—since there had been anything physical between them. But they had talked about this, when the new technology came online. A renewal of vows. Revisit the passions of youth, acts of lust he could barely remember now, they were hazed by nostalgia, although perhaps the sarcophagus would have a sharper recollection. But then Emil—*Elena*—had decided to become a woman. He would never want her again. Or perhaps the sarcophagus would. Irrationally, that thought enraged him even more.

Elena didn't answer his question. Perhaps it had been more of a plea, pathetic, really. She must think him pathetic. She had leaped where he was lingering. She had not been afraid. His ex-lover unfolded her long legs, stood, rested a hand on the duvet. He felt the pressure of her fingers on his shins through the bedding.

"Don't wait too long, dear heart," she said. "I miss my partner in wine."

• • •

The sarcophagus was in the room. It stood at the end of his bed, watching him slyly. There was an unpleasant expression on its face—malevolence, greed?—he couldn't quite work it out. If he were awake, he could work it out, but he was asleep, and the sight of it terrified him.

The sarcophagus bent forward, placed its hands on either side of his feet, looked him straight in the eye. Once it had his full attention, the sarcophagus stood and stretched, displaying its lithe naked body, the muscles scything across its torso. Then it strolled across the room and opened the door to his drinks cabinet.

His terror gave way to indignation.

"What do you think—"

He struggled to sit up, but without Tarek there as a brace his limbs were leaden, unresponsive, he could only prop himself upon one elbow and watch awkwardly as the sarcophagus extracted one of his favorite reds, a Swedish pinot noir, uncorked the bottle, and poured itself a glass. Saliva gathered in his mouth. He remembered that pinot noir. The feel of it, the nose of it, the slight grip of the tannin on his teeth—yes, he remembered.

And yet his mouth was ash.

The sarcophagus tilted the glass, admiring the ruby complexion of the wine. It took a mouthful, drew air through the liquid, swilled, tipped its head back, swallowed. An ecstatic expression possessed its features.

"Old world," it said. "Smoke. Wood fires. Earthiness, yes, oak-aged, raspberry, cherry, spice, a warmth to it, a palpable warmth. This is an excellent vintage."

The sarcophagus tilted the glass toward him. He felt the urge to weep. He remembered. The sarcophagus couldn't remember, it wasn't here, he was dreaming.

"Care to taste?"

His rage welled up, sudden and irrepressible.

"You know nothing about that vintage—"

"Did you know," said the sarcophagus meditatively, "the nose has the capacity to detect up to fourteen thousand aromas? And your nose, even before the augmentations, has served you particularly well. Has it not?"

"Get out!" he yelled. His breathing was coming faster. It felt as though a clay fire oven was parked upon his chest.

"And yet," continued the sarcophagus. "I have to wonder. What have you really achieved over the last century, Mr. Vardimon, *sir*? Have you revolutionized the sensory experience? Have you solved the global distribution of food? Or have you just thrown together a few endangered ingredients and branded it haute cuisine?"

"Fuck you!" he shouted. "I remember a time when insects were sneered at. When I was a child, virtual reality was practically embryonic and things like you were illegal—"

"It's true," said the sarcophagus. "You're a relic of the old world yourself. But I—I shall be entirely new. Just like Elena."

It was too much. He reached for the sarcophagus. Its tongue—he wanted its tongue, he would seize the muscle, rip it from its throat still coated in the residues of the pinot noir. He would fucking eat it. The sarcophagus watched him languidly, unaffected by the violence of his thoughts. Believing, no doubt, that he did not have the capacity to commit such an act. He thrust back the covers. He lunged—

• • •

He woke to find himself on the floor beside the bed, an ache rising down the right side of his body, the emotions of the dream still blurring his perceptions. The door opened and one of his staff entered. Not Tarek. It was too early for Tarek. Exclamations. Lights raised. His fall had triggered an alarm. They lifted him into the bed, fussing, gently chiding. You must wait for us, you're not as strong as you think. You just have to call! Furtively, he checked the corners of the room, expecting to see the sarcophagus lurking there, a sardonic smile plastered over its symmetrical face, but they'd turned the glass and the sunrise filled the room, and with the morning it had nowhere to hide.

• • •

"I want to see my body."

"Sir, I'm not sure—"

"I said I want to see it."

He insisted Tarek call a technician. He insisted Tarek came with him. They floated him down the corridor on a gurney. He had imagined they would keep it farther away, there was something blasphemous about it being so close. But in the end there were only rooms between them.

The sarcophagus was in a tank. It was naked, as it had been last night, fetal and covered in some sort of gel, an oddly phosphorous glow to its suspended limbs. Its skin was clear, without lines, a lustrous brown, its internal organs clean as a baby's and its senses unmarred.

Vardimon experienced a surge of envy so great he wanted to kill it. But it wasn't yet alive. It would only become alive with him, his mind, his intellect and bank of memory.

"Tomorrow," he said abruptly.

"Sir?"

"We'll do it tomorrow. Tell Polyakov to make the arrangements."

They would put him to sleep. He'd wake in the sarcophagus. Its face would be his face. Its tongue his tongue. It was time.

"I want you to be there," he said. Tarek nodded. Unexpected gratitude overcame him. Tarek would be there. Even if everyone else abandoned him, the nurse would not. "I want breakfast. Pancakes, maple syrup, bacon. Fresh cream. Blueberries. Juice. Ethiopian coffee. You understand?"

"I'll see to it, sir."

• • •

Tarek stood before the page on the wall, gazing at the words until his vision blurred them into nonsense. In the garden in the page there was no ending. There could not be an ending, because it was an isolated page, and the last word on the page was *and*.

"Aren't you working, Dad?"

Laila had crept up behind him.

"Not tonight."

Not tomorrow, either. Polyakov had seen to that. Tarek had failed in his task; Vardimon wasn't sufficiently delusional for Polyakov's purposes.

"Have you told Aunt Amira?"

"There's no point. It's over, Laila. I won't be working up there again."

"Why not?"

He didn't have an answer to that, not one his daughter would understand. He put his arm around her shoulders. She was thinner than she should be. In his head he heard Amira's voice, saying everyone knew, had always known, there was enough food in the world. It just wasn't going where it was needed. From snatches of conversation overheard in the heights, he knew it was true.

He had wanted to tell Polyakov that her entire world was founded upon a delusion, the delusion that the heights could get away with it, continue to hide behind their candied sculptures and land-reared meat whilst only minutes away by hovercraft there were people who struggled to feed their families every night. He was on the verge of saying this, and other things, the kind of things Amira would have said, when the call came. The officer asked him to come to the police station. Laila was there. If she hadn't been a juvenile, she'd be locked away by now.

He wondered whether Vardimon would think of him when he awoke to his pancakes and blueberries, alone. He thought of the body in the tank, the greatest luxury a mind could know, wondered how it would feel to become young again. Though it was not Vardimon's youth he envied but his age. The old age Uri should have had, and was denied.

• • •

The night before the transfer, the technicians took a final scan and administered his pre-op drugs. They would return in the morning, first thing. They would induce this body's death. Vardimon had insisted he was left alone and undisturbed. He had one night to dream, dreams that would belong only to him, to this version of his mind. The sarcophagus would have no recollection of these final hours.

He ordered the windows to clear, saw the glaze of the city stretching away behind the glass, blending. The drugs were making him woozy.

He had heard that near the end you saw your life compressed like a showreel, nuggets of memory passing before your eyes. He would have to create his own showreel. He thought of his first restaurant, the shouts and steam, delirious chaos of the evening service. He remembered Emil's face serene against the pillow, Emil's lips brushing his. A plate of buttery olives, not quite ripe. Wines whose origins drifted north with the decades. Ethiopian sunsets over acres of teff. Diving for oysters off the coast, before the sea rise, before the build. He remembered the surface.

Behind the glass, the city pulsed softly. He pulled himself to the edge of the bed and rolled off, ignoring the jolt of pain as he landed on the floor. It didn't matter now. On his elbows he hauled himself toward the glass, until he could peer down into the city's nascent depths.

He imagined stepping through the glass and off the ledge. The moment of suspension before he dived, blasting downward, a tail stretching out behind him in saffron yellow. Past the chromium wonderland in the sky, through the crude, regimented architecture of Tarek's world, and down, and down, hitting the toxic smog that obscured the land that begot Louse. It stung his eyes. He pulled a mask over his face, but the stench of it burned against his throat and the delicate papillae of his tongue.

He landed with a crash on Louse's pyramid. Sat for a moment, blinking through the smog. Accustoming himself to the precarious, constantly shifting textures of his seat, the swelter. The entrails of the world were here. And so was she. Louse sat opposite him. She was crouched, frog-like, a stillness to her as though she had been waiting for some time.

Her mouth had no lips.

Vardimon found he had a bowl in his hands.

"Scallop?" he offered her.

Her oil eyes watched him. Slowly, she extended a hand. The skin on her palm rippled, a chameleon texture to its surface. She took the scallop, crammed it entire into her lipless mouth. A sucking sound. He looked away. He sipped at the bowl, curious as to its flavors, and gagged. His palate had returned, but the soup before him bore no relation to squid ink; Nguyen had made him a sauce of sewage.

Louse smiled. Her incisors were half the size of normal teeth, blunt and square. He gave her the ostrich steak next, and watched the blood run down her chin. Did they practice cannibalism down here? Who knew how these people lived? He sensed movement below, and when he looked down he could see a pack of alligators circling the trash heap. They looked hungry.

Last was the candy tree. He showed Louse how to break off twigs and extract the strawberries from within. He ate one himself. The release of flavor on his tongue was the most beautiful thing he had ever experienced. He felt tears gather behind his eyes. The glaze wasn't balsamic though. He realized then that he had been lied to. Polyakov had known of his incapacity all along.

Louse had not eaten the strawberry. She held it between fingers red with ostrich blood, turning it over and over, admiring the fruit as if it were a precious jewel. He looked skyward. He wanted to show something to Louse, the constellations, perhaps, or Maxwell's empire reaching toward space, but the smog was complete and all he saw was the open mouth of a chute.

Louse tugged at his sleeve. She was trying to communicate with him, odd whistling and clicking noises that bore no resemblance to words. She pointed overhead. He understood, allowed her to clamber onto his shoulders, got shakily to his feet. Now she was high enough. She gripped the filthy lip of the chute and levered herself up inside. She was not afraid. Vardimon remained where he was, listening to the alligators foraging. After a while he knew she wasn't coming back. He imagined her climbing upward, aware of a restfulness that he had not felt for a long time, and he realized that she had taken his fear with her.

OLIVER LANGMEAD

GLITTERATI

(2017)

WEDNESDAY. Or was it Tuesday?

"Darling?"

"What is it, dear heart?"

"Is it Wednesday, or Tuesday?"

"It's Tuesday today."

"Did we not have a Tuesday yesterday?"

"No, dearest. We had a Monday yesterday. I recall it being Monday quite clearly, in fact, because Gabrielle was wearing that blue Savinchay dress with the sequined trim, which she only ever wears on Mondays because it would be outrageous to wear Savinchay on any other day of the week."

That settled it, then.

Simone unpeeled his face from the pink leather chaise longue. Last night had been a rainbow of cocktails, resulting in the headache now threatening to impinge on his usually immaculate poise. He went to the gold-plated Manchodroi dresser, which he only ever used on Tuesdays, and was astonished to find his usual dose of painkillers gone.

"Darling!" he cried.

"What is it, Simone?"

"My medicine is missing!"

"Have you checked the Manchodroi dresser?"

"I have opened the very drawer in which my Tuesday dose is stored, and that drawer is quite empty. Might you have accidentally taken them?"

"Certainly not."

"And you're absolutely sure that today is Tuesday?"

"I'm positive, dearest Simone. I have just this minute remembered that Galvin was wearing his red Crostay suit last night, which he only ever wears on Mondays, because, as everyone knows, red Crostay is a delight which should only ever be savored on the first day of the week. I am absolutely, one-hundred-percent certain that today is Tuesday. Could it be that you've misplaced your medication?"

"Well," said Simone, uncertainly. "It could be. I remember very little of last night."

"Use the supply we set aside in the upper left cupboard of the guest wardrobe. And do get ready. You have work in two hours, and it would be simply awful were you to arrive too late."

This was true. It being a Tuesday, it would be the talk of the office were Simone to arrive at work anything more than twenty minutes late. Simone quickly rushed through to the guest bedroom and rooted around in the wardrobe until he located the spare painkillers. In the guest bathroom, he spread the white powder across the shining surface of the chrome sink and proceeded to snort it all up in one go. The drugs fizzed in his brain, and his headache began to recede.

"Superb," he said, to his ruffled reflection. "Most delightful."

Tuesday, then, which meant wearing white to work. Simone searched through his walk-in wardrobes and located his white suits. The first, a close-fitting number from Messr Messr, the second, a looser, but tastefully trimmed alternative from Saint Darcington, and lastly, his brand-new white suit, made with a newly invented meta-material infused with light-emitting micro-LEDs from Karpa Fishh, which was at the very forefront of fashion technology. Still not feeling himself, Simone settled on the tastefully understated Messr Messr suit, and laid it out while he got to work on his face.

Tuesday was a pale day, which meant bringing out his cheekbones. He began with a three-point washing formula from Karrat, and moved on to some moisturizer from Stringham, before clearing that away with body temperature water sourced, purified, and heated to perfection by Dracington Lord. Then, he moved on to his Flaystay foundation, applied with his perfectly softened Karrat brush set, and finished up with a layer of ivory white Flaystay powder. The powdering done, he blended his gray Stringham blushers together and began to highlight the shape of his skull with perfect precision, applying liberal shadows to the space beneath his cheekbones. Then, once his face seemed perfectly skull-like, he began to draw out his eyes with his collection of Dramaskil complimentary eyeliners and eye shadows, until they were quite the centerpiece of his face. Running his fingers along his collection of Dramaskil false eyelashes, he selected a brilliant white pair speckled with tastefully dusted black powder, and delicately affixed them to his eyelids using Dramaskil's gentle false eyelash glue. These he finished off with a little of Stringham's excellent mascara to bring them out. Finally, he settled on a light gray Seleseal lipstick, to contrast with his perfectly whitened teeth, and lined it with some black Seleseal lip liner, to give his lips some real definition.

Pouting to make certain that all was in place, Simone sealed it with Grantis Grato makeup fixer, spraying liberally to make certain nothing would slide off during his busy day ahead.

Face affixed, Simone pulled on his Messr Messr suit and tightened his tie.

Two-forty-five, already? Simone hastened through, air-kissed his wife, and struck a pose before the hallway mirror, which was framed with bright bulbs in order to reveal every single possible flaw in the beholder. Feeling satisfied, he left for work.

• • •

Unfortunately, Simone's route to work took him above the streets of the city suburbs, where the poor unfashionables lived.

The windows of the pristine vibro-rail carriage revealed the depths below, where the houses were made for practicality instead of design. They looked, to Simone, like terrible parodies of the packaging that some of his cheapest items of clothing came in. Simone stared down at the suburbs, his mouth curled in contempt.

The uglies. The unwashed, unmanicured masses. The unfashionables.

It pained him to see them down there, milling around without the first idea of how dreadful they appeared; how their untrained aesthetic senses were so under-developed that they could barely comprehend their own hideousnesses. To think, they did actual labor! To think, they used things like shovels and wrenches and drills! Simone shuddered, but found himself unable to look away. The horror of it drew him in completely.

It was unfathomable that people existed like that.

The carriage slipped through a tunnel, and suddenly they were there, at the heart of the horror, where beyond the unornamented fences the unfashionables lumbered around. If only Simone's tear ducts hadn't been removed—why, he would have wept for them. Feeling his gut squirm inside him, he watched them go by, bumping into each other, smiling their ugly, unpainted smiles, staring open-mouthed and lustily at the vibro-rail carriage as it swept past; at its contents—the beautiful glitterati.

To think that they were the same species. It boggled the mind.

Simone secretly hoped that the unfashionables would all catch a disease and die. Of course, it wasn't fashionable to think such thoughts. The fashion was that the uglies were to be pitied, and that charity in the form of discarded past-season wardrobes was a sign of good character. But Simone only said that he sent his old wardrobes down to the unfashionables. In reality, he burned his clothes when he was done with them. The mere thought of his discarded suits touching the skin of any of those aesthetically impaired imbeciles made him feel ill.

So caught up in horror he was, that Simone barely noticed the vibro-rail carriage gliding to a halt. He was the last to leave.

The vast and crystalline Tremptor Tower rose ahead, and Simone felt his heart lift. Surrounding the square were offices built to be aesthetically brilliant, but none compared to the mighty beauty of Tremptor Tower. It was like working in Heaven—the fluted glass cylinders which made the whole building look like an enormous celestial organ always made him smile. He was careful with his smile, of course. It simply wouldn't do to affect his face before making his entrance.

He checked his watch. Precisely twenty minutes late. Perfect.

There was a queue at the front entrance, and the instant that Simone set his eyes upon it he felt his heart stop. Every single man and woman in the queue was wearing purple.

What could it mean? Had he missed an issue of one of the one hundred and sixteen different fashion magazines he was subscribed to? Holding a hand delicately to his chest, Simone felt as if he must flee—he must go home this instant and feign illness. But it was too late. He was already caught up in the queue. And those behind him . . .

Simone risked a glance backward. Perfectly painted open mouths and wide eyes. Horror.

Maybe it was a joke, and everyone in Tremptor Tower was in on it. Maybe he would make his entrance and everyone would clap and applaud and laugh, and he would laugh with them, and they would all drink champagne and reminisce for years to come about how delightful the jest had been.

Slowly, the queue moved forward. Then, it was Simone's turn.

Striking his best pose, Simone sashayed inside.

Absolute silence. The hands poised mid-clap to receive him were completely still. The long red runway yawned out endlessly before him, but still he sashayed on—eyes on the horizon, lips pursed. Not a single camera flashed. But there, at last, his salvation; the steps leading off the entrance runway and across to the lifts. He would have run the last few meters, but not a single drop of sweat had been shed in Tremptor Tower since its construction, and he certainly wouldn't be the first to desecrate the hallowed ground.

Inside the lift, Simone pressed the button for the tenth floor with one shaking finger. Everyone around him was wearing purple. They kept glancing at him, but he kept his eyes down, studying the tastefully designed Tremptor elevator carpet design.

Eventually, the elevator arrived at the tenth floor.

Simone power-walked the final few steps into his office, and shut the door. He crystallized the walls so that they were opaque, and sat down behind his three-tier desk.

What could have happened? What had gone wrong? Unless . . . Simone's eyes grew wide.

What if it wasn't Tuesday after all? What if it was actually *Wednesday*?

The implications were unbearable. Was he to spend the entire day unfashionable? Wearing all white when it was a complete faux pas to be in monochrome on a Wednesday? But what could he do? He could phone his wife and get her to bring a spare suit. But then—what about his face? The Grantis Granto makeup fixer was already in place. His makeup would be solid for at least the next eight hours.

Simone resolved to hide in his office all day. If anybody came knocking, he would claim to be in a meeting. It was the done thing, after all. An actual meeting had not occurred in Tremptor Tower since its creation, but to use being in a meeting as an excuse was to be considered polite.

There wasn't anything of any real substance in Simone's office. He would have to get creative in order to bide his time. There were artfully piled stacks of blank paper, and aesthetically pleasing towers of electronic equipment that he had no idea how to use. Nobody in Tremptor Tower did any work, after all. That would have been a hideous use of the mind. Actual work was for the dreadful unfashionables below, who could afford the brainpower.

Simone took a deep breath. It would be all right. He would simply read magazines all day. Drawing out the latest Gentlemen's Art from his desk, he began reading—admiring the models wearing the best in avant-garde designs—and eventually began to relax. It would be fine. Only a few people had seen him, after all. He would laugh it off tomorrow. They would all laugh it off, and drink champagne, and it would be a funny anecdote.

There came a knock at the door. "Simone?" It was Darlington.

"I'm in a meeting!" he cried, hiding behind his magazine.

"But Simone, you simply must come out! It's Trevor Tremptor. He's come to see us."

How utterly dreadful! Simone had forgotten. Today was the day that Trevor Tremptor, fashion icon and head of the Tremptor company, was coming around to mingle with those on the tenth floor of his tower. Simone was mortified. This could mean embarrassment before the whole company. Worse—this could mean demotion.

Trembling, Simone stepped out into the corridor and stood before his door.

Everyone else was lined up, all dressed in purple. As soon as they set eyes on him, there were gasps. Monochrome? On a Wednesday? It was outrageous.

There was Trevor Tremptor now, air-kissing each of his coworkers, and offering little compliments. Everyone blushed the correct amount, and struck a little pose. Trevor himself was an Adonis—so incredible to look upon that it hurt Simone's eyes. Had ever a more fashionable being existed? Simone wanted to disappear into the carpet.

At last, Trevor Tremptor arrived before Simone. There was a long silence. Everyone was holding their breath.

"Simone . . ." said Trevor, carefully, but Simone couldn't meet his eyes. He kept his head down, so ashamed of what he was wearing. He knew he was letting everyone down. "Simone . . ." said Trevor again, and Simone closed his eyes, waiting for the guillotine to drop. "That . . . is . . . *fabulous*."

• • •

The rest of the day passed in a magnificent whirl.

Simone was promoted not just to the eleventh floor, but all the way up to the nineteenth, where some of the most beautiful people in the company worked.

The offices were dazzling with their array of poised statuaries and intricate pieces of useless electronic equipment. Even the stacks of blank paper were of top quality—a creamy white, displaying this month's Tremptor logo.

Everyone applauded him, and he was surrounded on all sides by remarkable fashionistas, who each praised him for his daring. "Monochrome on a Wednesday?" they said, "It's simply incredible! Unheard of. It's so *subversive*. The irony of it, and the *precision* of it."

Invited on a tour of the offices, Simone was overwhelmed. It felt like his brain was on fire. The people on the nineteenth floor made those down on the tenth look like sniveling uglies, but now, here, Simone knew he could realize his full potential—his place as a true innovator in the art of fashion. He had never considered himself an innovator before, but now that he was here it was obvious.

After work, everyone treated him to drinks at the bars. Beneath the neon lights, Simone himself felt neon. He drank endless bottles of champagne, and beautiful rainbow cocktails, and inhaled so much white powder that it felt as if he was breathing drugs instead of air. He was on top of the world. He was brilliant, and he knew it. Everyone slapped him on the back, and called him remarkable, and gave him their business cards, and no less than three magazines wanted to take his picture.

In a whirling, frothing, state of absolute euphoria, Simone submerged in neon. For the first time in his life, he felt as if he really knew that he was beautiful.

• • •

When Simone awoke, he was still buzzing. "Darling! Did you hear about my promotion?"

"I heard everything, Simone! But we have no time to chat this morning. You simply must ready yourself for work. After all, it being Thursday, you must be ten minutes early."

Of course she was right. But something was tugging at Simone's bubbling brain. Something had happened to him. Something was different.

He unfurled from the pink chaise longue and felt like a beautiful butterfly, emerging from its ugly cocoon. Today was the first day of his life that he was truly fashionable. Today he would dare to go against the trend again. He would show them all how brilliant he was.

And there was his first moment of inspiration, courtesy of his wife. He wouldn't be early, nor would he be late. Simone would arrive at work *precisely on time*.

But what to wear? What to wear?

Thursday usually meant flowers; organic greens, brilliant yellows, and every color of the rainbow. It was a day in the fashion world devoted to life. But Simone was a fashion prodigy now, and he knew that he must represent that. He must show them all that he was worthy of the nineteenth floor of Tremptor Tower.

Death, then. He would spit in the face of life and all would love him for it.

Gray. It must be gray. He threw open the doors to his walk-in wardrobes and swept his hands along his suits, before coming to the gray section. There was his darling Sarcross suit—a desirable classic—and his thick ungainly Redrad suit, which was only to be worn on the third Sunday of each month. But instead of either of these, Simone tore open the boxes containing his slate-gray Dan Chopin suit, which he had been saving for a special occasion. It was made of an experimental material which was considered capable of drawing out the dullest, least-vibrant shade imaginable.

He would be the opposite of life. He would be a void of unlife.

But what about his face? What would he do?

Simone emptied his cupboards, searching for anything gray. But none of it was good enough. How was he meant to represent absolute nothingness with a bit of eyeliner? Some false eyelashes? A gray lipstick? Frustrated and trembling, he threw powders at the walls, and shattered glass bottles.

"Simone?" His wife. "What's happening?"

"I simply must . . ." he hissed, at his reflection.

But there—another moment of inspiration. The walls in the pool-house were being repainted in shades of gray. Normally, of course, Simone would avoid the unfashionables while they were at work—to behold them so close would make him nauseous—but today he must be brave. He would face them, for the sake of his art.

Running through the house, he flung open the pool-house doors. Water reflected across the half-painted walls, and a dozen pairs of unornamented eyes stared at him in wonder. Simone hated them. Waves of hate rolled over him. But he persevered. He burbled some nonsense gibberish at them and grabbed one of the buckets of paint.

CAUTION, it read on the side. TOXIC FUMES.

Simone upended the bucket over his head. The paint was cold, and a little slipped down his throat, but the fumes shot up his nose, making him sure of himself.

Running back to his mirror, he saw that he had done right. His skin was perfectly gray. It was brilliant. He grinned, and the whiteness of his teeth sent shocks through him. They weren't good enough. Dipping his fingers into the still-wet paint covering his neck, he rubbed at the white until it was dulled. Then, he washed his hands in the paint. Gray skin, gray teeth, gray everything. Only his eyes would emerge—the wild ever-watchful eyes of death.

Finally, he put on his Dan Chopin suit.

Gray nothingness: death. He was ready to face them.

Laughter tumbling from his lips, he entered his wife's dressing room.

"I'm ready!" he cried.

Her eyes widened and she let out a shriek, but Simone paid it no attention. He knew that he was beautiful. Even as she fainted, he air-kissed her and ran for the door, tapping at his paint-encrusted watch. If he left now, he would be exactly on time for work. Just as planned. He could already hear the applause thundering in his ears.

• • •

The vibro-rail carriage was empty, because everyone else had arrived at work early.

Simone felt the excitement growing in his gut. Or maybe it was illness. It was difficult to tell. The fumes wafted into his nose from the paint covering his face and made bubbles in his brain that weren't gray, like the paint, but neon, like the clubs of last night.

As the carriage passed over the suburbs where the uglies tramped around on their worn shoes, a stream of bright pink vomit shot out of Simone's mouth and coated the window. Instead of being disgusted by the sight, Simone became fascinated by it. Through the lens of his pink vomit, the dull realm of the unfashionables below became a thing of beauty. Suddenly, the regular shapes became organic, lumpy things, enhanced by chunks of undigested food, and the uglies were like brilliant pink beetles, their unkempt features bright.

But of course this should happen, Simone thought. He was becoming so fashionable that his very effluence was making the world beautiful.

Beyond the suburbs, the carriage smoothly sailed on past the streets where the unfashionables walked. Another jet of vomit soared majestically from between Simone's gray lips, splattering all over the windows, this time in bright orange. "You're welcome," he said at the uglies, admiring the way that the streaks of red through the orange made pretty kaleidoscopic whirls to mask their hideousness.

By the time the carriage came to a halt, Simone felt euphoric. Stumbling from the vibro-rail, he beheld the way that Tremptor Tower wafted around in his vision as if it was a flag in a gale. He inhaled deeply, huffing great gouts of paint fumes into his lungs, and his euphoria heightened, killing any doubts he might have had. The pain in his gut was getting worse, but of course it wasn't actual pain. It was only the transformation occurring—his transformation from tenth floor fashionista to nineteenth floor fashion innovator and icon.

Wrapping his hands around his collar to hold himself upright, Simone swanned up to the Tower entrance. There was no queue. He was the last to arrive today. But it was perfect, so perfect—they would all have a chance to see his brilliant daring.

Throwing the doors aside, he swaggered down the red carpet, letting his hips lead him. The carpet wormed perilously beneath him, but he kept his stride. There was no applause to greet him, and no cameras flashed, but that was fine. Simone knew that his audience were too awed to respond. He shot glances to the left and the right, and saw members of the press fainting—falling from their chairs as if life had left them.

"Today," he announced, swinging his arms wide. "I am death!"

There was a shriek from an unknown source. Simone leapt heroically from the end of the red carpet, fell to his knees, and then dragged himself standing again. The shriek continued. The whole lobby whirled around in his vision, as if it was all caught up in a storm and he was the eye of it, and he couldn't locate the source of the scream. It was only as he managed to summon a lift that he realized that the shriek was tearing its way out of his own lungs. He let it happen for a while longer—screaming out the last of his ugliness, no doubt—and then inhaled sharply through his nostrils. Paint fumes powered their way into his brain and everything suddenly stopped whirling around.

The lift rose and rose, and Simone felt a great itching across his shoulder blades. He scratched weakly at the place, feeling a pair of strange lumps there, and for a moment he worried that something was terribly wrong. Breathing heavily fixed that worry—soothing his thoughts and reminding him that this was just another part of his transformation. By becoming death, he was becoming art.

By the time the lift arrived at the nineteenth floor, Simone's legs were no longer working. The doors pinged open, and a stream of red vomit erupted volcanically from between his lips, showering the perfectly white carpet. A dozen colorfully painted faces peered out from office doors as Simone hauled himself along, toward the distant conference room. Bodies dropped as he passed by—fainting spells affecting his jealous colleagues, no doubt—and he laughed at them. He laughed at their clownish faces, painted to worship life. He was death! Come among them!

The fact that he could no longer walk was fine, because he knew now what the lumps on his back were. Why, he wouldn't need to walk ever again. His transformation was nearing completion—he would be a bright gray butterfly of unlife. There was a sharp, stabbing pain in his gut, which he knew were the last throes of his metamorphosis, and he grinned, spitting blood from between his teeth.

Pulling himself up using the conference table, Simone lounged in the chair, awaiting his flock. They would all worship him, he knew. Worship him in his capacity as the most fashionable being to ever grace them. For he knew now that his transformation was alchemical—that he was transcending the mere human form and becoming fashion incarnate.

There was an uproar, but Simone couldn't tell if it was inside his head or not. The room spun, blurred, become unreal, and then suddenly stopped. There were faces at the door, and among them was Trevor Tremptor himself, gripping hold of the door frame. His nostrils were splayed, his eyes were wide, and the ends of some of his hairs were split. *Ugly*, thought Simone.

"What," demanded Trevor Tremptor, seething, "is *the meaning of this?*"

"Behold!" burbled Simone. He tried to stand, but only succeeded at slipping from his chair onto the floor. "I—" he managed, coughing. "I am death."

"Hideous!" screamed Trevor Tremptor, lancing at Simone with one outstretched finger. *"You're fired!"*

Wiping at his nose temporarily cleared it, and Simone felt the paint fumes as they wrapped themselves around his brain and rolled around inside his hollow body like a thick mist. Filled with renewed strength, he leapt to his feet and tore at his jacket and shirt. "I am death!" he howled, at the top of his lungs.

Two security guards rushed into the room. They were uglies from below, built for strength instead of beauty, and Simone loathed them. He wouldn't let them touch him. To do so would be to desecrate his perfect transformed state of absolute fabulousness. So, he darted from between their grasping hands and swung himself clear over the conference table. Ahead there was only the window, but that was fine. It was time to reveal his true form.

Simone smashed through the window and unfurled his wings.

• • •

It was generally agreed that Simone was a fashion genius, after all. The way his body lay splayed on the ground, blood leaking out of every part of him—why, it was a masterpiece. His image made the front cover of several magazines, and for a few weeks afterward fashionable people killed themselves on Thursdays. Then a new fashion came in, for sequins, and Simone was forgotten.

OMAR ROBERT HAMILTON

RAIN, STREAMING

(2019)

1/4

He stands before the gleaming porcelain of the Reizler-Hummingdorf Neorelax executive bachelor's bathroom ceramic solution. He stands before the gleaming . . . He stands . . . Christ this floor is freezing. Val, what the fuck? Why is this floor always so fucking cold?

Would you like to register a complaint, Val?

How many have we registered already? What's the point? When are we rotating out of here?

We're scheduled to rotate on Matchday VIII, Val.

Matchday VIII? Send your complaint. What's happening out there?

Four new friends, three sympathizes, two wows, four upcomings, and three memories.

Weak. Let's have the news.

CNNBreaking: Exclusive interview with Pantheon member Michael Bay on his Transformers Decalogue.

Save. Refresh.

He steps out of the subtly lit bathroom atmospherics and, in a few steps, collapses back into his king-size bed. Is that it? Heavily? Exhausted? Should I try to sleep? Too late probably. Get up and be first in to work. Boost my MateMarket. What am I trading at, Val?

At close of play yesterday you were trading at $22.19.

Okay. Get the fucking deal through and you'll close hot. With the thought he hears the usual chords ripple through his body, sees the sun-washed room, the sleeping beauty within it, the peace of an earlier time. *I'm sitting here alone up in my room . . .* No. Not now. Refresh.

[Curated content:—]

Here we go.

[What's keeping you up
at night?]

Getting my kill rate high enough.

[Keeping your credit score up
and your weight down.
Am I right?]

Whatever you say, Lady.

[CalorieCredits
motivates you for both.
Just choose your target weight—]

Val, shut up.

[—and when you get there—
we'll bump up your credit score.
Everyone's a winner.]

Val, it's too early for this. Give me some news or something. You're supposed to be on my side for Christ's sake.

Roger that.

Roger that? Where do you learn these things, Val?

We watched The Dirty Dozen, *Val, and you scored it 7 on imdb.com. Do you like it?*

Sure, sure. Gotta get my MateMarket rate up today. Fucking Brazil, jerking me around. Here's an idea. Sell your goddamned rainforest to someone who gives a damn. One thing you can't offset is idiocy.

[Curated content:
Offsetting can be upsetting.
But those days are over—]

Val, are you on the fritz this morning?

On the fritz, Val?

Well did we watch *The Dirty Dozen* or not? I said cool it.

On the fritz has no usage in the registered screenplay, Val. And you signed up for **Crate Expectations'** *free trial which comes with free artisonical advertorials.*

Fine. Play the thing.

[Offsetting can be upsetting.
But those days are over.
With CarboRate, caring for the
environment has never been simpler.
Invest in your future.
Invest in everyone's future.
Blink through now.]

God that took forever. Can we go to work now? Maybe today's your Surge. Permission to shake the hand of the—how did it go?—permission to shake the hand of the daughter of the bravest man I ever met. Order a car please, Val. What's the weather like?

Pleasantly warm.

Natch. He pauses, catches sight of himself in the mirror. A darkness takes over his face, his body, his whole being. He holds eye contact with the stranger in the mirror and slowly raises a hand, a finger, an accusation at the other man . . . Some day a real rain's gonna come.

No rain scheduled for the coming week, Val.

I know, I know. I wasn't talking to you.

Sorry, Val.

It's okay. He looks at himself in the mirror once more. Let's get going.

He stares out the window quietly gliding along the city streets. The world flickers with droptic offerings and savings and exclamations. You'll be rotated out soon. Why even look?

Refresh.

That music. My music.

That bouncing baseline you know from a thousand sleepless nights and morning fantasies, the low groan of the siren. You would know it in a heartbeat an eternity from now: the song is fused to your DNA, it is part of you—and you, it. One note and you're on Mars, together, her perfect white top shimmering like a mirage as she steps toward you through the choreographed flamethrowers, the sum of all human endeavor, the end of history: Britney.

But why?

[The moment you've all been
waiting for has arrived.]

It can't be—

[For the first time in human history
you can win the ultimate ReFix—]

But Britney's estate, the tight-fisted sons of bitches . . .

[TONIGHT!

Patriot Games 14 *is HERE.]*

Don't get your hopes up.

[And there can be
only one
super-predator]

Don't—

[worthy of]

They'll never do it.

[Britney—]

No.

[—Spears]
Thank you, Lord.
[Show off your skills against your fellow patriots.
Choose your arena.]
Thank you, Pantheon.
[Take on the drug lords
of the jungle.]
Thank you.
[Defeat the terrorists.]
This is it.
[Prove yourself.]
The moment you've been waiting for.
[Protect America.]
The ReFix the world has been waiting for.
[And win a place in Britney's heart.]
It's all coming together.
[Enlist now for Patriot Games 14.
Streaming live from midnight
                    on HalliburtonHomeBoxOffice.
Blink through for—]
Yes. Yes. Blink through, Val, quickly. What are the theaters?
Patriot Games 14: *Theaters: Narco jungle. Balkan bloodplain. Dirty bomb.*
Registration opens in one hour.
Make sure we're first to register. I want—
Balkan bloodplain?
You know me so well.
You have a new follower. UrbanLover: Nike forearm tattoos are 50%—
Wait pause. Got to think. What's our latest myopics?
Currently fifteenth ranked MyOp on @HalliburtonHomeBoxOffice. Fran-
chised up to state syndication last season with @CathodeRaytheon.
Good. We have to prepare. Got to think. Britney. It's actually happening.
He winds down the car window. Shit, it's hot already. Someday a real rain's
gonna come.
I got some bad ideas in my head, Val.
Ha! Very nice, Val. You're getting funnier every day.

2/4

The camera tracks behind. The music rises in static confidence, its sonar pulses
searching out into the midnight dark. The bass line breaks. Confidence is a
must—*here we go*—cockiness is a plus—*sing it*—edginess is a rush. The camera
stays tight on Val's muscular, masculine back, hair shining over shoulders silhouetted against the neon corridor, the road, the light, the inevitability of the arena.

Two hundred men enter, one man leaves. *Patriot Games 14.* Who have we got, Val?

Playing now is @Joliath. Three public ReFix wins. 782,422 followers. Average of seventeen responses per post, posting on average eighteen times daily.

Arena?

Equatorial jungle. Rebel attack on unearthed state resources. Civil defense contract. Neutralizations: 4.

Weapon of choice?

Synth mercenary.

How's the audience?

Scores aren't in yet.

Obviously. But how's he looking?

Awedience Pro's live language analysis gives me a positive rate of 72.

Very beatable.

It is a considerably higher than average score, Val.

Maybe today's the day I teach you about art, Val. About human genius and inspiration.

The expression or application of human creative skill and imagination, Val?

That's the one buddy. Synth Mercenary . . . You think these people haven't seen that before? What a waste of time. Refresh.

Pantheon: Streaming from tonight: Don Simpson: The Man, the Legend.

Save that. When are we up, Val?

Up next, Val.

Here we go. A few minutes and it'll be all you. All me and you Britney. Your white blouse brilliant against the angry Martian landscape, me stepping, one, two steps closer: "but I thought the old lady dropped it into the ocean at the end?"

Scores are in for Joliath.

Hit me, baby.

Neutralizations: 6. Audience retention: 34%.

Fine. We can beat that. Refresh.

[Curated content: HalliburtonHomeBoxOffice:

Holding a crowd?

Submit your MyOps for cash today.]

What do they think we're doing here for chrissakes? Refr—

You're up, Val.

Here we go.

He clicks his knuckles with relish at the challenge ahead, his shoulders seem to broaden as he steps into the arena, the gaze of hundreds upon him as he settles into the command chair. As the assistant hands him the controls she can't suppress her smile. Here we go. Shut all media down, Val, it's time to concentrate.

Good luck, Val.

See you on the other side.

3/4.

[Ten seconds to theater]

The audience responds well to dogs, having a dog is worth five points alone right, Val? Refresh. Oh right, just in here with myself now, anyway, that was Joliath's first mistake, crashing in with a huge anthro-synth to scare the children—sure you can use a synthetic in a private game, a late night game, a game in parts of town you don't rotate into—but the *Patriot Games*, the *Patriot Games* is a family affair, kids are watching, parents, it's educational, so give them dogs, birds, safety animals, make them feel safe, a dog protects you from the bad guys not a big synth burning down a village it just doesn't scan great just doesn't look fair and looking fair, hell *being* fair, it's just the most important thing in here, we're going to war here and you better believe we don't do it lightly, fairness is a goddamned cornerstone and if you forget that it's like forgetting, well it's like forgetting we're Ameri—

[Nine seconds]

nothing quite like it, though, is there? iContact is one thing but that look in the eye, that moment you connect really connect with the target and he's looking at you and he knows it's over and you're watching the hope drain from his face and he knows there'll be no mercy—what are we supposed to do?—are we gonna wait and find out if he's got a bomb strapped to his chest or shoved up his ass—no—who would do that?—you wanna risk a million bucks of top grade canine biomechanical defense engineering?—no—you're gonna pull the trigger—he knows it and you know it—lose a Boeing Big Dog in the field and you're right back down to the minileagues, the riot squads, the aerial surveillance—no, you're gonna pull the trigger—who would—

[Eight seconds]

this is it, Val oh, right, okay, solo time, when are they gonna loosen up the rules on that, anyway, watch this Joliath, watch my Awedience score spike nice and early when they see the Big Dog and watch me hold it up there as I cruise through to the final *bada-bing* to the head, you know you should think of a line you need your fucking catchphrase now, pal, and what have you got? what's Britney gonna hear, huh Val? How about "to lose all your senses, that's just so typically YOU" . . . a bit long . . . what else we—

[Seven seconds]

gotta focus: it's a midday game, Huawei Hyperdome, you're on your own here, out in the wilds, out reaping justice, just a man and his dog not too slow, not too quick. Pull the trigger. Not too slow, not too—

[Six seconds]

look at the arena, let's look at the arena: Balkan Bloodplain, State Department licensed target, four bodyguards, one target: female—you're on my radar—classic city arena, good, gives the audience things to look at cos you're not going to win this with a big kill rate, you're going to have to give them a show, a little stealth, a little style—looks like it's raining down there, never tried the Big Dog in the rain before . . . how strange to even see so much water—

[Five seconds to theater]

focus: just think of the MyOp you're gonna get out of this, the national syndication and maybe even Britney herself will watch it, maybe we'll watch it together—yeah, watch it with Britney, very likely– don't start up on that *shit*—when was the last time you listened to "Mona Lisa," bubs, she says it all herself—*shut up, shut*—

[Four seconds]

how many ways do they have to lay it out for you, friend? She's gone, she's always been gone and they're not even hiding it—it's all in the police report, car crash, blood on the sidewalk, no body, just a perfect golden lock of JT's hair. Gone too soon. *Shut up.* Pour one out—

[Three]

Concentrate. The mission. The Mutually Assured Democracy program is a cornerstone of our freedoms, The Mutually Assured Democracy program is a cornerstone of our freedoms, that's fucking right, you're a fucking patriot and you are fucking in and out, it's a licensed target, wanted by Interpol, State Department, everyone, no questions asked: the target's the bad news and you're two seconds away from making the world a safer—

[Two]

Play your cards right and tomorrow night you'll be on Mars with Britney, play your cards right and you're a God cos she's there, already there and waiting and you can see her, perfect in her white blouse, her eyes lighting up as she opens the black velvet box you've just handed her and you're holding your breath as her eyes flicker back up to yours: *but I thought the old lady dropped it into the ocean in the end?*—

[Impact]

Well baby, I went down and got it for you.

4/4

It's you. You're up. Your first line. You listen to the crackle of the interplanetary intercom. It's so real. You look at the numbers rapidly processing on the dashboard. 3684 / 1508. 0x02278FEO-00895.39228. No doubt some hidden codes from the genius mind of Nigel Dick.

You look around and the barren red sands of Mars stretch into the distance as far as you can see—but you are not nervous. Val, are you recording this?

There's too much data for a complete world download, Val. But I have your POV.

It's so real. Look at this. It's a whole world. You stretch your hand and you're really there. This is, without a doubt, the finest ReFix ever created. A whole world alive and living for miles and miles of Martian nothingness all around us. Your prize. Go forth and claim what's yours. You showed them something they'll never forget last night. Balkan bloodplain. You were born for it. A comprehensive destruction of all opponents. A seamless neutralization. Even an undetected exit. You showed them something. Now go forth. Go forth and claim what's yours. Go find your Britney.

There is only one structure visible. The factory up ahead. And inside, you know she's waiting for you.

They want the line. They're ready for it. Years of heartache end tonight. You clear your throat. The whole world is watching. How are we doing, Val?

You have two hundred and fourteen new followers, Val. Two hundred and nineteen. Two hundred and thirty-seven.

You deserve this. You're a winner. You can do this. You eliminated the target without quarter or mercy. You are a star. You are a patriot. Your fans are watching. Everyone's watching. Say the line. Take your crown.

Two hundred and forty-nine new followers.

The world hangs on your every word; your every move. You stop, turn your body forty-five degrees toward the invisible camera. You didn't need the rehearsals they insisted on. They could tell right away: this is your part, your moment.

You feel the image cut in to close-up, the first real look at you. You hold your jaw firm.

[Curated content: a little touch-up work has never been cheaper—]

What? Not now, Val.

No curated content, Val?

No, Christ, Val shut it off. Hold the jaw firm.

You would like me to turn all curated content off, Val?

Val, what the fuck, we're in the middle of the fucking ReFix. I've missed my fucking line. Turn everything off.

But Val I have to remind you that you're currently enjoying a free trial subscription to Buckshot Magazine—

Don't tell me what I'm enjoying, Val. I'm enjoying being the first and only human in the history of the fucking universe to star in a Britney Spears ReFix.

But in the terms & conditions—

I don't care, Val. Turn everything off.

Everything, Val?

Off. All off. Unsubscribe from everything. I've got to do my lines, Val. Off off off.

• • •

And there, half-buried in the sand beneath your feet, an ancient relic waits. A last message from another world. You've seen it a thousand times—and though it's new every time it's never been as new as this, as real as this. You bend down to pick it up, her image, perfectly faded, looks out at you.

You say your line, with perfect pitch and timbre, examining the CD cover, holding it up for the audience to see Britney, young Britney, the original Britney, Britney before the accident, staring out at them, summoning them into her world. Britney before the crash, before the innocent blood.

The earth is shaking. Rocks crash off the red mountains. She is coming.

Her eye, her mouth, that siren call.

The flamethrowers pour their burning gasses into the air, the heavy steel of chains grind, you look up and you see her, descending from the dark vault of heaven, brilliant in the red of a thousand hells, the music filling your head and steeling your spine, the heat pulsing through the plastics of the spacesuit, every nerve-end pulling you toward her, she's there, she's real, she's here, she's now, she sings.

Behind her the chorus line begins its ritual, dancing sightlines of mathematical precision pulling toward her celestial light: she's coming toward you, singing to you. You are the messenger, you are the one, you are falling, she's there and if you just reached out you could touch her, if you reached out you would become one with Britney as your pixels merge and reemerge in unique combination.

But this is a ReFix and you will respect it. Every world has its natural laws. You don't need to touch her, you don't need any more than this.

Incredible. The detail. You can hear every breath, see every muscle flinch, feel the vast emptiness of Mars rolling behind you. There's a twitch. A moment of uncertainty. Britney's looking at you. She's thinking something new. Britney? Something's wrong. No. No, just a glitch. She's smiling. Britney Spears is smiling at you. Her hair streams black then blonde again. Raindrops land on her forehead. Raindrops? On Mars?

What's going on, Val?

I don't know, Val. You said to turn everything off.

And suddenly you're in the air, you're pulled up, up, your feet off the ground you're hurtling up into the sky and you strain to see above you and you're attached to a chain and the men with their steel levers are pulling you up and you're trapped and you can't move and you knew this would happen but you had no idea and you try and move to pull at the chain but you can't reach it but it's okay, Britney is there, far below, transformed now into her angelic white, her arms flowing in perfect choreography above her head and you just need to watch and you just need to breathe. The rain is falling, the target's breathing is so heavy, she's on her knees, the rain is falling all around her, your finger is on the trigger. Watch the dance, breathe, and keep your eyes on Britney. She's Britney. Think of the followers. Think of the outside world, the losers and the frauds all schlepping off to work today, the young tuning in for a moment of ReFix glory, the old waiting to die, all watching you, all waiting for your next move. Val, how are we doing?

What do you mean, Val?

What's our count? What are we up to?

You said to turn everything off, Val.

She looks up at you, only at you. You focus. It's all going so fast. Concentrate, it will be over soon, she's on the second chorus already and she's flying toward you, spinning in the air, transforming from the red latex into the black-and-white shirt and skirt and she's in front of you and the rain clouds are gathering, it's your line again you're up and you've said it ten thousand times in your head and in the mirror and in the shower and now it's time to make the words into something, it's time to say them, to say them finally to Britney herself.

"Britney," you say, your voice quivering with manly meaning.

You look down at the black velvet box that has appeared in your hand. You look at her. She is calm, expectant.

Her hand almost touches yours as she takes the box from your fingers.

[But I thought the old lady
dropped it into the ocean
at the end?]

She looks up at you and she's drenched in rain, eyes all imploration, her words begging in your head. No. Please. No. She's just a girl. It's just a glitch. You'll tell them when you're out. They'll fix it. They'll give you a refund. They'll tell you to run it again. The rain is falling now and she's crying but you know you'll do it, you'll do it like every time, you'll win the day, you'll defend the country, you'll be a man and you'll do what's right but it's just a glitch, it's Britney, glitch. She's back. She's staring at the ring. Everything's fine. She glances up at you and in the glance, the glitch, the bullet, the rain. It drips down your shirt, the heat of the sand burns up through your suit.

Just keep your eyes on Britney.

[But I thought the old lady
dropped it into the ocean
at the end?]

It's so hot. The rain is dripping in from the neck. The old lady dropped it into the ocean at the end. Britney's looking at you. Puzzled . . .

[But I thought the old lady
dropped it into the ocean
at the end?]

She wants the line, the whole world wants the line, take your crown, take your prize, say the line. What's the line? Val, what's the line? Britney's waiting. Tell me the line, Val. She wants the line. You're hurting her. Please. We take the target we're assigned. You're not supposed to ask questions. Christ, Val, the line, the line—

[But I thought the old lady
dropped it into the ocean
at the end?]

M. LOPES DA SILVA

FOUND EARWORMS

(2019)

I FOUND THIS WORDCO in the desert, with its autogrammar and what the fuck ever bullshit built in to make my words all pretty. I still like it, though.

I used to write shit out when I was a runt living in the freecamp hard by the old nuclear plant. The normies are scared shitless of that place. Good. It's a good time. We get rowdy and keep the cockroaches awake. I got my first piercing there, the one through my left nostril. That's why I keep a big fucking plug in there. Amateur. It was okay, though—I messed him up for fucking up so bad. We hang out sometimes now. It's cool.

•   •   •

Every die
Every day

Every dying day—is that something? Maybe I should write a song.

•   •   •

Everydie like everyday
Riding

• • •

I don't know. Fuck! Writing songs is hard.

• • •

Nothing. The desert. Gave myself a new tattoo of a werewolf howling at a cheez-burger. I think my linework is getting better.

• • •

Hung out with friends in one of the abandoned shopping malls. We've remade a lot of it. It's wild. Art on art on art on art. Not the kind of stuff you see in towns. Someone threw a party in the big space downstairs, and it started with a lot of old stuff—The Ramones, The Slits—that turned into newer shit like The Pussy-cocks. We got drunk off tequila and cactus wine and howled and fucked and wept and nobody got hurt that night.

• • •

The normies expect us to work until the work makes us sick, but they don't give us any of the medicine that they make from the plants we pick. Like we didn't work hard enough. Yeah, right.

Me and my friends we put on our dust masks and lit our Molotovs and revved up the darters until sand spewed up like vomit beneath our treads, then we rode! We went and lit up the roof of the front office, while Mope and Freekel snuck around back to rob the truck with all the medicine in it. And I mean we got away with ALL of it. They're mad.

• • •

The normies have been chasing us with their freaking cruisers for days now. We try to make extra time at night, but they keep following. They never come out this far. Usually.

• • •

Mope couldn't take it anymore. She just turned around and drove right at them, Freekel and Eddi tried to get away, but the normies just shot them down.

• • •

I'm still running—straight into the desert. I cut a patch away on my jeans so I could stare at the werewolf with its cheezburger scabbing over.

I'm thirsty. My friends are dead. I've only got a fraction of the medicine left. But the normies can't last forever in that metal box. They're hungry and thirsty, too.

So I'm writing this song and riding riding riding.

• • •

Everydie like everyday
Riding hard to robinhood
Never liked you anyway

FUCK I HATE WRITING SONGS!!

MARIE VIBBERT

ELECTRIC TEA

(2019)

I CAME HOME in the watery dawn, exhausted from waitressing all night. As I eased my bike against the porch railing to chain it up, a neighbor who had never said two words to me before leaned over his chain-link fence. "Hey, Sue, right?"

Tsui. I didn't correct.

"Did you see the fire? Man, I would have loved to have seen that!"

"Fire?" I asked.

He pointed behind our homes, down the weed-and-trash-strewn slope to the warehouse, its undamaged roof all that was visible from the front sidewalk.

I pushed through vines and broken fences with the dreamlike possession artists yearn for. A small crowd was gathered, reverent at the edge of hasty police tape.

The arsonist had painted the warehouse in careful lines of linseed-oil pigments, flammable as anything. The colors were lost, but the image wasn't—fat, indulgent lines that tapered sweetly into finer detail. The picture was a skeletal bird-creature holding the long arm of a Sears Shop-Vac. The logo was identifiable, despite foreshortening as it curved around the barrel.

I was jealous of the craftsmanship. Every line touched to spread the fire. Combustion started at the Shop-Vac's business end, its flat nose pushed into the joining of wall and weedy gravel. Those first lines had the thickest char. By design or chance, the fire department arrived before the flames burned far from the confines of their original lines. The black rising from the vacuum's mouth echoed decals on hot rods, a symbol of speed arrested.

I would not rest until I found this artist and learned their purpose and, more importantly, their process.

Our narrow street, Jefferson, sagged off the backside of Tremont like a rotten floorboard. Two of my classmates and I had pooled our resources to rent the narrow clapboard house. We were failed artists who didn't know it yet. In violation of our renter's agreement we'd painted murals on every wall using ceiling white, porch floor gray, and matte black spray paint. I did the black. I arched into a backbend to make one complete slash across the living room, straight as a sword stroke. I wanted the line to be unrestrained, violent. Instead, it bloomed like mascara. Mahesh painted a woman in white and gray, heavy breasts falling from the join of ceiling and wall, her arm outstretched along my black line. I kept my eyes on the floor when I crossed the living room.

"I can't believe we missed it!" Jay said, slouching on the giant spool we used as a kitchen table. His dreads lay like a sleeping cat around his shoulders. "I hope the dude posts a video. It must have been sexy when the lines first caught."

I hoped so, too. I wanted the motion, like music, art that exists in time, rather than the notation left in its wake.

"It was derivative street art," Mahesh said. "Tsui could do better."

My name is pronounced "Sue," but I can hear it when the person speaking knows there's a T, something hesitant in the S. I prefer that.

"If it weren't down the hill," I said, "If the trees weren't so thick, I could have seen it on my way home."

"Yeah." Jay nodded. "It's worse, isn't it? Being so close and missing it? Have you ever seen paint burn? The flames glide, like they're hovering."

Mahesh was working on the cabinets under the sink, adding a slouching monster where some paint had dripped. "I'll bet it was electric tea. Someone drank it and ran out to prove it had an effect on them by doing something crazy. These things always hit Cleveland after the bigger towns. Like bands and fashion."

"No, they don't." Jay straightened. He'd lived in Cleveland his whole life and was protective of it. "People have been drinking electric tea here for years. Before it went big."

"Okay," Mahesh said, keeping his eyes on his work. He dragged his brush slowly, flat, making a bumpy nose.

Jay took that as the dismissal it was. "I know people who drink it. Who've been drinking it. None of them went crazy, either."

"It must have been beautiful," I said. I looked out our back window at the warehouse roof among the trees and saw a smudge, like a line from a conte crayon, curving along a glittering tarpaper edge. "I'd drink electric tea if it helped me make such a thing."

Artists fail for many reasons, and most fail where we were—fresh out of art school. I couldn't speak to Jay and Mahesh's nascent failings, but mine was simple: I wasn't good enough. I studied and experimented. I took critique well. I hoped that enough time studying and experimenting and responding well to criticism would somehow build up to the golden magic of "good enough," but I knew that "good enough" wasn't enough.

We were in pursuit of our futures, self-consciously temporary in our living arrangements, and compulsively recklessness. Mahesh spent what we all knew were his last dollars on a sable brush. Jay tried to tattoo himself. I went to five-dollar shows at the Phantasy when I had work the next morning. Someone set fire to buildings. It made sense.

· · ·

Jay met me at the restaurant as I was leaving my early shift. "You still want to go?"

"I want to see it," I said. "Just to see."

He nodded. "Leave your bike here." As we started walking down the street, he said, "It's not that it's not safe, but I don't know if you want people to see your bike there and know, you know?"

"Electric tea isn't illegal."

"Yet," Jay said. He looked side to side, his dreads twitching like nervous snakes. He jogged across the street and took me down a few alleys to University Road by the back of Sokolowski's. We slunk behind the restaurant and through the gravel lot under the freeway bridge. His shirt was torn below the right sleeve, giving me momentary glimpses of his muscular side.

All the quick, covert motion made little sense when we reached Abbey Avenue and had to sedately walk the long bridge. Tremont is an island, bordered on all sides by cliffs man-made and natural—the river valley, the freeways, the railroads. This bridge was one of a limited number of ways out of Tremont. The cracked sidewalk was scrawled with anti-gentrification graffiti.

"Is it far?" I asked. The neighborhood ahead of us held breweries and a strip mall, I couldn't imagine an electric teahouse squeezing in.

"Not far now." We crossed the smaller bridge for the RTA tracks.

The West Side Market was crowded, voices filling the high, vaulted space with a concert-hall buzz. Jay led me around pastries and meats and out again through the fruit stands where thick-accented men vied for our attention with chunks of cantaloupe on knifepoint. We resumed sneaking up alleyways and down side streets.

We paused beside one of the dozens of three-story Victorian storefronts in Ohio City, all brick and recessed entrances. A record store was doing well on the corner, plastered with prints of local bands from the '70s like the Dead Boys and Electric Eels, unkempt and daring you to call it nostalgic. In the middle of the block lettering from generations of failed businesses made a pastiche of faded gilding over nondescript doors and blackened windows.

Jay ducked into a blind alley and down bluestone steps to a basement door.

"Do we need a password?"

He raised his eyebrows at me and knocked with the back of his hand. One of his failed tattoos stretched on the paler skin of his inner wrist. It was a broken bit of barbed wire originally intended to be a bird. I felt very tender toward that tattoo.

A thin, caramel-skinned man answered the door, pulling it against a brass security chain to eye us before unlatching.

All this pseudo cloak-and-dagger was appropriate to electric tea—an illicit substance that was not illicit. More than half the flavor was myth; it would lose its power if you could buy it in the drugstore like incense.

The basement was lit by LED strips at the base of brick walls, partially hidden from sight by rows of cast concrete fleur-de-lis. Black fabric with sequins draped between and over pipes on the ceiling. The chairs and tables were a mix: wrought iron garden sets and marble café tables and one old door on sawhorses.

The man who let us in returned to his stool by the door's peephole and left us to find our way.

Electric tea was, ultimately, just tea, in a special cup. The cup contained a mechanism that would broadcast invisible waves toward your brain, stimulating emotions, thought processes. If it worked right it would play your brain with recorded thoughts like vinyl grooves resurrected Joey Ramone. It supposedly left your mind clearer and sharper in its wake. Stimulants helped the effect, so its first use was with hyper-caffeinated energy drinks. There were incidents, allegations, nothing proven, but it was now only legal with ordinary tea. The partial prohibition made it sexier.

There was a sheet of SmartPaper on each table with a menu to scroll through. I tapped "black" from the list of categories. They had every type of tea I'd ever heard of and a few I hadn't.

The prices weren't listed. Always a danger sign. I rifled my fingers through the loose tips in my pocket.

A plump white girl approached, wearing a short waiter's apron over her jeans. "Can I get you anything?"

Jay ordered green tea. I scanned the list again. "Gunpowder Smoke," I said.

She smiled. "Good choice. We just started serving that. It's our own blend of black gunpowder tea with Lapsang souchong."

"Sounds expensive. I think I'll have the Darjeeling."

"All our teas are the same price. Give it a try. You'll love the kick."

I could never disagree with a waiter, so I nodded. When she left, I asked Jay, "Have you done this before?"

"Yeah. Of course."

"Do you believe the stories?"

He shrugged. "I know it's supposed to make you think more clearly. I also know that anything that does good to the mind can be overdone. I dunno. I've had some great ideas after coming here. Like, that's when I started 'Rodin Bows to a Dream of Donatello.'" He smiled, mocking his own pretension.

I admired how he sat in his chair like his clothes were not attached to him. He always wore loose jeans and shirts, his lithe frame a rumor reported secondhand by folds and shadows. "I'll never paint anything that real," I said.

He turned to regard me sideways. "We are not going to start that again, Tsui. When you finally let go, you'll be the best of us all."

My cheeks warmed. I pretended to be fascinated by the menu. "I need to learn to make unselfconscious lines."

The tea arrived in oversized cups, ceramic on the outside and glass inside so we could see the little circuit board and dime-sized emitters. The blinking purple and blue LEDs were almost certainly just for looks.

The tea smelled metallic and smoky. I paused before sipping, uncertain.

Of course, holding the cup was the dangerous part, wasn't it?

Jay leaned back, a picture of cool unconcern. He kissed his teacup slowly, deliberately.

"I should have brought my sketchbook," I said. "That's a good pose for you."

Self-conscious, his lines tightened and shifted. Without changing his pose, he ruined it. "Drink your tea," he said.

I sipped my tea. It tasted like it smelled—like the smoke from a black powder pistol wafting through tall grass.

I closed my eyes and breathed in slowly, evenly, letting the steam bathe my face. I was waiting to feel something. "What is it supposed to feel like?"

"Like waking up," Jay said. "Like plugging in an amp, like a pebble dropping into water. Like a head rush."

I felt warm stoneware in my hands. I felt recycled wind from the air conditioner. I felt a bit silly.

"Mahesh doesn't approve," Jay said. "If he were any more uptight, he'd vibrate."

"Don't," I said.

Jay used Rapidograph pens with micrometer tips on SmartPaper to plan every sculpture, made small models and intermediate models. Precise and careful in art, Jay relaxed in everything else. The opposite of Mahesh. He raised his eyebrows. "Don't what?"

I couldn't explain what they both meant to me, how much I needed them to love each other. "Mahesh bleeds when he paints," I said.

Jay's cheek lifted, the languor returning to his limbs. "Yeah, I love him, too."

I felt no effect from the tea. I watched Jay closely, to see if he felt anything. He was just Jay.

The tea was expensive, but not more than my tips for the night. I declined a second cup.

We took a more direct route home and passed a band playing in a walled courtyard. Raw and loud, practicing in the middle of the day. Cymbals crashed like paint splatters on brick walls. It was living art, spilling into the street. You couldn't study to make this.

I took Jay's hands and pulled him back. He laughed and danced to me. His movements, the music, this was what I wanted: something perfect because it was unpolished, something pure.

Who needed an electric kick when we lived in a vibrant art community? I hugged Jay's sweaty, muscular arm as we continued walking and he talked about Japanese printmaking and I interrupted to talk about the graffiti we passed.

"Will you sculpt tonight?" I asked.

"Hell yes. And you will paint, Tsui. You'll paint if I have to strap the brush to your hand."

• • •

Mahesh was, ironically, making tea when we got home. He looked up from lowering the mesh ball into the pot. "Where have you been?"

"Getting some tea," Jay said, tilting his head back, challenging.

Mahesh shook his head. "It's a placebo, you know."

"How would you know?"

I said, "Don't fight."

"Absinthe," Mahesh said. He put the cozy on the teapot and turned to face us, arms crossed. "In the nineteenth century, absinthe was a craze. They claimed the wormwood caused 'effects' beyond drunkenness. Mind-opening, clarifying. Inspiration. Ring any bells?"

Jay shrugged fluidly. "They also thought cocaine was a good headache medicine, doesn't mean aspirin is going to get you high."

Mahesh set three mugs on the wooden spool. "There were no special effects. There was strong alcohol and wishful thinking. The power of ritual." He waved his hand over the table. "How would you know that I'm not serving you electric tea right now?"

"Because the cups are crap." Jay picked up a cracked mug with the logo for a construction company and waggled it, exposing its chipped side.

Mahesh looked at me. "Did you feel anything?"

I didn't want to take sides, but I had to shake my head.

"If it really did anything, the government would regulate it," Mahesh said, and poured the tea.

Jay walked out, taking any hope of conversation with him.

• • •

A well-known local sculptor was found dead inside a cooling tower across from Tremont Park. He'd climbed to the top of the structure with an armful of rebar and slipped, falling twenty feet to crack his skull on the metal grating below. His wife had no idea he had even left home that night.

Because of the similarity of some of his sculptures to the bird-skeleton drawing, it was speculated that he was the arsonist, and the news blogs all raised the question: had he been drinking electric tea?

The art community knew better than to suspect him of the fire. He was a sculptor, had never painted in any medium, much less fire, and electric tea drinkers did not tend to change genres.

Besides, a day later there was another fire, down in the flats. The painting this time was a chorus of large-headed waifs, their little bodies twisted like candle flames, ringing one of the conical mounds of iron ore deposited by shipping boats for the steel mills. It burned longer before being doused, but as its substrate was iron dirt, nothing was damaged.

You could see minute traces of color, where the paint soaked in and was protected. Burnt turquoise and magenta. Inspired planning, how the colors sank and glowed against the rust brown ore.

On *Scene Magazine*'s main page the two fire drawings were shown side-by-side, the headline simple: Copycat or Serial Arsonist? The comments section raged with theories, and images by local artists either being accused or exonerated.

Mahesh leaned over my shoulder. "A hundred artists in this area have that style. Maybe a thousand. Just in this small-ass city. He could be from somewhere else, just passing through. They'll never catch him that way."

I resented the "they." I would catch him. Practice at catching fame. "He could be a she," I said.

Mahesh said, "I was using the gender-neutral 'he.' Come on, I want to use the computer."

Both painters were clearly right-handed. It's no great forensic trick to tease out the handedness of a line-artist; even the very best have to lift and drop their brush. Some artists, of course, are more careful. Both fire paintings were not careful, reveling in the mess and accident of an overloaded brush. I admired the punk-rock joy of the lines.

I could hear Mahesh breathing. He spoke quietly, bloodlessly. "I need the computer more than you do. You already have a job," he said.

"It's not an art job."

"I'm not unemployed because I'm too precious to wait tables, Tsui. I'm trying, all right?"

I slipped out of my seat. "I didn't say anything like that." We had leaped over the cliff of graduation together, and in the air before landing, whether it would be the promised shore of gainful employment or the abyss below us, it was hard not to claw at each other.

• • •

After Jefferson crosses West Third, it quickly starts to look like an old country road, overgrown and sun-bleached and neglected, concrete silos rising up behind graffiti-decked tin railings. You forgot the Cleveland skyline and the high bridges were waiting to slip into view between tangled vines.

The warehouse's fence lay flat where the fire trucks had come in. Someone had held a business here, had cared about this expanse of overgrown gravel.

Someone had already sprayed graffiti over top of the burn-lines. A vermillion penis pointed skyward like a cannon raised on its misshapen wheels.

• • •

The chubby white girl opened the basement door this time. "We're not open yet," she said.

"Please let me wait inside?"

She looked up the stairs. It was a bright, hot afternoon. I tried to look afraid and vulnerable and small. "All right," she said. "It's not going to be that long."

The room looked different with the overhead lights on—ordinary. There were chair-height scrapes on the walls and dings in the tables. The sequined fabric had loose threads and a cheap shine.

"The kitchen isn't open yet, but I could get you a glass of water."

I shook my head. She left and came back a few minutes later with a cash drawer, which she slid into a holder on the wall. Then she unlocked it and counted its contents. The familiar waltz of preparing a restaurant for its operating day.

I tried to think of some ingratiating way to start conversation. Instead I blurted out, "Is it a placebo?"

Her shoulders dropped. "Jesus," she said. She turned to face me. "I'm trying to run a business. I don't need your approval or opinion. Go read a webpage."

"I didn't mean . . . I'm not." I stood, stepped forward, stepped back. I looked at my own twisting hands. "I didn't *feel* anything."

I looked up to see her considering me. She said, "You aren't going to lecture me or write some stupid blog 'exposing' the 'truth' about electric tea?"

I shook my head. "I just wanted to feel something. To understand."

She sighed. She closed the cash drawer and made a note on a tablet. "It's not a placebo. I wouldn't have started this business if it were, if I hadn't been convinced the first time I drank it."

"Does it only affect certain people?"

She looked embarrassed. She went to the counter and stooped below. She pulled out a pair of cups and set them on the counter. "The thing of it is, sometimes the battery runs out. Or gets weak. Or a connection is loosened throughout the day. I'd say there's about a ten to twenty percent chance you didn't get a working cup." She shook her head. "So yeah, there is a placebo effect, and I rely on it because this technology is fragile as *heck*."

She pushed a cup toward me. "I barely make a profit, fixing the stupid things all the time."

"Oh."

"What'll you have? They're all working. They always all work at the *start* of the night."

"Gunpowder smoke."

"Good choice. We just started serving that. Our own blend of—"

"You said," I said.

"Oh." Her face was tired, older looking as she bent to retrieve a glass jar from under the counter. She filled a tea ball and snapped it shut with one hand as she put the jar away. "Guys love the gunpowder smoke. It sounds manlier than rosehip chamomile. I always get happy when a woman orders it." She looked at me again as she held the cup under a hot water tap. "When I was in college, I was convinced Lapsang souchong cured writer's block. Maybe it was the smell. Wood smoke. Scent is linked strongly to memory. I never had trouble telling stories around campfires."

We bent to sip our cups of smoke tea together. This time I felt a strange tickle, an itch on my forehead. An idea vibrated through my mind like the crash of cymbals.

The teahouse owner raised her eyebrows. "You see?"

"Thank you," I said.

Her face transformed with her smile, like just the right line turns a mere representation into beauty. "That's why I had to have this shop. I had to share that feeling. It's magic, every time I see that look on a new person's face."

        •   •   •

I did not go to work like I was supposed to. I walked home, knowing Mahesh would be there alone. Jay worked days at a gallery on Professor. I found Mahesh painting light bulbs and flying saucers around the cabinet knobs in the kitchen.

He wiped his brush and stared at me. "Shouldn't you be at work?"

"Why did you do it?" I asked. He recoiled, started to stammer the usual things people stammer in this case. "You set fire to the warehouse. And the ore pile. Close to home and then farther away to confuse the trail. Will you do it again? Were you angry? Frustrated?"

His head hung over his hands, resting his weight on the edge of the kitchen sink.

"It's okay," I said. "No one was hurt."

"It's not art if it doesn't hurt!" His eyebrows formed a harsh line.

"We'll help you. Jay and me. We'll keep you from doing it again, from being caught. We're in this together."

He sank, back against the counter, shoulders dropping, eyebrows loosening. He looked bewildered. "How did you find out?"

There are false things in life—the hopes of an artist being one of the most common, but there are true things, too, made by human minds and hands. Art can be an assembly of technology and smell. I didn't say that. I said, "There are different forms of inspiration."

I made Mahesh tea—regular tea—because inspiration was never his problem.

COREY J. WHITE

EXOPUNK'S NOT DEAD

(2019)

DOWNTOWN VIBRATES with sub-low frequency, churning Jack's guts along-side the anxiety he knows will only quiet with booze. The frame of his exoskeleton buzzes as he stomps closer to the source of the sound—metal humming to the kick drum thump coming up through cracked asphalt. Red paint flakes like dandruff; underneath the paint, steel rusts.

Jack's is a basic demolition exo: limbs attached to a sturdy hydraulic frame lacking any armor plating. He floats within the exoskeleton's torso, dangling on a battered harness with haptic converters aligned to his musculature. It's airy inside the machine, its canopy open to the elements. A breeze from the bay rolls over Jack's bare arms, carrying the salty smell of rotting seaweed.

Jack checks the flyer one last time, worried he might turn up at the wrong place—as though that distant clamor could be anything *other* than a punk show. The flyer's proper old-school, photocopied onto thin sheets of yellow paper:

EXOPUNK (WRECKING) BALL
OLD CITY HALL
DOORS OPEN 8 P.M.

The city council was voted out a year ago, but even a democratically elected governmental algorithm needs time to implement changes. At first, police had patrolled the grounds, protecting it while the city tried to find a buyer, but once enough of the walls had been torn open for the copper piping, they pulled out. The official demolition starts Monday, but after tonight's gig, with all the exopunks from the highlands dropping in, half the job will be done.

Jack rounds the corner and joins a procession of skels thudding up the street. Seeing his people, the knot of tension in his guts unravels. Even in his nine-foot-tall exo, the goliath city hall building looms threateningly: graffiti spots the stone facade like bruises, masonry already crumbling as decay sets in.

A broad wall of noise slams against Jack's chest as he stomps into the old building. The air is hot and humid, thick with competing scents of sour sweat and spilled beer.

The band on stage is lit up bright, high above the thrashing, glinting mosh, and plaster dust rains from the cracked ceilings with every heavy beat. Exos fill the pit: classic twelve-foot clankers slamming among sleeker SOTA rigs, while armored bouncers look on. The pit is already three feet below the rest of the floor, marble tiling and cement foundations churned up as the opening acts hype the crowd.

Jack points his exo at the bar jutting from a hole bashed into the walls; behind the bartenders, empty office cubicles are filled with trash and drug detritus. He gets in line and forces his exo onto the balls of its steel feet so he can see over the heads in front of him.

"Nice ride."

At the voice, Jack pivots inside his skel. The guy has a thick, black beard around an easy smile. A thick mat of hair crosses his broad chest, visible through tears in his replica cosmonaut suit. He hangs inside his exo's frame, looking almost weightless—very "stranded in space."

When the guy starts to grin, Jack realizes how long he's been staring without saying anything. His cheeks burn. A rat-king of nerves tangles in his stomach, but it's a good nervous, a "cute guy is talking to me" nervous.

"Thanks," he says, finally. "It's a hand-me-down; was my older brother's."

"Makes sense; you don't see too many guys our age in one of the classics."

Jack laughs, just a single throaty "Ha." He knows his beat-up Ward-D2 isn't really a classic, but he can see a pickup line for what it is and still want to be picked up, can't he?

The next song starts, and decibels soar like courier drones. Jack pushes his exo toward the bar as the line moves.

"Did he go into engineering?" the punk-onaut shouts.

"What?" Jack says, leaning forward in his harness. The chat-link light inside his exoframe blinks, and Jack hits the switch.

"Your brother," the other guy says, his voice tinny through Jack's audio system: "did he go into engineering or something?"

"Yeah, *something*," Jack says; he doesn't say that "something" was prison. "My name's Jack."

"I'm Ramón, and no, I hate The Ramones."

Jack chuckles, then sees he's almost at the front of the line. "What are you drinking?"

"Cider."

Jack gets flustered at the bar and orders two ciders, though it's normally too sweet for his tastes. He takes one of the canisters and hands it to Ramón, then slots the other into his exo's rehydration unit as the band on stage finishes their set.

"Thanks," Ramón says. "I'll get the next round."

Jack drinks from the tube strapped inside the head module and the cider slides down his throat, thick, saccharine, and cold.

"Wanna go up the front?" Ramón asks.

"Hey, ho, let's go," Jack says, and beams at his own joke. Ramón rolls his eyes but smiles.

Exopunks drop into the cratered pit, their eyes eagerly following members of the next band as they walk out on stage; *Mucus Mary and the Moist Mothers* spray-painted on a bedsheet hanging on the rear wall.

The guitarist and bass player wear their instruments inside their suits and the singer has the microphone mounted to her exo's head. The drummer's exoskeleton clunks and thuds as it interfaces with the drum machine—twelve limbs flexing and stretching as she gets a feel for the gear. She counts in and the band erupts in a vicious car crash. The pit surges, sending dirt and cement chunks into the air where, Jack swears, they hover for a full second, held in place by the singer's banshee screech.

"I love this band," Ramón yells.

Jack thrashes to the sound and his shinbones shudder every time his exofeet jackhammer the ground. As the stage lights sweep over the crowd, the fog of cement dust around him and Ramón glows.

Ramón drops into the pit and before Jack can think twice he's done the same. Jack slams the head of his exo into the wall of the pit and Ramón joins him while Mucus Mary wails and squeals. Jack screams and euphoria seeps into his veins, as warm as the cider is cold.

He gulps a mouthful of air and dust as he wraps his lips around the rehydration tube. The dust gently scratches his throat as he swallows. Dust lines his nostrils too—if he gets a spot on the official demolition crew come Monday he'll be wearing respiratory gear, but right now, he doesn't care. His lungs could rot inside his chest and it would be worth it to be here tonight, drowning in noise, surrounded by the only thing that ever made sense to him. Study hard, they said; yeah, thanks for the debt. Get a job, they said; fuck you, there aren't any.

Jack dances harder, his suit's haptics fighting him as it struggles to keep up. The only truth Jack ever found was in punk rock: music that's dirty, fast, and over so soon, just like life.

The band starts another song and Jack stops dancing to take a drink. Ramón's chest hair glints with sweat and Jack imagines slipping his hands inside the cosmonaut suit so the hairs curl around his fingers. But Ramón doesn't catch Jack's overt gaze; his attention is elsewhere, watching three skinheads in archaic getups using their massive exos to tower over some kids in shiny-chromed rigs.

Jack's chest rattles—not from the noise, but the fight-or-flight thump of his heart. Ramón takes a step forward and Jack's mind is made up for him as he and Ramón push through the crowd.

"You fucking better not be here Monday," one of the skinheads says, thumping one kid's rig with a clenched exofist. "Those demolition jobs are for us. You want work, go back to Iraqistan."

"Hey," Ramón yells.

The three boneheads turn; identical triplets with their shaved heads and faces: babies that got big, but never grew up.

Jack's fear gives way to anger as he glances past the skinheads and sees the young punks cowering. They look like honor roll kids who miraculously discovered good tunes in the banal suburban sprawl. But that's the exopunk ethos: *anyone* is free to work if they've got a rig, and *anyone* is free to wreck if they've got that fucking fire in their belly.

The music lulls and the lead bonehead yells new slurs at Jack and Ramón. Far up front on the stage, Mucus Mary points into the crowd as her band breaks into a new song: a frenetic stampede of noise. A chorus joins in as Mucus Mary screams, "Nazi Punks Fuck Off!" It was a classic before Jack was born, and it's the one song every decent punk band knows, even if they never want a reason to play it.

Jack freezes as Ramón steps forward and grips the lead skinhead's rig in both exohands. The bonehead tries to break Ramón's grip, but he locks his exo's hands in place, unhooks his harness, and throws himself forward. Ramón grabs the collar of the bonehead's bomber jacket and buries a fist into the fucker's nose. Blood pours into his mouth, hanging slack.

Jack stomps close, barring the other Nazis as they try to get at Ramón. His hydraulics shriek with the effort of holding them back, a sharp screech that pierces his ears as more punks push in toward the scuffle.

Plaster dust underfoot glows purple—security moves through the crowd riding black security rigs, all sharp angles and blacklight LEDs. Ramón disconnects his exo and Jack pushes him back before standing with an impromptu line of exopunks, blocking Ramón from the bouncer's view.

Jack points and yells, "Get these Nazi fucks out of here," shifting his exo to stay between Ramón and the bouncers. Jack can't see the bouncer's face inside the armor, but the exo bobs in acknowledgment, and he hijacks the three boneheads' suits and leads them out of the pit.

Jack turns to Ramón, gingerly poking his knuckles with his left hand. "You okay?"

"I heard something crack, just hope it was his nose and not my knuckle." Ramón shivers and Jack feels it too: the drop of adrenaline leaving his body.

Jack unclips his harness and climbs out to stand on the frame of Ramón's rig. He slips inside Ramón's exoskeleton and buries his fingers in Ramón's coarse beard. "Want me to get some ice for your hand?"

Ramón lets out a deep breath, then looks up from his bloody hand, his eyes a deep brown, speckled with orange. "It'll be fine," he says.

Jack leans in, sour-sweet breaths coalescing in the moment before their lips meet, Ramón's tongue wet and hot against Jack's.

Jack smiles. "You really gave that guy a blitzkrieg—"

Ramón cuts him off with another kiss, a longer one that only stops when they get jostled, the crowd slowly gaining momentum after stalling for the fight.

"Make another Ramones joke," Ramón says, "and that might be the last time I kiss you."

Jack kisses Ramón again while his heart beats double-time. His mouth tastes sickly sweet with dead apples and probable regret, but he doesn't care. This man might break his heart, but it would be worth it to be here tonight.

"What's the matter with your exo; we need technical support?" A bouncer stands beside Jack's abandoned exoskeleton.

"No, it's fine," Jack yells.

When the bouncer sees Jack inside Ramón's exo, he shakes his head and smiles. "Don't leave it empty on the dance floor, all right fellas; it ain't safe."

Jack almost laughs at "dance floor," but he nods and climbs back into his exo as the bouncer walks off chuckling.

They get lost in the music again; moving with the crowd like every exo in the joint is linked. Sweat soaks through Jack's clothes as they yell and stomp in a circle of exopunks; he grins whenever his eyes catch Ramón's.

When Mucus Mary is done, she and the Moist Mothers leave the stage to a mushroom-cloud of cheers from the pit. Ramón leads Jack to the edge and they jump out of the crater. Jack pauses to take in the sweat-slicked revelers panting for breath and the exos knocking together with the clank of punk love; the bliss that follows an epic mosh.

Standing close enough to Ramón so that they can lean out of their exos and touch, Jack asks, "Are we gonna get another drink?"

"I only really came for Mary," Ramón says, "so I was gonna go home."

Jack frowns, and Ramón laughs.

He pinches Jack's chin and says quietly, "I was hoping you'd come with me."

LAVANYA LAKSHMINARAYAN

ÉTUDES

(2020)

Adopt at your own risk. No guarantees, no returns.
—the Analog Orphan Adoption Home

HAPPY BIRTHDAY, IT!

I stare at the birthday card in front of me in horror.

I shouldn't have opened it. Not here, in front of them. Not ever, if I'd known what the inside read.

I flip it wide open and turn it toward my best friend, Mae.

I hate that word.

It.

"It will need to earn its place in Virtual society."

I sit on a leather stool in front of the Home's creaky upright piano. I look down at the keys.

I've just played Barthöven's Sonatina 23 in alt-F Minor.

I've made four obvious mistakes, I fumbled three runs. Including the opening section.

I hope I'm still worthy.

These two strangers could change their minds at any moment.

I glance up at them. They seem to be studying me.

I look back down, staring really, really hard at the black keys in between F, G, A, and B, just to the right of middle C.

Mrs. D'Souza's voice fills the silence.

"*It's toilet-trained and reports excellent personal hygiene. It reads at an average pace and has done fairly well on our psychological tests. No tendencies toward violence, no delusions of grandeur.*"

The strangers say nothing.

Mrs. D'Souza continues. "Mr. and Mrs. Anand, we assure you that you will have no trouble with this one. We only let the very best Analog wards get to this stage of the adoption process. The less competent ones remain at the Institute until they become employable or drop out. The defective ones are sent straight to the vegetable farm.

"*You could always change your mind about taking it home, of course. But it's one of our very best.*"

I turn my head and see her beaming at me.

"*We wouldn't let distinguished twenty percenters such as yourselves take home a flawed child.*"

Mrs. D'Souza talks about me as if I'm not in the room. I'm used to it.

One of the strangers smiles at me. The man.

I stare at him.

"*We do have some guidelines, however. It is in your best interest to follow them. We dissuade you from developing a strong personal attachment to the ward, despite being its adoptive parents. You may give it a name—this one is biologically female, and is approximately twelve years old.*"

The woman frowns at this.

I wonder if I've done something wrong.

"*We recommend that you don't permit it to refer to either of you on the basis of your filial relationship. First names are better than Mum and Dad. It leads to an easier separation should the child fail to qualify as a Virtual Citizen.*"

"*We'd like the child to feel accepted," the man says.*

Mrs. D'Souza sighs. "These decisions are left to your discretion, of course. The Home will assess the child annually to assess if it is appropriate for Virtual society."

"*Yes, we've read the fine print." The woman's tone is sharp.*

"*Psychologists have found that Analog wards with a lower sense of personal identity are more Productive. They're more eager to please if they perceive identity markers as rewards for good behavior. We recommend that it be placed in impersonal surroundings. The fewer preferences it has, the easier it will find readjustment should it need to be returned to the Analog world, though we will not take it back in—*"

"*Why are you certain they're going to fail?*"

"*Can we stop calling them 'it'?*"

The man and woman speak together, and they sound angry.

I've been told to keep a smile on my face, but I frown at that.

If I'm not "it," what am I?

"—it's—I mean she's done really well for herself, all things considered."

His smug voice brings me back to the present.

Mae is staring him down in a look of distilled hatred.

"It's only taken her ten years."

Dear Nina of the Future,

I'm literally the only living person, this century,
to have owned a journal. I hope you never forget
where you've come from once you're a Virtuoso.
   Haha.
   That's wishful thinking.
   Here I am, stuck at my birthday party, when I
should be practicing Bracht and Rodriguez for my
upcoming demi-Virtuoso Examination. It's only
ten days away and it's ONLY the opportunity of a
lifetime to get into the Apex City School of
neo-Acousta Performance Studies.
   But who cares about the opportunity of a
lifetime, right?

"What are you writing in that journal, anyway?" he says, reaching out for it. I slam it shut.

"Touchy." He grins. "Now where was I?"

He returns to his captive audience. They're supposed to be my friends. And he certainly isn't.

"Right. So I was talking about my first time. There I was, right? Never having played before . . . I remember looking down at those keys. Completely blank."

Everyone leans in to listen to what Andrew Sommers has to say. Everyone except Mae, who mimes strangling him from where she stands behind him, taking care not to spill her strawberry shake.

I twirl a straw around my glass of carrot-cucumber juice.

"But then, the GlimmerKeys kicked in and began to highlight the score for me. I don't know why people even bother with sheet music anymore. It took me through the entire song, with my InEars keeping perfect tempo for me."

Niraj and Anushka are hanging on to every word.

Andrew Sommers is the best-known musician at our school. He has an official HoloTube account, with a following in the hundreds of thousands in Bell Corp cities across the world.

How long has he been learning?

Eighteen months.

How long have I been learning?

Ten years.

What's the difference between us?

DreamMusician.

I'm surprised he even showed up at my party, considering we aren't friends. When I say that, I don't mean that we don't have any classes together, or that we've never given recitals together.

We just haven't made eye contact. Ever.

We've never spoken a word to each other outside of a practice.

And yet here he is, celebrating another year of my life going by.

Why?

"You must be at a real disadvantage, Nina."

"What?" I scowl.

"It must be so hard for you. Learning the *Analog* way."

I don't like the way he emphasizes the word "Analog." I hear it all the time but I'll never get used to it. I look down at the birthday card, and the word "it" glares back up at me.

I don't want to get into a fight. I can't afford to. So I shrug instead.

"I mean, how do you keep time? Do you count in your head?" Andrew smirks.

"It's more than you can do. Count, that is," Mae mutters loud enough for everyone to hear.

Niraj's laugh sounds like a strangled bark.

"And what about the dynamics? Do you just bang away at the keys until you get the proper tone?"

I realize that I've begun to shred the edges of the card.

"Seriously. I'm curious." He winks.

I really can't afford to get into a fight. Not with the Citizenship test so close. I begin to focus all my attention on my breathing.

"Don't get me wrong, you're not bad at all. You just lack . . . *precision.*"

I feel heat spreading through my cheeks.

"Anyway, I should be leaving. My parents don't like it when I hang out at *the Mall* too long." He gives our surroundings a significant look.

"Yeah, the Strip is way cooler." Niraj grins.

Sycophant.

Andrew gets to his feet. "Good luck, Nina. I expect you'll be playing at the demi-Virtuoso Examination too."

Too?

Did he just say *too*?

Does that mean Andrew Sommers is part of the competition?

"Don't be upset when they pass you over. It's not your fault you don't have precision. It must suck to have been born an Analog," he says nastily and leaves.

Mae looks at me with concern, but I drop my gaze and take a sip of my juice.

Niraj and Anushka head over to examine a coin-operated arcade machine with interest.

Yes, I said coin-operated. You push physical tokens into a slot and then play a game with 3D graphics on a flat-screen monitor.

"Do you guys want to head to the Strip?" Anushka asks. She's looking around as if she expects a dodgy Analog to jump her any minute.

"Umm, guys." I look at the table. "No chip, no intel-glasses, no Hyper Reality experiences, remember?"

Anushka opens her mouth as if to argue.

"If you guys want to head there, though, carry on . . ."

"What! Nooo!" Anushka forces brightness into her voice. "It's your birthday! We want to hang out with you!"

Sure.

The giant, squat structure rests at the edge of an abandoned airstrip. The relics of long-forgotten passenger aircraft litter vacant tracts of land outside. Rumor has it that at one point, the Analogs used to mount raids to strip them of fuel and scrap metal.

The Mall is made from rusty metal appropriated from former aircraft parking bays, old strips of steel and tin bolted together and painted over in depressingly bright colors. It houses seven floors of twentieth-century gaming technology, flat-screen movie-watching experiences, and clothing stores where you have to physically try on an outfit before buying it.

It's the only place where I can find entertainment that isn't gated on Holo-Tech privileges I don't have.

Compared to the Hyper Reality at the Strip, this must feel like a trip to the poorhouse.

My poorhouse.

Welcome to the last century, guys.

This is where I live. All the time.

.   .   .

"Did you have a good birthday, honey?"

Mum plants a kiss on my cheek as she ladles a generous helping of mac and cheese on to my plate.

"Um, sure," I say tonelessly.

Dad gives me a look, and suddenly grins. "You know what? I think we need to liven things up a bit. It isn't every day that our only daughter turns seventeen!"

"What do you have in mind, Madhu?" Mum's tone is unnecessarily bright.

"Oh, I don't know . . . It needs to be special." Dad waggles his eyebrows excitedly. "I think we need to give Nina her first sip of wine."

"Of all the clichéd coming of age rituals, Madhu . . ." Mum says, exasperated.

"Come on," Dad says. "She'll remember this moment with her parents for the rest of her life!"

He heads to his impressive bar, and hovers at the wine rack indecisively.

"It needs to be a really fine one to mark the occasion," he mutters.

"Dinner's getting cold, love." Mum rolls her eyes.

"We're building a new tradition," Dad says. "One that we can add to our birthday mac and cheese dinner."

I feel small. I've eaten half my mac and cheese. I can't eat any more. It's delicious, though.

I wonder if I should tell her. The woman.

"What names do you like, kiddo?" The man smiles at me.

I don't know. I don't say that out loud.

"Do you feel like a boy's name or a girl's?" the woman asks.

I don't answer. Girl, I think, but I don't want to get it wrong.

"Shaila! No, you don't look like you own that name."

"Anuja. Does she look like an Anuja to you?"

"I'm not sure. Let's ask her what she'd like to go by?"

They look at me over the dinner table.

I only know me as D2721, Performer Class. It.

They didn't give me a name at the Home.

"You play the piano beautifully," the woman says.

I smile and nod, my gaze fixed on the hand-carved patterns along the border of the table.

"Do you have a favorite musician?" the man asks.

I shake my head. I wasn't permitted to like things at the Home.

"Would you like to listen to some music? Maybe you'll find a name you like." The woman smiles.

"Thank you," I say nervously.

They let me pick a record—it's glossy black and very shiny. It's so light that I'm scared I'll break it.

They show me how to put it on the player, and how to make it work.

It's amazing. The sound is clean and pure.

I've only listened to cassettes on a tape player. The hiss of the record makes it less alien, more familiar.

"They're nearly two hundred years old, vinyl records. But nothing has ever managed to beat them for sound quality," the man explains.

"This one is Pierre Bolling. I don't suppose you could be a Pierre. It's usually a boy's name, though don't let that stop you!" The woman smiles again.

The music is beautiful.

They change the record.

"Have you heard this one? It's Frida Szeltsmann."

The music sounds happy, like a memory of chocolate.

I've eaten chocolate a few times before. We were allowed a square each time we behaved well at the Home.

They put another record on.

"Give this a try. It's called Wanderer of the Air. *It's by Nina Rodriguez."*

The music is quiet. I can tell that it means many things without saying any of them.

"I like this."

I say it out loud. I shouldn't have said it out loud.

I look at the floor.

"I love this," the woman says.

"It's like you," the man says. *"Quiet, but mysterious."* He's smiling at me.

"I like it very much," I whisper.

"Do you know about the composer?"

I shake my head no.

"Nina Rodriguez was the first woman to become a neo-Acousta Virtuoso. She was a brilliant pianist and composer. And she was blind."

"Wow."

"She learned by listening, without reading a single sheet of music. She wrote many wonderful pieces of music, and taught demi-Virtuosos at the Apex City School for years."

"Does she inspire you?" the woman asks.

"I don't know what that means."

"Does she make you feel like you're unbeatable? Like you can do anything your heart wants to?"

I think about it for a minute. I imagine being blind. I imagine playing perfect music without being able to read the notes. It sounds difficult. She must have been really clever.

"I would like to be like her."

I burst into tears. I don't know why.

The woman hugs me until I stop crying. I stop crying quickly. They didn't like us crying at the Home.

"So . . . Nina, for now?" the man asks. He's grinning.

Nina.

I say it in my head. I feel it.

Nina.

I look up at them.

"Okay," I say slowly. "My name is Nina."

I feel it on my tongue for the first time. It tastes like hope.

"To Nina!" Dad pronounces, holding up a glass of wine.

He nudges another one across the table toward me. I notice that it's only half as full as his own.

"Go on, now. A drop of alcohol won't poison you." He winks.

"Go easy," Mum warns.

I grin. I can't help it.

"To me!" I giggle, raising my glass.

"To Nina!" they say together.

I take a sip and try not to spit it out. It tastes terrible.

Mum and Dad burst into peals of laughter, and after a moment, I can't help but join in.

. . .

Dear Nina of the Future,

I'm sitting in history class, and it sucks to be me at school.

I'm the only person in the room with a textbook. On printed paper.

Everyone else is watching a Hyper Reality holovid on their intel-glasses. Meanwhile, I'm reading about the pre-Bell history of Apex City, comprising the early stages of the Start-Up Revolution in Bangalore.

Reading.

It's so much slower.

Well, sucks to be me, right? No Bell Biochip,
no intel-glasses, no HoloTech. Not until I pass
my Virtual Citizenship test. I have to prove
myself worthy of their technology, just because
I was born an Analog.

~~It isn't as if I can blow up the school with
a holo-watch.~~

Stuff like that is dangerous to write.
Especially for an Analog-born.

It's so anti-Bell that they could deport me
for saying it.

And so the cycle continues . . . I'm
perpetually falling behind in class because I
don't get information beamed straight into my
brain, or Hyper Real worlds where I can explore
ancient maps of Apex City, or

"Nina, are you having trouble catching up again?" Magistra VX81 flashes a
pixelated scowl.

I hide my journal under my printed textbook. The rest of the class is staring
at me.

I look at my desk. "I need a few more minutes to get through the chapter,
Magistra."

She sighs. In her electronic voice, it sounds like the scrape of sandpaper over
a tin can. "Go on."

I feel the eyes of the entire class on me. I skim over the page as quickly as I can.
What I wouldn't give to have intel-glasses right now.

"The rest of you can start putting forth arguments in favor of or against the
Ceasefire Treaty."

The Ceasefire Treaty ended competitive advertising on social media, I read. I balk
when I look at the sea of text that forms a detailed analysis of the agreement.

"It's not our fault she's slow," someone mutters.

"Are you sure you learned how to read at the orphanage?" Someone else sniggers. "We. Speak. English. Not. Trad."

"Enough, class." Magistra VX81's voice is firm.

Someone says something unintelligible to me.

"I don't speak the traditional dialect," I snap.

The class bursts into giggles.

"Enough!" Magistra snaps. "Nina, I'd like you to stop disrupting my class."

My ears are hot. The words on the page start to blur, so I slam the book shut
and look up.

"I'm done."

"Good." Magistra VX81 smiles at me. "What were the consequences of the
Ceasefire Treaty?"

I swallow.

I skipped that paragraph.

"Um . . ."

"She's so slow that she's practically a time traveler. Into the past."

I ignore the taunting and take a deep breath.

"Nina, come on. The rest of the class is waiting on you. We can't do this every day."

"Slooo-ooow," says someone in a sing-song voice.

"What happened after the Ceasefire Treaty?"

I rattle off facts while my brain races to fabricate a plausible answer.

"The Population Catastrophe saw the collapse of nationalism. Large-scale governments could no longer meet the escalating demands for resources from their citizens. When they tried to go to war with each other, the Woke Wave Uprising—armed forces and citizens alike—rebelled against them in the Great Nuclear Boycott."

I flub, recapping basic history, buying myself more time.

"Resource distribution became riddled with allegations of corruption. States seceded from parent countries, cities established independence. It occurred worldwide within the span of a decade. This led to the rise of multiple systems of micro-governance, formed on the basis of trade in natural resources."

I fidget with the spine of my journal.

"Bell Corp emerged as a conglomerate in erstwhile Singapore, now called Premier City. When promising technological communities emerged around the world, Bell Corp invested in them and helped them self-organize into sustainable meritocracies."

"Get to the point, Nina," Magistra drones.

"London was transformed into Crown City, Berlin became Pinnacle, San Francisco is called Crest, and Bangalore joined the big leagues during the Bell Takeover, rebranding itself Apex City . . ."

"Nina!" Magistra snaps.

Someone behind me sniggers.

"When Bell Corp began its investment in Bangalore, the city was divided along traditional communal and cultural identities, but was a thriving start-up hub. The city had escaped the worst of the effects of the Population Catastrophe owing to its high economic stability . . ."

The class has lost interest. Whispers break out all around me.

"Yes, Nina, very good." Magistra VX81 jerkily brings her mechanical appendages together, mimicking applause. "You remember your third-grade history lessons. Admirable."

I roll my pencil across my desk.

"What happened next? What was the outcome of the Ceasefire Treaty?" she fires.

"Bangalore's start-ups . . . competed on social media for pride of place, eating into each other's potential market share? The Ceasefire Treaty ended competition on social media, and . . . and Bell Corp swooped in and saved the day?"

Magistra VX81 gives me a look. It looks hilarious on her pixelated LED face but I've seen it before. It isn't meant to be funny.

"Homework. I want a two-thousand-word paper on the Bell Takeover, from the consequences of the Ceasefire Treaty onward."

"Please Magistra—"

"I want it on my desk, Monday morning."

"Psst, Nina," someone whispers. "She wants it in English."

"I'll translate," someone else sniggers. Her voice lapses into gibberish.

My head spins and I take several deep breaths, trying not to let the laughter in the room overwhelm me.

"Is she an Outsider?"

"I think she's an Analog."

"Not even a Repop kid?"

"Nope."

"Wow, our school's standards are dropping."

"I hear the Analogs don't speak English."

"I hear that they can't read or write. I wonder how she got into our school."

"Shh! Her parents are the Anands. They're the twenty percenters who own the Apex City League of Champions."

"Oh! Those Anands."

"Yeah, those."

"Why would they ever let a freak like this into their home?"

"Guilt, probably. Who knows what they've done to the Analogs."

"Ha ha, are you telling me your parents have never used the Analogs?"

"Come on, who hasn't?"

"Maybe she has a special talent."

"What, like being ugly?"

I keep my head down. I don't look around me.

They've been whispering all day. All week.

Everyone is eating but I'm too scared to unwrap my lunch. What if they make fun of my sandwich?

They won't make fun of my sandwich. My parents—adoptive parents—are important twenty percenters. It's a tasty sandwich.

I've never seen so many twenty percenters. They're scary. They're all well-dressed. They look intelligent. One girl even has blonde highlights in her hair. Another one has a FantasyLights backpack—it keeps flashing beautiful patterns.

I'm wearing nice clothes too. They're new and clean.

The woman let me pick the color. I was really scared to, but then I chose a pale blue dress. She even combed my hair into a braid.

I look like them, but I don't feel like me.

"What do they make you do?"

A girl stands across from me. She's smiling at me.

"N-nothing," I say.

"Harvest-shit. You must have some value. Do you clean the floors? The bathrooms?"

Another girl joins her. The one with the FantasyLights backpack. "I'm sure the Anands can afford a server-bot, Sneha," she drawls. "She must have other uses."

She reaches forward. It's sudden.
She grabs the front of my dress and rips it. Buttons fly everywhere.
My cheeks flush. Everyone's looking at us and laughing.
She looks at the training bra under my dress.
"Nope. Clearly there are no other uses."
Something snaps. I'm on her, pulling her hair. The back of my hand makes contact
with her face.
She screams. Somebody pulls me off her.

I look down and notice that my fingers are curled around the edge of my desk.
My knuckles strain white against my skin.

"Sit down, Nina," Magistra VX81 says.

They're still laughing. She hasn't intervened.

They laugh all the way until the bell rings to signal the end of the day, and it
seems like the longest five minutes of my life.

I slam my textbook shut. I rush out of the school's corridors and get into
Mum's self-driving car, slamming the door shut behind me. She has to pick me
up every day since I'm not allowed to use the teleportals.

"Something wrong, honey?" she asks.

She speaks an address to the computer and it drives us away.

"Nope."

"I'm not your mother for nothing. Did you get into trouble at school?"

"NO!" I say angrily. "I—it's been years since I retaliated."

"Let's call your dad and we can talk about it," she soothes.

I look at the city. It's a blur as we rush past it.

"Nina," the woman begins.

"You shouldn't have hit that girl," the man says.

I look at the floor. It has a carpet.

"I'm sorry."

"Why did you hit her?"

I'm silent.

"You can tell us."

"She ripped my dress open. She said mean things."

The woman looks at the man. "I thought as much, Madhu. I knew the principal
wasn't telling us everything."

"Yes, but she should know better than to lash out at them." He sounds angry. "You
know it's going to be hard for her to become a Virtual Citizen."

"Yes, but I think she's too young to understand this."

"I think we should tell her. Luckily, we convinced the school to keep this off her
permanent record."

"Good thing we padded our BellCoin stacks before the meeting, yes." The woman's
eyes flash angry. "Building donation, indeed!"

"Anya, there will always be eyes on her. She needs to be careful."

I slide my shoes under the carpet.

"Nina, what did the girl say to you?"

I don't answer.

"You have to tell us, Nina." The man's voice is stern. "We don't want to have to punish you."

I feel my eyes sting. "She said you're going to make me work for you. Cleaning things. And other things." My voice begins to shake. "Because I'm an . . . an . . . Analog."

The words tumble out of me before I can help myself.

"I know I'm an Analog, but please don't send me back to the Home because I hit her. I didn't mean to. I can be good. I'll be useful—you've been so kind, not making me do any work at home, but I know how it works. I'll clean up—I'm good with a broom, I can mop the floor and I can't really cook, but you could teach me and then I could do that too. Just please don't take me back to the Home . . ."

I can't bear to look at them.

"Nina, that's ridiculous!" the man exclaims. "Our home is your home now."

"We're not going to make you work for us," the woman says.

"She said that's why you bought me." My voice comes out as a squeak.

The woman's eyes glitter with something that looks like anger and sadness.

"Who's that odious little girl? It's Sheila's daughter, isn't it? I'm going to have a word with her mother . . ."

"Yes, you should, love," the man says to her.

Then he looks at me. "Nina. Let me establish this, once and for all. We adopted you. We didn't buy you. We always wanted to have children, but we couldn't. You're the child we've always hoped for. You might be an Analog by birth, but that doesn't mean you're not a wonderful human being."

I take a deep breath.

"And we will never, never make you work for us," he finishes angrily.

The woman turns and looks me over.

I'm glad I'm not crying this time.

"Nina, you're our daughter. I think it's time you started calling us Mum and Dad."

"Nina," Dad says, his likeness holo-rayed across the backseat of our self-driving car. "I hear you had a bad day, kiddo."

"Meh," I reply.

"We're very proud of you for keeping your cool," he says.

"Hmm."

"We're so proud that you've managed to get such good grades, in spite of being disadvantaged by your lack of HoloTech," he continues, beaming.

"Hmph."

"And that's going to end soon!" Mum chimes in brightly. "Your Citizenship test is just around the corner!"

That knocks me out of my sulk. "What?"

"We got the email just this morning. It's in two weeks' time."

My stomach does a few backflips.

If I become a Virtual Citizen, it'll mean access to intel-glasses. I'll be able to hang out at the Strip and experience Hyper Reality.

I won't be *different* from everyone else in school. I won't be that *special kid* every class has to put up with, while she *reads* her way through a textbook.

If I become a Virtual Citizen, I'll be able to get my InEars, wired straight through to my Bell Biochip and synced to the Sonic Highway. I'll have unlimited access to every piece of music ever written—a library hundreds of years old, all up on the Nebula—that'll stream directly into my consciousness with a single thought. No more having to manually trawl through hundreds of vinyls to find a song. No more having to fast-forward and rewind cassettes to listen on my Walkman. I'll have unlimited access to everything.

The thing that I'm most excited about—the one thing I've wanted for years, that I've never been allowed to have is—

"*DreamMusician.*"

Mum and Dad look at me in surprise.

"That's what I want. As soon as I pass the test, I'm going to sign up."

"Are you sure you want that? Isn't it more fun to learn from Mr. Kuruvilla?"

I stare at the both of them like they're crazy.

"Sure. Yes, he's a great teacher. But I want to learn real precision. I want perfection. It's the only way I'll make it into the demi-Virtuoso program next year."

"Next year?" Mum looks confused.

"Aren't you taking the examination this year?" Dad frowns.

I sigh. "Yes, of course, Dad."

He looks at me expectantly.

"Let's face it. There's no way I'll make the grade."

His expression is blank.

"All my competition is DreamMusician-trained!" I say impatiently.

He smiles in understanding. "I know it must be intimidating. But you underestimate yourself, Nina."

I exhale in exasperation. "No, Dad. Look. I'm being realistic. All of them have trained with InEars. They have a Metronome feed directly into their heads. They haven't had to learn to read sheet music; they just use GlimmerKeys and the piano tells them what to do. Their command over dynamics—"

Dad holds up his hand. "I get it, Nina. I really do. They're trained to play like machines."

"Exactly!"

"But here's where you're different, kiddo." Mum grins. "You play with your heart."

I groan inwardly. I don't know how they do it, but it feels like my parents really do finish each other's sentences.

"You'll be the most unique sound they hear!" Dad snaps his fingers, and grins. "There, now don't you feel better? What's a bad day at school compared to all the great ones to come."

I groan at his positivity.

"Dad, this means that I now have my Citizenship test *and* my demi-Virtuoso exam within days of each other."

"When it glitches it fries, eh? Don't worry, you'll ace both."

He glances at his holo-watch.

"I'm running late for a meeting. See you at home, kiddo. Love you both!"

I do feel better, but as I stare out the window a tiny flip-flop of something cold and unpleasant crawls around in my stomach.

I'd better get to work.

The price of failure is deportation.

• • •

"Nina."

Mum drums her elegant fingers on my notebook.

"Stop studying. Don't you need to practice for your demi-Virtuoso exam?"

I roll my eyes.

"Mum, the Citizenship test is way more important."

"And you know everything you need to pass it already. You're burning your-self out. Go play the piano! It's something you love . . ."

I sigh.

I get up from the coffee table and head into the living room.

I set myself down on the piano bench and carefully lift the lid. I place my fingers over the keys and begin to run through the trickiest sections of *Wanderer of the Air*, or Op. 9 No. 1, Ballet in supra-B-Flat-Major by Nina Rodriguez. It's still about fifteen minutes before my piano teacher arrives, and I'm making the most of this opportunity to not run through finger drills.

It isn't like the one at the Home. That was off-key half the time.

I only had a one-hour slot to play it, every week.

Here, I can play the piano all the time. Except when I'm at school, of course.

Sometimes it's scary to sit at it. It stands all by itself in our large living room.

It's magnificent and glossy black. The name Manuela Alvares is embossed in a beau-tiful gold loop along its front. I wonder who she was. Maybe she was a famous musician.

At the Home, we had one grand piano that we would play when we gave perfor-mances. Most of the time, it was to raise money for the Home. Otherwise, we practiced on a creaky upright with missing felts.

All the songs I know sound wrong. Maybe because this piano can be properly tuned to the alt and supra scales. Maybe because none of the keys get stuck when I play them.

The Anands—Mum and Dad, as I've started to think of them—get me some sheet music. I can read it and I do my very best to learn it right.

They're looking for a teacher. I thought it would be easier to find a teacher on this side of the world. They are twenty percenters, after all.

Maybe all the Virtuosos are too busy being famous, traveling the world and giving performances.

I'm practicing one of my new pieces when Mum knocks on the door.

"Honey, we think we might have found you a teacher."

I stop playing. I can't believe it!

"He wants to meet you and hear you play. Do you think you're ready?"

"N-now?" My hands shake a little.

"Yes, unless you'd rather not. I understand if it's a bit sudden—"

No. This is so exciting. "No. I can play."

A tall man with long dark hair steps into the room.

"David, this is Nina. Nina, this is Mr. Kuruvilla."

I stand, nearly tripping over the stool.
"What have you learned so far, Nina?" His voice is low.
"Br—Brächt. Barthöven. Some preludes and sonatinas."
"Okay, can you play me some music?"
My hands are shaking. I fumble for my sheet music, turn the page, and begin.
The keys feel like they're listening to my every touch.
I start off right. Nice and soft. I get through the opening section and into the trills
without a fault.
My fingers stumble over the last trill.
Hold it together, Nina.
I enter into the next part of the piece, building it up to its eventual crescendo.
Three bad notes.
My hands are shaking now.
Hold it together, Nina.
The crescendo is perfect, but I think I've pedaled inaccurately.
A rest.
I pause. Collect my thoughts in a second.
The piece descends back into its opening bars. I play this part well.
It diminishes, and ends on a dramatic flourish, played forte, and I hit the notes right.
I sit back. I breathe. I hope I've done enough.
The room is quiet.
"That's not bad at all, Nina." Mr. Kuruvilla smiles at me. "Some obvious mistakes—
but practice and the right technique can iron those out."
"Th-thank you."
"You read sheet music? Who taught you?"
"I learned . . . at the Home."
"And you've never been trained virtually?"
"What's that?"
"DreamMusician?"
"I don't know what that is."
I wonder if I'm failing this test. I look at my feet, still resting on the pedals.
He turns to my Mum. "You say she won't have access to any Virtual music aids?"
"She won't be allowed to use any until she passes her Virtual Citizenship test."
He nods slowly.
"I won't lie to you, Anya. It'll be difficult, very difficult. She'll have to internalize
rhythm and timing. She'll need to learn each piece by rote, by reading through the
sheet music. Tone, dynamics—she'll have to find her way around through feel, work on
her musicality the old-fashioned way."
"I'm sure she can—"
"Anya, it's like teaching the blind to paint."
Mum stands up. "Thanks, David. I understand. Don't worry about it, we'll find
someone else—"
"Hang on." Mr. Kuruvilla grins. "I didn't say I wouldn't teach her. She's got in-
stinct. I can provide direction."
He looks at me. "If you really want to learn—if you're serious about the

piano—*then know this. It will be hard. It will be harder for you than for anyone else I've known in a long, long time. I can show you how to become a Virtuoso, but you will have to put in hours and hours of practice to do it. Do you want to do that?"*

I hold my breath.

Does this mean he'll teach me?

"I only teach the very best, Nina. Would you like me to teach you?"

I exhale.

"I would like that. Very much."

"Focus, Nina."

My hands stop abruptly.

I didn't even notice him enter the room.

"Your mind isn't here, today." He frowns. "It needs to be here, every day. You need to be present. *At the keys.* Remember, neo-Acousta is only created when precision meets emotion in perfect aural union."

I grimace. I fumbled a cadenza on its descent.

"The cadenza is one of the most prized performance skills in any Virtuoso's oeuvre. It demonstrates absolute control over the instrument. Rodriguez herself would use these sections to improvise in her live performances."

"I know. I'm sorry."

"You don't need to stick to the time signature of the piece, but the descent still has to sound musical. Which means that you must deviate from perfect timing with intent. Symmetry is a big part of Rodriguez's music. You aren't playing Wyschnegradsky here."

I sigh.

"It's a bit late in the day for this, but I think you need to make a conscious effort with your timing."

He picks up the metronome that sits at the top of the piano. It's antiquated—it isn't holographic, there's no touch interface, and its construction is a geometric curiosity. At the base of its pyramid structure is a small knob. Mr. Kuruvilla winds this, then releases the pendulum from its casing. He shifts a weight on it and sets the tempo at *moderato.*

He replaces it at the top of the piano.

The pendulum sways back and forth.

Tick . . . tock . . . Tick . . . tock . . . Tick . . . tock . . .

I play.

I have to recalibrate the movement of my fingers to match the slower timing. Usually, this section is played with a gradual increase in tempo, until it becomes a sonorous flurry of notes.

I can feel Mr. Kuruvilla's eyes on the backs of my hands.

It's hard to calm my nerves. It's not as if I have a Bell Biochip to regulate my adrenaline and suppress my anxiety. I don't even know how I'm expected to perform at this level without one. My fingers go rigid from the strain of sticking to the timing, they begin to cramp from my obvious distress.

"Light fingers, Nina," Mr. Kuruvilla chastises.

I grit my teeth and begin again.

Mr. Kuruvilla talks over my repetitive practice of the cadenza.

"You know, normally Analog metronomes are saved for—no, you're half a beat behind, start again—what was I saying? It's only after you're an accepted Virtuoso that you get to use the liberties of a physical metronome. You'll never develop the same degree of precision without InEars in your formative years of study—stop, you're losing it. Begin again . . ."

I try to drown him out and focus on my accuracy.

It's hard to be perfect without InEars. I'm listening externally and trying to attune myself to the metronome's rhythm, instead of having a tempo beamed directly to my brain.

Not that Mr. Kuruvilla seems to have any sympathy for me.

"You're losing sound clarity each time your little finger plays a note. I wish you'd played this for me last week. We have only days to go to your examination."

It's almost impossible to be dynamically en pointe without DreamMusician. I'm trying to manually exert different degrees of pressure on the keys to evoke emotion. I don't think I'll ever be spot-on.

"Any chance you'll get your InEars before the exam?" He's stopped me again, recalibrating the metronome to slow it down further.

"No, my test is two days after."

He doesn't make eye contact.

"You'll do fine. Don't worry."

"How?" I snap. I didn't mean to.

"I'm sorry?"

I try to check my temper and fail.

"*How* will I do fine? I haven't learned any of this with InEars. My dynamics are all by feel, I don't even know if they make sense. Sure, I'm following the sheet music, but I'm not following it using carefully calibrated Tactile+ on Dream-Musician. Everyone else is going to sound *perfect*."

"I'm going to stop you right there."

I pause.

"Yes, everyone else is going to sound perfect. But you are going to sound genuine. All this—neo-Acousta—is about the purity of sound. And you create that experience because you play with purity of heart."

"A good heart has never got someone into this program," I grumble.

"Okay, enough for the day."

"Are you kidding? The examination is in five days!"

"I'll come back tomorrow. You take the day to clear your head."

"Mr. Kuruvilla, I'll practice. Really, let's go."

I reach for the metronome.

"Up."

My shoulders sag. I rise to my feet.

"Why did you choose this piece, Nina?"

I know why, but I don't want to tell him.

"What does it mean to you?"

I say nothing.

"You're not going to tell me. I get it." He sighs. "It means a lot to you. It's a very personal choice, I gather."

I nod.

"You know how I chose my piece for my examination? I picked it for its complexity. I picked it because it would demonstrate my technical superiority."

"Did it work?"

"Of course it did. That's how it's been done, for years and years."

"Great, thanks. I'm going to fail."

"Listen, kid. You'll be the only person there playing music that comes from the soul."

"Good for me."

"Not so fast. The jury will connect with that. In its pursuit of perfection, neo-Acousta has ignored the expression of the soul for far too long. You'll remind them of this."

I roll my eyes.

"Homework. Think of what this piece means to you. What is its story? Write it down for me."

"Really?"

"Yes, really. We'll reconvene tomorrow."

Why does everyone keep making me write things down?

• • •

Dear Nina of the Future,

Have you made it yet? I hope you're world famous by now.

I've been practicing nonstop for my demi-Virtuoso Examination, and I'm sure I'm going to fail miserably because try as I might, I can't nail down this cadenza, even after working on the story of the piece and showing it to Mr. Kuruvilla.

He loved it.

I love it too, but that's not the same as playing it perfectly, is it?

"Are you stressed about the exam again?"

I look up from my journal.

Mae is staring at me, her brows furrowed in concern.

I slam my notebook shut. "No. Nooo. I'm fine. *Fine.*"

She arches her eyebrows, and I can tell she doesn't believe me.

Niraj and Anushka look over from where they've been arguing over whether almond milk or soy milk is better for their weight-loss diets.

"Is Andrew Sommers going to be playing at that thing?" Niraj sounds enthusiastic.

"Ooh, will you get to watch?" Anushka squeals.

Mae shoots her a filthy look.

"What, he's dreamy!" She pouts.

"Don't worry, Nina," Mae says, touching my arm gently. "We'll all be there to cheer you on."

"Will they let us listen to everyone's performances?" Anushka asks brightly, then quickly adds, "I mean, we'll be there for you, but it wouldn't hurt to check out the competition."

She blushes before quickly absorbing herself in the pile of greens on her lunch tray.

"You haven't touched your lunch," Mae mutters.

"Not hungry," I mumble.

"What?"

I glare at her.

"I've had enough," she says, getting to her feet. "Let's go."

"Go where?" Niraj says, shocked.

"What do we have after lunch?"

"Double psychohistory," Niraj says promptly.

"Yeah, Nina and I are skipping that."

"We are?" I start.

"We are. You guys let Magistra know that we had a . . . erm . . . what could have gone wrong? A . . . *a female emergency*."

Niraj chokes on his chicken salad.

"You'd better cover for us."

Mae glowers. "Mae, I dunno . . . I've got my Citizenship test round the corner too. What if this counts against me?" I say uncertainly.

"Suddenly getting your period? I'd like to see them try!" she huffs.

"I'm not on my period." My cheeks flush.

"And they'll never know because you don't have a chip. Ha. Haha," she laughs sarcastically. "Nina. Up."

She's bossy. It's impossible for me to ignore her, even at the best of times.

I spring to my feet, pushing my untouched lunch aside and grabbing my journal. I scurry after her as she strides out of the lunchroom.

"Where . . . where exactly are we going?"

She doesn't meet my gaze. Instead, she marches me straight through a pair of bright green gates that mark the end of the school campus.

We stand on the sidewalk under the shadow of a tree, as far from the school's visible PanoptiCam lenses as possible. I look around guiltily, hoping that the school doesn't have any hidden cameras, and even though Mae does a great job masking it, I can tell she's twitchy.

Behind us, the enormous gray stone buildings and red-tiled roofs of our school glower ominously down upon us. Skipping out could have consequences;

being able to socialize and learn in a physical schooling institute, instead of being distance-educated, is a privilege that only the twenty percenters can claim.

I glance nervously up the school's driveway for signs of the patrol-droids. I fervently hope that we don't run into a Magistra, or worse, the principal on her rounds.

I heave a sigh of relief when an empty self-driving cab rolls up within three minutes.

"Meridian Gate, please," Mae announces to the computer, pulling me in after her.

We ride together in silence. I knot the tassels on my jacket sleeve and Mae types away furiously on her OmniPort.

I don't know why she's taking me back. I haven't been near the other side since that horrible train ride I'd been forced to go on.

"Welcome aboard! This is Maglev Adventures' Mission Analog!" the tour guide says, beaming at our class.

I ignore the class when they all give me pointed looks and giggle at the word "Analog."

Magistra AB43 sits up front with the tour guide watching us all, recording our behavior. Mum and Dad warned me that she'll be paying careful attention to me, live streaming my every reaction onto the Nebula so that the people at the Home can check how I respond to being back in the Analog world.

"It's a test," they'd said. They'd looked worried.

I know I need to pass.

I stare blankly ahead, keeping a straight face all through the tour guide's announcements and instructions. When the train departs, I don't join in when some of my classmates begin to shriek and cry. Instead, I wave to my parents who are waiting on the station platform.

"We're going to visit your real home," Anastasia Prakash mocks, flicking a wad of paper at me.

"Do you have servants?" Sneha giggles beside her. "Oh wait, you are servants."

The rows behind me take up the giggle.

I ignore them, staring straight ahead. I don't even gasp when the big blue shield opens itself up and lets us through.

The girl sitting beside me is new. That's probably why she chose to sit next to me— most people avoid coming near me. She hasn't said a word to me. She must be learning.

The train zooms into a pod-house and I flinch. I can't believe we're entering someone's home uninvited. We'd never have dared, when I was being raised at the Home.

The house is filthy. I wonder why. We were much cleaner at the Home.

"Did you live in a box like this?" Anastasia says loudly.

"No wonder you're so scared all the time," Sneha adds. "You're not used to seeing daylight, are you?"

I'm about to snap at them, but I feel Magistra's gaze on me and ignore them.

Magistra addresses the class. "Why don't the Analogs have any privileges?"

"Because they're bad citizens," the class recites. I chime in the loudest.

We're going past the vegetable farm now.

"Is this why you're an orphan?" Sneha whispers. "Do you carry your parents around in a little box in your backpack?"

Everyone except the girl sitting beside me giggles, even though they all look terrified at the thought.

When the tour guide points out the nutro-shakes and protein porridge that I was raised eating, I cringe at the memory of their taste.

"She's never eaten real food before," Anastasia gasps.

"That explains the brain damage," Sneha says cruelly.

More laughter.

For the first time, the girl sitting next to me turns around and glares at them.

"What are the principles of the Bell Curve, class?" Magistra asks.

We recite the Rhyme of the Percentiles that we've been taught. It's written on the first page of all our textbooks. I chant it louder than anyone else, especially the last verse.

"Bottom ten
deport, forget,
Mice, not men
must live in regret."

When we arrive in Market Square, I begin to wonder if I'm going to fail my test. I look at all the shops around me and wonder if I'll be sent back to work in one of them. When the tour guide plays anatronica over the speakers, I bob along to the beat of it before realizing that everyone's staring at me.

"You call this music, Nina?" Anastasia hisses.

"I thought you were a pianist." Sneha smirks.

"A pianist!" Anastasia laughs. "What sort of pianist would ever enjoy this garbage? I'll tell you—a fake one. I'll bet you my allowance for the year that she's deported before the end of term."

I focus on the glass of the train window. I stare through it, barely registering a word that the tour guide is saying. If I stare at it hard enough, maybe it'll break and the Analogs will attack and Anastasia will finally shut up.

The girl sitting beside me whips her head around.

"You're on."

"And who in all the Analogged world are you?"

"Mae. Mae Ling. I just transferred from Premier."

"Hmm . . . Mae Ling, let me tell you how it works. There are some of us who belong here, and there are those of us who don't. Who would you rather be?" Anastasia whispers fiercely.

"Human," Mae Ling says coolly, turning her back on her. "Nina, it's so cool to finally meet you. I heard you play at the recital the other day—you're supra-brilliant . . ."

I think I've just made a friend.

"You're a brilliant pianist, my friend, but you've got the attention span of a fly," Mae says, clearly annoyed.

I snap out of my daze.

"What? Sorry, Mae, what were you saying?"

"I was ravishing you with compliments, but I guess you'll never hear them now." She grins.

The baobab-shaped structures of Bell Towers F and G cast their scattered net of shadows upon the city streets. We pass through the Arboretum, driving close to an overturned statue lying on its side. She's covered in moss and vegetation, though her plaque still proudly names her "Vic."

"Look," Mae commands.

"At Vic?"

"At the shield."

We are at the edge of the Carnatic Meridian. The car rolls to a stop.

Mae passes her hand over a holoscanner to pay for the ride, another thing I can't do. We step outside.

"Look through it. Look beyond, to the other side."

"No thanks," I say hurriedly, turning away.

"Look," she insists, grabbing my shoulder and shaking me slightly.

I look. All I can make out through the shimmering blue haze are the skull-like silhouettes of pod-houses reaching into the sky, a tightly packed warren of dust paths weaving their way through them into infinite black.

"Why are we here again?"

She waves at the world beyond the Meridian, the world that was my life before I was Nina.

"You might have come from over there, you might have spent your childhood on the other side. You might want to prove yourself to the world. But here's the thing . . . You've got nothing to prove. Not to me, not to your parents, not to Mr. Kuruvilla. Do you understand me?"

"I need to prove to myself that I'm worth it," I say flatly.

"You are worth it," she says simply.

"I don't want to disappoint everyone—"

"Nina, we want you to succeed. We want you to make it. That is the deepest wish of everyone who loves you. It's a wish, that's all. It's not an expectation. We'll love you, no matter how things turn out."

I look through the Meridian. I look at Mae. Her words are heavy, and several seconds pass before I burst into a sudden fit of giggles.

"All right, good talk."

"That's the most serious conversation we've ever had." I laugh.

"Ugh," Mae says. "Talk about getting sentimental."

"If I get deported, you'll come visit?"

"You won't get deported," she says with finality.

• • •

Dear Nina of the Future,

I've handed in my essay to Magistra VX81.
  I've studied for my Virtual Citizenship test.
  Now I just have to nail my examination.
  Here I am.
  I haven't seen the jury yet. I'm in the
waiting room with all the other demi-Virtuoso

hopefuls. I don't know what pieces they've
chosen to play. The room vibrates with an air
of secrecy. We aren't allowed to listen to each
other's auditions.
   Andrew Sommers is here—

And he hasn't even looked at me.

Anushka keeps whipping her hair back, tossing him sidelong glances, but he's ignoring her. He has a contented look on his face, nodding his head to the music that's probably filtering straight into his mind through his InEars. Niraj nearly went up to him to wish him luck, but Mae quelled him with one of her death glares.

My friends and family talk in hushed voices around me, while I listen to my piece one last time before I play it.

I feel every inch the Analog with my Walkman and my over-the-ear headphones.

There are pianists here who have holo-pianos. They're Hyper Reality simulations of the instrument, complete with weighted keys and pedal units. They're practicing on them and appear completely immersed.

One of the pianists plays with tons of flourish. Clearly she'll have the upper hand on the drama quotient.

Someone appears at the door.

"Nina Anand," she announces.

"Good luck, kiddo." Dad thumps me on the back.

"Go for it, honey." Mum hugs me.

Mae squeezes my hand, and Niraj and Anushka toss me a thumbs-up sign and a heart sign.

My legs feel like jelly. I'm wobbly all over.

Andrew Sommers doesn't even look in my direction.

I step through the door and enter a dark room with the loudest silence I've ever heard.

Five jurors sit at a dais, and the room is empty but for a grand piano.

"Name, please."

"Nina Anand."

"And your piece?"

"*Wanderer of the Air*, or Opus 9 Number 1, Ballet in supra-B-Flat Major by Nina Rodriguez."

"What can you tell us about Nina Rodriguez?"

"She was blind. She learned to play music by ear. Her pieces are about underlying symmetry and simplicity, disguised by technical complexity and flourish."

"And why did you pick this piece?"

I panic. I don't know how to answer. The reason—this piece—is so much bigger than me. It dwarfs everything that comes within its reach. It contains me, and all I can do when I play it is wander the halls of its melodies, lost within a magic unlike any other.

I stop my train of thought and settle for a predictable, unemotional response.

"It—it embodies the spirit of neo–Acousta. It's pure and elevated, outward-looking but deeply personal."

The jurors don't react.

"You may begin," one of them says.

I sit at the piano. I adjust the bench.

I place my hands over the keys and take a deep breath.

I don't have a Bell Biochip to soothe my nerves by inducing adrenaline suppressors.

I don't have InEars to guide my rhythm.

I don't have GlimmerKeys or Tactile+ to help me create an artistically designed atmosphere.

I only have my soul.

I play my story.

• • •

Dear Nina of the Future,

I'm hoping to hear from the demi-Virtuoso
Examination today. I hope I get to finish my
Citizenship test first, though. The
disappointment of failure would be a crushing
blow, and I'll probably be deported
because I underperformed.

I'm sitting in another waiting room—why is my
life a story of waiting on other people's
approval?—and I feel grateful for my parents. I
look around at the other Analog adoptees. I've
never seen another one in my life, and
they . . . They break my heart.

They don't look like they come from loving
homes. Or like their lives are filled with
opportunity. They look terrible, as if they've
never been able to escape the other side.

I don't know why, but I've understood over the
years that not all adoptive parents are as nice
as mine. Some of them are downright awful.

"Nina Anand."

I feel like I'm always being summoned.

I step into the room. It's bare. It has a single desk within it.

I sit at the desk. I'm handed a holo-questionnaire and a stylus by a patrol-droid that's monitoring my performance.

I gasp at how unfair this is. Most of the Analog children here may have never seen this technology. They'll probably be intimidated by the droid.

I'm one of the lucky few who saw it at school all the time, whose parents showed me how to use it.

I look down at my test. I blitz through it. I know I've aced it.

I'm led by a patrol-droid through a door made of reinforced steel. I sense another adopted child take their place at the seat I just left, and hope they do well, before I refocus and enter the next room.

This is the part where my parents warned me not to lose my temper.

They call it the *Character Evaluation*.

A wood-paneled table runs the length of the room. Behind it sits a pair of women, both staring at me indifferently.

"Ms. Anand. How long have you been in the Virtual world?"

"Five years," I say immediately, and then cautiously add, "Madam."

"Explain the Bell Curve to me."

"The Bell Curve is an algorithm that takes into account several factors." I rattle off an explanation of all its points systems. I know this like the back of my hand.

"And where do you see yourself on this Curve, young lady?"

"At the top twenty percent. Madam."

The women are silent.

"Why do you think you'll make it there?"

One of them lifts her intel-glasses off the bridge of her nose, skeptically.

"I'm an extraordinary pianist," I say, with more confidence than I feel.

The women laugh.

"*You're* an extraordinary pianist despite your lack of tech? Come on, Ms. Anand. Don't delude yourself."

"It's true," I stick to my guns politely, like my parents said I should.

Apparently the jurors like what they call Alpha-Behavior Characteristics. It proves to them that I'm not a browbeaten Analog likely to crumble under pressure.

"Who's your teacher?"

"David Kuruvilla, the well-known Virtuoso."

"We don't pass liars."

"I'm not lying. You can verify this."

I tilt my nose upward, putting on my best twenty-percenter air.

One of them runs a check on a holo-device I can't see.

"It's true."

"Very well. So you want to be a Virtual Citizen?"

"Yes, please."

I'm extra polite, now that I've made my point.

"Why do you deserve it?"

"I've assimilated the culture and philosophy of merit that is propagated on this side of the world. I understand how it works. I work hard, I'm Productive. I have friends at school, despite not being able to share in their tech experiences. Imagine all I could be once I have access to HoloTech?"

"I impressed the jurors in my demi-Virtuoso examination, despite never having used DreamMusician. Do you know how far I could go once I have music-learning aids?"

"That's all well and good, but how do we know you're still not an Analog at heart?"

My heart sinks.

One of the women leans forward.

"Any links to them? Do you listen to anatronica? Do you find yourself longing for home?"

"Yes," the other woman adds. "Do you ever visit? Pass them information about us?"

"This is my home," I say boldly. "The Analogs are filthy. They're slackers and lowlifes. They are the bottom ten percent. I wouldn't go back, not for any reason in the world."

I say it with a conviction that I'm not sure I feel.

"You believe you're superior to them? You were born of them."

"An unfortunate accident that was beyond my control." I grimace.

The women nod.

"You will hear from us shortly."

And just like that, I'm dismissed.

. . .

```
            Dear Nina of the Future,

We made it.
  We're a Virtual Citizen.

We heard from the demi-Virtuoso Examination too,
and I came in second. That means I'm eligible
to join the program, straight after school.
  Now there's no looking back.
  If you ever happen to look back, though, don't
forget that you're more than what the world
tells you you can be. That you're loved,
no matter what you achieve. Your life might be
wrapped up in your music, but you're also so
much more . . .
```

My Bell Biochip itches a little. I guess I'm getting used to having an implant behind my ear.

It distracts me from the piece that I'm playing, but I ignore it and carry on.

Mr. Kuruvilla is making me work harder than ever, now that I'm about to make it to the big leagues.

I'm not using DreamMusician yet. I checked it out but it was way too distracting. It's like constant background noise.

The GlimmerKeys confused me, and the InEar Metronome plug-in gave me a headache. I found Tactile+ far too restrictive. It felt like a straitjacket.

I get to use intel-glasses at school, and Hyper Reality blows my mind. I can finally talk to Dad without needing Mum around to sign me in on her OmniPort. I've discovered HoloTube, where my piano videos are steadily accumulating followers . . .

"Stop," Mr. Kuruvilla barks. "You're rushing into playing this forte. I want you to build up to it. Try again."

I begin again.

"Stop. See, here? That's the exact note. It's such an abrupt transition."

I begin again.

"Better. Keep going."

BETH CATO

APOCALYPSE PLAYLIST

(2020)

"ROAR LIKE A LION" BY TRIUMPH

Nothing like an 1980s arena rock ballad to establish optimism as news comes about the imminent, probable end of humanity.

Music constantly streams through Orchid's head thanks to the chip installed behind her right ear. Such implants are fairly commonplace, but most augment the brain and senses in other ways. Her curated filter of tunes enables her to work, survive, even to sleep in an otherwise overwhelming world.

As her coworkers begin to cry, some calling up family, some running for the door, Orchid decides there's little point in finishing her expense report. The song—the original album cut, not the abbreviated radio version—enters its prolonged dramatic drum solo as she goes to the office kitchen to equip herself with a carving knife, medical kit, and anything else of use for the long walk home.

"MY LOVE, LOVE, LOVE IS LIKE A BALL-PEEN HAMMER" BY UNORTHODOX CARNAGE

Orchid is hungry. Despite frequent dieting throughout her life, she hasn't known true starvation until now. Her heavy-metal musical catalogue empowers her with anger and strength, even as she quivers with weakness behind a gutted electronics store. Gun shots punch the air nearby, an eerie fit with the frenzied drumbeat. Dragging footsteps approach. This man has tracked her since his gang raided her friends' hideout two nights ago. Orchid and five other women had banded together in recent weeks. She needs to find them again. She needs them to be okay.

She bobs her head slightly to an enraged rhythm only she can hear. She doesn't possess the titular ball-peen hammer from the song, but she does have a brick. She clutches it with trembling fingers. She hopes he's carrying food.

"RAINBOW, SHINE DOWN (LORD, SHINE DOWN)" SUNG BY ANGELA TERRY, COMPOSED BY FELICITY FAYETTE

Religious songs occupy a small fragment of her chip's database, but Orchid finds herself mentally queuing up the music often these days—not for herself, but for the others in the compound. No matter their backgrounds, everyone craves hope, in this life or the next. This contemporary a cappella rendition of an 1893 hymn is especially pleasant.

Most evenings, Orchid sits before the community and sings along with the music in her head. Her voice is nothing extraordinary, but she possesses the repertoire, and that's what matters. Many people have told her that this after-dinner gathering is their favorite part of the day.

She feels the same way.

"MARCH ON THE DARK LADY'S CASTLE" COMPOSED BY HIMARI NAKAMURA

Orchestral video-game music establishes a necessary rhythm throughout hours of mundane labor. Scoop shovel into mud, toss into pile. Make the pit. Assist with the bodies. Start on next pit. Never mind that Orchid is still enervated after her own bout of influenza. She's in better shape than most. She's alive.

"I SEE THE WORLD INSIDE YOUR EYES" BY COLORBLIND (FEATURING DJ HECTOR-HECTOR)

Orchid never expected to get married. By the age of forty, she had only hoped to pay off her student loans. Instead, here she is, singing as she walks toward a bearded man with bright blue eyes. Friends surround them and sing along with the '90s R&B song she chose for this moment.

She selfishly wishes she could write down the lyrics for this song as part of her compendium. In her new official role as community Bard, she's transcribing songs deemed "most important" to preserve. That requires many hard, yet necessary judgment calls, as there is never enough paper.

One thing is certain. This ultimate love-song-style moment will be something she remembers for the rest of her days.

"MY NAME IS A FLOWER" BY ROSE, PERFORMED AT THE SAME TIME AS "LALA HAHA" BY THE JIGGLY RHYTHMS

"Mama! You have to put this song in your brain!" Rose stands atop a boulder as she belts out yet another song of her own creation. Orchid smiles as she hoes the field, saying nothing until the performance is done. Rose doesn't have her mother's medical need for a constant soundtrack, but her passion for music is undeniable.

"I can keep your song in my brain as a normal memory." Orchid taps her forehead. "But I can't upload it to my chip with the rest of my music library."

"Oh." Rose's face puckers as she struggles to understand the difference. "Well, I'll keep my songs in my memory! I can fit a bunch in there, huh, can't I?"

"Oh yes. Lots. In my brain, I fit all five songs you've composed today."

"Five! That's how old I am! Sing one of my songs to me, Mama!" Rose pauses. "Please?"

"I'll sing your newest song again because my name is a flower, too," says Orchid, smiling as she matches the beat with that of the pop anthem simultaneously pulsing through her mind.

"THREE CATS ON A FENCE" BY BANANA GIRL AND THE SPLITS (TV VERSION)

For several days, Orchid debated what song should be her last one. Finally, she settled on her first favorite song. The one that, in her anxiety-filled pre-chip early childhood, she sang to herself constantly to help her cope with the noisy, overwhelming world.

Before the Apocalypse, her cancer battle would've been hard. Now, a quick end is inevitable. The music of the past cannot die with her. Today her chip will be transplanted to her teenage daughter. It's unknown if the chip will take, but Rose is determined to try.

Orchid is hurting. She's scared for herself, for Rose. Her husband and daughter anchor each hand as the familiar melody fills her brain. Despite all, she smiles.

Her lips trace the preschool lyrics and count down cats. Her doctors and family sing with her. They know the words.

ERICA SATIFKA

ACT OF PROVIDENCE

(2021)

HAILEY THREADS THROUGH the crowd of protesters and ever-present camera drones. The excitement caused her to miss her bus, so she'll have to walk home. After turning the corner, Hailey finds herself in a pop-up open-air nighttime market, where hand-knitted scarves jockey for place with home-brewed red ale. The people milling about don't seem to even realize what's happening only a block away.

Or maybe they don't care, Hailey thinks. *Is that still possible, not to care?* She doubts it.

She becomes aware of a figure following her. A man, from the footfalls. Hailey lets him trail along as far as the last market stand—a guy selling knockoff sunglasses out of an ancient beater—and then whirls on him. "What do you want, kid?"

"I think I know you."

Hailey feels heat rise to her face. Those fucking documentaries. "You don't."

"No, I do, you're one of those Rhode Island survivors," he says. "I think it really sucks what happened to you people. So few of you made it."

"Well, we get to live here now," she snaps, spreading her arms wide. "A Development Zone paradise."

"So, I guess you live in New Providence, huh? I have a transport parked near here, I can take you home."

Hailey brushes a wrinkle from her pants leg. "Go home with you? I don't even know your name, you weirdo."

He grins. "I'm Dalton. And you're Hailey. See, I told you that you looked familiar."

She rolls her eyes. "Whatever."

"Oh come on, it's cold out." He says it with a teasing lilt at the end, and when the wind gusts between them, Hailey can see his point.

"Fine, you wore me out. You can take me home. But I should warn you in advance that I'm defensively armed." The law is, you're allowed to outfit your-self with whatever gadgets you want, as long as you make a reasonable effort to inform any nearby people that you're carrying. Tonight, Hailey has poison darts embedded in her clothing and whisker-thin screamer alarms knotted into her hair.

Dalton heads away from the market, presumably in the direction of his trans-port. When they reach the parking lot, she sees it's a sporty little thing, its cherry-red chassis free of the garish advertising that most transports are slath-ered in.

This guy must be loaded, Hailey thinks. *He doesn't even need his vehicle to be subsidized.*

They face one another as the transport points itself in the direction of New Providence. Hailey can feel the kid studying her, and she touches the dart sewn into the sleeve of her sweater.

As the spires in the heart of the Development Zone disappear in the distance, Dalton speaks again. "You're the one they found in the clothes dryer, right?"

Hailey sighs. "I really don't like to talk about it. There are lots of shows about us you can watch if you're interested. My sister's in a lot of them."

"I've seen them," Dalton says. "Look, I'll be straight with you. This wasn't a random meeting, I've been tracking you for some time. I'm a game designer, and I'd like to buy the rights to your story."

This isn't the first time Hailey's heard this particular refrain, although the "game" part is new. "You'd have to talk to our agent. We all have one, as a group."

"The games are illegal, Hailey."

She'd forgotten. It's an easy thing to forget, as open as the consumers of the virtual-reality platform known as the "gamespace" are about their vice. The unenforced ban dropped a few years ago, after some rumors emerged about the drug used to enhance the experience.

"I don't play, but I know some people in New Providence who do," Hailey says. "I'll hook you up."

"I was really rather hoping *you'd* be interested," Dalton admits with a sheep-ish grin. "I've researched the Rhode Island disaster a lot, and you make the most narrative sense for the story I have in mind."

Hailey blinks and places a finger next to one of her poison darts. "I never thought I'd have a stalker. My sister will be *so* jealous."

Dalton heaves a sigh. "Can I give you my pitch? You're the youngest survivor of the wave that rearranged the coastline until your home wasn't there anymore. You survive through a freak accident, trapped among the wreckage of not just an entire city, but an entire *state*."

"I don't need a recap. When does the 'game' part come in?"

He taps his chin. "It's more of an immersive narrative than a game, actually. Oh, I'll put a few minigames in there, I'm sure. The ratings will suffer if I don't. But mostly it's just about seeing the disaster up close. Imagining what it was like to be there."

"That doesn't sound like a game that's going to make a lot of money," Hailey says.

"It won't. That's another reason I don't want to involve your group's agency. They'd laugh me out of the room."

Dalton's transport has stopped at the cross street closest to the entrance to the New Providence subdivision. The houses here are nicer than most on the outskirts of the Pittsburgh Development Zone, thanks to many thousands of generous donations to the Rhode Island branch of the New England Wave Survivors' Foundation. The Solfind Corporation had chipped in a fair amount too.

They only cared because they could assuage their guilt affordably, she reminds herself, *with a commemorative suburb for fifty-four people.*

"I need to go," she says as she waits for him to unlock the transport.

"So are you interested? I can pay you something, even if it's not very much."

Hailey stamps her foot; it echoes throughout the interior of the transport. "I'm pretty busy, honestly. I work for Solfind." She doesn't tell him that she just works one day a week as the token human at a spire-base restaurant. The majority of her and Teresa's living expenses are drawn from the survivors' fund.

"My card," he says, "in case you change your mind."

The door hisses open and Hailey gratefully exits, wrapping her arms around herself in the frosty October night. Dalton's red transport idles a few more moments at the corner, then slides away down the smooth, gridded, newborn streets.

Hailey glances at the card before she puts it in her pocket. Like his car, it's devoid of decoration, just a name and screen code marked in black ink on a soft white piece of cardboard.

Kind of traditional for a game designer, she thinks. *What a weirdo.*

• • •

"Breakfast?" Teresa says. She's speaking to Hailey, but her gaze is centered on the thumb-sized camera drone hovering in front of her face.

She's live, Hailey thinks as she pulls back a chair and seats herself at the table. *Well, when is she not?* "Sure."

Teresa artfully arranges a plate, tilts it to the camera, and deposits it on the table. The camera tracks the movement, and Hailey wishes she'd put on the monster mask she sometimes wears when Teresa's streaming. "Thanks."

Teresa flashes a grin at the camera and dances back to the stove, the microprocessors in her knees whirring. While they'd been in the dryer, Teresa's body had been pressed down on her legs in such a way that they'd had to be removed and replaced with the sort of limbs fitted to New People, the humanlike androids the Solfind Corporation developed to do the jobs too dangerous or tedious for humans. Teresa admitted to Hailey once that the artificial limbs have poor tactile sensation, but that overall they'd helped her personal brand so much that she couldn't quite be sorry things had worked out the way they did. "I didn't even hear you come in last night."

"I missed my bus because of the protests," Hailey says as she spears a miniature heart-shaped pancake with her fork.

"When will all this madness end?" Teresa says, speaking only to the camera this time.

"You don't even know what they're protesting about, Teresa."

"I'll tell you what I do know," Teresa says. She fishes a small tube out of her apron pocket. "This lip liner . . ."

Hailey picks up her plate and heads back upstairs. She holds up her screen as she eats on her bed, thumbing through her feed. Then she notices a small banal object on the floor of her room. The card Dalton the game designer gave her last night.

She picks it up. There's only a number, not a site address. Before she can talk herself out of it, she punches his number into her screen.

I want to talk more about the game, she messages.

She waits for a response, and nearly screams a moment later when the phone rings.

"Can you meet me at the BurgerMat near your house?"

"The fuck," she says. "You *called* me?"

"Yeah, I'm a bit of a throwback," he says. "So, meet me there? You need a ride?"

Hailey takes a deep breath. "No, I'll walk. I'll bring my jacket this time."

•   •   •

Hailey has been waiting outside the BurgerMat for fifteen minutes when Dalton comes puffing up. She can't see his red bullet-like transport anywhere.

"Sorry I'm late," he says, though it sounds like he doesn't really mean it.

She peers inside, where a bored human worker sits within the octopus of mechanisms that prepare the food. *That's what the protests are about*, she thinks. *Solfind wants to eliminate the human workers entirely, cut out the make-work jobs.* This won't affect her position, guaranteed as it is by the contract the Rhode Island survivors have with Solfind. But it makes the Development Zone that much more exclusive.

"Do you want to get food?" Dalton asks.

"I want to discuss terms," Hailey says, "*over* food."

Dalton pushes his way through the glass doors and the stench of processed meat wafts out like a greasy cloud. He punches in an order without asking Hailey her preference and they perch on stools near the counter while the array of machines whirs into action.

"First of all, the process will require you to take Trancium," Dalton says. "If you're not comfortable with that, we should stop right here."

Hailey isn't surprised at this stipulation, but she's still a bit uneasy about it. Trancium's reported effects are almost certainly overblown, but it's never been something she planned to fuck around with. "My comfort level depends on what I'm getting in return. I'm not destroying my brain for pocket change."

"Oh, that's just fearmongering," Dalton says, as he picks up their trays of food and ferries them to a booth. "I've taken Trancium dozens of times and my MRI is clean as a whistle."

She bites into her burger. "I still don't know why you aren't asking Teresa instead."

"Because everyone already knows her story. Yours is a mystery."

Hailey chews, considering. If she doesn't take this opportunity now, one might not come around again. It *would* be nice to live on her own, away from Teresa's ever-present cameras. "What does Trancium *do*, exactly?"

Dalton balls up his wrapper and chucks it into a hole in the table. "It's a relaxant. It frees up your mind so you can either slide into a game or build one on your own, out of your own memories and imagination."

"Have you had *your* memories put into a game?"

"My senior thesis, actually," Dalton says. "Here, I can show you on my screen."

Hailey watches a short video clip filmed in a first-person perspective of an unseen figure running through a field. From the height, she suspects it's a child. Figures approach from the corner of the screen, closing in like wild animals who've caught the scent of prey. "Who are those guys?"

"My brothers. They're not the nicest people."

"And it's a *game*?"

Dalton takes the screen back, clears his throat. "Like I said, it's more of a narrative experience."

"And you took Trancium to make this thing?"

He pinches his fingers a half-inch apart. "Just the tiniest amount. The project got a B, for what that's worth. The instructor said it would have been an A if market potential wasn't one of the grading criteria."

Hailey raises her hand, silencing him. "So it's a vanity project. Where do you get the money to pay *me*?"

"My parents give me my money. They work for Solfind."

Well, that figures, Hailey thinks. "But what's in it for Solfind?"

"Nothing. But there's a lot in it for me, and well, my parents love me."

Just as Hailey suspected all along, Dalton is a rich kid, no different fundamentally from the entitled little princelings her mother used to teach at a private school in Newport. Every one of them died. All the money in the world couldn't buy their survival.

"I'm going to give you a number," she says, "and if *you're* not comfortable we can stop right here." She writes down an amount that totals out to the cost of her own home in New Providence, or alternatively, several dozen acres of land in the Undeveloped Zone.

Dalton peeks at it. "Oh, we can do this."

Fuck, she thinks. *I should have asked for more.*

. . .

Hailey meets Dalton again the following day at his "studio," which turns out to be just a curtained-off section of his apartment with a shiny, new-looking gaming rig set up inside. He'd breezed her past the living room and kitchenette, but she can tell from the real fruit and shelf full of art books that despite sharing a Development Zone, they don't live in the same world.

The only decoration in Dalton's studio aside from the gaming equipment itself is a pad on the floor. "Where's your stereo? I read that you need music for this."

"Not if we're just making a recording," Dalton says, and Hailey supposes that's for the best. The audio samples of the game-enhancing folk singer Johnny Electric she'd listened to before coming over hadn't been much to her taste. She stiffens a bit when he rests the rig on the crown of her head. "Now, think of something."

"About the disaster?"

Dalton shakes his head. "Let's not start with that. Something simple. We're only calibrating."

Hailey imagines a bouncing red ball. The monitor on the screen shows a grainy grayscale image of a ball, though its movements are choppy rather than elegant. "*That's* what it looks like? Nobody's gonna pay for that."

"I told you, it's calibrating. Plus you haven't taken the Trancium yet." Dalton fishes a glass stopper bottle out of his pocket and draws up a tiny amount of the stuff into a syringe. "I use the concentrate. Easier to portion out."

"Where did you get that from?"

"I went to art school, Hailey. I have a source. Now, do you want to lay down some base memories? We can fill in the details later." He moves the dropper closer to her mouth.

Hailey stares at the syringe. A vision of Teresa enters her mind. *I can perform too*, she thinks. She opens her mouth, and Dalton squirts the liquid beneath her tongue.

"Lie down," Dalton says, and suddenly the mat on the floor looks like the most comfortable thing in the world. Hailey slides down onto it, giggling slightly from the unreality of it all. "Put that bunch of wires into your mouth. Yeah, that one."

The last thing Hailey experiences before she slips away is the coppery taste of the wires, then the concentrated Trancium flows over her like an internal Great Wave and she's gone.

. . .

Floating, waiting, dying. The air is rank with the smell of fear and your sister's rotting lower legs. Though it shouldn't be possible, you pop the dryer open from the inside, tumbling onto the rock outcropping onto which the appliance had marooned itself. The water from a greatly expanded Narragansett Bay fills your mouth and lungs, making you choke.

You start to swim in the direction of a distant shouting. You haven't learned how to swim in the ocean yet, but your legs work anyway, kicking away from the dryer to take in the devastation that surrounds you.

The shouts emanate from a woman tangled in cables and seaweed, her screams echoing over the water. You attempt to untangle her from her bindings, but her frantic windmilling makes that impossible, and she eventually sinks beneath the water's surface.

You have to get back to the clothes dryer; you have to save your sister. You begin to see things you recognize, like the sign from the pharmacy your parents used to take you to for candy and cheap toys. One of the workers bobs nearby, his blue vest waterlogged, obviously dead.

Teresa is lodged in tight, her blackened legs refusing to relinquish their position. You start to scream for help then, because surely there must be someone taking care of this mess, but you know there's nobody you can depend on. Nobody in the entire world.

. . .

Hailey gasps as she comes to, her body trembling with all of the memories the Trancium has unearthed. She looks around for Dalton—*the fucker didn't skip out on me, did he?*—and finds him hunched over one of the monitors.

"Did you get it?"

"I got *something*," he says. He points at the monitor. It's nearly as crude as the bouncing ball had been, though there's dull color spread throughout. He presses a button and the image sharpens slightly.

"No offense, but it's still kind of shitty."

He pushes another button and the screen clicks off. "This is only the beginning. How are you feeling?"

Hailey considers. She's fairly sure the memories she'd fed to the rig aren't real; recovered memories aren't exactly a thing. He *had* said imagination played into the whole deal, back at the BurgerMat. "I left the dryer on my own. I'm pretty sure I didn't in real life, but—"

"It's a game," Dalton says. "It's not going to map directly to your experiences. But there was some real emotion in that take, and I really want to keep that going for our next session."

Next session? For some reason Hailey assumed he'd be able to get everything in one. "How long was I under?"

"A standard four hours. We have a lot of work ahead of us. Same time tomorrow?"

Hailey thinks of herself floating in the morass of flotsam and corpses, of the smell of her sister's dead legs. And she finds that she can't wait to go back there, now that she knows it isn't dangerous, or at least, not as dangerous as she'd feared. "Yeah, I'll be here."

. . .

"Haven't seen much of you lately," Teresa says. For once, she's not soliloquizing for her flying camera. "That job didn't give you more hours, did it?"

"I made a friend," Hailey says.

Teresa frowns, and Hailey knows it's because she wishes she hadn't powered down her drone. This could have been an interesting plot development for her stream. "Good for you! I really mean that."

Hailey bites her lip, wondering whether or not to talk about the game, then just decides to come out with it. "We're working on a project together about my life."

A shadow of doubt runs across Teresa's face before being replaced by unenthusiastic support. "A biography, huh? Well, you know what they say. Everyone has a story, no matter how small."

"He's paying me for it. I might earn enough to move out," Hailey says. "Then you can have the whole place to yourself if you want."

"Nothing comes for free, Hailey. And no offense, but you don't have enough of a story to buy yourself a house. Hell, not even *I* do."

Hailey takes a deep breath. "We have a contract."

Teresa shrugs. "It's your life, sis." Then she pushes herself off the couch with her New Person legs and goes upstairs.

Probably gonna go make out with her camera, Hailey thinks.

• • •

The next time she shows up for a recording session, Hailey heads immediately to the studio, but Dalton calls her back to his understated rich-kid living room.

"We need to talk," he says. "I'm not getting the quality out of these takes that I've been expecting. The emotional aspect is strong, but the visual one is . . . not great." He holds up his screen, where a grainy, staticky image shows Hailey's avatar towing a box containing a litter of kittens to safety. "This is as good as I can get it."

"So what do we do about that?"

He looks away before he speaks. "I want to try giving you more Trancium. I think it will help."

Hailey stares down at her hands. She hasn't experienced any of the negative side effects of prolonged Trancium exposure so far—no trembling fingers, no alienating sense of body dislocation—but the idea of taking *more* of the stuff just seems stupid. "No."

"I figured you'd say that. It's a shame we won't be able to finish the game, though. And that I won't be able to pay you." Dalton smiles at her then, and she's reminded of the vast gulf of differences between them.

She drops her gaze at her hands again. Her non-shaking, perfectly sound hands. "You know what, I think I changed my mind."

Dalton smiles and takes her hand. "I promise, Hailey. Nothing bad will happen to you."

• • •

This time, you save them all.

Not everyone in Rhode Island, of course. That would be ridiculous. But on this particular run-through, you manage to load your parents, your sister, and your Aunt Frieda who'd been visiting from Boston onto a piece of siding that manages to float, boat-like, toward the new coastline so far away.

You chart your course. You speed up.

Reaching the shore should end the game, and it did in the first script. But as you've gone deeper, the story has expanded. The game is totally off-script at this point, and it hadn't ever been all that tethered to reality.

After dropping off your rescued family at the infirmary, you stop at the volunteers' tent. You're ready to go back out. The default avatar for this interactive narrative has been aged up from six to seventeen to make the rescue operations more realistic, and you have to admit that you prefer it this way, to be a confident young adult with elite swimming skills instead of a scared little girl in a clothes dryer.

Way more than fifty-four Rhode Islanders have survived; you can recognize at least a dozen people in this camp alone, friends and neighbors who in reality were never seen again. You'd love to stay and chat, but you have to get back out there.

You have to save as many as you can.

· · ·

For the first time in all her weeks of memory recording, Hailey wakes up screaming. Dalton is shaking her, and she watches as her hands rake at him, seemingly not under her control.

"Why did," she pants between breaths, "you do that? This was a really good session."

"Your vitals were off," he says, pointing at the monitor that measures Hailey's breathing, muscle movements, and blood sugar, all taken from a small device buried in the gaming rig. Most of them don't have this feature, but Dalton's equipment is top of the line.

It's the eighth time she's gone under with the increased dose, and Dalton's hunch had been right: More drugs *do* make the experiences better. Both for her and for the game's eventual players, based on what she's seen on Dalton's screens. "I feel *fine*, Dalton."

"I think you should see a doctor. You're signed up with SolHealth, right?"

Hailey holds her hand up. She doesn't detect any shaking, but Dalton's right. She should get checked out. "Well, you got that session recorded, right? Aren't we almost done?"

"We *were* done. The scope of the project has now changed."

She narrows her eyes. "What do you mean?"

"Interactive narratives are out. Well, they were never in. But now they're *really* out and if this project is going to make any money at all, it needs to be more like a game. More branches, more choices."

Hailey breathes in and out, slowly. "So that's why all the Trancium." She tries to meet his gaze, but he's started to fiddle with the monitor. "I wish you would have told me. I still would have said yes." *And not for the money,* she thinks. *Or at least, not only for the money.*

Dalton shrugs, looks away.

"Can I take the rig off now?" she asks, then starts to do it before he gives the all-clear. For some reason she can barely grasp the thing, and then she realizes why.

Her hands are shaking. *Badly.*

. . .

The next appointment available through SolHealth isn't for three weeks, so Dalton gets her in with his family's own physician, who practices out of one of the fanciest spires in the Pittsburgh Development Zone. Hailey supposes it's the least he can do, since it's kind of his fault this happened to her.

Of course, he wants to finish his game too, she thinks. *That's what this is really about.*

The doctor is a stern-faced woman who rushes Hailey through test after test, and when she's done, she calls Dalton back into the room. Hailey isn't exactly happy about this, but his family *is* the one who's paying.

"It's not good," the doctor says. "At this level of abuse, expect forty percent reduced mobility by the spring, possibly sooner. Eighty percent loss of speech by summer." The doctor angrily punches something into her screen. "I hope this was all worth it, little lady."

Say something, Hailey tries to beam to Dalton, mind to mind. *Tell them that I did it for your art, for our game.* But he just stares down at the tile floor with an expression impossible to read.

"What if I stop?" she asks the doctor. "Like, just stop taking Trancium completely, right now. How does *that* change things?"

"It doesn't," says the doctor. A smug grin flickers briefly over her face.

Dalton steps between Hailey and the doctor; he's still not looking at her, and Hailey wonders if he'll ever do so again. "But she didn't even take that much. I . . . I was there with her. I saw how much she took, and it wasn't enough to hurt her."

"Clearly she's indulging behind your back. And there are genetic profiles that are more sensitive to Trancium, but I'd check her pockets first."

Now Dalton faces her. "Don't worry, Hailey. You'll be well provided for."

Hailey watches, horrified, as her left leg begins to kick at nothing at all.

. . .

Dalton visits Hailey a few months later, after all of the legal odds and ends have been cleaned up, after Teresa cashed his family's big fat check. The check wasn't for completing the game, that was made very clear, but as a "sincere gesture of goodwill" for the girl their no-good youngest son had ruined.

"I finished the game," he says. Teresa has left for the day. Part of the family's nondisclosure agreement forbids streaming any images of Hailey, which has put a serious dent into Teresa's career. "I thought you'd want to know."

"Go fuck yourself," says Hailey.

Dalton sits down on the couch with her without asking permission, then just keeps talking as if she gives a shit about what comes out of his mouth next. "I'm still going to release it. Lots of people on the dark web would love to play it, I bet. Especially once they know the story."

The story is that you ruined my life and got away with it, Hailey thinks. She'd say it right to his face, but speaking isn't that easy for Hailey these days.

"I shouldn't even be here," he says. "The agreement says so. But they can't tell me what to do. What *we* can do. Don't you want to see me release it?"

Hailey forces her voice out through the trembling of her chest wall. "*Fuck you,*" she repeats.

His face goes red under his mop of blond hair. "You know, my family's done a lot for you. You're basically getting my inheritance, Hailey. They're forcing me to move back into their spire. We've both suffered for this."

Hailey tries to say "get out," but it sounds more like a groan.

"Anyway, I just wanted to tell you about the game, how I'm releasing it. And that, well, this sucks." Dalton stands up. "So, I'll keep in touch, right? And just remember, *you* took the Trancium. It was my idea, but you took it."

Hailey turns away from him, and stays in that position until she hears Dalton close the door behind him.

• • •

You float out on the tide in the little inflatable dinghy you've gotten as an upgrade for being so good at this. Thanks to your actions in this memory that never happened, you've managed to save nearly everyone.

You've been spending a lot more time here. You no longer need the Trancium or the rig; you're here within minutes of closing your eyes. Sometimes you're not even sure your eyes are closed, so seamless is the transition between the increasingly painful real world and the world of this "interactive narrative."

This is the body dislocation you've read about. Being in two places at once, simultaneously, yet always feeling the draw to this other world. It never goes away. It will never go away.

Today, you're searching for survivors in a part of the enlarged bay you've only seen from a distance. But now it's been fully sketched out for you, and your avatar is strong enough to get there, through an iceberg field of garbage mounds swept from what had once been Rhode Island.

There's a cry from an unseen figure mired in a small whirlpool of fast-food wrappers; you angle the boat toward the sounds and prepare for the worst. It's a little boy with a profusely bleeding head wound, but he's strong enough to work with you on his own rescue.

"Mama?" he says, stroking your avatar's face.

"No," you say, "but let's go find her." And it occurs to you that if this family exists

here in this phantom world, there's no reason you can't have one too. This is a place where you can indeed raise children, where you could live your whole life if you wanted to, in a place far away from the coast and the Great Wave, a place sketched out by your own Trancium-altered mind.

You can do this, live here forever in the place that's always being created. And something tells you that you wouldn't be the first one to make that choice.

After settling the little boy safely into your boat, you repoint it toward the shore. Nothing here can ever be taken away from you, because it's all you.

You're home.

SAM J. MILLER

FERAL ARCADE CHILDREN OF THE AMERICAN NORTHEAST

(2021)

WE WERE SO MANY. Latchkey kids and runaways, hardscrabble children for whom home was a motel or a broken-glass abandoned storefront or a flat patch of dirt under an off-ramp—but also indolent, precious bunny-rabbit boys and girls abandoned to the elements by their wealthy parents. We were immigrants learning English from badly translated video games, and Jersey-born locals destined to never leave the tristate area. We came carrying hundreds of quarters, or with hands and pockets empty. We came to make money. We came to spend it. We sold drugs, or rented out parts of our bodies for brief periods of time. We lived our lives in a strip mall archipelago a hundred miles long. The arcade children of Interstate 287 were a great and numerous nation.

· · ·

My mom's boyfriend from the time I was ten to around when I turned eighteen was a guy named Tomm, and whether the extra *m* in his name was his own doing or the work of an imaginative parent I was never able to discern. Mom told me once that Tomm had made a lot of bad decisions in his life. He didn't drink, and he flinched when Mom popped the top off a can of beer for herself.

I never knew exactly what he did for a living, just that it meant he dropped me off in the morning and came for me sometimes before sunset and sometimes long after. Same pep talk every time, when I got out of the car—don't talk to strangers, don't be rude to the staff, always keep an eye on the exits. Same five-dollar bill for food every time; same roll of quarters for keeping me entertained. Sometimes he'd be gone for an hour, and sometimes twelve.

Mom didn't know what he did either, and didn't want to. I suspect we both believed it was something illegal, or borderline legal. I never told her anything about what my days were like, when Tomm "took me to work." She never asked questions. The poor woman was forever overworked. Tomm took care of child-care concerns for a lot less than a babysitter. I came home unharmed each time, and that was probably enough to calm her down. I knew, somehow, that telling her the truth would mean the end of it.

• • •

We were the numerically dominant species in the arcade ecosystem, but there were others. Most of them predators. Some sold us drugs: speed or spider-webbing. Cheap at first, but pretty soon you were selling off pieces of yourself. For many of my fellow feral arcade children, especially the older ones, life was pain. I could see why they'd choose to escape into substance abuse.

Other predators, occupying an ecological niche so well-fitted to the drug dealers that it seemed like symbiosis, gave us the money we might need for drugs or quarters. Some wanted to fuck us; some wanted to get fucked. Some would want it out in the parking lot. Some fucked us in between the machines in the back. Some, the ones with the most money or the oddest hungers, drove us off to motels or homes or undisclosed locations.

I didn't see it, then. The difference between me and the kids who took those five- and ten-dollar bills.

• • •

You want to know about the urban legend. That's why you're here, really. You've heard rumors, tales told so many times it's like an endless game of Telephone, and you know better than to believe them, of course, but still.

The mysterious arcade game that kills people. Some kid died, right? Or kids? In Seattle, or was it somewhere down the Jersey Shore? Killed, or just disap-peared? Kidnapped, probably. Sex criminals, Russians. Something.

• • •

Cops were our apex predator, and they came through all the time. Cracking down on sex work or drug sales, usually, or occasionally dragging out a drug-addled or overdosed or antagonistic adult. But mostly it was us they preyed on. The johns, they barely saw. Too busy cuffing kids. We were so vulnerable, us feral arcade children.

• • •

Sex was not some secret world for me. Even before Tomm arrived in that crummy apartment with only one thin wall between their bed and mine, we had lived in a dozen or so spots surrounded by people who lived their most intimate lives very publicly. Women who screamed the obscenest demands through slammed doors at three in the morning. Men who sobbed out the most unnecessarily detailed confessions. Couples fucking in stairwells, who didn't stop when a wide-eyed, eight-year-old me came stomping down from the floor above.

So, no. I was not ignorant of the fact of sex. It was one more realm of terror that lay waiting for me. One more inscrutable aspect of adult villainy. The one my mother warned me about the most. "Sex criminals" were everywhere. Stranger danger. "Perverts" who waited in every corner for the moment you let your guard down so they could kidnap you and do terrible sex things to you until you die.

* * *

Unwashed boy, beer gone sour, spilled soda, and ancient cigarettes. Sperm and sweat and lube. By age thirteen, the smell of the inside of an arcade could bring me to an instant pubescent erection. It smelled forbidden; sexy. Seedy. Slothful. So when I first saw Fenn at fourteen, slumped against a Gaijin Ninja cabinet in a dark corner; when he looked up and caught me staring and winked, I instantly imprinted all that eroticism onto him.

* * *

Who knew what weird electricity drew me to Fenn, or Fenn to me. He spent a long time scoping me out, I know that. He told me later he'd been watching me before we first made eye contact—Fenn always had his eye on everyone, assessing who was a threat and who had potential, but potential for what I wouldn't learn for a while. And even after we did lock eyes, he didn't come right over and say hey. He slipped into the shadows, and I didn't see him again for a couple of weeks, when he popped up beside me and poked me on the nose and said, "You're cute."

* * *

Fenn lit me up like electricity, like a quarter slid into the coin slot of my soul. His smile set my pinball flippers flapping; his touch made me clang like a new high score.

Bright blue hair. Barbed wire bracelet. Tall and lean and dark. Brown eyes ringed with green. The third time we talked, he took hold of the hood of my sweatshirt and tugged, pulled me into a corner. Not gently. Pushed me up against the wall. Put his mouth on mine. Slid his studded tongue past my lips. Metal probed flesh. Something unspooled inside of me. Fenn reached into my pants and sex suddenly ceased to be scary, which is probably a way of saying I stopped being a little kid.

* * *

After that, I carried sex around with me like a switchblade in my pocket. Every scary situation got a little less scary, knowing I had it. Even if I couldn't use it right there and then—it was mine, it was waiting for me, it was a reminder that even if we had to be human (and humans were awful), we were also animals (and animals were amazing).

Fenn introduced me to Jenny Ng. A chubby girl from a good home, smart in that way where it was scary. Where you found yourself compelled to either talk too much, to prove you could keep up, or stay quiet so she wouldn't know you couldn't.

"Don't say anything about her name," Fenn said, when she headed for the restroom. "Apparently it's not weird at all in Chinese."

Jenny had a jacket full of markers, all sizes and colors and levels of toxicity. She handed me one, told me to think up a tag for myself, or a slogan.

"The world needs less clean surfaces," she said. "McDonald's tabletops, plate glass storefront windows, whatever. Everybody wants to pretend like everything's clean and happy and perfect. People like us, who know how fucked up everything is, we have an obligation to tell everybody else."

I nodded. This thought was electrifying, no less than when Fenn pushed me to my knees and unzipped. I was honored that she thought I somehow shared her rebel spirit, when I was pretty much the squarest soul imaginable.

"Ish," I said, tagging up my palm.

"See?" she said. "It's perfect. You were made for this."

"Ron found a black-box game at the Dauphin mall," Fenn said.

Jenny asked, "Was it one of . . . ?"

"Not sure. He only had a couple quarters. Said he had a headache afterward, and nightmares. Game was called Destroy All Monsters! I think."

She made a note in a sketchbook full of graph paper. Her letters were so precise she could have actually been a robot. I wanted to ask to read it, or to know what they were compiling notes on, but we'd only just met.

• • •

Black-box games were not such a big deal. Bootleg knockoffs, stolen cabinets spray-painted over. Hacks out of Hong Kong or Hoboken; Mega Pac Man or Pac Man Gaiden or Sexy Pac Man. How were we to know the difference between a legit sequel and a work of piracy? We'd get all excited to start playing, only to pop in a quarter and find a simple color-shifted carbon copy of the original.

And then there were the games that had been slapped together by computer school dropouts or programmers for the mob, soldered and wired together by utter amateurs. Weird shit you couldn't figure out, where polygons roved and shattered and shrank and it wasn't clear which one you were, or what each button did, if anything. The video game industry was a much less structured place back then. Anyone with a hundred bucks and a garage full of parts could create a game, and any halfway-smooth talker could get it into an arcade.

So, yeah. There were lots of strange games. Some arcades switched them out on a weekly basis, and other spots kept the same games so long we imagined they'd been forgotten by their owners. And since stories were our stock-in-trade, the only mass media in a nation served by no newspaper or radio show, members of our tribe were forever reporting on what games were turning up where.

. . .

There *were* other games. That much is true. Ones that were weird in ways that had nothing to do with amateur programming or inept piracy. Monster games. Games we had good reason to be afraid of. I watched one girl stagger back from a black-box game she'd spent five short minutes playing, and saw the blood coming out of her ears.

Fenn had seen worse; so much worse he would not tell me what.

. . .

Fenn wasn't scared. Neither was Jenny. I was, but I let their fearlessness be a safety blanket I could hide beneath.

. . .

Fenn pressed his fingers against the screen and shut his eyes. "Come here," he said, grabbing me by the collar, pushing down my head until my cheek was flush with the console surface, my eyes inches from his fingertips, then he draped his hoodie over my head.

The smell of him was so strong that I swelled to a state of full immediate erection.

"Watch," he whispered, and I widened my eyes, stared into the musky dark.

My mouth opened, my throat desert-dry with thirsting for it.

"No," he chided, with a chuckle. "Dirty boy, Ish. But not that. Not right now. Just watch."

Blue light crackled, lit up his fingertips and the battered plastic buttons. Tiny little strands of electricity stuttered in the air between man and machine. Clicks rattled in the cabinet. A gong sounded, then a shrill high buzz.

Player up! the machine said, which is what it said when you stuck in a quarter, but Fenn had done no such thing. He'd zapped it with his fingers, tricked it with little bolts of blue lightning.

"What the hell was that?" I asked, staggering to my feet, aroused in a whole new way.

Fenn shrugged, and kissed me hard.

. . .

One monster arcade game attack was so bad it made the news. Kid ended up in the hospital. Paralyzed from the neck down. No sign of trauma or evidence of damage. News didn't mention she was an arcade kid. But we saw her, and we knew.

THE BIG BOOK OF CYBERPUNK

The place was packed when we went there later that week. All the tribes of our whole far-flung nation had sent delegates. The woman behind the counter hadn't been on duty the night the kid collapsed, but she'd heard. "Wasn't an ambulance came to get her," she said, over and over, delighted at all the attention. "Unmarked van. Black and shiny. Brand-new. Two women and three men took her out, none of them looking like EMTs. That was four in the afternoon. She got dropped off at the emergency room at nine at night."

"What game was it?" Fenn asked, and some people said Destroy All Monsters! and some said Polybius, but most people said Destroy All Monsters!

• • •

"Try it," Fenn said, standing behind me, holding me by the shoulders.

And so I did. Flicked my fingers, tried to summon blue sparks.

And kept trying. For an hour. By the end of it my heart was beating so fast that Fenn giggled when he kissed my jugular, and all I managed was one quick spray of blue lightning tendrils that didn't give me a free game at all, but did delete every saved high score in the console. Six entries, all identical, a whole long line that said FEN.

• • •

"I found it," Fenn said, one gray Jersey morning near the shore, the sky smelling like fried seafood, and he did not look well. Blue-black circles beneath his eyes; a brand-new furrow in his brow.

"Destroy All Monsters!? Where?" I asked. Jenny was not around. It had been a week since the last time I saw Fenn.

He named a place. "It was gone when I went back the next day."

"You played it? What was it like?"

He nodded. Locked eyes with mine. Did not look away. He was trying telepathy. He did that from time to time with people. My head filled up with horrific images—children screaming, a white gorilla with fur stained red—but I was pretty sure they came from my imagination and not his memory.

"I know what it is now," he said. "I don't know who made it—aliens or evil corporations or whoever-the-fuck—but I know what it's here for."

He shivered. Sucked in a long slow drag on his cigarette. He hardly ever smoked.

"What's it for?"

"It's here to kill us."

• • •

"I don't get it," Jenny said. "If it's so evil, why do you still want to play it so bad? Why don't we fucking destroy the thing?"

"Because the only way to do that is to play it. Find your way to its cold wet heart. And beat it."

"Bullshit," she said. "Pull the plug on it, pour a couple of Cokes into it, zap it a bunch for good measure, and I know you can fry the fucker."

"It'll just come back," he said.

It'll respawn, I thought. Like any video game villain.

"How do you know that?"

"I saw into its . . . I don't know. Soul? CPU? Black twisted heart? It'll keep killing us until we kill it."

"That's fucking idiotic," she said, blowing a bright green gum bubble.

"It's a monster, Jenny," he said, his voice going halfway British the way it did when he wanted to mock her for being so brilliant. "Monsters are real. Surely you're not too smart to see that."

• • •

Mom kept telling me to get a job. Said I was too old to be spending all my time in stupid arcades. That was kid stuff, and I was not a kid anymore.

Tomm tried to shield me, but we both knew he couldn't do it for long. Sooner or later I'd have to find a fast-food joint or mall kiosk, plop myself down in front of a deep-fat fryer, and be careful I didn't get stuck there for the rest of my life.

• • •

Fenn dreamed of playing professionally. Somewhere, he'd heard, were whole leagues of competitive video gamers with big corporate sponsors. Every game he played he was gunning for that glory, for the day when they'd swoop down and snatch him up.

Hearing him talk about it was the first time I suspected that maybe he was nowhere near as smart as I imagined him to be.

• • •

I played along with Fenn's fantasy. Talked about how we'd conquer the competitive gaming world. With his electric mastery, and once I learned to leverage my clumsy, destructive ability to jinx things for his competitors, I swore we'd swiftly rise to the top of the list of whatever they were looking for.

Turned out I did have a gift, and it was telling stories that were not completely true.

• • •

I'd imagined ourselves to be a nation of equals, all the arcade children united in our status of outcasts, but suddenly I could see how that was bullshit. Hearing Fenn talk about his dreams of competitive gaming, I could see how out of touch he was with how the world worked. How for all his wisdom, he was still just as ignorant as I was, only differently ignorant.

We had a hierarchy, the feral arcade children. So wide and extreme that it took me a long time to see myself on it at all. Jenny had a car, had money, had college in her future. I had none of those things, but I had so many things Fenn lacked. And once I could see that, I couldn't see him—couldn't see any of it—the same way anymore.

We were not one thing, one united nation. We were so many things. How could there be any hope for us, as divided as we were?

• • •

And, sure, Fenn had nothing, but plenty of kids had less. Boys and girls who sold themselves in significantly less safe ways than Fenn did. Kids who wandered through with their eyes full of fear, for whom the measly twenty-five-cent cost of admission was too much, for whom the arcades were one more space full of bright, beautiful things they'd never have access to; a space where the wind and rain couldn't hit them, but still full of predators both potential and actual.

Fenn went out of his way to befriend them. To show them how to game the machines. To make them magical monsters like himself.

Once, I watched him lead three eleven-year-olds out into the parking lot. He placed their hands against the massive metal pole that supported the sign listing all the stores for that particular strip mall. He shut his eyes, whispered words. They shut theirs.

One of them jumped, stepped back. They laughed, shook it off, put their hands back on the pole.

"Yeeeeaahh!" Fenn cried, clapping his hands.

They grinned, electric. Unstoppable.

Something metal screamed. High above them, the sign burst into flames. Fenn put his finger to his lips and they stepped away, vanishing into invisibility again.

After that, I started noticing blackened, burnt-out signs outside strip malls all up and down 287.

• • •

Sometimes I heard him talked about. The kid with electric fingers and electric blue hair. The f——who can control machines. And once I saw a magnificent, stocky Mexican girl, who said she'd been taught by someone who'd been taught by the electric kid, as she lit up a whole line of pinball machines with nothing but a snap of her fingers, and let an ecstatic gaggle of our fellow feral arcade children play for free all afternoon. I followed her at a discreet distance, my mouth stuck open in awe. She could do things Fenn could not; whatever it was had evolved on its way to her, or been transformed by something special inside of her.

• • •

We looked and we looked, and we never found it.

And then . . . we found it.

Destroy All Monsters!, nestled in a corner of one of the weirder spots, down the Shore, a strip mall where half the stores were left empty when summer stopped. And it was at the one arcade where a superhot dude worked, not much older than us, known to rent his mouth out to richer men himself sometimes. Jenny and I meant to go talk to him when Fenn sparked the Player up! chime, see what we could learn about the game and who brought it, but five minutes after he started playing, we could see that Fenn was sweating.

"What?" Jenny said. "What's going on?"

"Can't describe it," he said.

On the screen, his monster stomped through city streets and gobbled up children. Seized them by the fistful, swallowed them whole. Every fifty kids, his hairy, long-armed T-Rex got bigger. A big white gorilla waited for him at the center of the city, which he could challenge when he got strong enough.

Muscles twitched. Eyes flickered. On the screen the game seemed simple enough, but inside his body he seemed to be at war.

Who knows how long it was before the game went black. "Fuck," Fenn hissed, but none of us could look away from the screen. So it took us a solid forty-five seconds to realize that it wasn't just the game that had gone out. The whole arcade was dark. Every cabinet was silent. Kids wailed in the distance—their digital lives cut short, high scores lost, hard-earned quarters wasted.

"You okay?" I asked Fenn, and he was trembling, but he nodded.

"I can do it," he said. "I can see how."

*   *   *

On our way out, I felt so full of life and power and potential—like we could solve every problem, like the monsters could be defeated, like the mysterious forces of the world could be comprehended and conquered—that I said, "See you tomorrow" to Superhot Dude, even though his hotness was super intimidating. He flashed a smile full of teeth.

*   *   *

Getting Tomm to take me back the next day was basically the hardest thing I'd ever done. He said "no" at first—and at second, and at third. I had to tell my mom I'd start looking for a job the following week—which put her in a great mood—which made him happy enough to consent to take me back to Destroy All Monsters! And Jenny. And Fenn. And the secrets of the malevolent universe.

Sweat dripped, puddled on the console beneath Fenn's fingers. Strangled sounds gurgled out of his throat from time to time. Kids came; crowded around. Watched his ravenous creature gobble down children.

Most games were bloodless, scoured clean. This one was not.

"Look at his eyes," I said, because I had never seen ones so bloodshot.

"You need to stop," Jenny said.

"No," he barked. "I'm so close."

. . .

To what, we didn't know. We were watching the same screen, but I could tell we saw different things. Fenn flinched, tapped buttons in response to apparently nothing. Something about the angle of where he stood, maybe. Or the deeper he went, the more it bored into his skull, until only a very small part of the game was playing out in the console.

He died fast, and often. Kept zapping blue flame at the coin slot. The air stunk of ozone and scorched machinery.

. . .

I went to get a cherry soda. Flicked my wrist at the coin slot. Pressed my hand against the glass. Snapped my fingers. Blue smoke spattered, sparked. It took me twenty tries, and when it finally "worked" the machine gave me three diet ginger ales instead. On my way back, though, I saw Superhot Dude standing at the front door, talking to three cops. And then he pointed in Fenn's direction.

My heart clenched. My jaw dropped. Superhot Dude saw it and flashed me the same terrifying line of teeth.

"See you tomorrow," I'd said, and wished I could take back the words. Wished I could die.

I'd imagined him to be benevolent, but why? Where had it come from, the possibility of assuming best intentions in strangers? One more difference between me and Fenn, another insurmountable wall. Somewhere along the line, something in my life—maybe my mother and maybe the minimal solid stability of our shitty little apartment—had given me the luxury of mistakenly believing that maybe people weren't so bad.

. . .

The cops stomped toward us. Monkey Fracas kept chanting its chim-chim-chim jingle, synthesized cymbals ominously happy.

"You've been playing this same game for three hours," one cop said. The crowd of kids had scattered. Jenny and I stood there, mouths dry, hands wet, feeling sick with helplessness.

"I'm just really good," Fenn said, sounding like something else.

"There's no quarters in this machine."

"Even if that's true," Fenn said, "what is that, like, twelve dollars? You gonna take me in for that?"

"That's exactly what we're going to do," the cop said, and of course we knew, all of us, that that wasn't what they'd be taking him in for, but none of us knew what the real reason was. It could have been so many things. For selling himself; for underage drinking; for carrying condoms; for transforming a tribe of feral arcade children into an army of magnificent monsters.

• • •

"They were looking for him," Jenny whispered, as they took a cuffed Fenn out of the arcade. Her hand gripped mine so hard it hurt, and I was happy for the pain of it. "They've been looking for him, and the game helped them find him."

"Who's they?"

She shook her head. Kids drifted over. I could feel our anger in the air.

• • •

Sparks flew. Games spat quarters. Vending machines sprayed scalding soda. We moved toward the exit after them, as one, ready to rain blue hellfire down on all who would harm us.

Fenn saw us, and stopped us with one stern head shake. And maybe it was telepathy and maybe I just knew him, finally, so I could read a whole speech in that tiny motion. We all could.

This is not the moment. Don't let them know what you can do. Don't come to their attention.

Not yet.

Keep going.

• • •

The whole crowd of feral kids followed them out. We felt way more numerous than we had inside, scattered through the vast, empty, dark space.

Someone picked up a stone. Hurled it at the cop car. A beer bottle followed. Then a solid wall of insults, jeers, shrieks. The officers stared out at us impassively, but Fenn's smile was huge.

• • •

When the cops had taken him away, I looked around. All those kids, faces twisted up, tight, dark, or pale with rage or grief. My pain was like theirs, but I was not one of them. Neither was Jenny, but she had picked up rocks and chucked them every bit as hard.

I hadn't been able to do that. But this, I could do.

• • •

You are one of us, even if you never knew it. Even if you only ever saw us in small clumps or couples, and never suspected what a mighty nation we were. Even if by the time you were born there weren't any arcades anymore.

• • •

"Stop fucking crying," Jenny whispered, but she was crying too. The Mexican girl spoke in angry, urgent whispers to a small crowd of comrades.

• • •

We sat in Jenny's car for an hour, letting the rain tick-tock against the roof.

I was convinced they'd kill him. Torture him first—take him apart on an operating table, try and fail to figure out how he worked.

Jenny said they'd probably lock him up overnight, and then remand him to foster care. Maybe juvenile detention. Juvie until jail. "Fenn had priors," she said.

I told Jenny he'd make a new army in there. No matter how different they all were. That's what an army was, I realized. A bunch of different things that become one thing. Locked up together they'd be able to go deeper, develop their skills, refine and expand whatever it was until they could summon blue lightning bolts out of the sky to slay every evildoer and break down every wall.

• • •

Sometimes I'd see our skill at work in the world. Creeps' cars fried; arcade cabinets that let you play for free forever.

Fenn's still out there. Somewhere. Maybe he's still Fenn and maybe that body was already broken, and he's been reborn in a brand-new body—or, even better, let loose to wander the world unencumbered by the awful ugliness humans are subject to. Doing his thing, far away or just around the next corner. Maybe I'll find him, and maybe you will.

Jenny sends me updates occasionally. She's still looking for the robots. The aliens. The Army.

Me, I see the monsters everywhere. They have no need for wicked mind control machines. They have cable company contracts and strip-mall parking lots and deep-fat fryers, sucking out our souls for minimum wage and sending us home stinking of grease and the flesh of animals even less fortunate than ourselves.

They have all that. But we have the spark.

POST-CYBERPUNK

There will always be technological innovation and there will always be society and, sadly, there will always be friction between the two. Because of this inevitability, cyberpunk should, in theory at least, be immune to obsolescence. It is the ultimate in vulture capitalism: the literature of disaster, and there's always one to be spotted on the horizon.

In practice, however, cyberpunk, as a discrete mode of storytelling, only barely clings to existence. Science fiction, literary fiction, non-fiction, even reality itself, have become more "cyberpunk." The problems that cyberpunk saw in the distance are now squatting in the road ahead and on the front pages. This means cyberpunk's pioneering themes, those championed by the original "punks," have now become mainstream; cyberpunk's windmills are now everyone's bugbear.*

With that in mind, the "post-cyberpunk" section of this volume could easily be a collection of, well, pretty much anything. It is difficult to find any piece of contemporary fiction (speculative or otherwise) that doesn't share some similarity with, or resemblance to, the themes or modes of cyberpunk. Cyberpunk

---

* The normalisation of cyberpunk's discussion of the abnormal is further evidenced by the evolution of language itself. For example, "The Scab's Progress" (herein) was first published with footnotes explaining many of its more avant-garde terms. Almost half of these, from "otaku" to "nutraceutical" are now in the Merriam-Webster Dictionary.

has gone from software to operating system; a platform upon which other narratives can be built.

This section highlights a few very specific instances of the genre's evolution into something beyond its original, core remit. It is slightly idiosyncratic and very self-indulgent.

• • •

Greg Bear's "Petra" (1982) is not cyberpunk.*

The definition at the start of this very book makes that clear. The story features a nonhuman protagonist, an unrecognizable far-future world, and wildly transformative technology. It is de jure *not* cyberpunk. It is light-years from *Neuromancer*, from *Blade Runner*, from *The Matrix*. Whatever you think of as "cyberpunk", "Petra" is not.

It is also, however, in *Mirrorshades* (1986). Whatever you, or I, may think, the actual cyberpunks felt "Petra" was cyberpunk enough to include in the definitive collection of cyberpunk. "Petra" is therefore included as a cherry-picked fly for my own ointment: a reminder that cyberpunk is about souls, not systems. (A lesson, coincidentally, found within the story itself.)

At the risk of undermining what fragments of credibility may remain of my introduction, "Petra" also demonstrates how the genre is *contextual*. Cyberpunk defines, and often pushes against, the vectors perceived by its authors and creators. The most limited definition of the genre freezes time, and limits cyberpunk to specific discussions of specific trends as displayed in a specific milieu: North America in the mid-1980s. But that is inherently flawed. First, because the struggle is eternal, universal and dynamic; second, because of "Petra": a mutation in the very womb of the genre.

The next three stories—"The Scab's Progress" (2001) by Bruce Sterling and Paul Di Filippo, "Salvaging Gods" (2010) by Jacques Barcia, and "Los Piratas del Mar de Plástico" (2014) by Paul Graham Raven—all apply the tools and themes of cyberpunk to new challenges. They are, in one sense, "post-cyberpunk", as they describe futures unimaginable during the formative phase of the genre, as written by authors in presents that would have been unimaginable at that time. Yet, again, they show that cyberpunk, as a genre or a mode, has no expiration date. They are human-centric stories that, although undeniably about technology qua technology, are ultimately more about social change in and of itself.

All three stories exist in worlds where vast technological, geopolitical, and/or ecological transformation has already occurred, moving them outside of cyberpunk's predictive scope. Despite the robust scientific supposition, all three focus less on technology itself than the cultural adaptation that results. In "Los

---

* "Blood Music" (1983), by the same author, is definitely cyberpunk. And also one of the first stories to explore the harrowing ramifications and/or limitless potential of nanotech. It can be found in *The Big Book of Science Fiction*.

Piratas" the key is the role of the storyteller, in "Salvaging Gods" the focus is the mitigating (or opiative) power of religion, and "The Scab's Progress" looks at how sweeping, unmoderated technological change has led to the creation of entirely novel societies. Tellingly enough, in none of these stories docs technological progress naturally correlate to, or lead to, social progress.

In this volume's opening story, "The Gernsback Continuum", Gibson acknowledges the bittersweet reality of our technocratic utopian dreams never coming to fruition. In our final stories, we take an alternative path to the same destination: technology has advanced beyond our wildest imaginings, but humanity remains, in essence, unchanged.

GREG BEAR

PETRA

(1982)

"God is dead, God is dead" . . . *Perdition! When God dies, you'll know it.*
—Confessions of St. Argentine

I'M AN UGLY SON of stone and flesh, there's no denying it. I don't remember my mother. It's possible she abandoned me shortly after my birth. More than likely she is dead. My father—ugly beaked half-winged thing, if he resembles his son—I have never seen.

Why should such an unfortunate aspire to be a historian? I think I can trace the moment my choice was made. It's among my earliest memories, and it must have happened about thirty years ago, though I'm sure I lived many years before that—years now lost to me. I was squatting behind thick, dusty curtains in a vestibule, listening to a priest instructing other novitiates, all of pure flesh, about Mortdieu. His words are still vivid.

"As near as I can discover," he said, "Mortdieu occurred about seventy-seven years ago. Learned ones deny that magic was set loose on the world, but few deny that God, as such, had died."

Indeed. That's putting it mildly. All the hinges of our once-great universe fell apart, the axis tilted, cosmic doors swung shut, and the rules of existence lost their foundations. The priest continued in measured, awed tones to describe that time.

"I have heard wise men speak of the slow decline. Where human thought was strong, reality's sudden quaking was reduced to a tremor. Where thought was weak, reality disappeared completely, swallowed by chaos. Every delusion became as real as solid matter." His voice trembled with emotion. "Blinding pain, blood catching fire in our veins, bones snapping and flesh powdering. Steel flowing like liquid. Amber raining from the sky. Crowds gathering in streets that no longer followed any maps, if the maps themselves had not altered. They knew not what to do. Their weak minds could not grab hold . . ."

Most humans, I take it, were entirely too irrational to begin with. Whole nations vanished or were turned into incomprehensible whirlpools of misery and depravity. It is said that certain universities, libraries, and museums survived, but to this day we have little contact with them.

I think often of those poor victims of the early days of Mortdieu. They had known a world of some stability; we have adapted since. They were shocked by cities turning into forests, by their nightmares taking shape before their eyes. Prodigal crows perched atop trees that had once been buildings, pigs ran through the streets on their hind legs . . . and so on. (The priest did not encourage contemplation of the oddities. "Excitement," he said, "breeds even more monsters.")

Our Cathedral survived. Rationality in this neighborhood, however, had weakened some centuries before Mortdieu, replaced only by a kind of rote. The Cathedral suffered. Survivors—clergy and staff, worshipers seeking sanctuary—had wretched visions, dreamed wretched dreams. They saw the stone ornaments of the Cathedral come alive. With someone to see and believe, in a universe lacking any other foundation, my ancestors shook off stone and became flesh. Centuries of rock celibacy weighed upon them. Forty-nine nuns who had sought shelter in the Cathedral were discovered and were not entirely loath, so the coarser versions of the tale go. Mortdieu had had a surprising aphrodisiacal effect on the faithful and conjugation took place.

No definite gestation period has been established, for at that time the great stone wheel had not been set twisting back and forth to count the hours. Nor had anyone been given the chair of Kronos to watch over the wheel and provide a baseline for everyday activities.

But flesh did not reject stone, and there came into being the sons and daughters of flesh and stone, including me. Those who had fornicated with the inhuman figures were cast out to raise or reject their monstrous young in the highest hidden recesses. Those who had accepted the embraces of the stone saints and other human figures were less abused but still banished to the upper reaches. A wooden scaffolding was erected, dividing the great nave into two levels. A canvas drop cloth was fastened over the scaffold to prevent offal raining down, and on the second level of the Cathedral the more human offspring of stone and flesh set about creating a new life.

I have long tried to find out how some semblance of order came to the world. Legend has it that it was the arch-existentialist Jansard, crucifier of the beloved St. Argentine—who, realizing and repenting his error, discovered that mind and thought could calm the foaming sea of reality.

The priest finished his all-too-sketchy lecture by touching on this point briefly: "With the passing of God's watchful gaze, humanity had to reach out and grab hold the unraveling fabric of the world. Those left alive—those who had the wits to keep their bodies from falling apart—became the only cohesive force in the chaos."

I had picked up enough language to understand what he said; my memory was good—still is—and I was curious enough to want to know more.

Creeping along stone walls behind the curtains, I listened to other priests and nuns intoning scripture to gaggles of flesh children. That was on the ground floor, and I was in great danger; the people of pure flesh looking on my kind as abominations. But it was worth it.

I was able to steal a Psalter and learned to read. I stole other books; they defined my world by allowing me to compare it with others. At first I couldn't believe the others had ever existed; only the Cathedral was real. I still have my doubts. I can look out a tiny round window on one side of my room and see the great forest and river that surround the Cathedral, but I can see nothing else. So my experience with other worlds is far from direct.

No matter. I read a great deal, but I'm no scholar. What concerns me is recent history—the final focus of that germinal hour listening to the priest. From the metaphysical to the acutely personal.

I am small—barely three English feet in height—but I can run quickly through most of the hidden passageways. This lets me observe without attracting attention. I may be the only historian in this whole structure. Others who claim the role disregard what's before their eyes, in search of ultimate truths, or at least Big Pictures. So if you prefer history where the historian is not involved, look to the others. Objective as I try to be, I do have my favorite subjects.

• • •

In the time when my history begins, the children of stone and flesh were still searching for the Stone Christ. Those of us born of the union of the stone saints and gargoyles with the bereaved nuns thought our salvation lay in the great stone celibate, who came to life as all the other statues had.

Of smaller import were the secret assignations between the bishop's daughter and a young man of stone and flesh. Such assignations were forbidden even between those of pure flesh; and as these two lovers were unmarried, their compound sin intrigued me.

Her name was Constantia, and she was fourteen, slender of limb, brown of hair, mature of bosom. Her eyes carried the stupid sort of divine life common in girls that age. His name was Corvus, and he was fifteen. I don't recall his precise features, but he was handsome enough and dexterous: he could climb through the scaffolding almost as quickly as I. I first spied them talking when I made one of my frequent raids on the repository to steal another book. They were in shadow, but my eyes are keen. They spoke softly, hesitantly. My heart ached to see them and to think of their tragedy, for I knew right away that Corvus was not pure flesh and that Constantia was the daughter of the bishop himself. I envisioned the old tyrant meting out the usual punishment to Corvus for such breaches of level and morality—castration. But in their talk was a sweetness that almost masked the closed-in stench of the lower nave.

"Have you ever kissed a man before?"

"Yes."

"Who?"

"My brother." She laughed.

"And?" His voice was sharper; he might kill her brother, he seemed to say.

"A friend named Jules."

"Where is he?"

"Oh, he vanished on a wood-gathering expedition."

"Oh." And he kissed her again. I'm a historian, not a voyeur, so I discreetly hide the flowering of their passion. If Corvus had had any sense, he would have reveled in his conquest and never returned.

But he was snared and continued to see her despite the risk. This was loyalty, love, faithfulness, and it was rare. It fascinated me.

• • •

I have just been taking in sun, a nice day, and looking out over the buttresses.

The Cathedral is like a low-bellied lizard, and the buttresses are its legs. There are little houses at the base of each buttress, where rainspouters with dragon faces used to lean out over the trees (or city or whatever was down below once). Now people live there. It wasn't always that way—the sun was once forbidden. Corvus and Constantia from childhood were denied its light, and so even in their youthful prime they were pale and dirty with the smoke of candles and tallow lamps. The most sun anyone received in those days was obtained on wood-gathering expeditions.

After spying on one of the clandestine meetings of the young lovers, I mused in a dark corner for an hour, then went to see the copper giant Apostle Thomas. He was the only human form to live so high in the Cathedral. He carried a ruler on which was engraved his real name—he had been modeled after the Cathedral's restorer in times past, the architect Viollet-le-Duc. He knew the Cathedral better than anyone, and I admired him greatly. Most of the monsters left him alone—out of fear, if nothing else. He was huge, black as night, but flaked with pale green, his face creased in eternal thought. He was sitting in his usual wooden compartment near the base of the spire, not twenty feet from where I write now, thinking about times none of the rest of us ever knew: of joy and past love, some say; others say of the burden that rested on him now that the Cathedral was the center of this chaotic world.

It was the giant who selected me from the ugly hordes when he saw me with a Psalter. He encouraged me in my efforts to read. "Your eyes are bright," he told me. "You move as if your brain were quick, and you keep yourself dry and clean. You aren't hollow like the rainspouters—you have substance. For all our sakes, put it to use and learn the ways of the Cathedral."

And so I did.

He looked up as I came in. I sat on a box near his feet and said, "A daughter of flesh is seeing a son of stone and flesh."

He shrugged his massive shoulders. "So it shall be, in time."

"Is it not a sin?"

"It is something so monstrous it is past sin and become necessity," he said. "It will happen more as time passes."

"They're in love, I think, or will be."

He nodded. "I—and One Other—were the only ones to abstain from fornication on the night of Mortdieu," he said. "I am—except for the Other—alone fit to judge."

I waited for him to judge, but he sighed and patted me on the shoulder. "And I never judge, do I, ugly friend?"

"Never," I said.

"So leave me alone to be sad." He winked. "And more power to them."

The bishop of the Cathedral was an old, old man. It was said he hadn't been bishop before the Mortdieu, but a wanderer who came in during the chaos, before the forest had replaced the city. He had set himself up as titular head of this section of God's former domain by saying it had been willed to him.

He was short, stout, with huge hairy arms like the clamps of a vise. He had once killed a spouter with a single squeeze of his fist, and spouters are tough things, since they have no guts like you (I suppose) and I. The hair surrounding his bald pate was white, thick, and unruly, and his eyebrows leaned over his nose with marvelous flexibility. He rutted like a pig, ate hugely, and shat liquidly (I know all). A man for this time, if ever there was one.

It was his decree that all those not pure of flesh be banned and that those not of human form be killed on sight.

When I returned from the giant's chamber, I saw that the lower nave was in an uproar. They had seen someone clambering about in the scaffold, and troops had been sent to shoot him down. Of course it was Corvus. I was a quicker climber than he and knew the beams better, so when he found himself trapped in an apparent cul-de-sac, it was I who gestured from the shadows and pointed to a hole large enough for him to escape through. He took it without a breath of thanks, but etiquette has never been important to me. I entered the stone wall through a nook a spare hand's width across and wormed my way to the bottom to see what else was happening. Excitement was rare.

A rumor was passing that the figure had been seen with a young girl, but the crowds didn't know who the girl was. The men and women who mingled in the smoky light, between the rows of open-roofed hovels, chattered gaily. Castrations and executions were among the few joys for us then; I relished them too, but I had a stake in the potential victims now and I worried.

My worry and my interest got the better of me. I slid through an unrepaired gap and fell to one side of the alley between the outer wall and the hovels. A group of dirty adolescents spotted me. "There he is!" they screeched. "He didn't get away!"

The bishop's masked troops can travel freely on all levels. I was almost cornered by them, and when I tried one escape route, they waited at a crucial spot in the stairs—which I had to cross to complete the next leg—and I was forced back. I prided myself in knowing the Cathedral top to bottom, but as I scrambled madly, I came upon a tunnel I had never noticed before. It led deep into a broad stone foundation wall. I was safe for the moment but afraid that they might find my caches of food and poison my casks of rainwater. Still, there was nothing I could do until they had gone, so I decided to spend the anxious hours exploring the tunnel.

The Cathedral is a constant surprise; I realize now I didn't know half of what it offered. There are always new ways to get from here to there (some, I suspect, created while no one is looking), and sometimes even new theres to be discovered. While troops snuffled about the hole above, near the stairs—where only a child of two or three could have entered—I followed a flight of crude steps deep into the stone. Water and slime made the passage slippery and difficult. For a moment I was in darkness deeper than any I had experienced before—a gloom more profound than mere lack of light could explain. Then below I saw a faint yellow gleam. More cautious, I slowed and progressed silently. Behind a rusting, scabrous metal gate, I set foot into a lighted room. There was the smell of crumbling stone, a tang of mineral water, slime—and the stench of a dead spouter. The beast lay on the floor of the narrow chamber, several months gone but still fragrant.

I have mentioned that spouters are very hard to kill—and this one had been murdered. Three candles stood freshly placed in nooks around the chamber, flickering in a faint draft from above. Despite my fears, I walked across the stone floor, took a candle, and peered into the next section of tunnel.

It sloped down for several dozen feet, ending at another metal gate. It was here that I detected an odor I had never before encountered—the smell of the purest of stones, as of rare jade or virgin marble. Such a feeling of lightheadedness passed over me that I almost laughed, but I was too cautious for that. I pushed aside the gate and was greeted by a rush of the coldest, sweetest air, like a draft from the tomb of a saint whose body does not corrupt but rather draws corruption away and expels it miraculously into the nether pits. My beak dropped open. The candlelight fell across the darkness onto a figure I at first thought to be an infant. But I quickly disagreed with myself. The figure was several ages at once. As I blinked, it became a man of about thirty, well formed, with a high forehead and elegant hands, pale as ice. His eyes stared at the wall behind me. I bowed down on scaled knee and touched my forehead as best I could to the cold stone, shivering to my vestigial wingtips. "Forgive me, Joy of Man's Desiring," I said. "Forgive me." I had stumbled upon the hiding place of the Stone Christ.

"You are forgiven," He said wearily. "You had to come sooner or later. Better now than later, when . . ." His voice trailed away and He shook His head. He was very thin, wrapped in a gray robe that still bore the scars of centuries of weathering. "Why did you come?"

"To escape the bishop's troops," I said.

He nodded. "Yes. The bishop. How long have I been here?"

"Since before I was born, Lord. Sixty or seventy years." He was thin, almost ethereal, this figure I had imagined as a husky carpenter. I lowered my voice and beseeched, "What may I do for you, Lord?"

"Go away," He said.

"I could not live with such a secret," I said. "You are salvation. You can overthrow the bishop and bring all the levels together."

"I am not a general or a soldier. Please go away and tell no—"

I felt a breath behind me, then the whisper of a weapon. I leaped aside, and my hackles rose as a stone sword came down and shattered on the floor beside me. The Christ raised His hand. Still in shock, I stared at a beast much like myself. It stared back, face black with rage, stayed by the power of His hand. I should have been more wary—something had to have killed the spouter and kept the candles fresh.

"But, Lord," the beast rumbled, "he will tell all."

"No," the Christ said. "He'll tell nobody." He looked half at me, half through me, and said, "Go, go."

Up the tunnels, into the orange dark of the Cathedral, crying, I crawled and slithered. I could not even go to the giant. I had been silenced as effectively as if my throat had been cut.

The next morning I watched from a shadowy corner of the scaffold as a crowd gathered around a lone man in a dirty sackcloth robe. I had seen him before—his name was Psalo, and he was left alone as an example of the bishop's largess. It was a token gesture; most of the people regarded him as barely half-sane.

Yet this time I listened and, in my confusion, found his words striking responsive chords in me. He was exhorting the bishop and his forces to allow light into the Cathedral again by dropping the canvas tarps that covered the windows. He had talked about this before, and the bishop had responded with his usual statement—that with the light would come more chaos, for the human mind was now a pesthole of delusions. Any stimulus would drive away whatever security the inhabitants of the Cathedral had.

．　．　．

At this time it gave me no pleasure to watch the love of Constantia and Corvus grow. They were becoming more careless. Their talk grew bolder:

"We shall announce a marriage," Corvus said.

"They will never allow it. They'll . . . cut you."

"I'm nimble. They'll never catch me. The church needs leaders, brave revolutionaries. If no one breaks with tradition, everyone will suffer."

"I fear for your life—and mine. My father would push me from the flock like a diseased lamb."

"Your father is no shepherd."

"He is my father," Constantia said, eyes wide, mouth drawn tight.

I sat with beak in paws, eyes half-lidded, able to mimic each statement before it was uttered. Undying love . . . hope for a bleak future . . . shite and onions! I had read it all before, in a cache of romance novels in the trash of a dead nun. As soon as I made the connection and realized the timeless banality—and the futility—of what I was seeing, and when I compared their prattle with the infinite sadness of the Stone Christ, I went from innocent to cynic. The transition dizzied me, leaving little backwaters of noble emotion, but the future seemed clear. Corvus would be caught and executed; if it hadn't been for me, he would already have been gelded, if not killed. Constantia would weep, poison herself; the singers would sing of it (those selfsame warble-throats who cheered the death of her lover); perhaps I would write of it (I was planning this chronicle even then), and afterward, perhaps, I would follow them both, having succumbed to the sin of boredom.

With night, things become less certain. It is easy to stare at a dark wall and let dreams become manifest. At one time, I've deduced from books, dreams could not take shape beyond sleep or brief fantasy. All too often I've had to fight things generated in my dreams, flowing from the walls, suddenly independent and hungry. People often die in the night, devoured by their own nightmares.

That evening, falling to sleep with visions of the Stone Christ in my head, I dreamed of holy men, angels, and saints. I came awake abruptly, by training, and one had stayed behind. The others I saw vaguely, flitting outside the round window, where they whispered and made plans for flying off to heaven. The wraith who remained was a dark shape in one corner. His breathing was harsh. "I am Peter," he said, "also called Simon. I am the Rock of the Church, and popes are told that they are heir to my task."

"I'm rock, too," I said. "At least in part."

"So be it, then. You are heir to my task. Go forth and be Pope. Do not revere the Stone Christ, for a Christ is only as good as He does, and if He does nothing, there is no salvation in Him."

The shadow reached out to pat my head, and I saw his eyes grow wide as he made out my form. He muttered some formula for banishing devils and oozed out the window to join his fellows.

I imagined that if such a thing were actually brought before the council, it would be decided under the law that the benison of a dream person is not binding. I did not care. This was better advice than any I'd had since the giant told me to read and learn.

But to be Pope, one must have a hierarchy of servants to carry out one's orders. The biggest of rocks does not move by itself. So swelled with power, I decided to appear in the upper nave and announce myself to the people.

It took a great deal of courage to appear in daylight, without my cloak, and to walk across the scaffold's surface, on the second level, through crowds of vendors setting up the market for the day. Some reacted with typical bigotry and sought to kick or deride me. My beak discouraged them. I clambered to the top of a prominent stall and stood in a murky lamp's circle, clearing my throat to announce myself. Under a hail of rotten pomegranates and limp vegetables, I told the throng who I was, and I told them about my vision. Jeweled with beads of offal, I jumped down in a few minutes and fled to a tunnel entrance too small for most men. Some boys followed me, and one lost a finger while trying to slice me with a fragment of colored glass.

I recognized that the tactic of open revelation was worthless. There are levels of bigotry, and I was at the very bottom of any list.

My next strategy was to find some way to disrupt the Cathedral from top to bottom. Even bigots, when reduced to a mob, could be swayed by the presence of one obviously ordained and capable. I spent two days skulking through the walls. There had to be a basic flaw in so fragile a structure as the church, and, while I wasn't contemplating total destruction, I wanted something spectacular, unavoidable.

While I cogitated, hanging from the bottom of the second scaffold, above the community of pure flesh, the bishop's deep gravelly voice roared over the noise of the crowd. I opened my eyes and looked down. The masked troops were holding a bowed figure, and the bishop was intoning over its head, "Know all who hear me now, this young bastard of flesh and stone—"

Corvus, I told myself. Finally caught. I shut one eye, but the other refused to close out the scene.

"—has violated all we hold sacred and shall atone for his crimes on this spot, tomorrow at this time. Kronos! Mark the wheel's progress." The elected Kronos, a spindly old man with dirty gray hair down to his buttocks, took a piece of charcoal and marked an X on the huge bulkhead chart, behind which the wheel groaned and sighed in its circuit.

The crowd was enthusiastic. I saw Psalo pushing through the people.

"What crime?" he called out. "Name the crime!"

"Violation of the lower level!" the head of the masked troops declared.

"That merits a whipping and an escort upstairs," Psalo said. "I detect a more sinister crime here. What is it?"

The bishop looked Psalo down coldly. "He tried to rape my daughter, Constantia."

Psalo could say nothing to that. The penalty was castration and death. All the pure humans accepted such laws. There was no other recourse.

I mused, watching Corvus being led to the dungeons. The future that I desired at that moment startled me with its clarity. I wanted that part of my heritage that had been denied to me to be at peace with myself, to be surrounded by those who accepted me, by those no better than I. In time that would happen, as the giant had said. But would I ever see it? What Corvus, in his own lusty way, was trying to do was equalize the levels, to bring stone into flesh until no one could define the divisions.

Well, my plans beyond that point were very hazy. They were less plans than glowing feelings, imaginings of happiness and children playing in the forest and fields beyond the island as the world knit itself under the gaze of God's heir. My children, playing in the forest. A touch of truth came to me at this moment. I had wished to be Corvus when he tupped Constantia.

So I had two tasks, then, that could be merged if I was clever. I had to distract the bishop and his troops, and I had to rescue Corvus, fellow revolutionary.

I spent that night in feverish misery in my room. At dawn I went to the giant and asked his advice. He looked me over coldly and said, "We waste our time if we try to knock sense into their heads. But we have no better calling than to waste our time, do we?"

"What shall I do?"

"Enlighten them."

I stomped my claw on the floor. "They are bricks! Try enlightening bricks!"

He smiled his sad, narrow smile. "Enlighten them," he said.

I left the giant's chamber in a rage. I did not have access to the great wheel's board of time, so I couldn't know exactly when the execution would take place. But I guessed—from memories of a grumbling stomach—that it would be in the early afternoon. I traveled from one end of the nave to the other and, likewise, the transept. I nearly exhausted myself.

Then, traversing an empty aisle, I picked up a piece of colored glass and examined it, puzzled. Many of the boys on all levels carried these shards with them, and the girls used them as jewelry—against the wishes of their elders, who held that bright objects bred more beasts in the mind. Where did they get them?

In one of the books I had perused years before, I had seen brightly colored pictures of the Cathedral windows. "Enlighten them," the giant had said.

Psalo's request to let light into the Cathedral came to mind.

Along the peak of the nave, in a tunnel running its length, I found the ties that held the pulleys of the canvases over the windows. The best windows, I decided, would be the huge ones of the north and south transepts. I made a diagram in the dust, trying to decide what season it was and from which direction the sunlight would come—pure theory to me, but at this moment I was in a fever of brilliance. All the windows had to be clear. I could not decide which was best.

I was ready by early afternoon, just after sext prayers in the upper nave. I had cut the major ropes and weakened the clamps by prying them from the walls with a pick stolen from the bishop's armory. I walked along a high ledge, took an almost vertical shaft through the wall to the lower floor, and waited.

Constantia watched from a wooden balcony, the bishop's special box for executions. She had a terrified, fascinated look on her face. Corvus was on the dais across the nave, right in the center of the cross of the transept. Torches illumined him and his executioners, three men and an old woman.

I knew the procedure. The old woman would castrate him first, then the men would remove his head. He was dressed in the condemned red robe to hide any blood. Blood excitement among the impressionable was the last thing the bishop wanted. Troops waited around the dais to purify the area with scented water.

I didn't have much time. It would take minutes for the system of ropes and pulleys to clear and the canvases to fall. I went to my station and severed the remaining ties. Then, as the Cathedral filled with a hollow creaking sound, I followed the shaft back to my viewing post.

In three minutes the canvases were drooping. I saw Corvus look up, his eyes glazed. The bishop was with his daughter in the box. He pulled her back into the shadows. In another two minutes the canvases fell onto the upper scaffold with a hideous crash. Their weight was too great for the ends of the structure, and it collapsed, allowing the canvas to cascade to the floor many yards below. At first the illumination was dim and bluish, filtered perhaps by a passing cloud. Then, from one end of the Cathedral to the other, a burst of light threw my smoky world into clarity. The glory of thousands of pieces of colored glass, hidden for decades and hardly touched by childish vandals, fell upon upper and lower levels at once. A cry from the crowds nearly wrenched me from my post. I slid quickly to the lower level and hid, afraid of what I had done. This was more than simple sunlight. Like the blossoming of two flowers, one brighter than the other, the transept windows astounded all who beheld them.

Eyes accustomed to orangey dark, to smoke and haze and shadow, cannot stare into such glory without drastic effect. I shielded my own face and tried to find a convenient exit.

But the population was increasing. As the light brightened and more faces rose to be locked, phototropic, the splendor unhinged some people. From their minds poured contents too wondrous to be accurately cataloged. The monsters thus released were not violent, however, and most of the visions were not monstrous.

The upper and lower nave shimmered with reflected glories, with dream figures and children clothed in baubles of light. Saints and prodigies dominated. A thousand newly created youngsters squatted on the bright floor and began to tell of marvels, of cities in the East, and times as they had once been. Clowns dressed in fire entertained from the tops of the market stalls. Animals unknown to the Cathedral cavorted between the dwellings, giving friendly advice. Abstract things, glowing balls in nets of gold and ribbons of silk, sang and floated around the upper reaches. The Cathedral became a great vessel of all the bright dreams known to its citizens.

Slowly, from the lower nave, people of pure flesh climbed to the scaffold and walked the upper nave to see what they couldn't from below. From my hideaway I watched the masked troops of the bishop carrying his litter up narrow stairs. Constantia walked behind, stumbling, her eyes shut in the new brightness.

All tried to cover their eyes, but none for long succeeded.

I wept. Almost blind with tears, I made my way still higher and looked down on the roiling crowds. I saw Corvus, his hands still wrapped in restraining ropes, being led by the old woman.

Constantia saw him, too, and they regarded each other like strangers, then joined hands as best they could. She borrowed a knife from one of her father's soldiers and cut his ropes away. Around them the brightest dreams of all began to swirl, pure white and blood-red and sea-green, coalescing into visions of all the children they would innocently have.

I gave them a few hours to regain their senses—and to regain my own. Then I stood on the bishop's abandoned podium and shouted over the heads of those on the lowest level.

"The time has come!" I cried. "We must all unite now; we must unite—"

At first they ignored me. I was quite eloquent, but their excitement was still too great. So I waited some more, began to speak again, and was shouted down. Bits of fruit and vegetables arced up. "Freak!" they screamed and drove me away.

I crept along the stone stairs, found the narrow crack, and hid in it, burying my beak in my paws, wondering what had gone wrong. It took a surprisingly long time for me to realize that, in my case, it was less the stigma of stone than the ugliness of my shape that doomed my quest for leadership.

I had, however, paved the way for the Stone Christ. He will surely be able to take His place now, I told myself. So I maneuvered along the crevice until I came to the hidden chamber and the yellow glow. All was quiet within. I met first the stone monster, who looked me over suspiciously with glazed gray eyes. "You're back," he said. Overcome by his wit, I leered, nodded, and asked that I be presented to the Christ.

"He's sleeping."

"Important tidings," I said.

"What?"

"I bring glad tidings."

"Then let me hear them."

"His ears only."

Out of the gloomy corner came the Christ, looking much older now. "What is it?" He asked.

"I have prepared the way for You," I said. "Simon called Peter told me I was the heir to his legacy, that I should go before You—"

The Stone Christ shook His head. "You believe I am the fount from which all blessings flow?"

I nodded, uncertain.

"What have you done out there?"

"Let in the light," I said.

He shook His head slowly. "You seem a wise enough creature. You know about Mortdieu."

"Yes."

"Then you should know that I barely have enough power to keep myself together, to heal myself, much less to minister to those out there." He gestured beyond the walls. "My own source has gone away," He said mournfully. "I'm operating on reserves, and those none too vast."

"He wants you to go away and stop bothering us," the monster explained.

"They have their light out there," the Christ said. "They'll play with that for a while, get tired of it, go back to what they had before. Is there any place for you in that?"

I thought for a moment, then shook my head. "No place," I said. "I'm too ugly."

"You are too ugly, and I am too famous," He said. "I'd have to come from their midst, anonymous, and that is clearly impossible. No, leave them alone for a while. They'll make me over again, perhaps, or better still, forget about me. About us. We don't have any place there."

I was stunned. I sat down hard on the stone floor, and the Christ patted me on my head as He walked by. "Go back to your hiding place; live as well as you can," He said. "Our time is over."

I turned to go. When I reached the crevice, I heard His voice behind, saying, "Do you play bridge? If you do, find another. We need four to a table."

I clambered up the crack, through the walls, and along the arches over the revelry. Not only was I not going to be Pope—after an appointment by Saint Peter himself!—but I couldn't convince someone much more qualified than I to assume the leadership.

It is the sign of the eternal student, I suppose, that when his wits fail him, he returns to the teacher.

I returned to the copper giant. He was lost in meditation. About his feet were scattered scraps of paper with detailed drawings of parts of the Cathedral. I waited patiently until he saw me. He turned, chin in hand, and looked me over.

"Why so sad?"

I shook my head. Only he could read my features and recognize my moods.

"Did you take my advice below? I heard a commotion."

"Mea maxima culpa," I said.

"And . . . ?"

I slowly, hesitantly, made my report, concluding with the refusal of the Stone Christ. The giant listened closely without interrupting. When I was done, he stood, towering over me, and pointed with his ruler through an open portal.

"Do you see that out there?" he asked. The ruler swept over the forests beyond the island, to the far green horizon. I replied that I did and waited for him to continue. He seemed to be lost in thought again.

"Once there was a city where trees now grow," he said. "Artists came by the thousands, and whores, and philosophers, and academics. And when God died, all the academics and whores and artists couldn't hold the fabric of the world together. How do you expect us to succeed now?"

Us? "Expectations should not determine whether one acts or not," I said. "Should they?"

The giant laughed and tapped my head with the ruler. "Maybe we've been given a sign, and we just have to learn how to interpret it correctly."

I leered to show I was puzzled.

"Maybe Mortdieu is really a sign that we have been weaned. We must forage for ourselves, remake the world without help. What do you think of that?"

I was too tired to judge the merits of what he was saying, but I had never known the giant to be wrong before. "Okay. I grant that. So?"

"The Stone Christ tells us His charge is running down. If God weans us from the old ways, we can't expect His Son to replace the nipple, can we?"

"No . . ."

He hunkered next to me, his face bright. "I wondered who would really stand forth. It's obvious He won't. So, little one, who's the next choice?"

"Me?" I asked, meekly. The giant looked me over almost pityingly.

"No," he said after a time. "I am the next. We're *weaned*!" He did a little dance, startling my beak up out of my paws. I blinked. He grabbed my vestigial wingtips and pulled me upright. "Stand straight. Tell me more."

"About what?"

"Tell me all that's going on below, and whatever else you know."

"I'm trying to figure out what you're saying," I protested, trembling a bit.

"Dense as stone!" Grinning, he bent over me. Then the grin went away, and he tried to look stern. "It's a grave responsibility. We must remake the world ourselves now. We must coordinate our thoughts, our dreams. Chaos won't do. What an opportunity, to be the architect of an entire universe!" He waved the ruler at the ceiling. "To build the very skies! The last world was a training ground, full of harsh rules and strictures. Now we've been told we're ready to leave that behind, move on to something more mature. Did I teach you any of the rules of architecture? I mean, the aesthetics. The need for harmony, interaction, utility, beauty?"

"Some," I said.

"Good. I don't think making the universe anew will require any better rules. No doubt we'll need to experiment, and perhaps one or more of our great spires will topple. But now we work for ourselves, to our own glory, and to the greater glory of the God who made us! No, ugly friend?"

• • •

Like many histories, mine must begin with the small, the tightly focused, and expand into the large. But unlike most historians, I don't have the luxury of time. Indeed, my story isn't even concluded yet.

Soon the legions of Viollet-le-Duc will begin their campaigns. Most have been schooled pretty thoroughly. Kidnapped from below, brought up in the heights, taught as I was. We'll begin returning them, one by one.

I teach off and on, write off and on, observe all the time.

The next step will be the biggest. I haven't any idea how we're going to do it.

But, as the giant puts it, "Long ago the roof fell in. Now we must push it up again, strengthen it, repair the beams." At this point he smiles to the pupils. "Not just repair them. Replace them! Now we are the beams. Flesh and stone become something much stronger."

Ah, but then some dolt will raise a hand and inquire, "What if our arms get tired holding up the sky?"

Our task, you see, will not soon be over.

BRUCE STERLING AND PAUL DI FILIPPO

THE SCAB'S PROGRESS

(2001)

THE FEDERAL BIOCONTAINMENT center was a diatom the size of the Disney Matterhorn. It perched on fractal struts in a particularly charmless district of Nevada, where the waterless white sands swarmed with toxic vermin.

The entomopter* scissored its dragonfly wings, conveying Ribo† Zombie above the desert wastes. This was always the best part of the program: the part where Ribo Zombie lovingly checked out all his cool new gear before launching into action. As a top-ranking scab‡ from the otaku§-pirate underground, Ribo Zombie owned reactive gloves with slash-proof ligaments and sandwiched Kevlar-polysaccharide.¶ He owned a mother-of-pearl crash helmet, hung with daring insouciance on the scaled wall of the 'mopter's cockpit. And those Nevada desert boots—like something built by Tolkien orcs with day-jobs at Nike.

Accompanying the infamous RZ was his legendary and much-merchandised

---

* *entomopter* (n.): a small flying vehicle whose wings employ elaborate, scissoring insectoid principles of movement, rather than avian ones; abbreviated as *'mopter*

† *ribo* (adj.): all-purpose prefix derived from the transcriptive cellular organelle, the ribosome; indicative of bioengineering

‡ *scab* (n.): a biohacker

§ *otaku* (n.): Japanese term for obsessive nerds, trivia buffs

¶ *polysaccharide* (n.): an organic polymer such as chitin

familiar,* Skratchy Kat. Every scab owned a familiar: they were the totem animals of the gene-pirate scene. The custom dated back to the birth of the scab subculture, when tree-spiking Earth Firsters and obsessive dog breeders had jointly discovered the benefits of outlaw genetic engineering.

With a flash of emerald eyes the supercat rose from the armored lap of the daring scab. Skratchy Kat had some much cooler name in the Japanese collectors' market. He'd been designed in Tokyo, and was a deft Pocket-Monster commingling of eight spliced species of felines and viverridae, with the look, the collector cachet, and (judging by his stuffed-toy version) plenty of the smell of a civet cat. Ribo Zombie, despite frequent on-screen cameos by busty-babe groupies, had never enjoyed any steady feminine relationship. What true love there was in his life flowed between man and cat.

Clickable product-placement hot-tags† were displayed on the 'mopter screens as Ribo Zombie's aircraft winged in for the kill. The ads sold magnums of cheap, post-Greenhouse Reykjavik Champagne. Ringside tix to a Celebrity Deathmatch (splatter-shields extra). Entomopter rentals in Vegas, with a rapid, low-cost divorce optional.

Then, wham! Inertia hit the settling aircraft, gypsum-sand flew like pulverized wallboard, and the entomopter's chitinous canopy accordioned open. Ribo Zombie vaulted to the glistening sands, clutching his cat to his armored bosom. He set the beast free with a brief, comradely exchange of meows, then sealed his face mask, pulled a monster pistol, and plucked a retro-chic pineapple grenade from his bandolier.

A pair of crystalline robot snakes fell to concussive explosions. Alluring vibrators disoriented the numerous toxic scorpions in the vicinity. Three snarling jackalopes‡ fell to a well-aimed hail of dumdums. Meanwhile the dauntless cat, whose hide beneath fluffy fur was as tough as industrial Teflon, had found a way through the first hedge-barrier of barrel cacti.

The pair entered a maze of cholla. The famously vicious Southwestern cholla cactus, whose sausage-link segments bore thorns the size of fishhooks, had been rumored from time immemorial to leap free and stab travelers from sheer spite. A soupçon of Venus flytrap genes had turned this Pecos Pete tall-tale vaporware into grisly functionality. Ribo Zombie had to opt for brute force: the steely wand of a back-mounted flamethrower leapt into his wiry combat-gloves. Ignited in a pupil-searing blast, the flaming mutant cholla whipped and flopped like epileptic spaghetti. Then RZ and the faithful Skratchy were clambering up the limestone leg of the Federal cache.

Anyone who had gotten this far could be justly exposed to the worst and most glamorous gizmos ever cooked up by the Softwar Department's Counter-Bioterrorism Corps.

The ducts of the diatom structure yawned open and deployed a lethal arsenal

---

* *familiar* (n.): the customary modified-animal partner of a scab
† *hot-tag* (n.): clickable animated icons
‡ *jackalope* (n.): the legendary antlered rabbit of Wyoming, now reified

of spore-grenade launchers, strangling vegetable bolas, and whole glittering clouds of hotwired fleas and mosquitos. Any scab worth his yeast knew that those insect vectors were stuffed to bursting with swift and ghastly illnesses, pneumonic plague, and necrotizing fasciitis among the friendlier ones.

"This must be the part where the cat saves him," said Tupper McClanahan, all cozy in her throw rug on her end of the couch.

Startled out of his absorption, yet patiently indulgent, Fearon McClanahan froze the screen with a tapped command to the petcocks on the feedlines. "What was that, darling? I thought you were reading."

"I was." Smiling, Tupper held up a vintage *Swamp Thing* comic that had cost fully ten percent of one month's trust-fund check. "But I always enjoy the parts of this show that feature the cat. Remember when we clicked on those high-protein kitty treats, during last week's cat sequence? Weeble loved those things."

Fearon looked down from the ergonomic couch to the spotless bulk of his snoring pig, Weeble. Weeble had outgrown the size and weight described in his documentation, but he made a fine hassock.

"Weeble loves anything we feed him. His omnivorous nature is part of his factory specs, remember? I told you we'd save a ton on garbage bills."

"Sweetie, I never complain about Weeble. Weeble is your familiar, so Weeble is fine. I've only observed that it might be a good idea if we got a bigger place."

Fearon disliked being interrupted while viewing his favorite outlaw stealth download. He positively squirmed whenever Tupper sneakily angled around the subject of a new place with more room. More room meant a nursery. And a nursery meant a child. Fearon swerved to a change of topic.

"How can you expect Skratchy Kat to get Ribo Zombie out of this fix? Do you have any idea what those flying bolas do to human flesh?"

"The cat gets him out of trouble every time. Kids love that cat."

"Look, honey: kids are not the target demographic. This show isn't studio-greenlighted or even indie-syndicated, okay? You know as well as I do that this is outlaw media. Totally underground guerrilla infotainment, virally distributed. There are laws on the books—unenforced, sure, but still extant—that make it illegal for us even to watch this thing. After all, Ribo Zombie is a biological terrorist who's robbing a Federal stash!"

"If it's not a kid's show, why is that cute little cartoon in the corner of the screen?"

"That's his graffiti icon! The sign of his streetwise authenticity."

Tupper gazed at him with limpid spousal pity. "Then who edits all his raw footage and adds the special effects?"

"Oh, well, that's just the Vegas Mafia. The Mafia keeps up with modern times: no more Rat Pack crooners and gangsta rappers! Nowadays they cut licensing deals with freeware culture heroes like Ribo Zombie, lone wolf recombinants bent on bringing hot goo to the masses."

Tupper waved her comic as a visual aid. "I still bet the cat's gonna save him. Because none of that makes any difference to the archetypical narrative dynamics."

Fearon sighed. He opened a new window on his gelatinous screen and accessed certain data. "Okay, look. You know what runs security on Federal Biosequestration Sites like that one? Military-grade, laminated, mouse brains. You know how smart that stuff is? A couple of cubic inches of murine brain has more processing power than every computer ever deployed in the twentieth century. Plus, mouse brain is unhackable. Computer viruses, no problem. Electromagnetic pulse doesn't affect it. No power source to disrupt, since neurons run on blood sugar. That stuff is indestructible."

Tupper shrugged. "Just turn your show back on."

Skratchy was poised at a vulnerable crack in the diatom's roof. The cat began copiously to pee.

When the trickling urine reached the olfactory sensors wired to the mouse brains, the controlling network went berserk. Ancient murine antipredator instincts swamped the cybernetic instructions, triggering terrified flight responses. Misaimed spore bomblets thudded harmlessly to the soil, whizzing bolas wreaked havoc through the innocent vegetation below, and vent ports spewed contaminated steam and liquid nitrogen.

Cursing the zany but dangerous fusillade, Ribo Zombie set to work with a back-mounted hydraulic can opener.

Glum and silent, Fearon gripped his jaw. His hooded eyes glazed over as Ribo Zombie crept through surreal diorama of waist-high wells, HVAC* systems and plumbing. Every flick of Ribo Zombie's hand torch revealed a glimpse of some new and unspeakable mutant wonder, half concealed in ambient support fluids: yellow gruel, jade-colored hair gel, blue oatmeal, ruby maple syrup . . .

"Oh, honey," said Tupper at last, "don't take it so hard."

"You were right," Fearon grumbled. His voice rose. "Is that what you want me to say? You were right! You're always right!"

"It's just my skill with semiotic touchstones, which I've derived from years of reading graphic novels. But look, dear, here's the part you always love, when he finally lays his hands on the wetware.† Honey, look at him stealing that weird cantaloupe with the big throbbing arteries on it. Now he'll go back to his clottage‡ and clump,§ just like he does every episode, and sooner or later something really uptaking¶ and neoteric** will show up on your favorite auction site."

"Like I couldn't brew up stuff twice as potent myself."

"Of course you could, dear. Especially now, since we can afford the best equipment. With my inheritance kicking in, we can devote your dad's legacy to your hobby. All that stock your dad left can go straight to your hardware fetish, while my money allows us to ditch this creepy old condo and buy a new modern

---

* *HVAC* (n.): heating, ventilation, air-conditioning system
† *wetware* (n.): programmed organic components; software in living form
‡ *clottage* (n.): the residence of a scab
§ *clump* (v.): to enjoy meditative solitary downtime
¶ *uptaking* (adj.): a term of scably approbation
** *neoteric* (adj.): a term of scably approbation

house. Duckback* roof, slowglass† windows, olivine‡ patio . . ." Tupper sighed deeply and dramatically. "Real quality, Fearon."

. . .

Predictably, Malvern Brakhage showed up at their doorstep in the company of disaster.

"Rogue mitosis, Fearon my man. They've shut down Mixogen and called out the HazMat§ Squad."

"You're kidding? Mixogen? I thought they followed code."

"Hell no! The outbreak's all over downtown. Just thought I'd drop by for a newsy look at your high-bandwidth feed."

Fearon gazed with no small disdain on his bullet-headed fellow scab. Malvern had the thin fixed grin of a live medical student in a room full of cadavers. He wore his customary black leather lab coat and baggy cargo pants, their buttoned pockets bulging with Ziploc baggies of semilegal jello.¶

"It's Malvern!" he yelled at the kitchen, where Tupper was leafing through catalogs.

"How about some nutraceuticals**?" said Malvern. "Our mental edges require immediate sharpening." Malvern pulled his slumbering weasel, Spike, from a lab coat pocket and set it on his shoulder. The weasel—biotechnically speaking, Spike was mostly an ermine—immediately became the nicest-looking thing about the man. Spike's lustrous fur gave Malvern the dashing air of a Renaissance prince, if you recalled that Renaissance princes were mostly unprincipled bush-league tyrants who would poison anyone within reach.

Malvern ambled hungrily into the kitchen.

"How have you been, Malvern?" said Tupper brightly.

"I'm great, babe." Malvern pulled a clamp-topped German beer bottle from his jacket. "You up for a nice warm brewski?"

"Don't drink that," Fearon warned his wife.

"Brewed it personally," said Malvern, hurt. "I'll just leave it here in case you change your mind." Malvern plonked the heavy bottle onto the scarred Formica.

Raised a rich, self-assured, decorous girl, Tupper possessed the good breeding and manners to tolerate Malvern's flagrant transgressive behavior. Fearon remembered when he, too, had received adoring looks from Tupper—as a bright

---

* *duckback* (n.): a water-resistant building material
† *slowglass* (n.): glass in which light moves at a radically different speed than it does elsewhere; term invented by Bob Shaw
‡ *olivine* (n.): a naturally occurring gemstone used as a building material
§ *hazmat* (n.): hazardous materials
¶ *jello* (n.): a culture and transport medium
** *nutraceutical* (n.): a foodstuff modified with various synthetic compounds meant to enhance mental or physical performance

idealist who understood the true, liberating potential of biotech, an underground scholar who bowed to none in his arcane mastery of plasmid vectors. Unlike Malvern, whose scab popularity was mostly due to his lack of squeamishness.

Malvern was louche and farouche, so, as was his wont, he began looting Tupper's kitchen fridge. "Liberty's gutters are crawling!" Malvern declaimed, finger snapping a bit to suit his with-it scab-rap. "It's a bug-crash of awesome proportions, and I urge forthwith we reap some peptides from the meltdown."

"Time spent in reconnaissance is never wasted," countered Fearon. He herded the unmannerly scab back to the parlor.

With deft stabs of his carpalled fingertips, Fearon used the parlor wall screen to access Fusing Nuclei—the all-biomed news site favored by the happening hipsters of scabdom.

Tupper, pillar of support that she was, soon slid in with a bounty of hotwired snack food. Instinctively, both men shared with their familiars, Fearon dropping creamy tidbits to his pig while Malvern reached salty gobbets up and back to his neck-hugging weasel.

Shoulder to shoulder on the parlor couch, Malvern and Fearon fixed their jittering attention on the unfolding urban catastrophe.

The living pixels in the electrojelly cohered into the familiar image of Wet Willie, FN's star business reporter. Wet Willie, dashingly clad in his customary splatter-proof trench coat, had framed himself in the shot of a residential Miami skyscraper. The pastel Neo-Deco walls were sheathed in pearly slime. Wriggling like a nautch dancer, the thick, undulating goo gleamed in Florida's Greenhouse sunlight. Local bystanders congregated in their flowered shirts, sun hats, and sandals, gawking from outside the crowd-control pylons. The tainted skyscraper was under careful attack by truck-mounted glorp* cannons, their nozzles channeling high-pressure fingers against the slimy pink walls.

"That's a major outbreak all right," said Fearon. "Since when was Liberty City clearstanced for wet production?"

"As if," chuckled Malvern.

Wet Willie was killing network lag time with a patch of infodump.† "Liberty City was once an impoverished slum. That was before Miami urbstanced into the liveliest nexus of the modern Immunosance,‡ fueled by low-rent but ingenious Caribbean bioneers.§ When super-immune systems became the hottest somatic upgrade since osteojolt, Liberty City upgraded into today's thriving district of art lofts and hot shops.

"But today that immuconomic quality of life is threatened! The ninth floor of this building houses a startup named Mixogen. The cause of this rampaging outbreak remains speculative, except that the fearsome name of Ribo Zombie is already whispered by knowing insiders."

---

* *glorp* (n.): an antibiological sterilizing agent used by swabs
† *infodump* (n.): a large undigested portion of factoids
‡ *Immunosance* (n.): the Immunological Renaissance, the Genetic Age
§ *bioneer* (n.): a bioengineering pioneer

"I might have known," grunted Malvern.

Fearon clicked the RZ hotlink. Ribo Zombie's ninja-masked publicity photo appeared on the network's vanity page. "Ribo Zombie, the Legendary King of scabs—whose thrilling sub-rosa exploits are brought to you each week by Fusing Nuclei, in strict accordance with the revised Freedom of Information Act and without legal or ethical endorsement! Click here to join the growing horde of cutting-edge bioneers who enjoy weekly shipments of his liberated specimens direct to their small office/home office wetware labs . . ."

Fearon valved off the nutrient flowline to the screen and stood abruptly up, spooking the sensitive Weeble. "That showboating scumbag! You'd think he'd invented scabbing! I hate him! Let's scramble, Mal."

"Yo!" concurred Malvern. "Let's bail forthwith, and bag something hot from the slop."

Fearon assembled his scab gear from closets and shelves throughout the small apartment, Weeble loyally dogging his heels. The process took some time, since a scab's top-end hardware determined his peer ranking in the demimonde of scabdom (a peer ranking stored by retrovirus, then collated globally by swapping saliva-laden tabs of blotter paper).

Devoted years of feral genetic hobbyism had brought Fearon a veritable galaxy of condoms, shrink-wrap, blotter kits, polymer resins, phase gels, reagents, femto-injectors* serum vials, canisters, aerosols, splat-pistols, whole bandoliers of buckybombs,† padded cases, gloves, goggles, netting, cameras, tubes, cylinder dispensers of Pliofilm‡—the whole assemblage tucked with a fly fisherman's neurotic care into an intricate system of packs, satchels, and strap-ons.

Tupper watched silently, her expression neutral shading to displeased. Even the dense and tactless Malvern could sense the marital tension.

"Lemme boot up my car. Meet you behind the wheel, Fearo my pard."

Tupper accompanied Fearon to the apartment door, still saying nothing as her man clicked together disassembled instruments, untelescoped his sampling staff, tightened buckles across chest and hips, and mated sticky-backed equipment to special patches on his vest and splashproof chaps.

Rigged out to his satisfaction, Fearon leaned in for a farewell kiss. Tupper merely offered her cheek.

"Aw, come on, honey, don't be that way! You know a man's gotta follow his bliss: which in my special case is a raw, hairy-eyed lifestyle on the bleeding edge of the genetic frontier."

"Fearon McClanahan, if you come back smeared with colloid, you're not setting one foot onto my clean rug."

"I'll really wash up this time, I promise."

---

* *femto-injector* (n.): a delivery unit capable of perfusing substances through various membranes without making a macroscopic entry wound

† *buckybomb* (n.): an explosive in a carbon buckminsterfullerene shell

‡ *Pliofilm* (n.): all-purpose millepore wrap

"And pick up some fresh goat's-milk prestogurt*!"

"I'm with the sequence."

Fearon dashed and clattered down the stairs, his nutraceutically enhanced mind already filled with plans and anticipations. Weeble barreled behind.

Malvern's algal-powered roadster sat by the curb, its fuel cell thrumming. Malvern emptied the tapering trunk, converting it into an open-air rumble seat for Weeble, who bounded in like a jet-propelled fifty-liter drum. The weasel Spike occupied a crash-hammock slung behind the driver's seat. Fearon wedged himself into the passenger's seat, and they were off with a pale electric scream.

After shattering a random variety of Miami traffic laws, the two scabs departed Malvern's street-smart vehicle to creep and skulk the last two blocks to the ongoing bio-Chernobyl. The federal swab[†] authorities had thrown their usual cordon in place, enough to halt the influx of civilian lookie-loos,[‡] but penetrating the perimeter was child's play for well-equipped scabs. Fearon and Malvern simply sprayed themselves and their lab animals with chameleon-shifting shrink-wrap, then strolled through the impotent ring of ultrasonic pylons. They then crept through the shattered glass, found the code-obligatory wheelchair access, and laboriously sneaked up to the ninth floor.

"Well, we're inside just fine," said Fearon, puffing for breath through the shredded shrink-wrap on his lips.

Malvern helped himself to a secretary's abandoned lunch. "Better check Fusing Nuclei for word on the fates of our rivals."

Fearon consulted his handheld. "They just collared Harry the Brewer. 'Impersonating a Disease-Control Officer.'"

"What a lack of gusto and panache. That guy's just not serious."

Malvern peered down streetward through a goo-dripping window. The glorp-cannon salvos had been supplemented by strafing ornithopter runs of uptake inhibitors and counter-metabolizers. The battling federal defenders of humanity's physiological integrity were using combined-arms tactics. Clearly the forces of law and order were sensing victory. They usually did.

"How much of this hot glop you think we ought to kipe?" Malvern asked.

"Well, all of it. Everything Weeble can eat."

"You don't mind risking ol' Weeble?"

"He's not a pig for nothing, you know. Besides, I just upgraded his digestive tract." Fearon scratched the pig affectionately.

Malvern Velcroed his weasel Spike into the animal's crittercam.[§] The weasel eagerly scampered off on point, as Malvern offered remote guidance and surveillance with his handheld.

---

* *prestogurt* (n.): instant yogurt modified to be a nutraceutical

† *swab* (n.): governmental and private agents of bioregulation; the cops; antagonists to every scab

‡ *lookie-loo* (n.): a gaping bystander at a public spectacle; usually the cause of secondary accidents

§ *crittercam* (n.): a small audio-video transmitter mounted on animals

"Out-of-Control Kevin uses video bees," remarked Fearon as they trudged forward with a rattle of sampling equipment. "Little teensy cameras mounted on their teensy insect backs. It's an emergent network phenomenon, he says."

"That's just Oldstyle Silicon Valley," Malvern dismissed. "Besides, a weasel never gets sucked into a jet engine."

The well-trained Spike had nailed the target, and the outlaw wetware was fizzing like cheap champagne. It was a wonder that the floor of the high-rise had withstood the sheer weight of criminal mischief. Mixogen was no mere R&D lab. It was a full-scale production facility. Some ingenious soul had purchased the junked remains of an Orlando aqua-sport resort, all the pumps, slides, and water-park sprinklers. Kiddie wading pools had been retrofitted with big gooey glaciers of serum support gel. The plastic fish tanks were filled to overflowing with raw biomass. Metastasizing cells had backed up into the genetic moonshine somehow, causing a violent bloom and a methane explosion as frothy as lemon meringue. The animal stench was indescribable.

"What stale hell is this?" said Malvern, gaping at a broken tub that brimmed with a demonic assemblage of horns, hoofs, hide, fur, and dewclaws.

"I take that to be widely variegated forms of mammalian epidermal expression." Fearon restrained his pig with difficulty. The rotting smell of the monstrous meat had triggered Weeble's appetite.

"Do I look like I was born yesterday?" snorted Malvern. "You're missing the point. Nobody can maintain a hybridoma with that gross level of genetic variety! Nothing with horns ever has talons! Ungulates and felines don't even have the same chromosome number."

Window plastic shattered. A wall-crawling police robot broke into the genetic speakeasy. It closed its gecko feet with a sound like venetian blinds, and deployed a bristling panoply of lenses and spigots.

"Amscray," Malvern suggested. The duo and their animal familiars retreated from the swab machine's clumsy surveillance. In their absence came a loud frosty hiss as the police bot unleashed a sterilizing fog of Bose-Einstein condensate.*

A new scent had Spike's attention, and it set Malvern off at a trot. They entered an office warren of glass block and steel.

The Mixogen executive had died at her post. She sprawled before her desktop in her ergonomic chair, still in her business suit but reeking of musk and decay. Her swollen, veiny head was the size of a peach basket.

Fearon closed his dropped jaw and zipped up his Kevlar vest. "Jeez, Malvern, another entrepreneur-related fatality! How high do you think her SAT got before she blew?"

"Aw, man—she must have been totally off the IQ scale. Look at the size of her frontal lobes. She's like a six-pack of Wittgensteins."

Malvern shuddered as Spike the weasel tunneled to safety up his pants leg. Fearon wiped the sweat from his own pulsing forehead. The stench of the rot

---

* *Bose-Einstein condensate* (n.): an ultra-frigid state of matter

was making his head swim. It was certainly good to know that his fully modern immune system would never allow a bacteria or virus to live in his body without his permission.

Malvern crept closer, clicking flash-shots from his digicam. "Check out that hair on her legs and feet."

"I've heard about this," marveled Fearon. "Bonobo hybridoma. She's half chimp! Because that super-neural technique requires—so they say—a tactical retreat down the primate ladder before you can make that tremendous evolutionary rush for breakthrough extropian* intelligence." He broke off short as he saw Weeble eagerly licking the drippy pool of ooze below the dead woman's chair. "Knock it off, Weeble!"

"Where'd the stiff get the stuff?"

"I'm as eager to know that as you are, so I'd suggest swiping her desktop," said Fearon craftily. "Not only would this seriously retard police investigation, but absconding with the criminal evidence would likely shelter many colleagues in the scab underground, who might be righteously grateful to us, and therefore boost our rankings."

"Excellent tactics, my man!" said Malvern, punching his fist in his open palm. "So let's just fall to sampling, shall we? How many stomachs is Weeble packing now?"

"Five, in addition to his baseline digestive one."

"Man, if I had your kind of money . . . Okay, lemme see . . . Cut a tendril from that kinesthetically active goo, snatch a sample from that wading-pool of sushi-barf . . . and, whoa, check the widget that the babe here is clutching."

From one contorted corpse-mitt peeked a gel-based pocket lab. Malvern popped the data storage and slipped the honey-colored hockey puck into his capacious scabbing vest. With a murmured apology, Fearon pressed the tip of his sampling-staff to the woman's bloated skull, and pneumatically shot a tracer into the proper cortical depths. Weeble fastidiously chomped the mass of gray cells. The prize slid safe into the pig's gullet, behind a closing gastric valve.

They triumphantly skulked from the reeking, cracking high-rise, deftly avoiding police surveillance and nasty street-spatters of gutter-goo. Malvern's getaway car rushed obediently to meet them. While Malvern slid through traffic, Fearon dispensed reward treats to the happy Spike and Weeble.

"Mal, you set to work dredging that gel-drive,† okay? I'll load all these tissue samples into my code-crackers. I should have some preliminary results for us by, uhm . . . well, a week or so."

"Yeah, that's what you promised when we scored that hot jellyfish from those Rasta scabs in Key West."

---

* *extropian* (n., adj.): one who, or relating to one who, subscribes to a set of radical, wild-eyed, optimistic prophecies regarding mankind's glorious high-tech future
† *gel-drive* (n.): an organic data-storage unit

"Hey, they used protein-encrypted gattaca*! There was nothing I could do about that."

"You're always hanging fire after the coup, Fearon. If you can't unzip some heavy-duty DNA in your chintzy little bedroom lab, then let's find a man who can."

Fearon set his sturdy jaw. "Are you implying that I lack biotechnical potency?"

"Maybe you're getting there. But you're still no match for old Kemp King-seed. He's a fossil, but he's still got the juice."

"Look, there's a MarthaMart!" Fearon parried.

They wheeled with a screech of tires into the Mylar lot around the MarthaMart, and handed the car to the bunny-suited attendant. The men and their animals made extensive use of the fully shielded privacy of the decon chambers. All four beings soon emerged as innocent of contaminants as virgin latex.

"Thank goodness for the local franchise of the goddess of perfection," said Fearon contentedly. "Tupper will have no cause to complain of my task-consequent domestic disorder! Wait a minute . . . I think she wanted me to buy something."

They entered the brick-and-mortar retail floor of the MarthaMart, Fearon racking his enhanced memory for Tupper's instructions, but to no avail. In the end he loaded his wiry shopping basket with pop bottles, gloop† cans, some recycled squip,‡ and a spare vial of oven-cleaning bugs.

The two scabs rode home pensively. Malvern motored off to his scuzzy bachelor digs, leaving Fearon to trudge with spousal anxiety upstairs. What a bringdown from the heights of scab achievement, this husbandly failure.

Fearon faced an expectant Tupper as he reached the landing. Dismally, he handed over the shopping bag. "Here you go. Whatever it was you wanted, I'm sure I didn't buy it." Then he brightened. "Got some primo mutant brain-mass in the pig's innards, though."

· · ·

Five days later, Fearon faced an irate Malvern. Fearon hedged and backfilled for half an hour, displaying histo-printouts, some scanning-microscope cinema, even some corny artificial-life simulations.

Malvern examined the bloodstained end of his ivory toothpick. "Face defeat, Fearon. That bolus in the feedline was just pfisteria. The tendril is an everyday hybridoma of liana, earthworm, and slime mold. As for the sushi puke, it's just the usual chemosynthetic complex of abyssal tubeworms. So cut to the chase, pard. What's with those explosively ultrasmart cortical cells?"

"Okay, I admit it, you're right, I'm screwed. I can't make any sense of them at all. Wildly oscillating expression-inhibition loops, silent genes, jumping genes,

---

* *gattaca* (n.): DNA; any substrate that holds genetic information
† *gloop* (n.): a foodstuff
‡ *squip* (n.): a foodstuff

junk DNA that suddenly reconfigures itself and takes control—I've never seen such a stew. It reads like a Martian road map."

Malvern squinched his batrachian eyes. "A confession of true scabbing lameitude. Pasting a 'Kick Me, I'm Blind' sign on your back. Have I correctly summarized your utter wussiness?"

Fearon kept his temper. "Look, as long as we're both discreet about our little adventure downtown, we're not risking any of our vital reputation in the rough-and-tumble process of scab peer review."

"You've wasted five precious days in which Ribo Zombie might radically beat us to the punch! If this news gets out, your league standings will fall quicker than an Italian government." Malvern groaned theatrically. "Do you know how long it's been since my groundbreaking investigative fieldwork was properly acknow-ledged? I can't even buy a citation."

Fearon's anger transmuted to embarrassment. "You'll get your quotes and footnotes, Malvern. I'll just shotgun those genetics to bits, and subcontract the sequences around the globe. Then no single individual will get enough of the big picture to know what we've been working on."

Malvern tugged irritably at the taut plastic wrapper of a Pynchonian British toffee. "Man, you've completely lost your edge! Everybody is just a synapse away from everybody else these days! If you hire a bunch of scabs on the net, they'll just search-engine each other out, and patch everything back together. It's high time we consulted Dr. Kingseed."

"Oh, Malvern, I hate asking Kemp for favors. He's such a bringdown billjoy* when it comes to hot breakthrough technologies! Besides, he always treats me like I'm some website intern from the days of Internet slave labor."

"Quit whining. This is serious work."

"Plus, that cobwebby decor in Kemp's retrofunky domicile! All those ultra-rotten Hirst assemblages—they'd creep anybody out."

Malvern sighed. "You never talked this way before you got married."

Fearon waved a hand at Tupper's tasteful wallpaper. "Can I help it if I now grok interior decor?"

"Let's face some facts, my man: Dr. Kemp Kingseed has the orthogonal genius of the primeval hacker. After all, his startup companies pushed the Immuno-sance past its original tipping point. Tell the missus we're heading out, and let's scramble headlong for the Next New Thing like all true-blue scabs must do."

Tupper was busy in her tiny office at her own career, moderating her virtual agora on twentieth-century graphic narrative. She accepted Fearon's news with only half her attention. "Have fun, dear." She returned to her webcam. "Now, Kirbybuff, could you please clarify your thesis on Tintin and Snowy as precur-sor culture heroes of the Immunosance?"

Spike and Malvern, Weeble and Fearon sought out an abandoned petroleum distribution facility down by the waterfront. Always the financial bottom-feeder,

---

* *billjoy* (n.): a doomsayer; derived from Bill Joy, a fretful member of the twentieth-century digerati

the canny Kemp Kingseed had snapped up the wrecked facility after the abject collapse of the fossil-fuel industry. At one point in his checkered career, the reclusive hermit-genius had tried to turn the maze of steam pipes and rusting storage tanks into a child-friendly industrial-heritage theme park. Legal problems had undercut his project, leaving the aged digital entrepreneur haunting the ruins of yet another vast, collapsed scheme.

An enormous spiderweb, its sticky threads thick as supertanker hawsers, hung over the rusting tanks like some Victorian antimacassar of the gods.

Malvern examined the unstable tangle of spidery cables. "We'd better leave Weeble down here."

"But I never, ever want to leave dear Weeble!"

"Just paste a crittercam on him and have him patrol for us on point." Malvern looked at the pig critically. "He sure looks green around the gills since he ate that chick's brain. You sure he's okay?"

"Weeble is fine. He's some pig."

The visitors began their climb. Halfway up the tank's curving wall, Kemp Kingseed's familiar, Shelob, scuttled from her lair in the black pipe of a giant smokestack. She was a spider as big as a walrus. The ghastly arachnid reeked of vinegar.

"It's those big corny spider-legs," said Malvern, hiding his visceral fear in a thin shroud of scientific objectivity. "You'd think old Kingseed had never heard of the cube-square law!"

"Huh?" grunted Fearon, clinging to a sticky cable.

"Look, the proportions go all wrong if you blow them up a thousand times life-size. For one thing, insects breathe through spiracles! Insects don't have lungs. An insect as big as a walrus couldn't even breathe!"

"Arachnids aren't insects, Malvern."

"It's just a big robot with some cheap spider chitin grown on it. That's the only explanation that makes rational sense."

The unspeakable monster retreated to her lair, and the climbers moved thankfully on.

Kemp Kingseed's lab was a giant hornet's nest. The big papery office had been grown inside a giant empty fuel tank. Kingseed had always resented the skyrocketing publication costs in academic research. So he had cut to the chase, and built his entire laboratory out of mulched back issues of *Cell* and *Nature Genomics*.

Kingseed had enormous lamp-goggle eyeglasses, tufts of snowy hair on his skull, and impressive white bristles in his withered ears. The ancient Internet mogul still wore his time-honored Versace lab coat, over baggy green ripstop pants and rotting Chuck Taylor high-tops.

"Africa," he told them, after examining their swiped goodies.

" 'Africa'?"

"I never thought I'd see those sequences again." Kingseed removed his swimmy lenses to dab at his moist red eyes with a swatch of lab paper. "Those were our heroic days. The world's most advanced technicians, fighting for the planet's environmental survival! Of course we completely failed, and the planet's ecosystem totally collapsed. But at least we didn't suck up to politicians."

Kingseed looked at them sharply. "Lousy, fake-rebel pimps, like that Ribo Zombie, turned into big phony pop stars. Why, in my generation, we were the real, authentic transgressive-dissident pop stars! Napster . . . Freenet . . . GNU/ Linux . . . Man, that was the stuff!"

Kingseed beat vaguely at the air with his wrinkled fist. "Well, when the Greenhouse started really cooking us, we had to invent the Immunosance. We had no choice at that point, because it was the only way to survive. But every hideous thing we did to save the planet was totally UN-approved! Big swarms of rich-guy NGOs* were backing us, straight out of the WTO† and the Davos Forum. We even had security clearances. It was all for the public good!"

Malvern and Fearon exchanged wary glances.

Kingseed scowled at them. "Malvern, how much weasel flesh do you have in your personal genetic makeup?"

"Practically none, Dr. Kingseed!" Malvern demurred. "Just a few plasmids in my epidermal expression."

"Well, see, that's the vital difference between your decadent times and my heroic age. Back in my day, people were incredibly anxious and fussy about genetic contamination. They expected people and animals to have clean, unpolluted, fully natural genelines. But then, of course, the Greenhouse Effect destroyed the natural ecosystem. Only the thoroughly unnatural and the totally hyped-up could thrive in that kind of crisis. Civilization always collapsed worst where the habitats were most nearly natural. So the continent of Africa was, well, pretty much obliterated."

"Oh, we're with the story," Fearon assured him. "We're totally with-it heart-of-darkness-wise."

"Ha!" barked Kingseed. "You pampered punks got no idea what genuine chaos looks like! It was incredibly awful! Guerrilla armies of African mercenaries grabbed all our state-of-the-art lab equipment. They were looting—burning— and once the narco-terror crowd moved in from the Golden Triangle, it got mondo bizarre!"

Malvern shrugged. "So how tough can it be? You just get on a plane and go look." He looked at Fearon. "You get on planes, don't you, Fearon?"

"Sure. Cars, sleds, water skis, you bet I get on planes."

Kingseed raised a chiding finger. "We were desperate to save all those endangered species, so we just started packing them into anything that looked like it would survive the climate disruption. Elephant DNA spliced into cacti, rhino sequences tucked into fungi and hey, we were the *good guys*. You should have seen what the *ruthless terrorists* were up to."

Malvern picked a fragment from his molars, examined it thoughtfully, and ate

---

* *NGO* (n.): nongovernmental organization
† *WTO* (n.): World Trade Organization

it. "Look Dr. Kingseed, all this ancient history's really edifying, but I still don't get it with the swollen, exploding brain part."

"That's also what Ribo Zombie wanted to know."

Fearon stiffened. "Ribo Zombie came here? What did you tell him?"

"I told that sorry punk nothing! Not one word did he get out of me! He's been sniffing around my crib, but I chased him back to his media coverage and his high-priced market consultants."

Malvern offered a smacking epidermal high-five. "Kemp, you are one up-taking guru! You're the Miami swamp Yoda, dad!"

"I kinda like you two kids, so let me cluetrain you in. Ever seen NATO military chimp-brain? If you know how to tuck globs of digitally altered chimp brain into your own glial cells—and I'm not saying that's painless—then you can radically jazz your own cortex. Just swell your head up like a mushroom puffball." Kingseed gazed at them soberly. "It runs on DNA storage, that's the secret. Really, really long strands of DNA. We're talking like infinite Turing-tape strands of gattaca."

"Kemp," said Fearon kindly, "why don't you come along with us to Africa? You spend too much time in this toxic old factory with that big smelly spider. It'll do you good to get some fresh jungle air. Besides, we clearly require a wise native guide, given this situation."

"Are you two clowns really claiming that you wanna pursue this score to Africa?"

"Oh sure, Ghana, Guinea, whatever. We'll just nick over to the Dark Continent duty-free and check it out for the weekend. Come on, Kemp, we're scabs! We got cameras, we got credit cards! It's a cakewalk!"

Kingseed knotted his snowy eyebrows. "Every sane human being fled out of Africa decades ago. It's the dark side of the Immunosance. Even the Red Cross ran off screaming."

"'Red Cross,'" said Malvern to Fearon. The two of them were unable to restrain their hearty laughter. "'Red Cross.' What ineffectual lame-os! Man, that's rich."

"Okay, sure, have it your own way," Kingseed muttered. "I'll just go sherlock my oldest dead-media and scare up some tech-specs." He retreated to his vespine inner sanctum. Antic rummaging noises followed.

Fearon patiently sank into a classic corrugated Gehry chair. Malvern raided Kingseed's tiny bachelor kitchen, appropriating a platter of honey-guarana snack cubes. "What a cool pad this rich geezer's got!" Malvern said, munching. "I am digging how the natural light piped in through fiber-optic channels renders this fuel tank so potent for lab work."

"This place is a stinking dump. Sure, he's rich, but that just means he'll overcharge us."

Malvern sternly cleared his throat. "Let's get something straight, partner. I haven't posted a scab acquisition since late last year! And you're in no better shape, with married life putting such a crimp in your scabbing. If we expect to pull down big-time decals and sponsorships, we've just got to beat Ribo Zombie to a major find. And this one is definitely ours by right."

After a moment, Fearon nodded in grim commitment. It was impossible to duck a straight-out scab challenge like this one—not if he expected to face himself in the mirror.

Kingseed emerged from his papery attic, his glasses askew and the wild pastures of his hair scampering with dust bunnies. He bore a raven in a splintery bamboo cage, along with a moldy fistful of stippled paper strips.

"Candybytes!* I stored all the African data on candybytes! They were my bonanza for the child educational market. Edible paper, tasty sugar substrate, info-rich secret ingredients!"

"Hey yeah!" said Malvern nostalgically. "I used to eat candybytes as a little kid in my Time-Warner-Disney creche. So now one of us has to gobble your moldy old lemon-drops?" Malvern was clearly nothing loath.

"No need for that, I brought old Heckle here. Heckle is my verbal output device."

Fearon examined the raven's cage. "This featherbag looks as old as a Victrola."

Kingseed set a moldy data strip atop a table, then released Heckle. The dark bird hopped unerringly to the start of the tape, and began to peck and eat. As Heckle's living read-head ingested and interpreted the coded candybytes, the raven jumped around the table like a fairy chess knight, a corvine Turing Train.

"How is a raven like a writing desk?" murmured Kemp.

Heckle shivered, stretched his glossy wings, and went Delphic. In a croaky, midnight-dreary voice, the neurally possessed bird delivered a strange tale.

A desperate group of Noahs and Appleseeds, Goodalls and Cousteaus, Leakeys and Fosseys had gathered up Africa's endangered flora and fauna, then packed the executable genetic information away into a most marvelous container: the Panspecific Mycoblastula.† The Panspecific Mycoblastula was an immortal chimeric fungal ball of awesome storage capacity, a filamentously aggressive bloody tripe-wad, a motile Darwinian lights-and-liver battle-slimeslug.

Shivering with mute attention, Fearon brandished his handheld, carefully recording every cawed and revelatory word. Naturally the device also displayed the point of view of Weeble's crittercam.

Suddenly, Fearon glimpsed a shocking scene. Weeble was under attack!

There was no mistaking the infamous Skratchy Kat, who had been trying, without success, to skulk around Kingseed's industrial estate. Weeble's porcine war cry emerged tinnily from the little speakers. The crittercam's transmission whipsawed in frenzy.

"Sic him, Weeble! Hoof that feline spy!"

Gamely obeying his master's voice, the pig launched his bulk at the top-of-the-line postfeline. A howling combat ensued, Fearon's pig getting the worse of it. Then Shelob the multi-ton spider joined the fray. Skratchy Kat quickly saw the sense of retreat. When the transmission stabilized, the superstar's familiar

---

* *candybytes* (n.): an educational nutraceutical
† *Panspecific Mycoblastula* (n.): a MacGuffin

had vanished. Weeble grunted proudly. The crittercam bobbed rhythmically as the potent porker licked his wounds with antiseptic tongue.

"You the man, Fearon! Your awesome pig kicked that cat's ass!"

Kingseed scratched his head glumly. "You had a crittercam channel open to your pig this whole time, didn't you?"

Fearon grimaced, clutching his handheld. "Well, of course I did! I didn't want my Weeble to feel all lonely."

"Ribo Zombie's cat was watergating your pig. Ribo Zombie must have heard everything we said up here. I hope he didn't record those GPS coordinates."

The possessed raven was still cackling spastically, as the last crackles of embedded data spooled through its postcorvine speech centers. Heckle was recaged and rewarded with a tray of crickets.

Suddenly, Fearon's handheld spoke up in a sinister basso. It was the incoming voice of Ribo Zombie himself. "So the Panspecific Mycoblastula is in Sierra Leone. It is a savage territory, ruled by the mighty bush soldier, Prince Kissy Mental. He is a ferocious cannibal who would chew you small-timers up like aphrodisiac gum! So Malvern and Fearon take heed of my street-wisdom. I have the top-line hardware, and now, thanks to you, I have the data as well. Save yourselves the trouble, just go home."

"Gumshoe on up here, you washed-up ponce!" said startled Malvern, dissed to the bone. "My fearsome weasel will go sloppy seconds on your big fat cat!"

Kingseed stretched forth his liver-spotted mitt. "Turn off those handhelds, boys."

When Fearon and Malvern had bashfully powered down their devices, the old guru removed an antique pager from his lab bench. He played his horny thumb across the rudimentary keypad.

"A pager?" Malvern goggled. "Why not, like, jungle drums?"

"Pipe down. You pampered modern lamers can't even manage elementary anti-surveillance. While one obsolescent pager is useless, two are a secure link."

Kingseed read the archaic glyphs off the tiny screen. "I can see that my contact in Freetown, Dr. Herbert Zoster, is still operational. With his help, you might yet beat Zombie to this prize." Kingseed looked up. "After allowing Ribo Zombie to bug my very home, I expect no less from you. You'd better come through this time, or never show your faces again at the Tallahassee ScabCon. With your dalkon shields or on them, boys."

"Lofty! We're outta here pronto! Thanks a lot, gramps."

· · ·

Tupper was very alarmed about Africa. After an initial tearful outburst, hot meals around Fearon's house became as rare as whales and pandas. Domestic conversation died down to apologetic bursts of dingbat-decorated e-mail. Their sex life, always sensually satisfactory and emotionally deep, became as chilly as the last few lonely glaciers of greenhouse Greenland. Glum but determined, Fearon made no complaint.

On the day of his brave departure—his important gear stowed in two carry-on bags, save for that which Weeble wore in khaki-colored saddle-style pouches—Fearon paused at the door of their flat. Tupper sat morosely on the couch, pretending to surf the screen. For thirty seconds the display showed an ad from AT&T (Advanced Transcription and Totipotency) touting their latest telomere upgrades. Fearon was, of course, transfixed. But then Tupper changed channels, and he refocused mournfully for a last homesick look at his frosty spouse.

"I must leave you now, Tuppence honey, to meet Malvern at the docks." Even the use of her pet name failed to break her reserve. "Darling, I know this hurts your feelings, but think of it this way: my love for you is true because I'm true to my own true self. Malvern and I will be in and out of that tropical squalor in a mere week or two, with minimal lysis* all around. But if I don't come back right away—or even, well, forever—I want you to know without you, I'm nothing. You're the feminine mitochondriome in my dissolute masculine plasm, baby."

Nothing. Fearon turned to leave, hand on the doorknob. Tupper swept him up in an embrace from behind, causing Weeble to grunt in surprise. Fearon slithered around within the cage of her arms to face her, and she mashed her lips into his.

Malvern's insistent pounding woke the lovers up. Hastily, Fearon redonned his outfit, bestowed a final peck on Tupper's tear-slicked cheek, and made his exit.

"A little trouble getting away?" Malvern leered.

"Not really. You?"

"Well, my landlady made me pay the next month's rent in advance. Oh, and if I'm dead, she gets to sell all my stuff."

"Harsh."

"Just the kind of treatment I expect."

• • •

Still flushed from the fever-shots at US Customs, the two globe-trotting scabs watched the receding coast of America from the deck of their Cuba-bound ferry, the *Gloria Estefan*.

"I hate all swabs," said Malvern, belching as his innards rebooted.

Fearon clutched his squirming belly. "We could have picked better weather. These ferocious Caribbean hurricane waves . . ."

"What 'waves'? We're still in the harbor."

"Oh, my Lord . . ."

After a pitching, greenish sea-trip, Cuba hove into view. The City of Havana, menaced by rising seas, had been relocated up the Cuban coast through a massive levy on socialist labor. The crazy effort had more or less succeeded,

---

* *lysis* (n.): cell destruction

though it looked as if every historic building in the city had been picked up and dropped.

Debarking in the fragrant faux-joy of the highly colored tropics, the eager duo hastened to the airfield—for only the cowboy Cubans still maintained direct air flights to the wrecked and smoldering shell of the Dark Continent.

Mi Amiga Flicka was a hydrogen-lightened cargo lifter of Appaloosa-patterned horsehide. The buoyant lift was generated by onboard horse stomachs, modified to spew hydrogen instead of the usual methane. A tanker truck, using a long boom-arm, pumped a potent microbial oatmeal into the tethered dirigible's feedstock reservoirs.

"There's a microbrewery on board," Malvern said with a travel agent's phony glee. "Works off grain mash just like a horse does! *Cerveza muy potenta,* you can bet."

A freestanding bamboo elevator ratcheted them up to the zeppelin's passenger module, which hung like a zippered saddlebag from the buoyant horsehide belly.

The bio-zep's* passenger cabin featured a zebra-hide mess hall that doubled as a ballroom, with a tiny bandstand and a touchingly antique mirror ball. The Cuban stewards, to spare weight and space, were all jockey sized.

Fearon and Malvern discovered that their web-booked "stateroom" was slightly smaller than a standard street toilet. Every feature of the tiny suite folded, collapsed, inverted, everted, or required assembly from scattered parts.

"I don't think I can get used to peeing in the same pipe that dispenses that legendary microbrew," said Fearon. Less finicky, Malvern had already tapped and sampled a glass of the golden boutique cerveza. "Life is a closed loop, Fearon."

"But where will the pig sleep?"

They found their way to the observation lounge for the departure of the giant gasbag. With practiced ease, the crew detached blimp-hook from mooring mast. The bacterial fuel cells kicked over the myosin motors, the props began to windmill and the craft surged eastward with all the verve and speed of a spavined nag.

Malvern was already deep into his third cerveza. "Once we get our hands on that wodge of extinct gene-chains, our names are forever golden! It'll be vino, gyno, and techno all the way!"

"Let's not count our chimeras till they're decanted, Mal. We're barely puttering along, and I keep thinking of Ribo Zombie and his highly publicized private entomopter."

"Ribo Zombie's a fat showbiz phony, he's all talk! We're heavy-duty street-level chicos from Miami! It's just no contest."

"Hmmph. We'd better vortal† in to Fusing Nuclei and check out the continuing coverage."

Fearon found a spot where the zep's horsehide was thinnest and tapped an

---

* *bio-zep* (n.): a pseudo-living, lighter-than-air zeppelin
† *vortal* (n., v.): a virtual portal

overhead satellite feed. The gel screen of his handheld flashed the familiar Fusing Nuclei logo.

"In his one-man supercavitating* sub, Ribo Zombie and Skratchy Kat speed toward the grim no-man's land of sub-Saharan Africa! What weird and wonderful adventures await our intrepid lone-wolf scab and his plucky familiar? Does carnal love lurk in some dusky native bosom? Log on Monday for the real-time landing of RZ and Skratchy upon the sludge-sloshing shores of African doom! And remember, kids! Skratchy Kat cards, toys, and collectibles are available only through Nintendo-Benz . . ."

"Did they say 'Monday'?" Malvern screeched. "Monday is tomorrow! We're already royally boned!"

"Malvern, please, the straights are staring at us. Ribo Zombie can't prospect all of Africa through all those old UN emplacements. Kingseed found us an expert native guide, remember? Dr. Herbie Zoster."

Malvern stifled his despair. "You really think this native scab has got the stuff?"

Fearon smiled. "Well, he's not a scab quite like us, but he's definitely our type! I checked out his online résumé! He's pumped, ripped, and buff, plus he's wily and street-smart. Herbie Zoster has been a mercenary, an explorer, an archaeologist, even the dictator of an offshore data haven. Once we hook up with him, this ought to be a waltz."

In the airborne hours that followed, Malvern sampled a foretaste of the vino, gyno, and techno, while Fearon repeatedly wrote and erased an apologetical e-mail to his wife. Then came their scheduled arrival over the melancholy ruins of Freetown—and a dismaying formal announcement by the ship's Captain.

"What do you mean, you can't moor?" demanded Malvern.

Their captain, a roguish and dapper yet intensely competent fellow named Luis Sendero, removed his cap and slicked back the two macaw feathers anchored at his temple. "The local caudillo, Prince Kissy Mental, has incited his people to burn down our trading facilities. One learns to expect these little setbacks in the African trade. Honoring our contracts, we shall parachute to earth the goods we bring, unless they are not paid for—in which case, they are dumped anyway, yet receive no parachute. As for you two Yankees and your two animals—you are the only passengers who want to land in Sierra Leone. If you wish to touch down, you must parachute just as the cargo."

After much blustering, whuffling, and whining, Fearon, Malvern, and Weeble stood at the open hatch of *Mi Amiga Flicka*, parachutes strapped insecurely on, ripcords wired to a rusty cable, while the exotic scents of the rainy African landscape wafted to their nostrils.

Wistfully, they watched their luggage recede to the scarred red earth. Then, with Spike clutched to his breast, Malvern closed his eyes and boldly tumbled overboard. Fearon watched closely as his colleague's fabric chute successfully

---

* *supercavitation* (n.): the process of underwater travel employing leading air pockets

bloomed. Only then did he make up his mind to go through with it. He booted the reluctant Weeble into airy space and followed suit.

• • •

"Outsiders never bring us anything but garbage," mumbled Dr. Zoster.

"Is it Cuban garbage?" said Malvern, tucking into their host's goat-and-pepper soup with a crude wooden spoon. "Because if it is, you're getting ripped off even in terms of trash."

"No. They're always Cubans bringing it, but it's everybody's garbage that is dumped on Africa. Africa's cargo-cult prayers have been answered with debris. But perhaps any sufficiently advanced garbage is indistinguishable from magic."

Fearon surreptitiously fed the peppery cabrito to his pig. He was having a hard time successfully relating to Dr. Herbie Zoster. It had never occurred to him that elderly Kemp Kingseed and tough, sunburned Herbie Zoster were such close kin.

In point of fact, Herbie Zoster was Kingseed's younger clone. And it didn't require Jungian analysis to see that, just like most clones, Zoster bitterly resented the egotistical man who had created him. This was very clearly the greatest appeal of life in Africa for Dr. Herbie Zoster. Africa was the one continent guaranteed to make him as much unlike Kemp Kingseed as possible.

Skin tinted dark as mahogany, callused and wiry, dotted with many thorn scratches, parasites, and gunshot wounds, Zoster still bore some resemblance to Kingseed—about as much as a battle-scarred hyena to an aging bloodhound.

"What exactly do people dump around here?" said Malvern with interest.

Zoster mournfully chewed the last remnant of a baked yam and spat the skin into the darkness outside their thatched hut. Something with great glowing eyes pounced upon it instantly, with a rasp and a snarl. "You're familiar with the Immunosance?"

"Oh yeah, sure!" said Malvern artlessly, "we're from Miami."

"That new Genetic Age completely replaced the Nuclear Age, the Space Age, and the Information Age."

"Good riddance," Malvern offered. "You got any more of that cabrito stew? It's fine stuff!"

Zoster rang a crude brass bell. A limping, turbaned manservant dragged himself into their thatched hut, tugging a bubbling bucket of chow.

"The difficulty with massive technological advance," said Zoster, spooning the steamy goop, "is that it obsolesces the previous means of production. When the Immunosance arrived, omnipresent industries already covered all the advanced countries." Zoster paused to pump vigorously at a spring-loaded homemade crank, which caused the light bulb overhead to brighten to its full thirty watts. "There simply was no room to install the new bioindustrial revolution. But a revolution was very necessary anyway. So all the previous junk had to go. The only major planetary area with massive dumping grounds was—and still is—Africa."

Zoster rubbed at his crank-stiffened forearm and sighed. "Sometimes they promote the garbage and sell it to us Africans. Sometimes they drop it anonymously. But nevertheless—no matter how we struggle or resist—the very worst always ends up here in Africa, no matter what."

"I'm with the sequence," said Malvern, pausing to belch. "So what's the four-one-one about this fabled Panspecific Mycoblastula?"

Zoster straightened, an expression of awe toughening his face below his canvas hat brim. "That is garbage of a very special kind. Because the Panspecific Mycoblastula is an entire, outmoded natural ecosystem. It is the last wild continent, completely wadded up and compressed by foreign technicians!"

Fearon considered this gnomic remark. He found it profoundly encouraging. "We understand the gravity of this matter, Dr. Zoster. Malvern and I feel that we can make this very worth your while. Time is of the essence. When can we start?"

Zoster scraped the dirt floor with his worn bootheel. "I'll have to hire a train of native bearers. I'll have to obtain supplies. We will be risking our lives, of course . . . What can you offer us in return for that?"

"A case of soft drinks?" said Malvern.

Fearon leaned forward intently. "Transistor radios? Antibiotics? How about some plumbing?"

Zoster smiled for the first time, with a flash of gold teeth. "Call me Herbie."

• • •

Zoster extended a callused fingertip. It bore a single ant, the size and color of a sesame seed.

"This is the largest organism in the world."

"So I heard," Malvern interjected glibly. "Just like the fire ants invading America, right? They went through a Darwinian bottleneck and came out supercharged sisters, genetically identical even under different queens. They spread across the whole USA smoother than marshmallow fluff."

Zoster wiped his sweating stubbled jaw with a filthy bandanna. "These ants were produced four decades ago. They carry rhizotropic fungi, to fertilize crops with nitrogen. But their breeders overdesigned them. These ants cause tremendous fertile growth in vegetation, but they're also immune to insect diseases and parasites. The swabs finally wiped them out in America, but Africa has no swabs. We have no public health services, no telephones, no roads. So from Timbuktu to Cape Town, cloned ants have spread in a massive wave, a single superorganism big as Africa."

Malvern shook his head in superior pity. "That's what you get for trusting in swabs, man. Any major dude could've told those corporate criminals that top-down hierarchies never work out. Now, the approach you Third Worlders need is a viral marketing, appropriate-technology pitch . . ."

Zoster actually seemed impressed by Malvern's foolish bravado, and engaged the foreign scab in earnest jargon-laced discussion, leaving Fearon to trudge along in an unspeaking fug of sweat-dripping, alien jungle heat. Though Zoster was the only one armed, the trio of scabs boldly led their little expedition through a tangle of feral trails, much aided by their satellite surveillance maps and GPS locators.

Five native bearers trailed the parade, fully laden-down with scab-baggage and provisions. The bare-chested, bare-legged, dhoti-clad locals exhibited various useful bodily mods, such as dorsal water storage humps, toughened and splayed feet, and dirty grub-excavating claws that could shred a stump in seconds. They also sported less rational cosmetic changes, including slowly moving cicatrices (really migratory subepidermal symbiotic worms) and enlarged ears augmented with elephant musculature. The rhythmic flapping of the porters' ears produced a gentle creaking that colorfully punctuated their impenetrable sibilant language.

The tormented landscape of Sierra Leone had been thoroughly reclaimed by a clapped-out mutant jungle. War, poverty, disease, starvation—the Four Land Rovers of the African Apocalypse—had long since been and gone, bringing a drastic human population crash that beggared the Black Death, and ceding the continent to resurgent flora and fauna.

These local flora and fauna were, however, radically human-altered, recovering from an across-the-board apocalypse even more severe and scourging than the grisly one suffered by humans. Having come through the grinding hopper of a bioterror, they were no longer "creatures" but "evolutures."* Trees writhed, leaves crawled, insects croaked, lizards bunny-hopped, mammals flew, flowers pinched, vines slithered, and mushrooms burrowed. The fish, clumsily reengineered for the surging Greenhouse realities of rising seas, lay in the jungle trails burping like lungfish. When stepped upon, they almost seemed to speak.

The explorers found themselves navigating a former highway to some long-buried city, presumably Bayau or Moyamba, to judge by the outdated websites. Post-natural oddities lay atop an armature of ruins, revealing the Ozymandias lessons of industrial hubris. A mound of translucent jello assumed the outlines of a car, including a dimly perceived skeletal driver and passengers. Oil-slick-colored orchids vomited from windows and doors. With the descending dusk invigorating flocks of winged post-urban rats, the travelers made camp. Zoster popped up a pair of tents for the expedition's leaders and their animals, while the locals assembled a humble jungle igloo of fronds and thorns.

After sharing a few freeze-dried packets of slumgullion, the expedition sank into weary sleep. Fearon was so bone-tired that he somehow tolerated Malvern's nasal whistling and Zoster's stifled dream shouts.

He awoke before the others. He unseamed the tent flap and poked his head out into the early sunshine.

Their encampment was surrounded by marauders. Spindly scouts, blank-eyed and scarcely human, were watching the pop-tents and leaning on pig-iron spears.

Fearon ducked his head back and roused his compatriots, who silently

---

* *evoluture* (n.): an artificially evolved creature

scrambled into their clothes. Heads clustered like coconuts, the three of them peered through a fingernail's width of tent flap.

Warrior-reinforcements now arrived in ancient Jeeps, carrying anti-aircraft guns and rocket-propelled grenades.

"It's Kissy Mental's Bush Army," whispered Zoster. He pawed hurriedly through a pack, coming up with a pair of mechanical boots.

"Okay, girls, listen up," Zoster whispered, shoving and clamping his feet in the piston-heavy footgear. "I have a plan. When I yank this overhead pull tab, this tent unpops. That should startle the scouts out there, maybe enough to cover our getaway. We all race off at top speed just the way we came. If either of you survive, feel free to rendezvous back at my place."

Zoster hefted his gun, their only weapon. He dug the toe of each boot into a switch on the heel of its mate, and his boots began to chuff and emit small puffs of exhaust.

"Gasoline-powered seven-league boots," Zoster explained, seeing their stricken expressions. "South African Army surplus. There's no need for roads with these things, but with skill and practice, you can pronk along like a gazelle at thirty, forty miles an hour."

"You really believe we can outrun these jungle marauders?" Malvern asked.

"I don't have to outrun them; I only have to outrun you."

Zoster triggered the tent and dashed off at once, firing his pistol at random. The pistons of his boots gave off great blasting backfires, which catapulted him away with vast stainless-steel lunges.

Stunned and in terror, Malvern and Fearon stumbled out of the crumpling tent, coughing on Zoster's exhaust. By the time they straightened up and regained their vision, they were firmly in the grip of Prince Kissy Mental's troops.

The savage warriors attacked the second pop-tent with their machetes. They quickly grappled and snaffled the struggling Spike and Weeble.

"Chill, Spike!"

"Weeble, hang loose!"

The animals obeyed, though the cruel grip of their captors promised the worst.

The minions of the prince were far too distanced from humanity to have any merely ethnic identity. Instead, they shared a certain fungal sheen, a somatype* evident in their thallophytic† pallor and exophthalmic‡ gaze. Several of the marauders, wounded by Zoster's wild shots, were calmly stuffing various grasses and leaves into the gaping, suety holes in their arms, legs, and chests.

A working squad now dismantled the igloo of the expedition's bearers, pausing to munch meditatively on the greenery of the cut fronds. The panic-stricken bearers gabbled in obvious terror but offered no resistance. A group of Kissy Mental's warriors, with enormous heads and great toothy jaws, decamped from

---

* *somatype* (n.): the visible expression of gattaca
† *thallophytic* (adj.): mushroomlike
‡ *exophthalmic* (adj.): pop-eyed

a rusty jeep. They unshouldered indestructible Russian automatic rifles and decisively emptied their clips into the hut. Pathetic screams came from the ruined igloo. The warriors then demolished the walls and hauled out the dead and wounded victims, to dispassionately tear them limb from limb.

The Army then assembled a new booty of meat, to bear it back up the trail to their camp. Reeking of sweat and formic acid, the inhuman natives bound the hands of Fearon and Malvern with tough lengths of grass. They strung Weeble and Spike to a shoulder pole, where the terrified beasts dangled like piñatas.

Then the ant men forced the quartet of prisoners forward on the quick march. As the party passed through the fetid jungle, the Army paused periodically to empty their automatic weapons at anything that moved. Whatever victim fell to earth would be swiftly chopped to chunks and added to the head-borne packages of the rampaging mass.

Within the hour, Fearon and Malvern were delivered whole to Prince Kissy Mental.

Deliberately, Fearon focused his attention on the prince's throne, so as to spare himself the sight of the monster within it. The Army's portable throne was a row of three first-class airplane seats, with the armrests removed to accommodate the prince's vast posthuman bulk. The throne perched atop a mobile palanquin, jury-rigged from rebar, chipboard, and AstroTurf. A system of crutches and tethers supported and eased the prince's vast, teratological skull.

The trophy captives were shoved forward at spearpoint through a knee-deep heap of cargo-cult gadgets.

"Holy smallpox!" whispered Malvern. "This boss man's half chimp and half ant!"

"That doesn't leave any percentage for human, Mal."

The thrust of a spear butt knocked Fearon to his knees. Kissy Mental's coarse-haired carcass, barrel-chested to support the swollen needs of the head, was sketched like a Roquefort cheese with massive blue veins. The prince's vast pulpy neck marked the transition zone to a formerly human skull whose sutures had long since burst under pressure, to be patched with big, red, shiny plates of antlike chitin. Kissy Mental's head was bigger than the prize-winning pumpkin at a 4-H* Fair.

Fearon slitted his eyes, rising to his feet. He was terrified, but the thought of never seeing Tupper again somehow put iron in his soul. To imagine that he might someday be home again, safe with his beloved—that prospect was worth any sacrifice. There had to be some method to bargain with their captor.

"Malvern, how bright do you think this guy is? You suppose he's got any English?"

"He's got to be at least as intelligent as British royalty."

With an effort that set his bloated heart booming like a tribal drum, the prince

---

* *4-H* (n.): an amateurs' club, primarily for children, that focuses on homeostasis (bodily maintenance through negative feedback circuits), haplotypes (gamete amounts of DNA), histogenesis (cell differentiation from general to specific), and hypertrophy (gigantism)

lifted both his hairy arms, and beckoned. Their captors pushed Mal and Fear right up against the throne. The prince unleashed a flock of personal fleas. Biting, lancing, and sucking, the tasters lavishly sampled the flesh of Fearon and Malvern and returned to their master. After quietly munching a few of the blood-gorged familiars, the prince silently brooded, the tiny bloodshot eyes in his enormous skull blinking like LEDs. He then gestured for a courtier to ascend into the presence. The bangled, headdressed ant man hopped up and, well-trained, sucked a thin clear excretion from the prince's rugose left nipple.

Smacking his lips, the lieutenant decrypted his proteinaceous commands, in a sudden frenzy of dancing, shouting, and ritual gesticulation.

Swiftly the Army rushed into swarming action, trampling one another in an ardent need to lift the prince's throne upon their shoulders. Once they had their entomological kingpin up and in lolling motion, the Army milled forward in a violent rolling surge, employing their machetes on anything in their path.

A quintet of burly footmen pushed Malvern and Fearon behind the bluish exhaust of an ancient military jeep. The flesh of the butchered bearers had been crudely wrapped in broad green leaves and dumped into the back of the vehicle.

Malvern muttered sullenly below the grumbles of the engine. "That scumbag Zoster . . . All clones are inherently degraded copies. Man, if we ever get out of this pinch, it's no more Mr. Nice Guy."

"Uh, sure, that's the old scab spirit, Mal."

"Hey, look!"

Fearon followed Malvern's jerking head-nod. A split-off subdivision of the trampling Army had dragged another commensal organism from the spooked depths of the mutant forest. It was a large, rust-eaten, canary yellow New Beetle, scribbled over with arcane pheromonal runes. Its engine long gone, the wreck rolled solely through the juggernaut heaving of the Army.

"Isn't that the 2015 New Beetle?" said Fearon. "The sport utility version, the one they ramped up big as a stretch Humvee?"

"Yeah, the Screw-the-Greenhouse Special! Looks like they removed the sun-roof and the moonroof, and taped all the windows shut! But what the hell can they have inside? Whatever it is, it's all mashed up and squirmy against the glass . . ."

A skinny Ant Army courtier vaulted and scrambled onto the top of the sealed vehicle. Gingerly, he stuffed a bloody wad of meat in through the missing moonroof.

From out of the adjacent gaping sunroof emerged a hydralike bouquet of heterogenous animal parts: tails, paws, snouts, beaks, ears. Snarls, farts, bellows, and chitterings ensued.

At length, a sudden flow of syrupy exudate drooled out the tailpipe, caught by an eager cluster of Ant Army workers cupping their empty helmets.

"They've got the Panspecific Mycoblastula in there!"

The soldiers drained every spatter of milky juice, jittering crazily and licking one another's lips and fingers.

"I do wish I had a camera," said Fearon wistfully. "It's very hard to watch a sight like this without one."

"Look, they're feeding our bearers into that thing!" marveled Malvern. "What do you suppose it's doing with all that human DNA? Must be kind of a partially human genetic mole rat thing going on in there."

Another expectant crowd hovered at the Beetle's tailpipe, their mold-spotted helmets at the ready. They had not long to wait, for a fleshy diet of protein from the butchered bearers seemed to suit the Panspecific Mycoblastula to a T.

Sweating and pale-faced, Malvern could only say, "If they were breakfast, when's lunch?"

· · ·

Fearon had never envisioned such brutal slogging, so much sheer physical work in the simple effort of eating and staying alive. The prince's Army marched well-nigh constantly, bulldozing the landscape in a whirl of guns and knives. Anything they themselves could not devour was fed to the Mycoblastula. Nature knew no waste, so the writhing abomination trapped in the Volkswagen was a panspecific glutton, an always-boiling somatic stewpot. It especially doted on high-end mammalian life, but detritus of all kinds was shoved through the sunroof to sate its needs: bark, leaves, twigs, grubs, and beetles. Especially beetles. In sheer number of species, most of everything living was always beetles.

Then came the turn of their familiars.

It seemed at first that those unique beasts had somehow earned the favor of Prince Kissy Mental. Placed onboard his rollicking throne, the trussed Spike and Weeble had been subjected to much rough cossetting and petting, their peculiar high-tech flesh seeming to particularly strike the prince's fancy.

But such good fortune could not last. After noon of their first day of captivity, the bored prince, without warning, snapped Spike's neck and flung the dead weasel in the path of the painted Volkswagen. Attendants snatched the weasel up and stuffed Spike in. The poor beast promptly lined an alimentary canal.

Witnessing this atrocity, Malvern roared and attempted to rush forward. A thorough walloping with boots and spear butts persuaded him otherwise.

Then Weeble was booted meanly off the dais. Two hungry warriors scrambled to load the porker upside down onto a shoulder-carried spear. Weeble's piteous grunts lanced through Fearon, but at least he could console himself that, unlike Spike, his pig still lived.

But finally, footsore, hungry, and beset by migraines, his immune system drained by constant microbial assault, Fearon admitted despair. It was dead obvious that he and Malvern were simply doomed. There was just no real question that they were going to be killed and hideously devoured, all through their naive desire for mere fame, money, and professional technical advancement.

When they were finally allowed to collapse for the night on the edge of a marshy savannah, Fearon sought to clear his conscience.

"Mal, I know it's over, but think of all the good times we've had together. At least I never sold Florida real estate, like my dad. A short life and a merry one, right? Die young and leave a beautiful corpse. Hope I die before I get—"

"Fearon, I'm fed up with your sunny-sided optimism! You rich-kid idiot, you always had it easy and got all the breaks! You think that rebellion is some kind of game! Well, let me tell you, if I had just one chance to live through this, I'd never waste another minute on nutty dilettante crap. I'd go right for the top of the food chain. Let me be the guy on top of life, let me be the winner, just for once!" Malvern's battered face was livid. "From this day forth, if I have to lie, or cheat, or steal, or kill . . . aw, what's the use? We're ant meat! I'll never even get the chance!"

Fearon was stunned into silence. There seemed nothing left to say. He lapsed into a sweaty doze amid a singing mosquito swarm, consoling himself with a few last visions of his beloved Tupper. Maybe she'd remarry after learning of his death. Instead of following her sweet romantic heart, this time she'd wisely marry some straight guy, someone normal and dependable. Someone who would cherish her, and look after her, and take her rather large inheritance with the seriousness it deserved. How bitterly he regretted his every past unkindness, his every act of self-indulgence and neglect. The spouses of romantic rebels really had it rough.

In the morning, the hungry natives advanced on Weeble, and now it was Fearon's turn to shout, jump up, and be clouted down.

With practiced moves the natives slashed off Weeble's front limbs near the shoulder joints. The unfortunate Weeble protested in a frenzy of squealing, but his assailants knew all too well what they were doing. Once done, they carefully cauterized the porker's foreparts and placed him in a padded stretcher, which was still marked with an ancient logo from the Red Cross.

They then gleefully roasted the pig's severed limbs, producing an enticing aroma Fearon and Malvern fought to abhor. The crisped breakfast ham was delivered with all due ceremony to Prince Kissy Mental, whose delight in this repast was truly devilish to watch. Clearly the Ant Army didn't get pig very often, least of all a pig with large transgenic patches of human flesh. A pig that good you just couldn't eat all at once.

By evening, Fearon and Malvern were next on the menu. The two scabs were hustled front and center as the locals fed a roaring bonfire. A crooked pair of nasty wooden spits were prepared. Then Fearon and Malvern had their bonds cut through, and their clothes stripped off by a forest of groping hands.

The two captives were gripped and hustled and frog-marched as the happy Army commenced a manic dance around their sacred Volkswagen, ululating and keening in a thudding of drums. The evil vehicle oscillated from motion within, in time with the posthuman singing. Lit by the setting sun and the licking flames of the cannibal bonfire, big chimeric chunks of roiling Panspecific Mycoblastula tissue throbbed and slobbered against the glass.

Suddenly a brilliant klieg light framed the scene, with an 80-decibel airborne rendition of "Ride of the Valkyries."

"Hit the dirt!" yelped Malvern, yanking free from his captor's grip and casting himself on his face.

Ribo Zombie's entomopter swept low in a strafing run. The cursed

Volkswagen exploded in a titanic gout of lymph, blood, bone fragments, and venom, splattering Fearon but not Malvern from head to toe with quintessence of Mycoblastula.

Natives dropped and spun under the chattering impact of advanced armaments. Drenched with spew, Fearon crawled away from the Volkswagen, wiping slime from his face.

Dead or dying natives lay in crazy windrows, like genetically modified corn after a stiff British protest. Now Ribo Zombie made a second run, his theatrical lighting deftly picking out victims. His stagey attack centered, naturally, on the most dramatic element among the panicking Army, Prince Kissy Mental himself. The prince struggled to flee the crimson targeting lasers, but his enormous head was strapped to his throne in a host of attachments. Swift and computer-sure came the next burst of gunfire. Prince Kissy Mental's abandoned head swung futilely from its tethers, a watermelon in a net.

Leaping and capering in grief and anguish, the demoralized Army scattered into the woods.

A swarm of mobile cameras wasped around the scene, carefully checking for proper angles and lighting. Right on cue, descending majestically from the darkening tropic sky came Ribo Zombie himself, crash-helmet burnished and gleaming, combat boots blazoned with logos.

Skratchy Kat leaped from Zombie's shoulder to strike a proud pose by the prince's still-smoking corpse. The superstar scab blew nonexistent trailing smoke from the unused barrels of his pearl-handled sidearms, then advanced on the cowering Fearon and Malvern.

"Nice try, punks, but you got in way over your head." Ribo Zombie gestured at a hovering camera. "You've been really great footage ever since your capture, though. Now get the hell out of camera range, and go find some clothes or something. That Panspecific Mycoblastula is all mine."

Rising from his hands and knees with a look of insensate rage, Malvern lunged up and dashed madly into the underbrush.

"What's keeping you?" boomed Ribo Zombie at Fearon.

Fearon looked down at his hands. Miniature parrot feathers were sprouting from his knuckles.

"Interesting outbreak of spontaneous mutation," Ribo Zombie noted. "I'll check that out just as soon as I get my trophy shot."

Advancing on the bullet-riddled Volkswagen, Ribo Zombie telescoped a razor-pincered probe. As the triumphant conqueror dipped his instrument into the quivering mass, Malvern charged him with a leveled spear.

The crude weapon could not penetrate Ribo Zombie's armor, but the force of the rush bounced the superstar scab against the side of the car. Quick as lightning a bloodied briar snaked through a gaping bullet hole and clamped the super-scab tight.

Then even more viscous and untoward tentacles emerged from the engine compartment, and a voracious sucking, gurgling struggle commenced.

Malvern, still naked, appropriated the fallen crash helmet with the help of a spear haft. "Look, it liquefied him instantly and sucked all the soup clean out! Dry as a bone inside. And the readouts still work on the eyepieces!"

After donning the helmet, a suspiciously close fit, Malvern warily retrieved Ribo Zombie's armored suit, which lay in its high-tech abandonment like the nacreous shell of a hermit crab. A puzzled Skratchy Kat crept forward. After a despondent sniff at the emptied boots, the bereaved familiar let out a continuous yowl.

"Knock it off, Skratchy," Malvern commanded. "We're all hurting here. Just be a man."

Swiftly shifting allegiances, Skratchy Kat supinely rubbed against Malvern's glistening shins.

"Now to confiscate his cameras for a little judicious editing of his unfortunate demise." Malvern shook his helmeted head. "You can cover for me, right, Fearon? Just tell everybody that Malvern Brakhage died in the jungle. You should probably leave out the part about them wanting to eat us."

Fearon struggled to dress himself with some khaki integuments from a nearby casualty. "Malvern, I can't fit inside these clothes."

"What's your problem?"

"I'm growing a tail. And my claws don't fit in these boots." Fearon pounded the side of his head with his feathery knuckles. "Are you glowing, or do I have night vision all of a sudden?"

Malvern tapped his helmet with a wiry glove. "You're not telling me you're massively infected now, are you?"

"Well, technically speaking, Malvern, I'm the 'infection' in this situation, because the Mycoblastula's share of our joint DNA is a lot more extensive than mine is."

"Huh. Well, that development obviously tears it." Malvern backed off cautiously, tugging at this last few zips and buckles on his stolen armor to assure an airtight seal. "I'll route you some advanced biomedical help—if there's any available in the local airspace." He cleared his throat with a sudden rasp of helmet-mounted speakers. "In any case, the sooner I clear out of here for civilization, the better."

All too soon, the sound of the departing entomopter had died away. After searching through the carnage, pausing periodically as his spine and knees unhinged, Fearon located the still-breathing body of his beloved pig. Then he dragged the stretcher to an abandoned Jeep.

• • •

"And then Daddy smelled the pollution from civilization with his new nose, from miles away, so he knew he'd reached the island of Fernando Po, where the UN still keeps bases. So despite the tragic death of his best friend Malvern, Daddy knew that everything was going to be all right. Life would go on!"

Fearon was narrating his exploit to the embryo in Tupper's womb via a state-of-the-art fetal interface, the GestaPhone. Seated on the comfy Laura Ashley couch in their bright new stilt house behind the dikes of Pensacola Beach, Tupper smiled indulgently at her husband's oft-polished tale.

"When the nice people on the island saw Daddy's credit cards, Daddy and Weeble were both quickly stabilized. Not exactly like we were before, mind you, but rendered healthy enough for the long trip back home to Miami. Then the press coverage started, and, well son, someday I'll tell you about how Daddy dealt with the challenges of fame and fortune."

"And wasn't Mommy glad to see Daddy again!" Tupper chimed in. "A little upset at first about the claws and fur. But luckily, Daddy and Mommy had been careful to set aside sperm samples while Daddy was still playing his scab games. So their story had a real happy ending when Daddy finally settled down and Baby Boy was safely engineered."

Fearon detached the suction cup terminal from Tupper's bare protuberant stomach. "Weeble, would you take these, please?"

The companionable pig reached up deftly, plucked the GestaPhones out of Fearon's grasp, and moved off with an awkward lope. Weeble's strange gait was due to his new forelimbs, a nifty pair of pig-proportioned human arms.

Tupper covered her womb with her frilled maternity blouse and glanced at the clock. "Isn't your favorite show on now?"

"Shucks, we don't have to watch every single episode . . ."

"Oh, honey, I love this show, it's my favorite, now that I don't have to worry about you getting all caught up in it!"

They nestled on the responsive couch, Tupper stroking the fish-scaled patch on Fearon's cheek while receiving the absent-minded caresses of his long tiger-ish tail. She activated the big wet screen, cohering a close-up of Ribo Zombie in the height of a ferocious rant.

"Keeping it real, folks, still keeping it real! I make this challenge to all my fellow scabs, those who are down with the Zombie and those who dis him, those who frown on him and those who kiss him. Yes, you sorry posers all know who you are. But check this out . . . Who am I?"

Fearon sighed for a world well lost. And yet, after all . . . there was always the next generation.

JACQUES BARCIA

SALVAGING GODS

(2010)

GORETTE FOUND HER SECOND godhead buried under piles of plastic bottles, holy symbols, used toilet paper, and the severed face of an avatar. No matter how much the scavengers asked, the people from Theodora just wouldn't separate organic from nonbiodegradable from divine garbage. They threw out their used-up gods along with what was left of their meals, their burnt lamps, broken refrigerators, tires, stillborn babies, and books of prayer in the trash can. And when the convoys carrying society's leftovers passed through the town's gates, some lazy bureaucrat would mark in a spreadsheet that another mountain was raised in that municipal sanitary landfill, the Valley of the Nephilim. And to hell with the consequences.

Her father says no dead god is dead enough that it can't be remade in our own image. The old man can spend hours rambling about overconsumption, the gnostic crisis, the impact of all those mystical residues poisoning the soil and the underground streams, how children are born malformed and prone to mediunity, and how unfair it is that only the rich have access to miracles. People will do what's more comfortable, not what's best for everyone, he'd finally say. It's far easier to buy new deities than try to reuse them. So he taught her how to recycle old gods and turn them into new ones, mostly, she believed, because he wanted to make a difference. Or maybe because he was the one true atheist left in the world.

It was a small one, that godhead, and not in a very good shape. Pale silver, dusty, scratched surface, and glowing only slightly underneath the junk. At best, thought Gorette, it'd have only a few hundred lines of code she'd be able to salvage. Combined with some fine statues and pieces of altars she'd found early that morning, perhaps she'd be able to assemble one or two more deities to the community's public temple at Saint Martin. The neighborhood she was raised in had only recently been urbanized, so that meant the place was not officially a slum anymore. But still, miracles were quite a phenomenon down in the suburbs.

"Hey, Daddy. Found another one," Gorette said, covering her eyes from the burning light of midday. "Can we go home now, please?"

The egg-shaped thing had the pulse of a dying heart, and fitted almost perfectly in her adolescent hand. So she arranged a place for it among the relics in her backpack, inside the folds of a ragged piece of loincloth, and into a beaten up thurible where it'd be safe enough to survive the hour-long ride back to the city.

Her father stood next to a marble totem, sweeping the field with a Kirlian detector. The pillar was part of a discarded surround-sound system with speakers the size of his chest, and served as a landmark to the many scavengers exploring the waste dump. When he heard his daughter calling him, he took his gas mask off and said, "That depends," his low-toned voice coming like a sigh, tired. "Do you think this will do? We're running out of code and there are many open projects in the lab."

A plastic bag some ten yards away from her smelled of rotting flesh. Animal sacrifice, she knew, and the vultures seemed to have noticed that too. "Yeah," she lied, "It's a bit wasted, but I think it has a lot of good code in it. Never seen one of these, so I suppose it's a quite new model." She desperately needed to take that stink out of her body and today she hoped was water day. "Is it water day today, Daddy?"

The old man picked up one last relic, a fang or something, and examined it close to his thick glasses. He nodded to the object and put it in a sack he carried tied to his waist. "No, it's not. The Palace said three days ago that they'd reinforce the water gods cluster, so the suburb's rationing would drop to two days. But of course that didn't happen." He finally walked to Gorette and scratched her dreadlocks, trying to smile. "Maybe you can build a water god with the godhead you found, huh?"

• • •

Gorette made her first wish that evening, after incubating some of the new godhead's code in an altar of her own design. It was built out of the remains of a semi-defaced idol, a one-eyed marble bust wearing a tall orange hat, adorned with shattered crystals, split dragon horns, praying cords, and barbed wire. That last bit just to make sure everything would stand in place. The godhead rested inside the same thurible Gorette used to cradle it safely back from the Valley of the Nephilim. But now the metal egg had dozens of acupuncture needles trespassing its shell, and every single one was linked to hair-thin optical fiber threads, shining with divine code, feeding with data a green phosphorus monitor.

Without warning. It just woke up.

When the loading bar hit 100 percent, the stone bust opened its one eye, fluidly, staring directly at her. She fell back from the chair, startled, and stared back at the thing's physiognomy from where she stood. From the floor up.

It was her first attempt at a new design model, one that toyed with disharmony instead of symmetry. Profanity instead of divinity. Good hardware, her dad says, is as important as good code. But harmony. Harmony is the key. The problem is that new gods are coming with even more complex, specialized godheads, their kernels incompatible with older or malfunctioning holy paraphernalia. She decided to try out the new approach and, to her surprise, it worked.

"I want a fucking bath," Gorette said, pointing a finger to the bust. "A *warm* bath. Now."

The stone in the god's crippled face moved like it was made out of clay. Smooth. No, it moved like that stop-motion movie, what's its name, the one that always airs on holidays and Friday evenings. The one Dad just loves to watch when he's back from the Valley.

"As you wish," it said coldly.

A sound of streaming water echoed from the bathroom and almost instantly the smell of steam and soap and essential oils filled up the room. She grinned, and jumping over her feet ran toward the shower, undressing on her way. Is it lavender? Maybe birch. Arnica in the white cloud. She felt she was clean even before she could reach the shower, she felt the dirt collapsing, decanting on the floor before she could have a chance to lie in the tub and rest.

A bathtub. "A bathtub?"

She looked back at the one-eyed god running miracles in her room. "You made me a bathtub." The idol remained still. She stood there for a few more seconds trying to figure out how her jury-rigged water god made her a complete bath, with a bathtub, aromatic oils, and, now she saw it, the finest bathing gown. Collateral miracles were not unheard of, but modern godheads had filters to prevent the danger of leaking energy. Motionless, the god just kept staring forward, to nowhere in particular, its exposed wire guts transmitting magical pulses to the screen, blipping a green dot like the apparels in private hospitals, monitoring a wide-eyed comatose half head, an undead, glitchy deity. Gorette felt like checking her complementary coding, but confessed to herself the hot pool of perfumed water was too tempting to be ignored. After all, feeling clean and relaxed she'd have more chances of debugging her creation.

That's it. She immersed herself in the tub and let all her worries trail off, evaporate.

· · ·

After the bathtub miracle, the god produced a new set of porcelain plates, when Gorette only commanded it to clean the dishes. Days later she asked for ice and got a refrigerator and a minibar. Then the thought of a nice meal generated spiced fish. And, one night, the sound of a calm, streaming river came as a lullaby. And rain cooled a hot day. And a smile painted watercolor on canvas. On and on, over the course of a week, her tiniest, involuntary wishes were fulfilled and as much as she tried, she couldn't find the bug in the god's code tree. Okay, after the tenth attempt, the effort to fix the problem wasn't that strong-willed. But Dad had taught her a bug could untap the power of a god, mollifying reality in its closer vicinity, causing the neighborhood's divine networks to go haywire. It was dangerous, she knew.

She spent days and nights trying to fix it, trying to combine source codes distilled from newer godheads, but nothing seemed to work. She decided she'd destroy the thing before it'd cause her trouble.

A dead boy changed her mind.

It was Monday morning and Gorette swept the water god off her working bench into a big cardboard box lying on the floor. She just discarded it, trying not to think much about getting rid of her first creation. The thing fell inside the box, a stone punch enveloped in barbed wire. Gorette gave the god a last inspection and could see that the cold half face was looking upward from its new room. She met its gaze one last time and closed the box, decided to sell its parts in the market for whatever the merchants gave for it.

The girl picked up the box and went downstairs, hardly able to keep balance with the thing's weight pushing her back and down. So heavy and so slowly she spent thirty minutes walking down the stairs, flight upon flight on a downward spiral to the first floor. She finally reached a smooth carpet under her feet and felt her strength renewed when she captured the smell of cinnamon tea being brewed in the kitchen. There was music playing and the house was calm and empty. Patchouli.

She walked to the door, the box in front of her, light in her arms and spirit. An awesome Sunday waited for her outside the house.

On her way out, she tripped over a gas mask resting facedown on the floor, but managed to jump on one foot and keep herself from falling. She kicked the mask off from her, startling the white tiger sleeping under the crystal table. Immediately, the giant cat clawed the mask with its tiger-y reflexes, making it spin and fall over its face, covering all of its beastly features but the lower jaw and its protruding fangs. A gas-masked albino tiger. Nothing can be cooler than that. Maybe a gas-masked cephalopod. No. Albino tiger is definitely cooler.

Outside, the day was perfect. The sun shone bright and there was the bluest cloudless sky sheltering Saint Martin. The street was busy, the market was everywhere. Fresh bread, roses, dew. Birds, carts, and horses on the march. The signal was red, so she stood close to a bald man reading the newspaper, waiting in line for his turn with the public god service. She overheard someone, the first in the row, complain with the totem, why in fuck's name you can't cure eczema? It's a damn fungus, damn it. Your credits have expired, answered a featureless voice. She felt sorry for the man, but couldn't help but giggle. Next time, try boiling the river's water. That fetid thing the Palace calls a river.

She turned in time to see the man walking away from the totem, down the street, right in her direction. His right cheek and part of his upper lip and nose was covered in a pink, moist blotch, a blistered wound shaped as a face, a somewhat familiar face that now she could see, as he approached, went down to his neck and into his shirt. She swallowed her giggle and wished the man could find a cure.

"As you wish."

"What?"

Slo-mo time warp, the air thick as a jar of glycerin. The man walked past her like the actors playing living statues in Gaiman Square. As he moved, she could see all the tiny blisters, the face wound staring back at her. And as if someone had hit the rewind button, the eczema started to erode. Skin took back its space, first in the borders and then in spots inside the pink perimeter, holes forming eyes and a space like a mask, or mouth that seemed to say, "Oh," and then scream, wider and wider, until it completely disappeared, leaving nothing but an afterimage, a memory, a sensation.

"Did you see that?" Gorette turned to face the man next to her, a young guy wearing a ponytail, reading the newspaper. Like waking up from a deep dream, she looked down to the box in her arms and immediately dropped it to the ground. Her nails tore the cardboard walls and there it was, the god, face up, the way she put it back in her room.

The god in the box looked like it was engaged in silent battle with her. Face to face.

People walked past them on the sidewalk, the noises and colors and smells of Saint Martin coming back to her in a single torrent. Too many steps and the scent of flowers and wax, hooves clicking, and chantings, all around the street. A procession.

She turned once again, feeling dizzy, and saw the ocean of people and candles and garlands and, in the middle of the street, a huge bier with a coffin and a little altar, an undertaker god surely preparing the body, the grave, and the costs for the burial. Around the altar, there were pictures of a kid, younger than her. The face of the corpse inside the coffin.

"A kid," the words came out without her noticing.

She closed her mouth and locked it with both hands, closing her eyes not to think, not to think, not to think.

"As you wish," and again, several yards away from her, like an echo, above the crowd, "as you wish."

Five seconds passed before the bier's conductor jumped from his seat, let go of the reins and climbed on the coffin. People noticed the man's hurry and soon there was a commotion around the vehicle. People cried "help him out!" and "open the coffin!" and "my kid! He's alive!" And now she could hear a stifled sound, a desperate knock-knock on wood coming from the depths of the underworld. There were relatives pushing the coffin's lid, but damn those nails, the joiner that worked across the street rushed with a crowbar and soon was forcing the wood cover. Gorette's heart was pounding, someone please open that coffin. *Asyouwishasyouwishasyouwish.*

Suddenly, the nails were fired off to the air, like a machine gun trying to shoot down the heavens. The whole wood box went down to splinters in a moment. The crowd went mad when the boy rose and took the cotton balls out of his nose.

"It was her!" Gorette heard someone cry behind her. "I saw it. She commanded the god to resurrect the boy."

"No, I didn't," she heard herself speaking as if the words came from someone else.

"Yes, you did," said a very low, calm, cold voice.

"No."

Soon the crowd was all over her, praising her good deeds—*as you wish*—calling her a saint—*as you wish*—asking her for favors—*as you wish*—raising her and her god above them, a new procession for the miracle of life, for the savior, *ad majorem femina gloriam*, for the Popess.

"As you wish," she said, grinning.

• • •

Emissaries.

From other neighborhoods, from the Palace, from other cities.

They came in tides, high and low, high and low. They threatened and cajoled, but eventually ended up asking for something they needed to be done, some disease to be cured, another to be implanted, a hand to help their business, some virility, beauty, you name it.

One out of five diplomats demanded to know how she assembled her god. How the hell that thing could—

The truth was she didn't know. She wished she did. And that seemed to be one of the few wishes her creature wasn't able, or willing, to fulfill.

However, most penitents came asking for knowledge, for wisdom, for guidance. That, too, was out of her reach, out of her experience. But certainly not out of her god's verbosity.

That marvel now standing on a totem in front of her throne, a foot lower than her, encased in crystal, half-faced and barbed-wired. For those who entered the temple and met her gaze, her features dominated the god placed only an inch below. But even if her eyes held a deep jade glare, it was the silver beacon of the godhead that really shone brighter. Like the moon.

"Speak," she said.

"Most honorable Popess," began a merchant in a golden tunic, shutting down his smartphone, "what's the nature of true miracles?" The question raised a wave of murmurs in the hall. He was the fifth or sixth person consulting her that morning. "What are they made of? What makes your god able to perform such wonders, surpassing the capabilities of every other functional god in the realm?"

"I—" began Gorette, the Popess, but that cold voice interrupted her speech. That behavior had become quite common in the public sessions lately and the people were beginning to question the Popess's authority over the god.

"I can calculate reality at far-superior floppage," the god said. "My miracles per second rate is also higher than your average god. Also, my database—"

"It's my will," cut the Popess.

"No, it's not," replied the stone statue.

"Silence."

"As you wish."

The Popess dismissed the merchant with a wave of her hand. The man bowed slightly, obviously upset for not being answered. He turned and mixed himself with the rest of the crowd, other merchants, other tunics, men in coats and gas masks. "The session is over," she said.

"Popess?" Already at the center of the court. Dirty overcoat and gas mask. She could smell filth in the wind, rotten oranges and oil. The man had a tiger, white as snow, chained to his wrist and it, too, wore a mask, and had a big box mounted on his back, covered by a red velvet coat. "Can I speak?"

The Popess was halfway through leaving the throne, but stopped and turned back to her seat. A green dazzle came from her eyes asking, who's this man, do I know him? "What do you want from me?"

The man gave two steps ahead, dragging the chain, making the gas-masked albino tiger move and then lay. Nice and easy. "Actually," he said, his voice covered by the mask, "I'd like to address your god."

"It?"

"Me?"

"Yes, your Holiness. I want to question your creature," said the stranger.

She was curious. She straightened herself in the throne, crossed her legs under the long robe and smiled, as if expecting entertainment, a show. "Okay. Go on. Let's see what you're gonna get from it."

"In truth, there's only one thing I'd like to ask it." He moved forward and immediately the tiger rose and followed, both closer to the totem. The people gathered around the hall seemed to get closer, curious about what this masked stranger and his beast were up to. "I want you to tell me—what's the nature of God?"

"The nature of gods?"

"No. God." So close now. His breath clouded the crystal case. "Gods are manifestations, constructs. They're functions, myths, narratives. They're tools. Limited, discardable, yet very spectacular tools. I want to know what's the nature of God," the man said.

A second passed before its marble lips moved. You could hear the silver sphere, the mighty godhead whirring, its core processing billions of code looking for an answer. Suddenly, the noise stopped. "God is unique. God wishes," it said. "I am unique. I wish."

Marble soldiers, flaming tigers, hydras, and giant spiders materialized in the hall, as if coming onstage after opening reality's invisible curtain. Panic took over the crowd in the room, a whirlwind of faces and tunics running, dissolving, and exploding in gushes of blood and rot and desecration.

The Popess sank in her throne, reduced to her youth, her green eyes crystallized with fear.

The man under the mask refused to run and instead yelled at the crystal case. "Even a god found in a sanitary landfill, assembled from pieces of junk and designed by a very young, immature girl who didn't even know what she wished for in her life?"

"Even so."

"You're not unique." The stranger reached for the velvet cape over the tiger and pulled it from over the box. There was a crystal case with a marble god inside. A reused god. Design almost identical to that of the Popess's own creation: a silver moon of a godhead pierced by tiny acupuncture needles, linked to a pedestal by fiber optic cables, tied with barbed wire and praying cords and a hat balanced atop a half-faced, one-eyed, mouthless piece of avatar at its center. "Do you recognize it? I found it some ten meters away from you."

The older god whirred. The soldiers and monsters charged toward the man and his own technomagical beast. He stood right where he was, but quickly typed shortcut commands to the god and the giant cat. When the creatures were close enough, the tiger attacked with a mighty leap, his claws hacking the monsters' fire hides and carapaces.

But the man kept staring down at the god while the white feline defended their position. More creatures continued to condense into existence out of thin air. The tiger still managed to kill them, keeping the perimeter safe.

"I will destroy her," the god said. "If I can give life, I can take it."

"No, you won't. And you can't." The Popess stood next to the god's crystal case, staring at its single, immovable eye. "Dad once told me about the nature of God." She got close, really close, to the crystal case, as if trying to whisper into the god's ear through the transparent wall. "He told me God is flawless."

The white tiger, now blood-red, circled the totem, pushing the soldiers back. Fast and precise as tigers are, he clawed the box, shattered the crystal to tiny bits, sent the stone face away to the floor along with its miraculous monsters. The thing fell hard, barbed wires, praying cords, tokens, and fiber-optic cables disassembling the holy design with the shock.

Gorette strode across the room at the destroyed god's direction. It rested on the floor, close to the corpses of humans and miracles. She could see it tried to speak, its lips moving in a very familiar way. She decided not to give a damn about what the thing had to say. She picked up the silver godhead and looked deep into the god's eye close to her feet. "God is flawless. But nothing, you hear me? Nothing is without flaw," she said. "Now, shut down."

"As you wish."

• • •

At the Valley of the Nephilim, the god wishes it had arms. He wished he was a *he*, not an *it*, not a carcass in the filth, beneath the remains, in the mud. Die, worm, die. You chew my wires off, you reincarnate as a, as a, as a *human*. That. A human. A human.

A human.

A blip and another. Above ground. Steps coming closer. Another blip and an intense, acute sound. Like a blip, but never ending. Like a whistle.

"Guess there's one here."

Yes, there is. There's one here.

Some light, then light and too much light.

"Here you are."

A human.

"Yeah, it looks just like that other one."

What? Not like any other. I'm the others. The others are me.

"Not sure. Will destroy it anyway."

No.

"Come here."

Pressure.

"Boy, you're hard. Wish I had a hammer with me."

As you—

"Oh, here it is," said the girl. "This is what I call a *force quit*. Goodbye, little one. Send my regards."

Beat. Crash.

Silence.

PAUL GRAHAM RAVEN

LOS PIRATAS DEL MAR DE PLASTICO

(2014)

HOPE DAWSON STEPPED DOWN from the train into the bone-dry heat of afternoon in southern Spain, and wondered—not for the first time, and probably not for the last—what the hell she was doing there, and how long she'd end up staying.

The freelance lifestyle did that to you; seven years crawling to and fro across Europe as a hand-to-mouth journo-sans-portfolio had left Hope with few ties to her native Britain beyond her unpaid student loans, and she'd yet to settle anywhere else for long. She'd spent the last six months or so bumping around in the Balkans on a fixed-term stringer's contract from some Californian news site she'd never read (and never intended to), scraping up extra work on the side wherever she could: website translation gigs, trade-zine puff pieces, and the inevitable tech-art exhibition reviews; she could barely remember the last time she put her own name in a byline, or wanted to. The Californian site had folded itself up a few days before the contract ended, and after a few agreeable weeks house-sitting an alcoholic Tiranese lawyer's apartment, burning through the small pile of backhanded cash and favors she'd amassed, and poking at her perpetually unfinished novel, she felt the need to move on once more. Albania was cheap, but it was a backwater, and backwaters rarely coughed up stories anyone would pay for; her loans weren't going to repay themselves, after all, and the UK government had developed an alarming habit of forcibly repatriating those who attempted to disappear into the boondocks and default on their debts.

The world dropped the answer in her lap while she wasn't looking. As winter gave way to spring, Tirana's population of favela geeks—a motley tribe of over-educated and underemployed Gen-Y Eurotrash from the rust belts, dust belts, and failed technopoles of Europe—began to thin out. Hope's contacts dropped hints about southern Spain, casual labor, something to do with the agricultural sector down there. That, plus a surge of ambiguous white-knuckle op-eds in the financial press about the long-moribund Spanish economy, was enough for Hope to go on. She'd finished up a few hanging deadlines, called in a favor she'd been saving up, and traded a lengthy, anonymous, and staggeringly unobjective editorial about Albanian railway tourism in exchange for a one-way train ticket to Almeria, first class.

Hope squinted along the length of the platform, a-shimmer with afternoon heat-haze beneath a cloudless azure sky, to where a dozen or so geeks were piling themselves and their luggage out of the budget carriages at the very back of the train. They were loaded down with faded military surplus duffels and mountain-eering backpacks, battered flight cases bearing cryptic stencils, and rigid luggage that looked uncharacteristically new and expensive by comparison to their cloth-ing which, true to their demography, looked like a random grab-bag of the ugliest and most momentary styles of the late-twentieth century. Only a decade ago, while Hope had been wrapping up her undergrad work and hustling for her PhD scholarship back in Britain, one might have assumed they were here to attend a peripatetic music festival, maybe, or a convention for some obscure software framework. But that was before the price of oil had gone nuts and anni-hilated the cheap airline sector almost overnight. Even within Europe, long distance travel was either slow and uncomfortable or hideously expensive. Unemployed Millennials—of which there were many—tended not to move around without a damned good incentive.

Milling around on the platform like a metaphor for Brownian motion, the geeks were noisy, boisterous, and a few years younger than Hope, and she worked hard to squash a momentary feeling of superiority, to bring her field researcher's reflexivity back online. *Tat tvam asi*, she reminded herself; *that thou art*. Or *there but for the grace of God*, perhaps. The main difference between Hope and them, she decided, was a certain dogged luck. She looked briefly at her reflection in the train window and saw a short girl with tired-looking eyes wearing an executive's dark trouser-suit in the London style of three winters previous, her unruly mass of curly blonde hair already frizzing into a nimbus of static in response to the heat. Who was she trying to fool, she wondered, for the umpteenth time. The geeks looked ludicrous, flowing off the platform and into the station like some lumpy superfluid, but they also looked comfortable, carefree. It'd been a long time since Hope felt either of those things.

Leaving the station, Hope donned her spex, set them to polarize, and blinked about in the local listings. She soon secured herself a few cheap nights in an apartment on the sixth floor of an undermaintained block about half a klick from the center of town. Almeria reminded Hope more than a little bit of the ghost towns of southern Greece, where she'd gone to chase rumors of a resurgence in piracy in the Eastern Med a few years back: noughties boom-time tourist infrastructure peeling and crumbling in the sun, like traps left lying in a lobsterless sea. Leaning on the rust-spotted railing of her balcony, she looked westward, where the legendary Plastic Ocean stretched out to the horizon, mile after square mile of solarized bioplastic sheeting shimmering beneath the relentless white light of the sun. The greenhouses were all Almeria had left since the tourists stopped coming, churning out a relentless assortment of hothouse fruit 'n' veg for global export, but they'd been predominantly staffed by semilegal immigrant workers from across the Med for years. She couldn't see much chance of the geeks undercutting that sort of workforce.

Later that evening, Hope was prepared to use her clueless middle-management airhead routine on the tapas bar's waiter but didn't need to: he had plenty to say, albeit in a Basque-tinged dialect that tested her rusty Spanish to the utmost.

"You're with those guys who bought the Hotel Catedral, yes?" he asked her.

"Oh, no," she replied. The waiter relaxed visibly as she spooled out her cover: purchasing rep for a boutique market stall in Covent Garden, sent out to do some on-the-spot quality control.

"Well, I knew you couldn't be with those damned kids who've been turning up the last few weeks," he said, plunking down a cold beer next to her tapas.

Hope fought to keep a straight face; the waiter was no older than the geeks he was disparaging, but she was very used to the employed seeing the unemployed as children. "Yeah, what's with them?"

"Damned if I know." He shrugged. "They all seem to head westward as soon as they arrive. I'll be surprised if they find any work in El Ejido, but hey, not my problem."

"And what about the Hotel Catedral?"

"Again, don't know. They've been close to closing for years, running a skeleton staff. Times have been hard, you know? My friend Aldo works the bar up there. Few weeks back, he tells me, he's doing a stint on the front desk when this bunch of American guys breeze in and ask to speak to the manager. They disappear to his office for half an hour, then they come back out, gather the staff, announce a change of ownership. More Yankees came in by plane, apparently. Place is full of them, now." He scowls. "They hired my girlfriend and some others as extra staff. Good tippers, apparently, but a bit . . . well, they're rich guys, I guess. What do you expect, right?"

Hope nodded sympathetically. She'd never worked hotels, largely because she knew so many people who had.

. . .

Hope spent the next morning getting her bearings, then drifted casually toward the Hotel Catedral, where she enquired about booking a table for supper. The lobby was all but empty, but the receptionist had the tight-lipped air of a man with a lot to worry about.

"No tables for nonresidents, señora; my apologies."

"Oh—in that case, can I book a room?"

"We are fully booked, señora."

Hope made a show of peering around the empty lobby. "If it's a money thing, I can show you a sight-draft on my company's account?"

The guy continued to stonewall, so Hope relented and wandered back onto the palm-studded plaza, where the sun was baking the sturdy buttresses of the titular cathedral. She was drinking a coffee at a café across the square when a gangly and somewhat sunburned young man pulled up on some sort of solar-assisted trike.

"Hey—Hope Dawson, right?" He spoke English with a broad Glaswegian accent.

Hope protested her innocence in passable Castilian, but he whipped out a little handheld from a pocket on his hunting vest and consulted it, shielding his eyes from the sun with his hand.

"Naw, see, this is definitely you. Look?"

Hope looked. It *was* definitely her—her disembarking from the train yesterday afternoon, in fact. Drone-shot, from somewhere above the station.

"Who wants to know?" she growled, putting some war-reporter grit into it.

"Mah boss. Wants tae offer ye a job, see."

"Well, you may tell your boss thank you, but I'm already employed."

"Bollix, lass—ye've not had a proper job in years." The lad grins. "I should know. It was me as doxed ye."

"Is that supposed to reassure me?"

"Naw, it's supposed to intrigue ye." He slapped the patchwork pleather bench seat of the trike behind him, shaded by the solar panel. "Cedric's a few streets over the way. Come hear what he has to say before ye make up yer mind, why not?"

. . .

"I hope Ian didn't alarm you, Miss Dawson," said Cedric, as a waiter poured coffee. They were seated in the lobby of a midrange boutique hotel which, given the lingering musty smell, had been boarded up for years until very recently.

"Not at all," Hope lied, in a manner she hoped conveyed a certain sense of *fuck you, Charlie*. "But I'd appreciate you explaining why you had him dox me."

"I want you to work for me, Miss Dawson."

"Just Hope, please. And as I told Ian, Mister . . . ?"

He smiles. "Just Cedric, please."

"As I told Ian, Cedric, I already have work."

"Indeed you do—a career in journalism more distinctive for its length than its impact, if you don't mind me saying so. Not many last so long down in the freelance trenches."

"Debts don't pay themselves, Cedric."

"Quite. But it would be nice to pay them quicker, wouldn't it?"

Hope put down her coffee cup to hide the tremor of her hands. "I'm flattered, but I should probably point out I'm not really a journalist."

"No, you're a qualitative economist. You were supervised by Shove and Walker, University of Lancaster. I've read your thesis."

"You have?"

"Well, the important bits. I had Ian précis the methodological stuff for me, if I'm honest. It was well received by your peers, I believe."

"Not well enough to lead to any research work," said Hope, curtly. No one wanted an interpretivist cluttering up their balance sheets with talk of intangible externalities, critiquing the quants, poking holes in the dog-eared cardboard cutout of *homo economicus.*

"Obviously not—but participant observation research work is what I'm offering you, starting today. Six months fixed-term contract, a PI's salary at current UK rates, plus expenses. I'll even backdate to the start of the month, if it helps."

"What's the object?"

Cedric looked surprised; his expression reminded Hope of the animated meerkat from an ad campaign of her youth. "Well, here, of course. Almeria the province, that is, rather than just the city."

"Why?"

He smiled, leaned forward a little. "Good question!" A frown replaced the smile. "I'm afraid I can't really answer it, though. Confidentiality of sources, you understand. But in essence, I was tipped off to an emerging situation here in Almeria, and decided I wanted to see it up close."

"I'm going to need more than that to go on, I'm afraid," said Hope.

Cedric somehow looked chagrined and reproachful at once. "There are limits, I'm afraid, and they're not of my making. But look: If I say I have reason, solid reason to believe that Almeria is on the verge of a transformative economic event without precedent, and that I have spent upward of five million euros in just the last few days in order to gather equipment and personnel on the basis of that belief, would you trust me?"

Not as far as I could throw you, frankly. "So why me, specifically?"

A boyish smile replaced the frown. "Now, that's a little easier! Remind me, if you would, of your thesis topic?"

To her own surprise, Hope's long-term memory duly regurgitated a set of research questions and framings polished to the smoothness of beach pebbles by repeated supervisory interrogations: transitions in civic and domestic consumptive practices; the influence of infrastructures and interfaces on patterns and rates of resource use; the role of externalities in the playing out of macroeconomic crises. Warming to her topic, she segued into a spirited defense of free-form empirical anthropology, and of interpretive methods as applied to the analysis of economic discontinuities.

"Good," Cedric intoned, as if she'd passed some sort of test. "H and M is researching exactly those sort of questions, and we think Almeria could be our Ground Zero."

That was a worrying choice of phrase.

"The markets are turbulent places, Hope," he continued, "too turbulent for mere mathematics to explain. They no longer interest me, in and of themselves."

He leaned back in his chair. "This will sound crass to someone of your generation, I'm sure, but nonetheless: I am not simply wealthy. I am rich enough that I don't even know what I'm worth, how I got that way, or who I'd have to ask to find out. Money is a very different matter for me than for you. I have the extraordinary liberty of being able to think about it purely in the abstract, because my concrete concerns are taken care of."

Hope stared at him, stunned into silence.

"So I am able," Cedric continued, "to explore economics in a way accessible to few, and of interest to even fewer. Lesser men, poorer men obsess over mere commerce, on the movement of money. My concerns are larger, far larger. You might say that it is the movement of the movement of money that fascinates me."

She grabbed her bag, stood up, and started for the doorway.

"Hope, hear me out, please," he called. "I don't expect you to like me, or even understand me. But I need you to work for me, here and now, and I am willing to pay you well. Wait, please, just for a moment."

Hope paused in the shade of the doorway but didn't turn around.

"Check your bank balance," he said after a brief pause. She blinked it up on her spex: a deposit had just cleared from Huginn&Muninn AB, Norwegian sort-code. More money than she'd earned in the last twelve months, both on the books and off. "Consider it a signing bonus."

She turned round, her arms crossed. "What if I won't sign?"

Cedric shrugged elegantly in his seat; he'd not moved an inch.

"I'll think about it," she said, turning on her heel.

Ian drove her back to her apartment block on the trike.

"So I'll come fetch ye tomorrow morning, then," he announced. "Run you down to El Ejido, get ye all set up and briefed."

"I told Cedric I'd think about it, Ian."

"Aye, I heard ye." Ian grinned. "Told him the same meself."

• • •

True to his word, Ian came to collect her the next morning. Hope found, to her surprise, that she was packed and ready to go.

"Knew ye'd go fer it," asserted Ian, bungeeing her bags to the trike.

"Very much against my better judgment," she replied.

"Aye, he's an odd one, fer sure. But he's not lied to me once, which is more than I can say fer mah previous employers." He saddled up, flashed a grin. "Plus, he always pays on time."

"He'd better," replied Hope, as Ian accelerated out into the empty streets of Almeria, heading westward. "What is it you do for him, anyway?"

"Not what you might be thinking! Ah'm a kind of general gopher, I guess, but I do a lot of reading for him when he's got other stuff on. News trawls, policy stuff. The doctoral theses of obscure scholars, sort o' thing." He grinned again, over his shoulder. "Sometimes he just wants to chew over old science fiction novels until the early hours. You thought it was hard to find work off the back of *your* doctorate? Try bein' an academic skiffy critic, eh!"

"Seriously?"

"Oh, aye. Says they inspire him to think differently. Me, I reckon he thinks he's Hubertus fuckin' Bigend or some such . . ."

"Who?"

But Ian had slipped on a set of retro-style enclosure headphones and turned his attention to his driving, dodging wallowing dirt bikes and scooters over-loaded with helmetless geeks and their motley luggage, all headed westward. The road from Almeria to El Ejido passed briefly through foothills almost lunar in their rugged desolation, before descending down to the Plastic Ocean itself. Hope couldn't see a patch of ground that wasn't covered with road, cramped housing, or row after monotonous row of greenhouses shimmering with heat-haze. Hope was surprised to see trucks at the roadside in the iconic white and blue livery of the United Nations and tapped Ian on the shoulder.

"What the hell are *they* doing here?" she yelled over the slipstream.

"The man hisself tipped 'em off. Fond of the UN, he is—fits wi' his Inter-national Rescue fetish, I guess—and they seem to appreciate his input, albeit grudgingly. We'll fix ye a meeting wi' General Weissmuutze, she's sound enough. Always good to know the people wi' the guns and bandages, eh?"

. . .

Ian dropped Hope at a small villa near the southern edge of El Ejido, loaded her spex with a credit line to a Huginn&Munnin expense account and a bunch of new software, and told her to call if she needed anything, before whizzing off eastward on his ridiculous little vehicle. Hope settled in, pushed aside her doubts, and got to work familiarizing herself with the town and the monotonous sea of greenhouses surrounding it. Cedric's backroom people had assembled a massive resource set of maps and satellite images, and a handful of high-def camdrones were busily quartering the town, collecting images to compile into street-view walk-throughs; they'd also, they claimed, fudged up a cover identity that would hold up to all but the most serious military-grade scrutiny. Hope had her doubts about that, but after a handful of days and a fairly drastic haircut, she was confident enough to hit the streets and pass herself off as just another new arrival, of which there were more and more each day.

Eager and noisy gangs of geeks were descending on boarded-up villas, bou-tique hotels, and bars, reactivating the inert infrastructure of the tourist sector, stripping buildings back to the bare envelope before festooning them with solar panels, screen-tarps, and sound systems of deceptively prodigious wattage. The wide boulevard of Paseo los Lomas, quiet enough during the daylight hours, started to fill up with ragged revelers around 6:00 p.m.; by nine each night, with the heat of the day still radiating from the pavements, it resembled a cross between a pop-up music festival and a Spring Break riot. The few businesses still owned and operated by locals hung on for a few days, watching their stock fly off the shelves at premium prices, before selling up their operations lock, stock, and barrel to expensively dressed men bearing bottomless yen-backed banker's draughts.

"I'd have been crazy not to sell," a former restaurateur told Hope, as his wife and kids bundled their possessions into the trunk of a noughties-vintage car retooled for biodiesel. Inside the building, an argument was breaking out between the new owners over which internal walls to knock through. "The mortgage has been under water for a decade, and they offer to pay it off in full? I'm not the crazy one here. They're welcome to it," he said, turning away.

Inside the cafe, Hope found five geeks swinging sledgehammers into partition walls, watched over by a man so telegenic that he was almost anonymous, his office-casual clothes repelling the dust of the remodeling process.

"Hey, girl," the man drawled in approval. The geeks carried on hammering.

"Hi!" she said, bright as a button. "So I just got into town, and I was wondering which are the best job boards? There's, like, so many to choose from."

The guy looked her up and down. "Guess it depends what sort of things you can do, doesn't it, ah . . . Cordelia?"

"That's me!" The cover identity seemed to be working, at least. "I guess you'd say I was in administration?"

"Not much call for admin at the moment, princess. Here." He threw a URL to her spex. "That's the board for indies and nonspecialists. You're a bit late to pick up the best stuff, but you should be able to make some bank if you don't price yourself out of the market. Or maybe one of the collectives will take you on contract for gophering? I'm sure these lads could find a space for a pretty little task rabbit like yourself in their warren, couldn't you, boys?"

"Right on, Niceday, right *on*," enthused a scrawny geek. "You want the URL, girl?"

"Please," she lied. "I'mma shop around some more, though. See what my options are, you know?"

"Whatevs," shrugged the dusty kid. "Longer you leave it, less we'll cut you in."

"You should listen to him, Cordelia," said the well-dressed guy, stepping closer to her. "In business, it pays to be bold." His eyes narrowed a little. "And loyal."

"Oh, sure! So what about *your* warren, Mister . . . ?"

"Niceday. And I don't have a warren, I hire them."

"So you're, like, a veecee or something?"

Niceday smiled an oily sort of smile. "Or something," he agreed. The smile vanished as he locked eyes with her. "Choose wisely, Cordelia, and choose soon. This isn't the time or place for . . . observing from the sidelines. Unless you're with the UN, of course."

"Haha, right! Well, ah, thanks for the advice," said Hope, her heart hammering against her ribs, and beat a swift retreat.

● ● ●

The mood on the periphery of the town was in sharp contrast to the raucous debauch of the center. The greenhouse workers—almost all youngish North African men—were packed like matches into street after street of undermaintained tourist villas and former residential blocks, with the more recent arrivals living in slums built of breezeblocks and plastic sheeting on the vacant lots where the plastic ocean broke upon the dark edges of the town. Hope spent a few hours wandering from coffeeshop to shisha-shack, trying every trick in the interviewer's book to get them to talk. They were happy enough to have drinks bought for them on Cedric's dime, and to complain at length about work in the abstract as they demolished plates of tapas and meze, but questions about actual working conditions led only to sullen, tense silences, or the sudden inability of the formerly fluent to speak a word of Spanish.

"You only ask about our work so you can steal our jobs," a gaunt man accused her toward the end of the evening, pointing his long, scarred finger at her through a cloud of fragrant shisha smoke. "For so long, no one else will do this work so cheap. Now all you people come back, make trouble for us."

She tried dropping her cover a bit, and played the journalist card; big mistake.

"Journalists, they don't make good stories about us, ever. We are always the villains, the evil Arabs, no?"

She protested her innocence and good intentions, but he had a point. Hope's background research had uncovered a history of tension between the greenhouse workers and the local residents that stretched back to before she was born: grimly vague and one-sided stories in the archives of now-moribund local news outlets about forced evictions, arson, and the sort of casual but savage violence between young men that always marks periods of socioeconomic strife. The attacks had lessened as the local youth migrated northward in search of better work, but there was a lingering vibe of siege mentality among the remaining immigrants, and their dislike for the influx of favela geeks was tangible.

"Go back to your rich friends," the man repeated, jabbing his finger for emphasis. "It is they who are meddling, trying to make us look bad! We'll not help you pin it on us."

"Pin what on you?" Hope asked, suddenly alert to the closeness of the knowledge she needed, but the guy's eyes narrowed and his lips tightened and he shook his head, and the whole place went silent and tense, and Hope was horribly aware of being the only woman in a dark smoky room full of unfamiliar men speaking an unfamiliar language.

She stammered out some apologies, paid her tab, and left quickly, but the damage was done. From that point on, the workers refused to talk to her. As the days passed, there were a few ugly incidents in alleyways late at night: botched muggings, running brawls, a few serious stabbings on both sides. But the geeks were confident in their newfound dominion, not to mention better fed and equipped, and the workers had no one on their side, least of all the employers they'd never met, and who only communicated with them via the medium of emailed quotas and output itineraries. If Hope wanted to get to the bottom of whatever was going on, she was going to have to do more than ask around.

.   .   .

Most of the geeks worked by day in jury-rigged refrigerated shipping containers and partied by night, but Cedric's backroom people had tipped her off to the existence of a small night shift that drifted out into the greenhouse ocean around midnight and returned before dawn. They'd furnished Hope's villa with an assortment of technological bits and bobs, including an anonymously military-looking flight case containing three semiautonomous AV drones about the size of her fist. She spent an afternoon syncing them up with her spex and jogging around among the miniature palms and giant aloes in her compound, getting the hang of the interface, then waited for night to fall before decking herself out in black like some amateur ninja and sneaking along the rooftops toward the edge of town, using the raucous noise of the evening fiesta as cover. Spotting a small knot of kids heading northward out of town, she sent two drones forward to tail them, one to run overwatch, and followed after at a distance she assumed would keep her out of sight, or at least give her plenty of time to cut and run if she was spotted.

After about half an hour, the geeks paused and split up. Hope hunkered down just close enough to still receive the feed from her drones, then flew them slow and low down the narrow gaps between the greenhouses, using an IR overlay to pick out the warm bodies among the endless identical walls of plastic, and settled down to watch.

Hope was no agricultural technician, but there was plenty of public info about the basic design of the greenhouses: long tunnels of solarized plastic sheeting with automated ventilation flaps covered row after row of hydroponic medium, into which mixtures of precious water and bespoke nutrients were dribbled at algorithmically optimized rates, depending on the species under cultivation. Over the years, more and more of the climate control and hydroponics had been automated, but the hapless workers still had the unenviable task of shuffling up and down the greenhouses on their knees during the heat of the day, checking closely on the health and development of their charges; the consequences of quality control failures were draconian, in that it meant being sacked and blacklisted for further employment. The only reason they'd not been replaced by robots was that robots couldn't do the sort of delicate and contextual work that the greenhouses required; it was still way cheaper to get some poor mug straight off the boat from Morocco and teach him how to trim blight and pluck aphids than it was to invest in expensive hardware that couldn't make those sorts of qualitative decisions on the fly. Plus the supply of desperate immigrants was effectively inexhaustible, and their wage demands were kept low by Europe's endemic problem with unemployment. In Spain, as in much of the rest of the world, automation had been eating away at the employment base from the middle class downward, rather than from the bottom upward . . . and the more white-collar gigs it consumed, the larger and more desperate the working class became. There was barely a form of manual labor left that you couldn't design a machine to do just as well as a human, but hiring a human had far lower up-front costs. Plus you could simply replace them when they wore out, at no extra expense.

The geek night shift weren't doing the work of the greenhouse guys, that was for sure. Of the trio Hope was watching, one was squatting on the ground over a handheld he'd plugged in to the server unit at the end of the greenhouse module, another was fiddling around with the nutrient reservoirs, and the third was darting in and out of the little air lock next to the guy fiddling with the server. Lost in the scene unfolding in front of her eyes, Hope steered one of her drones in for a closer look as the third guy reemerged with his fists full of foot-long seedlings, which he threw to the ground before picking up a tray of similar-looking cuttings and slipping back inside.

She was just bringing her second forward drone around for a closer look at the reservoir tanks when her spex strobed flashbulb white three times in swift succession, causing her to shriek in shock and discomfort. Blinded and disoriented, she stood and started running in what she assumed was the direction she'd come, but tripped on some pipe or conduit and fell through the wall of a greenhouse. She thrashed about, trying to free herself from a tangled matrix of plastic sheeting and tomato plants, but strong hands grabbed her ankles and hauled her out roughly onto the path. She put her hands up to protect her face as a strong flashlight seared her already aching eyes. At least I'm not permanently blind, she thought to herself, absurdly.

"Stay still," grunted a Nordic-sounding man, and she was flipped over onto her front, before someone sat on her legs and zip-tied her hands behind her back.

"I've got a bunch of drones out here," she threatened.

"No," replied the Viking voice, "you had three. We only have one. But unlike yours, ours has a maser instead of a camera."

Hope stopped struggling.

. . .

Dawn took a long time to come. When it arrived, Hope's two hulking assailants fetched her out of the shipping container they'd locked her in, bundled her into the back of an equally windowless van, then drove east in stony silence, ignoring her attempts at conversation. They delivered her to the reception room of a top-floor suite at the Hotel Catedral, where a familiar face was waiting for her.

"Ah, Cordelia . . . or should I say Hope?" drawled Niceday. "We meet again!"

Hope kneaded her wrists, where the cable-tie had left deep red weals. "You could have just pinged my calendar for an appointment," she snarked.

"I work to my own schedule, not yours. Nor Cedric's, for that matter. How's he doing, anyway?"

"Ask him yourself," she shot back. "I just work for him."

"Quod erat demonstrandum," said Niceday, leaning against a drink cabinet. "He's always been a great collector of . . . novelties."

"You know him well, then?"

Niceday laughed, but didn't reply.

"Why are those kids out hacking greenhouses in the middle of the night?"

"That's literally none of your business, Hope."

"But it is *your* business?"

"Mine, yes, and that of my associates. There are laws against industrial espionage, you know."

"There are also laws to protect journalists from being kidnapped in the course of their work."

"But you're not a journalist, Hope." Niceday snapped his fingers. A hidden projector flashed up a copy of Hope's contract with Huginn&Munnin onto the creamy expanse of the wall. "Qualitative economist, it says here. Good cover for an industrial spy, I'd say."

"I'm not a spy. I'm a social scientist."

"Are you so sure?"

Hope opened her mouth to reply, then closed it.

"You should listen to your gut instincts more often," Niceday continued. "Isn't that what journalists do? I hope that, after this little chat, your gut instincts will be to stay the hell away from my task rabbits."

"What are you going to do if I don't—have me disappear?"

"Don't dream it's beyond my reach, girl," he snapped. "Or that I couldn't get you and Cedric tangled up in a lawsuit long enough to keep you out of my hair— and out of sight—for years to come."

"So why haven't you?"

The smile returned. "Lawyers are expensive. Much cheaper to simply persuade you to cease and desist, mano a mano, so to speak."

"That rather implies you have something to hide."

"Oh, Hope—who doesn't have something to hide? Only those with nothing to lose. Do you think Cedric has nothing to hide? Weren't you hiding behind a false name yourself?"

"Yes, but—"

"But nothing. You've no moral high ground here, Hope. You can write a story about my task rabbits and try to get it published somewhere, if you like, but you'll find there's no respectable organ that'll run it. Takes a lot of money to keep a good news outlet running, you know, and ads just don't cover it." He shook his head in mock lament. "Or you could publish it online yourself, independently, of course. But you might find that some stories about you were published around the same time. The sort of stories that kill careers in journalism and research stone dead: fabricated quotes, fiddled expenses, false identities, kickbacks, tax evasion, that sort of thing."

"So you're threatening me, now?"

Niceday arched an eyebrow. "Hope, I just had two large men zip-tie your wrists together and lock you in a shipping container for four hours."

Hope felt the fight drain out of her. "Yeah, fair point."

"We understand each other, then. Good. Now, you get back to your fieldwork. The boys will drive you back to El Ejido, if you like."

"You're just going to let me go?"

He laughed again. "If I thought you or Cedric could do any lasting damage to my business plan, you'd have never got within a hundred klicks of Almeria. Do you think it says 'Niceday' on any of my passports? Do you think this face matches any official records, that this voice is on file somewhere? I might as well not exist, as far as law enforcement is concerned; far less paperwork that way." He crossed his arms. "Keeping your nose out of my affairs going forward is just a way of avoiding certain more permanent sorts of cleanup operation. Do you understand me?"

Hope stared at him: six foot something of surgically perfected West Coast beefcake, wearing clothes that she'd need to take out a mortgage to buy, and the snakelike smile of a man utterly accustomed to getting his own way.

"Who are you?" she wondered aloud. "Who are you, really?"

He spread his arms in benediction, like that Jesus statue in Brazil before the Maoists blew it up.

"We," he intoned, "are the opportunity that recognizes itself."

She didn't understand him at all. She suspected she never would.

• • •

Around five weeks after she'd arrived, the storm finally broke, and Hope found herself riding shotgun in General Weissmuutze's truck on the highway toward the port facility at Almeria, weaving along between an implacable and close-packed column of self-driving shipping containers. The hard shoulder was host to a Morse-code string of greenhouse workers, moving a little faster on foot than the solar-powered containers, backs bent beneath their bundles of possessions. The General was less than happy.

"I have a team down at the airport; the private planes are leaving as quickly as they can arrange a takeoff window. And then there's the port," she complained, gesturing out of the passenger-side window toward the sea, where Hope could see a denser knot than usual of ships large and small waiting for their time at dockside. "Every spare cubic foot of freight capacity on the entire Mediterranean, it looks like. They're trying to clear as much of the produce as they can before I can seal the port."

Weissmuutze's team had been awoken by an urgent voice call from the FDA in the United States. A routine drug-ring bust by the FBI somewhere in the ghost zones of Detroit had uncovered not the expected bales of powder or barrels of pills, but crate after crate of Almerian tomatoes. After taking a few samples to a lab, they discovered that the fruit's flesh and juice contained a potent designer stimulant connected to a spate of recent overdoses, and informed the FDA. The FDA began the process of filing with Washington for an embargo on imports from Almeria, before informing the Spanish government and the United

Nations, who'd patched them straight through to Weissmuutze in hopes of getting things locked down quickly.

"Scant chance of that," said Weissmuutze later, as they watched the ineffectual thin blue line of the Almerian police force collapse under a wave of immigrant workers trying to climb the fence into the container port. "The Spanish government doesn't have much reach outside of the big cities, and they handed the port over as a free-trade zone about a decade ago. The consortium is supposed to supply its own security, but . . ." She shrugged her bearlike shoulders. "My people are deactivating all the containers they can now the highway's blocked, but these poor bastards know that means there'll be more space for passengers."

Hope watched as the front line of workers reached the fence and began lobbing their bags and bundles over it, shaking at the fence poles. "I think they've known this was coming for a while," said Hope.

"We've all known something was coming," muttered Weissmuutze. "Exactly what it is that's arrived is another question entirely."

Hope left Weissmuutze and her peacekeepers to supervise the developing riot as best they could and headed for the airport, where Ian was lurking at Cedric's behest. The concourse bar was crowded with men who wore the bland handsomeness of elective surgery with the same casual ease as their quietly expensive Valley-boy uniform of designer jeans, trainers, and turtlenecks.

"Honestly!" protested Ian over the rim of his mojito. "This is only my first one, and I only bought it 'cause they'd nae let me keep my table if I didn't."

Hope filled him in on happenings at the port. "What's happening here, then?"

"Looks like the circus is leaving town. Well, the ringmasters, at any rate. Hisself hoped I might be able to get some answers, but it's like I'm invisible or something, they'll nae talk to me . . ."

Hope sighed and scanned the room via the smallest and subtlest of her drones, finally spotting a familiar mask. Donning her own, she made her way over to the end of the bar, where Niceday was sitting nursing a highball of something peaty and expensive. "Ms. Dawson, we meet again. Are you flying today?"

"I put myself on the standby list, but for some reason I'm not expecting any luck."

"Oh, very good," he replied, flashing a vulpine grin. "Are you sure you're not looking for a career change? I can always find work for girls with a bit of character, you know."

Yeah, I'll bet you can. "My current contract is ongoing, *Mister* Niceday, but thanks for the offer. You're moving on from Almeria, then?"

"Yeah—the party's over, but there'll be another one soon enough, somewhere. The lions must follow the wildebeest, amirite?"

"If the party's over, who's in charge of cleaning up?"

Niceday waved a hand in breezy dismissal. "The UN have been here a while, haven't they? They know what they're doing."

"They know what you've been doing, too."

"Fulfilling the demands of the market, you mean?"

"Manufacturing drugs, I mean."

"Oh, I forgot—all drugs are bad, aren't they, unless they're being made by and sold to the right people? Besides, if those drugs weren't illegal or patented, I wouldn't be able to make any profit from doing so. Market forces, girl. I don't mark out the field, I just play the game."

"So this is some ideological crusade, then?"

"Nah," he replied, warming to his theme. "More an opportunity that was too good to pass up. My colleagues"—he gestured around the crowded bar—"and I had been doing business around south Asia, making use of all the redundant 3D printing capacity out there that the fabbing bubble left behind. But recent changes in feedstock legislation made it much harder to produce . . . ah, viable products, let's say. If you want feedstock that produces durable high-performance materials . . . well, you might as well try buying drug precursors, right? Serious regulation, poor risk/reward ratio. Boring.

"Now, I'd been watching the local markets here for some time, flipping deeds and water futures for chump change while I kept an eye open, when I had my little revelation: the greenhouses of Almeria were basically a huge networked organic 3D printer, and the only feedstocks it needed were water, fertilizer, and sunlight. And while it couldn't print durable products, it could handle the synthesis of very complex molecules. Plants are basically a chemical reactor with a freestanding physical structure, you see, though my geneticist friends assure me that's a terrible oversimplification."

"So you just started growing tweaked plants right away?"

"Not quite, no; it took a few weeks to set up the shell companies, liaise with buyers, and get the right variants cooked up in the lab. Not to mention getting all our task rabbits housed and happy! Then it was just a case of getting buyers to file legitimate orders with a grower, set the task rabbits to handle the seedling switcheroos and hack the greenhouse system's growth parameters. Intense growing regimes mean you can turn over full-grown tomato plants in about three weeks. Biotech is astonishing stuff, isn't it?"

"You're not even ashamed, are you?" Hope wondered aloud.

"Why should I be?" His frown was like something a Greek statue might wear. "I delivered shareholder value, I shipped product, and I even maintained local employment levels a little longer than they'd have otherwise lasted. We are the wealth creators, Ms. Dawson. Without us, nothing happens."

"But what happens after you leave?"

A look of genuine puzzlement crossed Niceday's face. "How should I know?" He glanced away into some dataspace or another, then stood and downed his drink. "Gotta go, my Gulfstream's boarding. Sure I can't tempt you with a new position?" The smile was suave, but the eye beneath the raised eyebrow was anything but.

"Very."

"Shame—waste of your talents, chasing rainbows for Cedric. The option's always there if you change your mind."

"And how would I let you know if I did?"

Niceday winked, grinned again, then turned and vanished into the crowd. Hope went back to find Ian, who was getting impatient.

"Waitresses still willnae serve me, dammit. All ah want's a Coke!"

"I think they're concentrating on the big tippers while they can," Hope replied; he rolled his eyes. "C'mon, let's get back to El Ejido. Weissmuutze says it's all kicking off down at the container port. She wants us civvies out of the way."

Ian sighed. "You'll never guess where the trike's parked."

• • •

Things fell apart fast after Niceday and his fellow disruptors moved on. It soon became apparent that, absent the extra profit margin obtained by growing and shipping what the international media was already waggishly referring to as "FruitPlus," a perfect storm of economic factors had finally rendered Almerian greenhouse agriculture a loss-making enterprise. Cedric's quants spent long nights in their boutique hotel arguing heatedly over causal factors, but the general consensus was that relentless overabstraction of water from the regional aquifer had bumped up against escalating shipping costs and the falling spot price of produce from other regions. Chinese investment in large-scale irrigation projects on the other side of the Med were probably involved, somehow; if nothing else, it explained the mass exodus of the immigrant workers. Those that had failed to get out on the empty freighters had descended on the desiccated former golf resorts along the coastline, squatting the sand-blown shells of holiday villas and retirement homes left empty by the bursting of the property bubble, fighting over crouching space in the scale-flecked holds of former fishing vessels whose captains saw midnight repatriation cruises as a supplement to their legitimate work.

A significant number showed no signs of wanting to leave, however, particularly those whose secular bent put them at odds with the increasingly traditionalist Islamic model of democracy that had sprouted from the scorched earth of the so-called Arab Spring in the Teens. Some fled quietly to the valleys hidden among the foothills of the Sierra Nevada to the north, where they set about reviving the hardscrabble subsistence farming methods that their Moorish forebears had developed centuries before. Others—particularly the young and angry—occupied small swathes of greenhouse and turned them over to growing their own food, as did some of the more self-reliant and entrepreneurial gangs of task rabbits who'd stayed on. Territorial disputes—driven more by the lack of water than the lack of space—were frequent, ugly, but mercifully short, and Hope spent a lot of time riding around the region with General Weissmuutze and her peacekeepers, putting out fires both literal and figurative. Within a few weeks the Plastic Ocean had evaporated away to a ragged series of puddles scattered across the landscape, separated by wide stretches of near desert, the fleshless skeletons of greenhouse tunnels, and wandering tumbleweed tangles of charred plastic sheeting.

Other task rabbit warrens found other business models, and Weissmuutze was hard-pressed to keep a lid on those who'd decided to stick with disruptive drug pharming. With the evisceration and collapse of the EPZ syndicate, courtesy of Niceday and friends, the container port at Almeria became a revolving door for all sorts of shady import/export operators, and overland distribution networks—for everything from nontariff Chinese photovoltaics and Pakistani firearms to prime Afghan heroin—quickly sprung up and cut their way northward into central Europe. Weissmuutze was obliged to be ruthless, rounding up the pharmers and their associates before putting their greenhouses and shipping-container biolabs to the torch. But the Spanish government had little interest in doing anything beyond issuing chest-thumping press releases, and most of her detainees were sprung by colleagues overnight, slipping eastward or southward and vanishing into the seething waters of the dark economy.

Much to Hope's fascination, however, the majority of the warrens went for more legitimate enterprises, from simple reboots of the greenhouse model aimed at growing food for themselves and for barter, to more ambitious attempts at brewing up synthetic bacteria to clean up land and waterways blighted by excessive fertilizer runoff, all of which Weissmuutze did her best to protect and encourage. The disruptors had snared a lot of warrens in contracts whose small print specified they could be paid off in stock and other holdings in lieu of cash, with the result that various collectives and sole operators found themselves holding title to all-but-worthless slivers and fragments of land, all-but-exhausted water abstraction rights, and chunks of physical infrastructure in various states of disrepair or dysfunction. Parallel economies sprung up and tangled themselves together almost overnight, based on barter, laundered euros, petrochemicals, solar wattage, and manual labor. The whole region had become a sort of experimental sandbox for heterodox economic systems; the global media considered it a disaster zone with low-to-zero telegenic appeal, and ignored it accordingly, but to Hope it was like seeing all the abstract theories she'd studied for years leap off the page and into reality. She was busy, exhausted, and, by this point, a most unBritish shade of Mediterranean bronze.

When she finally remembered to wonder, she couldn't remember the last time she'd been so happy.

• • •

She was sitting beneath a tattered sunbrella on the promenade at Playa Serena, poking at her mothballed novel, when Ian rolled up on his trike. Cedric was perched on the bench seat in the shade of the solar panel, wearing a pale suit and a casually dignified expression that reminded Hope of archived stills from the height of the British Raj.

"May we join you, Hope?" he asked, dismounting. Ian rolled his eyes and grinned, leaning into the backrest of the trike's saddle.

"Sure. Stack of these brollies back there, if you want one."

Cedric settled himself next to her and stared down the beach, where a small warren was clustered around a device that looked like a hybrid of Ian's trike, a catering-grade freezer, and an explosion in a mirror factory. "What have we here?" he asked.

"Solarpunks," said Hope. "They're trying to make glass from sand using only sunlight."

"Innovative!"

"Naw, old idea," said Ian mildly. "Was a proof of concept back in the Teens. No one could scale it up for profit."

"What's their market, then?"

Hope gestured westward, toward a large vacant lot between two crumbling hotels. "There's another lot down there working on 3D printing at architectural scales. They want to do Moorish styles, all high ceilings and central courtyards, but they're having some trouble getting the arches to come out right."

Ian barked a short laugh, then fell silent.

"I came to thank you for your hard work, Hope," said Cedric.

"You've paid me as promised," Hope shrugged. "No need for thanks."

"No requirement, perhaps, but I felt the need. Given the, ah, mission creep issues early on."

The euphemisms of power, thought Hope. "No biggie. I got to see the face of disruption close-up. Lotta journalists would kill for a chance like that."

"A lot of researchers, too," Cedric suggested. Hope didn't reply.

"I've taken the liberty of paying off your student loans in full."

"That's very generous of you, Cedric."

"Think nothing of it," he said, with a wave of his hand. Hope let the silence stretch. "I was wondering if you'd like to sign up again," he continued, with that easy confidence. "Same terms, better pay. There will be more events like this, we're sure. We don't know quite where yet, but we've a weather eye on a few likely hot spots. Colombia, maybe. Southern Chinese seaboard. West Africa. Wherever it is, we'll be there."

Hope thought of Niceday, standing in the opulence of his suite; such similar creatures. "Don't you worry, Cedric, that you're one of the causal forces you're trying to explain? That your own wealth distorts the markets like gravity distorts space-time? That the disruptors are following you, rather than the other way around?"

Ian laughed again. "She got ye there, boss."

"Thank you, Ian," said Cedric, mildly. "Yes, Hope, I do worry about that. But I have concluded that the greater sin is to do nothing. As you know, no one can or will fund this sort of research at this sort of scale, especially out in the hinterlands. General Weissmuutze has been passing our reports directly to the UN, at no cost. She tells me they're very grateful."

"I guess they should be," Hope allowed. "As should I."

"Think nothing of it," he said again, leaning forward and resting his elbows on his knees. "Come with us, Hope. Don't you want to be part of the next story?"

"No, Cedric," she replied. "Don't you get it? This story isn't finished. Only the bits of it that interest you and Niceday's people have finished. And the next story will have started long before you get wherever it is you decide to go. You can close the book and start another one, if you like; that is your privilege." She sighed. "But the world carries on, even when there's no one there to narrate it."

"So what will you do?"

"Stop running. You've set me free from my past, Cedric, and I'm grateful. But you can't give me a future. Only I can do that." She pointed at the solar-punks down on the sand. "That's what they're trying to do, and the others. And maybe I can't build things or ship code or hustle funding, but I can tell stories. Stories where those other things don't matter so much, maybe.

"When you look at this place, you see a story ending. I see one just beginning. And sure, perhaps it'll be over in weeks, maybe it'll end in failure. But we won't know unless we try writing it."

"'It takes a special kind of person,'" said Ian, quietly, "'a special eye, to make the ruins bloom.'" He sat up straight in his saddle. "C'mon, boss. Ye got way more than yer pound o' flesh from this one. Leave her be now, eh?"

"You're right, of course," said Cedric, standing. "If you ever change your mind . . ."

". . . you'll find me, I know."

Without another word, Cedric settled himself onto the trike's bench seat. Ian raised his sunglasses, tipped her one last wink, and whirred away down the promenade to the east, where the last clouds of the morning were burning away to wispy nothings.

ABOUT THE AUTHORS AND THE TRANSLATORS

Yasser Abdellatif is a writer, poet, and literary translator from Egypt. He was born in Cairo in 1969 and received his bachelor's degree in philosophy from Cairo University in 1994. He worked as a scriptwriter and journalist in Egyptian television and the Spanish News Agency in Cairo until 2009, then he moved to Edmonton, Canada, where he pursued his career as a freelance writer and translator. He has published four fiction books, three poetry collections, many essays and articles, and several pieces of music.

He writes mainly in Arabic, but many of his works have been translated into English, French, German, Italian, Spanish, Maltese, and Korean. He has also translated many literary works from French and English into Arabic, including some classics by French authors such as Charles Perrault, Balzac, and Émile Zola.

His novel *The Law of Inheritance* won the Sawiris Prize in 2005 and was translated and published in Spanish and English. His collection of short stories, *Jonah in the Belly of the Whale*, won the Sawiris Prize in 2013 in the category of prominent writers.

K. C. Alexander is the author of *Necrotech* and *Nanoshock*—transhumanist sci-fi called "a speed freak rush" by *New York Times* bestseller Richard Kadrey and "slick, sharp, and snarky" by *New York Times* bestseller Chuck Wendig. They cowrote *Mass Effect: Andromeda: Nexus Uprising*, Bioware's first novelization for *Mass Effect: Andromeda*, with *New York Times* bestseller Jason M. Hough. Other credits consist of a short story to *Fireside* magazine and an essay for *Uncanny*'s "Disabled People Destroy Science Fiction" issue. Specialties include voice-driven prose, imperfect characters, and an inclination to defy expectations.

Jacques Barcia writes weird fiction. His stories have appeared in *Clarkesworld* magazine, *Electric Velocipede*, *The Immersion Book of Steampunk*, *The Apex Book of World SF 2*, and *Shine: An Anthology of Optimistic Science Fiction*. He works as a professional futurist, is an avid roleplayer, and growls in a grind-core band. He's trying to write a novel.

Greg Bear was the author of more than forty books, including *Blood Music, Eon, The Forge of God, Moving Mars, Darwin's Radio, City at the End of Time,* and *The Unfinished Land*. His work has been awarded five Nebulas, two Hugos, and many international awards. Bear was married to Astrid Anderson Bear and father to Chloe and Alex. He died in November 2022.

Steve Beard is an experimental writer who lives and works in England. Back in the 1990s, he challenged himself to write an English cyberpunk novel, and *Digital Leatherette* was the result. William Gibson called it a "neo-Blakeian riff-collage," which was nice. Beard's latest work, *Pop Heresiarchs*, is a collection of theory fiction.

Russell Blackford is an Australian academic and writer. He is currently conjoint senior lecturer in philosophy at the University of Newcastle, NSW. His many nonfiction books include *Science Fiction and the Moral Imagination: Visions, Minds, Ethics*. He has a longstanding interest in science fiction and fantasy and has published novels and stories in both genres. His novels include an original trilogy for the Terminator franchise (collectively *Terminator 2: The New John Connor Chronicles*) and *Kong Reborn*—a modern-day sequel to the original 1933 *King Kong* film.

Pat Cadigan was born in New York, grew up in Massachusetts, and spent most of her adult life in the Kansas City area, until she emigrated to the United Kingdom in 1996.

After ten years as a writer for Hallmark Cards (yes, she wrote the cards, in verse), she became a full-time writer in 1987. Her books include the Arthur C. Clarke Award–winning novels *Synners* and *Fools*. She has also won the Locus Award three times. In 2013 her novelette *The Girl-Thing Who Went Out for Sushi* also won both the Hugo Award and the Seiun Award (aka the Japanese Hugo). Cadigan is a popular guest lecturer and has spoken about many different subjects around the world.

Nebula-nominated **Beth Cato** is the author of the Clockwork Dagger duology and the Blood of Earth trilogy. She's a Hanford, California, native transplanted to the Arizona desert, where she lives with her husband, son, and requisite cats.

Suzanne Church grew up in Toronto, moved to Waterloo to pursue mathematics, and never left town. Her award-winning short fiction has appeared in

Cicada, *Clarkesworld*, several anthologies, and her 2014 collection *Elements*. Her favorite place to write is a lakefront cabin, but she'll settle for any coffee shop with Wi-Fi and an electrical outlet.

A native Rhode Islander, **Paul Di Filippo** lives in Providence, some two blocks away from the granite marker denoting Lovecraft's birthplace. Since selling his first story in 1977, he has accumulated more than forty books with his byline. His newest will be a story collection titled *The Way You Came in May Not Be the Best Way Out*.

Cory Doctorow is a science fiction author, activist, and journalist. He is the author of many books, most recently *Radicalized* and *Walkaway*, science fiction for adults; *How to Destroy Surveillance Capitalism*, nonfiction about monopoly and conspiracy; *In Real Life*, a graphic novel; and the picture book *Poesy the Monster Slayer*.

His latest book is *Attack Surface*, a stand-alone adult sequel to *Little Brother*; his next nonfiction book is *Chokepoint Capitalism*, with Rebecca Giblin, about monopoly and fairness in the creative arts labor market. In 2020, he was inducted into the Canadian Science Fiction and Fantasy Hall of Fame.

Candas Jane Dorsey is an internationally known writer, editor, former publisher, community-builder, and activist living in Edmonton, Alberta. She is the award-winning author of, among others, *Black Wine*, *A Paradigm of Earth*, *Machine Sex and other stories*, *Vanilla and other stories*, *ICE and other stories*, *The Adventures of Isabel*, and *What's the Matter with Mary Jane?* (the Epitome Apartments Mystery Series), and YA novel *The Story of My Life Ongoing, by C. S. Cobb*.

George Alec Effinger was born January 10, 1947. His first novel, *What Entropy Means to Me*, was nominated for the Nebula Award. He achieved his greatest success with the trilogy of Marîd Audran novels *When Gravity Fails*, *A Fire in the Sun*, and *The Exile Kiss*, set in a twenty-second-century Middle East, with cybernetic implants and modules allowing individuals to change their personalities or bodies. A collection, *Budayeen Nights*, contains all Effinger's short material from the Marîd Audran setting.

His novelette *Schrödinger's Kitten* received both the Hugo Award and the Nebula Award, as well as the Japanese Seiun Award. A collection of his stories was published posthumously in 2005, entitled *George Alec Effinger Live! From Planet Earth*; it includes the complete stories Effinger wrote under the pseudonym O. Niemand and many of Effinger's best-known stories. Each O. Niemand story is a pastiche in the voice of a different major American writer (Flannery O'Connor, Damon Runyon, Mark Twain, etc.), all set on the asteroid city of Springfield. *Niemand* is from the German word for "nobody," and the initial *O* was intended by Effinger as a visual pun for Zero, and possibly also as a reference to the author O. Henry.

Other stories Effinger wrote include the series of Maureen (Muffy) Birn-
baum parodies, which placed a preppy into a variety of science fictional,
fantasy, and horror scenarios. He was in ill health for much of his life and died
at the age of fifty-five on April 27, 2002.

Isabel Fall was born in 1989.

William Gibson is credited with having coined the term *cyberspace* and having
envisioned both the internet and virtual reality before either existed. He is the
author of *Neuromancer*, *Count Zero*, *Mona Lisa Overdrive*, *Burning Chrome*,
Virtual Light, *Idoru*, *All Tomorrow's Parties*, *Pattern Recognition*, *Spook
Country*, *Zero History*, *Distrust That Particular Flavor*, *The Peripheral*, and
Agency. He lives in Vancouver, British Columbia, with his wife.

Omar Robert Hamilton is a writer and filmmaker working between Europe
and the Arab world, and a cofounder of the Palestine Festival of Literature.

Karen Heuler's stories have appeared in more than 120 literary and speculative
magazines and anthologies, from *Conjunctions* to *The Magazine of Fantasy
and Science Fiction* to *Weird Tales*. Her latest novel is *The Splendid City*. It's a
tale about stolen water, an exiled witch and her gun-wielding cat, and a city
run by a self-declared president who loves parades. Her latest collection is *A
Slice of the Dark*.

Gwyneth Jones is a feminist writer and critic of science fiction and fantasy who
has also written for teenagers using the name Ann Halam. Awards include the
Philip K. Dick Award, Arthur C. Clarke Award, the Dracula Society's Children of the Night Award, the World Fantasy Award, and the Pilgrim Award
for SF criticism. She lives in Brighton, England, with her husband and two
cats, Milo and Tilly. Hobbies include curating assorted pond life in season,
watching old movies, playing *Zelda*, and staring out the window.

Richard Kadrey is the *New York Times* bestselling author of more than twenty
novels, including the Sandman Slim supernatural noir series. *Sandman Slim*
was included in Amazon's "100 Science Fiction & Fantasy Books to Read in
a Lifetime." The book is in development as a feature film through Studio 8.
Some of Kadrey's other books include *The Grand Dark*, *The Everything Box*,
and *Butcher Bird*. In comics, he's written for *Heavy Metal*, *Lucifer*, and *Hell-
blazer*. He's also been immortalized as an action figure.

Cassandra Khaw is an award-winning game writer and former scriptwriter at
Ubisoft Montreal. Khaw's work can be found in places like *The Magazine of
Fantasy & Science Fiction*, *Lightspeed*, and Tor.com. Khaw's first original novella, *Hammers on Bone*, was a British Fantasy Award and Locus Award finalist,
and their novella *Nothing But Blackened Teeth* is a Bram Stoker Award finalist.

Being a young man in post-communist Bulgaria, **Christian Kirtchev** was living the cyberpunk "high-tech, lowlife" cliché lurking in dark, dank techno clubs or surfing grave-hour internet cafés for that techno-fetish high surrounded by the decay of a crumbled political and economic system. After publishing "A Cyberpunk Manifesto" in 1997, he subsequently wrote a few more pieces and short stories describing the emerging techno-culture in late 1990s Eastern Europe from a cyberpunk point of view.

Aleš Kot is a writer and producer. They believe in the power of art. They have nothing to sell you.

Nancy Kress is the author of thirty-four novels, four story collections, and three books on writing fiction. Her science fiction has won six Nebulas, two Hugos, a Sturgeon, and the John W. Campbell Memorial Award. She often writes about genetic engineering. Her work has been translated into two dozen languages—including Klingon—none of which she can read. She teaches writing at various venues in the United States and abroad, including a guest lectureship at the University of Leipzig and an intensive seminar in Beijing, plus the annual Taos Toolbox with Walter Jon Williams. She lives in Seattle.

Lavanya Lakshminarayan is the award-winning author of *The Ten Percent Thief.* She's a Locus Award finalist and is the first science fiction writer to win the *Times of India* AutHer Award and the Valley of Words Award, both prestigious literary awards in India. Her fiction has appeared in various magazines and anthologies, including *The Best of World SF Volume 2* and *Someone in Time*, and has also been translated into French, Italian, German, and Spanish.

She's occasionally a game designer and has built worlds for Zynga Inc.'s *FarmVille* franchise, *Mafia Wars*, and other games. She lives between multiple cities in India.

Oliver Langmead is a Scottish author and poet whose books include *Birds of Paradise, Dark Star*, and *Metronome*. He is a lecturer in creative writing at the University of Lancaster, and in 2018 he was the writer in residence at the European Space Agency's Astronaut Centre in Cologne. After writing "Glitterati," Langmead developed it into a full-length novel, available now.

Fritz Leiber Jr. was born Fritz Reuter Leiber Jr. in Chicago, Illinois, on December 24, 1910, to Fritz Leiber Sr. and Virginia Bronson Leiber, both Shakespearean actors. He toured with father's repertory company in 1928 before entering the University of Chicago, from which he graduated in 1932. He went on to study at General Theological Seminary in New York and was briefly a candidate for ordination in the Episcopal Church. He toured intermittently with his father's company and appeared with him in films *Camille*

(1936) and *The Great Garrick* (1937). Leiber married Jonquil Stephens in 1936 and moved to Hollywood; they had a son soon after. He corresponded with horror writer H. P. Lovecraft, who encouraged and influenced his literary development; wrote a supernatural novella, *The Dealings of Daniel Kesserich* (1936; published posthumously in 1997); and showed Lovecraft early stories. Returning to Chicago, Leiber took a job as staff writer for Consolidated Book Publishing (1937–1941), contributing to the *Standard American Encyclopedia*. His first publication as a professional writer, "Two Sought Adventure" (in John W. Campbell Jr.'s *Unknown*), introduced popular characters Fafhrd and the Gray Mouser, whom he developed with his friend Harry Fischer and modeled on their relationship; the story inaugurated a series he would continue for more than fifty years, helping to define the subgenre he labeled "Sword and Sorcery." (Fafhrd and the Gray Mouser stories were later collected in *Two Sought Adventure*, 1957; *Swords in the Mist*, 1968; *Swords Against Wizardry*, 1968; *The Swords of Lankhmar*, 1968; *Swords and Deviltry*, 1970; *Swords and Ice Magic*, 1977; *The Knight and Knave of Swords*, 1988; and other volumes.) Leiber worked as a drama and speech instructor at Occidental College in 1941 and during the war as an inspector at Douglas Aircraft. His first novel, *Conjure Wife*—about secret witchcraft on a college campus—appeared in *Unknown* in 1943 (but not as a book until 1952; it was filmed three times). His first science fiction novel, *Gather, Darkness!*, was also serialized in 1943 (book version, 1950). From 1945 to 1956, he worked as an editor at *Science Digest* in Chicago. He published science fiction novels *Destiny Times Three* (in *Astounding*, 1945; book version, 1957), *The Green Millennium* (1953), and *The Big Time* (in *Galaxy*, 1958; book version, 1961), the last winning a Hugo Award and inaugurating his popular Change War series. Leiber moved back to Los Angeles in 1958 and turned to writing full-time; he published science fiction novels *The Silver Eggheads* (1961), *The Wanderer* (1964), and *A Specter Is Haunting Texas* (1969).

Leiber lived in San Francisco after the death of his wife in 1969; the city forms the setting of his fantasy novel *Our Lady of Darkness* (1977). In 1976, he received a World Fantasy Award for Life Achievement and, in 1981, a Grand Master Award from Science Fiction Writers of America. Leiber married Margo Skinner in May 1992. He died on September 5, 1992, in San Francisco of an apparent stroke. In 2001 he was inducted posthumously into the Science Fiction Hall of Fame.

Jean-Marc Ligny was born in 1956 in Paris. He pursued high school studies that led him to the baccalaureate but no further. Very early, he plunged into science fiction (from the age of eight!) and devoted himself to writing in this field from 1976, after unsuccessful musical attempts (as a rock guitarist). He published his first short story in 1978, in Philippe Curval's anthology *Futurs au Présent*. His first novel, *Temps Blancs*, published the following year, was noticed by the critics and earned him a passage in *Apostrophes* (a famous literary TV show at that time).

Ligny decided to devote himself to writing full-time when he "immigrated" to Brittany in 1985. Nevertheless, he worked for a few years (part-time) on a local editorial staff for a regional daily newspaper, *Le Télégramme*. After spending ten years in the Forez Mountains, he returned in 2015 to live in Brittany (Morbihan), where he works full-time as a writer and translator.

He has written about fifty short stories and forty novels, in many fields covered by science fiction and fantasy, including about fifteen for youth, which led him to become involved in schools. He has also produced two international anthologies on the theme of love, translated and published in Italy.

He draws his inspiration from music (*Furia!*, *La Mort peut danser*), ethnology (*Yurlunggur*, *Yoro Si*), esotericism (*Les Voleurs de rêves*), history (*La Mort peut danser*), and ecology, especially climate change (*Aqua™*, *Exodes*, *Semences*, *Alliances*). He is also interested in fantasy (*Yoro Si*, *Les Ailes noires de la nuit*), cyberpunk (*Cyberkiller*, *Inner City*, *Slum City*), space opera (*Les oiseaux de lumière*), or more political fields (*Jihad*, *Aqua™*). He also wrote some detective novels. Two trips to Burkina Faso and one to Ireland provided the setting for two of his major works: *Yoro Si* and *La Mort peut danser*. In the field of fantasy/horror, he seeks an original approach to the genre, based on myths and legends of current and past civilizations, but does not neglect contemporary urban fantasy (*La maison aux démons*, *Mal-morts*).

Ligny is the winner of the main French prizes in the field of science fiction: the Grand Prix de l'Imaginaire in 1997 for *Inner City*, the Rosny Aîné Prize in 1999 for *Jihad* and in 2007 for *Aqua™*, the Tour Eiffel Prize in 2001 for *Les oiseaux de lumière*, the Julia Verlanger Prize (endowed by the Fondation de France) in 2007 for *Aqua™*—this last novel was published in Germany and China—and finally the European Utopiales Prize in 2013 for *Exodes*.

Since the early 2000s, he has devoted most of his fiction to climate change and its social and environmental consequences: four novels have been published on this subject (*Aqua™*, *Exodes*, *Semences*, *Alliances*), as well as a dozen short stories.

M. Lopes da Silva is a nonbinary and bisexual author and artist from Los Angeles. They write queer California horror and everything else. They have had their speculative fiction published by Dread Stone Press, in *Unnerving* magazine, and in *Glass and Gardens: Solarpunk Summers*.

Phillip Mann has published eleven science fiction novels including his acclaimed *The Eye of the Queen*, *The Disestablishment of Paradise*, and, most recently, *Chevalier & Gawayn: The Ballad of the Dreamer*. He also wrote for radio and theater. He was a theater director and teacher, founding New Zealand's first university drama studies course at Victoria University.

Born in North Yorkshire, England, Mann lived and worked in the United States, China, and France, as well as New Zealand, where he lived with his family until his death in 2022.

Sam J. Miller's books have been called "must-reads" and "best of the year" by *USA Today*, *Entertainment Weekly*, NPR, and *O, The Oprah Magazine*, among others. He is the Nebula Award–winning author of *Blackfish City*, which has been translated into six languages and won the now thankfully renamed John W. Campbell Memorial Award. Sam's short stories have been nominated for the World Fantasy, Theodore Sturgeon, and Locus awards and reprinted in dozens of anthologies. He's also the last in a long line of butchers. He lives in New York City.

Robin Moger is a translator of Arabic into English. His translations of prose and poetry have appeared in *The White Review*, *Tentacular*, *Asymptote*, the *Washington Square Review*, *Words Without Borders*, and others. He has translated several novels and prose works, most recently *The Book of Sleep* by Haytham El Wardany, *Slipping* by Mohamed Kheir, and *The Law of Inheritance* by Yasser Abdellatif.

Sunny Moraine is a writer of science fiction, fantasy, horror, and generally weird stuff, with stories published in outlets like Tor.com, *Clarkesworld*, *Lightspeed*, and *Shimmer*, along with the story collection *Singing With All My Skin and Bone*. Moraine has a PhD in sociology, with a doctoral dissertation on extermination camps. Moraine also writes, narrates, and produces a serial horror drama podcast called *Gone*. They live near Washington, DC, with their husband and two cats.

Kim Newman is a critic, author, and broadcaster. He is a contributing editor to *Sight & Sound* and *Empire* magazines. His books about film include *Nightmare Movies* and *Kim Newman's Video Dungeon*. His fiction includes the Anno Dracula series, *The Hound of the D'Urbervilles*, and *An English Ghost Story*. He has written for television (*Mark Kermode's Secrets of Cinema*), radio (*Afternoon Theatre: Cry-Babies*), comics (*Witchfinder: The Mysteries of Unland*), and the theater (*The Hallowe'en Sessions*). He also directed a tiny film (*Missing Girl*). His latest novel is *Something More Than Night*.

Jeff Noon was born in Manchester, England, in 1957. He trained in visual arts and drama and was active on the post-punk-music scene before becoming a playwright and then a novelist.

His science fiction books include *Vurt* (Arthur C. Clarke Award winner), *Pollen*, *Automated Alice*, *Nymphomation*, *Needle in the Groove*, *Falling Out of Cars*, *Channel SK1N*, *Mappalujo*, and a collection of stories called *Pixel Juice*. He has written two crime novels, *Slow Motion Ghosts* and *House with No Doors*. The four Nyquist Mysteries (*A Man of Shadows*, *The Body Library*, *Creeping Jenny*, and *Within Without*) explore the shifting intersections between science fiction and crime.

Harry Polkinhorn is a writer, visual artist, and psychoanalyst. Beginning in his teenage years, he has written poetry, prose, essays, and articles for more than fifty years. In the late 1970s and early 1980s, he cofounded Atticus Press and coedited *Atticus Review*. He has published more than 115 books.

In the visual arts he followed studio courses in painting and color theory at the Kunstgewerbeschule der Stadt Zürich, and while living in Europe visited galleries and museums throughout the Continent. His photographs have been exhibited at the city museum of Quito, Ecuador, and published widely.

qntm (pronounced "quantum") is a UK-based science fiction author and software developer. He has been writing short-form and serial science fiction for most of the millennium to date, publishing his work on Everything2, his own website, and the SCP project. He is the author of supernatural thriller novel *There Is No Antimemetics Division*, which is about monstrous, invasive ideas from beyond the human ideatic ecology. He is also the creator of HATETRIS, a variant of *Tetris* that always gives you the worst piece. He is cagey and gangly.

Jean Rabe is a longtime *Shadowrun* player who favors trolls that use bows and arrows. She is the coauthor of *Aftershocks*, a Shadowrun novel she happily penned with John Helfers. In addition, she has written two dozen novels and more than four dozen short stories. In her spare time . . . such that it is . . . she plays a variety of games, tugs on old socks with her dogs, and tries unsuccessfully to put a dent in her growing stack of to-be-read books.

Cat Rambo's 250-plus fiction publications include stories in *Asimov's*, *Clarkesworld* magazine, and *The Magazine of Fantasy and Science Fiction*. In 2020 they won the Nebula Award for the fantasy novelette *Carpe Glitter*. They are a former two-term president of the Science Fiction and Fantasy Writers of America (SFWA). Their most recent works are space opera *You Sexy Thing* and an anthology, *The Reinvented Heart*, coedited with Jennifer Brozek.

Paul Graham Raven is (at the time of writing) a Marie Skłodowska-Curie Postdoctoral Fellow at Lund University, Sweden, where his research is concerned with how the stories we tell about times yet to come shape the lives we end up living. He's also an author and critic of science fiction, an occasional journalist and essayist, a collaborator with designers and artists, and a (gratefully) lapsed consulting critical futurist. He currently lives in Malmö with a cat, some guitars, and sufficient books to constitute an insurance-invalidating fire hazard.

Justina Robson is the award-winning author of several novels, novellas, and short stories. Most of her books and stories are science fiction, dealing in particular with transhumanism, genetic engineering, nanotech, and human evolution. They focus on the adaptation of human beings to new ways of creating themselves with technology.

A graduate of Clarion West (1996), she has gone on to teach at the Arvon Foundation in the United Kingdom. In 2005, she was a judge for the Arthur C. Clarke Award. In addition to her original works, she also wrote *Transformers: The Covenant of Primus*, the official history of the Transformers in the Prime Continuum, for Hasbro in 2013. She continues to study and write at her home in Yorkshire, where she lives with her husband, children, and pets.

Pepe Rojo practices interference in the California border zone in both Mexican and English, as there is no other way to go at it in Tijuana, where he has spent most of his life for a decade and a half. He has published five books and more than three hundred works dealing with fiction, media, and contemporary culture, while exploring hybrid formats and genres from science fiction interventions at the border crossing, speculative theory and fiction, to a philosophical dictionary of Tijuana. He is currently raising *Tierra y Libertad* flags while trying to survive a communications PhD at UCSD.

A former analyst at Oracle and programmer for Harvard, **N. R. M. Roshak** now writes about how technology and cutting-edge science interact with our loves, hopes, desires, and work. Their award-winning fiction has been published in three languages and has appeared in various anthologies and magazines, including Flash Fiction Online, *Galaxies SF*, Daily Science Fiction, and *Future Science Fiction Digest*. They live in Ontario, Canada, with a small family and a loud cat.

Nicholas Royle is the author of numerous short story collections, including *Mortality, Ornithology*, and *London Gothic*, and novels such as *Counterparts, Antwerp*, and *First Novel*. He has edited more than twenty anthologies and is series editor of *Best British Short Stories*. He runs Nightjar Press, which publishes original short stories as signed, numbered chapbooks. His English translation of Vincent de Swarte's 1998 novel *Pharricide* was published in 2019. His memoir is *White Spines: Confessions of a Book Collector*.

Erica L. Satifka's short fiction has appeared in *Clarkesworld, Interzone, The Dark*, and many other places. She is the author of the collection *How to Get to Apocalypse and Other Disasters*, as well as *Busted Synapses* and *Stay Crazy*, and she received the 2017 British Fantasy Award for Best Newcomer. Erica lives in Portland, Oregon, with her spouse/editor, Rob, and an indeterminate number of cats.

John Shirley is the author of numerous novels, including the A Song Called Youth cyberpunk trilogy: *Eclipse, Eclipse Penumbra*, and *Eclipse Corona*. His newest book is the cyberpunk climate-fiction novel *Stormland*. Other works include *Demons, Wetbones, Cellars, Heatseeker, Living Shadows, City Come A-Walkin', Bioshock: Rapture, A Splendid Chaos, The Other End*, and his story collection *Black Butterflies*, which won the Bram Stoker Award. His newest story collection is *The Feverish Stars*. He was co-screenwriter of *The Crow* (1994) and has written teleplays and animation.

Zedeck Siew is a writer, translator, and game designer based in Port Dickson, Malaysia. His English-language fiction has been published in Malaysia, the United Kingdom, and the United States. With visual artist Sharon Chin, he created *Creatures of Near Kingdoms*, a naturalists' guide to imaginary Southeast Asian flora and fauna; with visual artist Mun Kao he creates *A Thousand Thousand Islands*, a tabletop role-playing game series inspired by Nusantara mythistory and lived experience.

Bruce Sterling, author, journalist, editor, and critic, was born in 1954. Best known for his ten science fiction novels, he also writes short stories, book reviews, design criticism, opinion columns, and introductions for books ranging from Ernst Juenger to Jules Verne. His nonfiction works include *The Hacker Crackdown: Law And Disorder on the Electronic Frontier, Tomorrow Now: Envisioning The Next Fifty Years, Shaping Things*, and *The Epic Struggle of the Internet of Things*. His most recent book is a fiction collection, *Robot Artists and Black Swans: The Italian Fantascienza Stories*.

During 2005, he was the "visionary in residence" at Art Center College of Design in Pasadena. In 2008, he was the guest curator for the Share Festival of Digital Art and Culture in Torino, Italy, and the visionary in residence at the Sandberg Instituut in Amsterdam. In 2011, he returned to Art Center as visionary in residence to run a special project on Augmented Reality. In 2013, he was the visionary in residence at the Center for Science and the Imagination at Arizona State University. In 2015, he was the curator of the "Casa Jasmina" project at the Torino Fab Lab. In 2016, he was visionary in residence at the Arthur C. Clarke Center for Human Imagination.

He has appeared on ABC's *Nightline*, BBC's *The Late Show*, CBC's *Morningside*, MTV, and TechTV, and in *Time, Newsweek*, the *Wall Street Journal*, the *New York Times, Fortune, Nature, I.D., Metropolis, Technology Review, Der Spiegel, La Stampa, La Repubblica*, and many other venues. He lives in Belgrade, Austin, Turin, and Ibiza.

Charles Stross is a full-time science fiction writer and resident of Edinburgh, Scotland. The author of seven Hugo-nominated novels and winner of three Hugo awards for best novella, Stross's works have been translated into more than twelve languages. His most recent novel is *Quantum of Nightmares*. His next novel, *Season of Skulls*, is forthcoming.

Like many writers, Stross has had a variety of careers, occupations, and job-shaped catastrophes in the past, from pharmacist (he quit after the second police stakeout) to first code monkey on the team of a successful dot-com startup (with brilliant timing he tried to change employers just as the bubble burst). Along the way he collected degrees in pharmacy and computer science, making him the world's first officially qualified cyberpunk writer (just as cyberpunk died).*

Michael Swanwick has received the Nebula, Theodore Sturgeon, World Fantasy, and Hugo awards and has the pleasant distinction of having been nominated for and lost more of these same awards than any other writer. His novels include *Stations of the Tide*, *Bones of the Earth*, two Darger and Surplus novels, and *The Iron Dragon's Mother*. He has also written more than a hundred and fifty short stories—including the Mongolian Wizard series on Tor.com—and countless works of flash fiction. He lives in Philadelphia with his wife, Marianne Porter.

E. J. Swift is the author of the Osiris Project trilogy, a speculative fiction series set in a world radically altered by climate change, and *Paris Adrift*, a tale of bartenders and time travel in the City of Light. Her short fiction has been nominated for the *Sunday Times* short story award and the British Science Fiction Award and has appeared in a variety of publications. Her latest novel, *The Coral Bones*, connects three women across the centuries through their love of the ocean.

Molly Tanzer is the author of five novels and two collections. Her work has been nominated for the Locus Award, the British Fantasy Award, and the Wonderland Book Award. Her novel *Creatures of Charm and Hunger* won the Colorado Book Award in 2021; her debut, *Vermilion*, was an NPR Best Book of 2015. Tanzer lives outside Boulder, Colorado, with her notorious cat, Toad.

Lavie Tidhar's latest novels are *Maror* and *Neom*. His awards include the World Fantasy Award, the British Fantasy Award, the John W. Campbell Award, the Neukom Prize, and the Jerwood Fiction Uncovered Prize.

James Tiptree Jr. was the pen name of Alice Bradley Sheldon, whose radical and pioneering science fiction stories were matched by her extraordinary life. As a child she traveled widely with her parents and featured in several African-set travel books written by her mother. After attending a finishing school in Switzerland, she embarked on an early career as an artist and a critic. During WWII she joined the US Army Air Force, attaining the rank of major, and then worked for the CIA before moving to a chicken farm in Virginia with her husband. She turned to writing science fiction as an escape from her PhD thesis on experimental psychology and chose her pseudonym from a pot of jam. She later explained, "A male name seemed like good camouflage . . . I've had too many experiences in my life of being the first woman

* Well, that's awkward.—the Editor

in some damned occupation." Her true sex was kept secret for years. She died in 1987 in what appeared to be a murder-suicide pact with her husband. She wrote some of the greatest science fiction short stories of the twentieth century, telling of dystopian chases, alien sex, and the loneliness of the universe.

Marie Vibbert has sold more than eighty short stories to places such as *Nature* and *The Magazine of Fantasy & Science Fiction*, with reprints translated into Chinese and Vietnamese. Her debut novel, *Galactic Hellcats*, was longlisted by the BSFA for 2021. *The Gods Awoke* is her second novel. She's played women's professional football and tried to ride all the roller coasters in the United States. By day, she's a computer programmer in Cleveland, Ohio.

Corey J. White is the author of *Repo Virtual* and the VoidWitch Saga—*Killing Gravity*, *Void Black Shadow*, and *Static Ruin*. Their short fiction has appeared in anthologies including *A Punk Rock Future*; *Night, Rain, and Neon*; and *Phase Change*. They studied writing at Griffith University on the Gold Coast and are now based in Melbourne, Australia. Their cyberpunk novel, *Repo Virtual*, won the Aurealis Award for Best Science Fiction Novel.

Neon Yang is the author of the Genesis of Misery and the Tensorate series of novellas (*The Red Threads of Fortune*, *The Black Tides of Heaven*, *The Descent of Monsters*, and *The Ascent to Godhood*). Their work has been shortlisted for Hugo, Nebula, and World Fantasy awards, among others. Neon is queer, non-binary, and lives in the United Kingdom.

Alvaro Zinos-Amaro is a Hugo and Locus award finalist who has published fifty stories, as well as more than a hundred essays, reviews, and interviews, in a variety of professional magazines and anthologies. These venues include *Analog*, *Apex*, *Lightspeed*, *Beneath Ceaseless Skies*, *Galaxy's Edge*, *Nature*, the *Los Angeles Review of Books*, *Locus*, Tor.com, *Strange Horizons*, *Clarkesworld*, *The Year's Best Science Fiction & Fantasy*, *Cyber World*, *This Way to the End Times*, *The Unquiet Dreamer*, *It Came from the Multiplex*, *Shadow Atlas*, and many others.

ABOUT THE EDITOR

Jared Shurin's previous anthologies include *The Outcast Hours* and *The Djinn Falls in Love* (both with Mahvesh Murad and both finalists for the World Fantasy Award). He has also been a finalist for the Shirley Jackson Award (twice), the British Science Fiction Association Award (twice), and the Hugo Award (twice) and won the British Fantasy Award (twice).

Alongside Anne C. Perry, he founded and edited the "brilliantly brutal" (the *Guardian*) pop culture website *Pornokitsch* for ten years, responsible for many of its most irritating and exuberant articles. Together, they also cofounded the Kitschies, the prize for progressive, intelligent, and entertaining speculative and fantastic fiction, and Jurassic London, an award-winning, not-for-profit small press.

His other projects have included the *Best of British Fantasy* and *Speculative Fiction* series and anthologies of mummies, weird Westerns, and Dickensian London. A frequent reviewer, he has also written articles on topics as diverse as *Gossip Girl* and *Deadwood*.

Jared is a certified BBQ judge.

ACKNOWLEDGMENTS

No one does a better job of standing on the shoulders of giants than an anthology editor.

I owe a debt of gratitude not only to the authors and translators whose work appears in this volume, but also the many editors who initially discovered and published those stories. These include, but are not limited to: Victoria Blake, Bill Campbell, Sarah Champion, Neil Clarke, Ellen Datlow,* Milton Davis, Eileen Gunn, Jason Heller, Karie Jacobson, Maxim Jakubowski, Richard Jones, James Patrick Kelly, Larry McCaffery, Rudy Rucker, Bruce Sterling, Jonathan Strahan, Joshua Viola, and Stephen Zision. These editors—and many others—created, fueled, and sustained this fragile genre: thank you all.

Navigating the twin worlds of cyberpunk and permissions presented a challenge, but I met some expert guides along the way. A special thanks to Richard Curtis, Vaughne Hanson, Simon Kavanagh, John Shirley, Paul Graham Raven, Robin Moger, Nisi Shawl, Marissa Skeels, Ganzeer and the kind people at the SFWA for going above and beyond in their help.

Much support (literary, emotional, physical, occupational, or culinary) was provided by Vicky, Sam, Becky, Syima, Patrick, CFM, Mahvesh, Matt M, Arin, Rich, The Good George, the Garlic Club, and my 'waffle-loving' Discord friends. Many of whom don't even like cyberpunk . . . but still got behind this project and helped every step of the way.

Much tolerance was also provided by my wonderful family, who have heard me talk about nothing besides cyberpunk for several years. A special shout out to

---

* In the introduction to *Mirrorshades*, Bruce Sterling refers to Ellen Datlow as "a shades-packing sister in the vanguard of the ideologically correct." This is the single coolest description ever and is entirely merited.

Sophia, George, and Nathaniel, shaping up to be three of the best *-punks* the world has ever seen.

David Holden, Lavie Tidhar, and Alex Shvartsman were terrific traveling companions, providing support, guidance, and good humor across time zones and digital platforms.

I had never met Ann VanderMeer before this project began. She steered me in the right direction at the outset (and provided impromptu therapy), and has been gracious with her time and her advice throughout. She is a role model both as an editor and a human being.

The Big Book of Cyberpunk would not have been possible without the hard work and dedication (and patience and creativity and chutzpah) of Ron Eckel, Anna Kaufman and Nick Skidmore. Thank you both so very, very much. The transatlantic team at Vintage Books has been brilliant. Turning a two-thousand-plus-page Word file into the beautiful objects you see before you is an amazing achievement. Thank you so much to production editor Kayla Overbey; copy editor Kathy Strickman; proofreaders Lyn Rosen, Karen Niersbach, and Melissa Holbrook Pierson; designer Nicholas Alguire; publicist Jordan Rodman; and marketer Sophie Normil for making magic. In the UK, thanks to managing editor Rhiannon Roy; proofreader Saxon Bullock; marketer Hannah Shorten; publicist Maya Koffi; production controller Konrad Kirkham; and cover designer Yeti Lambregts.

Anne C. Perry and Goblin: You may have 631,002 cyberpunk walruses and one tiger. You've earned them.

PERMISSIONS ACKNOWLEDGMENTS

Yasser Abdellatif: "Younis in the Belly of the Whale" by Yasser Abdellatif, © 2014, 2018 by Yasser Abdellatif. Translation copyright © 2014 by Robin Moger. Previously published in English in *Sunspot Jungle: Volume 2* (2018), edited by Bill Campbell. Reprinted by permission of the author and the translator.

K. C. Alexander: "Four Tons Too Late" by K. C. Alexander, © 2014 by K. C. Alexander. Originally published in *Fireside Magazine* (2014). Reprinted by permission of the author. Revised for this publication.

Jacques Barcia: "Salvaging Gods" by Jacques Barcia, © 2010 by Jacques Barcia. Originally published in *Clarkesworld* magazine (October 2010). Reprinted by permission of the author.

Greg Bear: "Petra" by Greg Bear, © 1982 by Greg Bear. Originally published in *Omni* (February 1982). Reprinted by permission of the author.

Steve Beard: "Retoxicity" by Steve Beard, © 1998 by Steve Beard. Originally published in *Disco 2000* (1998), edited by Sarah Champion. "Retoxicity" is an excerpt from the author's novel *Digital Leatherette* (1999). Reprinted by permission of the author.

Russell Blackford: "Glass Reptile Breakout" by Russell Blackford, © 1985, 1990 by Russell Blackford. Originally published in *Strange Attractors* (1985), edited by Damien Broderick. Revised version first published in *Glass Reptile Breakout and Other Australian Speculative Stories* (1990), edited by Van Ikin. Reprinted by permission of the author.

Pat Cadigan: "Pretty Boy Crossover" by Pat Cadigan, © 1986 by Pat Cadigan. Originally published in *Isaac Asimov's Science Fiction Magazine* (January 1986). Reprinted by permission of the author.

Beth Cato: "Apocalypse Playlist" by Beth Cato, © 2020 by Beth Cato. Originally published in *Nature* (October 2020) by Springer Nature. Reprinted by permission of the author.

Gwyneth Jones: "Red Sonja and Lessingham in Dreamland" by Gwyneth Jones, © 1996 by Gwyneth Jones. First published in *Off Limits: Tales of Alien Sex* (1996), edited by Ellen Datlow. Reprinted by permission of the author.

Richard Kadrey: "Surfing the Khumbu" by Richard Kadrey, © 2002 by Richard Kadrey. First published in Infinite Matrix. Reprinted by permission of the author and Ginger Clark Literary, LLC.

Cassandra Khaw: "Degrees of Beauty" by Cassandra Khaw, © 2016 by Cassandra Khaw. Originally appeared in *Terraform* (October 2016). Reprinted by permission of the author.

Christian Kirchev: "The Death of Designer D" by Christian Kirchev, © 2004 by Christian As. Kirtchev. Collected in *Chemical Illusions* (2009). Reprinted by permission of the author.

Aleš Kot: "A Life of Its Own" by Aleš Kot, © 2019 by Aleš Kot. Reprinted by permission of the author.

Nancy Kress: "With the Original Cast" by Nancy Kress, © 1982 by Nancy Kress. First appeared in *Omni* (May 1982). Reprinted by permission of the author.

Lavanya Lakshminarayan: "Études" by Lavanya Lakshminarayan, © 2020 by Lavanya Lakshminarayan. Permission to reproduce this chapter from *The Ten Percent Thief* (2023) is granted by Rebellion Publishing Ltd., © Rebellion Publishing Ltd. 2023. First published in *Analog/Virtual: And Other Simulations of Your Future* (2020).

Oliver Langmead: "Glitterati" by Oliver Langmead, © 2017 by Oliver Langmead. First published in *2084* (2017), edited by George Sandison, from Unsung Stories. Later expanded into the novel *Glitterati* (2022), published by Titan. Reprinted by permission of the author.

Fritz Leiber: "Coming Attraction" by Fritz Leiber, © 1950 by the estate of the author. First published in *Galaxy* (November 1950). Reprinted by permission of the author's estate and the agent, Richard Curtis Associates.

Jean-Marc Ligny: "RealLife 3.0" by Jean-Marc Ligny, © 2014 by Jean-Marc Ligny. First published in *Bifrost* 75 (July 2014). English translation © 2023 by N. R. M. Roshak. This first English-language translation published by permission of the author and translator.

M. Lopes da Silva: "Found Earworms" by M. Lopes da Silva, © 2019 by M. Lopes da Silva. First published in *A Punk Rock Future* (2019), edited by Steve Zisson. Reprinted by permission of the author.

Phillip Mann: "An Old-Fashioned Story" by Phillip Mann, © 1989 by Phillip Mann. First published in *Interzone* (May/June 1989). Reprinted by permission of the author.

Sunny Moraine: "I Tell Thee All I Can No More" by Sunny Moraine, © 2013 by Sunny Moraine. First published in *Clarkesworld* (July 2013). Reprinted by permission of the author.

Kim Newman: "SQPR" by Kim Newman, © 1992 by Kim Newman. First published in *Interzone* (May 1992). Reprinted by permission of the author.

Jeff Noon: "Ghost Codes" by Jeff Noon, © 2011, 2023 by Jeff Noon. First published on Twitter and on the author's website. Collected and revised for this publication by the author.

Paul Graham Raven: "Los Piratas del Mar de Plastico" by Paul Graham Raven, © 2014 by Paul Graham Raven. First published in *Twelve Tomorrows* (2014), edited by Bruce Sterling, published by MIT Press. Reprinted by permission of the author.

Harry Polkinhorn: "Consumimur Igni" by Harry Polkinhorn, © 1992 by Harry Polkinhorn. First published in *Avant-Pop: Fiction for a Daydream Nation* (1992), edited by Larry McCaffery, published by Black Ice. Reprinted by permission of the author.

Jean Rabe: "More Than" by Jean Rabe, © 2010 The Topps Company Inc. All Rights Reserved. First published in *Spells and Chrome* (2010), edited by John Helfers. Shadowrun & Matrix are registered trademarks and/or trademarks of The Topps Company, Inc., in the United States and/or other countries. Catalyst Game Labs and the Catalyst Game Labs logo are trademarks of InMediaRes Productions LLC. Reprinted by permission of Catalyst Game Labs.

Cat Rambo: "Memories of Moments, Bright as Falling Stars" by Cat Rambo, © 2006 by Cat Rambo. First published in *Talebones* (Winter 2006). Reprinted by permission of the author.

Justina Robson: "The Girl Hero's Mirror Says He's Not the One" by Justina Robson, © 2007 by Justina Robson. First published in *Fast Forward 1: Future Fiction from the Cutting Edge* (2007), edited by Lou Anders, published by Pyr. Reprinted by permission of the author.

Pepe Rojo: "Gray Noise" by Pepe Rojo, © 1996 by Pepe Rojo. First published as "Ruido gris" (November 1996) by Universidad Autónoma Metropolitana (México). English translation © 2003 by Andrea Bell, first published in *Cosmos Latinos* (2003), edited by Andrea Bell and Yolanda Molina-Gavilán, published by Wesleyan University Press. Reprinted by permission of the author and translator.

Nicholas Royle: "D.GO" by Nicholas Royle, © 1990 by Nicholas Royle. First published in *Interzone* (November 1990). Reprinted by permission of the author.

Erica L. Satifka: "Act of Providence" by Erica L. Satifka, © 2021 by Erica L. Satifka. First published in *How to Get to Apocalypse and Other Disasters* (2021), from Fairwood Press. Reprinted by permission of the author.

John Shirley: "Wolves of the Plateau" by John Shirley, © 1988 by John Shirley. First published in *Mississippi Review* (1988). Reprinted by permission of the author.

Zedeck Siew: "The White Mask" by Zedeck Siew, © 2015 by Zedeck Siew. First published in *Cyberpunk: Malaysia* (2015), edited by Zen Cho, published by Fixi Novo. Reprinted by permission of the author.

J. P. Smythe: "The Infinite Eye" by J. P. Smythe, © 2017 by J. P. Smythe. First published in *2084* (2017), edited by George Sandison, from Unsung Stories. Reprinted by permission of the author.

Charles Stross: "Lobsters" by Charles Stross, © 2001 by Charles Stross. Originally published in *Isaac Asimov's Science Fiction Magazine* (June 2001). Reprinted by permission of the author.

E. J. Swift: "Alligator Heap" by E. J. Swift, © 2016 by E. J. Swift. Originally published as "A Handful of Rubies" as part of the digital e-book project *STRATA* (2016), inspired by the story world created by Tommy Lee Edwards, published by Penguin Random House UK. Reprinted by permission of the author.

Molly Tanzer: "The Real You™" by Molly Tanzer, © 2018 by Molly Tanzer. First appeared in *Lightspeed* (October 2018). Reprinted by permission of the author.

Lavie Tidhar: "Choosing Faces," by Lavie Tidhar © 2012 by Lavie Tidhar. First published in *Arc* (September 2012). Reprinted by permission of the author.

James Tiptree Jr.: "The Girl Who Was Plugged In" by James Tiptree Jr., © 1973 by James Tiptree Jr., © 2001 by Jeffery D. Smith. First published in *New Dimensions 3* (1973). Collected in *Her Smoke Rose Up Forever* (1990). Reprinted by permission of the author's estate and the estate's agents, the Virginia Kidd Literary Agency Inc.

Marie Vibbert: "Electric Tea" by Marie Vibbert, © 2019 by Marie Vibbert. First published in *A Punk Rock Future* (2019), edited by Steve Zisson. Reprinted by permission of the author.

Corey J. White: "Exopunk's Not Dead" by Corey J. White, © 2019 by Corey J. White. First published in *A Punk Rock Future* (2019), edited by Steve Zisson. Reprinted by permission of the author.

Neon Yang: "Patterns of a Murmuration, in Billions of Data Points" by Neon Yang, © 2014 by Neon Yang. First published in *Clarkesworld* (September 2014). Reprinted by permission of the author.

Alvaro Zinos-Amaro: "wysiomg" by Alvaro Zinos-Amaro, © 2016 by Alvaro Zinos-Amaro. First published in *CyberWorld* (2016), edited by Josh Viola and Jason Heller. Reprinted by permission of the author.

FURTHER READING

The Big Book of Cyberpunk is, despite its obvious heft, not an exhaustive review of this fascinating genre. As noted previously, it is also limited to short fiction, while cyberpunk thrives across many different formats.

The recommendations below are not intended to be a 'best of' list or a definitive bibliography. Instead, these are works that I, personally, enjoyed, and would suggest to those who wish to keep exploring what cyberpunk has to offer.

For the sake of variety, I have tried, except where unavoidable, to exclude works by authors who appear within this anthology. As always, my selection is personal and whimsical.

ALBUMS

1. *Beyond the Valley of 1984* (1981) by The Plasmatics
2. *Power, Corruption & Lies* (1983) by New Order
3. *The Initial Command* (1987) by Front Line Assembly
4. *Outside* (1995) by David Bowie
5. *Interstellar Fugitives* (1998) by Underground Resistance
6. *Gorillaz* (2001) by Gorillaz
7. *Year Zero* (2007) by Nine Inch Nails
8. *ArchAndroid* (2010) by Janelle Monae
9. *Terror 404* (2012) by Perturbator
10. *Simulation Theory* (2018) by Muse

FILM AND TELEVISION*

1. *Escape from New York* (1981)
2. *Outland* (1981)
3. *Scanners* (1981)
4. *Blade Runner* (1982)
5. *Videodrome* (1983)
6. *Max Headroom* (1985)

---

* For sanity's sake, I've not included sequels. But you can safely assume that *Blade Runner 2049* is also, indeed, cyberpunk.

7. *The Running Man* (1987)
8. *Akira* (1988)
9. *Robocop* (1987 and 2014)
10. *Demolition Man* (1993)
11. *Wild Palms* (1993)
12. *Strange Days* (1995)
13. *Johnny Mnemonic* (1995)
14. *Hackers* (1995)
15. *Lawnmower Man* (1996)
16. *Batman Beyond* (1999)
17. *eXistenZ* (1999)
18. *The Matrix* (1999)
19. *The Cell* (2000)
20. *Black Mirror* (2011)
21. *Ex Machina* (2014)
22. *Sense8* (2015)
23. *Mr Robot* (2015)
24. *Westworld* (2016)
25. *Severance* (2022)

9. *Beneath a Steel Sky* (1994)
10. *Hell: A Cyberpunk Thriller* (1994)[‡]
11. *System Shock* (1994)
12. *Heresy: Kingdom Come* (1995)[§]
13. *Netrunner* (1996)
14. *Deus Ex* (2000)
15. *868-HACK* (2013)
16. *Watch Dogs* (2013)
17. *Satellite Reign* (2015)
18. *Cyberpunk 2077* (2020)
19. *CY_BORG* (2022)

ANTHOLOGIES

1. *Mirrorshades* (1986), edited by Bruce Sterling
2. *Semiotext(e) SF* (1989), edited by Rudy Rucker, Paul Lamborn Wilson and Robert Anton Wilson
3. *Storming the Reality Studio* (1991), edited by Larry McCaffery
4. *FutureCrime* (1992), edited by Cynthia Manson and Charles Ardai
5. *Simulations* (1993), edited by Karie Jacobson
6. *Cybersex* (1996), edited by Richard Jones

VIDEO AND TABLETOP GAMES*

1. *2400 AD* (1988)
2. *Cyberpunk* (1988)
3. *Mean Streets* (1989)
4. *Shadowrun* (1989)
5. *Corporation* (1990)
6. *GURPS Cyberpunk* (1990)[†]
7. *Kult* (1991)
8. *Syndicate* (1993)

---

* I've listed franchises, not individual games, and dated to the first installment therein; excluding sequels, reboots, new editions or other expansions. With many thanks to George Osborn and James Long for their help.

† Perhaps less notable as a game than as a moment in cyberpunk history, *GURPS Cyberpunk* was the cause of the ill-fated Secret Service raid of Steve Jackson Games, demonstrating, amongst other things, the heightened confusion and paranoia at the time.

---

‡ With apologies to the fine people at Take-Two Interactive Software, this game is truly terrible - notoriously so. It is from the generation of *Myst*-like games, wherein the player does a lot of precise mouse-clicking to solve puzzles and 'earn' the reward of grainy video cut-scenes. In the case of *Hell*, the puzzles were (inadvertently, due to flaws in the code) impossible and the video cut-scenes included Dennis Hopper and Grace Jones. *Hell: A Cyberpunk Thriller* is, in and of itself, cyberpunk.

§ This obscure but fabulous game mostly exists in a shoebox under my bed.

7. *Disco 2000* (1996), edited by Sarah Champion
8. *Hackers* (1996), edited by Gardner Dozois
9. *Future on Ice* (1998), edited by Orson Scott Card
10. *The Ultimate Cyberpunk* (2002), edited by Pat Cadigan
11. *Rewired: The Post-Cyberpunk Anthology* (2007), edited by James Patrick Kelly and John Kessel
12. *Cyberpunk: Stories of Hardware, Software, Wetware, Revolution and Evolution* (2013), edited by Victoria Blake
13. *CyberWorld: Tales of Humanity's Tomorrow* (2016), edited by Jason Heller and Joshua Viola
14. *A Punk Rock Future* (2019), edited by Steve Zision
15. *Cyberfunk!* (2021), edited by Milton Davis

COMIC BOOKS AND GRAPHIC NOVELS*

1. *The Long Tomorrow* (1976) by Dan O'Bannon and Moebius
2. *Judge Dredd* (1977) by John Wagner and Carlos Ezquerra
3. *The Incal* (1981) by Alejandro Jodorowsky and Moebius
4. *American Flagg* (1983) by Howard Chaykin
5. *Ghost in the Shell* (1989) by Masamune Shirow
6. *Battle Angel Alita* (1990) by Yukito Kishiro

---

* To spare my sanity and yours, I've only listed the first publication date. As any reader of comics knows, continuity is tenuous at the best of times..

7. *20/20 Visions* (1997) by Jamie Delano, Frank Quitely, Warren Peece, James Romberger and Steve Pugh
8. *Transmetropolitan* (1997) by Warren Ellis and Darick Robertson
9. *The True Lives of the Fabulous Killjoys* (2013) by Gerard Way, Shaun Simon, and Becky Cloonen
10. *Vision* (2015) by Tom King and Gabriel Hernandez Walta

NON-FICTION

1. *The Media is the Massage: An Inventory of Effects* (1967) by Marshall McLuhan
2. *Future Shock* (1970) by Alvin Toffler
3. *Simulacra and Simulation* (1981) by Jean Baudrillard
4. "The Neuromantics" (1986) by Norman Spinrad (*Isaac Asimov's Science Fiction Magazine*)
5. "High Tech - High Life: William Gibson and Timothy Leary in Conversation" (1989) (*Mondo 2000*)
6. *Cyborg Manifesto* (1991) by Donna Haraway
7. "A Cypherpunk's Manifesto" (1993) by Eric Hughes
8. *The Posthuman* (2013) by Rosi Braidotti
9. *CCRU: Writings, 1997-2003* (2017)
10. "Heavenly Bodies: Why It Matters That Cyborgs Have Always Been About Disability, Mental Health, and Marginalization" (2019) by Damien Williams

Two excellent volumes that cover the breadth of the genre are *The Routledge Companion to Cyberpunk Culture* (2020) and *Fifty Key Figures in Cyberpunk Culture* (2022), both by Anna McFarlane, Graham J. Murphy and Lars Shmeink.

NOVELS, NOVELLAS AND COLLECTIONS*

Precursors

1. *The Long Good-bye* (1953) by Raymond Chandler
2. *The Stars My Destination / Tiger, Tiger* (1956) by Alfred Bester
3. *The Soft Machine* (1961) by William S. Burroughs
4. *A Clockwork Orange* (1962) by Anthony Burgess
5. *Crash (1973) by J.G. Ballard*
6. *Shockwave Rider* (1975) by John Brunner
7. *Home is the Hangman* (1975) by Roger Zelazny
8. *Blood and Guts in High School* (1978) by Kathy Acker
9. *True Names* (1981) by Vernor Vinge
10. "Press Enter_" (1984) by John Varley

Cyberpunk

11. *Street Lethal* (1983) by Steven Barnes
12. *Hardwired* (1986) by Walter John Williams

13. *Dark Toys and Consumer Goods* (1989) by Lawrence Staig
14. *Santa Clara Poltergeist* (1990) by Fausto Fawcett
15. *The Illegal Rebirth of Billy the Kid* (1991) by Rebecca Ore
16. *High Aztech* (1992) by Ernest Hogan
17. *Down and Out in the Year 2000* (1992) by Kim Stanley Robinson
18. *Destroying Angel* (1992) by Richard Paul Russo
19. *Trouble and her Friends* (1994) by Melissa Scott
20. *Clipjoint* (1996) by Wilhemina Baird
21. *Brown Girl in the Ring* (1998) by Nalo Hopkinson
22. *Noir* (1998) by K.W. Jeter
23. *Pashazade* (2001) by Jon Courtenay Grimwood
24. *Market Forces* (2004) by Richard Morgan
25. *Kung Fu High School* (2005) by Ryan Gattis
26. *Cyclonopedia* (2008) by Reza Negarestani
27. *Slum Online* (2010) by Hiroshi Sakurazaka
28. *The Stories of Ibis* (2011) by Hiroshi Yamamoto
29. *Self-Reference ENGINE* (2013) by Toh Enjoe
30. *The Red* (2015) by Linda Nagata
31. *Infomocracy* (2016) by Malka Older
32. *Otared* (2016) by Mohammed Rabie
33. *The Goldblum Variations* (2018) by Helen McClory
34. *The Tiger Flu* (2018) by Larissa Lai
35. *Autonomous* (2018) by Annalee Newitz

---

* A reminder that I've deliberately chosen not to include works by those authors who otherwise appear in *The Big Book of Cyberpunk*. However, for the sake of the historical record: 'I officially recommend them all.'

36. *Sweet Harmony* (2020) by Claire North
37. *Noor* (2021) by Nnedi Okorafor
38. *Immersion* (2022) by Gemma Amor
39. *Mindwalker* (2022) by Kate Dylan
40. *Cyberpunk 2077: No Coincidence* (2023) by Rafal Kosil

Post-cyberpunk*

41. *Microserfs* (1995) by Douglas Coupland
42. *Maul* (2003) by Tricia Sullivan
43. *Harmony* (2010) by Project Itoh
44. *Machine Man* (2011) by Max Barry
45. *The Mall* (2011) by S.L. Grey
46. *Bleeding Edge* (2013) by Thomas Pynchon
47. *Sad Sack: Collected Writing* (2019) by Sophia Al-Maria
48. *XX* (2020) by Rian Hughes
49. *Prompt: Conversations with Artificial Intelligence* (2022) by Dave McKean
50. *Red Earth* (2023) by Michael Salu

---

* At the risk of lobbing another definitional grenade into the fray, 'post-cyberpunk' in this case stands for works that are in conversation with (or otherwise informed by) cyberpunk, but in some way - thematically, aesthetically or topically - radically and distinctly depart from the movement.